Praise for The Tiger and the Wolf

'It's addictively brilliant! The protagonist is vivid and sympathetic – and I love both the story and the world Adrian has created. It's meticulously thought out and utterly believable'
John Gwynne

'A classically brilliant fantasy writer, a pusher of boundaries, a great storyteller'
Paul Cornell

'This is a satisfying read, a story you can really lose yourself in'
SFX

'Equally deft in the realms of science fiction and fantasy adventure, Adrian Tchaikovsky knows how to take you to a place, no matter the setting . . . the real strength of *The Tiger and the Wolf*, though, lies in the main character herself. Accompanied by a serpent priest and chased by a relentless hunter, Maniye Many Tracks is a fascinating character; layered, strong, torn, constantly developing and hugely empathetic'
SciFiNow

'Tchaikovsky has woven a richly textured world, brimming with difference and complexity'
SFReader

'A really good read with some incredibly unusual flights of fancy and very emotive writing. This is an author who can really make you feel the cold, the hunger and the despair of his characters'

Speculative Herald

'Tchaikovsky's writing is wonderfully evocative, bringing the wilds of Maniye's world to icy and fiery life . . . The first in the forthcoming Echoes of the Fall trilogy, *The Tiger and the Wolf* also works well as a standalone story. A beautifully fierce fantasy about our need to belong and the importance of our choices, this is a coming of age tale with bite'

Geek Syndicate

'A blazing new start to an epic series, the story unfolds with the grace of an old tale and the characters have a depth and dimension that speaks to Tchaikovsky's skill as a storyteller'

Pop Culture Beast

'Bleak. Brutal. Brilliant. *The Tiger and the Wolf* is a unique and powerful novel, where loyalties are defined by birth and where cultures clash with spectacular frequency. Adrian Tchaikovsky has succeeded in creating a novel with incredible scope and limitless vision; a vivid depiction of a world inspired by the cultures of our past and told in a style unique to this series'

Books By Proxy

The Tiger and the Wolf

Adrian Tchaikovsky was born in Woodhall Spa, Lincolnshire, before heading off to Reading to study psychology and zoology. For reasons unclear even to himself, he subsequently ended up in law. He has worked as a legal executive in both Reading and Leeds, where he now lives. Married, he is a keen live role-player and occasional amateur actor. He has also trained in stagefighting, and keeps no exotic or dangerous pets of any kind – possibly excepting his son. He's the author of the critically acclaimed Shadows of the Apt series, *Children of Time* and *Guns of the Dawn*.

www.shadowsoftheapt.com

By Adrian Tchaikovsky

ADRIAN TCHAIKOVSKY

The Tiger and the Wolf

Echoes of the Fall:
Book One

PAN BOOKS

First published 2016 by Macmillan

This paperback edition published 2016 by Pan Books
an imprint of Pan Macmillan
20 New Wharf Road, London N1 9RR
Associated companies throughout the world
www.panmacmillan.com

ISBN 978-1-4472-3457-9

5 7 9 8 6 4

A CIP catalogue record for this book is available from the British Library.

Map artwork by Michael Czajkowski

Typeset by Ellipsis Digital Limited, Glasgow
Printed and bound by CPI Group (UK) Ltd, Croydon, CR0 4YY

To Andy and Natasha Madgewick Connell, Dave Huxter,
Matthew Ledgerwood and David and Tamsin Moore

And to Christine Czajkowski, the Wilderness Dweller

Stone
Place

Winter
Runners

Laughing Men

Atahlan

Loud
Thunder

Shining
Halls

Horse
Post

Where the
Fords Meet

Tsokawan

The Tiger and the Wolf

1

The sound of the chase confirmed he'd been right: they were heading his way. No doubt the quarry was flagging by now, but still keeping ahead of the pack. Akrit was not as young or swift as he once had been, but strength came in many forms, and raw speed did not decide success in a hunt like this.

A big, broad-shouldered man was Akrit Stone River: weather-beaten skin like old tanned leather and his hair starting to grey. He had led the Winter Runner tribe of the Wolf for twenty years, and each one of those years had made his people stronger, extended their reach, brought more hearths into the Wolf's Shadow. If he showed weakness though, some challenger would step from the pack to face him. On days like this, he knew they were all waiting for it.

Akrit was sure that he could beat any of them if ever that day came. But he was not as sure as he had been five years ago.

If I had a son . . . and that *was* a weakness of his body, even if it was not one that slowed him in either the chase or the fight. If he had a son, then he would be unassailable. *But just a daughter . . . Am I less of a man? A daughter's better than nothing, isn't it?*

He scowled, thinking of that. *A* daughter, maybe. *His* daughter? He recognized little enough of himself in her. The fear that had grown in him, as the girl had grown, was that she was too much her dead mother's child.

There is still time. Aside from the girl's mother he had taken three wives, but none of them had borne him anything but excuses. This year, perhaps, he would find a fourth. *There must be a woman born within the Jaws of the Wolf who is strong enough to take my seed.*

As he crouched there, listening to the music of the chase, he thought of his daughter's dead mother, the one woman who had been that strong.

I should have kept her. I shouldn't have had her killed like that. But, once she had given him what he wanted, she had become too dangerous. A daughter had seemed ideal: from her a girl would serve his purposes better than a boy, and he had been young then, with plenty of time to sire a few sons to be true heirs. Who could have known that he would get no other issue in all those years since? Just that sullen, close-featured girl.

He could hear a shift in the baying as the chase neared – telling him exactly who had taken the lead, and who had exhausted their strength and fallen back. The quarry was giving them fair sport, that was plain: a good omen. The Wolf appreciated a good run.

Ten years before, Akrit Stone River would himself have been in the pack, keeping a moderate, confident pace, taking his turn to snap at the heels of the stag and then fall back. Nobody would have berated him that he was not at the fore when the quarry was brought to bear.

Now, though . . . now he was ten years older.

He heard the eager throats of his warriors as the quarry started to weary, imagined them coursing, a river of grey bodies between the trees with the stag's heels flashing before them. There was Smiles Without Teeth, Akrit's war leader and a man who would be his most dangerous challenger if he were not so loyal and devoid of ambition. There, too, was Bleeding Arrow's high call, jaws closing on air – no, a hoof delivered to the snout as he got too close. Then Amiyen Shatters Oak was next at the fore, the fiercest of his huntswomen. She was near as old as Akrit but still as strong as ever, and if she had been a man she would have challenged him long ago. Impossible to take to wife, though, and that was a shame. Surely she would have made a good mother of many sons.

Too fierce to share a tent with, Akrit decided. No pairing could survive the conflicting ambitions of two strong hunters. So it was that Amiyen bore sons for another man, who tended her hearth while she went hunting.

He braced himself, hearing the chase draw near. *All this struggle for a few more moments of life, and still I knew which way you would come*. The land spoke to him, its rises and falls, its skeins of little lakes and streams, its hard ground and its soft, the very pattern of the trees showing him where the quarry would turn, where he would leap, where the pack would turn him aside.

And the Wolf is with me for another year. He ran forward and Stepped onto all fours, his burly human frame flowing into the wolf that was his soul, his second skin. Bones, flesh, clothes and all, turning into the grey hide of the beast. Now he was building up speed, claws catching at the turf, bolting from the undergrowth almost under the hooves of the fleeing stag.

The quarry reared, panicked and turned aside, just as Akrit knew it would. Smiles Without Teeth took the chance to lunge for its haunches, tearing a gash with his claws but failing to catch hold, and the deer was off again, staggering slightly, and Akrit had shouldered his way to the front of the pack, fresh and strong and laughing at them.

They had no words between them, but he heard their thoughts in the snarls and panting as the pack fell in behind him. Smiles Without Teeth was chuckling, Bleeding Arrow was angry at being out-thought – but then out-thinking Bleeding Arrow was no great feat. Amiyen Shatters Oak was pushing herself harder. She wanted to show that if any woman had been allowed to challenge for leadership, then it would have been her.

The joy of the chase, and feeling the pattern of the pack shift to accommodate him, whether they liked it or not, was taking hold of him. Even Bleeding Arrow was moving to his will, falling out towards the flank to head off the quarry's inevitable questing there, bringing the stag back in line – and now they were forcing the beast into the denser forest, where their own lithe forms would slip more easily between the trees.

A good spread of antlers on that head, Akrit noted approvingly. If the quarry fulfilled his part then this would be a good year, with that fine tribute to place between the jaws of the Wolf. No need for a priest to read omens as fine as that.

One of the many lessons a warrior must learn was held in the great span of those antlers: *Do not let your strength become your weakness*. How proud was the stag of that broad spread of points, how he must have strutted before his women, and yet in the chase they were a weight that slowed him down, an encumbrance constantly in danger of being caught by briars or branches.

Akrit gauged his moment, then spurred himself forwards, snapping at the flanks of the stag, driving him sideways to where Smiles Without Teeth was waiting to rip his fangs across the beast's path. The quarry turned more quickly than Akrit would have expected, but the pack was closing in on him from all sides, offering a set of jaws wherever the stag turned: the only path left was deeper into the forest, to where the trees grew close.

There was a glade there that Akrit knew well, its bracken and moss long fed on old blood. The pack was already spreading, those hunters who had been hanging at the back regaining their strength were now drifting out to the side, and with a swift burst of speed began to move ahead.

The stag burst into the glade, ready to gain some ground over the open space, but the pack was already there before him, and he wheeled, rearing high, those mighty antlers clashing with the trees overhead: brought to bay at last.

The encircling wolves snapped and bared their teeth at one another, excitement running high between them, but they were waiting for Akrit's move. He had them for another year at least.

The stag lowered his antlers, threatening them with those

jagged tines, wheeling round and round, trying to hold all quarters against the grey tide. Akrit waited for his opening, bunching himself to spring. There was still a very real chance of getting this wrong if he was too impatient—

And there went Dirhathli, a boy out on his first hunt, unable to restrain himself, trying to earn a name. The antlers flashed, and the boy yelped and fell back, twisting to lick at his side, and then Stepping entirely from thin wolf to thin boy, holding his wound and crying out in pain. *No hunter's name for you*, Akrit thought sourly. *Or, if you're unlucky, you'll earn such a name as to make you regret this hunt all your life.*

Another two of the pack made abortive lunges at the quarry, more to drive it back to the centre of the glade than to harm it. They were still waiting for Akrit.

Then the quarry Stepped, and a moment later there was just a long-limbed man crouching in the centre of the clearing, one leg bloodied where Smiles Without Teeth had gashed him, his face twisted in fear.

A shudder went through the circling wolves, one of disgust and horror.

'Please,' said the quarry, hands held out in supplication, and Akrit felt a stab of anger, and fear too, for this was surely a bad omen unless he could turn matters around somehow.

He growled deep in his throat and Stepped too, a man amongst wolves, aware of the pack's eyes on him.

'Running Deer, this is no proper tribute. You know how this is done.'

'Please . . .' The man's chest was heaving with the exertion of the chase. 'I can't . . .'

'You know what this price buys your people,' Akrit told him sharply. 'You know what your cowardice will cost them. I give you one chance to face death as you should, Running Deer.'

'No!' the trembling man cried out. 'My name—'

'You are Running Deer from the moment you were chosen as tribute,' Akrit shouted at him, incensed that this wretched

5

creature should flout the traditions of the hunt. 'Your family I will see torn apart. I shall feast on them myself. Your village shall give its children and women as thralls. I offer you this one last chance to avoid that. You know the rules of tribute.'

But the man – such a proud stag, and yet such a wretched human being – only begged and pleaded, and at last Akrit tired of him.

He gave the signal, and the pack descended. For himself, he would not sully his fangs, and none would blame him for not lowering himself. There would be no trophy of antlers for the Wolf, and no doubt Kalameshli Takes Iron would have dire warnings for the year to come. All of the hunters would have to be cleansed of the dead man's ghost. The entire tribute hunt had become a travesty.

Akrit had an ambivalent relationship with omens. He was quick to make use of them, but well aware that they were a knife with two edges. So far, in his rule of the Winter Runners tribe, he had been able to ride out whatever the fates had in store for him, turning each year's predictions to his advantage. The priest, Kalameshli Takes Iron, was his friend of old and their partnership a long-standing and close one, but a year's forecast of bad omens might change that.

Akrit walked away from the kill, because there was no glory to be found there. He was already trying to think how this day might be seen as anything other than a disaster.

★★★

The people of the Wolf, and those of the Boar and Deer, considered themselves denizens of the middle world. Their dominion was over the wet, cold lands. To the north lay frozen uplands shouldering their way ever northwards until they were eaten by the mountains' glacial tongues. South, the land dried slowly into the vast, temperate plains whose peoples had all the warmth they might desire but of water, other than the river, almost none. If there was yet a south beyond that, known of only from travellers' tales and myth, it failed to skew their sense of centre. They

6

dwelled in the very heart, the perfect place, the Crown of the World, studded with lakes like gems, and filigreed with silver streams. Theirs was a land of thick woodland that went on forever, of rich but stubborn earth that the winter months froze, but the spring always thawed. A land of vast forests where dwelled the beasts that were their ancestors, their kin, their prey and, after death, their rebirth.

In Maniye's great-great-grandfather's day, the Winter Runner tribe of the Wolf people had been driven from their haunts further north, where they had been forced to snarl over scraps with their brothers the Moon Eaters, and where the Bear came down in the worst of winters and took what it liked, leaving everyone hungry.

The Winter Runners had found a land already sewn tight between Deer and Boar and Tiger, and they had fought their battles, and spread the Shadow of the Wolf wherever they won, and licked their wounds where they had lost. But the time of the Wolf had since been in the ascendant, and more and more they had won, and now that Shadow lay thick across the entire land, and had not lifted in a generation.

Her great-grandfather – Akrit's grandfather – had raised this mound that now stood at a crossroads of others, and what had been uncut forest back then was now speckled with herders' crofts and the huddled villages of the Runners' thralls.

Here was the ancient longhouse of that long-ago great-grandfather – for though the roof was re-turfed each year, and the walls re-daubed, and even the timbers sometimes replaced, still all knew it to be the same house that the old man had raised. As the village was the Shadow of the Winter Runners, so this hall was the Shadow of her father and his forebears. Outside it seemed almost a part of the mound, built right up against the edge so that the slant of its roof might have been a continuation of the steeply sloping bank of earth. Inside, the cavernous space was dark and warm with fire's trapped heat, grand enough for pillars to prop up a floor overhead that created a close, slant-walled space where food was stored and meat was hung and the rats could not reach.

Maniye claimed just this much of it: a little alcove at one end that she had appropriated and made her own, a cell fit for the child of a chief. In all the dominion of the Wolf, this small space was the Shadow cast by Maniye, Akrit Stone River's daughter. She had beads here, and hangings and furs, all she could manage to haul up to soften the confines of her world. Her favourite part of her lair was an absence, though. In the wattle and daub of the end wall there was a smoke-hole that she had widened to be her lookout on the outer world, a narrow slot in the wall. It gave her a view out towards the forest's dark edge, but surely not an escape. She was small for her age, but her bony shoulders could never have fitted through that space, twist as she might.

And if there were those who said that the wolf shape she might Step into would be such a scrawny thing that it could have wriggled through – well, the drop, down the longhouse's wall and then the almost sheer side of the mound, would surely have broken her bones. Neither wolf nor girl could have made the climb. There could be no possible basis for anyone thinking otherwise.

And yet here came Kalameshli Takes Iron, with his bony face full of suspicion. The scrape and rattle of his robe of bones had tracked his path through the wives' quarters below – the one other man allowed there. She had seen his shadow blot the fire-light, angular and angry even in silhouette, and she shrank back into her tiny bottled kingdom, holding her breath and trying to wish him away.

Her wishes had never had power, and how could they have had power over *him* who was the Wolf's priest and favourite, and who knew the secrets of the forge?

There was a ladder placed at a slant, leading up to her, and she saw his form shift and slide, Stepping onto four fleet feet to scrabble up, then back on two as soon as he had ascended.

8

There was not quite enough space, even at the highest point beneath the ridge-pole, for him to stand upright.

Still she breathed shallowly and pretended to be elsewhere. There was some magic, she believed, that could cast an echo of her spirit to another place, to send hunters chasing after their tails instead of chasing her. The other girls spoke of such things, part of their arsenal when they sought to deceive parents and meet lovers. If such a thing was possible, Maniye did not know the making of it. Magic was not something Akrit Stone River's daughter was fit for.

He was hidden from her by the hanging meat and switches of herbs, but she felt him Step again, abruptly, no longer a man in a robe of bones, but a lean, grey wolf, scarred and cunning. She heard him sniff, finding her out by her traitor scent, despite all the clamour of chicory and feverfew. He padded forwards, eyes glinting in the dim light, and when he Stepped back to the shape of an old man, he was standing before her as she huddled beneath her makeshift window.

'Your peers are all at their practice.' He pronounced each word precisely, as though he was worried about spitting a few more loose teeth out if he spoke too hastily. 'They fight, they run, they jump, they Step. But not you.'

Kalameshli was still strong enough to wrench her arm or slap her, and he had free rein to do so. She backed away as he stalked to the window. The sun caught the thousands of tiny bones sewn into the hide of his robe, playing over the intricate patterns. Standing there, he made the place his, took the sun from her. 'Not you, no: here you are. Why is this, I wonder?'

'Perhaps it's because they hate me,' she told him flatly.

'And holding yourself aloof from them will win their love, then? Will it so?'

'Then perhaps I don't need their love.' Bold words, she knew, for a girl who was working her shoulder blades into the wall to get further from him.

'*Wrong!*' he snapped, and she flinched away from his tone. 'If

9

the pack despises you, you will *die*. Or do you fancy yourself a lone wolf. Perhaps you would walk in the footsteps of Broken Axe, hmm? You'd like that, would you?'

He knew that there was one man she feared more than himself or her father: Broken Axe, who had killed her mother. Her father had ordered it done, and Kalameshli had begged the blessing of the Wolf, but Axe's hands bore the blood and everyone knew it.

'What will they dare do to me, to Stone River's daughter?' she hissed, although her voice shook.

When his face swung towards her, away from the window's view, she knew he had been waiting for those words.

'If you are to be Stone River's daughter, you must be within the Jaws of the Wolf. Or you are *nothing*. Or you will be *meat*, and perhaps it will be Broken Axe following *your* footsteps. You must be of the Wolf or nobody will *care* whose get you are.' His spitting anger, like storm clouds from a clear sky, was no surprise to her. It lurked beneath his cold surface always, and most especially when he spoke to Maniye.

She did not answer. In those flashpoints of temper any words of hers would be provocation, but his rage came and went as swift as hunting, and now he was calm again.

'Some of the hunters said that they found tiger tracks near our walls,' he remarked.

She held herself very still, waiting.

He was looking out of the smoke-hole again – no, he was examining the edges, with hands and with eyes, seeking for scratches and marks. 'I told them there are no tigers here any more, and that I wanted to hear no more of it. But I went to see for myself. They looked very like tiger tracks to me.'

'You should set traps then,' she told him.

His hard features turned towards her again. 'They were very small tracks.'

'Then set very small traps.' She knew her expression admitted to nothing.

For a long time he stood there, half lit by the window, trying to force his way past her guard. She had been working on that innocent face of hers since she was five years old. She had learned quickly that anything the world discovered about what she thought or felt was a knife at her throat.

At last, Kalameshli Takes Iron sighed and turned away, before creaking his way back down the steps in a shiver of bones.

Wherever the people of the Wolf claimed as their home, they raised their mounds, whether it was a low heap of soil that bore some shepherd's croft, or the vast steep-sided hills that marked their villages in those places where they had grown powerful.

The Winter Runners were one of many tribes, not yet the greatest but far from the least. Their village was a loose scattering of artificial mounds that dominated the surrounding landscape. If those hills marked your horizon, then you stood within the shadow of the Winter Runners and were subject to their law.

Maniye slunk sullenly from the longhouse of her father, doing her best to avoid all eyes. She was a small, strange child, friendless and different. It was a difference as deep within her as her bones. The other children had sensed it from an early age, as though they had the noses of wolves even then.

She skulked down the paths running between the mounds. Each hill that reared above her bore the dwellings of a family, their store-houses and their workshops, timber-frame and mud wall and heavy peat-clad roofs whose eaves slanted down to the heaped earth. On another reared the effigy of the Wolf, into whose burning jaws Kalameshli sent offerings, and the windowless longhouse that was the temple, its walls made with heavy stone because of the rituals of fire and hammer Kalameshli enacted there. The temple and her father's house claimed the two highest mounds. They were the twin seats of a power that reached out through the dark between the trees to all the tributary villages Akrit had brought within the curtilage of his influence:

the Winter Runners' contribution to the greater domain they called the Shadow of the Wolf.

The temple's grand mound also held the training ground where the hunters would cast their spears and loose their arrows, and the growing young would practise Stepping until they could pass fluidly from man to wolf and back to man as swift as breathing. Maniye did not want to think of the training ground. The Testing was coming and, just as Kalameshli had reminded her, her fellows were up there already, in their exclusive camaraderie, practising at being wolves.

There were seventeen others from the Winter Runners due to be Tested alongside her, and it was supposed to be something of a celebration, something of a game, something of a chance for the elders of the Wolf to laugh at the inadequacies of the young. Nobody *failed* the Testing. That was a point of faith.

Except that Kalameshli Takes Iron did not seem to have that faith, and he should have been an expert on the subject. Kalameshli had dogged Maniye's steps these last two moons and croaked out his warnings, like ravens circling overhead. At first she had thought it was just his cold dislike of her: that constant pushing and needling, the disapproval, the disdain. That was her due from the priest, so why should it be any different over the Testing?

But of course, Kalameshli and his priests oversaw the Tests. She had not thought of it that way until recently, but each Testing was set by the priests of the Wolf, and so Kalameshli could make them as hard or as easy as he wished.

She understood now that he had been biding his time, through years of loathing her and taunting her, until now when she would fall briefly, but totally, under his power.

Nobody ever failed the Tests, but everyone knew what would happen to someone who did. Exile, or worse – torn apart by the pack or even given as an offering to the Wolf. It was the common stock-in-trade of her peers' conversations, each outdoing the last with their lurid stories.

Even if those going into the Testing did not believe they could fail, none wanted to look a fool before the Wolf and the Wolf's people. As the priest said, they had been practising all this last month, a motley mob of them charging around the circuit of the training ground, under every eave and between every hall, a constant annoyance for their elders and yet a source of fondness too. All the adults remembered their own Testing; a little rowdiness could be forgiven.

Maniye trained also, but alone and out of sight. She avoided the other youths, who mocked her and whom she despised in turn, with not a hand's span of common ground between them. Her own training took place after dark or in secluded corners, or even in the forest looming beyond the fields: forbidden places, abandoned times, where she would not be spied on. But all of it would be for nothing when Kalameshli gave her an impossible challenge, set her a course nobody could have run. If she was lucky he would merely humiliate her, earn her another beating from her father. Otherwise . . .

There was a herder's hut that lay unused at the foot of the mound. Come winter, the sheep would shelter there along with their guardians, but in these last days of fall she could creep there unseen and practise. Rat bones were piled like brittle sticks in the corners, older than the spring and with no sign of living descendants for her to hunt and take as minuscule trophies. She ranged the ten feet of dark space enclosed between the walls, no room to run and nobody to fight. Instead she practised her Stepping, mastering this uncertain new instinct that had only come to her during this last year.

Essential, for this, that there were no eyes there to see her, for she faced challenges the others did not.

No, I have gifts the others lack, that is the truth of it, she told herself over and over. Yet every time she hid those *gifts*, because she knew they would see her denounced, she believed a little more that they were nothing but a curse.

After she had bored herself with that, she sat and brooded,

inventing dire fates for Kalameshli and Broken Axe and her father – and anyone else who crossed her mind – until she was jolted from her dark reverie by the sound of a horn.

They're back. For her father and his picked band of hunters had been off after tribute from the White Tails. She had been given a few blessed days when the only chain about her neck was old Kalameshli's, and now she would be loaded with Akrit Stone River's disapproval as well.

But she was out of her hole before the echo had died away, to watch them return. There would be omens, after all. Kalameshli would want to see the trophy that he would offer to the Wolf. The course of the next year would thus be decided.

She felt badly in need of omens.

The hunters would be returning down the northern approach. The Wolves built no roads, and yet the arrangement of the smaller mounds about the chief's own formed a rough cross, guided by alignments of the stars and the wisdom of the priests. If she hid herself in the narrow, earth-smelling gap left between this hut's sagging roof and the ground, she could watch the hunters return, and even hear what they said. Let her fellows run and fight and chase each other about like chickens.

Perhaps the old priest already had a presentiment that all was not as it should be, for he was coming down from the hill, descending the earthen ramp with care. 'Stone River, the Wolf runs beside you,' Kalameshli called out, but Maniye could hear the concern in his voice, his words almost a question.

Akrit Stone River was at the head of the pack, and Maniye felt that emptiness in her chest that she had grown used to when looking on her father. There was no love in her for him, any more than there was any in his breast for her. And yet, and yet . . . despite every blow and curse and frown, still that gap persisted, the hollow space where she was wretchedly aware *something* should dwell. *I cannot love my father*, she told herself almost every day, and yet, and yet . . .

14

Akrit picked up his pace and drew ahead of the others, loping over to the old man's side.

'Where is the trophy?' Maniye heard Kalameshli hiss. None of the hunters was bearing the antlers of a kill.

'The quarry was a coward in the end,' Akrit rumbled. 'Their greatest warrior? Either the White Tails are sick to death or they hold out on us. Whichever, they're due a reminder of whose Shadow they dwell in.'

'But . . .' She could imagine the priest's face suddenly gripped with alarm. 'No trophy . . . the omens.' A pause. 'Or something else to burn in the Wolf's jaws?'

Maniye went cold all of a sudden, the priest's fear and ire no longer a cause for amusement. *The Tests* . . . Had Kalameshli foreseen this? Had the Wolf whispered to him that a sacrifice would be needed from within the pack? Or had he already decided that she was *not* of the pack, after all?

'Oh, we have something more than that,' her father declared, sounding too jovial for a man who had come back from the hunt empty-handed. 'Smiles, show Kalameshli Takes Iron what we found creeping through the Wolf's Shadow.'

Smiles Without Teeth, her father's keenest bully-boy, shouldered forwards, dragging a stranger in his wake.

Maniye stared: she had never seen the like. The captive was older than Kalameshli, and completely bald, his neck scrawny as a turkey's, his limbs thin like sticks. He had a hooked nose and deep-set eyes, and if only he had been dressed for it, and walking free, she thought he would look like a sorcerer should. His robe was ragged and patched, though, and his skin was dirty, and beneath that so pale it seemed almost translucent. Shifting forwards, she could see the veins in his forehead, above the mottled blue-black bruise someone had given him. His hands were tied behind him and, of course, a knotted rope was about his neck.

'What do we have here, do you think?' Kalameshli asked thoughtfully.

15

'Snake,' Akrit spat. 'A Snake that dares the Wolf. Well, you've found the Wolf now, Snake. You've found his very den.'

The wretched old man bared his teeth – and Maniye was disappointed to see that they were just teeth, after all, and not the hollow fangs of his namesake. 'You do not dare raise a hand against a priest!' he hissed. 'Ill fortune will dog you all to your graves!'

Some of the hunters were hanging back – everyone knew that to harm a priest was to invite disaster – but Smiles Without Teeth slapped the man across the back of his bald head and drove him to his knees.

'We've seen your kind before, up from the south,' Akrit snarled. 'All Snakes say they're priests, every one. It can't be *all*, so none of you are. But you are come just in time for the Wolf, old man. You are very welcome by the Wolf. Until we found you, I feared his jaws would go empty. Now your thin carcass shall roast within them. How will the Wolf like that, Takes Iron?'

Kalameshli considered the scrawny old man thoughtfully. 'He shall like it very well, I feel. It is right that the Wolf should devour the Snake's get, wherever he shall find them.'

The captive hissed suddenly, driving most of the hunters a step or two back. 'If you do not release me, I shall lay the Serpent's Curse on you all! I shall have your crops wither in the fields, your children in their mothers' wombs. There shall be no strike of misfortune under your Shadow but you shall see my hand in it!'

'Gag him!' Akrit snapped, and Smiles gripped the old man's jaw, forcing it shut, and then shook him when he still wouldn't be silent.

'Something more, I think,' Kalameshli decided, businesslike now. 'The venom of the Snake is legendary, but it cannot bite if it has no fangs. Bring him to the forge and I shall fetch my smallest hammer.'

The captive's eyes widened in alarm, but Smiles Without Teeth was already wrestling him towards Kalameshli's domain, where the magic of iron was made, while hunters went whooping off ahead of him to call for the priest's tools.

Maniye watched them go, finding that she did not share their enthusiasm. The old man had been weak and thin, it was true, but he had been something new just for a moment. He had been her own omen, promising change in the year to come, a reversal of her fortunes. Now they would destroy him, as they destroyed everything, and so everything would go on just the same.

She did not want to watch, and returned to her hidden hole as the shrieks and screams started, Kalameshli Takes Iron methodically smashing out every remaining tooth in the old Snake's head. *Because what is a Snake without fangs?*

But one thought would not leave her. Her people – or those truly of her people – were born in the Jaws of the Wolf, they said. It was to prove this birthright that the Testing happened. The Eyriemen were born under the Wings of the Hawk, and the children of the Boar between his Tusks. So it went that each of the People had their sign and their badge that marked them out as who they were.

But nobody ever spoke of the Jaws of the Snake. Kalameshli had made a mistake, she realized, and the very thought of it sent a shock of hope through her. *In the Coils of the Snake, that is the saying. Better break all his bones, priest, or you may find he does not go quite so easily to his death.*

2

There were many wolves in Maniye's world. Out beyond the extent of mound and field, the lean grey beasts, her mute kin, coursed between the trees. They hunted and bred, and everyone she knew would one day go to join them, just as, in time, their spirits would be reborn to human mothers of the Wolf tribes. They were kin and yet they were the enemy, too. They raided the herds and they culled the weak, devoted to making the lives of men harder, so that the people themselves became harder, fiercer, swifter. That was the way of the world, and that was the way of the Wolf. Maniye could not help feeling a jab of pride at knowing that her father's kin ruled the Crown of the World almost undisputed, while the people of the Deer and Boar paid tribute.

There was also the wolf that ran in the sky, he who had slunk into the night above at the start of fall, lean and hungry and written in stars. He was chasing the herds out of the heavens, and soon he would hunt the cold winter skies, prowling above his people each night until he sniffed out the approaching spring and brought back life to the growing earth, laying it at their feet like a trophy.

Then there was Wolf whose people she was born to: Winter Runner, Moon Eater, Many Mouths and the other tribes within the Jaws of the Wolf, who were masters of the world. Wolf was a harsh god, but no harsher than life itself. He pushed his people, howling in the cold nights and sending them hardship, famine and enemies to fight. He taught them that together they were stronger than any of them could be alone. And, when they triumphed, as they had triumphed, Wolf was proud of them. Kalameshli himself said so and, for the Winter Runners, Kalameshli was the very voice of the Wolf.

For Maniye, the Wolf was breathing down her neck. She could not know how it was for her peers, those others of the tribe for whom a place within those jaws meant security and belonging. For her, the Wolf was with her everywhere: the one set of eyes she could not evade. Wolf was not proud of her; instead, he sniffed dubiously at her tracks. She could almost hear his low, suspicious growl as he lifted his head from them.

Not one of mine, the Wolf reproached her, as she crouched in her jealously guarded alcove above the hall. *You skulk like a coyote. You hide like prey.* Below them was all the bustle of a meal being prepared: Akrit's wives and kinfolk readying a feast for the returned hunters, who had brought back not a span of antlers but a true sacrifice for Wolf's endless hunger.

'I am yours,' she tried to tell the darkness. 'I am Akrit's get. I am born between the Jaws of the Wolf.' But even to her, the words sounded false. She was Wolf but she was also Other, and she had not let go of that part of her birthright. It would be like cutting away a limb.

The Testing comes soon, came the Wolf's dark chuckle. *We will see then how much of mine you are.* She felt his hot, rank breath. If she closed her eyes and reached out a hand, she could have touched those yellow fangs, each longer than her arm: Wolf – the true Wolf from whom all lesser wolves derived. He was vast, as large as the sky, as deep as the darkness between trees at midwinter. And yet he fit everywhere, even in this little hidey-hole she had dug for herself. There was no escaping him.

She did not know if others heard Wolf as she did. Kalameshli must, of course, but he was a priest and trained to it. She had a horrible suspicion that she was alone in this fearful communion,

19

because, of all the youths who were due to be Tested soon, only she was doubted. The Wolf had a keen nose for weakness.

Her makeshift window beckoned. Impossible, of course, that either girl or wolf could escape the hall by that means, but she would go nonetheless. Not yet, for she would be looked for at her father's elbow while he ate, obliged to hear the story of how he caught the Snake – a serpent that would grow longer and more venomous with each telling. She would sit there in an oval of perhaps fifty people, her father's kin and his favourite hunters and their closest family, and she would sense the presence of that other for whom no place was laid. The Wolf would watch his people eat, and prowl about the edge of their firelight. The rustle of his coat would speak of the advent of winter, and warn each one of them to do their part in staving off the worst of the season ahead: mend, stitch, gather, trap, trade, raid, each of them a part of the greater living thing that was their pack, their tribe. Then the Wolf would pause in its stalking, its furnace breath hot in her hair. *But what is this, and what use is it? Is it anything more than a mouthful?*

She would endure. She had always endured. Child of a murdered mother and an uncaring father, constantly under Kalameshli's barbed attention and the mockery of her peers, she had yet survived. She had built a secret life away from them: inside her head and in all the little spaces left vacant day to day, season to season. She had sometimes felt she was more Rat than Wolf. Once, when she was eight, she had even tried to build a tiny altar of vermin bones, an unthinkable act of heresy and rebellion. Then she had felt something move in the dark – not Wolf's familiar menace but something else, unclean and scuttling, and she had scattered the little bones and never done such a foolish thing again.

After the meal tonight, when she could escape the scrutiny of everyone save for Wolf himself, she would retreat up here, and once the cold dark had set in, and the chamber below was a carpet of sleeping bodies, she would make her secret way out and go hunting. Because, however wretched, dirty and washed-out the old man had seemed, there was something new in the world this night, and soon enough it would be taken away from her by Kalameshli's iron knife, by Wolf's fire-heated jaws. Before then she would speak to the Snake.

Let the Eyriemen talk about the might of the open sky, its storms and keening wings. Let the Deer and Boar tribes talk of the growing earth. Wolf was winter, which meant at the same time that Wolf was fire. Fire was ever hungry, so was Wolf; fire was life and death in one, so was Wolf. Fire had secrets; fire was a magic stolen from the sun by that star-coated wolf up in the heavens.

Kalameshli paused in his hammering, noting the results were good. He was old, and three young men had learned the secrets of fire from him to carry on his work. Yet he was still strong. A life of hammer and knife would do that for you.

His mind was full of calculations, counting the time of his hammer blows, but also counting forwards: the days until the Horse Society arrived to trade; his stock of new-made tools, the knives and axe-heads his apprentices had sweated over, that were so very valuable to barter with. It all seemed meagre, but then it always did and there was never enough to trade for everything the tribe would need, and they would make do. Wolf never stopped testing his people: Kalameshli had run alongside him long enough to know that.

Then there was their stock of the sacred wood, which was dwindling, and there would be precious little opportunity to get some more unless he traded his finished iron for it with another priest. The workers and the slaves who had been out in the forest felling and burning all summer were back now, yet surely they had brought in more than this last year? *Is it because I'm old, that nothing seems as good as it was, or are the years really getting harder?*

The omens last year had been adequate. Running Deer had given Akrit's people a decent chase and died in the proper form, so that his antlers had graced Wolf's jaws and the quarry's spirit had returned to the herd. The rack itself had not been of the best, but Kalameshli had seen cautious hope there. Now he wondered if he had fallen victim to complacency. What was Wolf telling him this year, with the remarkable sacrifice that had fallen into his hands?

Change. The forge's hot breath was the breath of the Wolf. In Kalameshli's great-great-grandfather's time, before ever the Winter Runners had come to these lands, Wolf had spoken secrets to his people, to reward them for their sacrifices, their perseverance, their refusal to bow the head despite living in the shadow of other tribes. Wolf had spoken of how to make the wolf-wood from normal wood, by the long, slow burning and his careful breath. Wolf had spoken of how the fierce heat of burning wolf-wood could draw iron from the red stone, and how it could turn soft iron into hard. All these things had become known over generations, but by Kalameshli's grandfather's time the bond between Wolf and priest and the secrets of iron was forged and closed.

In Kalameshli's grandfather's time, the Winter Runners had come south to challenge the masters of these lands. At first they had fought against the Tiger alongside Deer and Boar. Later, when they had carved out space for the Wolf's Shadow, they had shown those people their new masters. And while the Wolf might be a hard master, still he was not wantonly cruel as the previous lords had been.

In Kalameshli's own time, five times five years ago, when he had been younger and Akrit had been very young, they had warred with those old lords – the Shadow Eaters who were born between the Claws of the Tiger. Village by village, valley by valley, they had driven them back, their hard iron pitted against bronze and stone, their swift packs against the enemy's strong champions. The war had been fought by the Winter Runners here, by other Wolf tribes north and south, each summer seeing

22

a new offensive, new victories for the Wolf, new sacrifices for his iron teeth.

But there had been peace for a long time now. The Tiger had retreated to the high eastern places, its power shattered. The Deer and Boar accepted the yoke and sent tribute and thralls and workers to make the Wolf stronger. Life had been good.

That was the problem, Kalameshli guessed. A comfortable life was a weakening one. Now the Wolf sent them this message: *change or die*. When he came to read the future in the old Snake's guts, perhaps the omens would show that it was time for the Wolf to go to war once more.

Of course his predictions would be tempered by his own knowledge, for the *girl* was almost grown now, sullen and contrary creature that she was. Akrit's long-held plans for her could be put into action, which would indeed mean more war to extend the Wolf's Shadow into new lands. Odd how these things so often worked out.

But there was the matter of the Testing. The girl thought she was so clever, the way she slunk about the mound, appearing and disappearing as the whim took her. She thought she could keep secrets, but Kalameshli had keen eyes and a sharp nose. He knew precisely what she was about, and the direction her Stepping had taken her.

If she was to be any use to Akrit at all, then she must remain securely within the Wolf's jaws. Kalameshli had taken upon himself the responsibility of ensuring that this particularly lengthy forging could be plucked from the fire and put to work, and he would do so no matter how hard he had to hammer at the girl, to beat her into shape.

The meal was a fierce affair, each of Akrit's hunters striving to outdo the last with their stories of the chase. Nobody seemed to remember that the whole endeavour had ended in cowardice and failure, and yet nobody was boasting about the Snake much either. Maniye said nothing, because she had learned long before that drawing attention to herself always ended in pain or humiliation. She sat in her father's shadow, at his jostling elbow, and ate with a grim determination as though every mouthful might be taken away from her. As it might, of course, if she made Akrit angry. Just the sight of her seemed to do that, and she thought it was because he had sired no brothers for her, meaning she was all he had. He had not intended her as a successor, she knew: no get of her mother's would ever become strong within the Winter Runners. That was why, once Maniye had been born into this half-life, he had sent Broken Axe to rid the world of his captive wife.

Even the chief's household ate sparingly. Whatever excess the year had gifted them was being saved for the grand feast that would follow after the Testing. Then the tribe would devour everything that would not last through the winter, slaughter the animals that could not be fed, and eat fresh any meat that could not be salted. Preparations were already under way, she knew. Like so much else, it fell to Kalameshli to determine what was to be the Wolf's share, to be eaten now, and what would be set down for the cold months before the spring. He had already been making a round of the herds, the sheep and cattle, marking animals for the slaughter with his brand and scratching tallies into a flat stone. It was magic, Maniye knew: the Wolf's secrets taught only to those who had been chosen for the priesthood. At the same time, she had spied on Kalameshli for some years now, and she understood distantly that the marks he made were counting, numbers that existed outside of his head. The revelation, which had come to her last year in a muddled dream after a day's covert trailing of the priest, made the business seem at once both more and less magical.

Even now, Kalameshli's mind was at work. In between long spaces of careful chewing, being an old man solicitous of his teeth, he would murmur remarks to Akrit. Maniye caught mention of numbers, of beasts, of tribute, of the expected Horse Society travellers, and how much salt they might have for trade, or whether there were Coyote packmen nearby who would have some to offer. In times like these, when his mind was solely on the future of his people, she almost forgot how much she hated him. Then his cold eyes would flick sideways towards her, behind her father's back, and they would harden like stones.

They made a contrasting pair, Akrit and Kalameshli. The priest was much older, a spare, sinewy creature with five decades on him. He was a man much like the iron he worked, still strong but no longer flexible. In the heat of the hall he had stripped down to a woollen shirt worn open down the front, and Maniye could see his chest and belly, snarled with wiry grey hair, sagging just a little and criss-crossed by a few old scars.

Her father was also no longer young – and for pure spite she counted daily the inroads that time had made on him. His dark hair and beard were streaked with grey, and his face, broad and high-cheekboned like all of their kin, was creased now, the lines of his ill temper engraved deep enough that they could not be smoothed out. He was a big man, though, and burly, still the equal of any of his followers save perhaps Smiles Without Teeth, who had no ambition in him at all.

Stripped to the waist, Akrit's history was laid bare. He had fought to become chief fifteen years ago, and then fought off a handful of challengers in those earlier years, and the marks of each fight were still on him. There had been the war, too, when, as a young warrior and then a chief, he had led the Winter Runners against her mother's people and defeated them, banding with the other Wolf tribes to drive them north and east into the highlands. He had won a few more scars then, from blade and claw both, but neither challenge nor conflict had managed to topple Akrit Stone River in all the years of Maniye's life.

The hearth-keepers, those women and men who stayed behind to cook and clean and mend, passed about the hall serving and bringing yam beer, milk and mead. The hunters ate and talked, and the children ran madly back and forth, re-enacting the hunt, taking it in turns to put their hands to their brow and pretend to be Running Deer.

And Maniye let her eyes stray thoughtfully to Kalameshli again, and saw exactly the same pensive expression on his face that she had expected. He would be thinking of his sacrifice and wondering how Wolf would receive it.

The thought that perhaps the scrawny old creature might not find favour – that Wolf's displeasure might light on Kalameshli and her father – was almost reason to let the business go ahead and just watch. She hid the thought away for later like a strip of stolen meat. It was always an option.

But first she wanted to see him, this old Serpent man who had emerged from the stories and the south. This *something new* that had come into her life.

Then Kalameshli met her gaze and, without saying a word, he had put their whole past conversation back into the front of her mind. *Remember the Testing*, he seemed to say to her. *I am waiting for you to fail.*

As soon as she could slink away, she retreated to her make-shift cave nestling up against the roof and waited for the talk below to subside. Gradually hunters went off to their own hearths, while Akrit's wives and his thralls cleared away the platters and the furs. She saw the fires begin to gutter, that would bleed out their warmth over the course of the night and be embers by dawn.

At last, she could hear nobody awake within the hall, merely the ocean-murmur of sleeping breath. Below her, Akrit and his wives would sleep, their slumber curtained off from the rest of the hall. In the other half of the space, the thralls – and a handful of young hunters who had no mate or hearth of their own – would lie clustered around the failing fire.

Was Kalameshli standing down there amongst them, waiting for her to make her move? Or was he prowling the outside of the wall, a sleek grey shadow far swifter on four paws than on his two old human feet? If so, she would have to out-dance him.

She would have to trust to her own speed and stealth – to the gifts of her mother.

Maniye was small for her age, just as Kalameshli had insinuated when speaking of tracks: a skinny, bony girl half a head shorter than any of her peers. As a wolf, she was smaller still. It was not just for the view that she had scrabbled and scratched out the edges of her little window. Now she hooked her hands over the sill, feeling the uneven mess of mud and sticks that she had gouged into. She put her head out into the chill of the night air.

All was quiet out in the world, save for the faraway, lonely call that was some distant speechless kin of hers, lost to the human world and living the Wolf dream.

She ducked back inside, because she might as well make this a test of her abilities while she was at it. Beneath a tatty deerskin she kept a tiny stash of objects that she practised with, and now she dug them out and cupped them in her hands.

A bone fish-hook, a tiny wooden deer that had been a toy for her when she was young, a stone arrowhead, a bead of bronze.

She thrust her head out through the gap again, into the open air, twisting to make it fit. Her shoulders tried to follow but, narrow as they were, they were yet too broad.

She Stepped, making the shift of her form as slow and controlled as she could. Most of her peers would try to shift in an eye-blink, and so could she if she had to, but they all too often lost their footing or ended up on their backs with the sudden change of perspective and balance. Right now, she had no wish to fall.

The change rippled through her from her nose backwards, her bones and flesh and skin flurrying into new alignments, skull lengthening into a snout, ears stretching to points, shoulders shrinking in, body longer, legs shorter, a tail springing out from the end of her spine and a glossy dark coat eating up her tan skin and her deer-hide shift, swallowing the garment into her, *inhering* it so that her wolf's skin was just that little bit tougher than some unclad wild cousin's.

Her hands swallowed her fingers, bunching them into clawed pads resting on the edge of the hole. She concentrated fiercely on their contents, feeling the hook vanish into her, the wooden toy likewise. For a moment the arrowhead was slippery within her mind, on the point of falling from her shrinking grip, but then she had that as part of her too, the flint, the substance of the natural earth, finding an invisible home within her body.

Her wolf ears heard the rattle as the bead struck the floor, beyond her reach. Bronze was inherently unnatural, and to become sufficiently attuned to the metal to make it a part of her would be a long, hard labour.

She did not even want to think about *iron*. Learning to become iron's kin, to make it a part of oneself, was the secret of priests. Those young hunters and warriors who walked that path were put through agonies, her peers said. The Testing of the young was nothing compared to the ordeal of carrying iron.

And now it was time for her to be gone. She took in a deep breath through her nose, her mind inflamed by the sudden intensity of her senses. Her eyes were more apt for darkness, even if they were otherwise something less than those of a human, and her ears, her nose, every hair of her now flooded her with a world of new sensations.

If Kalameshli was lurking out there, she hoped that she would sniff him out. There was no trace of him, and so she pushed at the floor beneath her and wormed her lithe way out into the open air.

Moments later she was dropping down the outside of the hall, a primal fear leaping and yelping inside her, but she was ready for it, and in a heartbeat she had Stepped again, not to her skinny little human body but to her other birthright.

What skidded to a precarious halt at the base of the wall, staring face-down along the steep side of the mound, was a different beast altogether. Maniye had just Stepped from her father's tribe to her mother's.

Her tiger's eyes were better still for moonlight, harvesting every shred of silver light, so that the great cross that was the Winter Runner village stood out almost plain as day. Her claws were dug into the wattle and daub of the wall itself, for a tiger – especially such a small tiger as she made – could climb and cling where a wolf would only fall.

Her nose as a tiger was not so keen, but she still trusted her senses, and she could steal downwards, pad by pad, in utter silence. If there was anyone abroad, they would not know that the very image of their old enemies walked amongst them.

The 'Fire Shadow People', they called her mother's tribe, among other, harsher things. She passed from darkness to open moonlight and back into the dark, the changing light rippling along her striped back, and it would have taken eyes as keen as her own to discern her.

Her mother had been great amongst the Tiger, defeated and captured in the last battles between her people and the upstart Wolves who had come to rob her of her lands and subjects. Now Maniye was both the Tiger child and the Wolf chief's daughter, and soon enough she would have to cast off one form forever. Everyone knew that a halfblood could not hold to both heritages at once. That was what Kalameshli had been warning her of: choose the Jaws of the Wolf, not the Claws of the Cat, or she would be Akrit Stone River's daughter no longer. And, as much as the prospect appealed, that would make her the enemy. That would turn her into prey.

And yet she did not want to choose. She had lived the world on a wolf's swift paws, drunk the wind with its nose, seen the night through a cat's mirror eyes, danced up trees and sheer walls with its fluid grace. Each of these was equally a part of her. To choose one over the other would be like being asked to choose her left hand over her right, and then to hack the other away.

She knew where the sacrifice was being kept: there was a pit overlooked by the temple mound. Kalameshli would not have left the prisoner entirely unobserved, but Maniye guessed that the watchers would not be over-vigilant. The wretched old man would be secured, after all, so where would he go?

Sure enough, a couple of youths were pitched under a canopy, ostensibly watching the pit but, when she slunk close, she found one asleep and the other huddled close to the fire, feeding it twigs and trying to shield it from a biting wind that was just beginning to rise. If either had Stepped into their wolf forms then they might have smelled her out, but they were no older than she, and could probably not stay in their wolf skin for long.

That was the greatest lesson of Stepping, and it had come to Maniye very swiftly indeed. Standing on four paws, her body taut with a tiger's graceful strength, she did not think *I am a girl in the shape of a tiger,* any more than she had thought of herself as merely wearing a wolf's borrowed skin. She *was* the tiger. She *was* the wolf. That was the lesson everyone must learn eventually. Born a babe within the village or a cub in the forest, they were one and the same. Man became animal, animal became man. Each soul ran on two feet and four. Before she had quickened in her mother's womb she had been a beast of the wilds.

But which beast? Supposedly she should know by now – one form or the other should call louder to her and tell her where her soul belonged – but all she knew was that she was a child of three shapes, and could Step between them as naturally as thought.

The young hunters noticed nothing of her as she crept to the mouth of the pit and looked down.

The old man seemed to be sleeping, lying bunched up on his side, bony knees drawn up almost to his chin. She could see the dark stains about his mouth where his ravaged gums had bled after Kalameshli's ministrations. His hands were secured to an iron peg driven deep into the ground, and there was a rope halter about his neck to prevent him Stepping.

He looked so pale, so alien. His features were strange: a knobbly pointed chin, long face, broad nose, the taut skin of his hairless head hiding nothing of the shape of his skull. He had some sort of painting or tattooing about his cheeks and forehead, but she could not make it out.

His eyes opened, staring up at her. She froze, knowing that it was dark and that surely he, with his mere human gaze, would see nothing.

He saw her. She felt that shock of contact. Somehow he had found her, a shadow bitten into the circle of stars that was all they had left him of the sky.

Abruptly she was very frightened of him, however helpless he was. The strangeness of him, that had seemed such a good omen, was now a threat just by its very presence. She backed away, changing her mind. She did not want to talk to the Snake man. She did not want her life to change. She would return to her close-walled sanctum. She would strive to pass the Testing. Life would go on.

She retreated from the pit into the shadow of the temple mound, feeling the great weight up above that was the Wolf and its idol, all ready for the sacrifice. Sitting there, she Stepped back to the human, feeling the sharp cold through her shift, that had barely bothered her tiger self. In her hand were the hook, the toy, the arrowhead, conjured back from that inner place she had sent them.

She felt disappointed with herself, and yet relieved. She would go back. She would find the wolf within her, pad back to the foot of her father the chief's mound and howl to be let in. She must forget her tiger. She must cut it away.

Movement caught her eye: a solitary figure walking one of the long thoroughfares into the village: a tall, lean man with a deerskin cloak about his shoulders. *Familiar:* she knew that walk and it terrified her.

Kalameshli Takes Iron she loathed; Akrit Stone River, her father, she hated; but the man she *feared* was Broken Axe. He was not even one of the tribe's hunters: a wolf who walked alone, save when Akrit summoned him. Most years, as the nights grew long, he drifted in to find shelter from the cold with the Winter Runners. But Broken Axe was a lone wolf, a law unto himself.

Somehow, she had convinced herself that she would not see him this winter, but here he was, trailing into the village unlooked for, past midnight.

He was a tall, long-limbed man with narrow eyes and a broken nose, and if he had ever cared to challenge her father, then he could have been chief of the Winter Runners. Everyone knew, but nobody said, that he was the one man Akrit Stone River might fear. Broken Axe gave him no cause, though. He showed no signs of seeking to lead, and when Akrit had a task for him, no matter what, he named his price and performed it, without fail.

Such as killing Maniye's mother.

This was the same man. When the Tiger had given up a child into the world for Akrit's purposes, when the screaming and the spitting of the birth was done, this was the man who had taken her into the woods and murdered her. When no other would do it – Akrit would not invite ill luck by bloodying his own hands over the mother of his child, and Maniye had heard her mother was a priestess too, always bad fortune to kill – it fell to Broken Axe to carry out the sentence. He had done it without qualm or question, just as always. Everyone said there was something missing in Broken Axe, who feared no curse nor what any might think of him. He was hard as stone and iron together.

And here he was, and he would sit by Kalameshli and drink Akrit's beer, and his eyes would stray to Maniye, as they always did, as though comparing her growing face and form to his memories of the woman he had slain.

Abruptly she was a tiger again, without choosing it, and padding back towards the pit and its lonely occupant.

3

The history of the Crown of the World was a chronicle of the harsh land and brittle winters that either hardened the people there like old leather or drove them out. Winter Runners, Cave Dwellers, Shadow Eaters, Eyriemen, each had seized its chance to rule the rest, risen to its prime then fallen in turn. The Wolf were strongest now, but the Crown of the World was a mutinous kingdom. No tribe had ever mastered it for long.

In the Riverlands of the south they told a different story, about building and growth. The Sun River Nation, that had once been just an idea in the heads of a handful of River Lord chieftains, had pushed its own borders steadily eastwards along the banks of the Tsotec. All the other tribes had knelt before them, not destroyed or exiled but consumed with the voracity of the River Lords' own gluttonous totem, to be made a part of the body of the Sun River Nation that stretched out its length along the river.

That part of the river that was the Nation's heartland was known as the head of the Tsotec, with the fragmented islands of the estuary forming the teeth in her jaws. Above the falls that framed the River Lords' great city of Atahlan, where the river turned northwards and began gathering in its tributaries, this was the Tsotec's back – rough and uneven and cutting into the side of the Plains before her many tails split into the rivers and lakes and thousand streams of the Crown of the World.

On the back of the Tsotec, heading from the endless summer of the Riverlands north to where winter was already gathering, three boats moved. Long and narrow, hide stretched around wooden spars, they were sturdy enough to forge through the current with the sweat of their oarsmen, light enough to be carried over rapids and past falls where need be, and held steady in the water each by their single outrigger. These were the canoes of the Horse Society, though they were seldom found heading north into the teeth of the cold at this time of year. Most of their brethren in the Crown of the World would already be ferrying their rafts of timber back south, loaded with whatever goods and raw materials they had been able to barter for. These three boats did not carry traders, though, but passengers. Amidst the Horse people were two men of the south: Asmander and Venater. The one was an earth-dark River Lord youth with an easy smile, the other a burly, villainous-looking estuary man, far from home.

'The Horse people are saying bad things about you, because you will not row,' Asmander remarked. 'They say you cannot have been such a pirate as you tell them, if you will not set hand to oar.' He was bare-chested, beaded with sweat from his stint, dashing himself with river water before pulling on his thin tunic.

Venater eyed him balefully. 'I didn't see you accomplishing much.'

'I did enough to assuage my honour.' Their boat shifted as it ground its keel in the shallows; some of the Horse Society jumped out to steady it and haul it to land. Asmander let himself over the side, plunging to his waist in water that was blessedly cool after the long, hot journey north up the back of the Tsotec. He put his shoulder to the vessel's side with the assured joy of a man who didn't have to, and could stop doing so any time he liked.

Venater crouched beside him, not even bothering to get out, let alone put his prodigious strength to any use. 'Well, boy, your father has my honour by the balls, and until he looses his grip I'll be pissed on before I do anything for mere honour.'

'I don't believe you.' Asmander was gritting his teeth at the effort, but he was grinning around it. 'And I can see that me doing this work is eating you up: the soft young boy of the River Lords callousing his hands! Unheard of! Plainly this world is upside-down and mad.' He was tall and lean, with the dark, dark skin of all the River Lords, his hair cropped short save for a knot of it gathered at the base of his skull. His features were a good battleground for his customary expressions: amusement, mischief, melancholy. They had won him many hearts back home – he was a man who could have been married three times over, had he ever got round to returning any of his suitors' sentiments. He was the blade of his family, though, and wielded always – as now – to further the ambitions of his father. Dalliances and ready smiles were never allowed to turn into anything more serious. Asmander carried responsibilities.

'If those Horse girls didn't make eyes at you so much, you'd not care,' Venater snarled. 'Show off for them all you like.'

'They're not my type.' Asmander stepped back, clapping his hands together at a job well done. All three Horse craft were beached safely now on this foreign shore.

Three days before, they had left the northern edge of the Sun River Nation behind, no matter how optimistically one drew the maps. Since the river had taken them northwards, the land to the west had soared steeply away, rising to the heights that were the Stone Kingdoms. To the east lay the Plains, green where the land met the river, but so much of it uncultivated, where in the south there would be fields and irrigation canals to wring the absolute most out of every hand's breadth of soil. Here in the drier lands the people were fierce and unfriendly, that much was known. They held and tilled only the land around their villages, because anything beyond that was simply setting out a meal for raiders from other tribes. They fought each other incessantly, held no oaths sacred, followed gods who valued nothing but blood, and ate each other's children for preference. Or so it was said amongst the River Lords.

Asmander knew full well that his own people's gods were also partial to their ration of blood. If Old Crocodile liked his sacrifices to be public and ritualized, that still left the offerings just as dead as some heart-ripping festival of the Plains people. He was a young man cynical beyond his years, who could smile at a great many things that others held terribly solemn. He knew that above all the gods and totems of the world there was one great and controlling spirit, and it was named Expediency. Honour was all very well – and something he pursued incessantly – and yet he was sourly aware that if one refused Expediency its necessary sacrifices, then the goodwill of every other god, never mind all the honour in the world, would get you nowhere.

At last Venater deigned to step ashore, getting no more than his bare feet wet. He was a broad-shouldered creature, a man of close on twice Asmander's age. A skin the colour of wet sand was scarred by innumerable fights, then scarred again by the deliberate tallies of deeds his people kept, an intricate and secret history of murder, raid and private brawl written in jagged weals down the broad canvas of his upper arms. He wore his hair long and unkempt, framing a lantern jaw, hollow eyes hard like flint, a nose broken more than once.

One of the Horse Society passed them by as they stood on the bank. 'We must make a good showing for the Laughing Men,' he told them.

Looking at the Horse delegation, Asmander decided 'a good showing' consisted of prominently displayed weapons.

'Why are we even bothering?' Venater growled. 'Your father is sending us off to die in the north, not at the hands of these scum.'

'He is not sending us to *die* anywhere,' Asmander reproached. 'And we bother because the Horse trade here, and they must keep the locals happy. And, if we want to get any further north than this place, we must do as we're asked.'

The two of them were travelling light: easier to ship River Nation coin than to clog the boat with everything they might need. Both were warriors, though, and when the Laughing Men came down to the riverbank, they found in the two southerners as martial a display as they could ask for. Asmander had donned a quilted tunic, with a plate of flat stone sewn into each pocket to make it hard armour. A stone-toothed wooden sword – the *maccan* of the River People – dangled from a strap at one wrist, and there were jade spurs at his ankles.

Venater was already wearing a coat of sharkskin, which made him a fearsome opponent to grapple and an unpleasant figure to sit next to in the close confines of a boat. Bracers of tortoiseshell covered his forearms and the backs of his hands, and his weapon was the *meret*, the blade-edged club of greenstone which he kept thrust through the cord of his belt. His stance suggested that he would be only too glad if the Horse diplomacy turned sour.

The locals – the Laughing Men – were already making themselves known, sloping down the riverbank with an insolent disdain. They were all on four feet, and Asmander knew that arriving Stepped to a first meeting was common amongst the Plains people. It hid what weapons they might be carrying, locked within those lean-flanked animal forms. He could see the glint of bronze in their teeth, but there was no way to know if they might suddenly leap into human form with arrows leaving the string or spears taking to the air. Also, he had to admit, they were an intimidating sight.

'Pretty lot, aren't they?' Venater growled. Probably he was wondering about fighting them. Fighting people was, to Asmander's certain knowledge, one of the few subjects that really occupied the older man's mind. Travelling with him was like walking under a sky constantly about to storm: human mind and beast soul united in perfect bloody-handed harmony.

These things are known: you list his good points, Asmander told himself, with a slight smile.

The shapes the Laughing Men took were not like lions, nor like dogs, but some distant cousin of both, or neither. The largest had shoulders that would rise to the hollow beneath Asmander's

37

ribs, and the least of them would come up to his waist. They were made oddly, forequarters broadly muscled, and front limbs longer than the rear. A crest of hair ran down their spines and their pelts were tawny and spotted with ragged patches of black. Their heads were vulpine, heavy-jawed, with baleful dark eyes. When they yawned, they showed a nest of dagger teeth that would give even a River Lord pause. As they approached, one or another would let out a weird cackle unpleasantly close to a human laugh.

By standing there as they were, with all their weapons on display, the Horse were signalling that they came without deceit. Asmander wondered idly if that would work with these ferocious-looking creatures. There were few who lived along the head of the Tsotec who had any kind words for the Plains tribes, although perhaps that was just because the only examples that came their way tended to be raiding parties.

For a moment, while the Horse stood firm, the Laughing Men coursed around them, sniffing and heckling, thrusting their noses at their visitors and baring their fangs in disconcerting grins. Then they had drawn off a little, though still in a loose crescent that penned their visitors against the water.

They Stepped lazily, seeming to stretch out into human form as though waking from dreams of blood and carrion. There were more women amongst them than men, Asmander saw, and certainly it was the women who had made the larger beasts. They had the long limbs and spare frames of the Plains people, and that skin like bright copper. The men had heads shaved to the scalp, but the women just cut theirs at the sides and sported coxcomb manes dyed in patterns of gold and black and red. There was a lot of metal worn at necks and wrists and ankles: copper, bronze and gold set into plates of bone and horn.

Many of the women had armour of stiff cotton panels, though the men wore no more than loincloths and cloaks of hide. Long-headed spears and javelins were much in evidence, and Asmander could sense Venater tensing, readying himself for a fight much as another man's mouth might fill with saliva at the scent of food.

'Are we not welcome?' The Horse people's Hetman, Eshmïr, spread her hands. She was the only one amongst the visitors not armed at all. 'Perhaps your Malikah may wish some talk with us – or with these, our guests?'

The leader of the Laughing Men, the oldest-looking of the women there whose skin bore the memories of many fights, nodded easily. They all smiled readily, these Plains people. Everything seemed to amuse them, and no doubt killing these new arrivals would just make them smile more. Asmander liked that honesty about them.

'Who are these, your guests?' their leader asked.

The Hetman offered Asmander a small nod, letting him know that the Laughing Men expected visitors to speak for themselves.

'I am the First Son of Asman,' he announced. 'I am a Champion of the River Lords.' He watched their faces to see if that meant the same to them as it did to his own people, and was satisfied to see that it did: enough widened eyes and thoughtful glances there to know that they understood him. He looked to Venater, who was scowling and plainly not about to play along, leaving Asmander with the difficult job of introducing him. *He would rather I humiliate him than he has to do it to himself.* 'This man is Venater, sworn to my family.' It was the kindest way to say it, for all that he probably owed his companion no kindness. Better than, 'a notorious but ultimately failed pirate', certainly.

'A little trade, a little talk, gifts.' The Hetman displayed her open hands. 'Friendship between the Laughing Men and the Horse Society. Friendship between the Laughing Men and the friends of the Horse.'

The woman who led these Laughing Men regarded them haughtily for a moment, as though contemplating driving them back into the river. Then she laughed, and the sound was just as they had made when Stepped into their animal shapes – wild and mad. 'Come, then. The Malikah likes gifts, and her mates like trade. Friends? We shall see.'

Dwellings of the Sun River Nation tended to be at least half underground, digging into the cool earth to ward off the daily height of the sun. The village of the Laughing Men, however, was all in the earth, barely rising above the level of the ground. Although their goat and cattle pens stood out, Asmander saw little sign of an actual settlement until they were nearly upon it, and he realized that the thirty or so raised mounds of dry grass were actually roofs. They lived in pits, did the Laughing Men, a scattering of holes in the ground, secluded and sheltered, with no fear of flooding in this dry land. He thought it all looked barren and primitive, but then the Plains life was not about showing your wealth to the sky. When they had come to the biggest hut, and descended the steps carved into the packed earth, he found the area within was surprisingly spacious, three-levelled and with the largest room being the deepest. The day was ebbing, and at first Asmander was just stepping down into darkness, twitchy with a sudden sense of danger. Up above though, children were already letting down pots of flame, suspending them by ropes from the spars that supported the roof, making an elaborate constellation that cast a thousand patterns of light and shadow all about the curving walls. There were paintings there, intricate and complex: human and animal figures, abstract designs, mountains and rivers. A hundred legends had been sketched out and intermingled in bright colours around the confines of the Malikah's home.

Most of the Horse party were being hosted elsewhere. Only the Hetman, her chief trader and her two southern guests had the honour of meeting the ruler of these Laughing Men. The trader became almost immediately ensconced with a pair of the locals, falling to discussing commodities for the coming year with an ease that told Asmander that all this threat and show was a ritual path both sides had trodden many times before. It

40

was the first such sign: till then he had begun to wonder if these Plains people were sharpening their bronze knives for the throats of their guests.

The Malikah of the Laughing Men was a woman as old as Venater, and just as battle-scarred. She wore a cloak striped with many colours, and a leather headband set with the teeth of lions rested in her tawny hair. She had a fierce beauty about her, as did so many of these Plains people. Every sign of the hunt and the fight that had marked her skin only added to her sense of presence, and now she fixed Asmander with a frankly acquisitive stare.

'Champion of the River Lords,' she addressed him. 'But you are no more than a boy.'

'I am as you see me,' he replied, sitting across the floor from her. 'So young and yet a Champion.'

'Asmander, First Son of Asman. Your father must be proud.'

He kept his smile steady, although for a second it was difficult. 'The honour of our family rests in me, Malikah.'

'And so he casts it away?'

For a moment he wondered what she had been told, but no . . . she was simply fishing, dangling a paw in the water to see what she might catch. 'The cold north calls to me. I would see the snows of winter.'

Her eyes turned to his companion. 'And you must be a young man too, even with your old face. Venater,' making great play with the end of his name, that juvenile suffix, 'your father, is he proud also?'

'I am all of my house.' Venater met her gaze steadily.

'But you have found a new father in the River Lords? How kind of them.'

'I piss on the golden doorsteps of the River Lords,' the burly pirate told her.

'These things are known: he does,' Asmander confirmed wryly.

Her eyes had narrowed, but she seemed content not to peel back Venater's past any more than that. 'Men come to us from

41

the south, sometimes. Men who offer us bronze coin to fight. Do you offer us coin to fight, Champion of the Riverlands?'

'No.' An easy shrug, and he had guessed that there would be some from the Nation who had sought mercenaries here. After all, why else was he himself heading north, if not to try and tempt the fabled Iron Wolves to support his prince, his childhood friend?

As always, thinking on the man his family had sworn allegiance to, Asmander felt a point of pain as though the knife was at his own chest. His honour and his family duty were both stretched tight about the success of this mission. He only hoped that the two did not part company, or he would be like a man caught with each foot on a different boat.

Thinking on his father, he was grimly aware how honour and family seldom shared the same house these days.

Eshmir the Hetman spoke then. She was a foundling of the Horse, with the flat features and snub nose of a northerner but the ruddy skin of the Stone People, and she danced carefully through a conversation with the Malikah that elegantly checked and repaired all of the ties the Society had built here. While she spoke, the subdued, slope-shouldered men who were the Malikah's mates – or slaves, or both – passed back and forth with gourds of a liquor that made Asmander's eyes water. Venater, he saw, was putting the stuff away with gusto.

'Champion of the River Lords.' He snapped back to himself as the Malikah addressed him. 'When you return to your lands in triumph, no doubt you will lead your own house.'

'Many things are possible,' Asmander allowed.

'Before then, will you drink your fill of the women of the Crown of the World, and cause them to lament your leaving them?' She had a cruel smile on her, as she toyed with a necklace of horn and gold.

'Even this, even this is possible.'

'They are cold, up in the Crown of the World. They have no fire such as we have here.' It was plain what she was after and it was because he was a Champion, that rare and special thing. The Laughing Men had none, he had heard, but their enemies of the Lion did, and perhaps she foresaw his seed and her womb breeding a hero of the next generation. In truth, there was a power to her that was greatly attractive, as power always was, but he shook his head regretfully.

'Alas, I am sworn to my father. My loins are not my own.'

She snorted at that, and Venater muttered a snide, 'This much is known,' which made Asmander want to hit him.

'Do none of my beautiful daughters catch your eye, for just one night?' the Malikah asked him, and that made him sad for a moment. The space that was between them was not contained merely within the interior of her hut; it was the years between his youth and her age. There was no sign of it on her face, but her words showed that she felt it.

'You honour me.' The most polite of all refusals, contained in the tone and not the words, and she did not press him further.

4

To navigate the sides of the pit, Maniye Stepped to her tiger shape again, descending with the beast's agility but human fore-thought. All the while the Snake's cold eyes were fixed on her, and not a muscle of him moved. Only when she had descended to his level did she realize that she had given him a weapon against her: she had revealed her mother's shape to him, that she had hidden so assiduously from everyone she knew.

For a moment she froze, close enough to the huddled man that she could have dug her claws in him. Had he enchanted her somehow, that she had made such an error? Where had her habitual caution gone?

Then she understood: *he is dead*. She was already thinking of the Snake as a dead man, the Wolf's due. Why hide secrets from a corpse?

She stared at him challengingly. Only his eyes moved to meet hers, that and a slight shivering. His breath plumed in the night's chill.

He could not reach her with his hands, and he could not Step. He might have tried to kick her, but it would profit him nothing, and he was such a feeble, used-up-looking creature that she would hardly feel the blow: a Snake without fangs.

She fell back into her human form, Stepping to leave herself with her back up against the pit's earthen wall. The stone, wood and bone pricked at her hand, and she shoved the trinkets into the waistband of her shift.

The old man still said nothing. Close to, she was struck even more by the two sides of him: strange and pale and foreign, and yet so dirty and ragged and thin that even Coyote would call him starved.

She had a hundred questions, but what came out was, 'Are you really a southerner?'

His withered lips moved, and then he spat, not at her but at the ground, clearing his mouth of old blood. 'Compared to you,' he got out.

'I thought southerners were burnt black by the sun.' She had heard it from the Horse Society, who travelled further than anyone else she knew.

A smile's ghost brushed the corners of his mouth. Those eyes – as pale and moon-coloured as the rest of him – wrinkled a little. 'Mosht of 'em are,' he got out, fighting the words. 'I'm sh . . . sh . . .' A spasm of annoyance rippled his features, and he made the sibilant by drawing breath sharply inward across the roof of his mouth. '*Ss-pecial*.'

Something small and mean turned within her, seeing him momentarily pleased at overcoming his limitations even by that small degree. 'They're going to sacrifice you to Wolf.'

He nodded once, the smile gone.

'Do you know how they'll do it?' she pressed. 'The stone face of Wolf has iron teeth – more iron than you've ever seen. They'll tie you between his jaws and light a fire in his throat, and the teeth will get hotter and hotter until you roast in his mouth.' It felt horrible to say the words, but at the same time it was a weird release, a catharsis she could not quite pin down.

Another bleak nod, and he even managed a shrug.

She had more hurting words already crowding her mouth. She wanted to make him see the utter despair of his position and, even as she opened her mouth, she understood the petty hand that gripped her. Here was a creature lowlier than she,

45

without even the meagre freedoms of a thrall. Here finally was someone she could hurt without fear of reprisal.

She stopped the words, killed them in her throat and disowned them, and instead the two of them just stared at each other for a long while.

'What issh your name, child?' came his soft, mumbling voice.

'Maniye.' She said it without thinking. A moment later – a moment too late – she was wide-eyed with wondering whether he could work some magic on her, simply by knowing her name. Filthy and wretched as he was, surely he still had a curse or two to spare for a foolish girl who did not keep her name close.

'I am Hessprec-Esh . . .' He made a determined effort, 'Hesprec Essen Skese.'

It was a great deal of name for this dried-up stick of a man. 'Are you really a priest?'

Again that guarded nod.

'When they kill you, will you curse Kalameshli Takes Iron – our priest? Will you curse my f—the chief?'

His eyes were fixed on her, and she realized that she had not seen him blink once since she came down to join him.

'Your father, Tiger girl?'

Abruptly she was frightened of him again – even dying in the Wolf's jaws he might betray her, after all. She wondered briefly if she had the courage to kill him here and now, whether as wolf or as tiger, but knew that she did not.

'Why did you come here?' she demanded.

And he laughed. It was a sound as weak and pitiful as he was, but his narrow shoulders shook with it. 'Ssh-eeking the wishdom of the north, to sh-*ss*-peak with your prieshts.'

'Then you're a fool.'

'I cannot deny it.' He sighed. 'How many yearsh have I ssheen, and yet I am a fool.' He spat again. 'When will it be?'

'The day after tomorrow is the Testing,' she told him, and the thought sent dread coasting past her like the north wind. 'The day after, there will be a feast, and you will die. Aren't you going

46

to ask me to free you?' The words came out without her ever forming them in her mind. Once spoken, she clamped her hands to her mouth, but too late now to call them back.

He regarded her coolly, then shifted his body sinuously, tucking his knees even higher, holding as much warmth as he could to himself. 'Why would you do that?' Not bitter but a question posed with genuine interest, and it sank its hooks into her. She found herself thinking of reasons immediately, each one more appealing than the last.

Is he doing this to me? Am I doing this to myself? Abruptly she had used up her stock of daring. Being in this forbidden place, with this terrible, tragic old man, was more than she could bear. She Stepped back to the tiger and raked her way up the side of the pit, hoping that nobody would examine it too closely on the morrow and see where her claws had been. At the lip she paused, hunched low and looking for the watchmen, but by now they were both asleep. They did not fear that the old man would escape, and nobody had even thought about some wilful girl deciding to go down *into* the pit.

She Stepped again into her wolf, her smallest shape, and padded swiftly back towards the foot of the chief's mound.

She thought of him often during the next day, as she stayed out of the way of everyone. *Hesprec Essen Skese*: that awkward foreign name had lodged indelibly in her mind. She decided she would creep out to speak with him again that night. After all, it was not as though she would have many more chances.

By that evening, though, the Testing had grown to encompass her entire horizon. She could think of nothing else. All day, Kalameshli had been giving her his cold looks, as if to say, *Just you wait . . .* And Broken Axe had been seated just a few places from her, a guest at the chief's fire as he always was. He went wherever he willed but, whenever he came home to the Winter Runners, there was no more popular man than Broken Axe. It was a popularity born of fear, she knew. Oh, they hardly feared him like she did, but there was fear there nonetheless. Here was a Wolf who needed no pack: a taboo-breaker, a lone-walker. A gift of food and shelter might buy him for a little while, but here was a man who might be capable of anything, severed as he was from the ties of hearth and family.

And his eyes had strayed to her more than once, as he ate. He had eyes like nobody else, did Broken Axe: pale blue like spring ice set in the gaunt brown leather of his face.

She did not dare sneak away from her lair to seek out the doomed Snake that night. She had the unshakeable thought that she would find Broken Axe out there, waiting for her.

What does he want with me? There were few possibilities, none of them pleasant.

And the next morning they were preparing the ground for the Testing, and all the mad energy that had infused her peers over the last month was abruptly gone. She stepped out into the chill morning, and saw them standing about as though someone had died. They were afraid. This was the day their lives had been leading to, and they all of them feared now.

Theirs was a different character of fear to her own. They feared bruises and welts, and the humiliation of making mistakes before the whole tribe. None of them was going to be singled out by Kalameshli Takes Iron, after all. None of them ran the risk of ending the day without family and tribe, cast out from the Wolf and destined to burn in his jaws. She remembered now the perverse glee that had gripped her as she described the old man's fate to him. Somehow she had overlooked that it might also be hers.

Up on the temple mound, before the forge where Kalameshli laboured, lay the training ground. Usually it was a place of young hunters and warriors running, wrestling, casting spears and Stepping. Now the whole tribe thronged around its edges, down to the meanest Boar or Deer thrall, and a course had been laid out with painstaking care for the boys and girls who would end this day as men and women of the Wolf.

48

Each year it was different, this course, but the intent was the same. The youngsters would be harried from one end to the other, and to make a swift progress past all the obstacles they must Step from child to wolf and wolf to child, until at last their final transformation would be into an adult. There were stretches of open ground where a wolf might break away from its tormentors, and there were obstacles that a swift youth might vault over. There were logs to balance along and narrow holes to dive through.

The crowd was already in high spirits. For the young triallists this might be a day that would stand by them for the rest of their lives, for good or ill, but for everyone else it was sheer entertainment. All the adult Wolves – the old especially – were hoping for a good crop of embarrassments to laugh at and retell later. The lucky few that Kalameshli had chosen were already standing by with rocks and rotten yams and sticks, quite ready to make the triallists' lives an utter misery for the handful of minutes in which they were being Tested.

Maniye had been trying to retreat into the crowd without thinking about it, pulling her usual trick of being overlooked. Without warning, her father was at her elbow, one hand gripping her shoulder painfully.

'Go,' he told her flatly, giving her a shove towards where the others were already gathering at the head of the course.

She cast what she hoped was a fierce glance back towards him. It had no discernible effect.

There were over a score of others to take the Test today, every youth of Maniye's age in the whole of the Winter Runners. Seventeen she knew by name but the rest had gathered from everywhere under the Runners' Shadow. They stood, all of them naked except for a loincloth, backs braced against the punishment they knew was coming.

Now Kalameshli was striding forwards, the thick staff in one hand ridged with the blades of flints that the wood had grown around before it was cut. The myriad bones stitched to his robe – animal and human – clattered and chattered.

He singled out one of the hopefuls wordlessly, a boy. There were some calls of encouragement, rather more jeers and mockery. That was the way, part of the ordeal.

Kalameshli barked out permission, and the youth was off, springing instantly onto all fours but stumbling a little, having to compose himself before he could master the transformation. Already the handful of beaters were throwing missiles: Maniye heard a wolf's yelp as the boy's hindquarters were struck by a stone. He flinched back as he reached the felled trees, knowing he should Step to two feet to clamber across it, yet fearful of being struck.

The beaters were already moving in behind, though, with staves and rods. Any contender who hesitated too long would soon regret it. When Maniye was ten, she had seen one boy frozen with fear – of pain, or of failure – until they reached him, hailing blows upon him until they drove him forwards, meeting every obstacle unprepared. He had been bruised and bloodied by the end, barely standing, unable to meet the glowers of his people.

He was a hunter now, though. He had survived, and grown stronger.

She watched the youth Kalameshli had chosen, knowing that he was at a disadvantage, the first to discover the course and its ways. Then he was struck full on by a rotten yam, and he would be dubbed 'yam-head' for at least a month after, his shame written in the tribe's collective memory, a joke that might hound him all the way to old age unless he accomplished something remarkable to wipe it out.

Then he was through, having run and crouched, jumped and balanced his way to the far end. Now his parents and uncles and aunts went to him, showering him with congratulations, welcoming him to the world of adults, giving him gifts.

There will be no one there for me, Maniye reflected, but even to think that far presupposed that she would survive the course.

The others were picked out at Kalameshli's discretion, and Maniye was not remotely surprised to find herself being left till last. All she could do was watch the others, learning what she could from their mistakes. Some of them were slow, some too timid, others reckless. They fell, they were struck, they tripped, they rebounded off the obstacles. One girl was hit with a stone so hard it shocked her out of her wolf shape, leaving her kneeling on the ground, clutching at her bloodied scalp and wailing, and yet she got back on her feet and went on, because to let the beaters catch up with her would be worse. One boy forgot himself so much he left his loincloth behind as he Stepped, arriving at the far end completely naked, for a moment horribly abashed, but then – realizing that he had passed the important test – strutting and whooping with his adolescent manhood dangling and dancing between his legs.

Then they had all gone, all of them except Maniye.

She watched the last of the pack, a girl she didn't like, haring off, Stepping from human to wolf with the confidence of those who have seen the game played out plenty of times before. Even the beaters seemed content to let these last go with only a desultory barrage. Everyone was waiting for what came next. Everyone was waiting for *her*.

She fixed Kalameshli with a stony gaze which he met readily enough. From his expression, he might be looking at his worst enemy.

He shouted out an order, and something was brought out from behind the temple. His three acolytes, brawny young men all, were sweating and straining to manhandle it, and the crowd eddied aside to let them through.

It was a wall, she saw. A wall of logs lashed together, rising ten feet straight up, and the acolytes dragged it to the middle of the course, securing it by ropes to the other obstacles. The crowd surged forward on either side until it formed a completely impenetrable barrier that divided one half of the training grounds from the other.

The assembled tribe had gone very silent. No beaters had come forth for her, but every one of them fixed her with their eyes. She saw plenty of dislike there – those that felt she somehow wallowed in unearned privilege, and who were sufficiently mistaken to envy her relationship with the chief. They saw this as yet more special treatment, some sign that she was being accorded a special status.

How about tomorrow's sacrifice? Is that status special enough?

Kalameshli gestured imperiously, jabbing his staff at the course, and she walked over with deliberate, mulish slowness.

Remember, his eyes seemed to say.

She clenched her hands into fists. She had no wish to come so close to him, but no choice either. She could smell him distinctly, even with her human nose: smoke and sweat and hot iron.

He held out his flint-ridged staff and one of his acolytes took it from him, handing him instead a razor-edged switch three feet long. She saw the sunlight glint off it, and knew that there would be stones bound into the last few inches.

'I will be right behind you,' he said softly. 'Now, run.'

She was not going to give him the satisfaction, until he cracked the switch, the flexible greenwood making a sound like branches snapping. The fright of it had her Stepping to wolf without thinking, because the wolf was the fastest, and abruptly she was running from him, retreating back ten feet and leaping up the first low barrier before she dared to turn and look.

With no great hurry, Kalameshli was walking after her. His steps were slow, and yet every one of them seemed to eat up the ground between them. The stone-toothed branch twitched at his side. There was no expression whatsoever on his face.

She turned and ran, coursing swiftly, in her wolf shape, across the clear ground and putting distance between them. Then there was an earthen barrier to scramble up – human

52

hands better than animal paws for that – and the tree to balance over, but she did it without thinking, without a moment's hesitation, and all the while Kalameshli was following patiently and without hurry.

Then the wall was before her, seeming twice as high now as when the acolytes had brought it in. The crowd thronged at either edge, watching her eagerly.

She backed off, casting a look over her shoulder. Kalameshli was just reaching the tree.

The wolf could never make it, she knew, but it could still jump surprisingly high. She took a few more steps back and then dashed forwards on all four feet, leaping up and then Stepping even as she hit the wall, scrabbling for purchase, feet kicking, fingers clutching at the slick trunks.

She fell back heavily, Stepping to wolf before she hit the ground and twisting to get her paws under her.

Kalameshli was close now. Impossible, surely, with all the lead she had won herself, but there he was. Seeing he had her attention, he cracked the switch again, making that broken sound.

She faced the wall, feeling her heart speed. She tried scrabbling at it as a wolf, getting nowhere. She Stepped to human, Stepped back, dashing to either side, hurled back by the animosity of the crowd.

And within her, the tiger was awake and demanding its hour. She would be up and over the wall in seconds with its claws. It knew no walls or bounds. It was proud and fierce. It wanted to show them all just how fierce it was.

Again the switch lashed, and this time she felt the breeze of it, whirling round and backing away from Kalameshli's steady progress, her tail between her legs, snarling at him in terrified defiance. His expression was disapproving but not really disappointed. After all, surely this was what he had planned. Perhaps he had nurtured the thought of this moment for years, knowing that a time would come when not even her father's name would shield her from his hatred.

She had no idea why he loathed her so, only that he always had. Something in him had looked on her, at the moment of her birth, and judged her unfit, as if their spirits had been enemies in past lives, human or animal or both.

Her back, her human back, was against the wall, and the voice of the tiger was loud in her ears, demanding to be released from the prison of her flesh. Before her stood only Kalameshli.

His face twisted in a nameless expression she had never seen before, on his face or any other's, and he struck out at her.

She screamed and flinched aside, and the switch scarred the wood beside her head. *That could have been my face. That could have been me.*

He drew back his arm again. Everyone there, the entire tribe, was silent, almost reverent, watching their priest at his work, driving weakness from the Wolf.

She found that she could do nothing. She would have Stepped to tiger then, if she could, because she was beyond any thought of her future in the tribe, but fear of Kalameshli had frozen her in a strangling grip against the wall.

Then he lashed out again and the flint-barbed head of his whip tore into her arm and shoulder, splashing blood across the wood behind her, and he was already preparing for another blow.

She let out a sound that was girl and wolf and tiger all at once, all in pain, and was up the wall, finding purchase from nothing, scrabbling and kicking with her breath coming in shuddering sobs. At her heels, the switch descended again, striking splinters just below her heels.

And she was at the wall's summit, crouching there and staring down at him, and for a moment she had no idea *what* shape she was in, or where her Stepping might have taken her.

But those eyes with which she now glared down at Kalameshli, they saw the world in human colours, and what held her to the wall were her human fingers and toes, crooked into every little crevice and crack she could find, bleeding from the rough wood, her nails ragged and broken.

And Kalameshli looked up at her, and where she expected to find bitterness was instead a kind of triumph, for she had mastered the personal Testing he had set her, and somehow the tiger remained caged. He had made her his creature, a thing of the Wolf only.

She slipped down over the far side of the wall, feeling numb. The rest of the course, she walked. Nobody threw anything at her. Kalameshli did not follow any further. His point was made, and he was satisfied.

At the course's end, nobody was there to greet her and exult with her, but she had expected that. By then her shoulder was agony, and she went to make a poultice to bind over it that would dull the pain. It would be grim work, one-handed, but nobody would do it for her, nor would she trust them to.

Later, when the tribe had begun the raucous celebrations that came after the Testing, Smiles Without Teeth came for her, and told her that her father demanded her presence.

5

Asmander was awakened by the sounds of fighting.

He and the Horse delegation had been gifted one of the smaller huts to curl up in, presumably leaving some of the more wretched Laughing Men to shiver outside in the dark. With so many sleepers laid out close together around the circle of floor, like interlocking pieces of a puzzle, the cold of nightfall did not touch them; and besides, Asmander had a gift for sleeping well, yet waking when he needed to.

He was on his feet in an instant – some of the Horse were already about, judging from the vacant spaces on the floor, and there was no sign of Venater at all. No surprise there: from the sound of it, Venater was one of those doing the fighting. The pirate had been awake still when Asmander retired, conversing in guarded, hostile tones with the Malikah of the Laughing Men. Asmander was only surprised it had taken the man so long to get into trouble.

In nothing but a loincloth, his stone-toothed *maccan* sword in hand, Asmander hurried up into the morning light.

There were three of them pitched against Venater. Three men, though, and it was plain that amongst this tribe the men were given no place of honour or respect. Nonetheless, they were game fighters, from what Asmander could now see, teaming up to try and bring the big southerner down.

It was all in friendly contest, that much he saw. When they

were in human form, their hands were empty of weapons. Still, the Laughing Men possessed jaws that could grind bones, and fights like these were seldom won or lost without blood being drawn.

Seeing that there was no real danger to Venater, and that the Laughing Men had not decided to butcher their guests, Asmander just stood back and watched his companion fight.

He moved like strong waters, this old pirate: deceptive when he was still, unstoppable once he struck. Sometimes he wore his human shape, with sallow skin gleaming in the bright sunlight. More often he was Stepped into the true form of his soul, the savage creature he called the dragon. Long and black, he was, as heavy and powerful as when he walked on two legs, and his scales were like black pebbles. His blunt head gaped wide in threat, showing a horrific array of curving fangs, and he could rush with a terrible swiftness even on those sprawling, ungainly looking legs.

The three Laughing Men tried to surround him, to nip at him from behind while he chased whoever was before him, but Venater was an old warrior, wise to such tricks. More than that, there was no part of him that was easy to attack. Asmander winced as one would-be ambusher was lashed across the muzzle by the sharp whip of Venater's tail, while one of the others got too close and was hooked about the foreleg by the monstrous lizard's claws. Instantly Venater was a man again, lifting the startled hyena up and flipping the animal over his shoulder. The Laughing Man Stepped in mid-air and managed a creditable landing on hands and knees, whereupon Venater kicked him in the stomach and sent him rolling away. The third hyena leapt for him, aiming to connect with his chest, but Venater had Stepped again, dropping down to his lizard shape so that his enemy sailed overhead.

With calculated indolence, Venater turned to face them, blue-black tongue lashing at the air. Then he was a man once more, trying to lure them closer, and Asmander met the stone force of his gaze, recognizing the challenge there and waving it aside. *Another time, perhaps.*

Seeing him there, Asmander was swept up in the memory of when he had first set eyes on the pirate; remembering when the two of them had fought.

Back then, Asmander's father had taken a warband of the clan's warriors out with the specific intention of ridding the Tsotec estuary of its most troublesome pirate. The Dragon were ever-troublesome vassals of the Sun River Nation, and more than one had turned outlaw and raider in the past. Venater had been the boldest in living memory, striking even within sight of the prince's own palace at Tsokawan.

The warband had tracked the pirate Venat – as he was known when his name was still his own – to one of the innumerable estuary islands. There, they approached under cover of the murky water, Stepped into the long, ridge-backed shapes of crocodiles. There were two score of them, and the pirates were less than a dozen, and mostly drunk. The fight as a whole was no great victory to carve on the walls of the mighty, but Venat . . .

Asmander remembered him leaping up, roaring his defiance, the stone blade of his *meret* cleaving spears in two and splitting shields. He had been as drunk as the rest, but that had not stopped or even slowed him. And Asmander, who had newly found his role as Champion of the River Lords, knew that the moment had come to test the shape of his soul against this foe.

He had Stepped into that fleeter form, the obsidian of his *maccan* becoming his teeth, the jade of his spurs his claws, and he had rushed from the midst of his father's warriors to do battle. They had wanted to stop him, but he was a Champion. They dared not lay hands on him, not even Asman his father.

And the fight – so fierce a contest! Venat had struck at him with his bone-breaking tail and claws strong enough to tear open bronze. He had snapped his teeth against the scaly quills of Asmander's hide, which were reinforced with the cotton and stone of the armour he wore. A shallow bite would have been debilitating, a deep one fatal, for the dragons of the estuary were venomous as well as merely savage. Legend said that dark spirits of the early world had created them to be as inimical to all other beasts as it was possible to be.

Asmander had let speed become his ally, leaping to drive his claws into the great lizard's back, always a step aside, a step ahead. He had known exactly the risks he ran, and he ran them gladly. He had never *lived*, as when he had lived next to the death that dwelled in Venat's jaws.

And at last the man was beaten, sprawled bleeding and cursing, shifting from writhing lizard back to man, and eventually just staring up at Asmander with hate-filled eyes, expecting nothing but death. And death was what he deserved: no noble robber of the stories, he, but a villain, a murderer, a rebel against prince and nation.

Asmander had placed one clawed foot on his defeated enemy's neck and waited for his father's command.

It had not come, and for a moment he had thought – he remembered this clearly – *Is he dead? Am I Asman now?* along with all the little attendant thoughts that whirled and spun in the wake of that huge one. But then he had cocked his head, while keeping one eye on his prize, and seen his father standing amongst his men, staring at his son with such an expression . . .

Pride, yes, but there had been depths to that expression, as clouded as the river. Anger that Asmander had so risked himself; calculation at how this proven asset that was his son might now best be used. And *envy*. Asmander remembered that plainly. The envy never left his father's face, from that moment on, that his son should be so honoured by the gods as to be a Champion, whilst he . . . he grew older and no stronger, and some day this boy before him would bear his name.

But Asman was a man of politics, above all. He had lived his life navigating the hazardous waters of the Sun River Nation's powers and factions. Not for nothing were his people known also as the Patient Ones.

'What, then?' he had asked his son. 'Will you stay your hand?'

In his Champion's shape, the youth could not answer, but he bobbed his head once, indicating his submission to his father's will.

'Notorious pirate,' Asman declared, 'you are defeated, your followers slain.' Around them, their corpses stood as mute witness, some stabbed with jagged spears, others ripped by long jaws. A couple of the victorious attackers had retained their crocodile forms, coasting silently through waters now red and salty with blood.

Venat had glowered murder up at him, but Asmander's talons were tight and sharp about his neck, holding him to his human form, a great sickle-claw poised ready to descend on his face.

'You will be bound and noosed,' Asman declared. 'You will be brought before Tecumander, heir to the Daybreak Throne. There, you will die in the pool of the Crocodile, ripped into pieces by our mute brothers.'

The pirate's mouth twitched, as though he wanted to spit, but was too wary of that hovering claw.

'Or, as you are a man of skill and courage, however misused, you may suffer yourself to be stripped of all you are – yes, even your name – and sworn to the service of my clan, to earn back your honour until such time as you can once again call yourself a man. Think on that choice as we carry you back to Tsokawan.'

'I'd rather die,' Venat had finally got out.

But he had not. Despite his defiance, when they had stood him before Old Crocodile's pool, he had bowed the knee and relinquished his name. Even then, he had stared at Asmander with a blood-red promise of revenge. The look he gave the youth now – these few years later, during which everything within the Sun River Nation had changed – was its close cousin.

Asmander was glad. It was a melancholy truth, but he had always been more at ease with hatred than with love. He knew where he was with antagonism, with challenge, with people who would rip out his throat if he bared it to them. He liked the Laughing Men on first sight for just that simple, honest quality. It was people who smiled and simpered and flattered him that meant him the more harm, he knew well.

Some day, he reflected, as Venater returned to his fighting.

'Have them wash their wounds well after,' he advised the spectators. 'He has filthy teeth.'

Later, he came upon Venater as the man washed. 'Finished with your playing?' he asked.

The pirate gave him a sour look. 'Travelling with the Horse is piss-dull. I like these people. They live well.'

Asmander smiled a little, hearing his own thoughts mirrored. 'They cut you a little, I see.'

Venater's bared chest and back bore a scattering of fresh scratches, a few of which still bled. For a precious moment he looked almost shifty, but then he laughed.

'Not them. It'd take more than those dogs.'

'Then . . .' Asmander reassessed the damage: trophies of a different sort of combat. 'You lay with the Malikah?'

'Only because you were too scared of her.'

'Not my type,' said Asmander, and then he grinned, shaking his head. 'Where did that come from?'

'She appreciates a strong man. They don't seem to have any around here.'

'And you?'

Venater shrugged, then winced ruefully. 'These things are known: beware a woman as strong as you are. I never ended a night with so many bruises. Are the Horse finally finished talking?'

Asmander had seen the Society delegation gathering, and he shrugged. 'Something's happening, anyway.'

The pirate growled. 'I never thought I'd find a people who talk more than you River Lords do. We should just take one of those boats and go.'

'And then you'd paddle? Or would that be just me pressing on the oar upstream, all the way to the Crown of the World?' Asmander asked him wryly. 'No, they know the back of the Tsotec, and we do not. And they will sell us fit clothing for the cold, once we are there. All lives interweave, as the Snakes tell us.'

Venater spat to show exactly what he thought of that but, soon afterwards, Eshmir the Horse Hetman was approaching.

'We've exhausted the hospitality of the Laughing Men?' Asmander suggested brightly. 'No more chuckles; they want us gone?'

Her expression was awkward. 'Something of the opposite.' Seeing the tense anticipation that descended on him she was quick to add, 'Not trouble, but they have invited you on a hunt.'

'Me?'

'Others as well, but the Malikah very much wishes for you to run with her hunters.'

'She wants to see the Champion,' Asmander divined.

'I am sorry,' she confirmed.

'Why?'

'You do not seem to wish to show it. Since leaving Atahlan, you have not Stepped . . .' Her face was a study in concentration as she tried to navigate the hidden reefs of Sun River custom.

'It is not for play,' he told her. 'Most certainly it is not to *impress*. The Champion of the River People is a shape not lightly taken. But for a hunt? Yes, a hunt is serious business. It is fitting.'

Her relief was palpable. 'I was not sure . . .'

'We are a complex people in the Nation and we care about many things,' Asmander said softly. 'But the Champion knows what is important in life. And sometimes that makes living with the cares of people difficult. Especially the Patient Ones.'

The Laughing Men hunted many types of prey, singly and in packs, but the great prize of the Plains was the wild aurochs. They had been tracking a solitary bull for days before the hunt, an old beast without a herd, yet strong and aggressive enough to warn off even lions. Now it stood in the chest-high grass, brooding and chewing, lifting its great head at every flight of birds or change in the wind. Looking on it, Asmander had the sense that the beast knew well what was to come, and welcomed it. The soul in that hulk of a body wished to move on with honour, and preferably with some blood upon its horns.

Venater did not care for the hunt, but the possibility of Asmander making a fool of himself was eternally attractive, and so he had come – with the Hetman and a handful of the Horse Society – just to watch. A good score of the Laughing Men were there too, half a dozen of whom would hunt alongside the southerner. These were the young and the strong, four women and two men, their skin fresh painted with streaks of white and gold.

'How do I look?' Asmander asked, grinning. He had the same adornment, the colours particularly striking against his darker skin.

'Like a badly decorated pot,' the pirate replied. 'All you need is a little red, but that's what those horns are for.'

The Malikah sent a stern glance towards him and, to Asmander's astonishment, Venater fell silent. The entire venture was almost worth it just for that.

'There was a tribe, once.' The ruler of the Laughing Men drifted closer, her eyes fixed on their wary quarry. 'They were the people of the Aurochs, and they were strong and fierce in battle.'

'So what happened to them?' Asmander asked, as was obviously required.

'They betrayed their own souls. They took their mute brothers and penned them, and kept them for their meat, and so they grew weak, and we fell upon them and destroyed them. But now we have cattle, and so do all the peoples. All of life is profiting from the misfortunes of others.' She grinned, feral and fierce. 'In your hunt, Champion, know that the souls of the Aurochs live

63

still, forever reborn into these mute bodies, forever knowing that they once had language and understanding. Know that, by shedding this old one's blood, you move him one step further on in his journey. Perhaps one day he will be born as a man again, when his soul knows that he has atoned for the mistakes of his people.'

Asmander nodded, eyes fixed on the great beast in the middle distance. Did he feel a shock of contact, meeting that far gaze?

'My hunters will drive him and channel him, but the honour of the kill is yours – if you can take it.' The Malikah was watching him intently.

Asmander rolled his shoulders. He was here bare-chested and without armour. Stone mail would not save him against the sweep of those horns, only speed of action.

There was no signal, but abruptly the Laughing Men hunters had all Stepped and were racing off into the grass, where their progress was visible as a rushing tremor cutting a curving path that would overshoot the bull, then draw back to herd the beast towards Asmander. The spectators were slowly falling away, abandoning him to his skills.

He looked back once, meeting Venater's gaze. The pirate's expression said eloquently, *Well, look what you've got yourself into.*

His *maccan* was a comforting weight dangling from its wrist strap. He saw the bull's head come up, scenting the approach of the hyena pack, and yet one dark eye was fixed on him alone.

'Old Crocodile, fill me with your peace, let me wait in the calm of your waters, let my strike be sudden,' Asmander murmured to himself, because soon words would be denied him. The high yipping cackle of the hunters carried to him over the grass. Abruptly the bull was in motion, just an amble at first, shaking his head in irritation, but then the pack must have appeared from another quarter, warding the beast away from his escape, and abruptly he was gathering speed.

'Serpent, you who pass below all,' Asmander said, now hurrying the words a little, 'guide my prey's soul swift to its new birth.

64

Or my soul. Or mine.' Then there was no more time for prayer, and he Stepped.

The Malikah and some of her people had stayed close enough to witness this moment, but he was oblivious to their reaction as his human form lunged forwards into that of the Champion of the River People. As he had said, it was not done for show.

He was no larger than human, in that form, and lower slung, his body canted forwards and balanced by the long stiff spine of his tail. His hide was something like scales, but longer, more delicate, and if he shook himself just so, they would rattle like a snake's tail, like the coursing of the rain.

He stepped forwards on two feet, each with its killing claw held delicately off the ground to keep it sharp. His hands – and they were still hands, just – were also barbed weapons, as was the deep bite of his jaws. There was something of the crocodile to him, and something of Venater's dragon-lizard, but mostly he was himself, an impossible animal. No man had ever hunted one such as he. His was a shape that existed only as a thought in the mind of the world, a memory of the great spirits for whom the span of all human years was an eyeblink, and irrelevant.

The bull was coming on fast now, with the pack nipping at its heels, infuriating it. Asmander stalked forwards with all of Old Crocodile's patience, with the Serpent's steady gaze. Inside, he felt as though he was only partly in control: the Champion was a second soul in him, passing through his life for the brief spans that he called upon it. No man could truly hope to own these killing limbs, this speed, this strength.

The dreadful anticipation that rose within him was that of the Champion, and to Asmander it was a like drug, a joy, a truth. The Champion saw the world so much more clearly that, each time he took this form, he did not want to let it go.

The bull saw him, that sleek reptile shape knifing through the grass, and turned its path away, tossing its head at a hyena unwise enough to get too close and sending the hunter yelping away. The aurochs was fast, moving at the limits of the pack's ability to herd it, but Asmander was faster. And he could leap. There was nothing else in the world that could leap as he could.

Three long steps towards the aurochs' turning flank and then he sprang, sailing clear above the grass to tear into the animal's hide, hanging there with four sets of claws before ripping a long, shallow gash down the bull's ribs and kicking himself away. He landed in a crouch and the bull turned on him, in fury, in recognition, its horns lowered. Asmander faced it down, head thrust forwards and jaws agape, screeching out his challenge.

For the length of a drawn breath, the world stood still: the aurochs and Asmander, whilst the Laughing Men looked on in wonder.

Then the bull charged without warning, its colossal weight and strength in furious motion, horns like lances and the ground shaking under its approach. Asmander felt a thrill of anticipation – never fear, for the Champion did not know it – and then he was skipping aside, leaving that sinuous motion to the last possible moment, and another leap carried him to the bull's hindquarters where he tore another patchwork of bloody lines. Still he did not bite: to bite was to commit, to fix himself in place to a quarry that could still very easily kill him.

He jumped off again, and this time the aurochs lumbered onwards, following the line of its charge until the Laughing Men materialized out of the grass to head it off. When it turned, it was wearier than before, its dark hide painted with blood.

It met Asmander's yellow gaze.

Once more, my friend. This was why Asmander had valued the rage and hate of Venater more than the words of his own clan or his prince's court. This was the kind of honesty that he sought in a crooked world. The bull wanted to kill him. The bull wanted to live. Asmander valued its hostile regard more than gold.

With the hideous cacophony of the Laughing Men at its back, it stamped and scuffed at the ground beneath it, and then it came for him, without hope but with honour – and how many men could say as much in their last moments?

This time, Asmander almost left it too late, seduced by the sheer power and beauty of the behemoth bearing down on him. The Champion knew its place, though, and swung him to the bull's forequarters, one sickle-claw dug into its throat, one hooked behind its shoulders. And, as the bull bucked and plunged to dislodge him, he brought his jaws down upon the back of its great neck with all their strength, shearing through the dense thickness of muscle and severing the chain of bone along which ran the aurochs' life.

When they reached him, the spectators, the Malikah, Venater, they found him in his human shape again, with the other hunters keeping a respectful distance. He was sitting by the huge mound of the bull's body, one hand on its bloodied side, feeling as though he had lost a friend.

6

Compared to the evening cold without, the air inside the chief's hut practically sweated with heat from the central fire, smoky enough to sting Maniye's eyes.

Tonight the tribe was fasting. She could hear distant yelps and howls as packs of the young – the recently Tested and their siblings and relatives – ran wild between the mounds, chasing after each other in mock hunts, engaging in brief, snarling fights. She had no wish to join them, to inevitably become the hunted and be reminded of her lot. Just for once, she had wanted to sit all alone and know that she had passed; that she had succeeded in this thing that had been looming over her for so long. She had scaled the wall!

And now Akrit her father had sent for her.

He was seated facing away from her, staring at the fire. Stripped to the waist, there were no war-scars on his back, for he was a man who faced his enemies whenever he fought them. Instead, she saw the set of savage, puckered marks left by some ordeal or initiation, a double row of livid blemishes flanking his spine.

Kalameshli sat nearby, watching her closely. Otherwise the hall was empty, even the thralls had been sent away.

At last Akrit turned. There were several gourds strewn nearby, the air ripe with the scents of honey and fermented yams, and she realized that he was drunk, or at least a little. Normally that would have her fearing his fists even more than usual, but tonight he was drunk in some new way, some way that made him happy rather than fierce and angry. He regarded her uncertainly, as though he had never seen her before.

And he hasn't, in a way. I am a new creature now. For once she felt she could meet his gaze without fear. She had something to hold her head up for.

'Kalameshli wasn't sure that you would pass,' her father said to her thoughtfully.

Kalameshli would have been delighted had I failed, was her instant thought, but she kept it to herself.

'I knew, though,' Akrit went on. 'You're my blood, after all. Of course you've mastered yourself. You're Stone River's child. It could be no other way.'

The unfairness of that – as though he was taking the credit for all she had done – stung her a little, but his next words wiped that resentment away.

'It's good. It's as it should be. It's good.'

Praise, of a sort? And he had not exactly been forthcoming with such in the past – nor had anyone else. And his expression, as he looked on her, was something warmer than the doubt or annoyance she was used to seeing.

'You're of the Wolf, now,' he told her. It was little enough, giving her what she had already earned, and yet, all of a sudden, fourteen years of bottled emotion began rising up in her. She fought them back desperately, a battle as hard as climbing the wall had been, because she would *not* appear weak before *them*. She was Wolf, and the Wolf was fire and winter, and did not know tears.

'When the year turns, it's time,' her father continued, more to Kalameshli than herself.

The old priest nodded. 'I suppose it is.'

'A purpose has been laid for you, since before you were born.' Now Akrit's eyes were back on Maniye. 'Everything was waiting on today. I had to know for sure you were *mine*, not . . .' The thought went unfinished, but she read it in his face.

Not my mother's. Not the Tiger's.

She felt the great cat stir again within her, at that, but it felt very far away, and buried deep. She was losing it: she was Wolf now. That was what was proper, what she had wanted, wasn't it? Suddenly she fitted in, she had a place amongst the Winter Runners, within the Jaws of the Wolf. And, if one must live so, how much better to be the teeth that tore, rather than the flesh they ripped into.

Will I be a hunter? she wondered. *Will I be a raider? What will you make of me?* It was as though a hanging had been drawn aside, and she could look into a different world, the world she had never realized would be opened to her. *I am the Wolf. I am the voice that calls in the night. I am that which hunts in a pack.*

Akrit sat, dropping straight down into a cross-legged position, with a small grunt of effort, and gestured for her to do likewise, as one adult to another, a chief to one of his tribe.

'Before you were born, we went to war,' he remarked. 'You know this, even you. Back then, the Tiger was strong, and we all lived in his Shadow. But the Wolf gave us iron claws and iron coats, and the Boar and the Deer rose with us, even the Bear and the Eyriemen, a little. And we broke the Shadow Eaters; we drove the people of the Tiger into the highlands. You have heard the stories of these things?'

'I have heard them.' Her voice even sounded different, not a girl's any more, and yet more of her father's daughter than before.

'You know that your mother was of their tribe.'

There was a hard edge to his tone, but when she answered, 'I know it,' without any hurt in her voice, that seemed to satisfy him.

'She was trouble, an evil woman. The Tiger are ruled by their women. You know this?'

'I have heard it spoken.' She was waiting for some stab of

70

anguish to engulf her over her mother, but she was Wolf, and she was calm. *I have no mother*, she could tell herself. *I have no tiger within me.*

'They called her the Tiger Queen when she was still free – before I took her,' Akrit explained. 'Even with a rope about her neck, too much trouble.' He gestured vaguely, shaking his head. 'But we were hoping this day would come, when a child of hers would come of age, and be of the Wolf. And here you are.'

A slow uncertainty was stealing over Maniye. The last thing she had expected was so much talk of her mother. She had stood before Akrit, feeling that half of her cut away, and now he was fumblingly trying to join it back onto her.

'I am of the Wolf,' she said carefully.

Akrit nodded animatedly, and in that rapid motion she saw just how drunk he really was. 'But you are *her* daughter.'

'I am *your* daughter.' It was not something she had ever wanted to be, before, but suddenly it was very important to her.

'But you are *hers*. That is how they do things, among the Shadow Eaters. The mother rules, and then the daughter.' Akrit grinned abruptly. 'So it is time we bare our teeth again! This spring the Winter Runners shall go to raid the highlands and draw the Tiger out. And when we have their attention, when we have bloodied them a little and reminded them of the strength of the Wolf, we shall show you to them: the child of their queen.'

She was just watching now, saying nothing.

'And they will kneel, because you are their dead queen's get. And you will bring them under the Wolf's Shadow. You will bring them under *my* Shadow, and they will league with the Winter Runners, and we will be the strongest of the Wolf's children, eh, Kalameshli Takes Iron?'

She felt as though she was tracking something through the forest, print by print, scent by scent, and now she stood before its lair, understanding what it was she had been hunting. She wondered how much of this might have been couched differently, had he been sober. Akrit's words for her were normally few and hostile, but her passing her Test, her denying the tiger within her, had been for him the culmination of many years of scheming. Apparently he felt that he was allowed to relax his guard just this much.

There was a High Chief of the Wolf, the first and only Chief of Chiefs. Seven Skins of the Many Mouths tribe held that honour, made such by the acclaim of his peers during the war with the Tiger. He had masterminded the uprising of the Wolf, when her father had been just one war leader amongst many, albeit one who had taken more risks and won more victories than most.

Seven Skins was old, though: years past Kalameshli's age. The time would come when he would pass into the forest, and if there was to be another High Chief, who knew who that might be? If Akrit could make the hated Shadow Eaters bow the knee, then none would deny him.

This was the purpose he had contrived for her. It was a grand plan, and one that might have failed at so many points, but Akrit and Kalameshli and the will of the Wolf had made it work. Here she now was, poised to stand before her mother's people and lead them into the Wolf's Shadow.

She reached within herself to see what she thought of this. She had never realized that the Tiger were so bound to their bloodlines that some bastard child of their last ruler might come and usurp control of their whole tribe. For all she knew, Akrit was entirely wrong about that. They might just tear her apart.

Or she might bring him a grand victory for the Wolf. She might prove herself Akrit's daughter.

She had not ever thought that *being of use* was something she might aspire to. She had spent her childhood being as contrary as possible, as a reaction to finding herself without friends or place or even parents who cared about her. The harsh hand of Kalameshli had seemed almost more paternal than that of Akrit. And yet all that time she had been in his thoughts: if not as his child, then at least as his weapon.

If he had asked for her agreement, she might have said yes, and been forever after bound by her own word. He took her consent – her subjugation to his plan and his will – as a given though. He never asked, and so never extracted that agreement from her.

And then he added, 'And we must find you a mate, of course.'

She went still at the thought.

'If the Shadow Eaters are to be driven into the Wolf's Shadow, they will need a firm hand holding the switch,' he went on, and the image made her think of Kalameshli, so that for a terrible moment she thought that the old priest was somehow being put forward as a suitor, against his vows and all prior custom.

'I will rule them for you,' she said, but Akrit barely seemed to hear her.

'You will need a man, a hunter, to govern you,' he told her, 'even if the Shadow Eaters will want to hear his words in your voice.' He frowned. 'Someone who will do what he's told.'

Something inside her was turning sour, as though she had been drinking and the liquor was curdling in her stomach. Yes, so many of her peers had lived a life of speculation over who they might be mated to, recounting the names of the fine young hunters or hearth-keepers of the Wolf tribes. For Maniye, how-ever, it had never been a consideration. She had made a virtue of necessity. She had lived a future in her mind in which she was self-sufficient: a tribe of one.

'I would match you to Smiles Without Teeth,' Akrit went on, forging deeper and deeper into this appalling new territory and dragging her along with him. 'I would want him always at my side, though. And he is . . . not the cleverest.'

Maniye had begun to shake, very slightly. She thought of big, brutal Smiles Without Teeth, a man without humour or imagin-ation, but very quick to strike out whenever the complex world frustrated him. He had already taken one wife, Maniye recalled, but the woman had been seen too often with bruises about her face, and she had cast him from her hearth. Smiles had been searching for a new wife ever since, but no woman would look at him.

But her father continued talking, the drink drawing the words out of him, and Kalameshli listened complacently. Nothing of the conversation even required her contribution or consent.

'But then I thought,' Akrit went on, 'there was one I need by my side for the fight, and nothing I've done for the ungrateful cur has ever bound him to me enough to keep him here whenever spring comes. But if I give you to Broken Axe, that must be enough. He must know his wandering days are done, and become my warrior.'

Maniye sat motionless, because she knew this game: this was the game she herself had played every day up to today, up to the Testing. This was the game she had thought she would never need to play again. This was *show nothing on your face*. This was where she sat and pretended that nothing that she heard or saw affected her, because if the world knew that it could hurt you, then hurt you it would.

Matched to the man who killed my mother. And it was obvious that her father saw nothing objectionable in this thought at all.

All at once she had made up her mind and knew what she must do.

'What good are you?'

The moon was overcast tonight, so the darkness of the pit was near total. She stared challengingly at the pale smudge that was the Snake priest, Hesprec Essen Skese.

'Tell me,' she hissed, feeling inexplicably furious at him, just for his being there, as though he was to blame for her predicament. 'What's the use of you? What's a Snake priest for?'

'I know many things,' he said carefully.

'What things? Priest things? Magic?'

'Ssome magic, yesh.'

'You have friends here in the Crown of the World? Friends who will help you?'

He was silent. That meant no.

'These things you know, they're valuable? Or you can make people do what you want, or . . . ?' Her words tailed away to nothing. He was bound, haltered, kept in a pit. If his knowledge gave him genuine power, would any of those things be true? 'What good are you?' she repeated.

She heard him take a deep breath and then he spoke as clearly as he could, fighting to speak around his raw gums. 'The wise of the north might value what I know, those who lust for blood less than do the Wolf. The Horse people will honour me. And I can live in many lands.'

'You're no hunter.'

'You need no hunter to trap or to fish.' His patient, quiet tone was maddening.

'You'll die,' she spat at him, striving to keep her voice low despite her desperation. 'If my father hadn't taken you, you'd be a frozen body out in the woods, or prey for our mute brothers.'

'And yet I crossed half the world to get here.'

She thought hard. She felt as though there must be some magic combination of words that would somehow cut the whole knot of her problem open, and present her with a simple and certain way out. Instead she had herself, and she had this ragged, wretched creature.

She was leaving, she had decided. She was abandoning the tribe. It wasn't unknown. Broken Axe had done it, become a lone Wolf and made his mark on the world. Much as she did not want to think about him, perhaps in this he would be her inspiration.

Of course, Broken Axe – or the youth he had once been – was not wanted by the chief for some mad plan to conquer the Tiger.

'What troublessh you, girl?' asked Hesprec Essen Skese softly.

She glared at him. She would give him no blades to hold to her throat, nor secrets to cut her with. She had crouched in her alcove under the roof of the chief's hall and counted over her options, forced herself to examine precisely why she was going to cut herself loose from her own people. The bitterness of it was that she had finally been given something to stay for, after all. She had passed the Testing. She had proved herself a Wolf. If he had only left her alone after that, she would have been Akrit's most loyal supporter. She could have taught herself to love him, despite all, even to love Kalameshli because he was the voice of the Wolf, her Wolf. But that was not what Akrit had wanted from her. He did not want *her* at all – not Maniye. He wanted a tame Shadow Eater cub with the Tiger muzzled within her, so as to twist her mother's people into paying him tribute and strengthening his name. That was all she was: a thing to be used. And to keep her on a leash, he would marry her to Broken Axe. That ought to be the worst of it, but in truth it was that sense of being used, as a *thing* is used: that cut deepest.

And even if the old Snake died in the cold, in the snow, in the woods, still she would be striking one grand blow against her father and against Kalameshli. Not only would she be taking herself out of their grasp, she would be robbing the Wolf of his sacrifice. The thought made her breathless with fear and daring. If the Wolf would not accept her as herself, then she would not hesitate to steal from his hearth. She would turn her back on him. Perhaps she would choose the tiger in her once she could put off that choice no longer.

The thought hurt her: making that choice between the two souls within her was like seizing briars. She knew she would eventually have to, lest her soul split in two and drive her mad, but she put the thought off one more time.

'You said the Horse – you came from the south with the Horse Society?' she told the Snake.

'I did.' Still so polite and conversational, though she could hear him shivering.

'Would they take you south again?'

'When I am done in the north.'

'Done what? Done being sacrificed?' she goaded him.

'If the Wolf will not sspeak to me, there is still the Deer, the Eyrie, the Bear, the Tiger. Sss-somewhere I will find wisdom in this cold land.'

She was about to demand that, as the price for his life, he take her south immediately, but then his words sunk in, and she thought . . . *the Tiger?*

'Will they receive you?' she asked. 'Or will they kill you? How do you know you won't be met like this wherever you go? We have no kind tales about the Serpent.'

'I don't know.' He let out a long sigh. 'I have to hope. It's very important.'

And she found she was decided, just like that. She had a flint blade in her hand and was stepping forwards, feeling him flinch.

'If I cut loose your collar, can you Step? Can you climb?'

'Better than a tiger.' His voice, so close to her, made her shiver.

'You must travel with me. I know these lands.' A gross exaggeration from a girl who, a moment before, had despaired of finding any use for this wreck of an old man. Now, though, he was all she had. She needed to keep him with her.

'Agreed.'

She had her hands at his throat, the razor sharpness of the flint against his skin. She could have killed him then and there, another way of stealing him from Kalameshli.

She seized the rope they had haltered him with, the noose that held him to his human shape, and sawed at it, tugging him back and forth, until the tough fibres parted and abruptly he was free.

Instantly she jumped backwards, Stepping so that she could see him with her tiger's eyes. For a moment he was just the same stiff old man, hands tied to a stake driven into the earth floor. Then, with the impression of immense relief and release, he Stepped. It was a fluid, elegant motion, one that ceded nothing of his age and stiffened joints. In an instant he had no arms nor hands, and the ropes had fallen away. Before her eyes he

77

squirmed into the form of a serpent as long as she was tall: a lithe, dangerous-looking creature. For a second she froze, aware that he could strike at her easily within the close confines of the pit.

But, of course, he had no fangs, thanks to Kalameshli. He could only threaten. She could sink her own claws into this reptile and rip him apart.

Then he was lifting up his head, weaving up the pit's vertical side, and she waited for him to drop back down and yet he never did, just ascending and ascending in a lazy zig-zag, somehow clinging to the earth with the very scales of his belly until his head had looped over the edge and he was fully up.

She realized that she was being left behind and followed suit, scraping and raking herself up, with far more effort than he had shown.

At the top, she thought she had lost him. Crouching low to the ground and relying on the cloud-coated sky to hide her in its shadow, she could see no sign of either snake or man. Then something moved almost under her feet and he was there, lifting his arrow-shaped head, the forked tongue flicking.

She had hidden a pack nearby: a hide bag of stolen food and clothes that she reckoned she could strap about her and carry either as wolf or tiger. Now she crept towards it, waiting to see if either of tonight's sentries was more alert, or whether they were still drinking to celebrate the successful Testing.

At her heels, the serpent followed. Unfanged or not, the thought made her shiver.

7

For the people of the Crown of the World, fall meant a time of sacrifice. Winters came hard enough to kill experienced wildsmen as well as just the old and the young. If a tribe had miscalculated or had suffered a poor year, or if vermin got at the stores, then winter was a killing time. None knew it more than the Wolf, and those that died in winter were the Wolf's due. Offering sacrifice as the nights grew long might persuade the Wolf to act as messenger to the greater powers of storm and snow and cold, and thus persuade them to stay their hands. Such intervention could make the difference between a winter that took only a few of the weak and one that took all but the strongest.

Journeying with Hesprec Essen Skese was not easy, Maniye had discovered. It was not like travelling with some sorcerer priest of the mysterious south. It was like travelling with an old, old man, and one with far too many quirks that slowed them down.

For a start, and while it was still dark – their best chance to put distance between themselves and Akrit's hall – he had called a halt, lurching into his human form and shivering in the thin robe they had left him, out of all his belongings. She had been forced to Step likewise and delve in her pack for what little she had brought for him: soft hide shoes that would surely not last long before wearing through; an old sheepskin jacket, much mended; a very thin woollen cloak. He struggled into them all gratefully. The first spots of rain were lancing down from the louring clouds above, and she had to watch as he sat and fought with the shoes, forcing his too-big feet into them, then fumbling with the bindings. And all the while their time was wasting, and they were still close enough that she felt tethered to the Winter Runners and her home.

About that time Maniye realized that she had not really been heading anywhere in particular. In fact, she had been taking them north, into friendless climes where the weather would get no kinder. What had drawn her there was the treeline. The cover of the woods lay closest in that direction, for the uneven landscape made felling difficult. Now she would have to pretend that was her plan, or else lose what little faith the Snake priest might have in her.

It made some sense: get into the shadow of the trees, then curve east, because she was heading for . . .

'You said the Horse men would listen to you . . .' She frowned. 'What are you doing?'

The old man had torn up the hem of his thin robe, exposing his bony ankles, and was binding the ripped cloth about his bald head with meticulous care.

'Sshowing due deference,' he told her, and he was certainly taking his time about it, no matter how his hands trembled in the cold, or how blue his lips were. That was the first time she wondered if he might just die on her; if she would leave his emaciated corpse behind her, not enough meat on him for a Coyote's belly.

'I don't know what you mean,' she said flatly.

'It is our way,' he told her.

'The Horse men, will they do what you ask?' He had nothing to barter with, but she was desperate. If he had told her that he could magic them to obey his will, she would have believed him readily.

'The Horse Society, yes, they might,' he agreed, closing his pale eyes. 'If I can promise them enough profit in the south, they might.'

'And can you get them to take us away from here?'

His eyes flicked open. 'I am not ready to leave.'

'I don't care. My f—Stone River will be searching every span of Winter Runner land for us.'

'I came here with a purpose,' he protested mildly.

'Then you have failed in your purpose,' she snapped, scowling down at him as he sat on a stone and fiddled with the bindings about his brow. 'I freed you so you could help me.'

'Is it ss-so?' At last his hands were still, indeed all of him was still: a Snake that might strike at any moment, if only it had teeth.

'Yes, it is *ss-so*,' she retorted, mimicking his mumbled speech. 'And I swear that, if you betray me now, if you will not take me to the Horse and beg their aid to get away from my people, then I will abandon you. I will leave you for the cold or for the Wolf, whichever finds you first.'

'Do you even know where you want to go?' he asked her, still calmly, but the words stung.

'Yes, I . . .' And now she must name somewhere, but she did not know where. *My mother's people*, but she found that she was almost as afraid of that idea as of going back to the Winter Runners. She had no image of her mother, no connection at all to them save her Tiger soul, and she could not even say for sure that she would possess *that* for much longer. Perhaps the Wolf inside her would overcome it soon, maybe even before the end of winter, and then where would she be?

'What about south?' she asked faintly. '*Your* south?'

'You have no idea what that is, nor how far away, nor what you might do if you should find yourself there.' The weight of those words seemed to exhaust him.

'Take me where I ask or—'

'I know, I know.' He sighed. 'Let us find the Horse Society.' He plainly insisted on the formal title, however hard it was for him to say. 'Let us see what my little stock of influence may buy.' He stood up, wincing. 'Go, lead on.'

She Stepped to her wolf and ran for the treeline, because the rain was beginning to turn from a few light spots to something fiercer. *All the better to hide our scent*, she tried to tell herself, but the sheer misery of having to be out in such a downpour outweighed any such advantages.

Whenever she turned, he was even further behind. Sometimes he was a man, stumbling along in her wake. Sometimes she had to hunt back to find the snake winding its laborious way across the uneven ground, half lost amid the grass. It seemed to take forever for him to reach the trees.

'You need to move faster,' she told him, when he finally arrived and Stepped into his gaunt, bony human body.

'Is it sso?' he got out.

'As man or as snake. You can't just hobble along like that. They'll catch us easily.' It had all seemed such a good idea before. She had envisaged a swift flight across the night-time country, greeting the dawn somewhere far away from Akrit's hall. She had not considered how old he was, how pale and ill-looking. He looked like something sent by fate to slow her down so that her father's hunters would be able to amble along her trail and find her standing over the old man's frozen corpse. She had never seen someone so ill-suited for travel.

'How could you even get so far from your home?' she demanded, almost in tears. 'How did you not die before I ever saw you?'

'Warmer clothes and setting my own pace,' he replied tightly. 'If you will leave me, leave me now. I cannot go faster. I cannot get warm.'

'You'll die here.'

'It ss-seemss likely.' He shuddered. Then his head jerked up, his eyes wide and fixed on her. 'Or perhaps you will trust me?'

She regarded him cautiously. 'Trust you how?'

'Your little pack, that your wolf can carry. Let me ride there, between your shoulders, girl. I will weigh sso little, and I will be warm . . .' There was a dreadful longing in his voice.

The thought made her squirm. 'You . . . want to ride me like a beast, a horse?'

'We must be swift. You are swift on four feet, as I will never be.'

'But . . .' She remembered his serpent form – slender, yes, but surely too large to coil itself into her small bag. 'You won't . . .'

'I can Step into a shape as thick around as a strong man's thigh, or slender as a whip,' he told her. 'We are not so rigid as you, where I am from.' His expression was naked, stripped of the wise humour he had pretended to in the pit. 'Please, if we are to move on . . . Or leave me.'

She recalled that he would not have been fed in the pit – growing weaker and weaker because the Wolf would not care, when he ate the old man's soul, how thin the sacrificed body had been. Perhaps Hesprec Essen Skese had been fit to wander at his snail's pace across the Crown of the World, wearing snug clothes and relying on the hospitality of strangers. Now, though, he was at his lowest ebb, with neither strength nor wit enough to save himself.

His life was in her hands, just as it had been when she came to cut him loose. And yet she needed his intervention with the Horse if she was ever to get far enough from her father to be free.

She had abandoned her kin and thrown herself on the world's mercy, so perhaps mercy was what she should show.

'Step,' she told him. 'Step, and climb into my pack if you can.'

'I cannot bite,' he told her, misinterpreting the pause. 'You need not worry.'

'Old man, I do not fear you.'

To her surprise, that brought a thin smile. 'Brave child,' he whispered, and then he was gone, gathering his clothes close to him and Stepping down into something ribbon-thin, a patterned snake perhaps half as long as she was tall. Even then she thought he must be too bulky to do what he had claimed, but when she opened the bag he slid into it, and on into it, feeding each hand's breadth of his slender body further in until the delicate line of his tail had vanished inside, and he was gone completely from her sight.

She picked up the bag, feeling his unfamiliar weight, and feeling strange to know that the man she had been speaking to was now entirely tucked within. The thought was an uncomfortable one. She felt that somehow she was giving him power over her, for all that he had put himself entirely in her hands.

When she first felt him move sluggishly within the bag, she almost dropped it. It took her three tries before she could secure the bulky pack on her back. Then she Stepped to her wolf form and contorted her jaws until she could draw the strings tight, still feeling that unwelcome and unfamiliar weight. It was all too easy to imagine the thin lash of his body drawing itself about her neck, strangling her slowly to death no matter what shape she might try to fight him in. Yes, such an action on his part would make no sense, and yet he was a foreigner, and a priest of a foreign god-spirit, so how could she trust him? None of her own people's stories about Snake were happy ones.

But he had called her 'brave child', and she must be brave. Forcing down her qualms, she set off into the woods, passing swiftly as a wolf walks, hearing the rain beat on the overhanging needles above and drip all about her, scenting the complex book of the forest and its myriad denizens, that was written afresh each night and blotted out by the raindrops.

Fasting and drinking were a powerful combination. In the predawn there were only a handful up and out in the rain to witness what Maniye had done.

At first neither Akrit nor Kalameshli had made the connection. The priest had been furious that his prisoner had somehow escaped, storming back and forth and beating the two luckless sentries mercilessly with his flint-studded staff. Yes, their job had been pure formality, because no sacrifice had ever made it out of the pit before, but, still, theirs were the eyes and they were responsible. He stopped only when he had clubbed them both to the ground and broken one's arm.

By that time, half the tribe had been awakened, but few felt much like venturing outside.

Kalameshli had stood there with the rain streaking the half-done paint on his face – the start of his preparations for the day's festivities and ritual. By that time someone had roused Akrit, who could still drink all night and yet be up with the dawn. The chief of the Winter Runners stormed over, wrapped in a bearskin, with a seal cloak over it to keep out the wet. He surveyed the scene grimly, standing at the brink of the pit and noting the absence.

'How can he be gone?' he demanded.

Kalameshli did not answer. Whatever thoughts snapped and danced within his mind did not show themselves on his face.

Akrit looked up at the low leaden sky, wondering if any trace of the old Snake's scent might remain. 'He was old. How far can he have got?' He stared at the handful of his people who had braved the elements and Kalameshli's wrath. 'Get me every hunter fit to track! He could still be coiled up somewhere in the village.'

'He's gone,' the priest said softly, even as the spectators ran off to do their chief's bidding.

'You don't know that. He was frail,' Akrit argued. 'How long could he last out there, with winter coming on? He'll stay by the warmth.'

'He wasn't alone,' Kalameshli pronounced carefully.

'What do you mean?' Akrit's eyes narrowed. 'A rescue? Is there a whole nest of Snakes in the Wolf's Shadow?'

Abruptly, Kalameshli had Stepped, his wolf form lean and strong, like the younger man he had once been, the chains of his years left behind. Without even glancing at Akrit, the beast went padding away, nose kept low, moving round the pit in widening

85

circles. Akrit watched, wondering what the priest could possibly find, and yet the wolf was moving with a purpose, looking for *something* specific.

A few of his hunters had arrived by then, including the reassuringly loyal presence of Smiles Without Teeth. Akrit had not even begun to think about what this meant, the theft of a sacrifice on the Wolf's own day. As omens went, it could hardly be worse – and then he needed to think what that meant for his continuing rule over the Winter Runners, and where he would stand when the High Chief died. None of it was good. It was events like this that could break even a strong man like Akrit Stone River.

By then Kalameshli had Stepped again, kneeling thirty yards from the pit, gesturing for Akrit to join him.

He had found some tracks that the rain had filled but not yet washed clear. Akrit himself might have missed them, hunter as he was, but the priest had known. Somehow he had divined the truth as though the Wolf had breathed it into his ear.

'Tiger,' he stated, for Akrit's hearing only.

For a moment the chief was on the edge of the wrong conclusion, picturing some warband of the Shadow Eaters come down from the high places to attack their enemies. Would not stealing the Wolf's meat be the sort of coward's revenge they would try?

But then Kalameshli said simply, 'A very small tiger,' and Akrit finally understood.

Even then he did not want to believe it. He Stepped to his wolf shape and rushed back up to his hall, headed inside and then up the shallow incline of the ladder to the store where Maniye had made her lair. She was gone, and so was some of her clutter. She was *gone*.

He raced back to Kalameshli, springing back onto his human feet even as he reached him.

'I don't understand . . . she passed the Testing. You . . . you tested her yourself, you made sure . . .' He was perilously close to accusing the priest, stretching the bonds of their alliance.

86

For his part, Kalameshli seemed more than ready to pull against him. 'And you saw what I saw: there was nothing but the Wolf in her after she finished the course.' His words were hard like stones, quiet enough that nobody but Akrit would hear. 'But then you called her in when you were in your cups and told her far too much all at once.'

'Because she was supposed to be *ours*, then,' Akrit hissed, but before he could say anything that might strain the space between them to breaking point he held up his hands. 'You truly believe my daughter has taken the sacrifice and run off with him?'

A single sharp nod confirmed it.

Akrit stared past him for a moment, feeling the wound tear within him. Not a wound of love, no: what he felt for the girl had never borne that name. A wound to his pride, though. For any hunter of the Wolf, pride was a tender organ. Especially for a chief, for a man who would be Chief of Chiefs. Bad enough that Akrit had no sons to strengthen his name. Now even his daughter had turned against him. Who would follow a chief that could not rule his own blood?

Seeing Kalameshli's derisive expression he snapped, 'I'll send Smiles into the Roughback lands to take some of the Boar. They've been left alone too long. The Wolf won't go hungry.'

The priest's look showed how inadequate he thought the gesture would be.

By then his hunters were up, no matter how hungover, and were ready to do his bidding. His first instinct was to simply send them out immediately to all quarters, without any plan. Even with the rain hammering down, her trail would be out there. Having his people charging back and forth like ants would make him more of a fool, though, and what did the girl know, truly? How long could she really survive in the wild and the wood, either as woman or wolf? But she was cunning, and cunning would lead her to where there were other people. There were villages of the Boar and the Deer, the small homes of farmers and herders, and there were trading posts of the Coyote and the Horse. With or without the old Snake, she would make for somewhere that offered food and shelter.

He delivered his orders, giving each man a destination. His pride wanted to limit word of this disgrace to the village, but such secrecy would only aid Maniye's escape. He must spread word of the girl, and let everyone know that her return would buy the gratitude of the chief of the Winter Runners, a rich commodity indeed.

As he had promised Kalameshli, he dispatched Smiles Without Teeth and two warriors to attack the Boar, because the Wolf must have something to grind between his burning teeth, even if it was just thralls and farmers. The meal would not be as rich as they had both hoped – neither the antlers of Running Deer nor the skinny body of that foreign trespasser – but Akrit needed to husband all the goodwill he could manage.

And last he turned to Broken Axe, who had been waiting patiently there, never mind the rain. The lean man was already dressed as if to set off into the wilds, cloaked against the weather and with a sack of food tucked under his belt. His cold, pale eyes met Akrit's stare in that manner unique to him: neither a challenger nor one ready to submit to another man's will, self-sufficient in all things. And yet a hunter and a tracker without peer.

'You know what has happened here?' Because by now the word would be in the ears of every Winter Runner. Akrit had coloured the tale in the telling, saying that the old Snake had freed himself, through magic perhaps, and had enchanted his girl, stolen her away. The truth could look just as convincing when turned backwards and inside out.

Broken Axe nodded. What he believed, or even if he cared enough to believe anything, stayed hidden behind his closed expression.

'Track them down,' Akrit instructed him. 'Find the girl, bring her back here alive. If the Snake is with her . . .' Akrit shrugged. 'Use your discretion. But I must have my daughter back.' He almost said more, because of course Broken Axe would know why the girl was so important. He would remember the mother, and Akrit's orders all those years ago. But, no, perhaps some things were best left unsaid.

The hunter weighed Akrit's words, looking away for a moment, and then back with a questioning glance.

'Whatever you ask, within reason,' Akrit promised him. 'Perhaps more than you could ever think of asking for.' Because this was still the most advantageous match for Maniye, once the girl was safely back. The girl would bind Broken Axe to Akrit's plans, just when he might have most need of such a man. Similarly, Axe would no doubt tame the wild cunning in her, even if he had to whip it out of the girl.

At last, Broken Axe nodded, eyes still weighing Akrit and his gratitude against future need. A moment later he had dropped to all fours and Stepped into the shape of a gaunt, pale wolf with dark hackles raised about his shoulders. Without a moment's hesitation, he was padding off with so much certainty that Akrit wondered if he had already scented the trail out before presenting himself here.

8

After the hunt, only Venater would come close. Nobody needed to ask why Asmander did not Step to his Champion form for trivial purposes. The Laughing Men regarded him with that mix of awe and envy that he was used to, even from his own family. The shape he had been gifted with had no mute brothers in the world; the eyes of men had seen no other beasts that strode on those two sickle-clawed feet. There was something intangible but undeniable that hung about that shape: deep and fierce and demanding of respect.

If only this gift had fallen to Tecumander and not me. Asmander pictured his childhood friend, into whose young retinue old Asman had schemed so hard to place his son. And it had worked: the two boys had been inseparable, no stronger comrades in mischief to be found in all the Sun River Nation. When they had been young, it had not mattered that one was the son of a mid-ranking clan head, and the other was the son of the Kasra – the lord of all the Riverlands.

Had it been young Tecumander singled out by the gods for this honour, then a great many difficulties would never have arisen, and Asmander would not even now be heading towards the inhospitable north.

Back at the Laughing Men village, the Horse Society had already bundled up its belongings, ready to depart. The intact return of their Hetman and their two passengers was greeted with poorly hidden relief. They decamped to the river shortly afterwards, with the Malikah and a party of her people coming to see them off.

'Champion,' the Malikah of the Laughing Men addressed him, as the Horse people loaded their canoes, 'you must know, we hear much news of your nation here, by land and water.'

Asmander's manner suggested this topic of conversation was no great matter to him. 'Indeed?'

'You are not the first guests we have entertained here. Some were not heading north,' she murmured in his ear. 'Some came solely to seek my attention.'

He shrugged. 'No doubt you showed them the same good hospitality with which you have honoured us. Perhaps they were here to trade.'

'In their own way. They sought to trade for the use of our spears. It is an odd thing, but the wind tells me that there is strange weather in the Sun River Nation since the old Kasra died.'

'We are a complex people,' he said. 'Will you tell me of your response to them?' They could not be Tecuman's emissaries that had come to her, that much seemed plain. And if they had not come at the behest of Asmander's friend, they were likely his enemies.

'Will you tell me of your prince?' Her breath was hot on his cheek, her voice scarcely more than a whisper.

'He is a paragon of honour. From his youngest days he was marked to rule, by his own manner and by signs and portents noted by the priests. All who saw him knew him as he on whom the mask of the Kasra must surely fall,' Asmander recited.

'I think not,' the Malikah said softly, 'for if it were as you say, then I would not have visitors from the south seeking the spears of the Laughing Men to come to Atahlan.'

'And what did you tell them, these visitors?'

Her yipping laugh was so loud and sudden in his ear that he

91

started away from her with a curse, the Champion's soul stirring briefly in him.

'Champion, the Laughing Men do not take sides,' the Malikah declared. 'We wait, and we mark those who are weak, and those who have lived too long, and those whose time has come to pass on. Merely hope, then, that your prince is strong.'

Then she turned from him and gripped Venater by the arm, hard enough to make him bare his teeth. 'You, you old Goat-Eater, you are a villain.' But her look was fond. 'If your young River Lord is too soft a master, come back here. There is always work for a man to do.'

He twisted his arm from her grasp and sent her such a look – that of a man who truly does not know how to take the measure of the woman before him. Despite the grim conversation he had just endured, Asmander summoned a laugh from somewhere.

Then the Horse were pushing their boats out into the water, and it was time to leave.

Just as Asmander swung himself over the side of the nearest vessel, another figure splashed out towards them. For a moment he thought it was the Malikah herself, but it was a different woman of the Laughing Men, much younger, a sack and two spears in one hand and a cloak of aurochs hide over her shoulders. The Horse Hetman made room for her in her own craft, with an ambiguous look towards the southerners.

'Seems you impressed them too much,' Venater said, staring at the woman with suspicion. 'Looks like they want to keep an eye on you.'

Asmander had half expected as much, given what the Malikah had said. When he looked at the new arrival, he found her gaze on him already. She had her hair cropped close at the sides, with a tawny crest on top, and there were bars of red highlighting her cheekbones. Like so many of her fellows, she had a startlingly *alive* quality, a flame of the moment for which the weights of old history and future prospects that troubled

Asmander's people simply did not exist. It made her beautiful, as fire was beautiful even as it destroyed.

The Plains tribes were becoming aware of changes in their southern neighbour. Some would seek to profit from it; others might be dragged in despite themselves. And the Laughing Men would always be ready to pick over the bones.

Or these waters may yet grow calm, he reminded himself, not for the first time. There were no battle lines yet, no declarations of war, no accusations or claims. But Tecuman had gone to the fortress at Tsokawan that secured control of the estuary islands, whilst in the capital of Atahlan . . .

But nothing will happen before the new year's floods. Surely nobody is so eager to shed blood and break down walls? They will talk and talk, and the Serpent's priests will meet, and nobody will lift their hand in anger, not yet.

It will not come to that. There will be bellowing and splashing and a showing of teeth, that is all. The Sun River Nation cannot war against itself.

That was his mission to the north, of course: the same that had sent other emissaries to the Laughing Men. He was going to fetch more teeth, better teeth. He was going to entice the Iron Wolves of the Crown of the World to come and stand by Tecuman's side. Surely that would be enough.

He felt the gaze of the Hyena girl fixed on him keenly, as though she was waiting for him to die.

It was the same when they drew up to the bank to make camp. When he looked for her, she was busy setting out her own blanket away from the Horse Society and the rest, laying out the brightly striped cloth with an air of great ritual. She was still watching him, though: when he turned his head away, her eyes were like points of faint pain in his mind.

It was a game, he knew. She wanted to draw him to her. The Malikah had tasked her with learning about the southern travellers, perhaps, or at least about their quest in the north. Probably the two of them would fight at some future time, her mission and his reaching their distant crossing point from which only one would walk away.

So he smiled to himself and made a great point of ignoring her, and thus sought to draw her to him, to force the questions from her. It was an old game amongst the Patient Ones of the Riverlands. His father had played it like a master, using silence like a killing edge to savage his enemies – and his own family.

It was one of Asmander's deepest-buried secrets, the thing about his father. He himself was the dutiful son, the paragon of his clan, the boy who did everything that was expected of him.

But the Champion's soul did not like his father. It loved the prince Tecuman as Asmander did, but his father, no. That fierce, proud soul bucked against the man's hand, bared its teeth at his orders. And who was Asmander to say that it was not right? It saw so many things more clearly than human eyes could.

And another smothered secret thought was just this: *If I were not his son, would I like him? Or would I loathe him as a dangerous, ambitious creature?*

Just as well I'm his son, then. And just as well he supports Tecuman, for I could not make that choice, not blood kin against bound brother.

'She says she's Shyri.' Venater dropped down beside him heavily.

Asmander closed his eyes. The delicate game that had been coming together between him and the girl was abruptly in ruins, and one more source of entertainment on the journey north was gone. 'You have no soul.'

'I have a Blackteeth soul,' Venater replied robustly. The Blackteeth were his tribe amongst the people of the Dragon, one of three equally vicious and disreputable clans of villains. To Asmander's knowledge, he had abandoned any close loyalty to them long ago, but he was still proud of bearing the violent stigma of their blood.

'So what is this Shyri and why do I care?'

'I thought you were sweet on her, from the way you weren't looking at her,' Venater leered.

'Oh, really?'

'These things are known: Asman's First Son has a reputation,' the pirate goaded.

'Not known this far into the Plains, I hope.' Asmander managed a wan grin. 'And no, not interested, save in what she wants from us.'

'She says she's the Malikah's daughter,' Venater stated. 'Not sure if that's actual daughter or just one of her tribe.'

'Well, if she can bear your breath, she's all yours,' Asmander assured him.

Venater gave him a crooked look. 'Not likely. Lay the mother, then the daughter? That's inviting ill luck.' His broad shoulders twitched. 'Besides, one woman of the Laughing Men is quite enough. Enough for a lifetime.'

This time Asmander laughed outright. Glancing over at the Hyena girl, he caught her predatory stare, just for a moment. Sitting away from the fire, away from the dozen Horse Society travellers already sharing a skin of something and telling one of their circular and recursive stories, she seemed as estranged as he was, even though this was her land.

The attack came two days later. The mechanics of it were simple: two ropes strung across the course of the river at a narrow point, sagging low enough that two of the canoes had passed over the first without noticing it. Then the trap was sprung, and abruptly both lines were pulled tight, catching the lead pair of boats between them, and almost flipping the last craft over as the line sprang up beneath its bows. Then there were warriors leaping down from the east bank, brandishing spears and bows.

The terrain here was rugged, the river grinding a canyon through the dry land that grew steeper the further north they travelled. The west bank rose in sheer cliffs, accessible only through occasional landslips or the odd path that had been painstakingly carved into the rock. The eastern shore was less severe, but still a ragged tumble of rock and scrub, sometimes rising to ten feet over the water, sometimes closer to twenty. The eroded, rocky ground offered plenty of hiding places, and in the first seconds of the attack Asmander felt that the whole bank was suddenly transformed into leaping, whooping men and women.

They were tall and long-limbed, some unarmoured and wearing only cloaks and tunics, others with cuirasses made from strips of thick grey hide. Most of the men amongst them sported headdresses of feathers, stiffened hair and grass that surrounded their faces, standing out in a ragged mane on all sides like the rays of the sun. Their faces were painted with white darts, like teeth.

The handful that had bows were already loosing arrows in shallow arcs over the water. One of the Horse men in Asmander's boat was struck at once, the shaft piercing deep into his arm. Others were scrabbling for their own weapons or trying to shelter under the gunwales. The lead canoe had struck the forward rope and skewed off towards the bank, the eddy of the current taking it right towards the attackers, as had obviously been planned.

The Hyena girl, Shyri, was in that first boat, and Asmander saw her crouching there, one spear in her off hand, and one cocked back ready to throw.

'Shall we?' Asmander called to Venater.

The pirate nodded, his face gone hard as stone. A moment later he had Stepped, from human to a great lizard coiled within the boat. Lunging over the side, he almost upset it entirely. Then he had vanished into the water, nothing to be seen of him but a sinuous wake.

Some of the Horse were now sending back arrows, using their deceptively small recurved bows that were supposed to be the best in the world.

Asmander bunched himself and then dived over the side of the boat into the water, Stepping even as the cool river hit him, so that what moved beneath the surface with a powerful thrashing of its tail was Old Crocodile, the long, ridge-backed shape of the River Lords. Instantly he was alive with new senses, feeling the liquid medium pulse and surge around him with every movement, scenting blood and fear, and letting the tremors and currents inform him. His whole body rippled with muscular ease, surging him forwards with all the speed he could muster, mastering the current that was trying to drag him away. His eyes broke the surface, seeing the confusion of movement that was the attackers. More than one of them had gone in ankle-deep or more to snare the lead boat.

His lunge was perfect, wholly unsuspected, his great jaws thrusting from the breaking water to clamp across the calf of one of the warriors there, filling the hungry void of his mouth with blood. A spasmodic twist of his tail and his yelling victim was dragged into the deep water. Here was where Asmander's mute brothers would hold the prey until it drowned, then tear it apart, working their jaws against each other's. He had no such desire or luxury of time, and so he wrenched himself sideways, spinning his body as if he was trying to tear off a mouthful of flesh and making a horrible ruin of the warrior's leg. A second later he had released his hold – fighting his Crocodile soul, which wanted only to slake its gluttony – and whipped himself back towards the shore. The river would finish what he had started with his prey.

This time he did not ambush from the water's edge, but turned his burst of speed into a leap out of the bloody wash that had him Stepping straight into his Champion's form, landing on two clawed feet with a shrill shriek of challenge.

The enemy nearest him had been about to cast a spear. She Stepped as she saw him, dropping into the heavy body of a lioness. Her amber eyes were wide and her ears flattened back, though, and she retreated from his stalking shape, swiping at him with a paw.

Asmander took a moment to take stock, despite the fierce need of his soul to seek battle. There was Venater's long, black-scaled body locked in a murderous embrace with a young lion, his jaws closed on the beast's throat, his hook-clawed feet sunk into its hide. On the other side, where the boat was, a handful of the Horse were fighting savagely with spears and long-handled dagger-axes. Two were down already, and then another Stepped, rearing up as a stallion and bringing bronze-hard hooves down on the heads of the attackers.

He heard a shrill cackle, and caught sight of Shyri, a hyena snapping and dancing as she led on a lion almost twice her size. She seemed terribly outmatched, and yet the bigger beast's hide was bloodied, and she was always just outside its reach. Then she was a woman again, whipping her cloak across that great muzzle and then driving her spear towards it, bloodying the claws it put out to snare her.

Asmander could hold himself back no longer. Three steps and a leap took him into the midst of the band that was pressing in on the Horse men, ripping a claw down one woman's ribs and bowling over a couple more. Instantly he was surrounded by lions, snarling and baring fangs, but the Horse took their chance, driving at their enemy with their long weapons, cutting themselves space.

Asmander had fought the Lion before and knew them well. A big male cat was heavier and stronger than his Champion form, but nowhere near as swift. More, the Lion were always coura-geous on the attack, far less so when forced to defend themselves. They liked easy conquests and were too wise to fight against the odds. With that in mind, Asmander unleashed a flurry of strikes, nothing that would kill or raise more than a scar, but he got a claw into all three of the beasts close to him and they sprang away, hurt and startled.

By then he had the Horse backing him, and Shyri slunk in

on one side with her teeth grinning red, whilst Venater was approaching along the waterline with a slow, insolent, tail-dragging pace.

The Lion raiders reformed partway up the bank, some as humans, some as beasts. They still outnumbered the travellers by more than two to one, but the presence of Shyri and the two southerners was plainly an unwanted complication.

Then one of them stepped forth: a man bigger than his fellows, his chest bare and gleaming like copper, hatched with scars and painted with thick white dagger-blades. He wore no mane of grass, and his face seemed misshapen, heavy-jawed and brutish. He had a short-hafted axe in each hand, the blades of chipped flint.

A pair of the Horse were getting their wounded on the boat as calmly as possible, making no sudden moves. Asmander Stepped abruptly to human, to draw the Lions' attention.

Shyri followed him. 'He's—' she started, but Asmander cut her off with a sharp nod. A Lion Champion this, no doubt of it. He could feel the presence of the man like a tangible thing, something more than the mere bulk of him could account for.

It was an unlooked-for prize, to pit his soul against this man's. Asmander squared his shoulders, feeling within him that thrill of anticipation that was both his and not his.

Then Venater had unfolded into his human shape as well. 'This one's mine.'

Asmander glanced at him. The pirate was grinning, just a little, showing his brown and yellow teeth. He was shorter than his opponent, broader at the shoulder but surely more than ten years older.

'You're sure?'

For answer, Venater stepped forwards, pointing the stone blade of his *meret* at the Lion Champion. 'Hey, fat boy!'

Shyri yelped in amusement, sitting back on her haunches.

In an instant the Lion had dropped to all fours and Stepped, undergoing a monstrous shift as his bulk bloated out and forwards. His cat shape was stub-tailed, heavy-shouldered. He was half again the size of the largest lion Asmander had seen, fangs like swords curving from his upper jaw. Every line of him demanded fear and awe. Here was a monster that lived only within the soul of the Lion; no beast like this walked the earth.

The Champion roared, the sound rolling across the rocks like thunder. Everyone else held motionless as he padded forwards, his steps almost delicate. Venater stood waiting, still as stone.

He had his tricks, though, did the old pirate. The first was that sudden shift of stature, from big man to the low-slung bulk of a lizard. Venater was moving even as the Champion increased his pace and, when his enemy pounced, he was ducking, lunging forwards into his reptile form as though he was a thrown spear. The whip of his tail raised a welt across the Champion's ribs, and then they were both turning, the Lion faster, Venater just fast enough. The Champion smacked out with a paw, the claws skidding off his opponent's pebbly hide to leave a smear of blood. Venater's sharkskin coat lent a thousand tiny blades to his lizard scales. Then the Lion's terrible jaws were gaping wide, insanely wide, about to drive those killing teeth down into him. Venater writhed aside, taking a gash across the shoulder that peeled even his tough skin, and dragged his own regiment of fangs across the Lion's foreleg just as he twisted away.

Then the two of them were circling, or at least the Champion was circling and Venater was mostly staying still, just shuffling round to keep facing his enemy. Blood welled sluggishly from his opened shoulder.

The Champion went for him again, a smooth transition from stalking to leaping that caught Asmander by surprise. The old pirate had been waiting for it, though, rearing up onto his hind legs and then abruptly becoming human, trying to vault over the swift bulk of his enemy. He almost made it, too, but the high crest of the Lion's back knocked him aside, sprawling him on the ground.

Asmander was aware of many eyes flicking towards him, wanting to know when he would intervene to save his companion. He wanted to – moment to moment he wanted to – but it was not his place. Venater would have cursed him for it.

Venater was up on one knee, breathing heavily under the yellow gaze of the Champion. He drew the greenstone of his *meret* up to his mouth and licked its edge as though seeking the taste of blood there. He stood up slowly, watching the Lion pace, weathering the fire of the Champion's presence. He looked like a man waiting for execution.

Then the Champion was rushing down on him again, but three steps into his charge the Lion stumbled, his wounded foreleg folding unexpectedly. Venater was on him immediately, seeming for a moment to be grappling the creature, and then he had brought the dense weight of his blade down across the Lion's back and ribs with a single solid stroke.

The Champion yowled in pain, knocking Venater flat with a blow of his paw but not following up, instead backing away, limping and favouring one side. For a second he was a warrior again, staring at Venater in bafflement: *Why aren't you dead yet, old man?* Asmander knew that look well enough.

Then they had both Stepped back to their fighting shapes, but this time it was Venater who was advancing implacably, and the Champion fell back, one uncertain step at a time. The venom in the Lion's veins was not enough to kill, but the great beast's strength was being sapped moment to moment. He would need a quick victory over Venater, and yet, when courage was most needed, the man was failing.

Asmander found himself silently urging the Lion on, Champion to Champion, willing the man to stand and fight. *What would I do, if I were he?* Of course he would like to think that he would go on until the death. Was it really true though? Surely every man's courage was a rope of uncertain length, hauled hand over hand out of clouded waters. Who knew how suddenly that rope's end would whip up into the air?

Then the Lion Champion was a man again, standing impassively, staring at the black length of the dragon lizard before him. He closed his eyes, letting his axes fall, and then he had dropped to one knee – not submission so much as being unable to stand any longer. A current of anguish and despair murmured through the Lion raiders as they saw it.

Venater regarded him, bluish tongue flicking. He took another lethargic step forwards.

'Back,' Asmander told him. 'Enough.'

A shudder of annoyance rippled down the lizard's body.

A fistful of threats came to Asmander, invocation of the powers his clan had gained over the defeated pirate, the oaths of fealty that had bought him his life. In the end, though, all he said was, 'No doubt you will enjoy your fill of Champion's blood, old man, but not today. Your chance will come.'

Venater was abruptly human again, staring back at him. Asmander's meaning was heard and understood. When he had won his name back from the First Son of Asman, there would be a settling of scores.

'These things are known,' he growled, and Asmander nodded.

The Lion raiders were retreating back up the ragged rocks on the bank. One of the Horse Society was dead, two injured but not in imminent danger. Venater moved his torn shoulder, wincing and feeling for the damage.

'Let them see to it,' Asmander advised. He thought the pirate would refuse, but then a tired expression came to Venater's eyes and he nodded wearily.

A familiar pressure came to Asmander then, and he looked about to find Shyri still sitting at the water's edge but in her human form now. This time she did not look away.

'You would have killed him, of course, or let Venater kill him,' he observed to her.

She shrugged. Seeing that the Horse had brought all their boats to shore and were cutting away the two ropes restricting the river, he abruptly sat down beside her.

'How far has your mother sent you, Laughing One?'

'What makes you think I am sent?' Her stare was intrusive, like a prodding finger.

'How far will you go, then? All the way to the cold?'

'Wherever I wish, however far I care to.'

'And will you follow me?' he asked her.

Her eyes flared wide. 'Longmouth, you flatter yourself,' and she was suddenly up and stalking over to the boats, leaving behind only Asmander – and Venater's faint laughter.

9

What surprised Maniye was how well she could run. For all her life she had been tethered to Akrit's hall and to the scatter of mounds that was the village of the Winter Runners. At best she had gone as far as the treeline perhaps, or ventured between the fields and pens that spread out beyond the mounds. She had never known what it was like just to run, to give her paws free rein and let them tear up the miles.

The wolf inside her knew, though. It had been born to the wilds and, from the first time she had Stepped, those wilds had been planted in her like a yearning that grew and grew.

She had the best of both worlds. A true wolf would have felt the cold far more, but she had swallowed up three layers of wool and deer hide when she Stepped, and carried that extra warmth with her, husbanding her strength rather than spending it profligately on fighting the chill.

If she had been traversing the forest on two feet, with only the senses of a human girl to aid her, then she would have become lost very swiftly, gone in circles and never known it until her father's people caught up with her. The wolf in her could not get lost. Her nose was the gateway to a world of a thousand thousand clues, where every tree was a wealth of information to navigate by. With each inhaled breath the world told her where north was, with the promise of snow borne on white wings. She knew instantly the paths her mute brothers the wolves used when they crossed the forest, and knew to avoid them. She knew where the boars had rooted, where the deer had run. Her nose marked where the owl had stooped and the sinuous track the marten made. She knew the grave of every mouse, the buried hoards of squirrels. Every moment told its story, and all those myriad stories joined together in her mind to weave a picture of countless threads, telling her exactly where she was and which way she must go.

She never ventured deep into the forest, but kept the edge of the trees at the periphery of her attention, hiding from view and yet cutting the shortest path. Sometimes she forgot the burden on her back that no natural wolf would bear. Sometimes, for short spaces, she even forgot what she was running from. The running had become an end in itself.

She surprised small animals, even birds. She killed a young deer, bursting out on it in a moment of mutual surprise and then lunging forwards, hooking her teeth into its haunches and tasting the sudden salt rush of blood. She brought it down in a furious struggle, clumsy and panicking at first, but then riding her instinct to rip at the kicking beast's throat. Afterwards, her wolf jaws fed ravenously while her human mind commended her prey's soul to its totem to be reborn anew, perhaps as a mute beast again, or perhaps as one of the Deer's tribe.

As she ate, Hesprec Essen Skese slithered from her back and Stepped into his old human bones. She regarded him warily because, if he wanted to talk, she might have to join him in that shape, and she did not want to. The wolf was warmer than the girl might have been. The wolf was freer too.

He tore himself a little meat, in tiny scraps that he could swallow raw – certainly nothing that he might have needed to chew. What he ate would not have sated a stoat, and yet it seemed to be enough for him. Perhaps the serpent in him needed little sustenance, slim as it was.

After she was fed – and resisting the sudden urge to find somewhere to curl up – she whined at him urgently. He was squatting on his heels, watching her thoughtfully, apparently just as grateful as she not to resume their sparring of before. Now he Stepped once more, back to that little sliver of sliding shadow that must be the smallest snake he could become.

This time, taking his place in her pack, his cold ridged body climbed up her flank to get there. This did not seem as objectionable as she had expected and, once he was in place, his weight between her shoulder blades was almost familiar. Perhaps she would even have missed it, had he been left behind.

She followed her nose, in the end, and her sense of the sloping ground. She had travelled this way once before, many years ago, when the Horse had first established a trading post in Winter Runner lands and her father had taken a hunting party to go and impress them. She had been too young to Step back then, denied all these clues to help her find her way, but she had still possessed eyes and a mind sharp enough to remember. Now she could analyse those memories and know that she must scent out running water, for the Horse had made their camp on the banks of the Sand Pearl river. Even such meagre clues were enough to guide her to where she wanted to go.

When there was smoke on the air, she turned away from it. Since leaving the Winter Runners she had not seen anything that wore a human shape except the Snake priest, and the more she looked on him, the less sure she was that he was entirely human. Seeing him in daylight had been a shock, because he had hardly any more colour to him than he had under the moon. She had not seen him close up when her father had brought him in, and memory had smudged the edges of her recollection. Now she saw that his skin really was white, as though all the blood and colour had been drained from him, save where old tattoos crossed his sunken cheeks and high forehead, faded diamonds of orange and purple making a snakeskin trail that led across to his covered scalp. His eyes were almost colourless, the skin around them pinkish and unhealthy-looking. She had never seen eyes so wide and round before; they looked as though, should he ever be truly surprised by something, they would pop from their sockets entirely.

They had stopped to let her rest and to eat a little more of their dwindling provisions. Seeing her critical regard, he smiled thinly. 'You must ssee few travellers here in the north. I cannot imagine why.'

She looked disdainful at that, especially as the Crown of the World was not *north*. North was the highlands and the mountains, the Bear and the cold. North was the Crystal Valley People of the stories, so beautiful that no traveller who saw them ever wished to return home. 'We have the Horse,' she pointed out. He looked quite different from the Horse people, though, and for a moment she felt very small when thinking on how far he must have walked to reach the lands of the Wolf.

And what a wasted journey, in that case. But, after all, if not for him, where would she herself be? Perhaps he had been sent by Wolf or Tiger or by some greater invisible power that had chosen to meddle in her life.

He was carefully adjusting the cloth about his head, pulling the strips tighter, but his pale eyes were smiling still. Rested and warm, she could hardly equate him with the desperate creature of that previous night, who had begged her to carry him.

'You have a plan, of course,' he observed, 'for when you reach wherever you wish the Horse to take you?'

She did not rise to the bait. No, she had no plan – or rather the plan was just *away*, and any finer details would have to wait.

'Why do you wrap your head?' Always better to turn the questions back on him. 'Have you hurt it?'

He gave her an amused look. 'History and reverence.'

'You have a lot of long words that say nothing.' She put her hands on her hips, wondering if she should demand proper answers, or else refuse to carry him in the pack again.

He gave a croak of laughter. 'Stone River's daughter, you are a fierce huntress. Will you track down all my old man's habits

107

and tear out their poor throats?' His words were still soft about the edges where his teeth should have shaped them, but he was working hard on compensating for the loss. 'As Serpent dwells under the ground – under the ground everywhere – so we hide ourselves likewise. To go bare-headed under the sun where our god cannot would be disrespectful.'

'If your Serpent is under *this* ground, he is frozen.' She was not sure why exactly she wanted to dent his comfortable composure, but the urge was strong in her.

'No doubt you are right.' Her words glanced off him and left no wound, but they left him thoughtful nonetheless. 'I am a long way from home and, though I know that he is with me, that he moves in the earth even here, sometimes it is hard . . .' His next smile was touched with pain. 'Perhaps we should be on our way?'

She followed the scent and sound of fresh water until she found one of the innumerable streams that laced the Crown of the World like filigree. Running alongside the water took her to what she guessed must be the Little Sand Pearl, a swift-flowing river still fierce and angry after its journey from the highlands before it joined its big sister. Her best judgement had taken her downstream, and now she was rewarded with a tangle of smoke from a score of fires, and the unmistakable sight of the Horse trading post.

Actually seeing it there, a testament to her impromptu navigation, gave her a sudden surge of hope. She was just a girl, a pup, a cub, and yet she had travelled for two days on fleet paws, and found herself arriving exactly at the target she had set. Which of her father's hunters could have accomplished the same?

Almost all of them, came her own caustic response, but she shook it off, bounding along the Sand Pearl's banks with fresh energy.

I will sleep under cover tonight, and in my human form, she told herself. Save for brief rests and the odd word with the old

Serpent, she had held to the wolf's form almost entirely. *And we will get food and warmer clothes.* For the air was just starting to fill with falling snow and she was starting to feel the chill through her pelt and the clothes inhered beneath it.

And Hesprec will make them take us away from here, she thought.

And then ... and then ... To get out from under the Wolf's Shadow, that was enough. What choices there were she would make as a free woman and without her father's heavy hand twisting her course.

The Horse Society post was not like anything else in the Crown of the World. They did not raise hills to build on: instead there was a wooden wall of stakes encircling their compound, with a gap opening on to the river and another, opposite, on to the land. Within, the Horse had built round houses of sticks that were set up on stilts high enough that, as a child, she had crawled under one.

Although the walls would plainly allow the Horse men to defend what they had, the effect of the whole was curiously meek and unimposing. Without a grand earthen mound, such as the least of the Wolf dwellings was set up on, the trading post did not dominate the landscape but seemed almost to hide in it. Despite all that heavy wood, and the work and time invested in the construction, the trading post had a curiously temporary air, as though the Horse might at any time simply pack it up and haul it elsewhere.

Outside the walls were a motley assortment of tents and the smoking remains of campfires. She remembered there being more when she had travelled here as a child but, with winter coming on, the itinerant traders of this land would be heading home, whether they had obtained what they sought or not.

By the time she had trotted closer, the snow was thickening and the air had grown cold enough that she wondered if even the swift Sand Pearl might see some ice. She walked between the tents cautiously, spotting almost nobody. The traders themselves would no doubt be hurrying to conclude their business within the palisade, and their wives and hearth-husbands had laced the tents shut against the weather.

Nobody stopped her from entering the trading post, although she drew plenty of looks as people satisfied themselves that she was Stepped, and not some bold little animal come in from the woods to steal a supper.

Although that may yet be necessary. She was aware that, no matter how much she had excelled so far, she would now be at the mercy of her companion. She had nothing to barter – or nothing she was willing to barter – that might gain her anything from the traders of the Horse Society.

She slunk around the wall of the nearest propped-up house until she was out of the wind and the worst of the snow. Stepping into her true shape meant immediately feeling the bite of the cold, as her fur was stripped away.

Shivering a little, she placed her pack on the ground and prodded it with her foot until the snake reluctantly emerged. For a moment the little reptile just coiled in upon himself, writhing against the chill, but before he could grow sluggish, Hesprec Essen Skese Stepped out from its twisting loops and hugged himself, mouth twisted in a toothless grimace.

'You're glad we're going to head off south *now*, aren't you,' Maniye told him grimly.

He managed to raise a smile, even then. 'Ssave me from women who must always be *right*.' He took a deep breath, and the following exhalation plumed on the air. 'Let us seek out some dignitary of the Horse and petition him. At the least, let us hope they offer us the hospitality of a roof, even if it is just for as long as our words with them last.'

There were still a few people about despite the snow, and they quickly found a couple of Coyote traders heading back for their tents, satchels bulging with whatever the Horse had bartered to them. The Coyote were a familiar sight all over the Crown of the World, mocked as a tribe that would be Wolves if

110

they only could. Still, Coyote himself was a clever trickster, and his people survived the winters and the Wolves' disdain equally well.

Hesprec held out a hand to attract their attention, bringing it back vertically to his lips in an odd, ritual gesture that must have been a habit of his homeland. The two Coyote men stared at the mismatched pair and exchanged glances. Maniye was uncomfortably aware that they probably thought she was the old man's thrall, or worse. Hunched in his borrowed sheepskin jacket, Hesprec asked them for directions without ever really speaking, his hands talking for him, and one of the traders singled out a hut with a jab of his finger.

In the flurrying snow they could see little of the place but a shadow, so they worked their way around its curving wall until they found the three layers of hung skins that were keeping the weather out. Inside it was absurdly warm, the heat of a central fire combining with the bodies of almost twenty people to make the air thick and heavy with the reek of sweat. There was barely room there for two more, even a skinny girl and a skinnier old man, but with a little shoving and some half-hearted curses they managed to get themselves inside with the furs falling closed behind them.

Most of the press were outsiders, here for the last few days of the trading season. She saw plenty more Coyotes, short, thickset men and women who could have passed for Wolf if only they'd strutted more. Most of them had peeled back their clothes and were sitting relishing the fire, with sweat glistening on their skin. Maniye saw a couple playing a game she knew, bones balanced on the backs of their hands and then flipped up for catching – or perhaps to seek a glimpse of the future in the way they fell. One pair, a man and a woman, were entwined in an embrace, fumbling ardently despite the spectators.

She saw a couple of Crows down from the Eyrie: small wiry men who were the only friendly ambassadors those heights produced. Each had half his face painted or tattooed with intricate

111

curling patterns of black, and they stared at the newcomers using one eye at a time, tilting their heads to either side just like birds.

There was a raised platform at the far end of the hut, and it was there that the Horse were conducting their business. There was a man up there who seemed to be in charge, broad-shouldered and broader-waisted, and yet probably as tall as Hesprec if he stood. He wore a thin beige robe of some material she didn't know – certainly not the wool she was used to. It was richly ornamented at the hems with stitching of many colours, and she thought it was one of the finest garments she had ever laid eyes on. Above it, around his neck, was a torc of copper, polished to gleam in the firelight. The sight of it made her uncomfortable – too much like the halters that thralls wore to prevent them Stepping. The metal did not meet at the front, and was presumably a symbol of rank and importance, but she could not shake the feeling that there was a touch of servitude there, even so.

There was a Horse woman sitting up there behind him, dressed more plainly in a long woollen shirt, and she was making marks in a clay tablet to tally whatever the man was bargaining for, and occasionally interrupting to give her opinion. She had the same coppery skin as all the Horse people, with a pointed face and a curved nose, and Maniye thought she looked very exotic and elegant. She had heard the Winter Runner men talk often enough about the grace and beauty of Horse women.

Another of the Horse had hopped down from the platform as soon as they came in, and he kicked and pushed his way through the gathered throng to speak to them. He was long-boned and much younger than the Hetman doing the bargaining – enough to be the wide man's son – and he wore a jerkin of hard leather scales over a wool robe that fell to his knees. Like all the Horse she had ever seen, he had a calm strength to him that went beyond merely his strong frame. His eyes were flecked and tawny, like polished stones.

His attention skipped from one to the other, resting mostly on Hesprec and plainly not sure what to make of him. 'You come to trade?' he asked, a flick of his gaze taking in their other visitors. 'What goods have you?' It was only through hearing his voice, and the strangeness of the way he spoke, that Maniye noticed the absence of anything similar in Hesprec. For all his odd choices of words, the Snake spoke as though he had been born to the Crown of the World. Except now, when he matched the Horse man's accent perfectly.

'Special goods for those heading south before the ice comes. A trade that comes along once in two span of years.' Hesprec's smile was broad, but without teeth it could never quite aspire to looking friendly. Still, he did his best.

The tall Horse man gave him a doubting look. 'You may be best to come next morning with your special trading, white one. There are many here to barter before you.' His eyes moved to Maniye again, and he surprised her with a smile. 'But our fire is warm. I offer that to you at least,' and then he was striding and shoving his way to return to the platform.

Up there, their chief was just concluding a trade, finishing with some grinning remark that had the Coyote woman opposite laughing – evidently a good deal for all concerned. As she hopped down and began to make her way towards the door, the tall man clambered up and had a murmured word with his superior.

The man in the torc seemed to doubt him, but then looked over and caught sight of Hesprec with almost exaggerated surprise. Maniye felt his eyes as they shifted to her and stayed there longer than she was happy with. With a few words and a gesture, the Hetman had sent his man back down to Hesprec and Maniye.

'It seems you're more special than you think,' he explained, a little exasperated by this turn of events. 'Come . . . come with me.' He reached upwards, and Maniye saw that there were struts overhead that projected out from where the walls met the

113

eaves, sloping up along the line of the roof but leaving a gap where various bundles had been stowed. From there, the tall Horse dragged down a heavy leather coat trimmed with fur and pulled it about himself. 'The Trading Master wants to speak about this special trade of yours, but somewhere better fit for it. Come with me.'

They struggled out into the snow again, which was now settling steadily. Hurrying almost on the heels of their guide, neither Maniye nor Hesprec were in any position to watch out around them, nor did they have any animal senses to call on.

From between two of the Horses' round huts, a wolf watched them, pale enough to be almost invisible in the snow, save for the darker fur about his shoulders. Narrowing his eyes against the thickening flakes, Broken Axe considered his next move.

10

The hut they were led to was smaller, and empty, with the embers of a central fire retaining just enough warmth for comfort. A raised platform furthest from the door bore a mess of furs and woollen blankets for sleeping on.

The tall young Horse man clasped his hands together before him. It meant nothing to her, but Hesprec echoed the gesture.

'I am Alladei, hand-son of the Trading Master Ganris, who directs all you see,' the Horse announced, although he wore a slightly complicit expression, as if to say, *Yes, grand words for so little*. Maniye found herself warming to him, perhaps just because he was the first person to show them some kindness.

'I am Hesprec Essen Skese, priest of the Serpent and one who has travelled far. Perhaps too far.' The old man spoke with a careful dignity that Maniye knew was to hide his ravaged gums. Again, his accent matched that of the man he was speaking to.

'My hand-father wishes to speak with you without many ears to hear. I shall find you food and drink and all else you might require.' Again he brought his hands together, and then he was backing out of the hut. All that time his attention had been only on Hesprec, but his eyes sought out Maniye just as he was leaving, and she thought she caught a smile in them.

'What is a "hand-son"?' she wondered aloud. She had almost thought he'd said 'handsome' at first.

'He will not be of this Ganris's blood, but adopted into his family. In the Horse, they do all things their own way.' Hesprec was sending birdlike glances about the interior of the hut, and now he hobbled over and sat on the platform, drawing one of the furs about him.

Maniye frowned. 'They take care of the orphaned – who does not?'

'No, no, they *buy* them.' Seeing her expression the old man cackled. 'The Horse buy children – some say steal them, but this I do not believe. It can be a good life, to be of the Horse. When there is no food, where a child might die otherwise, sometimes it is done to sell them to the Horse.'

'But . . . when they learn to Step . . . ?'

Hesprec shook his head. 'There are ways, rituals . . . you know this, surely? They sever them from their totems, then find them new Horse souls, so that they become Horse tribe in truth.' He said it very matter-of-factly, but Maniye cringed at the thought.

'That's horrible! How can they . . . ?'

'What is in here that makes us *us*, it survives the loss of the soul. It is only if no new soul comes that there is danger. The Horse is generous, it has many souls to spare, no doubt.' The old man stared at her pensively. 'Wolf girl, Tiger girl, you must know that *you* too will have to wield that knife.'

For a terrible moment she thought he meant he would sell her to the Horse. Then – more terrible still – she understood. She had two warring souls within her. One day soon she would have to sever one and cast it away. Tiger or Wolf: it was the choice that had lurked in ambush for her since the day she was born.

'I don't want to . . .' she began stubbornly, hopelessly.

Hesprec opened his mouth to say something, whether reassuring or prescriptive she did not know, but the words failed him and he said nothing. Pity looked wholly out of place on his pallid countenance.

116

Then Alladei was back, ducking into the hut to spread out another skin by the fire. On it he placed leather bowls: berries, dried meat, quamash meal. His big, long-fingered hands worked with exaggerated delicacy.

'Please, eat,' he invited them. 'My hand-father is coming.' Maniye had hoped he himself would stay, but he was already on his way out, backwards again with his hands clasped together. This time she mimicked the gesture.

She had a berry halfway to her mouth when the broad man, Ganris, arrived. 'Welcome to my home!' he boomed. 'Greetings, strange travellers with special trades to make.' He was so loud he seemed to fill the whole hut. 'You, old grandfather, may the sun warm your bones! And you, little daughter, swift be your hunting and let the winter smile on you!' His congratulatory smile was more for himself, Maniye felt, for so thoroughly putting his guests in their place.

He wasted no time in sitting down by the food, one hand already reaching for it without the need to look. From somewhere he produced a skin of something, and he unlaced it and took an ostentatious sniff at the contents.

It turned out to be goat milk, when it reached Maniye, although warmed and spiced with something. Once she had tried it she was highly reluctant to surrender it back to Ganris. Hesprec, for his part, had taken the tiniest sip, just enough to be a good guest, before passing it on.

'Now, speak of your special trading,' Ganris invited them. 'Out of the great respect I have for the Sun River Nation and its revered priesthood, I will listen.'

'Out of the respect I have for the Horse Society and its traditions, which is no less, I shall speak,' Hesprec agreed, twisting his thin lips to get the words right. 'Winter has come to the Crown of the World, as all can see. This is no time for the civilized and the sensible to let themselves freeze here. You must be ready to travel south for the Plains, and two such as we would

117

hardly slow you, on land or water. It would be a grand honour to travel with the Horse.'

Ganris nodded self-importantly, his manner indicating that such would indeed be a grand honour for them. 'I would hesitate to inflict the hardship of our travels on two so distinguished travellers. No doubt you would find our ways coarse, our hospitality mean, compared to what you are used to.' He took in Hesprec's mismatched clothing, and the general feel of dirt and weariness that hung over the pair of them.

'We are hardy, we will endure,' Hesprec replied unflappably.

'And this is not all, surely?' Ganris prompted. 'Two such as you would not trouble yourselves for such a meagre matter.'

The old man took a deep breath, and in it Maniye saw just how tired he was. Her feet had carried them here from the Winter Runners, but the sheer effort of talking was wearing him down.

'We would impose on your hospitality for new clothing, perhaps, and I am sure the matter of provisions need not even be discussed, so sumptuous are your riches.'

'Sumptuous.' Ganris rolled the word over his tongue, plainly pleased with a new acquisition. 'But the gratitude of the priesthood of the Sun River Nation would no doubt put what little aid we can render into shadow.'

Maniye felt a tightness within her. Now they were talking about what Hesprec had to bargain with. That had always been the hole in their plan. If the old man was as ragged and wretched as he looked, then they might as well barter for the sun and the moon as for some new clothes and passage south.

'Opulence,' Hesprec said precisely, 'shall be yours when you return this son of the south to the Serpent's coils.'

'And the girl, too?' Abruptly the florid-speaking Ganris was gone, and someone shrewd and calculating was in his place.

Does he think I'm a slave? Maniye thought, tense and growing tenser, tiger and wolf both clamouring to rise up and reshape her. *Will he offer to buy me?* And then: *Would Hesprec sell me?*

After all, she had travelled with the old man for just a few days. She did not know him. She could not trust him.

'The girl, too,' Hesprec agreed firmly.

'She is not of the south,' Ganris observed.

'Her soul has flown far from its last resting place,' the old man revealed. 'Why else would one such as I travel so, save to return to my home a soul dear to the Serpent that has been born into the cold jaws of the Wolf?' He said it with utter assurance.

Ganris, finding the skin back in his hands, took a deep draught from it. 'Remarkable,' he gasped, at the end.

'Such are the ways of souls. Even a priest such as I cannot be said to understand all things.' Hesprec managed his thin smile. 'Can we be said to have a bargain?'

Ganris's mouth twisted. 'The gratitude of priests . . .' he prompted.

'Gold, jade, obsidian, greater than all of these is the gratitude of Serpent for those that restore one of his own.'

'And the girl . . . ?'

'We are inseparable,' Hesprec confirmed politely.

Ganris nodded, then stood up smoothly, rising from crossed legs despite the bulk of him. 'Well, I am only a humble Trading Master, barely Hetman in anything but name. I must speak to my people and plead your case, to persuade them that our journey south shall be observed by strangers.'

'The Serpent's eyes are hooded. He sees only that which is wise,' Hesprec pronounced – overly mystically in Maniye's opinion.

'Even so.' Ganris did the same thing with his hands as Alladei had, and then he backed out.

Maniye locked eyes with Hesprec, studying him just as he was studying her.

★★★

Amiyen Shatters Oak was one of the Winter Runners' greatest hunters, and for that, she was bitter. Though Smiles Without Teeth might be stronger, and Hare Killer might be fleeter, there

119

were few who could so claim to have all the gifts of a hunter in one body. Perhaps there was none.

In her human form she was stocky and powerful, her bristling dark hair cut close to her scalp to afford no purchase for grasping fingers. As a wolf she was the equal of any of them in size and ferocity. Stepping could be a great equalizer.

Yet she would never be chief of the Winter Runners. She could prove herself as good as any man, or twice as good, and the honour would still be barred her. That was what made her grind her teeth.

She had sons, though. The honours denied to her, she could still secure for them. She had taught them ambition and patience, how to stalk with care, then to seize the prize in their jaws and not let go.

And sons were something Akrit did not have, take as many wives as he liked. Only one woman had borne his get, and he'd had her killed the moment the squalling creature was pulled from her womb. Amiyen was willing to wager he was regretting that now.

She had two sons – two more than Stone River would ever have. Rubrey was the elder, not the best of hunters and yet to earn a name for himself, but he was blessed with a dogged determination to see things through, and already had a following of young hunters. Her younger son, Iramey Arrow Taker, had earned his name after he had gone off into the highlands to take a tiger skin, and come back with a shaft in his leg to mark his recklessness. He had learned little from the experience, to Amiyen's frustration, least of all that enthusiasm was no substitute for planning and forethought. It was to cure him of his foolishness that she had brought him here with her.

Rumour amongst the traders placed the girl here – or at least identified the old Snake, who was more easily spotted. She could not have said what prompted her to take Iramey and run swift-pawed all the way to the trading post: one of those decisions she made mid-hunt, little hunches and suspicions leading her to an elusive quarry.

And now the quarry was Akrit's own daughter. Now *there* was a hunt worth exerting herself for.

If only the girl could be mated to one of Amiyen's sons, that would solve so many problems. Akrit had scoffed at the idea when she had brought it up, though. He had other plans, it seemed. Any man who became Maniye's mate would be in a strong place to become chief after Stone River. Amiyen had no interest in anyone gaining such an advantage over her own brood when the time came.

The Horse Trading Master was all polite niceties, at first committing himself to nothing, asking for a more detailed description of the girl, Maniye. Then at last the fat man was admitting to having heard some rumour, perhaps seen some glimpse . . . ? Yes, they had been here. Yes, perhaps they were still here – he did not know. Except that he *did* know. He was just trying to find a way to betray a guest without sullying Horse honour. In the end he had said nothing, yet at the same time told her everything. Amiyen stood up and stretched, tugging at the collar of her hide jerkin to show she was too hot, and ducked outside with Iramey padding at her heels.

***

'Did you mean what you said?' Maniye asked, after letting the silence between them stretch out as long as it could without snapping.

Hesprec cocked an eye at her and said nothing.

'You said,' she went on, 'that you came all the way here, to the Crown of the World, for me. Because of my soul.' In the face of his closed lips, the words tumbled out of her. 'And why would you be here? Why travel so far? And . . . and you're a priest, a magician. You might see . . .' She was disgusted by the hope in her own voice.

Would some southern madness result in everything she had done, all those lonely years of childhood, gaining a significance

121

and justification it had always lacked? Until that moment she had never quite realized that such a hole existed in her.

But Hesprec was just shaking his head slowly. 'I am sorry, Maniye, it was just a story.'

'You're lying.' She was clinging to a sinking boat just one moment longer.

'It was simply something to say, to the question Ganris asked me. I apologize if my powers of invention have misled you. And, while I cannot claim any grand destiny led me to you, believe me when I say I am very, very grateful that blind fortune nonetheless did.'

Then Alladei was thrusting his way back into the hut with a sack over his shoulder.

'Get up,' he ordered them tersely. 'You have to leave here.' He upended the bag and shook loose a wad of bundled clothing. 'Get these on. They will warm you more than what you have. Especially you, old Serpent.'

There were fleece-lined sheepskin robes there, and fur hats and boots, all fashioned in the Horse style. None of it fitted overly well – too large on Maniye while too short and too wide on Hesprec, but they donned them hastily. There was a bag of food too: dried fruit, nuts and shreds of meat jerky all mixed together.

'What is going on?' the Snake priest asked mildly, as he pulled on a boot.

'The Winter Runners are here in the camp,' Alladei told them tersely. 'They are seeking you. You are our guests.' Every line of his body was urging them to hurry. 'We do not take sides, and we do not know why they want you, and we do not want to be a part of a war within the Winter Runners, still less some business between them and the south. So: we clothe you, we invite you to leave. We tell them you were here but – ah! – gone now, who could have thought it?'

'And then?' Maniye asked him.

'They track you, they do not track you. They catch you or

they do not catch you,' he said. 'But it is not here inside our walls that it happens. Our duty as hosts is not breached. For what value I can give my wishes, I hope you stay a step ahead, all the way to where you are going. And perhaps, if this turns out to be the right thing to do, you will remember your friends of the Horse Society in a better year.'

'And where should we go?' she demanded.

'How can I say?' He shrugged. 'But downriver in Swift Back lands there is a larger trading post, big enough that we keep people there all year.'

For a moment, Maniye wanted to be angry at him, but she saw that it could just as easily have been Akrit's hunters bursting in on them, and that would probably have been the safer course for Ganris's people. And Alladei seemed sincere when he wished them well. She could read in him that he wanted to do more, but he was caught by the bonds that laced him to his people and his hand-father.

'We will go,' agreed Hesprec. He was fully attired now – perhaps the two of them could even have walked through the trading post and passed as Horse people, with the falling snow to shadow their features. Their disparate heights would betray them though – such a small girl, such a tall, gangling man – too suspicious not to draw a closer look. There was only one way to go.

'In the bag, old Serpent,' she instructed, far more bravely than she felt.

Hesprec Stepped into that same reptile form and slithered into her satchel, and she slung it over her shoulders.

'Our thanks,' she told Alladei. 'My thanks.'

He nodded soberly. 'Swift roads and fair forage,' and then, 'and look out for us in the spring.'

Then she had shifted her own form, reducing down to that small wolf that lived within her, tugging at the bag's strap with her teeth to tighten it. And there was nothing for it but to nose past the hanging furs and out into the same snow that must even now be falling on Akrit's hunters as they searched for her.

For a moment, surrounded by the scents and structures of men, she could not get her bearings: no idea which way was north, which south – all her wolf senses bewildered. Then she found the river that the trading post was built against, cluttered with the log rafts and canoes that the Horse Society would soon use to carry themselves and their goods south for the winter.

South was where she needed to go too, and for a moment she paused at the water's edge, cringing back from the boots of the Horse men and women who were already loading tightly bundled packages on their boats. Should she leap aboard and find some place to hide herself? But the Horse men had not given Hesprec their agreement – she would be like a thief, uninvited and outside any protection of hospitality. She could be dumped in the river as quick as thought once they discovered her, and all their fair dealings with Alladei, their talk with Ganris, would mean nothing. She did not know these people well enough, nor could she trust them.

She would have consulted with the old Snake if she could, but he was coiled inside her pack and she did not dare take her human form, not now she was being hunted. There was no escape here, save the water, and that was cold and swift enough to be more than a match for her ability to swim it. Mind made up, she was darting off, heading for the landward gate of the trading post.

Everything was a shadow in the swirling snow until she came within a few yards of it. Save for the labouring Horse people, there was nobody abroad, and she hoped that any of Akrit's people were similarly resting out the weather under Horse Society roofs. She dodged and scrabbled around the curved walls of the Horse huts, hunting for the way out into the open.

She spotted the other wolf all too late.

He had been waiting patiently, standing quite still as though he had somehow known she must come this way. She was going fast enough that she almost ran straight past him, within reach of his jaws. As it was, she scrabbled and slipped in the piling snow, skidding over onto her side as she desperately tried to stop.

He stared at her, head high. She recognized him. Man or beast, she would know Broken Axe.

Her guts turned to ice within her, and for a moment she could not move, shocked rigid with fear as he began to step calmly forwards, lifting his feet fastidiously to reach over the drifts.

His eyes – pale and clear as no wolf of the wilds would own to – lanced into her, and her mind was flailing frantically, wondering whether he would seize her in his jaws or Step into his lean, hard human body with axe already in hand.

Something broke inside her. Either she fought down her fear or it consumed her utterly, but she was on her feet, under his very nose, and launching herself off, one of her rear feet raking a claw across his muzzle as he lunged forwards.

She zigged and zagged, hoping to gain enough distance that the snow would lose her. She felt no breath at her heels, and guessed that he was already trying to flank her, to head her off – and that he would appear before her any moment, lunging out of the weather like a nightmare.

She dashed around the wall of another hut, seeing an openness before her that she hoped was the gate, and an arm caught her about the throat, dragging her off her feet, tight enough around her neck that she was ripped straight into her human form, hauled kicking and yelling into the wind-shadow of the hut.

Something cold pressed at her cheek. She knew it for iron instantly – no child of the Wolf would not: the long, narrow chill of a knife blade.

'If it's not Stone River's child,' a woman's voice said softly in her ear. Stripped of the speed of her wolf shape, Maniye was suddenly terrified in a quite different way – worse even than almost running into Broken Axe's open jaws. Her human hide seemed far more fragile and vulnerable than any animal's, and with the arm close about her neck she could not Step away, like a thrall wearing a collar.

Another wolf crossed her view: not Broken Axe but a young male – and a moment later she recognized his slightly awkward loping as that of Arrow Taker, Amiyen Shatters Oak's youngest. Which meant that the voice and the arm belonged to . . .

'Amiyen,' she got out, 'please . . .' No more than that, for what could she say? What did she have to barter with, after all? Yet still the hopeless words emerged. 'Not back to my father, please.'

The huntress chuckled in her ear. 'Is that your last true wish, Stone River's child?' The knife moved, just a minor readjustment but it had all of Maniye's attention. Abruptly the edge of it was at her throat.

'But he . . .' Her world lost what little balance it had left. Through all of this, she had been convinced of one thing: the fate she was fleeing was that described to her by drunken Akrit that evening after the Testing. She was fleeing Broken Axe. She was fleeing her part in her father's plan to use her to somehow bludgeon the Tiger into his service. What she had not thought she was fleeing was death itself. Oh, death for Hesprec, certainly, but he had been staring that in the face already. Death for herself had never been a possibility. Until now.

'Oh, your father . . . your father will not be chief forever,' came Amiyen's sharp-edged voice. 'Your father has no sons, Stone River's daughter. But he has you, and while he has you, who knows what might happen after he is gone? But without you . . .'

Maniye actually felt the steeling of the muscles that was Amiyen drawing together the will to kill her chief's flesh and blood. She was not the only one.

Something thin and hissing reared furiously past her shoulder, striking with gaping jaws at Amiyen's face. The huntress shrieked, fearing the venom, no room in her head for the memory that the old Serpent had been thoroughly de-fanged. She fell back with

126

her hands out to shield herself, her head striking hard against the wooden side of the hut and the knife falling away.

The arm was gone from about her neck, and Maniye Stepped instantly, racing past Iramey and away, feeling the shifting and sliding of weight that was Hesprec being jolted back into her pack.

The gate was ahead, and she bolted for it, seeing Iramey's sleek-furred form at the edge of her vision as he moved in on her flank with fangs bared to bite. She shied away from him, feeling his teeth catch at her fur. He was forcing her away from the gate, even if he could not get his fangs in her. Amiyen must be close behind. In their Stepped shapes, with their blood up, they would tear her apart.

Then he was gone with a yelp, tripped or stumbling, and she dashed ahead and out, beyond the palisade and into the furious teeth of the snow – but still better that than the teeth of the Winter Runners.

Amiyen had been a handful of heartbeats behind, just a few moments reeling from the knock to her head, Stepped back into wolf form but still groggy. When she got to the gate, there he was, and she felt a terrible, ripping sensation within her.

Her child, her youngest, her reckless Iramey.

He lay, human, curled into a ball, and the snow about him was melting red with his blood. He was still alive, just, shivering and shuddering.

Maniye had torn open his leg – the inside near the groin, where the blood ran fierce. Amiyen had seen enough people and animals die to know it.

She crouched beside him, on human knees now, feeling dead and cold in her heart. The loss was like a hammer raised, waiting to come down and spark her rage.

'Mother.' He clutched for her, but she drew back, shaking her head. It was very, very important.

'Iramey, listen to me, you must Step. You *must*.'

'Mother, it hurts! Please . . .' And he was twisting, trying to reach out for what comfort she could offer, despite the agony. She wanted desperately to gather him in her arms, but she needed him to obey her this one last time, for his own sake.

'My son, listen to me.' Her voice shook with the same erratic rhythms as his ravaged body. 'Iramey, son, please. You lived within the Jaws of the Wolf, so you must end. *Please*, Iramey, please, this one last time.' Tears left freezing trails down her cheeks. She could see Iramey fighting for another breath, another heartbeat.

'Mother . . .'

She opened her mouth, and knew that no words would come out, that it would be a sound of grief and loss – and all the more so if he died like this.

And then the dying boy was a dying beast, whimpering and trembling, Stepped at last into the form that all Wolves must hope to hold to, as they passed away. To die human was to deny the soul its exit, to trap it within the decaying corpse. Thus were ghosts made, tormented and twisted spirits denied rebirth.

Now she went to him and cradled his wolf's body in her arms, whispering in his ear, telling him it would be well, that he would live again, be born again, as man or as beast. Her words jumped and shuddered with her grief and his faltering breath.

The girl would be getting further away, she knew, and the snow would hide her tracks. This was more important though. Family always came first.

But even if she lost the trail now, she would find Stone River's daughter over winter, or in the spring, or in twenty years of searching, and she would tear open that girl's throat and gorge on her blood.

In her arms, Iramey faded at last, and she felt that moment when the soul fled from him. In that instant she had Stepped, because human grief was shallow and pale compared to the grieving of a wolf. She flung back her head and howled out the incandescence of her anguish and her fury.

11

Twin rivers were the bonds that tied the cold north to the warm south. In the east, the Sand Pearl fed into the Marl, which coursed southwards until the dry plains swallowed it up. To the west a skein of rivers mustered their forces to become the back of the great Tsotec. Neither the inhabitants of the Sun River Nation nor those of the Crown of the World truly understood how these rivers linked their worlds. Few had realized that the freeze and thaw of the northern winters caused the flooding of the Tsotec that inundated the fields of the south, bringing another year's prosperity and life.

But what they did know was that the river was a road. To walk from Atahlan to the lands of the Wolf would take many moons and expose the traveller to all manner of dangers, natural and human. Even the roads that the Horse Society had trodden out were safe only for large and well-guarded parties. The rivers were the swifter, safer path between north and south throughout the heart of the year, when they were not frozen or running mad with meltwater. So it was that travellers on the Tsotec heading north into the first days of winter must always hurry, for the ice would not wait.

Where they could, the Horse drew their boats up on the western shore, hauling them by main force up little trails or else the treacherous inclines left by rockslides. Across the river the Plains began, and the Horse seemed to have no more friends there that they were anxious to visit.

The western shore of the Tsotec's back was in the Shadow of the Stone Kingdoms, whose people lived closed lives, on the stepped plateaus of the high ground.

There were men and women of the Stone Kingdom in Atahlan, in some numbers. They came to work, and they stayed because they were paid well and valued. They were craftsmen and quarrymen, whose understanding of the moods and movements of the earth was unparalleled. Moreover, they were the arm of the Kasra: foreigners without ties to any of the great clans, they made perfect enforcers of the laws. Recruiting the Stone men to be the shield and the sword of the Sun River Nation's ruler was an old tradition. In return, the Snake priests had made their way even into the Stone halls, conquering ancient enmities with cunning words.

All of which was relevant to Asmander's purpose for one reason: this outside force, these spears hired from beyond the Nation's borders, would be a key factor in what happened next. And for all he hoped desperately that the near future would be one of peace succeeding peace, he did not believe it.

Hence his mission to the north, and he was not alone. Even as his prince, his beloved Tecuman, sent out trusted men such as Asmander, so there would be others . . .

When there was enough wood for a good fire, the whole travelling party clustered about it, and the chief entertainment then was telling stories. Everyone took their turn. The Horse told stories about far places, everywhere but their own home. So it was that one would tell a tale of the Crown of the World, how some hero tricked the sun into returning, and yet offended it so that it would always go away again. Another would tell some familiar Riverlands myth, or perhaps there would be a badly remembered history of the coming of the Pale Shadow, a myth Asmander had heard recounted far better by the Snake priests.

When his own turn came, he felt embarrassed. He was no

great storyteller: his voice would always go dry, and he forgot key parts of the tale so that the whole made no sense. When he had demurred enough, and everyone else – Venater and Shyri too – had made it plain he had no choice, he had lamely fallen back on one of the old children's stories, about the Crocodile and the Serpent. He muddled through it, how Serpent had come to the river and sought passage on Old Crocodile's back, and been refused three times. Who, after all, would carry a venomous reptile willingly? Here, Asmander found himself mimicking his long-ago tutors, bringing their expressions and gestures to life, sparking smiles from his audience. *Simpler tales for simpler times*, he thought. At the last, of course, Old Crocodile is tricked into carrying Serpent across anyway, and when he gets to the far side he's very surprised that the snake has not bitten him. More, Serpent has guided him to a new place where the herds come to drink. And so Old Crocodile learned to trust Serpent's guidance, just as Serpent had trusted his strength. Asmander thought he had done quite a good job of the telling, for all it was just a fable for the very young. When he had been that young, the world had seemed fit for such tales.

What will they tell about us, after we are gone?

After that, Venater wanted to give a blood-and-butchery retelling of some act of pointless villainy, but Asmander elbowed him sharply, and instead another of the Horse told a midnight story of the Old Kingdom – the first dominion of the Stone People – and how it had been eaten away from the inside by the Rat Cult, by poison and disease, and of the ruins still standing today where none would dare go again.

'I've seen them,' Shyri declared at the end of that, when everyone was pleasantly frightened by the idea of terrible things done far away. 'I've been there.'

That seemed to be in bad taste as far as the Horse were concerned, but she had a smug look on her face that said the Laughing Men did not care about the taboos of others. 'They are close to here. We will pass through their Shadow before we reach the north. If you were brave, any of you, you could follow me up there and see where the Rat gnawed the bones of kings.' She was grinning fiercely at their discomfort, plainly very satis-fied with herself.

Asmander knew where he stood with the Horse Society. He knew exactly how his relationship with Venater pivoted: duty and resentment, love and hate. In the days of their journeying together, he had come to no understanding of Shyri at all. She remained a cipher.

And so he announced: 'I will go with you.'

She had not been fishing for this, and his offer caught her off guard.

'We shall not have time,' the Hetman started. 'We will see ice on the river soon . . .'

'We will go at night, Laughing Girl,' Asmander suggested, seeing her eyes go gratifyingly wide. 'Or are you not laughing any more?'

'If you can keep up, longmouth.' But she was quieter now, far less delighted with her own wit.

'I have not known many of the Stone Men,' Asmander com-mented, reaching out for another handhold. 'I know they live shoulder to shoulder in their high places, or so I'm told. Perhaps I don't believe in this ruined kingdom.'

He was speaking to cover his own nervousness. The very path they followed gave the lie to his words. It was steep, but the steps of worked stone were still evident, rounded by time. Hardy trees and bushes had forced a foothold with their roots, making for easier purchase. The moon was close to full, too, but while that pale light showed them their way, Asmander did not like the way it seemed to make the rock stairs glow faintly.

Shyri, ahead of him, just grunted, concentrating on her own ascent.

'There are many places along the Tsotec where men once lived until disaster or bloodshed destroyed them. Now those

132

places are lived in again, by others. Nobody would abandon such a place forever. If it was good to live there, it will be good to live there still.'

'No doubt you're very wise,' she cast back at him. 'But there are places on the Plains, the old forts of the Horn-Bearers, which are sealed still. We do not go there.'

'And why?'

'For the same reason the Stone Men don't come here now. Because of what they let in, all those years back. Places where bad ideas have arisen; places where the people have consented to their own degradation and death; where the bones of the dead have been gnawed in such ways . . .' She paused ahead of him, and he glanced up and saw she had reached the top.

Clambering up beside her, he remained silent. There were indeed ruins. None of his rationalizations could wish them away.

An archway cut into the stone stood twice the height of a man, and through it, just a short distance off, he could see a broad and moonsplashed space, littered with tumbled stones.

Shyri was watching him with a mocking smile. 'So brave, Champion?'

'You have stood inside there?'

'In daylight.'

'How courageous of you.' In truth he found he did not want to venture in. A dreadful silence had its hand on the place. He had reasons, though, for coming up here with Shyri. That deserted arena within would serve his purposes. *The mission first*, he reminded himself.

She twice hesitated to walk into that dark passage, before she finally Stepped and skittered through on four legs. That seemed a good idea to Asmander. When he followed her, it was without hesitation, clawed feet clicking on the stone. The Champion was always a ready antidote to fear.

They resumed their human forms inside, staring about them at the dead city of the Old Stone Kingdom. Here was a canyon, sheer sides reaching far above them, with a trickle of a stream still snaking its way down its centre. The walls had been worked from top to bottom, cut into rooms one on top of another, not an inch wasted, so that the stone around them seemed to have a hundred vacant eyes on both sides.

'They go straight into the rock,' Shyri told him. 'I don't know how far. They go down, too. There are shafts like great wide wells that just go down . . .'

Every bare wall had been carved. They saw what had been human figures there, large and small, but everything vandalized. The faces, especially, had been smashed away, and most of the hands too: all the imagery that might have told them who those lost people were and what they had been about.

'Did you go in?' Asmander pressed. The look she gave him provided enough answer: no, she had not.

His curiosity was more than satisfied. It was time to talk.

'I will have words with you now.'

She did not mistake his tone, and perhaps she had been waiting for this. 'So,' was all she replied, but there was abruptly more distance between them than before. Asmander still stood between her and the way they had entered, and the Champion was faster than she was, whatever form she might assume.

'I do not understand why you are here,' he told her flatly.

'Some southern boy's foolish dare,' she said, hands on hips.

'You know what I mean. Why is one of the Laughing Men inviting herself to the Crown of the World?'

'I like to travel.'

'Plains people do not travel.'

That struck real anger. 'You know nothing, longmouth. I have travelled many places. Never to the north. Not yet.' She had started loud, but lowered her voice before she finished. The window-riddled stone around them had made something unpleasant of the echoes.

'Why did the Malikah send you?' he pressed.

'I was not sent.'

'If you are here to prevent me carrying out my mission, I will

134

kill you.' He was ready to fight now, right here. This place reeked of death. One more victim would make no difference. At the same time, he knew that the thought was shot through with dishonour. To turn the Champion loose upon this woman for such a reason would be mean-hearted and vicious. He felt his intentions tilt in the balance, waiting to see what excuse she would give him.

She was still angry, hands balling into fists, over and over. 'I don't even care what your mission is.'

'You know.'

'If you want to fight, longmouth, then let's just fight.' She had a bronze knife in her hand swift enough that he had not even seen her draw it. In the echo of her words, he sensed that something else stirred. For a moment he was imagining little feet rattling troves of old bones; flooding through the buried halls where the ancient Stone Men had gone off to die.

Looking into her eyes, he realized that she had imagined exactly the same thing, and so perhaps neither of them had imagined it at all.

'What I know is what everyone knows,' she said, quieter now. 'I know the Kasra is dead. I know there is no new Kasra, or two of them, and you cannot have two Kasra of the Riverlands. Everyone from the south tells a different story. What do you say, longmouth?' When he would not answer, she prompted, 'You spoke of your prince to the Malikah. I heard you say . . . what was his name?'

'Tecuman.' It seemed a betrayal, to give voice to that name in this place, but at the same time it brought a little strength along with it. 'Tecuman, my prince.'

'And he's going to be Kasra, is he?'

'I've heard it said.' *My father has staked a great deal on it.*

'But there's the girl, that's what they say. If he's Tecuman, then she's, what, Tecume?'

'Tecumet.' He had been listening to Shyri's voice, letting his ears search for the hidden intentions he had felt sure must be

135

there if she was here with an ulterior motive. He had heard nothing.

'Two children, one name, right. We may not be River Lords, but even we know that's not right,' Shyri told him. 'One has to find a new name. The other one's the Kasra.'

He realized he had taken his eyes off her – what should have been a fatal mistake. She had stepped closer, but the knife had been put away.

'So this matters a lot to you,' she observed. 'Enough to try and kill me.' The anger had gone along with the knife. In its place came something like sympathy, unlooked for in a Plains woman of the Laughing Men. 'You know this Tecumet?'

'From my earliest days.'

'And?'

'She is beautiful,' Asmander replied honestly, seeing a shadow of displeasure pass over Shyri's face. 'She is noble, wise and brave. She would make a good Kasra.'

'And your Tecuman?'

'The same – all of it the same.'

She regarded him, perhaps doubtfully, but he could not read her expression: the moon did not touch it. In the gap of her silence, the greater silence of the place around them crept in, until Asmander's ears began hearing sounds that might not even have been there. The scurrying and the scrabbling, as though the faint echoes issued from chasmed wells and long-lost chambers, winding their way to the surface by the ranks of empty sockets that lined the canyon.

'Come.' Abruptly he was turning, passing a panel of defaced inscription to the nearest squared-off hole that might have once been door or window. Beyond was only the darkness, and a faint, cool breeze that bore something disagreeable upon it. 'Come here.'

He heard the scuff of her feet as she approached him warily. He had one foot up on the edge of the hole as though about to descend into the unseen abyss beyond.

'The Stone People never returned to this place?' His voice echoed into the black depths below.

'Do you see them here?' She was at his shoulder, but tense and suspicious.

'Those I saw in Atahlan, they were no fools. Sober, serious – strong and not easily scared.'

'I told you, nobody will go where the Rat has raised its standard. Once a people have fallen to that despair, their home is lost forever. But you must tell the Rat stories, even on the River.'

'The Serpent priests do.' She had been waiting for him to do it, ready to hurl herself away from him, and still he was quicker. In an instant he had her, one hand at the back of her neck, the other gripping her right arm where she had drawn it back. The point of her dagger gleamed close to his eye. She was stronger than he had thought. They fought a silent battle over the precise distance between her blade and his face.

'These last three years, I have been hearing of the Rat Cult,' he told her. They were now teetering on the brink and she stopped trying to stab him only because it might have toppled them both. 'In out-of-the-way places, isolated villages, in old tombs, they say, the followers of the Rat are gathering within the Nation. The priests hunt them. I have seen Rat worshippers die an unclean death by the rope because their flesh is not fit for Old Crocodile, and their spirits must be penned within their human bodies. This is because my Nation stands at the edge of the fall, even as this place fell, as your Horn-Bearers fell. Wherever there is fear and doubt, the Rat creeps in and gnaws. This is what waits for us, if we descend into division and war between ourselves.' He was speaking too loud, and partly it was to drown the distorted echoes of his earlier words.

He forced himself to stay calm, to lessen his grip a little. She did not try to break free. Perhaps that was because she had another knife, for a tiny flint blade emerged between the fingers of her left hand to graze a bead of blood from his waist.

'That is why I cannot allow you to harm my mission. That is

what is at stake,' he told her. 'Tell me, what do the Laughing Men swear by, Shyri?'

'Tell me what you wish me to swear, Asmander.'

He almost felt that he did not need to ask her. That exchange of their names seemed to have sealed something between them.

'Swear that you are not sent to work against me.'

'By my mother's life. But beyond that I will swear nothing. I do what I will. I go where I will.'

'And where will you go?'

'For now? With you.'

For a moment he stared into her dark eyes and tried to find truth there, or anything he recognized. At last he said, 'You remind me of Tecumet.'

'Your enemy?' she demanded.

'Even so.' He paused, and perhaps should not have done so, for at that moment something else sounded from the cold depths beside them. A shifting stone, or something similarly innocuous, save what could be down there to shift it? Instantly they both sprang away from the edge, as frightened as children.

She put a body's length between them – fighting distance, save that her knives had disappeared again. 'What now, Champion?' she asked, and it was a direct challenge to that part of him she had witnessed killing the aurochs on the Plains.

Tecuman, forgive me if I am failing you in this. The two tines of the fork had him pinned: his duty to his prince and his personal honour. 'Now I trust you.' With those words he was walking towards the narrow archway by which they had entered, forcing her to trot at his heels.

'Just like that?'

'Even so.'

If they left with more haste than they had entered, well, the night was cold and growing colder. It was surely not the echoes of that dead place that drove them.

As they emerged from the shadow of the arch into a healthier kind of night, Shyri made a sound of amusement.

'You said she was beautiful,' she noted. 'And some other flattery too, but mostly that.'

'What of it?' He turned and found she was eyeing him with the same predatory gaze as the Malikah.

'Nothing of it.' Then, as they were descending the worn steps, 'But you know what everyone will think, now you've come back with me rather than without my corpse. You'll never persuade them that we haven't lain together.'

There was an unmistakable invitation in her voice, and for a moment he stopped, not so much from temptation as because he was wondering if he had misread her by *that* much. Was that all there was to it? He could not believe so.

He said nothing and continued descending. The look in the eyes of Venater and the Horse woman on watch said exactly what Shyri had predicted.

At last they were far enough north, and the year far enough advanced, that there was ice floating on the river. The evening after, Asmander asked Eshmir if they were close to their destination, and she shrugged. 'We come off the water soon, first chance we get. There should be a trading post of my people somewhere near. When we see it, we'll leave them the boats for the summer. Overland, from then. The water's too dangerous.'

'I can't believe it can all just freeze solid.' The first sight of jagged plates of ice tumbling in the flow of the river had greatly impressed him.

'Go far enough and everything does, I've heard,' she confirmed. 'But the rivers here won't, only they'll be cluttered with ice. The boats'd get torn open, and you don't want to find yourself sunk in water that cold.'

He nodded vigorously. Already he was well swathed in woollens and a fur-edged coat, gifts of the Horse. Annoyingly, Venater seemed to care less about the cold, or else he was just suffering in silence purely to vex Asmander. He had been sleeping with one of the Horse women, too, which meant that his nights were notably warmer.

Eshmir had been studying Asmander. 'I travel to the Many Mouths, Champion. They rule the Wolf right now. I am sent to strengthen their friendship with the Horse.' She had not spoken of her own mission before, and Asmander had been so wrapped up in his own that he had not enquired. Passing through the Plains she had been a model of calm authority, but now she seemed uncertain, a woman reaching out too far.

'You've not travelled to the north before?' he asked.

She shook her head. 'Family business, though, like yourself.'

'These things are known: one's clan is the river in which a man swims all his life,' Asmander quoted, hearing his own voice and its petulance.

'Your father's a big man, adviser to the throne, yes?'

When there was someone on it, at least. But he just nodded.

'Mine is a Low Malik of the Horse Society. He has eleven children, each expected to bring glory, and to repay his investment in us. So I go north, to strength our links with the tribes.'

It was only in hearing those words, and only for a moment, that he realized how much she had not wanted to undertake this journey; she had kept such feelings hidden all this time, and done her duty.

'I understand.' It was an understatement.

'So, Champion, where does your own path take you?'

'To the Wolves I must go. These Many Mouths sound suitable. They rule the others, like a Kasra? Or are their tribes at each other's throats, like the Plains dwellers?'

'Something in between. The High Chief is listened to. Each tribe is its own.'

He nodded again. 'You would like me to travel there with you?'

'You will gain credit in the eyes of the Horse Society.' She did not say: *I will feel safer with you there.* 'That can mean many things in a hard land. Well?'

140

'It is good,' he agreed. 'You shall have me and Venater.'

'And the Laughing Man girl, she will come at your heels, no doubt.' The Hetman gave him a look.

'I am not responsible for her.'

Her expression showed that she was pointedly declining to comment.

The next day they saw the first Horse raft travelling south, a great construction of logs that encompassed its own commodity, that northern timber that the Sun River Nation could never get enough of. The handful of Horse people who were poling it clear of the riverbank called out greetings to Eshmir's canoes, and this brief exchange told them that the trading post was close enough that, if they paddled hard, they should reach it around nightfall.

Asmander found he did not want to leave the river. While they travelled these waters, no matter how far north they went, there was still an unbroken line connecting him with home. The moment he headed inland, no matter that the north was said to be a place of lakes and streams and rains, he would be cut off from the lands that he knew.

The riverbanks were already pale with snow, and each night he huddled ever closer to the fire. The days were scarcely warmer. He was entering an alien and hostile land. He was stepping within the Crown of the World at last.

12

Battered by the driving snow, the air around her was robbed of all other scents and sounds. As soon as she was out through the gates, Maniye shouldered her way off into the wind, searching her mind desperately for a picture of how the world around her was put together. The infallible orienteering she had used to find the Horse post had been stripped from her just a yard outside its walls.

Downriver, was the only thought in her mind, and yet as she stumbled onto the bank – nearly blundering straight into the swift and icy water – she was somehow upriver of the post, already out of her way and with her enemies between her and her destination.

She would have to make a wide circle around the trading post, she knew, and hope that neither Amiyen nor Broken Axe chanced upon her. She would also have to trust that, with no visible landmark, she could even accomplish such a feat without going in circles or straying off course entirely.

No sane human being would be out in this blizzard, no matter what form they could assume. Even if she could turn into a great bear, she would be holed up and sheltering somewhere. The idea was so tempting: find some hole to crawl into and set off again after the weather had cleared. Except that would be fatal. The *falling* snow was the foe of trackers, obliterating scent and prints with a liberal hand. But already-fallen snow would speak of her passing to any eyes that cared to look for it. Yes, she would be one set of wolf tracks in the Shadow of the Wolf, but it was just as Kalameshli had said: they would be very *small* wolf tracks. She did not think for a moment that her pursuers would not recognize her tread.

So she turned herself around. Now the wind was behind her, mockingly speeding her steps even as it chilled her, raking her coat the wrong way and getting under the layered fur to her skin. She leapt and loped through a thickening morass of white, knowing that here again her size would betray her. *Why can I not Step like Hesprec does, and be a wolf of whatever size I choose?* But, for the people of her totem, the beast echoed the human that took its shape.

She thought there was a shadow to her left that must be the palisade wall of the trading post, and pulled away from it, losing it amid the blowing curtain of flakes. Or else it had been just some trick of the weather, and she was ploughing away from the river entirely. Or else she had never been anywhere near the river to start with. Something within her was already losing hope. All that confidence and bloody-mindedness that had carried her this far was being sapped from her by the cold, by the constant struggle to make headway.

She wanted to go home at that moment. If Amiyen had not made it plain that the return of a living Stone River's daughter was part of nobody's plan right then, she might even have surrendered herself. She was just a foolish girl, or at least she could have maybe convinced her father of that. She could even claim that Hesprec had enchanted her somehow with his Snake sorcery. They would believe many bad things of her, so why not that she was stupid and that she was weak.

And Hesprec would die, of course: either under Kalameshli's knife, or of the cold if she abandoned him out here. In that moment, when she was at her lowest, she could not bring herself to care.

She realized that she had been heading for somewhere for the last few heartbeats. Her eyes had found something to focus on in the maddening whiteness and, with no other point of reference, she had made it her beacon – just a shadow in the snow, but she was starved for any kind of darkness, trapped in the blizzard's all-encompassing pale fist.

It was darkness she found. There he was, waiting for her, hackles up against the cold and his pale coat dusted with snow, but with no other sign that he was sharing the same storm that she had fought her way through.

Broken Axe.

Abruptly she did not want to go home. Not if it meant Broken Axe. She had come to a dead stop as soon as she realized who she was looking at, and for a moment the two of them stared at one another, wolf to wolf. She bared her fangs in her best intimidating snarl, and he did not even dignify her with a single shown tooth.

Then he Stepped, and she shrunk backwards. The man was worse than the beast, so much worse. He stood, lean and hard and with a sheepskin cloak snapping and rippling fiercely about his shoulders like a living thing.

He moved towards her, hands out slightly, reaching. She felt a pinioning terror at just being this close to him, crouching with her belly to the snow, still showing her teeth and yet every line of her body signalling abject submission.

Could I attack him? The thought found her mind somehow. She was in her wolf shape still, and Wolf's grown children all had fangs and claws, be they never so small.

She could not make herself even consider it. She felt that if she touched him, even to tear at him with her jaws, then she would die. The death that he had visited on her mother would leap across to her and strike her down.

His face was very calm, a slight frown over those narrow black eyes. She could discern every hair of his stubbly beard, the scar on his cheek.

Her fear saved her, as it had before. Abruptly she had leapt up into the air, all four feet off the ground, and twisted to come down facing away from him and, even as he lunged for her, she was away.

She knew that he would Step a moment later, and come hounding down her trail after her. Still, she put as much distance between them as she could, sending out her pleas to the spirits of weather and wind that the snow would shroud her just enough to be out of his sight. She let her path take her left and then right, sharp turns taken blind into the snow. Suddenly she needed no sense of north or south, upriver or down. The only direction she needed to concern herself with was *away*.

She ran, and once again she was amazed at how she could run. Even though the snow conspired to drag at her; even though her muscles burned. She did not look back: that was not an easy luxury for wolves. In her mind, Broken Axe's jaws were forever an inch from closing on her haunches.

Then the white carpet was thicker and thicker, and more than once she tumbled into a sudden snow-filled dip or a drift that threatened to bury her. Worse, always there was the creeping chill that she tried to keep at bay with each instant's burning exertion. No pelt, no inhered winter clothing could keep this early winter at bay forever. However swift she was on her wolf legs, on good ground, this heavy going was killing her by degrees.

She did not believe that it would slow Broken Axe in the same way. She did not believe that anything could slow him, not even the great spirits of winter.

For a moment she Stepped to her human form, stumbling and tripping on two feet, but the chill seized her instantly in its jaws and shook her, and she knew that she could not survive – that all Broken Axe would find of her would be a cold corpse. It was as a wolf again that she ran on.

She was not sure exactly when she had reached the trees. Numbly, she recognized their shadows around her, and understood that the lessened snowfall was because of their sprays of needle-edged boughs above her, already growing heavy with white.

Am I north, or east? She must be north, again, for there was no river in sight. North and west – so back the way she had come.

By that time there was nothing more left to her. The well of energy that had whipped her all the way from the hall of her father had run dry. Her bones were cold and her strength used up.

Here, below the patchwork shelter of the trees, she knew she must find somewhere to rest. Under the smothering cover of the clouds, the day had already expired. She would follow its example if she did not find somewhere to hide up and lick her wounds.

And if Broken Axe found her . . . ? If he tracked her even through the snow? If he was staring at her even now?

She could muster only the feeblest flicker of fear. She had revised her opinion; the weather was the greater god. Not even the Wolf's most deadly son would willingly have subjected himself to this.

Soon after, she found a tree that some past storm had pushed over, leaning into two of its fellows with half of its roots wrenched up out of the soil. There she huddled, out of the wind and its cold burden, a small wolf in a small space that would not have admitted the girl, let alone Broken Axe in any of his forms. Outside, the diligent broom of the snow smoothed over her tracks.

She could not know that, while Broken Axe had been harrying her, Amiyen and her remaining son had guessed at her intended destination and set off swiftly downriver for the further Horse encampment, with murder on their minds. She would not hear their howls of rage once they realized their mistake.

At last, after such a fierce chase, she slept.

She woke.

She was bitterly cold but in her mind was an understanding that she had felt colder in the recent past. The hole about her was now snug with her body warmth, kept in by the enfolding arms of the snow itself. She was ravenously hungry.

There was light, pure white light, emanating from where the snow lay thinnest, and she could only be thankful that her hiding place had been here in the lee of the ruined tree, or she might have been buried and dead before now.

I wasn't thinking. There hadn't been much room left in her for thought at the end.

She scrabbled and pushed with nose and paws, breaking out by mere inches, then scenting the air.

The snow had extinguished the rich tapestry of the forest's memory, wiping it clean. She could only scent what had transpired since the storm had blown over. There were squirrels, her nose told her, and there had been a boar come foraging close not long before, and in the distance she reckoned she caught a whiff of bear.

No wolves though – nor men.

She would trust to her nose and dare to believe that Broken Axe had been left behind in the snow. No guarantee that he would not find her again – that he would not find her *soon*. Once she moved on, the snow would turn traitor and tell any curious eyes where she had gone. Still, no Broken Axe right *now*. No Amiyen. No Kalameshli Takes Iron. No vengeful father.

She wriggled her way out into the open and stood, blinking at the still, white world. There was a fragile and unfamiliar silence to it, and it struck her that she had never known a winter without having the walls of Akrit's hall to shelter her.

And yet I live, she told herself fiercely, whilst knowing that this was just the winter's very first flourish, and she had barely survived even that. In the back of her mind had been the fond fiction that she would simply live out the cold as a wolf, if she had to: hunting the small creatures of the forest and taking the shelter that nature provided. Her mute brothers did it, needing no better and having no human form to assume, so why not her?

She now had the first understandings of why not. The true wolves of the forest might have human souls, but they had grown and lived as beasts, and knew all the ways of the wild. And even then, save for a few, they lived in packs. Facing the ice season alone was a fool's game for men and women older and more experienced than she. Moreover, she was hungry and weary from her long run, and her wolf paws were tender from so much ground covered. If she kept pushing herself, seeking distance, she would wear out her ability to run until she was crippled by her own determination.

There were villages, she knew. If she followed her nose, she might be able to find a community of the Deer or the Boar who lived under the Wolf's Shadow. Perhaps she could even talk them into taking her in for the winter, threaten them with the Wolf's power or beg their indulgence and hope they were kinder than her own kin would ever be. But then every morning she would step outside and wonder if the face that would greet her first would be Broken Axe's or Amiyen Shatters Oak's. Or her own father's.

Deep in the forest she heard a sharp crack of breaking wood: the boughs all about her were weighed down and sloping under their cold burden. Elsewhere she heard the slumping thud of a branch shedding its load and springing back up. Other than that, nothing – as though the world had been rid of every human thing but her.

She felt the need to see more. Her hackles prickled with the fear that the silence hid some presence that was stalking her. In one smooth transition she Stepped to her tiger form – kept buried these last few days – and leapt up the nearest tree, raking her way up, bough to bough, in search of a vantage point.

What she had forgotten was her satchel, that did not shift with her and had been made with the narrow frame of girl or wolf in mind. As a tiger, she was broader about the chest and, two branches up, one strap tore away, leaving the bag swinging about one foreleg.

What fell from it was the tightly coiled shape of a serpent, which dropped like a stone and vanished into the drifts at the base of the tree, barely leaving a mark. What sprang from the snow with a squawk of outrage was Hesprec Essen Skese, the man, flailing and stumbling, in snow up to his knees and with his fur cap half over his eyes.

For a second Maniye was horrified. In the next instant she found herself sitting on the same branch in human form, because she could not laugh at him from a tiger's mouth.

The old man glowered up at her, lips twitching over his empty gums a couple of times as he sought some suitable reprimand. At last his shoulders sagged and he seemed to accept that he had become a figure of fun.

Maniye had already stifled her laughter, horribly aware of how the sound of it would carry in this grave-still forest. Now she clambered down, inadvertently showering the Snake priest with more snow and trying to look penitent.

'I trust that the view was worth it?' Hesprec asked her, trying to seem arch. He carefully adjusted the fur cap the Horse had given him, tapping it down more firmly on his bald head. 'Now I know why they say not to travel during the winters of the north.'

'This is not winter. This is not the north,' Maniye rebuked him. 'In the north this would seem like a summer.'

He rolled his eyes. 'This much is known: that the smallest whim of a great spirit can mean a lifetime of trials for a man. We have many troubles in my homeland, but at least the world is ordered so that the bringer of snow does not visit us there.'

Maniye blinked at that. 'What happens there in the winters?'

'Winters are a barbaric invention of the north, and we have no time for them. In the mighty Sun River Nation there occurs no such foolishness as this.' A sweep of his mittened hand indicated the snowbound forest around them. His expression was one of exaggerated outrage, and she realized that he was playing at mocking himself in the hope of amusing her.

Well, he needs me, she told herself. *He needs me more than I need him.* It was a mean thought, but she was still unsure of him, this pallid foreigner with his faded scale tattoos.

He wrapped his arms tightly about himself, shuddering and more serious now. 'What place is this?'

Maniye didn't answer, but he plainly read the truth in her face.

'I see you don't know.' He grimaced.

'We will find water and follow it downstream.'

'Back to where we were? And if your enemies are still there?'

'What is *your* plan, wise one?'

He exhaled deeply, pluming the air. 'Alas, I was separated from my plans by your so-hospitable people. I fear I will never get them back.'

More clowning from him, but she was wondering, *And just what were those plans?* Because he had never made them plain. She was ashamed to find that a part of her still yearned for that odd tale he had made up for the Horse: how he had come to find *her*. That she was special to the world as something other than leverage for her father to use against her mother's kin.

Hesprec had taken a few steps, and now he paused in thought. 'Until it snows once more, or until it thaws, what a tale we will tell wherever we go. Your hunters, they will be looking, I think, for the tracks of a little wolf? Or else the tracks of a man and a girl walking together.'

She nodded.

He appeared to come to a difficult decision. 'They will not be looking for one man on his own, perhaps. One set of tracks. They will not wish to go hunting every lost traveller or woodsman.'

Maniye stared at him. 'What do you mean?' Was he abandoning her? Did he think he would stand more of a chance alone in this cold and alien land, and go unhunted?

It cut her, and deeper than she would have imagined. She almost opened her mouth to beg, to demand . . . but she had

150

been born in the Jaws of the Wolf. The Wolf endured, no matter what. She drew herself up straight, confronting him adult to adult.

'Well, if that is what you think, we should part.' Her voice did not quaver at all.

He regarded her levelly. 'I was about to suggest that I carry you.'

She said nothing.

'You have carried me, after all, for some long distance. And, although the keen noses of your people may scent you out anyway, the deception seems worthy of the attempt.'

At last she broke out, 'You couldn't carry me, old Serpent.' She put a lot of scorn into her voice, but only to disguise the relief she felt.

'Not as a girl. Perhaps as a wolf, perhaps for a while. I would be denied the joy of your conversation, but that would be only another burden for me to bear.'

He carried her as she had seen shepherds bring in lambs, her lean wolf body draped over his shoulders, his hands resting light on her legs to steady her. He made slow progress of it, plodding through the snow, and she could only hope that if one of their pursuers came across his single track, they might persuade themselves to ignore it.

It was a faint hope, she knew. Better to hope that her foes were nowhere close at all. There was a lot of forest, after all – stretching from here all the way into the uplands, to the foothills of the *real* north.

Hesprec stopped to rest frequently, but he managed to bear her on his shoulders for most of the day. They ate some of the Horse Society's food but made no fires and, although the sky through the trees was white as the old man's skin, no more snow fell. When they were moving again, Maniye let her nose guide them still, pointing out the way for Hesprec. When she caught even the faintest trace of wolf – for all that it was not familiar Winter Runner wolf but just her mute brothers – she urged him away. When the breeze brought a hint of running water she guided him towards it. It was still her hope that somehow she could follow a stream leading to the Sand Pearl; that those hunting them might be gone from the Horse post; that there would still be a path south.

Alladei and his people would be already gone though, that much she knew. She would need to seek downriver into Swift Back lands for any of the Horse at all. Most likely, by the time she arrived there, they would not be travelling. There would be no movement on the river until the summer. And staying by the river, or with the Horse, was just an invitation for the hunters to find her.

And yet she had nothing and nowhere else. Only now with the luxury of hindsight, draped over Hesprec's narrow shoulders, did she realize just how little she had thought matters through. In her mind a hundred scenarios played out, and she had constantly to fight a nagging voice saying that life in her father's shadow would not have been so bad. To betray her mother's people, to become the mate of terrifying Broken Axe, these things could be endured more easily than the killing cold and hunger of a winter spent alone.

That night she found another hollow to sleep in, repairing her satchel as best she could to provide a bed for Hesprec. She did not dare try for a fire, but felt mournfully sure that she would not have been able to start one anyway. She had the understanding of how to do it, yet not the skill.

The next day she travelled on her own four feet, and he still on his two: too weary now to carry her further and yet too proud to beg a ride just yet. They passed the time in silence, with Maniye shackled to Hesprec's slow pace. That morning they finally found the stream that her nose had been telling her about. The land here was broken, worn snarls of rock pushing out of it like bones, the lie of it tilting up into slopes that were the edge of the uplands. She guessed that she had wandered even further north in her search for it, but here it was: falling in

152

a fierce, unfrozen torrent from the higher ground and carving its stony channel, a line free of snow.

She Stepped, needing a human mouth to speak and human eyes to read his face properly. 'Downstream will take us . . .'

He nodded. 'I know, I know.' For a long while they shared an uncertain stare. Downstream was a direction and a destination, two things they had bitterly felt the lack of since finding themselves in the forest. And yet every step would increase the chance that the Winter Runners would discover them.

'Can you fight at all?' she demanded.

'Threats only.' He tapped at his lips. 'And when they see he has no teeth, who shall fear the serpent?'

'I mean *you*, can you do . . .' even as she asked it, she felt like a child, '*magic* at all?'

He looked at her not with derision but with a great sadness. 'How I would like to say yes. And yet, if I had such magics – if there were any such in the world – would I have been where you found me?'

She could not refute the logic.

Then they found where the stream led: not to a river but a lake. She should have thought of it: the Crown of the World was dotted with a thousand such. The still body of water had been here forever, since the world was made, and yet to her it seemed just one more unnecessary impediment designed to wear her down.

She looked out across it, still with a skin of ice in its centre, even if the water was clear about the edges. The snow of its shores was trampled at many points, by deer and other animals coming to drink.

'We must go about its edge, this way.' She was recovering her orientation enough to know which was the southern shore. 'We will find where the water leaves it, and follow that.'

Hesprec nodded. He was looking drawn and his skin was almost bluish, even huddled in the heavy robes of the Horse people. When she set off again she held to her human shape, trying to match his pace and not forcing him to hurry.

The stream they found was broad and swift-flowing, winding off through a gully into the forest. Perhaps there would be more such lakes, Maniye considered, but there must eventually be a river, and that river would lead them *somewhere*.

Always assuming *somewhere* was where they wanted to be.

And then the voice, not Hesprec's, called out: 'I have a name for you. They should call you Maniye Many Tracks.'

She froze rigid on hearing it. At her side, Hesprec shifted slightly, his hand reaching for hers.

Broken Axe stood on the far side of the stream, so still against the snow that she had not noticed him. He must have been watching them approach around the lake's edge all this while.

She wanted to scream at him. She wanted to demand how he could always be there ahead of her. She would have believed, in that moment, that Axe was more of a sorcerer than Hesprec could ever be. Her voice stayed locked in her throat though, save for a tiny whine of fear.

She could Step now onto a wolf's paws, and dart away. She would be abandoning Hesprec, but then Broken Axe wanted her and not the old man. Or at least her *more* than the old man.

'I am here to take you home,' Broken Axe informed her, taking two casual steps forwards. Maniye was as aware of the lessening distance between them as she was of her own rapid breathing.

'You are here to kill me.' She was amazed she could even say the words.

'Not I.' And another step, his feet seeming to move without the knowledge of his face, which was trying, along with his voice, for earnest honesty. 'I will not say that your father worries about you. We'd both smell the lie in those words. But, still, you will be better in his shadow than dead in the jaws of winter.' And she could sense the tension coiling in him as he inched nearer, and still she could not move. He was two steps from the stream bank on his side; she was three steps from it on hers.

'What about him?' Maniye asked, and Hesprec's hand finally closed on her wrist.

'I don't care about him, Many Tracks.' She saw Broken Axe shift the set of his feet.

'Go,' whispered the Snake priest, and his bony fingers drove into her skin, the sudden shock of it breaking the spell and freeing her. But only to flee, once again, craven as a coyote.

Not knowing what he would do, she Stepped in that instant, dropping into the wolf shape that seemed almost more natural than the form she was born into. When she Stepped, it was always into the feet of each form, and so she had a desperate vision of Hesprec just collapsing into the coils of his serpent, and being left behind. His grip never left her, though. Somehow he cast himself up the arm that was touching her, so that when he whipped into the slim cord of his smallest shape, it was already coiled about her. There was a horrible moment when she felt him throw himself about her shoulders and neck, heartbeats from dragging her back to her human form, but then he had himself settled somehow, twisted about the knotted straps of her satchel, and she was dashing away, then twisting back to see.

In his native shape, still, Broken Axe took his final two steps and jumped, kicking off from the bank to cast himself across the stream. He Stepped in mid-air, the strength of his human legs lending the pale wolf more distance than it could ever have leapt across itself. In an instant he was almost alongside her, and once again she turned and ran.

13

The Horse people at the trading post on the Tsotec were surprised to see them. Asmander had the impression that, give it another two or three days, they'd none of them still be there. There was one final raft of logs rocking at the crude quay, and they were busy loading it with everything that could be carried, leaving just the hollow stockade behind.

The local Hetman, another tough and compact little Horse woman, obviously thought little of Eshmir and her journey. Asmander learned a great deal by watching the two of them talk, as the new arrivals enjoyed the fire's warmth in the post's only hut. It was not about what was said – all of which was very comradely – but about the way they sat and the distance between them, the attitude of their arms and shoulders. *Rival clans*, Asmander knew, without any doubt at all. The Horse Society's strength was its unity, that was what everyone knew about them: a network of trade and talk and travel from the northern ice to the southern banks of the Tsotec. It was fascinating to see the cracks.

At last, some northern natives were located and brought forward. They looked a sorry lot. On the one hand, a man and woman in furs and wool, each with a pack that looked half as big as they were, and neither of them looking young enough to be tramping through the wilderness in winter. The third was a small man with half his face tattooed or painted black, so that one eye stared out of that mask like a mad, trapped thing, while the other was creased with sardonic humour. He wore dark clothes: a woollen robe that looked almost priestly, with a heavy quilted cloak over it. All three had those flat northern faces: skin the colour of wet sand, high cheekbones, and eyes that seemed constantly suspicious of everything.

'The man and his trade-wife are Coyote,' Eshmir explained. The other's Crow, from the Eyrie. They're better than nothing.'

'How much?' Asmander asked her.

'Enough. They will guide us to the Many Mouths. Failed traders who got here too late, after all the pickings had gone. They're luckier to get us than we are to get them.'

'You fill me full of confidence,' he remarked.

At his shoulder, Venater snorted. 'They're no fighters.'

'I hope we shall need no fighters. With winter coming on, there will be few others abroad, I'm assured.'

'Assuming these natives don't lead us into an ambush,' Asmander put in, almost cheerily.

Eshmir gave him a pained look. 'We leave come the morning,' she informed him.

Everyone else was leaving under the same dawn. The local Horse traders cast off their final raft after a stilted exchange of well-wishings with Eshmir. The new arrivals were left in sole control of the stockade.

Eshmir and her people wanted to leave at once, but the three guides had apparently been conspiring, and they insisted that everyone sit and talk over the journey, which meant heading back into the hut.

The Coyote man, who had perhaps the least trustworthy face Asmander had ever seen, was their main speaker, and his given name was Two Heads, which turned out to be short for Two Heads Talking, in that peculiar northern fashion for names.

Even though he had already sworn his agreement over

157

guiding them, Two Heads was suspicious. First he wanted to know why Eshmir wanted to go to the Many Mouths, who he claimed would not be pleased to see her.

'Everyone is glad of the Horse Society,' she replied implacably.

'Wolves from all over the Crown of the World have come to the Many Mouths,' Two Heads went on. 'You have chosen an unlucky season. You should come next year.'

'We're here now,' Venater grunted, ignoring a look from Eshmir that said she wanted to do the talking. 'Piss on next year.'

'Seven Skins, the High Chief . . . he passes,' the Coyote explained, spreading his hands helplessly. 'Not a good time for strangers to come near the Jaws of the Wolf, or anywhere in the Wolf's Shadow. Me and mine, we go where we will, but Horse . . . ? And these?' An incredulous nod towards the southerners.

'Put up or piss off,' was Venater's sharp response.

'Nonetheless, we must travel.' Eshmir tried unsuccessfully to talk over him. She glanced at Asmander. 'We all have our duty.'

'Of course we will take you.' This was the Crow man with his half-darkened face. Currently he was eyeing them with the unpainted half, the other eye glowering past them at the sloping roof. 'You must have gifts for the road, though. You Horse, you always carry gifts.'

'You've had your price,' Eshmir told him flatly. The currency had not been coin, which apparently was something alien to the cold north, but in future favours from the Horse.

'We? Yes, yes.' The Crow bobbed his head. 'There will be others.'

'The Hetman said nobody travels in winter,' Eshmir stated, nothing in her face acknowledging how foolish that made her own mission sound.

'Winter?' The Crow chuckled deep in his throat. 'This is not winter. If we are not with the Many Mouths when true winter comes, then you will all die.'

158

'And you?' Asmander asked, not as a challenge but from genuine curiosity.

'I, Black Man? I shall fly away.'

There were only two steeds left for them, so Eshmir and one of her people would get to ride, and the rest must walk. Their supplies – a reluctant gift from the outgoing Horse Hetman – were distributed over every set of shoulders that would consent to bear them, which meant everyone except Venater.

'How do *you* get to go without?' Shyri asked him, then she cast a look at Asmander, with a flash of white teeth. 'You have a disobedient slave.'

Venater lunged for her, utterly without warning, and yet she slipped beyond his clawing grasp. 'Are you not his slave?' she asked delightedly, her voice bouncing back from the inside of the stockade.

'I'm no man's slave,' the pirate spat.

'Then what are you, old man?'

Asmander watched with interest as the pirate tried twice to answer her, murder glinting in his eyes.

'He is mine,' the Champion announced at last, when Venater had suffered long enough. 'That is all.'

'For just so long,' Venater got out. 'And then I will be my own again, and I will have my name back, and then I will kill you, boy. I *will*!'

The others – especially the three northerners – stared, because what was going on was something they simply did not *do*, not here where names were cheap and they did not understand. Chiefly they could not understand the sudden warmth of Asmander's smile.

'You will try,' he agreed. 'And who knows, perhaps this time you will succeed.'

Venater's stony eyes flicked away from him to their audience, then to Shyri. 'So what? You'll make me your pack dog?'

'Never,' Asmander assured him, his smile still there but hard.

159

'I've loaded you with so much weight already that another grain of corn might break you.'

He never knew the precise limits of Venater's temper – surely there was a point where the man would just snap, fly into the mad rage he had once been famed for, and so give up any chance of reclaiming his name and his soul from Asmander's keeping. For a second, those eyes seemed desperate, hunted, lost. The look in them was such that Asmander regretted his words, because he had never been one to find joy in torture.

Then, incredibly, the man's teeth were bared in a hard crescent. 'Oh, boy, I'm stronger than you know.' And the hurt was gone, and they were grinning at each other. *Look at what we've learned about each other.* 'But I'll still not carry for you.'

The expressions of the others, when Asmander looked around at them, were utterly bewildered, profoundly disturbed. All except Shyri: she had been mightily entertained, he saw. The Laughing Men did not care about understanding others: that was her secret. He envied her the contentment it must bring.

Once on the road, he placed himself at the front – beside Two Heads Talking and his trade-wife, whatever that was. They regarded him warily, as though he might suddenly do . . . anything, he supposed. He was the alien in their midst, a man of different skin and shape and customs.

'But tell me,' he addressed them, 'if the Wolves are so dangerous to outsiders, why go there yourself? Surely the Horse's favour cannot be worth endangering your skins? Or are coyotes enough like to wolves for you to avoid their wrath?'

Two Heads regarded him morosely. 'We need to be somewhere for winter. We came to the Horse too late, and now home's too far. At least your Horse woman will get us in amongst the Many Mouths. Winter has more teeth than all the Wolves in the world.'

'Never say a Coyote is a Wolf,' his wife spoke up. 'But in their

160

eyes we're not worth shedding blood for.' She grinned ferally. 'Not when they've got you.'

The attack came three days later, when they were all worn down from journeying and numb from the cold. There had been snow the day before, though light enough that Two Heads Talking had advised simply pressing on. On the morning that they fought, the sky was utterly clear – a pale blue that Asmander had never seen before.

Their guides were earning their keep. Whilst Two Heads led the way, his trade-wife – her northern name was Quiet When Loud – was forever straying off and coming back with game or even fish. The Crow cooked and tended the fire, and while they were camped he sometimes sang, strange wordless songs that made the hairs stand up on the back of Asmander's neck. He went by the name of Ragged Sky, but by now Asmander had worked out that they each of them had another name, a real name, that they did not share with mere strangers. They were an untrusting people here in the Crown of the World, keeping their names in darkness.

That day, Asmander had noticed a number of large birds dark against that strange sky, but had thought nothing of it. In truth, he needed most of his concentration focused on the ground. This Crown of the World was the most jagged country he had ever seen, as though great spirits had broken it apart with hammers in ancient times, and then some of it had grown over with grass and thick stands of slope-boughed trees. Water wormed through it everywhere, and much of the time their path was along the cut of some streambed. Right now they were ascending, in steps and lurches, along the channel that a river had carved into a steep hillside, the water's work making the unscalable into the merely laborious. The flow of water itself had atrophied to little more than a brook, the result of the oncoming freeze creeping down on them from the north.

With the rocky ground rising away from them on both sides, this was the obvious point for an ambush. Even before the trouble started, Asmander found himself feeling tense. Ahead of him, the stomping form of Venater already had his *meret* to hand, weighing its comforting heft with every step.

Then Ragged Sky appeared alongside Eshmir's horse, tugging at her boot as she guided the animal over the uneven ground.

'You should have your gifts ready,' he advised. 'You will need them.'

Two Heads Talking shot him a sharp look and then cocked an eye towards the sky. He put his fingers to his mouth and gave a piercing whistle. For a moment Asmander thought he was actually calling down the ambush there and then. Only Quiet When Loud came at his summons, leaping and bounding down the slope in her skinny little dog-like shape, before Stepping back to human form beside him.

Asmander took up his *maccan*, resting the flat of the toothed wooden blade on his shoulder. Their three guides were plainly tense, but not enough to suggest that they were about to fight for their lives.

'Pirates,' Venater declared, and Asmander nodded. That was the business with the gifts, of course. Whoever was about to make themselves known could apparently be bought off.

At that moment there came a sound out of the sky, starting just beyond the limit of hearing and building swiftly into a saw-edged shriek that split the ears. Asmander looked about wildly, ducking aside as one of the horses started stamping and plunging, its rider sliding off it but still holding tight to the reins. Some of the Horse had their bows strung, but the strange sound ripped into them, making them cluster together, fumbling their arrows.

Another high-pitched, savage voice joined the throng, and then a third. They came from above and all around, and Asmander saw those winged shapes passing and re-passing, stooping from on high and then climbing back into the cold and cloudless heavens.

Abruptly they started dropping down on all sides of the travellers, to end up perched on rocks and outcroppings overlooking the riverbed. They swooped with negligent speed, the nerve-shredding screaming arriving with them, stopping as they stopped. They came down as hawks but, when they landed, it was as men.

They were harsh-looking and barbarous creatures, to Asmander's eyes. They were still northerners, but their faces were craggier, with sharper noses and mad staring eyes. Like Ragged Sky, each had half his face painted, but they had used jagged patterns of black and red and white, so that when they glared with the eye on that side, it seemed to be at the centre of a storm. They wore surprisingly little despite the cold: cloaks and breeches, their bare chests painted with designs of lightning and wings and eyes. Some had bracers and greaves and long hauberks all made of ranks of bones laced together. For weapons they carried spears, and curved war-clubs with vicious bronze beaks. Many had odd lengths of wood strapped to their ankles, cut with holes, like flutes. With a sudden understanding Asmander realized that these must be the source of that terrifying sound as they dropped through the air.

The Horse had formed a solid group, standing back to back. Asmander, Venater and Shyri were each on their own, looking for room to fight. Eshmir stepped forward, apparently to address the newcomers, but Two Heads Talking quickly gestured for her to stop.

'Do I see Yellow Claw?' he called out to the newcomers, and then, 'These are his warband, are they not? Where is he?'

For a moment all fell still, the newcomers staring at them from their painted eyes, spears and clubs at the ready. Then a shadow passed over them all, and a vast winged form circled close overhead before displacing one of the raiders to claim his perch. It was white as the snow, and whilst the hawk shapes of

163

the others had seemed smaller than their human forms, this bird could have looked Asmander in the eye. It was surely large enough to carry away a man in its talons.

A Champion among birds, he realized, awed by the thought. When it fixed a single orange eye upon him, he had to work hard to face up to that burning regard.

Then it was a man in armour of bones and claws and quills. Curving struts of wood, thick with feathers, jutted above his shoulders, so that even standing on human feet he was winged.

'You sully my name, old dog,' he reproached Two Heads, and then, as a kind of formal announcement to the rest of them: 'I am Yellow Claw. I swoop on man and bear alike. In the wake of my wings I hear the cries of my enemies, the wailing of their women.'

Venater made a small sound that was a surprisingly subtle indication that he was not over-fond of Yellow Claw.

'Yellow Claw, these travellers of the Horse Society are not enemies of the Eyrie,' Two Heads went on, speaking quickly. 'They simply pass through these lands, as the Horse often does. I know even the Eyrie trades with the Horse.'

Yellow Claw cast a sour look towards Ragged Sky, who had been staying very still and silent. 'Let the Bone Pickers do whatever they wish. That we permit them to reside under the shadow of our wings is more than they deserve.' He hopped to another perch, his men moving around him, watching for his lead. 'But these are not my enemies, you say?'

'No indeed, Yellow Claw.'

'What can they be then?' He thrust out a bare foot and walked onto thin air. In that instant he had Stepped, his colossal wingspan blotting out the sun for a moment as he ghosted down to them, becoming a man again as he reached the ground. The buffeting of his wings rocked the travellers.

'Friends, with gifts,' Eshmir explained, but Yellow Claw looked through her as though she was not there. Only when Two

Heads echoed her words did the Eyrieman appear to hear them.

'Show me these gifts.' He was easily close enough for Asmander to attack him. Worse, he was close enough for Venater to do so, too, which seemed more likely. There was a confidence about the man, like stone, though. He stood there before them fully armoured in his belief in himself, in his status as a Champion.

If I Step . . . ? But Asmander knew the answer to that. *It would be a challenge to this Yellow Claw that he could not ignore. And I don't think even my vaunted honour will give me wings to match his.* He had no idea how these Eyriemen lived or what flaws held them back from being a power like the Wolf. Or perhaps they were so, in other parts of the Crown. He was finding his ignorance pressing in on him from all sides.

The gifts were some goldwork from the south, some turquoise and jade. None of it seemed notable to Asmander's eyes, but he guessed it seemed exotic enough when brought to these cold places. Yellow Claw looked at it all derisively, but he nevertheless snatched it from Two Heads Talking in a single swift motion. Then he went stalking over to stare at the southerners.

'Black man,' he noted. 'Why are you here, Black Man from the south?'

'Drawn by the wonders of the north,' Asmander told him.

Yellow Claw stared at him, first with one eye and then the other: war; peace; war; peace. He turned back to Two Heads. 'You have many women here, Two Heads Talking,' he noted.

The Coyote held himself quite still. 'Not really so many.'

'More than enough for an old man. Too many perhaps. Gifts, you said.'

It was not reassuring to see the sudden hunted expression appear on their guide's face. Ragged Sky had started shuffling away from the others, too, as though trying to deny any connection.

'Yellow Claw . . .' Two Heads started. His hand reached out and found his wife's.

'I know Quiet When Loud. She is funny,' Yellow Claw observed. 'Quiet when loud, loud when quiet. I know her. I do not insult you, to suggest I seize on her. But so many women. Horse women. Plains women.'

'Yellow Claw knows .the ways of the Horse Society,' Two Heads said carefully.

'You walk under my skies, Two Heads. This is a hard season for travelling. It is good that you have gifts. Gift me a woman, Two Heads Talking. Then you may have the blessing of the Eyrie for a year and a day.'

Two Heads' eyes flicked from Yellow Claw to Eshmir. 'They are not in my gift.'

'If they are not yours, then they are for the taking,' Yellow Claw suggested, his voice softly dangerous.

'Surely one so great as Yellow Claw has many mates already,' Shyri's voice broke in. When the Eyrieman did not seem to hear her, she prompted, 'Tell him that, dog-man.'

Stuttering a little, Two Heads did so.

Yellow Claw laughed, flashing bright teeth. 'Ah, yes, my nest is well feathered. But I have many followers, and some must return to a cold bed. Look at them.' A broad gesture towards the predatory gathering around them. 'Have pity, Two Heads, and share your bounty.'

'Have him pick one such, and I shall wrestle him,' Shyri intervened. 'If he beats me, say I'll go with him. If he cannot beat me, he's no man and I'll have none of him.'

The Coyote opened his mouth, but that boast was apparently too amusing for Yellow Claw to ignore. He regarded Shyri with his disparate gazes and laughed again. 'Oshkyr, come down here. Your wife wants to know you.'

One of the Eyriemen – younger, but still a broad-shouldered, strong-framed man – jumped up, Stepping at the apex of his leap and then feathering his way down to stand as a man by Yellow Claw's side.

'You'll go with him, will you?' Asmander murmured to Shyri.

166

'We don't all have your honour, Champion, nor do we all keep our word,' she growled back. 'You're lucky that I don't intend to lose.'

She strode forwards: a match for this Oshkyr in height, but more slender.

Yellow Claw clapped his protégé on the back. 'Go teach your wife,' he told him.

The man leapt at Shyri in that moment, obviously planning to make a quick end of it. She threw herself aside, Stepping for an extra burst of speed, and then regarded him again from out of reach. There was a current of jeering laughter from among the Eyriemen.

'Watch out, she has an ugly side!' one of them called.

Oshkyr scowled, and then he darted forwards again. Even as Shyri came to meet him with teeth and claws, he himself had Stepped, rising above her and then plunging down. For a moment he had his claws hooking at her back, but she Stepped sinuously back into her human shape, his talons merely gouging her coat. Briefly, he was snarled there, beating his wings hard enough to yank her off balance. Then she slipped out of it, down to a sleeveless tunic, and he wheeled away, almost clashing his wings against the rocky ground and Stepping down to face her, man to woman.

There were more exclamations from the Eyriemen, some mocking their fellow, others in loud speculation about how much more of Shyri would be revealed by the end of the contest. After his initial rash onslaught, Oshkyr was apparently learning some wisdom, keeping his distance, even backing up along the side of the river channel. A moment later he had kicked off, Stepped and was diving on her again with wings outstretched.

The first time she Stepped and warned him off with her bared jaws, forcing him to pull up awkwardly, faltering in the air. Yellow Claw found it hilarious. 'We'll need a collar and a muzzle for her, when we get her back,' he called out.

Then Oshkyr dropped back into his human shape even as he fell on her, trusting to his greater weight and the speed of impact to break her. For a moment Asmander thought he had succeeded, as Shyri seemed to fall beneath him, but then they were grappling, and she was holding him off, matching strength for strength, to Oshkyr's obvious astonishment. He grimaced and put his all into the next shove, trying to force her off balance. To Asmander, the Eyrieman's youth and inexperience practically screamed out.

Shyri had been waiting for it. She melted away before him, kicking his front leg out as he shoved, so that Oshkyr hurtled head over heels past her, tumbling into the shallow draught of the river.

She was on him instantly, smacking his face into the water and then reaching an arm about his neck. For a second there was a winged thing struggling for flight there, but then she had her hold, and he was a man again, straining and struggling to remove her arm. Asmander watched thoughtfully as she locked her legs about his waist and began the careful business of strangling him. He had thought Yellow Claw would make some move to halt the fight, but either he reckoned Oshkyr was due for some humiliation, or the spectacle of one of his warriors being beaten by a woman had rendered him speechless.

Strange are the ways of the north ... or of the Eyrie, anyway, he considered. Not unique, certainly, but the traditions of the Laughing Men were certainly a rude shock to these locals. From what Asmander remembered, the men of that tribe had been allowed little enough to laugh about.

Oshkyr had gone purple, eyes bulging, and abruptly his body went limp, head lolling. Shyri released him, then kicked him over, none too gently, to keep his face out of the water. 'This is no man,' she announced. 'You have sent me one of your children.'

For a moment all was still, and Asmander could read something of Yellow Claw's conflicting thoughts: his desire to avenge

168

his people struggling against the deal he had made openly before them.

At the last he laughed, although it sounded forced. 'Another year before you earn your name, Oshkyr.' Though that surely fell on deaf ears. The other Eyriemen sent up a half-hearted murmur in support.

'Go, Two Heads Talking.' Yellow Claw waved dismissively. 'Take your amusing wife and your amusing friends. Take them far off.'

The Coyote nodded hastily, looking as though he was surprised to still be alive and, under the stern regard of the Eyrie, the travellers got under way with as much haste as they could muster.

14

She tried to break south, heading away from the lake, but Broken Axe was a man who had lived a hunter's life, two feet or four. He was already putting on a burst of speed that would lead her into his jaws as she tried to veer away from the water, cutting a long, curved line as though he and the lake together made a pack that was closing her in, shutting down her options just like the prey she was.

She was fast, but she was hungry and tired and carrying a burden. Broken Axe loped along, sparing his strength, knowing that no matter how she dodged and turned, he would run her down with a wolf's patient endurance.

The sheer impersonal calm of the man was more frightening than slavering rage might have been. The chase was nothing special: just one of hundreds for him. When he brought her down – to tear out her throat or to drag her home – he would not exult, nor even much care. One more quarry, that was all she was.

This thought gave her access to a hitherto unsuspected surge of strength, and she pulled ahead, springing away from the water and into the trees, hoping she might lose him again. But this time there was no enshrouding snow to aid her. Even if she could put enough trees between them, her tracks would be his road towards her.

And he was still on her heels. She could hear the regular

panting of his breath, almost feel the heat of it on her haunches. The crisp thud of his footfalls in the snow were so very close. There was panic in her heart and she could not but give it rein, letting it whip her faster and faster. She would tire, she knew, but she did not have the ability to pace herself. That was a luxury so seldom granted to prey.

She twice tried to cut back south, desperately hoping to barter a brief burst of speed into something that would do her some good. He was there both times, mouth open in a wolf's easy grin, heading her away, making all the decisions over where this chase was going.

Somehow she was able to form the cogent thought: *He knows the ground already.* There was not a hand's span of the Crown of the World that had not known Broken Axe's tread. Even with the snow masking the tell-tale scents and muddling the scenery, he knew where he was. He was forcing her to head exactly where he wanted her, as a shepherd would nip at the edges of his flock, and she could do nothing to stop him.

The going was harder now, and she understood that Broken Axe was forcing her uphill, tiring her out further while he himself just dipped into what seemed an inexhaustible well of ready strength. The ground underfoot became more uneven, riven by stones and outcroppings of rock that the snow turned into ankle-breaking traps for the unwary. She kept her eyes ahead, legs still pounding away as she leapt and shouldered her way through the snow, burning with exhaustion a little more with each breath. The skew and disposition of the trees ahead were a hidden language telling her where the rock lay, where the ground was earth and roots. She spurred herself on, scrabbling and darting. Every time a tree passed on either side, she cast herself that way, trying to put obstacles in his path.

He did not seem overly concerned. Sometimes he was almost abreast of her, his sinuous progress at the corner of her vision, on the left or the right, steering her adroitly by the menace of his

171

very presence. For him, the trees and rocks might almost not have been there.

Then she saw, ahead, where the land would call a halt to the chase; where she, exhausted and terrified, would be brought to bay against a wall of upthrust grey stone. As though a god's stroke had severed the earth, the shallow, uneven rise that he had been hounding her up met with a weathered and cracked cliff face three times the height of a tall man. The barrier extended on either side as far as she could see, a grey gash in the white expanse of the world. Only now did she know how close she was to the uplands, because here they were. This was where the Wolf's Shadow grew fainter. Here were the first few jagged points that lined the northern edge of the Crown of the World.

Here was where Broken Axe sought to break her.

He was even slowing down, letting her dash herself against the rocks; letting her drive out the last few sparks of defiance that still burned in her.

She increased her speed, and for the first time had the sense that she had caught him off guard. The stone loomed over her, as though it would crash down and obliterate all trace that there had ever been such a thing as Maniye, Stone River's daughter.

A plan formed in her head: a mad plan, but the sane ones had all failed her. There was no wolf-test at which she would better Broken Axe, but she could do something he could not. *This cannot work*. But she guessed that Broken Axe had not been interested in the Testing. Certainly he was not the sort to engage in idle gossip with the Winter Runners, and there were drawbacks in being a man alone.

But it was very high, and she had never tried something like this.

She Stepped. For a moment her pounding paws became feet in Horse-gifted hide boots, going far too fast for a human, about to trip over herself and plant her face straight in that rough spread of stone.

She jumped, kicking off with all her strength, and as soon as

172

she had cleared the ground she was a wolf again. It was Broken Axe's trick to leap the stream. The distance her human strength would throw her human body was far less than it would throw the smaller wolf that she became. For a second she was a terrified animal, scrabbling at the rockface.

She had already worked through the sequence in her mind. In the next eyeblink she let her tiger out, its claws already hooking at whatever chink or fracture the rock would grant her, finding impossible purchase for a half-breath that would let her rake her way higher up the stone. She sensed Broken Axe at her very tail, leaping up with jaws bared, but falling away, falling short of her.

Her satchel strap snapped, and for a moment she felt sure that she would lose Hesprec again, and that he would fall into the waiting teeth of the hunter. Something like a chill whip coiled about her shoulder, though, and she knew he had lashed himself close to her for all his old snake body was worth.

Then her battle with the stone and with the yawning pull of the earth below consumed all her attention. She was fighting for a hold with all four feet, lurching upwards in uneven bursts, knowing that to fail was to fall. Her enemy was waiting to tear into her the moment she allowed him to.

But it was for her to allow. For the first time she was in control: she would succeed or fail by her own merits, not merely fall victim to Broken Axe's long-learned skills.

Then, halfway up, she lost her purchase and felt herself parting company with the treacherous rockface, almost as if it was shaking her off. She felt herself in fierce contention with its stone spirit, the stubborn and uncooperative entity that slumbered within it. Then it had shuddered, like a vast beast that feels the itching of some insect on its hide, and she was falling.

She twisted as only a cat can twist but, instead of poising herself to fall on her feet, she thrust herself away from the stone, imagining Broken Axe watching her arc overhead with a blank stare.

The outer branches of the pine tree whipped at her, and her

weight shattered them as she half leapt, half fell. Then she hit a branch that was solid enough to bear the small tiger that she had become. She flailed madly at the bark, claws digging in wherever they could. The trunk bent under her, but she gave it no time to realize the lunacy she had inflicted upon it. She scrabbled and scratched up another six feet, shifting her weight to lean in towards the cliff, and then let the tree spring away as she jumped again. Below her, Broken Axe jumped away from the explosive shower of snow she released.

This time she had spotted her target – the higher reaches of the cliff were riven and messy with roots and grass. For a moment she thought that only one set of claws had caught – not enough to keep her anchored there – but then both hind feet had found just enough roughness in the rock to boost her up, and it needed only three heaving breaths' work to see her over the top.

She turned, then, to look down. It was not exactly a gesture of defiance, and when she collapsed into a crouch it was because she was shaking too much to run any further. Still, she faced her hunter, and in doing so shook off the role of prey, at least for now.

The pale wolf that was Broken Axe looked up at her. She had thought he would Step to his human form and try to coax her back again, but there was just the beast below with his pale eyes and his dark shoulders. He sat back on his haunches and stared, and she tried to read many things into the language of his lean body, and could not be sure of any of them.

Then he stood and shook himself and trotted off along the line of the cliff, his intention plain. It would take more than the intervention of the earth itself to put him off his hunt.

She thought about trying to climb down then, but *he* was still there, somewhere below, and, if she thought of it, so might he have second-guessed her, as he seemed so apt at doing. Instead, when she had recovered her breath, she turned and set off again away from the fractured side of the earth. She returned to her wolf shape, but by now she had no clear destination left to her. The pursuit itself was the only thing that was keeping her moving.

When she grew tired, worn down by covering the broken ground, she sheltered wherever she could find, hunching in whatever nook the land would give her: under rock shelves or in the wind-shadow of trees. Hesprec made no appearance, having stowed himself back in her satchel. She felt as lonely and lost as if she was the last soul on earth.

Sometimes she went uphill, because she hoped Broken Axe would assume she would go down. Sometimes she went downhill, because she was tired and it was easier, and she was not thinking. The wind remained cold but the snow did not return, and the weakening sun began to eat into that which had already fallen, slowly restoring the world to her, and erasing her tracks.

On the third day, Broken Axe still not having caught up with her erratic wanderings, she broke into the clearing, and halted.

In one sinuous movement, Hesprec unwound himself from her satchel and Stepped into his old man's body, drawing his robe tight about him.

'What is this place?' he hissed, one hand making a quick gesture at the sight ahead of them, as if to ward off some hostile and very present power.

She had been running tired for some time, her head low, implacable feet drawing her on despite the bone-weariness in her limbs. She had not noted all the stumps of felled trees that had lined her path towards this place. She had not realized that, out of the domain of the wilds, she had come to a place of man.

There were no men here now though: the start of winter had driven them lower to warmer ground. She wondered if they were thralls of the Winter Runners or if she had wandered close to some other pack's territory – the Moon Eaters perhaps. Whichever, this was Wolf tribe work. No others did this.

Here, the felling of trees had cleared a great circular space containing the wreckage of a dozen mounds. Where the snow had melted, she could see the char of ash left behind, and there was plenty of half-burned wood scattered about, the shell that had been peeled away when the thralls had dug at the treasure within.

She had always known that the Wolf had marked her – and probably as prey. Here, she felt his presence keenly, his spirit lingering even after his work was done.

When she Stepped again, exhaustion fell on her like a hammer and she sagged to her knees. 'This is a sacred site.' She felt that she should be very scared to intrude here – as Hesprec must be, for certainly he had sensed the god of his enemies hanging about the place. Instead, though, she felt unnaturally calm. The Wolf was watching her but had yet to bare his teeth, and she was too sapped by her long run to show either deference or defiance.

'What do they do here?' the old Serpent asked, eyes narrowed.

She should not tell him, she knew. No child of the Wolf should divulge such secrets. But the rebellious streak that had driven her so far flared up again, and she looked the invisible Wolf right in its eye and said, 'This is where they make the magic wood. Kalameshli has scores of thralls employed for it. They do something special in the burning of it, and this normal wood becomes magic wood, the Wolf's wood.'

She glanced at him to see what he might make of that, and noticed a thoughtful expression under the shadow of his hood. 'This is the iron-magic?' he guessed.

'It is the iron-magic,' she confirmed. She did not know the secret, of course; only Kalameshli and his acolytes – and their counterparts in other tribes – could claim that knowledge. She knew the magic was only the Wolf's to use, though, a secret knowledge that had seen her father's people cast down her mother's, and that no outsiders must ever know. The iron was that unnatural, terrible metal that made tools that could shatter stone and weapons that could crack bronze; iron that no man could attune himself to and carry with him while Stepped, without going through terrible ordeals as secret as the metal's working.

'Your god is here.' Hesprec's voice seemed remarkably steady. 'Or one of them, at least. How does he look upon you, tell me?'

Wolf filled the clearing, towering high as the sky, his sightless paws planted as far apart as the furthest trees. She felt his vast attention on her, watchful and considering.

Well, O Wolf? she asked, inside her head. *Speak to me of your disapproval.* She knew the stories of those who betrayed the pack: hearth-husbands who were greedy when food was scarce; chiefs who led their people astray; hunters who were clumsy or over-proud; kinslayers – most of all kinslayers. In the stories, they found themselves in the wilds and they came face to face with Wolf, and they were judged.

There were many qualities Wolf despised, but many that he valued, too. Not all his people ran with the pack. Some walked alone, after all.

Wolf weighed her and scented her and marked her trail – all of her trail all the way back to Akrit's hall, and she felt no condemnation, not yet. Wolf was waiting to see how she would survive, now she had cast herself into the wilderness. She would know his judgement: it would be expressed in her living until spring, or in her frozen corpse being buried by the winter snow. Wolf despised betrayal and cowardice, but she felt neither of those rods descending upon her back. Instead, she knew that Wolf valued determination and perseverance, the endurance of the long chase, the will to survive the lean season of the ice.

'He is waiting,' she said softly. 'He wants to know what I will do next.'

Hesprec sighed and sat down beside her, stiffly enough that she heard his joints creak. 'And what *will* you do?'

'Survive.' The word came to her unbidden.

'Excellent. Always it is good to have a plan.'

177

She glanced angrily at him, but saw the slight smile there, the sign that he was baiting her.

'And you have a plan too, O Serpent?'

'It may be so. This is not my land but these things are known: what we have just lived through was the least hatchling of winter's brood, no? When the season comes in earnest, we will die.' He saw her stubborn expression, and amended that to: '*I* will die – of that I am sure.'

'I hear no plan,' she told him curtly.

'We are reaching the far bounds of your people, here? I had always thought that the highlands were not Wolf lands?'

'The Wolf walks where he wills,' she replied archly, but then: 'I think we must be at the very edge of the Wolf's Shadow here, though. This camp may even mark it. The Wolf-wood takes much normal wood to create, I think, so the camps are far spread.'

Hesprec closed his eyes and bowed his head. 'Let us head north, then.'

'Further north?' she asked, wide-eyed.

'North, into the highlands proper,' he confirmed. 'Use that nose of yours to sniff out some habitation that is not Wolf tribe. Let us claim some right of hospitality, and hope that whoever dwells here is kinder to a wandering priest than your kin were. Seek out the scent of smoke, and let us then trust to the power of our words to win us a place for the winter.'

'That is no plan,' she decided.

'It is my only plan. And yours is . . . ?'

She tried to sense what the Wolf might think. Was it craven to creep into some stranger's good graces just to ward off the chill? Should she not brave the utmost winter to show how she was the Wolf's child?

Except that she was not only the Wolf's child and, anyway, even the Wolf told stories of the clever as well as the strong and the swift. Wolf valued the crafty even as he valued the mighty.

She half felt that Hesprec's suggestion was doomed anyway.

Surely they could wander all over the highlands and not find a single campfire kept burning. But there was no harm to scent the wind for the taste of smoke, after all. In the end, even if the Wolf did disapprove, she wanted to live. A stranger's hearth was better than a cold grave.

It rained soon after, adding a new misery to the rest. As well as the wet chill that soaked into her pelt, they had run out of the food gifted to them by the Horse, and the hunting here was meagre. With the world's scents washed away and its creatures under cover, they might as well be in a desert, for all the prey she could scare up. This time it was Hesprec who saved them, setting little traps of thread unpicked from his robe edge so that a dozen small creatures – squirrels and mice – were caught overnight while they slept.

'The Serpent has other ways to be fed than all this chasing about,' he explained in that manner of his that trod the line between dignity and self-mockery.

He kept a single mouse for himself and let her take what meat she could from the rest of the diminutive catch. His own meal he swallowed whole and raw, Stepping into his snake form to digest it. He had explained that he could live for a week on such a repast, if he needed.

She had not thought she would come to rely on him. In the pit of the Winter Runners, he had seemed such a frail and helpless creature.

Later it snowed again, overnight, so that the white world was waiting for them once more when they awoke. By then, Maniye felt her ribs tight against her skin, her skin loose over her shrunken belly. She could not live on a mouse every handful of days, nor could Hesprec save himself from a freezing death without her wolf-warmth each night. Their co-dependence would not be enough to beat back the encroaching winter.

But that very same day, even as the sky was purpling, bruising down towards sunset, she scented smoke.

The taste of it, that lone evidence that she and Hesprec were not the sole surviving humans in the whole of the world, set her feet bounding and scrabbling through the snow, even as a fresh feathering of white began to descend. Someone had lit a fire. A fire meant warmth. A fire meant food. A fire meant home. Right then she was prepared to kill a stranger for those things, if only she found the strength for it.

She was not so maddened with hunger that she just went charging right in: when she spotted the fire's red eye, deep off in the forest, she Stepped to her human form and shook her satchel until Hesprec awakened and slung his coils out, spitting and cursing at the chill the moment he resumed his bony old human shape.

A simple pointing finger was enough to bring him up to speed.

'A campfire, I think,' he murmured, squinting into the twilight. 'Some other wanderer, perhaps. Who would be abroad this night? The dangerous and the desperate, none other.'

'You're having second thoughts?' she demanded.

He tucked his gloved hands under his armpits. 'Let us go anyway, and hope they are dangerously hospitable and desperate for company.'

'On these feet?' she asked, meaning: *In these shapes?*

'It would seem best,' he agreed weakly. 'I mean no slight, but who welcomes a wolf to their fire?'

They approached carefully, treading as lightly as possible through the snow and squinting into the dark at the burgeoning reddish glow that was fast becoming the focus of their world. Maniye had thought of Stepping to her tiger form to scout the strangers' camp, but if any of the fire-makers were resting in an animal shape, then they might pick up her scent. Worse, if she was spotted skulking about the edges of their camp, and if one of them had a bow or even a good spear-arm . . .

Closer, and the tantalizing scent of cooking drifted to them:

fish was not common fare in Akrit's hall, but even a human nose could not mistake it.

'Do the rules of hospitality hold, so far to the north?' murmured Hesprec. He had withdrawn his arms entirely from the sleeves of his robe, huddling his way along with them wrapped inside it about his skinny body, and in constant danger of falling over.

Only one way to find out, Maniye realized, but her own teeth were now chattering too much to say it.

The fire had been set in a hollow cleared of snow, to hold in as much of its heat as possible, so they were obliged to creep very close before they could get sight of its master. When they did, lifting their heads over the dip's edge, Maniye caught her breath in shock.

The fire itself had been laid within a half-cairn of stones to shelter it and to direct its heat. The structure was constructed intricately, a veritable work of art in dry stone, each piece interlocking with its neighbours elegantly – and all the more remarkable because its builder was a giant.

Even sitting at the fire, he would have been able to look Maniye directly in the eye. Standing, he would have loomed at least head and shoulders over Hesprec and, rather than being lanky like the Snake priest, he was massive, vastly broad across the shoulders, wide at the waist, lumpy with muscles like boulders. He wore a robe of overlapping, stitched-together hides and the garment itself probably weighed more than Maniye could lift, perhaps even with Hesprec's help. Over that he had a cloak of coarse wool that would have made a tent for a man of more modest proportions. His black hair was long, plaited into two thick braids that rattled with bone rings alongside his cheeks. His beard was the size and shape of a spade-head.

At his side sat a pair of muscular grey dogs, wolf-like but most certainly not wolves, and behind them, covered with a skin, was a sled. The dogs' attention was entirely fixed on what their master was doing. He sat cross-legged with a fist-sized ball of earth before him, and with a gentle tap he cracked it open, revealing a curled fish inside that had cooked in the heat of his fire. The smell was unbearably delicious.

Maniye spared a glance for Hesprec, who was plainly not going to last much longer without that fire. For herself, she felt that she would not last much longer without the fish.

Her stomach made the decision and pushed her forwards, one hand snagging the old priest's flapping sleeve to draw him after her.

As they half stepped, half slipped down into the hollow, she expected the huge man to leap up, outraged at these intruders, but apparently the two of them were not so very alarming as all that. Instead, their hoped-for host leant back, one eyebrow raised quizzically, and one hand moving over to rest easily on the haft of an enormous axe she had not noticed before. It was as long as she was tall, with a head of copper held to its arm-thick shaft by three sockets, and yet it seemed barely adequate for the man's huge hand.

'What's this now, hrm?' That last was a sound from deep in the man's throat, a growl that sent a shiver of fright through Maniye's bones. His voice was very soft, just as his stance was very calm and still, but there was a well of strength behind both.

Maniye had no idea how to address one of the Cave Dwellers – for he could be nothing else. The sheer bulk of him had struck her silent, mouth opening but her words afraid to venture forth.

'Kind lord,' came Hesprec's voice at her ear, 'we are but travellers in this land, who saw your fire from afar, as if it were a star to guide us.' His voice shook and shuddered from the cold, but he managed a stiff bow, and Maniye wondered if this was how people actually talked where he came from, or whether he was just making things up again.

The Cave Dweller grunted.

'Even I,' Hesprec went on gamely, desperately, 'who first saw the sun in a land far distant, have heard of the welcome generosity of these, your cold lands. Wherever life is harsh, there life is precious, that is what they say. Even for two strangers such as we . . .'

The huge man raised a hand abruptly, and Maniye found herself flinching back from him, even though he sat halfway across the fire from them.

'Share the fire, why don't you?' he suggested quietly, with a touch of exasperated humour. 'Leave all those words out in the dark, though.'

Now it was Hesprec who was lurching forwards and dragging Maniye after him, almost falling into the fire in his eagerness to get warm. Once he was sitting, shivering uncontrollably, she reached over and pulled his robe open a bit, against his protests, so that the fire's heat could get to him through all those layers.

Their host poked at the fire with a stick and excavated another clay lump. The look he gave his guests was distinctly put-upon. 'You'll be hungry, of course – all sorts of cold and hungry.' He looked mournfully at the ball before him. For him, they were very small fish.

'I will survive,' Hesprec said, 'but my friend has been doing much of the walking.' He pressed on with sudden abandon. 'I am Hesprec Essen Skese, a priest much respected in civ—in my own land, and the girl here is Maniye.' The exchange of names was an essential element of the bond between host and guest, as everyone knew.

The big man stared at him for a moment, his sullen expression almost a child's, then he shrugged. 'Loud Thunder,' he rumbled, striking a fist at his chest. A hunter name was better than nothing, Maniye knew, although not quite so potent as a birth name.

There were six more fish still in the fire, and they were able to watch the precise tilting of greed and conscience in Loud Thunder's face as he cracked the earthen balls all open and considered how to divide the spoils. In the end, Hesprec got half of one, Maniye the other half, and the smallest one of the remainder. Two went to the dogs, the huge man filleting the fish neatly with a thin blade of flint and then letting the animals snap and squabble over the meat. Nobody complained. The taste was surprisingly rich, flavoured with the herbs the fish had been wrapped around before being encased in clay.

Loud Thunder watched them as he ate, his knuckle-sized teeth making surprisingly delicate work of it. His expression was a little puzzled, a little resentful, but mostly that of a man withholding judgement.

Then, just as Hesprec had finished picking flesh from bone, one of the dogs lifted its head from the last scraps of its food, ears pricked high.

'Who is it that travels with you?' Loud Thunder growled suspiciously.

For a moment Maniye could not understand what he meant. A second later, she *knew*, without any doubt, who it must be.

In a thought she became a tiger, turning away from the fire as she Stepped, her keen eyes paring away the darkness, hunting out what the dogs had sensed.

There was a man out there, standing still as a tree amongst trees, and it was Broken Axe. There was no mistaking him. His image was branded on her mind.

The shock of seeing him jolted her back into human form, and she turned to see the Cave Dweller staring at her with almost comical surprise.

'Please,' she got out. 'Please, we are being hunted. There is a man out there, a killer. He is sent by my father to murder me. Please.'

Loud Thunder's expression told her that this went beyond any contract between host and guest, and his great head shook slightly. Then Broken Axe, human still, stepped carefully into the firelight with his hands empty.

The Cave Dweller's hand was resting on his axe again, but with no obvious intention of using it. Maniye felt her innards freeze up, the fear clenching her there hard enough to hurt.

'Please,' she forced out, 'he killed my mother. Please. He killed my mother.'

Now she had the absolute attention of all three men as the Wolf hunter approached.

'Well,' Loud Thunder murmured, taking a deep breath. For one mad moment she thought he would take up his axe and defend her, stranger though she was. She had a dream-vision of that heavy copper blade cleaving through the Wolf without slowing, just a single blow that would end forever her nightmares and her running.

Then the Cave Dweller nodded. 'Axe,' he hailed the newcomer, with evident familiarity.

'Thunder,' replied Broken Axe and, at a small nod from the big man, took a place at the fire.

15

'Amiyen Shatters Oak is returned,' Kalameshli announced.

Akrit was out on the training ground, pushing himself hard, working up a sheen of sweat despite the cold. First he had been wrestling with a few of the younger hunters, showing them just how little youthful vitality was worth against experience. Then he had called out Smiles Without Teeth, the biggest man there, whom none of the youngsters had yet dared challenge. Akrit knew Smiles well, though: big and strong but without imagination.

And loyal, in the bargain. Too loyal, perhaps, to show up his chief before the tribe. There had been a time when Akrit had known he could beat Smiles easily, matching his skill and speed to the man's strength. Now he beat the man, throwing him twice and then forcing him into a grunting armlock, and yet there was a nagging doubt in his mind that would not be silenced. *How much of this is he giving you? How much could you truly take by force?*

The fear – and the anger that always followed on its heels – made him twist Smiles's arm more savagely than he had intended, and he cast his henchman sprawling on the hard ground. For a moment he wanted that other kind of fighting, the serious kind. He wanted to get his teeth bloody. He stared about him at the hunters there – who had killed in their time, both as beast and as man. He found that he was desperate to be challenged, desperate to be brought to bay now, while he was still young enough and strong enough to tear the hide of any upstart who tried it. What were they all waiting for? Didn't they want to be chief?

And yet he knew what they were waiting for, any one of them with a drop of ambitious blood in them. They were trailing him like a good hunter should, letting him tire and tire as the years rolled by beneath his feet. Why attack the buck when he is full of pride and life when you can run him to his knees and then open his throat?

Now, with Smiles Without Teeth struggling back to his feet, here was Kalameshli with news.

Akrit did not ask the obvious question, not here, not before everyone. *Is the girl with her?* He could see it, anyway, from Kalameshli's expression. Amiyen had come home without her quarry.

He glowered about at the younger men, and they dropped their eyes gratifyingly, none of them wanting to confront his wrath. With that brief, petty satisfaction, he dragged his cloak about him and stormed off to his hall. Kalameshli would bring Amiyen to him, he knew.

'Out, all of you!' he bellowed as he entered, scattering thralls and wives. 'Underfoot and listening, every one of you!' He slapped a young Deer tribe slave as she tried to scurry past him, sending her tumbling to the floor. 'Out!'

For just one moment, old habit prompted him to go and root *the girl* out of her den up above, as he had been forced to do on other occasions when he wanted quiet counsel with Kalameshli. But, no, of course there would be no need now.

Nobody had mentioned her since she fled. Or nobody had dared do so to his face or within earshot, which was not the same thing. He had no doubt that his errant daughter had become the talk of the Winter Runners behind his back – and probably the news had got as far as the Moon Eaters and the

Swift Backs by now, for that matter. In his own sight, though, it was as though Maniye, his sole daughter, had never been.

He kicked a couple of bearskins together and sat down, hunching himself towards the embers of the fire. Now he was not wrestling, the cold seemed to make a sudden leap at him. And it *was* cold: the winter was coming on fast. It was the cold and not the years that made him shiver beneath his cloak.

Kalameshli and Amiyen entered, the priest settling the door-hanging carefully to keep the heat in. Akrit fixed the woman with a baleful look.

'Well?' he demanded.

Amiyen did not lower her eyes. The angry stare of her chief did not cow her, but was instead swallowed up amid her own sour and festering anger. 'She's gone,' the huntress spat.

'Where?' Akrit hissed.

'She went to the Horse, and when they gave her up, she fled. A storm ate her tracks. I went downriver halfway to the next Horse camp, but there was no sign.'

'You failed.' Akrit was trying to disentangle the knots of her expression. 'How hard did you search, Shatters Oak?'

'Oh, believe me, if she could be found, I would have found her,' Amiyen spat viciously. 'She killed my son, my Iramey. Come the spring I will go hunt her again.'

Akrit could not afford to show the shock he felt, holding his face carefully impassive. *Killed . . . ?* True the girl was a wild one, but he could not imagine her besting even Amiyen's younger, not as woman nor wolf . . .

But as tiger . . . Akrit remembered well how fiercely a tiger could fight when cornered. He recalled those battles, in the days when the whole of the Crown of the World had risen under the Wolf, and when men like Akrit had forged futures for themselves . . .

Simpler times, better times . . . But living in the past was for older men than he.

'Tell me,' he ordered, and Amiyen recounted it all, how she

188

had almost caught the girl at the Horse camp, but lost her in the snow. How she had then searched for days before the snows returned, and she and Rubrey were driven before the advancing cold all the way back to the stronghold of the Winter Runners. And since that first storm there had been no sign at all of Maniye or the Snake priest.

And her son . . . She spoke very little of her younger son, save to report his death. She kept the grief all inside.

Looking her in the eye then, Akrit knew that if the Winter Runners would consent to being led by a woman, then she would have called him out right there. Her mood was ugly and rebellious, and it was the blood of his blood that had spilled her own.

'What about Broken Axe?' Akrit demanded.

'There was no other,' Amiyen declared. 'Just the winter and me.'

Once she had gone, Akrit sat in silence for a long while, with Kalameshli seated across the fire from him, like his reflection in a dark pool.

The people of other totems pretended horror at the Wolf, especially those milksops of the Deer and the Boar who lived within the Wolf's Shadow. They claimed that a chief of the Wolf ruled only until a stronger beast tore his throat out. They told themselves that the Wolf were cruel – stronger than them, but only at the expense of some moral refinement. They did not understand, and that was one reason that those peoples had always come second: the playthings of whatever predator was stalking at the edges of their villages, be it Bear or Tiger or Wolf.

In truth, mere fighting skill won no chieftainships. What made a chief was the confidence of his tribe. A challenger without the backing of the pack would not even be allowed into the circle. A chief facing the loss of his tribe's support would back down without baring his teeth, knowing that the battle was lost. Only if the tribe was divided, only if the race was close, would it come down to bloodied fangs.

Akrit could feel that confidence in him slipping away. He was still chief; the Winter Runners would still follow him, but for how long? How long with one as respected as Amiyen gnawing away at his support like an old bone? He thought about her older son, Rubrey – a popular youth but unproven still. A bare handful might stand with him if his mother put him up to the challenge. A bare handful *this* winter but what about the next, when he had one year's more strength, and Akrit a year's less?

Therefore take a warband against the Tiger, capture some thralls, shed some blood, show the world that Akrit Stone River remained a power to be reckoned with. He had faith that his hunters would be up to the task, and there was always some skirmish, some theft or intrusion from the edge of the highlands that needed avenging. And, yet, just such a small venture was the meat and drink of young challengers: somewhere they could prove themselves. The shedding of blood was ideal for binding a new pack together about some emergent leader. Was Rubrey, son of Amiyen, that man?

When he himself was a young man, Akrit had known large dreams. The Wolves and their allies had thrown off the Tiger yoke, and he had caught the enemy ruler – taken that proud woman from the midst of the fray. He had already challenged for the leadership of the Winter Runners – he was the hero of a dozen battles and the tribe loved him. In covert conference with the new priest, Kalameshli, he had aimed his arrow higher. The Wolf tribes were choosing a High Chief, already planning their own hegemony over the Crown of the World. Akrit and Kalameshli had been looking to the future, assessing the chance that power over the Tiger might bring the Winter Runners into dominance over everyone born to the Jaws of the Wolf.

And it had seemed such an easy thing: get a child on the Tiger Queen. A child of two souls who would wear the Wolf's skin but still provide enough leverage to make the Tigers bow. And a girl-child too, as it turned out. What more could he have asked for? She was destined to be just one of his numerous brood.

190

He had since wondered if lying with the Tiger woman had not poisoned him, somehow, soured his seed within him. Each night he lay with one or other of his Wolf wives, yet not one of them bore his child, for all the charms and old wisdoms they resorted to.

More recently, he had begun to wonder if it was not the girl herself, Maniye, who had cursed him. That child, born of violence, sullen and resentful, sitting up in her nook like some malign ghost: who was to say that her mother had not given her some Tiger magic at her birth to ruin the man who had conquered her?

And yet, even though she was a girl-child, even though she was a wretched, hating creature who looked on nothing with kindness and had none who would call her friend, she was still of Akrit's blood. She was his only blood. He did not like her. Most certainly he felt no real father's love for her. She was the sole sign of his potency, though. She at least showed him to be a man in that vital way.

And she was out in the cold, and this year's winter promised to have teeth that would make even the Wolf back down. Even a strong hunter would not willingly live through the winter with only his pelt to keep him warm. How would the girl survive at all?

And with her death, Akrit would lose both his chance to mount his grand campaign against the Tiger, and the sole issue of his loins. With Maniye dead, how long could he ever hope to hold on to the Winter Runners? If not young Rubrey, then there would be some other.

'There is always Broken Axe,' he murmured. He knew too well that Axe could live through any number of hard winters, and did not always choose to shelter with the rest of the tribe when the snows came. So long as there was no sign of the man, then Akrit could believe he was still hunting Maniye.

Kalameshli was staring at him, his lined face solemn, a bruised look in his eyes.

191

'What?' snapped Akrit. 'You think this is how I wished it?'

'I think that you sent away her from the village as readily as if you gave her the order,' the priest replied, his tone quiet and clear. 'Your mouth, your words. And I think our people have gone to every village and camp, and come back with empty hands. And I think that the winter has no soft heart for girls just past their Testing, when caught in its teeth.'

Akrit scowled at him ferociously, but inside he felt a cold trickle of fear, because the moment that Kalameshli turned from him, then he could start counting the days. He and Kalameshli had always been two wolves running abreast on the hunt, knowing each other's movements and working together without fail. He had always been able to rely on the priest to intercede for him, both with man and with god.

But a priest's true loyalty was to the tribe and not its chief, not even to Wolf. If Kalameshli was losing faith in him . . .

'She was tested, she was tempered,' the priest whispered. 'I had struggled with her two souls for all her life, to drive her into the jaws of the Wolf. And now . . .' A tilt of his head to convey all of the cold, white world outside.

'You mourn your lost work as if it was *your* lost kin,' Akrit told him harshly. Kalameshli's head snapped up again, and for a moment the two men just stared at each other, the balance of power shifting between them. Akrit felt as if he was grasping a rope, putting his whole weight on it, seeing if it would part suddenly and betray him. But better this now, when it was just the two of them here in the hall, than on some other occasion before the whole tribe.

But it seemed Kalameshli was not quite ready to break with him, not yet.

'There is always Broken Axe,' the old man echoed, still seeming cut to the heart about the girl's desertion. 'There is no other like him in the hunt. We must hope that Wolf has found our sacrifice sufficient, and smiles on us.'

*

192

Winter had already prowled into the northern reaches of the Crown of the World by then, and daily it stalked south, doing battle with the sun and extinguishing its fires. The Winter Runners, as with all the people of that land, withdrew into their village and trusted to their stores of yams and wood, quamash bulbs and salted meat. Winter, that great god, was driving his warbands towards the coveted warmth of the southern lands. Some day, so the stories said, he would not permit spring to end his campaign, and would cover all the world in ice. It was not a story that any except children believed, and yet at the same time Akrit knew it to be a parable, a tale of what the Wolf might accomplish if it could bring all the Crown of the World together under a single banner. The world could belong to the Wolf.

There were still some travellers abroad. The snows were not so fierce, yet, and the better-trodden paths were clear. A few late Coyotes arrived with goods – or in some cases just to beg. A Crow trader down from the Eyrie braved the mockery and disdain of the Winter Runners in order to trade a welcome bag of salt for meat. And there was a messenger, too.

She rode in on a Horse Society mount, a stern-faced woman of the Wolf swathed in furs and with a woollen scarf drawn up past her nose to ward off the cold.

A woman, but a hunter, too, no doubt about that. She travelled with two spears holstered behind the saddle and a bronze axe at her belt, and she rode as easily as the Horse men themselves, swinging herself off the back of her beast to stand before the Winter Runners.

She was recognized quickly, an older man and woman from the Runners coming forth to greet her. All the Wolf tribes were connected by bonds of kinship, and it was common for messengers to be sent to where they might expect blood relatives to vouch for them. Strangers could find an uncertain reception in Wolf lands.

Her name was Velpaye Bleeding Feathers, of the Many Mouths tribe, and the spray of quills she wore in her hair had come from Eyriemen raiders that had fallen to her spears. She had come to speak to Akrit and, by the time that was known, the entire tribe was aware that something important was afoot. Nobody would send out a messenger at the dawn of winter for small matters.

Akrit received her in his hall with his wives and thralls, with Kalameshli and a score of other households represented. He wanted Bleeding Feathers to go back home with the right impression of the Winter Runners.

The news she brought must wait, of course. First there was food and drink laid before her, and she ate with careful politeness, sampling everything, her eyes on the people about her. Now she was their guest, and they her hosts, and a curse be on whoever might act to break that bond.

All through the ritual, Akrit's mind was busy. The High Chief of the Wolves spoke for the Many Mouths. Word from that quarter could mean many things. Was it war? Were the tribes being called together for some great campaign? Was it time at last to storm the Eyrie and put those thieving cowards in their place? Thinking of the possibility made Akrit feel like a young man again, or closer to one than he had felt in a long time. What a chance that would be to impress other tribes with his strength and cunning, laying the groundwork for his ambitions!

He found that he would greatly welcome any rumours of war.

At last the woman stood before Akrit's fire, ready to impart her news.

'Stone River of the Winter Runners,' she announced, 'I bring the word of the Many Mouths.'

Kalameshli shifted beside him, and Akrit nodded, frowning – the two of them were working together, as they were used to, faced with this intrusion of the outside world: knowing each other's thoughts without needing words. *Word of the Many Mouths, indeed? And yet not the word of their chief?*

In that moment, the true meaning came to Akrit, but he

shook it off, still clinging to his fond hopes for the opportunities that conflict might bring.

'Maninli Seven Skins, he who forged the iron of the Wolves, Tiger-killer, war chief, father of hosts, great chief of the Many Mouths and High Chief in the Jaws of the Wolf,' Velpaye recited, 'now he feels the breath of the Wolf indeed.' She told it like a story, as such news should be told, and a stir went through the listeners. It was winter: the breath of the Wolf was only cold. The words meant one thing, dress them up as the speaker might.

The High Chief of the Wolves knew it was his time to pass on.

Too soon! Akrit thought, though he revealed nothing of it in his poise or face. *Give me a year, maybe two, and the girl to use as I will, and then let Maninli walk off into the winter. But not now!*

'Maninli is strong yet,' he declared. 'I remember him when we broke the Tiger at the Field of Many Waters, his bear-killer sheathed in blood. None could face him.' And yet Akrit himself had been young, so young then, and just coming into his own strength. Maninli had been the man who brought the tribes together, who roused the whole Crown of the World with his victories and his mad courage, a man chasing death into the Tiger's very throat. And even then he had not been a man in the first of his youth.

And he was old, now. Old enough to fear the death that comes in sleep. Old enough to feel the Wolf's breath.

'Never was there such a war leader,' Akrit went on, because such a eulogy was expected. 'Never was there a man to follow but Seven Skins. Fierce he was, swift as storm winds, strong as the rivers in thaw.' He found that he was genuinely sad, mourning not for the lost man but those lost days. 'Do the Many Mouths call?'

'Will the Winter Runners hear?' More ritual exchange. She meant that old Seven Skins was turning his back, walking away from all that he had known and been, walking into the wordless dark. A hunter or a hearth-keeper might call to immediate family. A figure greatly admired might call upon a whole tribe. Seven Skins, High Chief of all the Wolves by the agreement and support of the leaders of every tribe, called upon the whole Crown of the World to witness his passing.

There was a fulcrum moment in which Akrit Stone River's world hung about his trust in Kalameshli Takes Iron. He cocked a sidelong glance at the priest, who was already nodding, an unspoken, spontaneous plan of action coming to both of them simultaneously – one that would require Akrit to put the utmost faith in the old man.

They had argued over Maniye's loss; indeed the priest seemed to take the business far more personally than Akrit thought reasonable. In the end, though, they were still like brothers, as they had been when they led the warriors of the Winter Runners against the Tiger to cut them some new stripes.

'The Winter Runners hear,' Akrit announced. 'Akrit Stone River, their chief, he hears also.' The words quietened the murmur of discussion that had arisen around him. The Winter Runners would not just send an emissary, some blood-kin of the Many Mouths, to honour the High Chief. Akrit himself would make the difficult journey. He would witness the old man's passing with his own eyes. He would spend the winter amongst another tribe, and Kalameshli would guide the Winter Runners in his absence. If there was some conspiracy, some ambitious challenger prowling at the edge of Akrit's firelight, that would be their time. If Kalameshli was not loyal, Akrit might find the tribe turned against him when he returned.

But he trusted Kalameshli. Despite harsh words, he found that a world without the priest by his side was beyond his imagining. And he would take Amiyen's elder son with him in his retinue, when he travelled. *There* was one who badly needed to be separated from his mother.

Velpaye Bleeding Feathers stared at him, keen-eyed, as though she was hunting for hidden motives. And of course, there *were* hidden motives. Placing himself amidst the Many

Mouths at Seven Skins' passing would put Akrit's name on many lips, and if he ever hoped to be High Chief in turn, then the love of other tribes was essential. The honour he showed them would be remembered and respected. And he would be able to see who the other tribes sent, and who his competition might be.

And all this, supposing that his plan could be brought to fruition, that Maniye even still lived, that she could be brought back under his control with the Tigers whipped into service. Without that, who was Akrit Stone River but just one man among many, and a man without sons?

But, aside from all such concerns and even in the midst of such feverish plotting, Akrit Stone River found that he was also a man who wanted to say a last farewell to a mentor and a friend.

16

For a long-drawn-out moment nobody spoke. Maniye's mouth was crammed with objections but she had frozen up, unable to move, unable to look at the man now sitting almost within arm's reach.

The only real movement came from the dogs. They did not bark – she had not heard them bark at all yet – but they were agitated, standing now, fidgeting back and forth, uttering almost inaudible whines through their teeth. They had plainly not liked Maniye or Hesprec much, but Broken Axe was something else again, like a figure out of their nightmares. Those born in the Jaws of the Wolf kept no dogs, and wherever their Shadow fell, dogs remained only on sufferance. It was something done often if a tributary village of the Deer or the Boar had displeased Akrit in some mild way that did not merit the shedding of human blood: a band of hunters would go forth and come back with the pelts of their sheep-dogs and their watch-hounds and the swift rabbit-catchers. Hardly worthy prey, but it taught a lesson: *next time it's you.*

Dogs possessed souls, albeit small souls that would not bear the weight of a human body. Although their mute minds could not know what Axe had done, perhaps they sensed their kin's blood on him somehow. Or perhaps it was just that long enmity between the Wolf and the Wolf's tame bastard. Whichever, Maniye clutched desperately at it, for Loud Thunder's dogs perhaps had some influence on him. Was he guided by their instincts? All this was faint hope when he plainly *knew* Broken Axe somehow. But then Axe travelled all over the Crown of the World and beyond. Perhaps everyone knew him, and knew to fear him.

'There's no more fish,' the huge man blurted out suddenly. 'Didn't think there'd be such a grand gathering.'

For an instant his forlorn expression made her feel guilty: the fish he had shared out had been intended for his stomach only. Then another ember of hope flared within her. She had some claim on him, under the laws of hospitality. He could not feed Broken Axe, so surely he would have to take her part against the man, no matter what their previous association?

But Broken Axe had a bag at his belt, and he stripped off his gloves and dug inside it, coming up with bundles of meat, not much but fresh, the remains of some luckless creature he had happened on along the trail.

Loud Thunder nodded appreciatively. 'Good, very good. You are welcome to my fire.' He almost snatched the flesh from Broken Axe and quickly put it on bone skewers propped over the flames. 'So,' he went on, this task accomplished, 'Broken Axe, the Wolf who walks by himself, and not seen in these lands for . . . two years?'

'Three.'

'So long, is it? And now here you are.'

Maniye was hanging on every word, trying to comb out what manner of shared past united the two men. Both were of an age, and both were plainly quite happy with the company of the wilds. Was that it: some chance meeting in the forest years before? She sensed they were more than simply passing acquaintances.

'You always knew I'd be back this way some time,' Broken Axe said easily.

'And now here you are,' the big man repeated.

Not scared of him but . . . scared of what his being here means, perhaps?

199

'It's a small matter.' The Wolf hunter's tone was almost flippant, but Maniye could tell he was choosing his words carefully.

'Long way to come for a small matter,' Loud Thunder muttered. 'This pair now, they come to bother me as well, eat my fish, disturb my dogs. All sorts of strange, they are. Did you ever see such a man as this in the Crown of the World?'

'Not in the Crown of the World.' Broken Axe's face wore a mild, polite smile, his hands still resting in his lap. Maniye had the sense of him stalking: a measured and delicate approach into striking distance.

'And in such company,' the huge man fished.

Broken Axe just shrugged. 'A small matter.' Somehow, in his nod and intonation, he was plainly referring to Maniye – little Maniye sitting on the far side of Hesprec and feeling cold to the core, where the fire could not reach.

'Ah.' A neutral sound from Loud Thunder at having the situation confirmed.

'She is far from home,' Broken Axe explained pleasantly. 'She is looked for there.'

'Is it so?' Loud Thunder nodded, as though reflecting on the fecklessness of young girls.

Maniye made a noise. It was meant to be a word, a denial, but instead it was just a noise. Still, the big man cocked a shaggy eyebrow at her.

'Hrm?'

He will kill me. He killed my mother. Her mouth was open, but the dark stone gaze of Broken Axe transfixed her, and all that came out was a sort of croak.

'Why do you care?' Thunder asked the hunter, as if any sane man would let runaway girls die out in the snow to teach them a lesson.

'For myself, why should I? But her father cares.'

That was too much. At last Maniye found her voice.

'He doesn't!' Her squeak of protest seemed to echo about the hollow. 'He's never cared except to use me.' And it was a bizarre

200

relief to put her new understanding of her father – and her whole life – into words. 'I've been nothing to him, ever, but a thing, a tool.'

If she thought that revelation would somehow wring compassion from the giant's heart, her hopes were broken in the shrug of his massive shoulders.

'Life,' he grunted, 'is hard. Why make mine harder? I don't want to know any of it.' And yet he was still not letting go. Maniye pictured the two of them in their Stepped forms, teeth sunk in her body, tensing themselves to pull.

'Just so,' Broken Axe agreed, and he too was obviously still aware that he had some work to do. 'But I am sent, and she is her father's daughter, and he is chief of the Winter Runners. So I hunt her.' And a tacit threat, perhaps: *that is who you will make an enemy of.*

Loud Thunder sighed enormously, voicing a mountain of sorrow at all the ill ways of the world. 'And him?' A cock of the head towards Hesprec.

'I don't care about him.'

'Probably no one does,' Thunder agreed.

The old Serpent sighed. 'If I were permitted to speak, I would say that I am a priest much beloved of Snake – who moves beneath us all – and when I was last within the Crown of the World there were yet some who knew that to harm a priest was to open the way for a hundred curses.'

Loud Thunder shrugged again. 'So Little Feet here is a runaway and Many Words is all sorts of lost, and proud along with it, and you're doing the Winter Runners' running for them.' He began taking the meat from the fire, obviously satisfied with its condition. The dogs got fed first, and then he cut strips for everyone, a swift and equitable division. 'Tracked her a long way,' Thunder got out, around a crammed mouthful. 'Good hunt, that. Good run from her too. Till now.'

'Until now,' Broken Axe agreed.

Thunder glanced at Maniye, meeting her gaze, seeing her

201

unable to eat, sitting there with her hands crooked into claws, rigid with tension.

'Said you killed her mother, too,' he observed idly.

'It's not true,' came Broken Axe's smooth reply.

'Liar!' She spat out the word too fast for her fear to stop her, and the rest followed. 'You took her and killed her, when my father had done with her! Everyone knows it. I've seen it in his face, and in your face every time you visited his hall! It was the first thing I ever knew about my mother, that she was dead – and by your hand.'

Broken Axe made a wry face: *Listen to the foolishness of women!* 'Thunder, you know me.'

'I *do* know you.' And it was a pronouncement that came down on neither side of the argument.

'You think—?'

'When we were young and we roamed with a warband, strange lands, strange faces . . . we saw many things. Some terrible things. Some that were made so by our own hands. Do I know what you've done or not done, since? How can I?'

'And do you care? This is a matter for the Wolf to bother himself with.'

'I saw how she was a tiger when she Stepped,' Loud Thunder said carefully. If these two men had been wrestling or brawling, this would be the moment that a blade was drawn. Broken Axe went very still.

'Loud Thunder,' he said softly, 'this need be no burden to you. It is a trouble of the Wolf.' And, seeing the bigger man's raised eyebrow, 'and the Tiger, if you wish. None of yours.'

'And yet now I'm curious,' Thunder replied implacably. His eyes flicked from the hunter to Maniye herself.

'He will kill me,' she got out.

'Not true,' Broken Axe put in quickly.

'Amiyen—'

'I am not Amiyen.'

A wave of Thunder's hand, the big man obviously not wanting to deal with the names of any not actually there with him. 'Tiger,' he stated flatly, and then, 'Wolf,' as though he were weighing up the two names. 'No, this makes me all sorts of curious. Tiger and Wolf had their war, yes. Yet both sides've kept beating that same drum ever since. You think *we* don't hear it?'

Broken Axe closed his eyes, summoning his strength. 'Do I care about the war? I do not. But I am tasked with bringing this girl safe home, and I will do it.'

'Will you?'

'Thunder, you don't care.'

'I'm curious,' the huge man said again, more forcefully. 'Tiger. Wolf. And this thing, whatever he is . . . Snake . . . thing.'

'A sacrifice,' Hesprec said sibilantly, 'but saved from that death by the girl. A priest bound for sacrifice, did you ever hear such a thing?'

'And worse,' Loud Thunder grunted. 'Sounds like Wolf work to me, yes. Take *him* if you want.'

'I don't want him. You can keep him, but I'll have the girl.' And Maniye could see the tension deep inside, drawing Broken Axe taut like a bow. He sat just the same, appearing easy, and with his hands in plain view, but in his fire-shadow she could see the wolf poised to pounce.

Loud Thunder looked deeply disappointed with himself. 'No, I'm curious. She and I will talk.'

'Thunder—'

'No.'

And they had Stepped, the both of them, in the same instant. Even though Maniye had been waiting for it, the moment caught her unawares. Broken Axe was a pale wolf with dark hackles, teeth bared and his whole body bunched to leap. And Loud Thunder . . .

He was huge even as a man. As a bear he was head and shoulders again as tall, and surely three times the weight, a vast red-brown mountain of furred flesh, his claws gleaming copper in the firelight, his axe swept up into the mountain of his animal form. He stood four times Maniye's height, bellowing and with his arms outstretched as though he would encircle the world, and the sky and the stars too.

Before him, Broken Axe seemed tiny, but he gave no ground. He snarled a warning, pale eyes fixed on the bear's throat, showing every indication that he would leap over the fire and attack, no matter the difference in size.

Hesprec had been bowled into her when Broken Axe Stepped, and now she wriggled out from under him, shifting her own form through sinuous wolf to burlier tiger and then to wolf again, her shape dancing with panic as her mind flitted between fight and flight. The dogs were going berserk by then, not wanting to go anywhere near Broken Axe, but barking fiercely: deep, chesty sounds that were a savage threat to Maniye's animal ears.

Of them all, only the old Serpent kept his human form. A toothless snake was hardly going to be of use here, and if he left the fire he would freeze. Instead he just huddled, one arm protecting his head.

Broken Axe and Loud Thunder locked eyes. The wolf showed his fangs, feinting forwards, trying to spark a reaction. His teeth were the dark iron of the axe he wore at his belt. The bear slammed down onto his forepaws and bellowed again, right across the fire into the wolf's face. Maniye could feel her two souls both struggling for control over her, fighting as though they were imprisoned together inside her, scratching and clawing and biting at her innards. The sheer proximity of bloodshed was sending the pair of them into a directionless frenzy. She did not know what to do. Too much choice now, and too little understanding.

Then Broken Axe Stepped again: nothing but a man once more, his hands out for peace. And for all that she hated and feared him, more even than her father or Kalameshli the priest, she could not help but be struck by the courage that must have taken. Loud Thunder had reared back onto his hind legs, and a single swipe of his paw would have smashed the Wolf hunter beyond recognition, for in Axe's human form he could neither fight nor dodge such a force of nature. And yet Thunder stayed his hand, and Broken Axe waited, sparing his words until there were human ears again to hear them.

At last the gigantic bear became the man – seeming diminished now, for all that he was still the biggest man Maniye had ever seen. 'So,' he pronounced.

Maniye herself was a wolf at that moment, and a wolf she remained in case this should turn against her. Hesprec carefully reached out a hand and laid it gently on her back, and she knew he would be able to come with her if she chose to run.

'Speak,' Thunder prompted, crouching down to put a hand out to his dogs, letting them sniff at it, quieting them.

'I see winter upon us,' Broken Axe observed, as though the seasons had shifted during their confrontation.

'Looks that way,' Thunder agreed.

'No time to be travelling south with a girl to look after,' the hunter observed reasonably.

The Bear tribe giant grunted.

'I will return for her, come the thaw,' Broken Axe stated.

'Will you?'

'I, Liosetli Broken Axe, say this.'

Maniye realized she had never heard anyone mention his birth name before now. It made it a powerful thing to swear by.

'You expect me to play host all through the winter?' Loud Thunder frowned, just the simple man once more, faced with unwanted complications.

'Or I shall take her now. Or else the winter will have her, and keep her.'

Thunder's head swung in Maniye's direction. 'Well?' And, when she wouldn't Step into a form that could answer him: 'One yap for yes, two for no, is it?'

Reluctantly she came back to herself, human voice and all. None of the three options before her was overly attractive. The Bear might kill her, and Broken Axe could also be intending to finish Amiyen's work. Winter, though . . . She had come a long way, but all her journey had done was teach her that she was not ready to face the winter alone and without shelter.

'I'll come with you,' she told Loud Thunder, knowing that she could be making a fatal mistake. What did she know of him, save that he was a sometime comrade of Broken Axe? In her mind were all the fates that he might have in store for her: enslave her, tear her apart and eat her, sacrifice her at some Bear tribe altar . . . She knew so little.

But of her father's people and Broken Axe, she knew more than enough.

'You too, I suppose?' Thunder rumbled at Hesprec resignedly.

'Kindness in a strange land to a chosen priest shall not go unrewarded,' the old man replied, regaining his feet, but not quite his dignity.

'So many words,' Thunder complained, mostly to Broken Axe. 'And the fire's going out now. Get some wood, if you're here for the night.' Just like that, it seemed the men were friends again, or at least no longer about to kill each other.

'I'll not disturb your dogs further,' Broken Axe said, sounding sad. 'I can find my own shelter, make my own fire.'

'The Wolf that walks by himself. Good, good,' Thunder agreed. 'Just like always.'

Maniye glanced between the two of them, sensing the edges of their shared history, however long ago it had been.

Then the hunter's dark eyes were turned upon her, and she did her best to face up to him bravely, easier to do so now that he was departing.

'Farewell, Many Tracks,' he told her, seeming almost fond. 'I shall find you come spring, if you still live.' And he had tracked her so indefatigably, so far, that she had no cause to doubt it. It would take more than a harsh winter to discourage Broken Axe.

Only after he had gone did she consider that he seemed serious about the name, her hunter name. *Many Tracks*. Despite its source it felt like a garment that fitted her body well. *Maniye Many Tracks*.

★★★

Her people called the Bear tribe 'Cave Dwellers', and indeed the back chamber of Loud Thunder's home was dug into a hillside, its walls of packed earth shored up with props that had once been tree trunks. The rest of his hall was built of timber, logs stacked on logs and the cracks between them stuffed with moss and mud. The roof sloped so as to shrug off the snows and not break under the weight, and the whole was set so deep within the dense-packed trees that it could hardly be seen until they were right on top of it. Thinking about it later, Maniye realized this concealment was hard won: Thunder must have hauled all the logs in from far off, rather than cut down the trees conveniently close.

She had travelled as a wolf from the cooling campsite, Hesprec tucked in her satchel once more. The choice was not just for his benefit either: Loud Thunder set a swift pace, his dogs hauling the sled between them and the big man striding through the deepening snow as if it was not there. Only as a wolf could she keep up with him, and even then it was hard going, floundering through the drifts and constantly in danger of falling behind.

The door into the Cave Dweller's hall was low and wide, and the skins hanging across it were pinned to the ground by large stones. After he had rolled them away, Thunder's dogs bounded inside joyously, racing about the interior and then returning to leap up at him. Ignoring his guests entirely, he made much of the beasts, congratulating them for bringing the sled home, then wandering inside with the animals trotting at his heels. Maniye hovered unhappily at the threshold. The interior smelled very strongly of bear, which was a scent like Loud Thunder's own, but with an added overtone of threat. *You'd have to be mad to go readily into a bear's den* . . . But they were the Bear's guests, or else his prisoners, or something . . .

Hesprec slid across her shoulders and managed to Step into human form before the snow could chill his scales. 'These things are known: there are worse places to endure the winter,' he murmured, and then called out at the hanging skins, 'My gracious host, might we enter?'

'Gifts.' Maniye shook her shoulders, newly human again, feeling the cold reach out for them. 'Have we any . . . ?'

'Food? Not that would feed a rat,' Hesprec admitted sadly.

Abruptly, Loud Thunder's broad face appeared at the edge of the hangings, stooping in the doorway to stare at them. For a second it was as though he had never seen them before, but then memory apparently returned. 'What, then?'

'Can we . . . ?' The thought of simply walking in, as though of right, was a breach of everything she knew. To sit in the Horse Society hut to talk terms, or share a campfire for a night, that was different. To come to the house of a stranger and accept his shelter and his food, but have nothing to render in return, was inviting ill fortune. In her present position, bad luck was something she wanted absolutely no more of than necessary.

The Cave Dweller's eyes cast about, trying to see what the problem was. Then he grunted.

'As you're standing there, fetch wood, get water. Someone needs to break the ice on the stream. Some wood left, just a little, out in the store.' And he vanished inside again.

It was not exactly a princely contribution, Maniye knew, but it would satisfy custom.

In the end she had to perform both tasks. Hesprec was not even strong enough to crack the ice. Perhaps he did not fear bad luck, or perhaps they did things differently wherever he called home. When she asked him, he assured her that the mere presence of a Serpent priest was gift and blessing enough, and she could not tell if he was being serious.

Inside, Loud Thunder was feeding the dogs. He barely glanced at his new guests as they entered, despite his stand-off with

Broken Axe in order to get them here. But then the winter would be long, and they would have quite enough of each other's company, one way or another, before its end.

17

To travel in winter was no man's first choice but, of all the tribes of the Crown of the World, the Wolf took to it most easily. This was the hungry season when their totem walked the field of stars above them. When deer and boar stayed close to their homes, when horses would founder and get lost, the wolves ran free and taught all others exactly why the winter was to be feared.

Akrit Stone River and most of his band had not taken human form since they left their own village. The road to the Many Mouths was long and hard after the snows came. Anyone trying it on two legs would freeze to death, or be brought down by the hunger of their mute wolf brothers.

He travelled with a half-dozen of his hunters and with the messenger, Bleeding Feathers. The Many Mouths woman alone had Stepped back as a human into the cold each night, taking it as her duty to build a fire that the pack could huddle round, the animals profiting from the work of human hands.

They made good time, a fleet flurrying of grey across the snow-clad slopes, over the ice of rivers and lakes, taking prey where their noses led them to it, and otherwise trusting to the deep-buried reserves of strength and endurance that let a wolf run and run.

When Akrit spotted the mounds of the Many Mouths ahead of him, at first seen just as the darkness of cleared earth against the white horizon, he stopped and threw back his head, howling out his presence. His pack joined in, each adding a voice to their chief's. The Many Mouths would know they had visitors long before they saw them.

Let me not be too late, was the most human thought in Akrit's head at that point. The idea had to fight for dominance by then. Travelling so long as a wolf, without ever Stepping back, clouded the mind. The thoughts of the animal became ever stronger, until such concepts as high chiefs and wars with the Tiger were harder and harder to hold on to. There were many tales of those who had simply let go of all that human baggage, their souls returning to a native state out in the wilds, heedless of the kin they had left behind. They were sad tales, but the lament was for the abandoned, not the abandoner. There were worse fates.

When the time came for him to finally Step, it took an effort of will. A welcoming party had come cautiously out from the village, a score or so on two legs and four. The burgeoning part of Akrit's mind that was solely wolf told him to veer away, to get clear of these human haunts. He shook it off and came back to himself. Bleeding Feathers was already Stepped by then, and his hunters followed one after the other, some more reluctantly than others.

The man before him was familiar: surely this was Otayo, the first son of Maninli Seven Skins. He was a lean man, close to Akrit's own years, but no hunter nor warrior. When the war with the Tiger had raged, he had minded his father's people, guided them and advised them. He was a hearth-husband: once he had a mate who bore his sons. Now she was dead and Otayo kept the hearth of another widower, a strong hunter who had been his friend from childhood. All the Many Mouths spoke of Otayo's wisdom, but he had never cast a spear and he would never be chief of the Many Mouths, let alone High Chief of all the Wolves.

'Is it Stone River I see?' Otayo called out.

'None other,' Akrit agreed. He could not come straight out and demand, 'Am I too late?' and so he read the other man's face, seeing there a sadness, but not a final sadness. Maninli

211

Seven Skins had not passed on yet. 'I am come to give honour to my great friend, Seven Skins.'

Otayo nodded, surely well aware that more than mere sentiment had brought Akrit all this way, but he threw wide his arms and declared, 'I give the Winter Runners welcome in my father's name. Your hard journey honours us. Will you guest with us this winter?'

'Our journey is no more honour than the High Chief deserves, and we would gladly be your guests.' Formalities, always formalities, but amongst a people like the Wolves it was wise to reinforce such traditions whenever possible. They would be given food now – sealing the pact between host and visitor, binding them both to fair dealings and good conduct.

The village of the Many Mouths was a little smaller than Akrit's own, and it would be a lean winter for the tribe because his people were not the only guests. He spotted Moon Eaters, so the news of Seven Skins' time had spread that far. *Competition*, Akrit realized sourly, but a quiet question put to Otayo revealed that the other tribe had not sent their chief, just respectful ambassadors.

Otayo fed them in his own hall, which had been built in the shadow of his father's. *A fit image for the man's whole life*, though he did not seem to begrudge his role. Seven Skins had not been wanting for children, Akrit knew. Four sons and three daughters he had sired who had survived to adulthood. Akrit remembered his second son well, a fierce warrior who had led the fight against the Tiger many times, until they had caught him and killed him slowly. The third son, Water Gathers, had also fought, but only in the war's final year, a youth who had been desperate to win some small slice of glory for himself. He would likely be the new chief of the Many Mouths, thus the man Akrit would have to outmatch.

Water Gathers has at least one son already, Akrit thought sourly, his thoughts straying briefly to his own troubles. *If the girl is dead in the snow, I will have Kalameshli beg the Wolf to torment her soul, to rend it into pieces. I will have him bind her ghost into a rattle.*

Who else aside from Water Gathers would be a challenger for High Chief? The man who governed the Moon Eaters was older than Akrit, a clever man but not a fierce one. He would be someone to woo, perhaps, with gifts or with promises. The Swift Backs chief was new, a young hunter who had come away unexpectedly victorious from a challenge; rumour said his own people were already rebellious, and that he might not last long. Still, the Wolf was plainly with him, to raise him up so swiftly . . . and a strong challenge for dominance over the other tribes could be what he needed to secure his position . . .

Otayo granted Akrit and his fellow hunters space in his hall, and Akrit let his people go out into the village, trusting that they would bring him any useful news they heard. He himself had waited long enough. It was time to call upon Maninli Seven Skins. It was time to pay his respects.

He had expected the High Chief's great hall to be bustling with well-wishers, slaves and family. Instead, there was just a woman kneeling before the door, who Akrit thought must be Maninli's wife, the new one, after the Tigers had killed his first. He remembered her as young, but she was grey now, and solemn.

'Stone River,' she greeted him.

For a moment he paused, unsure of what to say, but then: 'He must be close to his time.'

She nodded, lips pursed. There was that love that Maninli had always inspired in kin, in friends, even in strangers. Akrit had never known another man his equal for it. Seven Skins could stand up before a hostile crowd and calm them simply with a wave of his hand. He could take the dispirited and the broken and turn them into hard warriors.

'You are remembering him,' the woman divined.

Akrit found that he was smiling slightly. 'I am. I would like to see him.'

'He may not know you. He is on the Wolf's trail much, these days. Best that you Step, if you do go in.'

Akrit nodded, and shrugged down into his wolf shape, the world twisting around him as his senses shifted: colours dimmer, sounds sharper, a world of scents rushing in from all sides.

Mostly, as she held aside the skins that covered the entryway, he smelled the sickness of Seven Skins. It was a sour, stomach-turning scent, that of a man too long in the world and whose body had begun to fail. It was a smell of rot, of things gone bad, of excrement and stale urine.

It was a man-scent, though, not a wolf-scent, and within the hall was a wolf. Akrit padded in, seeing the old grey beast lying on a pile of skins before the embers of the last night's fire. At the intrusion, Maninli pushed himself to his feet, hackles up and his yellowed teeth showing.

Akrit knew the form: he, who had not needed to bow to anyone, man or wolf, in a long time, now ducked his head low, angling it so as to show his throat. He stayed still as the older beast stalked over, shaking out the stiffness in his legs. For a moment he thought that Seven Skins would truly not know him, that he was too far gone into senescence or down the Wolf's trail.

Then Maninli had Stepped, and was sitting before him with his back to the fire, a wondering expression on his face. He had a hand out, almost touching Akrit's muzzle.

'Can it be?' he asked softly.

Old – he was *old*. Akrit took a moment before Stepping also, because he could not show Maninli a human face with that look of shock on it. The strength that the beast within retained was always deceptive. It could even hide a weak, hollowed-out man like this.

Here was Maninli Seven Skins: the man who had brought the war host of the Wolf together and beaten the Tiger out of the heartlands of the Crown of the World. Yes, he had burned through his best days to do it, but he had always been strong, unbreakable. And yet the years since Akrit had last seen him had broken him. His skin was jaundiced and he looked as though he had not slept forever, the white of his eyes pink with misplaced blood. He trembled constantly, as though simply sitting there and holding his head up was taking all the strength he had. He was thin, the furs they had clad him in to keep him warm just hanging off his skeletal figure.

'I know, I know.' The roaring voice of Akrit's memory was a hoarse whisper. 'Look at me, old friend. I know.'

And Akrit forced himself to look. He owed Maninli that much.

'It's good to see you one more time. And you braved the winter for me. That's a thought to take with me when I go.'

Akrit reached out gingerly and laid a hand on his arm, feeling it bone-hard, bone-cold, fragile as a stick beneath his touch. 'You're waiting for midwinter?'

Maninli shuddered. 'I've waited too long already. I should have gone before the snows. I'm the wolf almost all the time now. The wolf isn't cold or tired like this. The wolf doesn't hurt like this. The wolf can *eat*, even. Only, when I become a man again, I cannot keep it down.' When he shook his head, it seemed to sway loosely on his neck. 'Eat . . . ? I'm being eaten, Akrit. It's the death that comes to us, the gnawing death picking at these bones. But it's difficult to let go . . . Even though I make things worse for everyone, the longer I stay, it's hard.'

Akrit had always thought that, when the time came, he himself would go bravely and be no burden. That was the hunter's way after a long life or a crippling injury. Now, looking at Maninli, he did not know for sure. Seven Skins had always been a brave man. If even this carious human existence was precious to him, what could Akrit truly know?

'I will retell your stories,' Akrit said softly.

'There are few left who can.' For a moment a new expression came upon the old man, a sly alertness that was something of the past creeping back. 'Otayo tells me you will raid the Tiger next summer.'

'Does he?' Akrit held his face still.

'They say he should have been a priest, that one,' Maninli managed a thin chuckle. 'They say the invisible world whispers to him. They don't realize all you have to do is listen and think, and you can predict the future well enough. So, will you?'

Akrit had not planned to talk about such things with anyone beyond Kalameshli, but here he was, and he could not just refuse his old friend. 'We have unfinished business,' was all he said. Besides, if Otayo was thinking of a mere raid or two, then he was thinking too small.

If the girl is alive. If the girl is brought back to me.

He shook off his doubts angrily.

Maninli was watching him from under half-lowered lids. 'Too late, too late. I would have been glad to have a few more of the Tiger given to the jaws of the Wolf before my passing. It would sweeten my path, surely. What meat would he savour more?'

'When chance brings me one of their warriors, then the Wolf will have that meat, and in your name,' Akrit promised.

The gap-toothed smile he received was almost senile in its bloodlust. He could see the focus draining out of Maninli's eyes, and so he straightened his shoulders. 'Old friend, do not spend all your strength before your time.'

A terrible, hunted look came to the old man's face, and in the next moment he had Stepped: not even a farewell, just a flight to the refuge of a wolf body that still had some strength in it. The animal stared at Akrit with yellow, unblinking eyes, and he could not say whether it knew him or not.

Akrit had assumed that Maninli intended to hold out for midwinter to pass on. Having seen the old man, that seemed unlikely now. The Many Mouths were holding themselves in constant readiness. Each night the cold's grip on the Crown of the World tightened, and surely their chief must simply wish to let go and leave them. And yet he held on, a little of the man clinging within him as if fearful of the great dark that was waiting for

216

him. His soul had grown used to his hands, was the saying that Akrit heard most often.

He and his Winter Runners settled down for a stay of uncertain duration, penned in by the growing strength of winter.

In truth, there was little to do save talk. The people of the Many Mouths told stories, while their hunters contested in races and wrestling. Akrit stalked about their village, constantly skirting the circle of influence maintained by Water Gathers, who seemed just as conscientious in avoiding him. The mood soured slowly. Nobody seemed to know what Maninli was holding out for.

'But it has to be something,' Otayo explained to Akrit one evening. 'You have seen our new priest, Catch The Moon, who the Wolf chose after old Singing Branch passed on? He is young but he has many visions. He has spoken to my father much. There is something yet to come.'

'What?' Akrit demanded in a hushed voice. They were the last two still sitting awake by the fire. Most of Otayo's family was asleep.

His host gave him a calculating look. 'He will not tell me – and do not think I haven't asked. I do not believe he has told Water Gathers either, which eats at my brother.' A slight quirk of the lips: it was no secret that the sons of Seven Skins did not always see eye to eye. 'Who would he tell then . . . ?'

The next morning Akrit went to visit Maninli one last time.

It was hard to persuade the man's wife that he should be allowed a second audience. She was terrified that her husband might die in human form, and so prevent his soul from passing on. There was a fragility about her eyes that made Akrit wonder if it was not the prospect of Seven Skins' angry ghost haunting the family hall which most frightened her.

When Akrit finally talked his way in, he approached the old grey wolf as warily as before. This time, though, Maninli did not Step, but just turned away and settled down by the fire, shifting mournfully every so often in an attempt to find a kind of comfort that time had stripped from him.

Akrit settled down beside him in human form, knowing that now he must talk and hope the wolf ears would still convey his words to a human mind. He recounted what Otayo had said, fishing for some sign that his suspicions were right, hoping that the bond of one-time comradeship between them would be enough.

But he had more to say than that, when the wolf remained a mute animal beside him. It was time for Akrit to share his own dream with Seven Skins: a pledge to the Wolf that the old man could carry with him when he passed on.

'I will take the Tiger,' he explained softly. 'Not just raids. I will bring them into the Wolf's Shadow at last. After that, perhaps the Eyrie will bow to us, or we will starve them out. The work you began, old friend, is not done. The people of the Wolf have a destiny.'

There was a sound beside him, and Maninli was sitting there, old head loose on his neck, eyes almost closed. He looked measurably older than when Akrit had seen him before.

But he spoke, and Akrit leant closer to catch the mumbled words.

'Catch The Moon has seen it. There is a time coming, a Great Dying Time.'

Akrit shivered to hear it, and the failing man's sour breath suddenly seemed to bring with it a chill, the sense of invisible presences looming near. Maninli's soul seemed perched on his very lips, clinging to the last threads of his human existence as his body consumed itself. There would always be spirits hovering close at such a time. Many of them would be wicked, and some would hope to poison Maninli's soul if it was trapped in a man's dead flesh, to turn it into something that would sicken and corrupt all of the Many Mouths, even all those of the Wolf. But such spirits whispered prophecy to the dying, too. The words of a man this close to passing on were pregnant with divination.

'Catch The Moon has seen a shadow that might stretch all

the way to the world's end. He says that those who do not submit to it will pass from this world. Whose shadow can that be save for the Wolf's? That is what it must be.' He coughed thinly, a feeble and miserable sound. 'Water Gathers, my son . . . he thinks that the world will never change through all his lifetime, that every tomorrow will be as yesterday once he is chief. But you can see further. You know the Wolf must grow stronger. I should have sent for you before. The Wolf has guided you to come to me.'

Akrit sat very still. Was this what he had been seeking? Yes, surely, and yet how much more weight did it place on his shoulders? How much more important that he become High Chief and that he bring the Tiger into the Wolf's Shadow? And for this, for all of this, he needed the girl Maniye, who might already be dead . . .

He leant close to Maninli, despite the reek of the man's decaying body. 'My friend, is this what you have stayed for? Know that you may go, you may pass on. You need not torture yourself in this flesh any more.'

The shake of Seven Skins' head was barely perceptible. 'There is one more I must see,' the withered lips moved again. 'They are coming to us now, those who can help this destiny to come to pass. When they are here, then I shall know my time is right. Strangers, Akrit. Strangers in winter. Mark them. It may be their deaths that you need, or it may be their lives. Make your decision wisely.'

A day later, a band of the Horse Society stumbled into the Many Mouths village, led by two Coyotes and a Crow, and in their midst were three strange figures, two southerners and a Plains woman – and Akrit knew the time had come.

18

'I expected tents, for some reason,' Asmander remarked. 'Or maybe huts.' His eyes flicked over the artificial hillscape before them, studying the earthworks raised by the Many Mouths.

'Or holes in the ground,' Venater said, easily loud enough for Shyri to hear, but even he sounded slightly impressed. There were plenty of northerners outside and staring as the travellers approached, and a handful of sleek grey wolves were trotting to either side of the newcomers as an impromptu honour guard, but to Asmander this did not look like a place where real people lived. The mounds that the northerners built upon had the same sense of ancient weight and scale as the ruins of the Old Stone Kingdom. This felt more like a place for the dead to be interred rather than for any sane human beings to inhabit. *Of course, the cold rather adds to that. I wonder if dead northerners actually get warmer after life departs.*

'It's not Atahlan,' he said bravely, 'but I confess it's quite a sight.'

'No fear among them, either,' Venater stated.

'You mean no walls?'

'They don't care about keeping men out, nor beasts. I reckon any who come uninvited would find out why.'

'They say the men of the Crown of the World believe that only the blood of their enemies will bring spring again,' Shyri declared.

'If it would do that, I'd open some throats myself,' Asmander responded.

The crowd was growing, even as they wound their way between the smaller mounds. Ahead of them was one far greater than the rest, the domain of a leader as plainly as was the Kasra's palace at Atahlan.

'What has brought you to the Many Mouths at such a time?' enquired a Wolf man, stepping forward from the pack. 'Or do the Horse go wherever they wish across our lands?' There was a confrontational tone to his question that Asmander found himself warming to.

Eshmir pressed her hands together. 'I come to honour the High Chief of all the Wolves. I come with gifts from the Horse Society.'

The Wolf spokesman spat, apparently placing little value on this. Asmander was watching the rest of them though, seeing that this man spoke for some but by no means all of them. He sensed divisions, factions, observing the way that the northerners clumped and eddied.

Two Heads Talking kept his shoulders hunched, avoiding the massed Wolf gaze as though this would make him invisible. He leant in towards Eshmir and murmured, 'This one is Water Gathers, son of the chief.'

'We know your father must pass on,' the Hetman said simply. 'We bring the respects of the Horse, as one so great makes his last journey.'

There was precious little grief in Water Gathers, Asmander reckoned, but at least this seemed to be the right thing to say. The majority approved, and the chief's son went along with them, giving ground grudgingly.

The Horse people had brought their own tents, and that would apparently have to be enough. Under Two Heads' direction they pitched them at the foot of one of the smaller mounds, whose residents were known to him. His trade-wife made the climb up to the hall above to barter for news and for hospitality.

Asmander was keenly aware that they were not quite guests, not yet, nor strangers either. He had a sense of having only a tenuous place in the world here, surrounded by unseen laws that he might break with the least mis-step.

That night, he huddled about a fire with Venater and Shyri. 'Our hosts do not like us,' he noted.

'That's fine,' the pirate growled. 'I don't like them.'

'You don't like anyone.'

Venater shrugged.

'Yet these are the fabled Iron Wolves,' Asmander considered, 'and here we are.'

The pirate grunted. 'Good luck, then.'

'I think we'll not just throw out a purse of coin and buy ourselves a warband or two. I think it doesn't work like that here,' Asmander decided.

'Worked that much out, have you?' Venater's look was derisive. 'Let me guess, old Asman didn't give you much to go on.'

'My father has faith in my initiative.'

This time Venater said nothing. Shyri looked from one to the other.

'Someone tell me what you're both not saying,' she said at last.

'It's a small matter.' Asmander made a dismissive gesture.

'With so many enemies around us, no matters are small matters.'

'So you think them enemies too?'

She laughed, uttering a brief high yap of a sound, always disconcerting to hear from a human throat. 'Of course they're enemies. Everyone's an enemy until you make them a slave or a friend. And friend's harder.'

'How lovely it must be to be a Plains dweller,' Asmander remarked. 'Such carefree lives of constant happiness.'

'Happy indeed,' she agreed. 'For it is not I who am sent here to beg. Such security you southerners must know, that you invite in even the Wolf to keep the peace.'

'These things are known,' Venater murmured.

'Enough from you,' Asmander told him, more sharply than he meant, but the older man just chuckled.

Because he could not sleep, the night found him later outside their tents, in a chill that seemed to have banished even the Wolf tribe to their hearths and halls. Above, the sky had the hallucinatory clarity of a scene viewed through a drop of water. He felt that he could count every star.

When he heard the scuff of someone approaching behind him, he was not surprised to find Shyri there.

'I begin to think I must have killed you back in the ruins,' he said softly. 'No ghost ever haunted a man more diligently.'

'Yes, yes, it's all about you,' she replied dismissively, arms folded. But then her next words were, 'So, the father who sent you, he loves his children, yes?'

'It is a great honour to have a Champion for a son.'

'He takes great pride in it, no doubt.'

'He is a proud man,' Asmander told her.

'Having a son greater than yourself, that sounds like the sort of honour that could rub badly against a man's pride,' she observed. Her attempt at an innocent expression was pitiful.

'You have been listening to Venater too much.'

'He doesn't like your father.'

'Being liked is not my father's aim in life.' Asmander immediately wished he had not said it. The cold here seemed to draw words out of him as though speaking hard truths was the only way he could keep warm. 'Venater has his reasons. My father took his name from him.'

'I thought *you* did that.'

'Well, Venater doesn't like me, either.'

She regarded him doubtfully, taking a step closer. She reminded him of someone stalking small game, trying to get as close as possible before it spooked.

'Let me guess, your own father is a paragon of mercy and kindness,' he suggested.

She snorted. 'Mercy and kindness are things the Laughing Men have no use for, longmouth. And it's the least of a girl's worries, where I come from, to know her father.'

'I envy you,' he murmured.

'Then you don't know my mother. I'd trade her for your father any day.'

He found he was grinning, despite having come out here with the express purpose of indulging his melancholy.

Then: 'Lie with me,' she said.

He gave her a very appraising look, and she laughed at him.

'Longmouth,' she said, 'it is freezing, and the Horse tents are worth nothing. Come lie down, and share your warmth, at least, instead of pissing it out into this big sky. Or do I go fit myself into Venater's armpit instead?'

'Ah, romance,' he said drily, and took her hand when she extended it to him. 'Let the three of us entwine ourselves then. Perhaps we can scandalize the locals.'

Akrit *knew*, somehow, when he awakened. There was something about the pale, flat light of morning that told him so, as certainly as if a spirit had whispered the knowledge in his ear.

'Today.' As he broke his fast with his own hunters and Otayo's family, the knowledge would not be kept inside. 'It will be today.'

Seven Skins' oldest son nodded soberly.

By the time the sun had cleared the horizon, most of the Many Mouths had gathered. The foreigners were there, too, standing in a close-knit group with their guides a few steps away, as though ready to deny any association with them at a moment's notice.

Coyotes and Crows, Akrit thought derisively, but even such scavengers had their uses.

Casting his gaze about, he met the eyes of Water Gathers, Otayo's younger brother. The hunter was staring at him with a flat, patient dislike.

Good. We understand one another. It must have soured the cub's milk when Stone River had come to pay his respects. No doubt Water Gathers reckoned himself as great a man as his father, fit to live in his hall and call himself High Chief. Akrit wondered whether Maninli's son had it in him to kill a guest of his tribe. Would he brave the ill fortune that such an act would bring, if it would secure his future?

Would I, if he were in my hall? Akrit gave the thought some honest consideration. *I would broach it with Kalameshli, at least.*

There would be a great gathering of the tribes at the equinox. Perhaps the Wolves would kneel to a new leader then. Akrit tried to weigh the odds: a tested warrior and chief backed by a respected priest, set against Seven Skins' son with his youth and his children.

They will not choose. He could already see how it would go. *They will hold back and the longer they do so, the further apart they will grow, until no man will kneel to a High Chief at all. Then all that work in bringing the Wolf together must begin again.*

So I must prove myself: I must either win the fealty of the Tiger or destroy them. I must do this even if the girl is gone. And it must be this year. Another winter will be too late.

Up on the chief's mound, Maninli's wife emerged from his hall. Seeing her face, Akrit knew it must be time. A ripple of that grim knowledge passed through the crowd. The man they had respected and loved would not be leading them into another spring.

He himself emerged into the cold air, padding past the woman who had been his wife and lifting his shaggy head to sniff at the morning. As a man, he had been cadaverous, eaten away by time and the curses that time brings. As a wolf he was old, but still sound. As the years had bent his human body, withered it and gnawed at it and crippled it, his soul had stayed strong, and all the winters that had burdened him had slid off its grey flanks. The beast whose shape he had Stepped into was in its prime, broad-chested, heavy-shouldered. There was a pack

225

out there in the fields of winter whose chief would face a hard choice tonight, to fight or to yield. Akrit would stake a great deal on that yield, for Maninli was a leader no matter what form he took.

For a moment, as he passed his wife, Seven Skins Stepped back, revealing an eyeblink of a stooped, shuffling old man, his naked form showing every fold and crease, the fragile cage of his ribs where the skin was stretched over them, the belly distended and lopsided with the tumour of his disease. His fingers trailed through his wife's hand: one last touch, one last moment of humanity, before he passed.

Then he was on four feet once more, descending from the mound and already moving to a subtly different beat: not the Stepped man but the mute beast. Within him, Akrit knew his human mind would be sloughing away. All the likes and dislikes, the memories, the thoughts that had made him Maninli Seven Skins would unravel like loose threads until only his true soul, the core of him, would be left. By the time he reached the mound's foot he was moving faster, a beast that finds itself trespassing in a human place, eager to be gone.

His people made way for him, and the grey wolf that had once earned the name Seven Skins bolted for the outskirts of the village. He did not look back, but was away over the snow in an easy lope: free from pain, free from care. Akrit had expected harsh grief, but instead that sudden bounding progress lifted his spirits. His old friend's soul was finally free of its mortal prison.

'My father has passed!' It was Water Gathers' voice that disturbed his thoughts, of course. Maninli's hunter son was striding into the empty space left by his father's passage. 'He has gone to join his mute brothers! Shall his soul go alone? Or shall the Wolf watch over him, and bless him in his new life?'

Akrit's eyes were narrow, and his hand was on his knife-hilt. This was a bold move from Water Gathers, but then he was just as much in need of deeds as Akrit himself. While the chief of the

Winter Runners had concerned himself with the ritual of passing, it seemed his rival had been making plans.

'My father was a great man!' Water Gathers went on. 'He defeated the Tiger. He subjugated the Crown of the World and brought it under the Wolf's Shadow! Shall he pass on like any common man, or shall we send a message in blood, so that the Wolf knows to watch over him – so that the Wolf knows how we value him?'

And how far are you going with this, boy? Akrit wondered, feeling that familiar tightening within him that spoke of bloodshed. So Water Gathers wanted to wet the Wolf's jaws with blood. Very well, and it was his right to call for it. But whose blood was another question. *Do you dare try me here, boy?* And he knew that he should stop thinking of Water Gathers in such a way – the 'boy' was not so much younger than himself. It was a boy's strategy, though: brash and heavy-handed. Akrit found that he was more than ready if Water Gathers called him out. *And ill luck, for sure, to send a son after his father in such a way, but I'll do it gladly if you make me.*

For a moment, their eyes met, and Akrit could see him working up courage, finding out whether he had it in him to try and send Stone River to the Wolf. They sensed together the precise moment that Water Gathers' resolve failed him, and instead he cast about him, looking for another victim.

Naturally enough, his eye lit on the little band of the Horse Society. 'See!' he called out. 'See what Wolf has delivered to us. The Horse come to us with gifts. Let them make a gift of blood for the Wolf's jaws!'

It was a stupid idea, Akrit knew. Why alienate the Horse Society when their traders might make the difference between life and death? But some of the Many Mouths were already calling out their support. Their faces were hard with grief for their lost leader, the man who had guided them for two generations. Time and old age were enemies they could not offer to the Wolf in sacrifice, after all.

Otayo was not happy, but he was not a hunter either. Being Water Gathers' older brother would count for nothing. Even the young priest, Catch The Moon, was nodding along.

The foolishness of it was goading, and perhaps that was even part of the plan. Akrit would not speak out – it was not his place, not with so many of the locals set on the idea. And perhaps this was what Seven Skins had meant when he said the foreigners were important. Perhaps their blood in the Wolf's jaws was all that the future needed.

So should I cheer them on? But Akrit stayed silent and watched.

Water Gathers' hunters were closing in on the foreigners, who had bunched together, hands reaching for weapons. It surprised Akrit just how many were in the impromptu warband. Certainly most of Seven Skins' own followers were making their new allegiance plain.

His own retinue were looking at him, but he held them back with the smallest gesture. *Let this play out . . .*

There was a flurry of motion. The Crow man that the Horse had brought with them was abruptly in the air, a confusion of black wings as he bolted for the skies. For a moment Akrit thought he had made it, but someone had a bow to hand, and a moment later the heavy bird had jerked in the air under an arrow's impact. He lurched to one side, one wing still beating madly, and then spiralled to the ground, spilling feathers. The Many Mouths tried to bind his neck to keep him from Stepping, but what fell to earth was already a corpse, the man's spirit flown where his body could not.

The two Coyote, the foreigners' other guides, were keeping their heads down, quiet and submissive and making no protest about the imminent demise of one of their patrons. *Wise, wise, but then Coyote were always survivors – and cousins of a sort, just enough to be more 'us' than 'them'.*

'I leave the choice to you, Horse woman,' Water Gathers was shouting. 'I give one of yours the honour of going to the Wolf as a gift of blood and fire, so that he will watch over my father in his new life. But choose swiftly. My pack are hungry.'

One of the foreigners was coming forward, pushing his way out of his fellows. It was the dark youth, the most exotic of them.

'You may have my blood.' It took Akrit a moment to understand what he was saying: he spoke the language but in a strange way. 'You may have my blood, yes, but only if you fight me for it. It must be taken, not gifted.'

'What makes you think you can set terms?' Water Gathers demanded.

'Do you know what a Champion is in these lands?' the southerner demanded. 'I am a Champion of the River Nation. Come, which of you will take my blood?'

Akrit stayed silent, but his pulse quickened abruptly. *Seven Skins' vision: is this what he meant?* And before he could think too much of it, he was calling out, 'It's only right, is it not? Challenge is the lifeblood of the Wolf.'

Water Gathers' head snapped round, glowering. 'What say have you? I am chief here.'

Akrit grinned, or at least he bared his teeth, because of course the man was not chief *yet*, and abruptly his support was ebbing away, his hubris suddenly unpopular.

'I have no say, of course. I am but a guest,' Stone River went on. 'But I have led the Winter Runners for many years and I know what it means when a man refuses a fight.' The trap closed neatly, leaving Water Gathers inside it. There were many things that would lose a man the confidence of his people, but none cut so deep as cowardice.

***

Asmander held himself very still, waiting. Either he was going to have to fight, or all of them were – and they'd most likely die if it was their little band against the whole of the Many Mouths. This other chief of theirs seemed to be winning some of them over, though, enough that the certainty of a bloodbath was now becoming something muddled and unclear. For a moment nobody seemed to know what would come next, and the old chief's firebrand son had lost his momentum. Then a burly hunter was stepping out from the throng: a big, scarred man of Venater's age.

'I will fight the black man,' he stated. 'I will give his blood to the Wolf. For Seven Skins I will do this.'

'Sure As Flint,' the chief's son named him. 'You were my father's fiercest warrior. Fitting the honour should be yours.'

'You have any idea what you're doing?' Venater growled in Asmander's ear. 'Only, I heard you were supposed to be recruiting this mob. Just let them have a Horse girl to cut up.'

'Honour,' Asmander told him. 'You wouldn't understand.'

Venater rolled his eyes, but then gave a sharp nod, and Asmander saw the chief's son, the angry one, approaching, sizing him up.

'Champion,' he spat, glaring at Asmander.

'You have such warriors, among the people of the Wolf?'

A sneer. 'We are all Champions. Prepare your soul, Black Man. When you are dead, your friends will go with you to the altar of the Wolf, *all* of them.'

'Oh, well done,' Shyri remarked, as the man stalked off.

'You'd just have thrown them one of our number, would you?' Asmander asked her, genuinely interested.

'Harsh seasons, harsh measures.' She shrugged. 'There are a lot of them. It won't be fun fighting clear of here, once your corpse hits the floor.'

'Such optimism!'

'Well, you're the one come to buy their service, because they're such terrifying warriors,' Venater pointed out. 'We get to see just how good, then? That was your plan?'

'Plans are overrated.' Asmander shrugged. 'Get my armour. I don't know much about souls but I'll prepare my body.'

So he pulled on his quilted cuirass, with the plates of obsidian nestling in each diamond panel. About his waist went his belt of twisted cloth, with a panel of layered cotton to guard his groin. He had a bracer of interwoven hide strips for his left forearm, and greaves of the same make for his shins. A little tortoiseshell buckler slipped over the knuckles of his right hand. So he donned all the fragments and pieces of his life, and the ritual was a comforting, centring one. At his heels went his sickle-shaped jade spurs, and in his hand his stone-toothed *maccan* sword.

Sure As Flint was coming now, having made his own preparations, no doubt just as much a ritual, drawing the spirit of the Wolf about him just as Asmander had cloaked himself in the invisible influence of Old Crocodile.

Venater's low whistle of appreciation was the only sound. The watching Wolf tribe had gone reverentially quiet. *Here* was what Asmander had come to find. Here was one of the legendary Iron Wolves whose fame had spread as far as the Riverlands.

He wore a wolf's pelt, cut so that the beast's head topped his own, fitting over a cap of leather and fur. The dead beast's hollow sockets seemed to fix Asmander with a judging stare, and he wondered if the creature's soul was bound inside there, a spectral ally for the man who bore its skin.

Sure As Flint had bracers from wrist to elbow that were leather set with bronze discs. Above that was his coat, which fell from neck to knee. Asmander had never seen anything like it. It was a coat of iron hairs, all twisted into curls and interlinked with each other. Wires, he realized, like a jeweller might draw from gold or silver, and yet who would ever have made armour out of wire?

But this was the Wolf-iron; this was the magic these people guarded so carefully. He felt almost privileged.

In the man's hands was an axe with a curved blade that gleamed like the moon.

'Black Man,' said Sure As Flint, shrugging his shoulders a little to shift the weight of his iron-hair coat. 'You have a name?'

'I am the First Son of Asman.'

'Let no man say the Son of Asman lacks courage,' the Wolf stated. 'I promise you a good death.' His eyes twitched to cover the other travellers, an acknowledgement that the same consideration would not be extended to them.

Asmander let himself settle into his fighting stance. 'Come then. I'm sure we both have other business to attend to.'

Even as he spoke, he Stepped, letting the Champion's soul well up within him, falling forwards into its clawed embrace as if into the arms of a lover. He had a brief sense of a ripple of shock passing out through the watching Wolves, but after that he was the Champion, and the Champion did not care.

For a moment, Sure As Flint paused, but he was not awed, just made cautious. He took two steps back and then dropped to all fours and was a great black wolf, heavy-built and snarling.

They circled each other, the wolf padding softly, his yellow eyes fixed on his opponent. Asmander's met them, unblinking.

He leapt. He had not fought wolves before, but he reasoned they would be little different from lions or hyenas, and this big sack of hair was surely not so very quick.

Sure As Flint *was* quick. He flinched aside from Asmander's pounce, snapped at him to keep him back, and then lunged for his leg, one fang dragging across the Champion's quill scales as they parted. Pushing for the initiative, the wolf was following him up immediately, taking advantage of Asmander's surprise.

The surprise was feigned. The Champion kicked off from the ground just as those jagged jaws lunged towards him. He came down askew across the wolf's shoulders, ripping in with the curved claws of his feet, about to bite.

His talons just scraped harmlessly off the beast's hide. Beneath that hair he felt the shifting links of Flint's iron coat.

Then the wolf had shaken him off, sending him sprawling and then darting after him, ripping at his opponent's stomach. Asmander got a rake across the wolf's nose that discouraged the beast, scrambling to his feet and putting some distance between them. He could feel a dull knuckle of pain in his gut: a little

232

blood drawn, and his own stone and cotton armour had barely slowed the wolf's metal fangs.

What he chiefly felt was exultation: not just at the ferocity of the fight but at the knowledge that, should he survive this clash, he had found what he had been sent to find. Whether or not his father had truly believed in this myth, here was the supernatural strength of the north condensed into this alien metal.

He made another two sudden sallies, relying on his speed to keep his hide intact. Both times he leapt, caught the wolf in the flank and hung on for a second or two, and yet his enemy's hide was impervious. Trying another tack, Asmander darted in, twitching aside from the hunger of those iron jaws, and then Stepped to human for the moment it took for him to lash his *maccan* along his enemy's spine. The force of the blow staggered Sure As Flint, and yet all it achieved was to strip half the teeth from Asmander's sword.

There was a chant now building amongst the people of the Wolf. It was not the name of their fighter, but an invocation of their god. 'Jaws of the Wolf! Jaws of the Wolf!' they were shouting: the same phrase to cover where they came from, and where they sent their foes.

Then Asmander was slightly slower than he should have been, and abruptly there was a bloody tear across one thigh, and now Sure As Flint was following him, pacing himself, driving his prey in a wide circle with red in his grinning mouth.

And slower still now. Asmander was aware that he needed to bring matters to a close: he was wounded, and the weight of iron his opponent carried would not slow him down as a wolf, for all that it made him as invulnerable as a magical hero from the stories. *And how do they kill such heroes, in the stories? Burn them, drown them, bury them. Hardly practical.*

But if I cannot pierce his hide . . .

For a brief while they were circling, and Asmander was the faster, but the circle they fought in seemed to be growing tighter and tighter. He was running out of room and time. The chanting of the crowd was loud in his ears, voicing their concentrated desire for his death. They hated him: as a foreigner, as a creature of alien shape, as their lawful prey; they bayed for his blood. He took strength from it, from the pure-water honesty of it. He fed on their loathing and made it a part of him. And somehow it revealed to him how he must fight Sure As Flint.

Then the wolf was rushing on him, assured of its victory, and he sprang sideways from it, and kicked out with all his strength, slamming his clawed foot solidly into the animal's flank. He felt the jarring shock of hard contact, but the Champion was strong, and all that concentrated force was like a giant's hammer-blow. He felt something give beneath that metal skin, and the wolf yelped, bowled over.

Instantly he was on top of Sure As Flint, raking and lashing at his belly, finding the same shifting hardness there, but not trying to cut it now. Instead he held on with one foot and jabbed the other over and over into the writhing creature's body, bludgeoning and bludgeoning. Then Sure As Flint was up, with Asmander leaping backwards to skitter away.

Now the wolf was pacing around the far side of their circle, that seemed to expand and expand until it might have been the whole Crown of the World. Now Sure As Flint was limping, his hide intact and yet something within him broken.

And what, though? I have not the teeth nor the claws to open his throat, and I will break my own bones before I finish him this way.

But even as he had the thought, something landed at his feet, a sure cast from Venater's hand. He saw it, and abruptly he had stooped into his human form to take it up. The sight of it, the intent of it, made him sick, but how could he deny the pirate's logic?

Such an innocent thing, a string of stones in twisted cloth, with a short wooden bar at each end. A pretty thing meant to go about a throat: the 'red necklace' they called it in the Estuary.

For, of course, all the people of the Estuary were filthy killers who knew nothing about honour, and of all of them the tribe of the Dragon were the worst, and Venater the most villainous even of them.

And Asmander Stepped back towards the Champion and approached Sure As Flint, who snarled at him, teeth gleaming with steel and strings of saliva. The wolf lunged but Asmander was on him, at first hanging on with tooth and claw, then with hands and locked legs as he fumbled for the beast's throat.

The wolf was quicker than he had thought: in a moment it was an armoured man he was grappling with, and Flint got an elbow in his face and flung him off, and then was on him in human form even as Asmander found his feet. He had his axe in his hands, but he was too close for it, and Asmander got his hands on the shaft and twisted it towards the other man's thumb, ripping it away and casting it aside.

He almost missed Flint's dagger: a short iron blade driving up at his stomach in a gutting strike. His right hand drew out his own stone knife and he fell into a parry that Venater had shown him, as nasty a piece of work as any pirate ever knew. Lunging in, he pushed the thrusting dagger down, holding his knife with a hand either side of his enemy's blade. In a single twisting motion of his wrists the hard flat surface of his weapon was crushing his enemy's thumb against Flint's own dagger hilt.

The Wolf warrior howled then, but Asmander had not finished with him, wrenching the man's trapped hand up behind his back so that the dagger blade cut a gash out of his cheek, and that only because Asmander had not quite managed to drive it into the base of his skull.

For those seconds, Sure As Flint had been too blinded by the pain to Step, but he seized control of himself just long enough, now mad to escape, and Asmander felt the hideous wrenching snap as his opponent spasmed into the shape of a wolf whose arm would simply not bend in such a way.

He failed in his resolve then: the sensation of Flint's shoulder shredding itself as he transformed sent a lash of revulsion and weakness through him, and he abandoned his grip, the dagger falling away. Flint, an iron wolf again, collapsed, then struggled up on three legs, and Asmander knew he must still finish the fight. This could only end with a death.

He shouldered forwards, and this time he had Venater's necklace in his hands, dragging it about the throat of the wolf so that the stones dug in, then twisting and twisting, twining the handles together so that it grew tight and then tighter. Flint was a man again instantly – a prisoner of his human flesh the moment his neck was caught. He clawed weakly at the necklace with his one good hand, choking and gasping as the grip of the stones became ever more unforgiving.

And Asmander knew this was it: this was the moment. The Many Mouths would remember him. Perhaps this was even the best way to win them: to kill one of their own in such a way, and wear his tormented ghost like a tattered shawl. Sure As Flint would die a man, and his soul would never pass on. He would haunt Asmander forever. For some that was a thing of horror, but there was a certain breed of hero in the stories who carried chains of ghosts dragging behind them as a tally of victories.

Now the crowd were not whooping. Now the Many Mouths watched Sure As Flint's face darken towards death, and the only sounds were moans of despair.

I will have them now, Asmander knew, but he also knew he would not take them at such a price. His honour and his duty warred within him, and this time honour won.

Abruptly he let go, loosening the handles, tearing away the red necklace, so that Sure As Flint jackknifed away from him, hacking blood first from a human mouth, then from the jaws of a wolf. As he Stepped, Asmander gathered up the dropped dagger and struck downwards with all his strength.

The iron bit the iron, as though he had solved some magician's riddle and found the one weapon that would truly kill his foe. He stabbed and stabbed, exhausting himself in rending that hide with gash after gash. By then, Sure As Flint was long dead, his soul flown free to find another birth, another life.

19

At first, living in Loud Thunder's shadow was fearful. His home was not large, and he filled it, so that Maniye was constantly cowering, scurrying out of the way as he stomped past. In the early days, he seemed to forget that he had guests with each new dawn, regarding them every morning with a surly and suspicious scowl. They were in his way, that look constantly said. They were breathing his air, cluttering his house, eating his food, upsetting his dogs. Any moment, it seemed, he might throw them out into the killing cold or Step into his monstrous beast shape and devour them.

Maniye's answer to this was to make herself useful. She would fetch water from the stream, breaking the ice with stones and then filling the Cave Dweller's clay pots and leather buckets. She would cut the firewood into billets, sweating and grunting with effort as she wielded a flint-headed hatchet she had found, wearing herself down as she learned through trial and error how the task was best accomplished. She once tried to cook, too, and that adventure had been the first time their host had actively deigned to notice them. He had hunched blearily out of the buried chamber that was his bed to find her at the morning fire, trying not to char some squirrels.

'What are you doing?' he had demanded. 'You have burned it and you have not cooked it enough, all at the same time!' He took one off the fire and hung his broad nose over it, inhaling deeply. 'It smells of nothing but fire. Never do this again. This is a terrible thing.'

At the time she had thought he was going to strike her, but instead he just busied himself with rectifying the damage, his anger – if he had really been angry at all – passing from him like water through loose-knit fingers.

Often he left them in sole possession of his hall and went wandering off into the snow, sometimes with the sled and sometimes without. He always took the dogs, though. Yoff and Matt they were called, and at no time did they really warm to either Maniye or Hesprec. Their looks to their master seemed to say, *You may have been fooled but we know a wolf and a snake when we smell them.*

Loud Thunder would leave for a handful of days at a time, coming back with fish, or with great loads of firewood for Maniye to cut up. It was that last which told her he was starting to accept his guests. Since she started that duty, he never stirred to attempt it himself, tacitly accepting her work as part of the host's due.

One day, with Thunder gone for two dawns, she emerged into the bright, cool sun of a crisp morning and Stepped, padding off as a wolf into the trees.

She was on her guard, expecting the worst. The silent forest might hold anything, and she was constantly scenting the air for any sign of danger, whether it came on four feet or two. At any moment she expected Loud Thunder to suddenly appear and drag her back home. He had bargained for her, after all.

And yet she passed, swift and quiet, through the brooding shadows of the forest, leaving behind her a trail of small prints. No terrible fate befell her. Out there, with the cold still world stretching on every side and no master but necessity, she was free. Knowing that, she realized that she had never felt free before.

Her first jaunt was brief, returning before the sun had trekked far across the sky. A few days later she was out again, and then again, sometimes as wolf and sometimes as tiger, as the mood took her; sometimes even as no more than a human girl.

Sometimes she found the tracks of other winter-dwellers abroad in the snow. She ran down a deer, a young stag just short of earning its antlers, coursing alongside its blundering flight on wolf paws and then springing as the tiger springs to bring it down.

When he saw the carcass hanging in his meat store, Loud Thunder just made a slightly surprised noise, and nothing was said of it. By then, she had begun to get used to the ways of this man who sought a life where human contact was the exception and not the rule. Saying nothing did not mean he was not marking each action.

Before that, there was a time he had arrived home before her, and was standing at the entrance to his hall as she padded out of the trees. She had frozen, obscurely ashamed, waiting to see how he would react. And he had reacted just the same as he did to almost everything else: a moment's blank stare, and then nothing. She was free to come and go as she chose.

Later, the wolf pack came.

She encountered them when she was toiling back from the lake with a bucket of water, the stream having frozen, then been chipped away to nothing by her depredations. There were five of them, rib-thin and hungry. She knew wolves enough that she could see they were not mad-starving yet, but this was the leanest of lean seasons. They advanced from between the trees, spreading apart a little as they closed: not on the attack, not yet, still cautious of a human, but they were five and she was only one.

She took two steps back, the bucket dropping heavily into the snow. For a moment she was convinced these were her people come to find her. They were mute, though. One day they would be reborn as human children, but for now they were only animals.

The Step to her own wolf form came instinctively, baring her teeth furiously, but it did not slow their steady approach. They were five and she was one, and smaller than the least of them. They would not hunt her now, but they would hunt these lands, and she would have to stay out of their sight and move on. That was the world's way.

Or she could join them. For a moment, the wolf soul in her felt the loneliness of the solitary hunter, an unfamiliar, powerful sensation. If she met them with the correct etiquette, deferred to their leader – or challenged him! – she might be accepted. She could run with the wolves for a winter, feast and starve as they prospered or pined away. It had been known: need or grief or simple alienation from human society had driven many to it, and many heroes of the stories were counted amongst their number.

But that moment passed. She knew well how she could lose herself that way, the wolf soul growing until not only the tiger but the girl was cut away. She was too young to make that choice.

Instead, she knew that she must put her tail between her legs, keep her head low, break eye contact and retreat. They would let her go, magnanimously. She need only cede the wood to them.

Without warning, her wolf soul was forced aside by the tiger inside. She would not back down. This was *her* territory, and it was these interlopers who must move on. Maniye watched the contest within her with something close to detachment, feeling the swelling of an anger she had not realized was part of her.

Even as the wolves drew closer she Stepped again, and this time they halted in their tracks. As a tiger, she was a hair's breadth larger than the greatest of them, burly and compact. She opened her jaws wide, snarling and yowling and hissing, her coat standing on its hairs' ends to bulk her out further. The wolves paused, milled a little, each looking to the others. There were five of them, still, and had they been any more desperate, then likely they would have attacked, coming at her from all sides in a coordinated strike she could not possibly ward off. She could hurt them, though, with teeth and claws both. Winter

241

was no time to be injured, to become the wolf who slowed the pack.

And she would not give ground, feeling a fierce possessiveness over everything about her: the snow, the trees, the sky. It was *hers*, not these intruders'. Let them brave the tiger if they dared!

And they wavered and they whined, but in the end they did not dare. As one, an unspoken decision made, they turned aside from her and padded off, away from the invisible boundaries of Loud Thunder's home.

Only when they were out of sight did she feel the fear, the soured excitement curdling in her stomach and making her realize what a dangerous thing she had done.

When she returned to Loud Thunder's hall that day, he looked at her a little differently, and she did not know if it was from a change in her or because he had somehow seen or learned what had gone on.

At the start, she had been most worried about Hesprec. She was working hard to earn her keep, but the old Snake would not so much as step out into the cold most days, spending his time huddled by whatever was left of the fire, his Horse-made coat hugged tight about him.

She had assumed that Loud Thunder would grow tired of him very quickly, but instead their host seemed to show Hesprec a wary respect, just as he might offer a real serpent. Probably it was the man's claim to be a priest, for she guessed the Cave Dwellers put more stock in that than her own people had.

But Hesprec did start to earn his keep, and how he did it was to talk.

Loud Thunder had certainly made it plain that the old man used far too many words, and was quick to shrug off his more florid utterances, so Hesprec's campaign to win him started with the old Serpent telling stories to Maniye. He did so as they sat about the fire after dark, the smoke coiling about the sloping eaves above them. Sometimes Loud Thunder was there, sometimes he was already in his cave at the back, but Hesprec had a trick he used, where his voice seemed to carry wherever he wanted it, not loud but always clear. He was playing his games with words, too, so that the more he spoke, the more the stresses and accents of his speech resembled their host's.

He would talk of the River Lords of the south, of how their heroes and their princes had divided the world between them, and then fallen out over the division. He would give the flawed rulers different voices to illustrate their shortcomings, and sometimes Maniye would hear, like an echo, a deep chuckle that escaped from Loud Thunder, no matter how straight-faced he seemed. Then Hesprec would tell Serpent stories of how the heroes of his people had gone into the dark, buried places of the world to learn wisdom. Sitting in the Cave Dweller's lair, surrounded by the earth, his words carried a particular resonance. Maniye fancied she felt the god's coils moving slowly all about them.

Another time, Hesprec spoke of what he called the Oldest Kingdom. Why was it called that, Maniye asked, and Hesprec would gather his dignity and frostily explain that it was the very oldest, the first time ever that many things had been done. Also, came the apologetic sequel, because the great fallen dominion of the Stone People was called by them the Old Kingdom, and so Hesprec's people had to make plain to them that their own lost empire was older still. He called it the Land of Snake and Jaguar, where his people had ruled the world, the first people to set stone on stone and to till the soil. He spoke of this Oldest Kingdom often, weaving it into all his other tales.

So it was that eventually Loud Thunder's voice rumbled out from close by, 'So, what happened to this Snake–Jaguar place?'

Hesprec glanced up, as if surprised that their host had even been listening. 'Gone, more generations ago than even my people can count,' was his answer. 'Gone, and we are scattered – to carry our wisdom wherever we can. The Pale Shadow People came from the sea, fair in person and with fair words, but they were without souls and they seduced the men of the Jaguar and turned our own warriors against us. The Pale Shadow rules there to this day, and we may never return.' And his voice had grown wintry and distant, not like his usual voice at all, carried a little too far off into his own soul by the thoughts of that lost and ancient place that perhaps had never been real.

From that night on, there were three sitting at the fire when the tales were told, and Maniye was surprised to find that Loud Thunder could tell a tale as well as the old man himself. He did not tell of myths and ancient heroes but of his own exploits: escapades in the Crown of the World as it must have been before Maniye's birth, or venturing south to the Plains. There was a wistful look in his eye while speaking of those days and his comrades. One of them had been Broken Axe, at that time just one more warrior whose tribe needed fewer mouths to feed and fewer aggressive young men.

She tried to imagine that man as young, her own age. It was not uncommon for bands of youngsters to leave a village for a few years, to go seeking blood and trinkets and the chance to hone their skills. Those that returned frequently became great hunters, even chiefs, and certainly they found themselves good wives or hearth-husbands. Had Broken Axe himself ever really been the sort of rough, bright-eyed chancer that Loud Thunder described? She found it hard to believe.

And then at last, one night, Thunder turned to her after finishing an innocent-enough story, and told her, 'Your turn.'

She blinked, as panicked in that instant as if he had grabbed her by the throat. 'What?'

'Your story.'

'But I haven't . . . you want a Wolf story?' She knew it was not what he meant.

'I want a story of *you*.'

'But I'm . . . You're both older than me. You've done more . . . I haven't . . .'

'You've done one thing, at least,' Loud Thunder told her, and she knew it was time: the time she had been putting off ever since Broken Axe had slunk off into the trees.

Before their combined gaze, and with the weight of the guest-bond on her, she could not refuse.

So she told them: about her mother, her father. She told them what Akrit had revealed to her, of the destiny he had planned for her as his obedient wolf-child from before she was even born. She recounted every word she could recall, not like a storyteller but in a quiet, dead-sounding voice.

The worst thing was listening to herself, hearing these things set out properly, in a coherent fashion. Since she had left her father's shadow she had been hunted, she had been attacked. A woman had tried to kill her, and so had the weather and the world. 'And,' she said, in just a whisper, 'should I . . . ? Was all this the right thing to do, only for *that*? Surely people endure far more, and they survive. Would it have been so bad to stay? What would it have cost me?'

'Well, I for one applaud your bold decisions,' Hesprec said drily.

'Your tiger soul, it would cost,' Thunder considered.

'But . . .' She did not need to say it. She had passed through the Testing now. She had one soul too many within her body, each of them growing and warring between themselves. Choose, or go mad.

As the days grew shorter, and the cold locked them ever tighter into the cramped space of Thunder's hall, Loud Thunder took to sleeping longer – sometimes for whole days and nights. When he awoke it would take him longer to recognize them or, in turn, become a person that they recognized. At his worst he would blunder about the interior of his home and ignore them completely, or just shamble past and head straight outside, Stepping to his bear form and leaving the hall to an uneasy truce between Hesprec and Maniye on one side and the dogs on the other.

245

Then he was gone for three nights running, so that Maniye began to wonder if he was coming back at all. On the third night, though, she heard distant sounds on the still, cold air: singing and whooping, and distant roars and bellows. Then she knew that Loud Thunder had gone to be with his own people, the first time all winter that he had sought them out.

'It is the longest night,' Hesprec murmured. 'Hard to calculate, with all these clouds you are so fond of, but I think it must be midwinter. Shorter nights and longer days from here, and warmer, I sincerely hope.'

Thunder came back the next night. When he stripped off his robe, she saw the marks of claws and teeth on his skin, all shrunk and puckered compared to the broader gashes they would have made on a bear's hide. One ear was torn, and there was a welter of bruises across his face and shoulders. He seemed unbothered by it. Certainly she had no sense that he had been defeated in any way. Instead, this was what the Bear tribe did. She wondered if, in fighting each other, they were fighting off the winter.

He was drunk, too, soaked in sweat and the sweet smell of mead. Despite looking dead on his feet, he did not sleep all through that night but built up the fire until it blazed high, then drank some more and sang. They were long, strange songs about fallen warriors, the passing on of great men, souls being reborn, and the turn of the year. To be with him then, to share that space with him, was almost impossible. It was not the fear of him but that he had brought the Bear with him, the unseen spirit of the Cave Dwellers crowding out everything else in its battle against the cold season.

After that, he slept – and it looked plain that he would be sleeping for days. He had eaten almost everything they had, but by now Maniye had learned a little of trapping from Hesprec, a little of ice fishing from Loud Thunder himself. She wrapped herself up as warmly as she could and set out to restock the larder.

It was then, wandering far afield to look for tracks in the snow, that she found the campsite.

The smoke caught her wolf's nose first, impossible to ignore. When she got there, the fire had long burned out, with only a little heat clinging to the ashes. It had been built in a sheltered hollow beneath an overhanging stone, not too far from the lake. She could see where hides had been hung to enclose the space and contain the warmth.

There was a single set of tracks leading away from it. Wolf tracks. Half a day old, and the snow did not hold his scent well, but she knew whose they must be.

She had thought he had gone back to spend the winter with her father before setting out again. After all, who would simply wait out the winter like this? Who was that patient and that determined?

Broken Axe. Broken Axe could fight even the highland winters to a standstill. All this time he had been there, keeping his distance, holding to the word of promise he gave to Loud Thunder.

But that word cut her as much as him, for midwinter was past now, the year climbing back towards the warmth of the sun. Spring was on the distant horizon and, with spring, he would come for her.

20

After midwinter and the secret revels of the Cave Dwellers, a change came over Loud Thunder. Never talkative, there was a despondent character to his new silence. Often he would just sit staring into the fire, a dog either side of him, brooding on something. Only Hesprec's stories could bring him back even a little bit, and their charm was clearly lost soon after the last word was spoken.

'Let me tell you about the time that Mongoose and Serpent tried to out-trick each other,' the Snake priest would begin, and the tale would be swift and convoluted as the two rivals sought ever more ridiculous means to outdo the other. And Loud Thunder would laugh, a rumble big enough to fill the inside of his home. But then the story would be done, and he would grunt and nod, and Maniye would almost see the mirth draining from him, down some hole he was powerless to stopper.

Or: 'This is a story of Sees Forever, whose eyes knew neither darkness nor mist, and who went beneath the earth and rescued the Corn Sister with Serpent's aid.' And the tale would be one of sudden ambush, of impossible guardian monsters, of a man pitting himself against the greater spirits, and prevailing. Then Loud Thunder would become inspired, and grin, and his hands would twitch whenever Sees Forever fought, as though some ghost of the myth-hero touched him. But in the end his great shoulders would shrug, all the purpose sloping off them as if to say, *It was all very well in those days, but now we have other worries.*

They were inching through the second half of winter, and nothing of any great import would stir while the white season held its dominion in the frozen world outside. Like a distant star, though, spring was coming. Loud Thunder feared the spring.

One morning she was bold enough to ask him, 'Is it because Broken Axe will come?'

He glanced at her, frowning. 'Is what what?'

'The thing that troubles you,' she pressed. 'Only, I think he was your friend, and I know he will come for me.'

'That's *your* doom,' he replied harshly. '*You* plan for that. When he comes, am I to stop him?'

'But . . .' Something lurched within her, as if a chasm opened up under her. 'I thought that you . . .'

'You have been my guest, this winter,' Thunder told her ponderously. 'Until winter's last day, you are my guest still, and Broken Axe will keep his distance. But you are his to hunt once the days have grown long enough to challenge the nights again. And, when that time comes, I'll not be a man to have guests.'

'What is it?' she asked him. Her own need was hammering within her, but she fought it down.

'Nothing . . . maybe nothing.' But it was plain he did not believe so.

'Your own people?' she divined. He just stared at her, but she saw in his expression that she was right.

Over that winter she had many nightmares. Her twin souls were turbulent within her, sometimes one ascendant, sometimes the other. She had dreams where her tiger was carried away from her in the waters of a furious, icy river. She woke with a start from a sense of having leapt up a cliff, as she had done to escape Broken Axe, only the wolf had been left behind, the threads that bound it to her snapping abruptly.

She had made no choice. To take one would be to betray the other, and they were both *her*. And yet she could feel a roiling instability within her, a loss of control. She would go mad, she knew. In the end those two souls would fight, and perhaps she would lose them both and have no shape to Step to at all.

So it was that she found a night when Loud Thunder slept but Hesprec was still alert, performing some devotion before the empty gaze of the fire. He had a hundred of these little rituals: burning things, burying things, drawing spiral patterns in the ash. She wondered if he was trying to catch the tail of the future, so that he could know what the new year would bring. Or perhaps he was speaking with his subterranean god, feeling its movements through the frozen earth.

She knelt on the other side of the fire from him, head down to show a due deference that was a marked change from her usual manner towards him, and waited for him to finish. She had a sense of him casting a pale eye at her, ever curious, but he carried on with his secret business, whispering to the flames, then watching them leap as though he saw an answer in their dancing.

At last his conversation with the fire was done, and she was itching to ask him what it had all been about. He would not have told her anyway, and her questions would have made him defensive and irritable, but normally that would not have stopped her. This time, though, she was going to ask for something perhaps bigger than anything before. She was trying to approach him with the reverence that she imagined his own people might show.

'Hesprec . . .' No doubt there was some title for a Snake priest in the River Nation, but he had never mentioned it.

He regarded her alertly, perhaps warily, as though something of her purpose had already reached him. Perhaps the fire had told him.

'I cannot choose,' she said simply.

He nodded soberly. 'These things are known: your dreams leak out of your mouth, most nights.'

'I need help.'

That cautious look of his returned.

'Hesprec, I cannot choose,' she repeated. 'I cannot let either of them go to please the other, and they fight – they fight inside me. So I thought of another way, a new way.' It was a terrible thing to think, worse to say, but now she squared her shoulders to confront it.

'Perhaps you will tell me?' he invited.

'You said with the Horse . . . how they took in children and gave them new souls. Made them belong in their tribe.'

'It is a shocking thing, but no less true,' he agreed.

'And I thought . . . I thought that if the Tiger will not let me be a Wolf, and the Wolf will not let me be a Tiger . . .' She faltered, then pressed on, desperate to get to the part where she actually asked him: 'Make me a Serpent.'

He froze, mouth slightly open, staring at her as though she bore a dreadful wound and he did not know how to heal it without hurting her even more. 'It cannot be,' he said at last, in just a whisper.

'*Please,*' she insisted. 'Whatever I need to do, I'll do it. I'll make offerings. I'll swear oaths. I'll give myself over to your god and learn all your things that you do. It must be possible.'

'But it is not.' His face creased in pain. 'What did I say to you, one of the first ever things? We of the Serpent are special. We are the scions of the Oldest Kingdom. There is no becoming one of us.'

'Why? What don't I have?' she demanded. 'I'll work, I'll take your trials, whatever—'

But he held a hand up, and that hand signified finality. 'It is not done. It has never been known. I cannot do it,' he insisted. 'If there is some way, then it is a secret held by some other priest, one closer to Serpent than I am.' A toothless grimace. 'I am sorry, Maniye. I cannot describe the sorrow in me that this thing cannot be, but you must seek elsewhere for your answer.'

She had a horrible sense of being a very ignorant girl asking something very stupid, and that he was being far too kind in his mild response. Facing that old, old gaze she felt callow and foolish. Before he could say anything else comforting, she stood up abruptly, almost kicking the fire, and struggled outside, dragging her Horse coat around herself.

She cut wood. It always needed doing and the work involved no thought. She was good at it now: the winter had taught her all sorts of skills that her life in the Winter Runners had not gifted her with. She could see with the benefit of hindsight, that her father had always had her in mind for someone's hearth-keeper, someone's wife. There was no dishonour in that: to gather and tend, to clean and stitch, to raise children, to meet with the other wives and hearth-husbands and make the hundred small decisions a community relied on. These were valued tasks and many, and yet she had tasted the wilderness now. She had run with the vanguard of winter. She would never be content to keep a hearth.

After that, she still did not feel she could face Hesprec, and so she took the leather bucket and headed for the lake. She was so wrapped up in her own embarrassment – and a kind of dawning horror as she imagined what she might have felt had he somehow said *yes* – that she did not realize she was not alone until the lakeshore became visible through the trees. Only then did the quiet get to her: not even those muted animal sounds that full winter could not stifle. She was advancing into a world already plunged into that still silence that spoke of the fear of man.

And he was there when she looked for him; not even keeping pace but just standing a little ahead of her, as though he had been waiting there all night or all winter. Broken Axe.

She started back, dropping the bucket. She could only think that she had miscounted the days, that the spring was already come, that it was time.

Then she Stepped, first to wolf, backing away with bared teeth, then to tiger, bulking out as big as she could, snarling and hissing and bristling every hair.

He remained very still, looking at her. If he had Stepped to his wolf shape, then she would have fought or run. She could not have said, right then, which course she might have taken. He remained human, though, with no weapon to hand.

'My oath still stands,' he said.

There was sufficient distance between them that, if he lunged for her, she would have time to find a form in which to meet him, or so she hoped. She knew she should simply flee, but here he stood, Broken Axe, and between them the iron barrier of his word.

She let go of the tiger within her, and her human feet took a single step back, widening the distance just that little bit more. 'And you've never broken an oath before, is that it?'

'Only once.' Ill fortune dogged the oath-breaker, just as it would the treacherous host, the ungracious guest, the kinslayer. These were the great crimes that even the most powerful took note of. But then he was a lone wolf, a man who ran without a pack. The stories agreed that such hunters were broken inside, so that their word was a twisting and slippery thing.

'I won't go with you,' she told him.

'You think so.'

'You bring back my corpse, or nothing at all.' Even as she said it, she wondered if she herself was making oaths she could not keep.

'Many Tracks, you're young still. Is it a happy thing to fall back into your father's shadow? No, but neither is it the end of the world. There are worse fates.'

'My father will never have me for a daughter.' She realized that something had shifted in her over the winter, something learned from Loud Thunder or from Hesprec, or from her own two warring souls. She would be as good as her word: she would not go quietly, nor become the meek daughter. 'And if there are worse fates than being Stone River's get, how about Broken Axe's mate?'

She caught the flinch in his expression, swiftly disguised. *He doesn't know!*

'My father promised it – or threatened it – to punish me. To bind you.'

For a long time he stared at her, and she could read precisely nothing of his thinking in his expression. Those eyes of his seemed to anatomize her, and eventually his silence became the most fearful thing about him, growing and growing until it filled the world.

'He will have *you* for his dog,' she said. She had meant it as a barb, but the silence had got to her, and it came out closer to a whisper.

'That is between Stone River and myself,' he said at last. 'But you cannot be my mate, not even if either of us found it a thought to rejoice in.'

It was her turn to frown but say nothing.

'Many Tracks,' he reminded her mildly. Through all this speech he had not moved, not so much as to shift his balance.

At first she could not see what he meant, and he was plainly willing to wait until the world froze over before saying more. Then the revelation descended on her like a storm, so that she actually staggered slightly. A hunter would take a mate to keep his hearth. Yet on the shores of the lake, when he had caught up with her, he had given her a hunter's name.

Many Tracks? She had not believed he had meant it. She'd thought it was just the mockery of a man who believed he had caught her.

He must have seen the leap of hope in her face. 'Do not mistake me,' he warned her. 'When the last day of winter dies, then I will come for you. This I swore, even as I swore to Loud Thunder that I would wait just so long. But of your father's plans for you – or for me – then know that you shall be spared the fate of being the mate of Broken Axe.'

'And you shall not be bound to my father's hearth.'

'Just so.'

There were parts of her that were still urging that she flee, but she mastered them. 'You have lived all the winter here, without even a roof.'

A nod from him.

'Why do you even bother with the tribe or with my father? A man who can triumph over winter should need nothing from them. If I could do that myself, I'd just . . .'

'Go into the wilds? Live as the wolf lives?' he asked her.

'Why not?'

'I wish I were that strong. But the call of kin, of blood, of company, it gets to you, if you give it long enough. It's easier to live alone when there are people you can live alone away from.' His small smile made him young just for a moment: the youth who must have shared adventures with Loud Thunder long ago. 'Perhaps one day you'll be stronger than me.'

'I'll do it.'

'Good luck to you. But do it after I've brought you back to Stone River. After that you're no longer my concern.'

And it was the strangest thing, but she could detect the falsehood there. She *was* his concern, somehow. It was not any desire for her – she had seen that plain enough when she had told him Akrit's plans. There was something else, though . . .

My mother . . . Was there some guilt there, that he had been the one to take her mother out into the woods and cut her throat? Surely guilt was for men other than Broken Axe.

Then he moved, and even though it was away from her she was instantly a wolf, skittering away from him.

'I'll be with you soon enough,' he called back to her. 'You must know that Loud Thunder will not stand in my way again. You've run well, and you've made good use of your chances, but where can you go now? What will you barter with next, for just a little more time?' And he seemed almost to be inviting her to think of something. *Is it that he enjoys the chase and wants to prolong it?*

Abruptly he had Stepped, becoming the pale wolf with the

dark mane, and went loping easily off through the trees, lost to sight in moments.

Her head was so filled with Broken Axe's words and their veiled implications that she just ran back towards Loud Thunder's home, taking no care and keeping no watch. So it was that she was caught completely by surprise as a huge hand fell on her shoulder, arresting her almost by its very weight so that her feet skidded out from under her. For a moment she was falling, but the hand closed tighter on her, an immovable anchor that held her upright – but then would not let her go.

Her instinct was to pull away but the grip could not be broken. Even when she Stepped to her wolf form, it had her by the scruff of the neck, dangling her off the ground. For a few pointless moments she snarled and snapped and twisted. Then he had shaken her once, not even very hard compared to the heavy, solid strength she could feel in that arm, and she lurched back to her human form, toes just touching the ground, twisting to look at him. And look up at him, and further up.

Another Cave Dweller, no doubt of it. Loud Thunder was broader and more massively built, but this newcomer was taller, towering so far above her she half thought there should be a white snowcap to him, far up the slopes of his body.

He was close to clean shaven, just a fuzz of stubble about his jowls and chin and neck, and he stared down at her dolorously, as though she was some poor omen. He wore hides, like Loud Thunder, but over them was a fur-lined, sleeveless robe of some fine material, coloured a green that Maniye had never seen before, and faintly edged with gold. Threadbare and ancient it was, but only amongst the Horse had she seen anything so fine. Hanging over his chest was a pendant of stones, flat and oval, black and painted with white lines, each of them the size of her open hand and all of them strung on a cord so thick it was almost a rope.

'What do you want,' she got out, trying to keep her voice

steady. He had this in common with Loud Thunder: in the silence his attention seemed to wander, so that only with her speaking did his eyes and face remember her. His hand, though, never forgot.

'You go to the cave of my brother,' he told her sonorously. 'Tell me then: what are you to him?'

She wondered what he might have guessed. Slave, perhaps? 'A guest,' she said forcefully.

'Hrm.' The same dubious growl that Thunder had made that first time. 'Guest of my brother then: take my words to him. Tell him that his brother is here. Bid him let me in, for I have words for him from our mother.'

She tugged to escape his hand, and he released her with a frown of surprise, as though he had not expected to find her there at the end of his arm. Retreating from him, she tried to think of some alternative to doing what he had just instructed. Loud Thunder's home was her only point of reference though. She backed away another few steps, keeping her eyes on him, and then she was a wolf again, bounding off over the hard-packed snow as swiftly as she could.

She knew, even then, that this was the thing that Loud Thunder had been fearing, this personal doom he had been hiding from. Even as the year turned towards spring, so it was waking up and remembering its grievances. Broken Axe would come for her, and Loud Thunder's brother had already come for him.

21

'Water Gathers has a journey he will take. He will go to the Stone Place when spring comes,' Otayo confided to Akrit, two mornings later.

'To the priests?' The chief of the Winter Runners rubbed at his chin thoughtfully. 'But will it help him, do you think?'

Seven Skins' eldest son regarded him with a humorous expression. 'My brother has every chance of following our father and becoming chief of all the Wolves,' he pointed out. 'You think the priests will not welcome him?'

'And yet here you are talking to me.'

'Even so.' Otayo's Deer tribe thralls had brought them food: hard cheese and smoked meat and dried fruit, a slice of what the winter had left them.

'You and he are no great friends.'

'If I were chief, I would guide the tribe away from his path. But I am no hunter.'

For the space of a moon, the nights had been long, grappling with the sunlight and strangling it before its time, but now the days were regaining their strength, wearing down their enemy until there came a time when they were evenly matched, like two brothers. On that day, on that night, the priests of many people would gather to read omens, to share knowledge, united briefly in a bond that was supposed to know neither tribe nor shape. Kalameshli would travel there, if he could, and Akrit knew he would meet with Deer and Bear, the farseers of the Eyrie, even with the blood-priests of the Tiger. There would be sacrifice, contest, ritual combat and invocation, each of them trying to control the fortunes of the coming year.

Those who came there without the aegis of a priesthood took their lives and futures in their hands. The spirits of the Stone Place could curse, the priests could kill, but some might come away blessed, the star of the hero shining above them. Water Gathers sought the benediction of the priesthood to strengthen his claim – after that disastrous business with the southerners, he needed something more than just his bloodline to recommend him.

As for Akrit himself, he had not thought to go there, but Otayo had achieved his aim in making the idea irresistible. The benediction of the Wolf priests would speak loudly of Akrit's virtue, and surely Kalameshli held some influence over them.

And, while there, he could seek the omens for his campaign against the Tiger, and perhaps plant some seeds of his own. When the time came to raise a war-host, how much better if there were those, priests especially, who were already thinking fondly of such an idea.

'Will I go?' He shrugged, in a great display of indifference. 'All things may come to pass.'

'You have made no friends amongst the Many Mouths,' Akrit pointed out. The little camp of the southerners was considerably shrunken now. The Horse Hetman woman and her people had left immediately after the fight, plainly sensing the expiry of their welcome. Such a *cautious* people – which explained why they seemed to end up everywhere and profiting from everyone, of course. And yet sometimes a man had a venture, a bold and grand venture, where caution might only be an impediment.

The two Coyote who had come along with them were still slinking around somewhere, but they were seldom seen consorting with those they had guided here. Thus far, the Many Mouths had found no way to express their anger, for their man Sure As Flint had been killed in a fair fight, and one of their making. The Coyotes could sense that this could not last forever: a handful of foreigners who had roused the ire of the Wolf could not be safe for long. Akrit knew that the priest Catches The Moon was already talking with Water Gathers and some of the elder hunters, trying to find some interpretation of recent events that would justify revenge.

The black man, the Champion, looked up at Akrit and smiled brightly. 'I am not good at making friends,' he admitted cheerfully. 'People say so everywhere I go.'

'These things are known,' rumbled the big man beside him – another southerner, but of some different breed, with yellow skin and blue-black hair that was long and lank. Their third was a Plains woman, young and very fierce – as more than one of the Many Mouths hunters had discovered.

'Why are you here, First Son of Asman?' Akrit asked him.

'I come to learn about the Wolf.'

'And what do you learn?'

'That he fights. I hear that he wears the Crown of the World about his brows, and ventures into the Plains as he wishes, and fears nothing.'

Akrit shrugged. 'Sometimes the Wolf goes south, sometimes the Dog Pack comes north. And any man who fears nothing is a dead fool. But there is some truth in what you say.'

'You are not of the Many Mouths, I think?'

'I am Stone River, chief of the Winter Runners, come to witness the passing of my friend Seven Skins.'

'Are the Winter Runners any better at making friends than the Many Mouths, I wonder?' the son of Asman enquired.

Akrit examined him, thinking on Seven Skins' words. The dying man had taken the arrival of these strangers as a sign, and yet desperation made a sign of anything. Water Gathers had taken that sign and made it into a thing to destroy, to overcome. That had not gone well for him.

'I shall depart soon for the Stone Place,' Akrit informed the southerners. 'There we will see the spring in, and hear the signs read, for there the wisdom of the Crown of the World is gathered.' Because Kalameshli would be there too, and right now Akrit felt a keen need for his counsel.

'Wisdom is a thing I always lacked, my father said,' the southerner remarked. For a moment Akrit thought he would ask to accompany the Winter Runners there, although no doubt they would slow the wolves considerably. The man's dark face was unreadable, though, thoughts moving unseen behind it like dark waters.

And yet, later, Akrit saw the black man speaking with the two starveling Coyotes again, and it was plain that he was negotiating some service from them. What else could it be? Perhaps this First Son of Asman was wise enough not to arrive at the Stone Place in Akrit's shadow, but he would go there nonetheless. Akrit had a sense of great things moving invisibly in the sky, of the spirits of the world bending low to take notice of human affairs. Always such times were fraught with danger, but out of hard days were hard men made, and great ones.

★★★

Maniye delivered the stranger's message word for word. Even though she felt safe within the home of Loud Thunder, beneath his roof and at the mouth of his cave, the presence of the new Bear hunter was like a pressure at the back of her head. He was out there still, and she could not ignore it.

Loud Thunder stared at her from the deep shadows of his cave, his gaze like a trapped animal's. He still had the fug of winter about him, which made him ill-tempered and clumsy and only half present, but her message had aroused his fear again.

'I'm sorry,' she told him, and those great rounded shoulders shrugged.

She had expected him to have her invite the stranger in, but Thunder just hunched in on himself even further, a man clinging to the few barricades he has left before the enemy arrives.

Soon after, she could hear a voice calling from outside: 'Your brother is thirsty! Will you leave him to parch at your very gates? Come, fetch a cup for your brother who waits for you!'

There was something ritualized about the words, and something lonely too. If it had been night outside then Maniye's thoughts might have turned to ghosts and spirits, those who died locked in a human shell, cut loose from their animal souls and forced to wander forever seeking succour.

Loud Thunder's head had lifted sharply at the voice, and his face twisted in resentment. She had thought he would ignore the call, but a heavy gesture to her indicated the waterskin hanging from the ceiling.

Outside, the new Cave Dweller had seated himself on a mat laid out in the snow, sitting patiently as though nothing was more usual for him. She handed him the cup and he drained it in one, giving her the barest nod. She had the sense that he did not really see her, or at least as nothing more than Thunder's agent.

'Please,' she whispered, still somewhat in awe of the sheer bulk and height of him, 'he doesn't want to come out.'

No anger from the visitor, only a brief, disinterested glance. 'He is my brother.'

She retreated inside and tried to busy herself with some small chores, but the presence of the stranger seemed to deform the very ground outside, as though he had a weight to him that pulled down the land about him: her thoughts were constantly sliding away towards him.

She was not alone in that, and eventually Loud Thunder shambled out of his cave to squat by the fire and cast angry looks at everything and nothing.

'Once there was a man,' he told them, 'who travelled too far and saw too much.'

He poked the fire with a stick, and his dogs whined at his dark mood.

'This man came from a hard land of winter, where his people

lived a hard life of winter, and they were few but strong. Seldom indeed did they find the need to venture to other lands and meet other people, for they knew all the ways of their home, and it provided for them,' Loud Thunder addressed the fire. 'But there was a son of this land who found even so few too many, and for whom the land of his birth was yet not hard enough, and so he took to his feet and left his mother and travelled south into the bowl that men call the Crown of the World.'

'Brother!' came the abrupt call from outside, and to Loud Thunder it might have foretold a death. 'Your brother is hungry! Will you let him starve at your very gate? Come, a meal for your brother who waits for you!'

Loud Thunder gave a long sigh, like a man waking up none too willingly. Wordlessly he found smoked meat and berries, sweet chestnuts and a pot of salted deer fat, then looked again to Maniye.

She went outside – the sun was gleaming bright on the snow, and all around her was the sense that the world was turning, new life stirring itself in an orgy of change. The Cave Dweller regarded her solemnly as she brought him the food.

'He wants you to go away,' she told him. Although she had no place here, she still felt as though she was playing a role in some great story she had no understanding of.

'He is my brother,' the huge man said again.

Back inside, Loud Thunder shook his head. 'This man,' he went on, for obviously the fire needed to know, 'visited many other people and lands, because his own were not enough. He lived amongst the Deer and the Boar, he fought alongside the Wolf. He went to where the land is flat and open as the sky, and where the Plains people have their battles and their hunts. He took strange brothers amongst the people of those lands.

'He saw more than any man of his tribe, in all living memory,' Loud Thunder told the fire and the walls and the timbers of his home. 'But home remained like a hook in his thoughts, and so at last he went back to a people who did not want to hear his stories of what he had seen. But it was his home, and that was where he knew he should be. And those stories were like another hook in his mind when he went home, so that he could not just settle there and forget. And so he made his home at the very edge of where his people lived, and he lived alone, as his people did.'

'Brother!' came the call again, and this time Maniye had been expecting it. 'Your brother is cold! Will you let him freeze at your very gate? Come, a roof for your brother who waits for you!'

And Hesprec said quietly in the silence that followed, 'For they are strong and solitary, all of them. Each could mean the death of another very easily, by intruding into a den without welcome. And so they call, and build the bond of guest and host between them most carefully, don't you think?'

'But what does he want?' Maniye asked.

Loud Thunder looked at her, and it was as though he had not seen her properly for a long time. Abruptly he was *here* and *now* again in a way that had been lacking since before midwinter.

'And this man who had travelled was shunned by his own people –' and he had stood up – 'because they could no longer understand him, for all the things he had seen.' He reached the door in one stride. 'And yet he knew that one day the world would change so that even those who dwell in caves must be aware of it. And on that day they would come to him and offer . . . and offer . . . things he did not want.'

He pushed his way outside, and in the same moment he was Stepping, looming up and outwards into the vast form of a bear, now standing out in the waning cold and shaking itself. For a moment he was on two legs, a tower of dense flesh and bone and claws. Then he fell forwards and slouched forth on all four paws, head held low.

The stranger had stood as soon as he came out, and Maniye saw him also Step, almost lazily, stretching up into an equally massive beast.

Maniye scrambled out to see Loud Thunder slope towards

him, feeling that a clash between them would level the forest for miles around, would be heard all the way back to the Horse post, even to the village of the Winter Runners.

When they were close to each other, they both pushed themselves up as tall as they could go, tottering on their hind legs and bellowing into each other's faces, great yellow teeth bared like swords. The echoes of their roaring came back to them from the forest, from the mountain peaks, resounding from the sky itself. Each of them was on the very point of mortal violence, cuffing at the other with blows that would have shattered every one of Maniye's bones. They dropped down, snarled and circled, bawling murder at each other, stamping and clawing at the snow. Then they were up again, grappling, measuring weight and strength, each always an inch from sinking his teeth into the opponent's throat.

And yet, after three of these exchanges, not a drop of blood had reddened the snow, and Maniye thought of what Hesprec had said, how they could destroy each other. The newcomer could simply have torn open Thunder's carefully constructed home to get at him. They could have flayed each other with their claws, bloodied their fangs on each other's lifeblood.

It was an argument, she saw: an argument between brothers who happened to be bears.

And, at the end, Loud Thunder had dropped down again, seeming almost baffled and shaking his head. He had not lost – indeed Maniye thought he had got the upper hand, older and heavier than the newcomer. He had not driven the other bear off though. It had endured the worst of him, and was still there.

Loud Thunder turned, then, and stomped back towards his home, Stepping from brooding bear to brooding man as he did so, and the newcomer followed suit, walking almost in his tracks.

He was called Lone Mountain, she discovered. He was not Loud Thunder's brother by birth, but a cousin. The aunt they had in common was the Mother of all the Bears.

Hesprec was listening intently, as though this all made perfect sense to him, but for Maniye it was hard to follow. The Cave Dwellers did not live together as a tribe, like all the other people of the Crown of the World that she knew. They lived here in this harsh country, and they spaced themselves far across it, allotting to each one or two or few a territory. They were a tribe, though, and they had their ways, their gatherings and meetings. And they had their mother. Of all the powerful women born within the Arms of the Bear, one was acknowledged as pre-eminent, by secret ways that were obviously as much of a mystery to the two Cave Dweller men as they were to Maniye. What marked out the Mother of the Bear people was her strength, but also her wisdom. The Mother saw many things, Maniye understood. What the Mother asked for, the Mother usually received.

'And she has asked for you,' Lone Mountain declared. 'You must go to the Stones once spring comes. You have been apart from your people long enough. Many have said it.'

Loud Thunder merely grunted, and stared at the fire.

'Did you think a son of the Bear could live always on his own, one such as you?' Lone Mountain did not seem entirely pleased about this whole business himself.

'I do not want it.'

'Your wanting does not matter,' Lone Mountain told him.

'It should be *you* she calls for.'

Maniye looked from one to the other, trying to decipher what they meant.

'I had always thought so.' Mountain scowled. 'But the world is changing. Her dreams and seeing have led her to call your name, so you must go.'

'What is it? What are you talking about?' Maniye demanded. She fully expected to be ignored – too small and insignificant for these two vast creatures to notice. Loud Thunder glanced at her, but said nothing. It was Lone Mountain who graced her with an answer.

'Mother has said that the Bear seeks a war leader.'

'War?' Now it was Hesprec chiming in. 'War against the cold? Against the trees?'

Lone Mountain shrugged ponderously. 'This is what Mother hears from the Bear. And of all of the hunters in the Bear's Shadow, it is your name she speaks. And you must go.'

'I will say no.'

'Say it to her face, if you dare,' Lone Mountain challenged. 'But go to her you shall. None will then say I did not do what was asked of me.'

What irked her was the change in Hesprec. He had been like a grey shadow all the winter, until she was convinced that he would not see the spring. Aside from his stories, there had been nothing to be got from him: as if he had retreated to the last spark of warmth inside himself and shuddered his way through each cold day, each long and freezing night.

Now a new brightness had come into his eye, and it was not just the promised spring. He was looking *smug*.

'This was what you wanted all along, wasn't it?' she accused him. 'It's the real reason you were here in the Crown of the World – seeking wise counsel or whatever. Did *you* make this happen?' She would have believed it, too, for who knew what the minions of the Snake could accomplish, or how their magic worked? Perhaps everything following her rescue of him from sacrifice had been twisted into place by the movements of the Serpent's coils.

'Does it suit my purpose? Yes,' he agreed. 'Can a poor, worn-down stub of a priest bring such things about, no matter how the Serpent favours him? Such things defy possibility.' And, when she still looked on him with suspicion, 'And does this not serve your purposes too, little hunter?'

'How can it?' she demanded.

'Before spring comes, our host here must set out for your Stones, or else risk offending his Mother,' Hesprec pointed out. 'What was your plan for the coming of spring? To flee into the

267

wilderness until the hunter tracks you down? Better travel with Loud Thunder. Seek for your new escape amongst the people who will gather at this place. You shall find more chances there than amongst the trees.'

She pictured Broken Axe on her trail again. He would follow her all the way to the Stone Place, but that was a magic place at a magic time. The division between spirits and ghosts, totems and men, it was frail there. The priests of many tribes met and held back their hatreds. A rash act in that company could curse the culprit for life or mark them out for the greater spirits to torment.

In her heart she did not feel that such considerations would dissuade Broken Axe any more than the winter had.

22

Maniye had assumed that Lone Mountain would travel with them, to ensure that Loud Thunder did not go astray. Apparently either Thunder's word was unquestionable or the Cave Dwellers were simply not people who lied to one another. As soon as Thunder had agreed to travel, Lone Mountain was already departing. He strode to the shadow of the trees, then cast a single look behind him before Stepping into his great-muscled bear form and loping off.

Loud Thunder looked unhappy. 'Mother calls for me. She should call for Lone Mountain. He is the better man. He is the one who stayed to serve his kin, not me. But it is my name on her lips, and I must go. You should go also.'

'Where?' Maniye demanded.

Thunder shrugged massively, the vague gesture of one hand describing the great expanse of the world.

'I . . .' Now that she must leave, she found herself far more attached to this little house, this ice-locked glade, than she would ever have thought.

'Will you come to the Horse with me?' she asked Hesprec uncertainly.

Hesprec looked solemn. 'I had a purpose that drew me to the north.'

'You were looking for wisdom. I thought you'd worked out there wasn't any.'

Loud Thunder snorted at that, and she glared him into silence.

'These Stones, this gathering . . .' Hesprec explained. 'This was the lure that drew me here so long ago. I had not imagined the path would be so long, to get me there. Or so cold.' He grimaced, showing his scarred gums. 'But I would go with Loud Thunder. If the Serpent preserves me from this cold, and from these people, then I shall gather what wisdom I find and carry it home.'

She nodded. 'Then I come with you: to the Stone Place and then to the south. After all, were you going to *walk*? Or did you think Loud Thunder would carry you in his pocket or about his neck, old Snake?'

★★★

'So, man-with-a-child's-name,' Shyri said, letting her long stride take her close to Venater, 'why have you not cut his throat yet?'

The old pirate cocked an eyebrow at her then glanced ahead at Asmander, who was walking with their Coyote guides.

'It must be simple living on the Plains,' was his only reply.

Around them, the Crown of the World rose and fell, as though once the land had rolled like the waves of the sea, and then the gods had put out their hands and frozen it in place.

'In the Plains, we know that life will set enough burdens on us, without our inventing more of our own,' the Hyena girl pointed out.

Venater's expression made it clear that ignoring her was a tempting option, but then he rolled his shoulders irritably. 'You mock me for my name, so you know how it is between us.'

'And what would you do with your name anyway?' she answered. 'If he should hurl it at you, like a bone thrown to a dog, do you even know what you would do?'

'I would kill him.' The words came out with a certainty and suddenness that seemed to surprise even Venater. Then, the qualification: 'I would try.'

Shyri was silent for a handful more steps, and a fresh flurry

270

of fine snow blew past them, drifting onto white ground that already bore scars of bare rock and the first shoots of green.

'You do not give him much incentive to free you,' she noted diplomatically.

'These things are known,' the pirate grunted, that oft-used saying of the south. 'But no doubt you're glad of it.'

'Why is it mine to be glad of?'

'You're sweet on him, aren't you?'

She gave a quick laugh at that, although he had a nasty, knowing expression on his face – and it was a face made for just such a look.

'Steer clear of him,' Venater cautioned, with his brown teeth grinning back at her. 'You're not what he's looking for in this land. And, even if you were, he'll be promised to some Croco-dile girl by his father, just like his father pulls all his strings.'

'I have no interest either in him or his father.'

'Well, then, why haven't *you* killed him? Feeling the loin-pain for him's the only thing I can think of that balances out how annoying he is,' Venater said disgustedly.

Her laughter at that sally was more natural, less forced.

'And what are you looking for, in this land?' She made herself grin at him, just to see if he would bite.

'Girl, I had your mother.'

'The Malikah's not my mother – not in that way.'

'Enough so for me. I've no wish to go sticking myself in the Hyena's Shadow any more than that.'

'Is this honestly the best topic of conversation the two of you could come up with?' Asmander called out from ahead. Shyri started, missing her footing, and would have skidded off down towards the abode of the local river god had not Venater caught her arm in a tight grip.

'Oh, and he has really good ears, the malingering bastard,' the pirate added with some satisfaction, before setting her back on her feet.

Meanwhile, Asmander himself just shook his head and then

271

took a handful of quick strides, to catch up with the two Coyotes.

'What was that your friend was saying?' Two Heads asked him.

'Just that he wishes to kill me.'

'That's normal, where you come from?' Evidently nothing would surprise the Coyote about the barbarous practices of other lands.

'It's normal for *him*.' He grinned abruptly. 'Do you have no such friends where you come from?'

'None we stay near to.' Two Heads rolled his eyes. 'There is a lot of wide open world, and no reason to stay in any part of it that displeases you, let alone to fight another for it. If only all men realized this truth, then the world would be a good place to live.'

'And nobody would ever spend two nights in one place.'

'Also no bad thing.' The Coyote shrugged. 'Roots are for trees.'

'You fill me full of envy.'

Two Heads glanced at him in surprise. 'Yet here you are, more of a traveller than we have ever been.'

'If you're not where you would like to be,' Quiet When Loud pointed out, 'then just keep moving. There will be a better place.'

An oddly comforting philosophy. And yet in Asmander's mind there existed something like a knot: a snarl of relationships and decisions that had brought him here. Travel as far as he might – to the highlands above the Crown of the World, to the jungles of the Pale Shadow People – he could not escape the tether that led him back to the Sun River Nation. Here was Tecuman: his friend, the man who would rule the Riverlands. Here was the sharp-edged snarl that was his father, the Patient One, a man leathered by the sun until nothing was left in him but desire and ambition. And here . . . here, like a hot coal in his head, was Venater's name.

He had thought often of speaking it aloud and returning it to its owner. He had imagined that moment as a scene from legend,

272

when the hero utters the names of the great spirits and unleashes them. He had pictured something invisible but unmistakable returning to the pirate's long-jawed face, to his stony eyes.

And then they would fight, as they had fought before, only this time Venater – *Venat* – would not be hungover or caught unawares.

The thought made Asmander shiver. Always the same astonishment: *How did I ever beat him?*

And now, without his name, that fire was lessened within him. Not Venat, but merely Venat's son, as Asmander was Asman's. If he died as Venater he would go to the Dragon as a boy – no deeds, no glory, no bloody-handed history – and only Asmander could give him back the name he had surrendered. How the hate must be stoppered up within him like a beast penned. Asmander found himself staring at the lock of its cage, over and over, and knowing he held the only key.

'I've never really moved at all,' he said, voicing the trailing end of his own thoughts, but the two Coyote seemed to understand him. *I'm like the river. I seem to be driven ever onwards, and yet here I am always.*

***

Loud Thunder travelled with his sled, Matt and Yoff pulling it swiftly over ground that was still deep with packed snow. He travelled on his human feet, and Maniye loped alongside him, outpacing him and coming back for him, with Hesprec sleeping or plotting inside her pack.

The bear would have moved faster, she reckoned, and, when they camped on the first night, she asked Loud Thunder if he stayed human because of the dogs.

His face took on one of those slightly embarrassed expressions of his, a big man making a small admission. 'The bear, it gets distracted: smells, hunger . . . and it doesn't care about time. It's been on lean pickings all winter, or it's slept. It needs more to eat than a man. If I Stepped, I'd be foraging all the time. I'd forget.'

273

She stared into his face, understanding that, living alone, he must hear the call of his bear soul asking him to give up his hands and his language and walk off into the wilds forever. It was the fate of the old and the grieving. Before now she had not thought of it as the fate of the lonely.

She guessed that there were not so many Cave Dwellers compared to the people of the Wolf or the Deer or the Boar, and perhaps that was one reason why. She tried to imagine what it would be like to have such a powerful totem as the Bear, and to be able to take on a body of casually superhuman strength and endurance. The temptation never to return to human form must grow strong in these harsh places.

Most nights, Loud Thunder fell asleep as soon as the camp was laid, trusting to the fire to keep away inquisitive beasts. Maniye and Hesprec were both more concerned about inquisitive *people* – and of course Broken Axe would be trailing them, invisible and silent and yet always present in her mind. The equinox, at the Stone Place, would mark the end of his promise, the return of his hunt. She could only hope that he would not try to seize her in front of all the priests of the Crown of the World. It might seem an act to invite bad fortune, but Broken Axe was a man who would dare anything.

They shared the watches, the two of them. Her keen wolf nose alternated with whatever alien senses a coiled serpent could muster; that was all they had against the hostile world. When it was her turn to sleep, she tucked herself against Loud Thunder's slumbering bulk for warmth. When it was Hesprec's, he slid his sinuous form into her pack and curled up there.

Most nights, when she was left the only one awake, she tried to think of what best to do. Living in Loud Thunder's shadow, she had not needed a plan, and each day had drawn in the next without any concern save to survive the winter. Now she was forced to confront the fact, once again, that she had no thought for the future save to move on into it and never retrace her steps. She was aware that everything she did only bought her a little more sunlight. That night must close on her was inevitable: whether it was captivity or death at the hands of her own people, or the inexorable rift between her souls.

But, while I can run, I'll run.

***

Elsewhere, following his own path, Water Gathers and a band of his hunters travelled on wolf feet towards the Stone Place.

He had already lost valuable time because he had bid his retinue lie in wait for Akrit Stone River. It was plain that the shedding of one man's blood now might spare the lives of many others later, if the Wolf should find itself tearing at its own.

But Stone River was a canny hunter, a man who had grown old and cunning during times of war and peace. He had found another route, even here in the heart of Many Mouths territory, so that Water Gathers had waited in vain.

The southerners and their guides had passed by, and he had been on the point of ordering an attack on them, remembering the death of Sure As Flint and the humiliation that it had brought with it.

Recollection of that yellow-eyed monster which the black man had turned into had stayed his hand. Who knew what losses such a creature might inflict; who knew what the black man's friends could do? He had been burned before by not knowing. Now he found that something else held him back. He would not acknowledge it as fear, so perhaps it was wisdom.

Every tribe of the Wolf, indeed every tribe of the Crown of the World, would have eyes present at the Stone Place. Water Gathers would speak to them all there, one by one, in the name of his departed and respected father. He would court the Swift Backs and the Moon Eaters, and he would tell stories of Stone River's weakness. What was a man without sons, after all? Be he never so great a warrior or a hunter, how could he call himself a man when his seed was weak?

***

Akrit Stone River was leading his pack through the dense forest, following a curving path towards the Stone Place. He had seen the look in Water Gathers' eyes, and he had weighed the odds. Seven Skins' son could bring more warriors than he himself had, certainly, but could he bring the strength of will? The chance of turning that suspected ambush back on itself was tempting, just to rid the world of his strongest rival.

But, in the end, he set his path away from the easy trails leading from the Many Mouths village. He told himself he did not like the odds. He told himself that if Water Gathers escaped, then there would be open war between their tribes and that would profit nobody except the Tiger.

Akrit's people travelled armed and armoured – the weight of iron and bronze did not slow down the wolf in them once they had shed their human shapes. They took the nights without fires, huddled together for warmth. They brought down what game they came across, and stayed as briefly as they could to gorge on it before setting forth again. Young deer, they took: bucks too reckless to know fear, too slow to escape. And some of the deer they took were men: errant herders and foragers caught unawares between the trees. All were as one to the Wolf.

They travelled by night and by day, breaking to sleep at irregular intervals, two or three days apart, making up in speed what they lost by their tortuous route. Always one or two were ranging further from the pack, pushing themselves ahead or stringing outwards to the sides, keeping a sharp eye out for the Many Mouths.

It was not Water Gathers' people who eventually found them. Towards the end of their journey, after many days travelling, a familiar figure was abruptly pacing Akrit, loping easily alongside him as though he had never left.

Akrit fetched to a halt, his people forming an uncertain scattering behind him. For a moment he looked into the pale eyes of the wolf before him and fully expected a challenge. *What has changed since I was last home?*

276

But then the newcomer Stepped, hands open to signify peace, and Akrit followed suit.

'Broken Axe,' he named the man. 'How goes your hunt?'

23

Where three rivers and the run-off from a score of hillsides met, the land was boggy all throughout the year, and the first melt of spring transformed it into a great swamp so vast and hungry it could have swallowed the world. No tribes lived here, though the swamp was rich and fecund enough that many came to gather and fish. And sometimes they died there, when the shifting ground ebbed suddenly from beneath their feet. It was said that the quicksands did not even let animal souls escape. True or not, enough had died there in their human shapes, smothering in the mud, that the swamp was crowded with ghosts. Priests travelled there to draw secrets from that buried mother-lode of the dead. On some nights even the least sensitive could see the lost souls drifting over the treacherous ground, glowing with pale fire.

In the heart of the swamp there was a great island: no natural thing, it had been raised by the hands of men in an earlier age, earth set upon earth until they had conquered even the hunger of the swamp. Those ancients had raised a causeway towards it, a narrow processional path that was the only fixed and safe road through the quagmire. They had fetched the stones, the monoliths of bluish rock hewn from the mountains of the north. They had hauled them over the miles of rugged, broken ground, and they had floated them across the marsh, and then had set them upright on the island.

Knowledge of whose hands had wrought all of this was lost.

Every tribe claimed the marvel for their own forebears. Looking down the causeway's length to that island, Maniye felt an abrupt certainty that it had been not one tribe but many. Somehow there had been a time, forgotten over the generations, when the peoples of the Crown of the World had come together united. And when they had stood together in one place, not even the earth nor the seasons nor the great spirits had been able to curtail their ambitions. They had remade the world.

That thought came to her almost with the force of a physical thing, stopping her in her tracks so that Hesprec and Loud Thunder walked on a little and then turned, each wearing his own frown. For a moment she felt that she had come upon an absolute certainty, although she could not have mustered a single argument to defend it. She felt that some invisible ghost of the marsh had whispered a secret truth to her.

She also had no intention of exposing herself to the mockery of either of the men, and so she skipped along to catch them up, and would not respond to their questions.

There were others travelling to the Stone Place, but not so many. This was not a gathering for all the tribes, just priests and their retinues. She could see tents set on the island already, in separate little huddles. There would be plenty of old rivalries there around the ring of the stones. Everyone would be very careful not to draw down the ire of the spirits, not to foul the coming year for themselves and their people. But, at the same time, everyone would keep one hand close to a knife hilt while the priests indulged in their contests of magic, riddles and lore.

If the other two had shown the faintest reluctance, then she would have allowed herself second thoughts. Loud Thunder just kept shambling along as though he had not noticed where they were, though. His dogs trotted at his heels, with the empty sled dragging behind them.

And Hesprec . . . a change had come over the old Serpent ever since they had reached the edge of the marsh. She wondered what he saw now with his priestly eyes. For him, did the waters hold the empty faces of the drowned dead? Did the air glow palely with the power of this place? His spine was straighter than it had been, his head held high. A look had come to his face that she did not like: hard and cruel and *old*, in a way he had not looked old before. Old like stories. Old like the Stone Place itself.

Then he caught her looking at him, and something in her expression made him smile and shrug, just the same old vagrant she had fled across the Crown of the World with. But that other look returned once he thought she was not looking.

'What will you do?' The sound of her own voice seemed an intrusion, and she felt the still waters soak it up and resent it. She needed to break out of her own thoughts though. She had never counted herself as someone sensitive to the invisible world before, but their approach to the Stone Place was weighing on her in a strange way.

'I must speak to my Mother,' Thunder muttered sullenly. 'But perhaps there is somewhere I can take you, before then?'

There was pitiful hope there, as he seized on any excuse to put off his own duty, but she could think of no answer. She had hoped that she might just tag along with him. Apparently that was not an option.

'There are people Hesprec must see,' she announced proudly, trying to show off at least a little reflected glory. Then she caught the Serpent's expression and flinched from it. 'What?'

'Little one,' he told her carefully, 'I seek the secret wisdom of the priests, if they will part with it. To my ears alone they may speak.'

A shock of betrayal went through her. 'Then what am I supposed to do?'

'I would ask that you wait for me.' He had the grace to look embarrassed. 'I am sorry, but you are no priest. These matters are deep and terrible. Happier for you that you do not know them.'

'So it's better for me to know that something "deep and terrible" is going on, but not what it is?' Maniye demanded.

Loud Thunder chuckled. 'I think she is more than ready for your secrets, old man.'

Hesprec hissed in exasperation. 'If I go as a priest from the River, and alone, then perhaps they might speak to me – if they do not kill me. If there is any respect left in all of this cold land. If I go with a fugitive Wolf girl, then they will see me as part of their feuds and rivalries and little wars, and they will judge me, and close their minds against me, and I shall learn nothing. And they will have one more reason to do harm to me. I have travelled—'

'For a thousand years over a hundred mountains and twenty deserts and under the earth, and all the rest of the nonsense,' agreed Thunder. 'Girl, when I go to my Mother, I will find you a hearth amongst her people. They will feed you and shelter you, while I do what I must do there.'

Maniye took a few quick steps until she was ahead of him and could look up into his face. 'Why?'

He smiled a little – which was as much as he ever really smiled. 'Why are you not dead in the snow, Many Tracks?'

The words, and his using Broken Axe's name for her, made her skitter backwards, until her heels were at the causeway's very edge. 'What do you mean?'

'Why are you not back with your kin, as their prisoner? Why did I not cast you into winter's teeth after you outstayed your welcome?' Still he was smiling, but for a moment she could not read him, or square his words with that expression. Then he made an expansive gesture, taking in himself, and her, and invisible connections to the rest of the world. 'Look at you: how you will not give up, you will not go away. Everything in the world you take between your teeth and shake it, to see what use to you it will be. You are a fierce little hunter, Maniye Many Tracks. You remind me of why I went south when I was young.'

She saw Wolf tents on the island, several groupings of them. The sight had her creeping in Loud Thunder's shadow, almost under his feet. Of course there would be Wolves here: the Moon Eaters lived close, and she saw banners that she thought were Swift Backs, too. And the Winter Runners, of course. Her home was south of here, but not so very far. Most likely Kalameshli himself would be present.

Would he try to seize her, even here, under the stern gaze of the invisible world? If he could catch her alone, she guessed he might, but not as long as she stayed in company. Likewise Broken Axe, who must surely either be here or be close behind her. They would have to wait until the gathering was over.

She thought this, and then she examined her own thinking. Kalameshli Takes Iron was a cruel man, the tormentor of her childhood, the man who drove her before him with a switch. He would not be here alone: a handful of hunters, at least, would have come as his pack. Would he not just take what he wanted, as the Winter Runners so often did?

And yet she did not quite believe it. It was the aura of the Stone Place; the air was thick with it. She could feel the tenuous balance of this place, and she knew nobody would wish to disturb it, to have it lash back across them like a bowstring. *I am more of a priest than you know, old man*, she thought, remembering Hesprec's dismissive words.

There were other little camps too. One was just a single ungainly tent composed of overlapping hides stitched over a round frame that stood almost twice Maniye's height. There were a couple of hearths set out in the open nearby, and some mounds of fur that Maniye assumed were just piles of hides. Then one of them moved, and she realized that she was looking at the Cave Dwellers.

There were no more than half a dozen there, and all of those she saw were men. There were none quite as big as Loud Thunder nor as tall as Lone Mountain, but every one of them was huge, nonetheless.

'Old man,' Loud Thunder said, as they drew near, 'you had best come meet my Mother. If you are looking for wisdom, then she is more wise than any other in the Crown of the World. If I ask it, she will speak with you – and probably not kill you.'

'How kind,' Hesprec replied faintly.

They arrived among the Cave Dwellers in a flurry of dogs. As Matt and Yoff drew close, there were a dozen of them already on their feet and barking uproariously. Thunder's dogs were no better, the pair straining at the sled's traces until he let them run free. Maniye feared the animals would tear each other apart, but it was simply that she had never lived with dogs before. The yapping chaos was resolved as simple greetings, Matt and Yoff renewing their acquaintance with their relatives. The Bear tribe themselves had a rather more reserved greeting for their way-ward son. One by one, the big men stood up, faces closed and sullen, staring as Loud Thunder drew near. Then, with shocking suddenness, they were all bears, standing tall on their hind legs. Maniye remembered then how he and Lone Mountain had fought when they met, and she stopped walking and started backing away. Hesprec was right beside her.

Loud Thunder Stepped as well, but did not slow his pace, and then all of the Cave Dwellers were bellowing at him, some dropping down on all fours, some standing as tall as they could. They seemed to be working themselves up for a fight, and Maniye could not imagine how Thunder imagined he might win against so many. He just ambled on, though, and they roared and shook their jaws at him, and yet none of them quite stood directly in his way. Then one got too close, and Thunder cuffed the smaller bear across the muzzle, sending it loping off sideways. The defiance of the others petered out slowly, until Loud Thunder reached the middle of them and sat down, blithely unconcerned, scratching at his belly. One by one, the Cave Dwellers gave up their show of protest, returning to their hulking human shapes and grudgingly giving the newcomer room. Maniye had the impression that the natural Cave Dweller demeanour was dour to the point of sulking, a people slow to demonstrate their emotions and slow to act. Looking at them now, the gathering together of such a weight of muscle and dense bone, she was glad of it.

'This girl has my protection,' Loud Thunder declared, directing a broad hand at her. 'The old Snake, too. My hearth is their hearth. They are my guests.'

That went down as poorly as she had anticipated but, now that he had arrived and established his place amongst them, his word obviously carried sufficient weight. When she moved to sit by the fire, they regarded her with dull curiosity, but made room.

'Now you wait,' Thunder advised the pair of them. 'Now we all wait. Mother will send for me, and she and I will have our talk, at last. She will tell me how the world is going to be, and what it wants with me.'

'Serpent guide you,' Hesprec said softly.

'Old man, this is the Mother of Bears. She could break your Serpent in one hand. Only thank your god that he drew out your years long enough to see the Stone Place and its business.'

The Snake priest lowered himself down beside Maniye and closed his eyes. She wondered if he was preparing himself for his own promised meeting, whenever that might happen, and tried to imagine how formidable this woman must be. Certainly all the Bear tribe were keeping a respectful distance from that single tent.

'Will you tell her your stories of Serpent?' she asked Hesprec.

The old priest shrugged his bony shoulders. 'Who can say?'

'Tell me.'

'Stories of Serpent?'

'Tell me what you've come here to find. Tell me what you think she knows. Make me understand.' Because the unseen was pressing on her eyes, and she felt it was trying to tell her something beyond her comprehension.

But Hesprec just hunched his shoulders and began coughing again, long enough to leave him weak and gasping.

Thereafter he was plainly too deeply lost within his own priestliness to have any more time for her, so she got up from the fire and padded over to where she felt the edge of the Cave Dweller camp must be. The sky was darkening now, and a little stubborn snow was feathering down to become one with the chill waters of the marsh. Little fires had sprung up everywhere around the island, save for the darkness between the stones themselves. A grand bonfire was set there, she had seen, but plainly it was for other purposes than keeping anyone warm.

She narrowed her eyes, examining the other supplicants arrived here for the equinox. There were broad, heavy-set Boar people, all layered hides and necklaces of teeth and tusks. She saw the long limbs of the Deer tribe, a familiar sight to her. Antlers graced the brows of their priests, and at the neighbouring fire a handful of them were stepping through the movements of a dance to the low patter of a drum.

A handful of Wolves passed nearby, and she forced herself not to shrink back. They were Moon Eaters, from their paint and clothes, and talking quietly amongst themselves. One of them barked out a brief laugh as they passed, but none spared her even a glance. Crossing from the other direction came a trio of Eyriemen, and there was a tense moment when one or other needed to give way, and neither group would. Then some unspoken accord was reached, and both bands took an exaggerated step aside, and in the space now between them was the secret of this place, the same spirit that hung about the stones, strong and wise and unforgiving.

There were other camps, too, and in the growing dusk it was hard to make out who kept which hearth. One drew her eye, though, as if there was a presence at her elbow pointing it out. The figures there seemed to be warriors, armoured in bronze polished to a gleaming shine that threw back their firelight. Somehow she knew they were priests as well. She saw gold glinting at their wrists and, wherever the fire picked out their skins, it found them striped with painted shadows.

People of the Tiger. And a spark was lit in her then that would not go out.

'How long will you wait?' she asked Loud Thunder.

He shrugged morosely. 'Always, with Mother, it is others who do the hurrying.'

'Days?'

'Most likely.'

She looked across the island, sounding out her own daring. This was the Stone Place. This was the still centre in the roiling turmoil that was the Crown of the World.

The voice of the invisible sounded strong within her. It told her to go explore, to step out from the Bear's Shadow. The island seemed alive with it, with a host of sightless entities that wanted her to move amongst them so that they could see her better. She could almost feel their spectral fingers trailing across her skin.

At first she meant to wait until morning. The sun was falling to earth in a welter of spilled red, and soon there would be darkness, with the treacherous marsh on all sides.

And she could not sleep anyway. She lay there, with Hesprec's bony body curled up on one side of her, and the vast snoring mountains of the Bears all around, and her mind was like a leaf bobbing in the waters, constantly dancing and dancing. It came to her then that she had no plan for the future. Hesprec's south was a fool's dream to hold on to, and one that the old man himself would surely never attain, let alone some vagrant Wolf girl he might choose to bring along with him. It came to her then – or at least she finally admitted it to herself – that Hesprec would die soon. He was hard and stubborn enough to fend off the winter, but the Crown of the World made all its guests work hard for the privilege of their keep.

She had come to a place where priests of every tribe were peering into the mists of the marsh to know the future, while she just looked ahead and saw a void. She was a creature of the moment, fleeting and transient.

She Stepped to her wolf's shape and rose silently, slipping between the bulky shapes of her hosts, and out into the night.

At first she intended heading straight for the Tigers' fire. Perhaps – she had not totally decided – she would even walk straight up to them, show them what shape she could assume, show them that *I am of you*. She imagined it all, daydreamed it in detail even as she left the Bears' hearth. She assured herself what it would feel like to step from under the Wolf's Shadow and into the embrace of a different god. Even while she wore the Wolf's own shape, she thought it. Perhaps that was why her feet led her astray.

Despite the fires, it was very dark in the Stone Place. Above her, the stars were shrouded, mocking those below who might seek to fish the future from their pond. Her wolf nose was battered by a multitude of scents: the bodies, fires and food of a dozen tribes. Abruptly she found that she could not tell which of the leaping lights of the island were nearby, and which were all the way across it.

Trying to shake off her uncertainty, she pushed forwards with a sudden flurry of speed. Ever since leaving the Winter Runners, she had raced through the world as though distance itself was a cure for all ills, and now it betrayed her. Abruptly the land was clear on either side, just the packed earth of this artificial hill . . . and then there were the stones.

They rose above her, to the left and to the right, great dark sentinels that she sensed more than saw. In a convulsive moment she felt as if something had gripped hold of her – intangible and irresistible, stripping her skin from her, nose to tail. A moment later she was in her tiger shape, its keener eyes harvesting distant firelight so as to make out the tall, still monoliths rising before her. For a brief moment she felt that the wolf was gone, totally gone, and scrabbled with unexpected panic within her, searching out all its old haunts one by one. Then she had it again, cowering at the very back of her mind, while the tiger in her was so bold . . .

She had almost run straight inside the circle of stones. She had almost crossed into the eye of the Stone Place, where the spirits watched all the time. Only priests went there and, though she had pretended to herself that she felt like a priest, now she knew she was nothing but a fugitive girl. If she had taken another handful of steps . . .

Who could know? But she would be marked forever. To stand before the greater spirits even a priest must purify himself and sacrifice and beg.

Her eyes caught the approach of more lights: a line of torches emerging from one of the camps, and she froze, torn between the desires to flee and to spy.

Their own fires picked them out for her, and her tiger's heart jumped – for it was her people, her own people, the ones she had never known.

A woman led them, who wore mail of bronze squares and an ornate helm with a feathered crest. The skin of her cheeks was raised in thin lines that the torchlight turned into dancing shadow-stripes. Behind her followed two men, their faces solemn. They had some of the look of the people Maniye had grown up with, but with something else as well. Their eyes were angled, their faces longer. There was a mystery written into them. To Maniye, they were beautiful.

She followed their progress, crouching close to the base of the closest stone. They were tracing a curving path, and she knew they were making for some special point, some invisible path known only to the Tiger, by which the circle could be entered.

Turning to keep them in view, she realized her error.

She traced the line of the stones with her eyes. The circle was simple, just a ring of irregular, jutting fingers with a single squat altar in its very centre. As the torches neared, many of the stones leapt into relief, casting their shifting shadows across the ground, across the circle that they enclosed.

The circle that she was *inside*. She had bounded straight into it, and only been brought to a halt by the stones on the far side.

She knew then that it was the coming of the Tiger to these stones that had Stepped her into this shape. If she had just been some hapless Wolf girl, then surely she would have been punished: struck blind, driven mad, killed on the spot. The spirits could do such things.

With this new knowledge, though, she could not stay. Half-belong as she might, she could not trespass within the circle during a Tiger ritual. There was reckless, and there was outright foolhardy.

She held her breath as she backed out between the stones, between the same two pillars that she'd thought had been keeping her from going *in*. Casting a glance behind her, she saw the three Tigers now enter the circle, their priestess at the fore.

Moving further away, she could see more. Her eyes caught a deeper darkness between the fires, and after a moment she identified it: spies, other spies. Of course, any who chose to look up the hill towards the Stones might see something of what passed between the Tiger and their god, but these – whoever these were – they had drawn closer.

Still clad in her tiger shape, she circled them, closing carefully, wondering who it was that took such an interest in her people.

Yet who else but her *other* people? She stopped dead-still because she had recognized a face she knew. Yes, yes, there was Kalameshli Takes Iron, and the sight of him sent a jolt of fear and hatred through her, a short lifetime's worth of taunts and goads flurrying through her head like snow. A moment later he was almost forgotten though.

Akrit Stone River was here too. He knelt on the ground, a man with patience to spare, and stared at the stones and the three votaries within. The two Shadow Eater men were singing now: one low and one high, an eerie counterpoint that seemed to rise up into the clouded sky and resonate through the earth.

Their torchlight barely touched Akrit's eyes, lurking there as the faintest of angry embers.

She began to back away. Their attention was fixed on the ritual. The spirits had blessed her this much: that she had spotted them first.

It was the fur of her flanks that told her of the other: not her nose, nor eyes nor ears. When she twitched away from him, he was close enough to reach out and take her by the scruff of the neck.

Broken Axe regarded her expressionlessly – no, not quite: there was a slight twitch to his lips, a token amusement at having found her yet again.

She had frozen in shock, and she saw his eyes flick towards the gathering of Wolves and to the Tiger ritual beyond. A shout from him would bring Akrit and Kalameshli both down on her back. She was caught, helpless and immobile, torn between leaping and fleeing.

Then that seed of a smile grew a little, and he shrugged and turned away, strolling over towards the other Wolves, not a hint of hurry in his steps.

She fled then, but he never called the alarm, and her father never knew she had been there.

24

The Tiger ritual had been disconcerting: a familiar message yet written in an alien tongue. The woman who stood in for their priest, and her two eunuch servants, they had gone through strange steps, made unfamiliar offerings, and yet Akrit felt he understood. Watching from out in the dark, he had seen an urgency in those motions, an invocation of martial preparedness. The Tiger tribe, too, were readying for conflict.

'There is a time coming,' Kalameshli confirmed, later. 'The spirits speak of it. My dreams – the dreams of many priests here – are disturbed by it. So the Tiger hear the same voices. They do not know your plans.'

Akrit had never concerned himself that the Tiger might be readying themselves to defend against him. He was struck by the sudden thought that his own plan – the plan he had been nursing all these years – might not be *his* plan at all. What if it had merely been gods and spirits working through him? He knew many who might be proud of playing such a role, but not he. Akrit Stone River was, above all, his own master. The Wolf wished no cringing thralls amongst those born in his Shadow.

The morning after, and keyed up by Kalameshli's words, he went to speak with the priests of the Moon Eaters, who were here in force. He needed to present himself to them, to win their blessing. He needed to have them thinking of him as the next High Chief.

And yet, when he reached them, it seemed he was a man come second to the feast. The hard, derisive eyes of Water Gathers stared out at him from the midst of the priests.

'Stone River,' began the son of Seven Skins, 'who would have thought to find you here? What purpose can you have, so far from home?'

Catches The Moon, the young priest of the Many Mouths, was lurking in his shadow, and there were plenty of sidelong glances shared between the Moon Eaters.

'I have told these wise men of the passing of my father,' Water Gathers explained expansively. 'All agree he departed from his tribe as a strong man, a warrior, should.'

'He did,' Stone River agreed. 'He was a man we shall not see again for a generation. Would that more were like him.'

The twitch at the corner of Water Gathers' mouth was slight, and utterly unamused. 'I have told them also of my father's last words to me: how he bid me follow in his tracks, how he marked me for greatness. I am my father's son, his heart, his all. I was his joy, when he still lived amongst us; to see me in my strength was what gave him the strength to leave his people in my care.'

'So much he told you.' Akrit could sense Kalameshli right behind him, the old man urging him silently to hold his temper. 'And yet I guested with your brother, a fine man and a wise one, and it seems your father had said not a word of this to him.'

'My brother Otayo is no hunter,' Water Gathers replied contemptuously. 'He brought my father neither joy nor solace by tending hearth while his mate sought prey.'

They are already with him more than with me, Akrit thought, letting his peripheral vision inform him of the Moon Eaters' disposition, even as he kept his eyes fixed squarely on his opponent. He knew what he wanted to say, and also he knew that those words could never be taken back. They would fan the hatred of Water Gathers into a high burning fire that might consume either or both of them.

And he realized that he was going to say them anyway. He

was losing face moment to moment. No man would follow a High Chief who turned his back.

'I, too, spoke with your father before his passing,' Akrit said softly, making them lean in to hear more clearly. 'It is true he said much of you. You were uppermost in his thoughts. But he was also my friend, my teacher, like unto my own father. We began the rising against the Tiger that drove them into the high places, and we finished it, he and I. Who else can boast the same that lives now?' *Not Water Gathers, certainly.* 'He spoke fondly of Otayo but, like you, he lamented your brother's choice to keep a home rather than to lead the hunt. For, if your brother had taken up the bow and the spear, your father would not have to lament your becoming chief of the Many Mouths.'

The Moon Eaters had gone quiet and still, recognizing that moment in a fight where wrestling and blows are no longer enough, and the knives are drawn.

'He was a honed blade, your father. Even in his last days he had a keen edge to him. Even sick, he was a man I would follow into the fire. And you are no blade, but a maul. You are a blunt striker, without wisdom or subtlety. You are not the man to follow Maninli Seven Skins.'

The words struck home like arrows, but Water Gathers was still standing firm, braced against them. There was only one brief moment when his mask cracked, and Akrit could see into his soul. He saw there more self-knowledge than he had expected. He saw that Water Gathers knew all of what his father had thought of him, and that becoming High Chief in Maninli's place was the only way he could erase the burning venom of that knowledge.

'And yet I am a man,' Water Gathers spat. 'I say my father loved me, and he saw himself in me. And in my sons, Stone River, my sons who shall carry the blood of Seven Skins down to their own sons. We have heard the wind of your words. Now show us your sons. Show us what the loins of the Winter Runners can fruit.'

293

'I will show you,' snarled Akrit, and yet he had none, and not even the girl to bring before them. *And if I had her, I'd tell them precisely what I would bring for the Wolf, with her at my side. If I had her, I'd have her here to beat them with. If . . . If . . .*

Amongst the Stones was a bad place to be, Asmander had decided. They all felt it: the northern spirits of place bending their gaze upon the three travellers. Shyri was skittish, jumping at shadows. Venater brooded and glowered, his flinty eyes stabbing out at anyone who looked his way, meeting the savagery of the north with savagery of his own.

A spirit place. And of course the Riverlands had such places of their own, but most of them had been built upon, weighed down with stone and garlanded with priests until they became something else, something that was a part of the Sun River Nation. Asmander had no sense that this place was a part of the Crown of the World in the same way, if for no other reason than there *was* no single Crown of the World. Just like the Plains, this was a fragmented place where men had never learned to live together. And just like the Plains, it was a foolhardy place to venture unprepared.

Asmander felt unprepared. He had come to treat with the heart of the north, but found it had no heart. The invisible presence that swathed this place like a miasma, and pricked up the hairs on his arms, was a divided and many-faced monster.

The two Coyote had left them as soon as they crossed the causeway, as though being seen with the southerners would be bad for their own reputations. The pair were priests, he had realized. All this time travelling with them, thinking of them as itinerant pedlars, when they had come here for their own devotions. Asmander tried to work out just who had used whom the most, in getting here.

'Wishing you'd not come?' Venater's rough tone grated in his ear.

'The lucky man's wishes are ignored by the world. The luck-less man's are granted,' Asmander replied, the old saying falling from his lips by rote.

'You'll go hunting this Stone River, if he's even here?'

'He's here,' Shyri's voice broke in. 'I saw one of his people – one of his warriors from the Wolf place. And he was watching us.'

'We cut such fine figures, who would not?' Asmander re-marked drily. The three of them were indeed attracting a lot of attention. Leather-skinned northerners stared at them as though they were ill-loved figures from legend, stopping in their tracks to glower at the three travellers. More than that, though, there was a constant pressure about them, a flexing of the air, a brist-ling of the ground. The Stone Place did not know them; the Stone Place did not like them.

'First things first: we will set a fire,' Asmander directed. 'In the morning, we shall see what we can accomplish.' He looked up at the louring sky, feeling that same great presence bear down on him. He wanted to fight it. He wanted to run. He wanted to shed his human form.

'I will not perform for you,' he whispered.

The next morning he woke slowly. Whatever the northern spring might be like, the world was still bitterly cold, and none of the Horse Society's gifted clothing could change that. The fire had died, and the three of them had been huddled close together, Shyri curled into him, and Venater's broad back against his own.

He had not slept well, waking often to stare up at a sky full of scudding clouds, at the cold and distant constellations. He could pick out plenty that he had a name for, but they seemed differ-ent here, refusing to acknowledge him. This was a northern sky and, like the Stones, it did not know him.

And he knew that the local people would be the same, unless he did something about it. If he just went from hearth to hearth and badgered them for aid, then it would not matter what he promised them. He first needed to cut himself a place in their world. And not just the craggy, boggy, freezing hell that was the Crown of the World. He needed to engage with the world of their traditions and their observances. He needed to touch the invisible here at the Stone Place.

With a chill, clouded dawn clawing at the eastern sky like a corpse from its grave, he kicked the other two awake.

'I am about to do something reckless,' he informed them.

'What's new?' Venater responded promptly, but the old pirate's eyes flicked towards the jutting fingers of the stones, and Asmander nodded.

'What if you die of it?' he asked – not quite an angry demand, yet certainly nothing as human as concern.

'If the locals kill me, I expect you both to go down valiantly before their blades in an attempt to prolong my life,' Asmander told him, eliciting a snort of derision. 'If I am struck down or driven mad or whatever by . . . by the powers here, then you're just plain out of luck, Child of Venat.'

'You're serious? You're going to piss on their gods?' Shyri demanded.

'What? No!' Asmander snapped back. 'That is how you go about things on the Plains, is it?'

'Certainly it is. We find a holy place of another tribe, piss on it's the least we do. How else to keep our enemies' gods weak?'

Asmander shook his head. 'Well, thank you. Suddenly this desolate place seems somehow more civilized in comparison.' He was about to go marching off towards the stones, when she snagged his shoulder.

'Wear this.' It was a necklace of polished discs, weirdly textured. He had seen it on her sometimes. She had a bag of similar pieces and swapped between them, for unspoken reasons of her own.

'If this is another pissing-contest thing, then I won't.'

'This was passed to me by my mother – my real mother, and

she had it from hers. The horns it is cut from belonged to a tribe wiped from the Plains in the story-times, the long-ago times. Like the Aurochs, they have gone back to their beasts, and my people drove them to it. So: this is strength, this trinket. This is triumph. I lend you the strength of the Laughing Men through all the years. We know no masters and there is nothing we will not do. That is our creed. Wear this, and carry our strength to the northern gods.'

Genuinely touched, Asmander took the cord and looped it over his head. The horn discs were an unfamiliar burden on his chest, heavy in a way their mere weight could not account for.

'That's a fine creed, girl,' Venater said softly.

'One your people would recognize,' Asmander noted, and the pirate nodded solemnly.

Then it was time: the sun was dragging itself clear of the horizon, a finger's breadth at a time, as Asmander strode towards the stark pillars at the heart of the island. The other two fell in behind him and, both at once and yet with no spoken signal, they Stepped, so that he approached the heart of the north with a spotted hyena padding to his left, and a sprawling, whip-tailed dragon on his right, the dawn light glittering on its black scales.

They stopped on reaching the stones themselves, though. It was only Asmander who stepped through into that circular space, to drop to his knees before the altar. By then, a great many eyes were fixed on him.

He bowed his head: not in reverence but merely as an aid to concentration. With his eyes closed, he could feel the hostility surging in on him in waves from all sides, from every stone. It was not a personal dislike, not the price of anything he had done. It was the place itself reacting to the child of another land, of different gods.

So, here I am, he addressed the stones in his mind.

I am the First Son of Asman. But that will mean nothing to you. Why should you care who my father is, after all?

I am born of the clan of the Bluegreen Reach – and on the banks of the Tsotec that is a good thing to be. But it is nothing to you, and who would blame you?

I am a Champion of the Sun River Nation. I am a scion of Old Crocodile, bearing a warrior soul within me, a soul from out of time. I can Step into a shape you never saw, a beast of the myth-times that no man ever hunted.

Ah, I have your interest, then? For he could feel the vast, invisible attention of the place shifting around him, like great stone blocks.

I have come a long way to stand before your people. You are mighty and I am but a man, yet I have seen sights that most of your people cannot dream of. I have seen Atahlan the beautiful and fought pirates amongst the estuary islands. I have hunted with the Laughing Men, and have stood in the dead city of the Stone People.

With his eyes closed, it was easy to believe that a ring of people surrounded him, close enough to touch. Perhaps they did. Perhaps killers of the northern tribes had crept up to avenge this slight offered to their holy place. The temptation to open his eyes, to reach out for them, was like a fire under his skin. To do so would ruin everything though.

I have earned my place here, he told the stones. *I have fought Sure As Flint, champion of the Many Mouths tribe, and I have sent his soul onwards to be reborn amongst the wolf packs. As who I am means nothing in this land, recognize me for my deeds.*

And he stood up smoothly, with his eyes still tight shut. One hand found the steel dagger he had killed Sure As Flint with, and he drew its blade across the back of his arm, feeling the sensation as cold more than pain. He held the metal in place there, letting his blood slick it, turning it so that both sides were greasy with redness. Then he laid it on the altar. *What belongs to the Crown of the World, I return to it. Take it, take my blood. Know me and recognize me.*

Stepping away, the sudden absence of that fierce pressure

almost made him stumble. He felt a gathering of powers knotting with the louring clouds above, twisting and coiling across one another.

There was thunder, but it was distant as the mountains, dismissive like the shrugging of gods. Nothing struck him down. He felt no curse descend upon him. The north did not have to like him, but it had withdrawn its enmity a little, giving him some time and room.

He turned and walked back to the other two, meeting none of the northern gazes that lit upon him.

'Who knows?' he told them, as he made that last step, the one which took him out of the circle, out of the direct focus of the Crown of the World. *Who knows what I have accomplished?*

Venater twitched his head sideways pointedly, and only then did Asmander see a third figure there, lurking in the shadow of one of the stones at the outer edges of the circle. His eyes went wide when he saw what manner of man the newcomer was.

A Serpent priest: just about the last man Asmander would have looked for here in the cold north. An ancient Serpent, his skin gone pale and brittle, grey beneath his eyes and in the hollows of his sunken cheeks crossed by the faded snakeskin tracks of his devotion. He wore Horse Society cast-offs, just like Asmander and his fellows, but here was a withered old man of the south, nonetheless.

'You dare more than I would, Champion of the Riverlands,' the priest said softly. For a moment the hair stood up on Asmander's neck, that this man should know him and his soul so quickly. In the next, he guessed that such information had come from the loose lips of Shyri or Venater.

He realized that he had tensed up, waiting for some terrible pronouncement from the old man, but the priest merely shook his head slightly.

'My name is Hesprec Essen Skese, and I have been travelling a long time, and it is good to see faces that I recognize. Let me be a guest at your hearth, just for a brief while, and I will ask the blessing of Serpent for you, and then we may talk of warmer places.'

It was close to midday the following day when Loud Thunder's Mother finally sent for him. Lone Mountain ambled up, and Maniye wondered if the pair would start fighting again, but they just stared at each other until Thunder nodded and sloped off towards the single tent. Maniye tried to trail in his wake but he turned and looked at her in a way that told her she was not welcome there. This was the heart of the Bear's mysteries and not for outsiders.

Lone Mountain now sat down almost exactly where Thunder had been, looking as disconsolate at being kept out as the other man had been unwilling to be called in. She went and sat near him, and tried to think of some way to open a conversation. The great brooding bulk of the Bears warned her off, though. They were all of them built on a different scale to her; they could smash her with a single ill-thought gesture.

Then he glanced towards her, expressionless, and she blurted, 'I like your robe,' before she could stop herself.

He grunted. A moment later she read the sound as amusement. 'I traded many skins for it, to a Horse man. I thought it would make me . . . different.'

She nodded warily. 'Because you want . . .'

'It is not to me she listens,' Lone Mountain said softly. 'It is to the spirits: to Winter and Storm and the Bear. In another season, in a different year, I would be enough. She would call me, and tell me to become war leader, because all the wars would be small wars.'

Maniye felt a curious cold feeling run down her back. 'Wars . . . ?'

Lone Mountain's voice dropped lower, until it became a whisper for her ears only. 'Mother is old. For ten years now we have thought she would soon pass on and leave her human shape behind her. She is close to the spirits, as only one of so many years can be. But is she wise now, or has she gone beyond wisdom into the foolishness of age?' He was not looking at her, but talking as if to order his own thoughts. 'She speaks of a great war and a time of broken laws. She says it will be soon now. She says she has looked in the sky and the water and the earth, and they tell her Loud Thunder must be war leader, or none at all.' His broad shoulders rose and fell.

Maniye was peripherally aware of a low rumble of voices from within the tent, deep enough that she almost felt it through the ground. Now one voice was raised, angry and insistent: as resonant as Thunder's own but a woman's voice nonetheless. Lone Mountain shifted uncomfortably. The other Bear men were paying no heed, some sleeping, one feeding sticks to a fire with a child's all-consuming focus, another knapping a flint with careful, measured strokes. Only Mountain himself seemed to detect the shift of mood. She had the impression that he had travelled more than the rest, spent more time with human beings of other tribes.

She wondered if he had been trying to be like Loud Thunder.

She could hear Thunder's slow tones sounding as though he was patiently explaining something. The other voice cut him off in mid-flow. There was nothing to the rhythm of their speech that suggested they would be finished any time soon. Maniye put a hand briefly to Lone Mountain's arm, a tiny gesture of commiseration, and then backed away from that solitary tent, seeking somewhere where the air was less taut and tense.

There was quite a milling of people in the space between the fires. She saw a handful of the Coyote had laid out blankets, setting out their stock in trade. This would not be their usual goods and gear that they had hawked between villages of the Crown of the World from spring to fall. Instead, here were their special wares: scrimshaw from the Wetback people of the coast; translucent sharp-edged stones stolen from the earth; blades of black glass; glittering statuettes of jasper and greenstone and shining grey false-iron stone. These were trade goods fit for priests, objects of ritual, and the men and women who had brought them here were not pedlars but votaries playing their part in the great dance between spirits and men.

She watched the acolytes of a dozen tribes crouching to pore over the assembled wares, as though divining the future in that scattering of items on the blankets. Everyone here was consumed with purpose, desperate to lure the favour of the coming year. There would be propitiations and ceremonies, dancing and drums. Some would don masks, others would paint their faces. There would be promises made, and sacrifices of precious things. Perhaps the Deer people would have a crowned year-king whose reign was come to an end, or the Eyriemen a girl-child clad in gold to become their messenger to the other world, or the Boar would bring the makings of a god-feast. Every tribe of the Crown of the World had come here with its own traditions and ways, but nevertheless they were all seeking the same thing.

Her eye lit on one particular piece amidst the ceremonial clutter. From somewhere, after how long a journey, had come to the north a carving in a rich green stone. Its shape was foreign, a twined and knotted serpent that seemed to tunnel in and out until it had honeycombed the material that it was composed of. She knew instantly this must be southerner-work, some token of Hesprec's own faith. Although she had nothing to trade for it, she drew closer, thinking what a fine gift it would make for him.

When she had squatted there long enough, knowing that she was wasting her time and yet fascinated by the delicate workmanship, she looked up and found herself staring into the eyes of Kalameshli Takes Iron.

The priest of the Winter Runners had plainly noticed her in the very same moment. For a moment they just stared. She was close enough that he could have reached out and grabbed her, and she felt every muscle tense, ready to Step, ready to spring away.

A terrible expression appeared on his face. It was not what she expected – not the anger that she almost demanded as her

302

due: *here I am – I ran away, I disobeyed.* But Kalameshli had only shock and alarm to offer her. It was as though she had become a figure of fear somehow for the man who had tormented all her growing years.

His hands twitched, but almost to shoo her away rather than to reach for her. And then it was too late. There was another man at Kalameshli's elbow, and it was her father.

Akrit Stone River saw her and his face went dead, every vestige of him withdrawing from it and leaving her no window into his thoughts at all. He was frozen, his body battling itself, and she was still there, still caught on the very point of flight, and around them everyone else continued about their business.

It was the Stone Place, she understood: the sacred place where no man raised a hand against another, save in the name of religion. It was as she had been told: so long as she remained here, and so long as the days of the equinox held, she was safe from the merely worldly ambitions of her father.

But there was a dark and angry look coming to Stone River's face as he stared at her, and she saw Kalameshli raise his hands in warning, not touching his chief, but trying to draw his attention and tap his ire. By now a few of the traders around them had sensed something amiss. She saw one old Coyote flip his blanket over and bundle his goods away hurriedly.

'Girl,' her father got out. 'Come with me.'

She shook her head, finding that she had no words left when facing him. She remembered the weight of his hand, the quick fire of his rage, the coldness of his regard. These had been the milestones of her years. They were her memories of home and family and childhood, and she had shed them like snakeskin when she had absconded with Hesprec.

'You are mine,' Stone River hissed. 'Come with me.' Still he would not actually reach for her, but his head twitched, tugging at her with his authority, demanding that she come meekly to heel.

There was a word rising within her. She felt it coming like a

303

nauseous wave and tried to fight it down, but it flooded her mouth with bile and forced its way out of her lips.

'No,' she said.

And then she had Stepped, because she saw that word impact on Akrit Stone River's composure and tear it open. He lunged for her then, with Kalameshli calling out his name to stop him, but all he got was a handful of hairs from her tail.

Then he had Stepped himself and went pounding after her.

25

The Snake priest stood up abruptly, ritual words forgotten. Asmander stared at him uncertainly. Hesprec Essen Skese had been seeking the Serpent within the earth, digging deep with his mind to find and wake his buried god. He had been speaking softly: familiar words of faith that left Asmander oddly homesick. Strange how he had not really felt that strained tether that was trying to draw him back south until he had run into this reminder of that other invisible world. Until then, he had felt more as if he was running away.

Now the old man was on his feet, benediction forgotten, staring off towards the Stones.

'Messenger,' Asmander addressed him formally, 'has the Serpent spoken to you?'

'Something is wrong.' It emerged as just a murmur from those withered lips, but he caught it.

Without warning, the old priest was off, hurrying away and leaving Asmander caught between a desire to follow and the old understanding that there were deeds of priests that other men were best not knowing about.

In the end he followed though. Even as he set off he felt as though the ground beneath him was suddenly treacherous, as though the swamp itself was rising to reclaim it. He felt a great and unseen fracture threatening in the sky.

Hesprec was hurrying – or as much as he could – to where a

scattering of huge men loomed around a tent. They were all on their feet, looking puzzled and sullenly angry, but uncertain, too, glowering around for whatever had disturbed them. One or two of them Stepped, surging into even larger forms that grunted and shook their heads and bared their fearsome teeth at each other. Asmander had never encountered a bear, but he knew one when he saw it. The stories he had heard about the north did not do them justice.

The flap of the tent rippled, and then a woman shouldered her way out, as big as the men and clad in a vast robe of hides that was sewn all over with bird skulls. Her broad, flat face was turned up to the clouds, and Asmander saw her sniff the air. Her expression was unreadable, totally closed to outside scrutiny.

Hesprec stumbled to a halt, head turning left and right but plainly not finding what he was looking for.

Then Asmander saw a flurry of movement over towards the stones themselves: a fleet, low shape skimming the ground: a small, grey-pelted wolf with a greater beast behind it. He took it for a ritual: a mock-hunt invoking of the greater Wolf they set such stock on here.

Hesprec let out a sharp hiss, and Asmander understood that this was no piece of religious theatre.

The smaller wolf tried to break away towards them, but its pursuer got in front of it, herding it away, driving it towards the stones themselves. Hesprec took a deep breath and began to hurry towards them, but Asmander could see that the hunt would be at an end long before the Serpent could intervene. And here, old and frail and far from his own places of power, what could he do anyway?

Then the little wolf was at bay, trapped with its back to the ring of stones, and Asmander saw it shift into a girl, and its pursuer turn into Akrit Stone River.

By then, Venater and Shyri had caught up with him, both of them equally baffled by what was going on.

'Wondered when he'd show his face,' the old pirate grunted.

'You going to ask him to lend you some warriors? Looks like a perfect time.'

'Stop your lips flapping for once,' Asmander told him tautly. 'Can't you feel it?'

It was plain that Venater couldn't, but to Asmander it was as though the entire island, all the invisible, roiling presences that had gathered here, were bending close to see what the two Wolves would do next.

Maniye could feel the stone circle at her back, like a fire. Her heart was hammering as though she had run herself ragged for two full days. Before her, her father appeared like a monolith himself, as heavy and intractable as the stones.

She could see careful movement as the others fanned out to ensure she did not try to slip aside. There would be Smiles Without Teeth and her father's other hunters and old Kalameshli – all the antagonists of her childhood.

'Child, come here,' Stone River ordered her flatly. He was holding his temper by a thin thread, but he still held it.

She bared her teeth, those silly, blunt human teeth. 'I'm not a child. I passed my trials.'

'You are my blood. You are my tribe. You are born within the Shadow of the Wolf,' he told her. 'You have a purpose, for the Wolf and for me.' He threw a hand out towards her. 'Come here.' It exerted a terrible gravity, that hand. It tugged at her and at all her memories, reminding her of every time she had tried to defy him; reminding her of why she had gone from day to day trying to stay out of even the corner of his eye.

But she fought against it. 'I am Maniye Many Tracks. I hunt alone.' She did not say, *Like Broken Axe*, and she was uncomfortably aware that Broken Axe himself was nowhere she could see.

'You are no hunter.' And he was a step closer, not with a sudden movement, but just a casual shuffle, till that hand was within a lunge of grabbing her. She could feel the Stone Place's presence all about her. She felt as though the whole island held its breath.

'I am Maniye Many Tracks,' she repeated. 'I do not accept you as my – chief.' She choked off the word 'father'. 'I leave the Winter Runners. I am a tribe of one alone until I choose another.' She did not know how she knew the words so well. When had she ever heard them recited? Still, they were the correct words. They were the words of her rights, as one born to the Wolf. Let her leave her tribe: they might hunt her, they might drive her away or even kill her, but they could not force her to be one of them.

But she saw from her father's face that this was not his understanding, and that in his mind she was still a possession of his. He had his use for her, and he would not let her go. She learned then how fragile tradition was when set against human ambition. He was the chief of the Winter Runners, so who would gainsay him?

'Girl,' he said, and then he had lunged for her, the hand darting in to claim its property, and she Stepped and ran in the only direction he had left to her. She fled inside the circle, and he followed on his own wolf feet.

The feeling was like a hammerblow, like running into a gale. She had made a terrible mistake. She was no priest, able to run through the eye of the gods like this. She was cursed, surely she was cursed.

Time seemed to stretch, her dash across the stone circle becoming a trek of hours. She could feel them all and their sharp-edged scrutiny: the hungry, drowning spirit that made this place its own; the killing cold gaze of winter; the impassive distance of the mountains; the vast expanse of the sky; the stars; the moon. Beneath all these, the little huddle of totems that actually recognized the people of the Crown of the World seemed terribly small. Still they were closer, close enough to touch. She sensed their hostile regard, their outrage: Bear, Deer, Boar, Seal, all of them drawing back in horror, preparing their condemnation of her.

Beyond them, two others circled, always at opposite edges of the circle, constantly stalking one another: Wolf and Tiger. For a terrible moment she thought they might make her choose then and there. But, no, they kept at their pacing, watching her. They waited to see what she would do.

There was a groaning weight of fear on her shoulders, the moment she understood what she had done, and yet Tiger and Wolf just circled and watched. She was at the very centre of the circle, and her legs wanted to give up. She was ready to lie down on her side and simply die. This was the will of all the great and distant spirits. A speck had crossed into their sight, and they wanted it gone.

She faltered, mis-stepping, feeling something clench about her heart like a clawed hand. The inside of the circle became like a maze of unseen walls. Abruptly she had lost her bearings. She could not find her way out. The hot breath of Akrit Stone River behind her seemed infinitely less frightening that what she had blundered into.

But there seemed to be a line across the ground, within her sight. A crooked line, but a path nonetheless. It was picked out by a shadow, as though something long and twisted was coursing beneath the earth. A foreign presence, as unwelcome as she was, and yet, though the Wolf might dig and the Boar root, they could not bring it into the light.

Her feet lit on the track of that shadow and then she had found her stride again. Akrit's teeth closed on thin air, and she was out of the circle.

She had only seconds. The other Winter Runners, Akrit's entourage, had split on either side of the stones to flank her, and Akrit was right at her back still. She had been driven away from the Bear camp – as if they would have aided her – and surely at any moment Broken Axe would appear before her to head her off. It was what he did, after all. He was the hunter who knew the mind of his prey every time.

And then there was a sudden flurry of violence behind her, and Akrit was no longer at her back. On her left, Smiles Without Teeth veered away to help his chief, and she cut across where his path would have taken him, pulling away from her pursuers on the other side. She had a brief, blurred glimpse of Akrit and another wolf tumbling over and over, snapping at one another's throats.

Akrit had seen the brief blur of motion from the corner of one eye, even as he was about to edge into a final burst of speed and overrun the girl. Something in that flash of grey told him everything he needed to know: not one of his people coming in to head Maniye off, but an enemy. An enemy born also in the Shadow of the Wolf. There was only one man it could be.

He veered away, so that Water Gathers' fangs just grazed his flank instead of latching onto his leg, and then he had twisted to lunge back, the two of them rising briefly to their hindlegs to snarl and snap at each other, before going down, locked together, forepaws tearing, muzzle twisting past muzzle, as they tried to get their teeth around something vital of their opponent.

He must be mad, to dare this! Akrit was now on the defensive, giving ground and stunned by the sheer presumption. Impressed, almost: he would not have thought that Water Gathers had the warrior's courage to brave the taboos of the island like this.

Another thought came, and he lost another handful of paces, retreating from his antagonist, knowing that some of his people were hanging back around him, unsure whether to aid him or not – or kept back by Water Gathers' own bodyguard.

What if he isn't the transgressor?

What if it's me?

There had been Kalameshli plucking at his sleeve, trying to restrain him, but the girl had been right in front of him, and she had disobeyed him: she had the temerity to tell him *No*. She was his daughter, wilful runt that she was. She was *his*, to do with as he wished.

He lunged without warning at Water Gathers, a brief low duck, as though he was about to submit, and then jaws agape at the other wolf's neck, forcing him back.

And yet the girl was an adult now. By the Wolf's ways, she was free to take up the lone life, and to come and go as she pleased – to live or die by her own meagre skills, if that was what she chose.

But Akrit *needed* her. He needed her as his weapon against the Tiger. In his mind his three prizes circled and circled like distant hawks in the sky: the high chiefdom; control of his daughter; final victory over the Tiger. He had lost track of which he wanted most. He knew only that these three goals were inter-dependent, and that he was Akrit Stone River of the Winter Runners and he would have them all. The Wolf was always hungry. The Wolf was never satisfied.

With that, he gained an access of strength and speed, leaping on Water Gathers and drawing blood about the other wolf's snout, tearing with his teeth, heedless of the claw-raking that he took in return. Then Water Gathers Stepped, a human in an instant, his hand coming down and the morning light gleaming on his axe-blade. Akrit matched him shape for shape, catching the arm and wrestling him over the weapon, the two men staggering back and forth, now one of them in control, now the other.

There were voices, he knew; he heard them distantly. Voices of men, though, and right then he was not interested in their opinions. Priests were calling for them to be stopped, but the warriors of both Wolf tribes were guarding the fight, the decision coming upon them all at once that this personal conflict had become something more, something divine. The chiefs of the Winter Runners and the Many Mouths were mad for each other's blood, here at the Stone Place, and surely this was the gods' plan.

311

Then Water Gathers had twisted away from his grip, with the axe cocked back to strike or to throw. Akrit sent a kick thundering into the hard muscles of his opponent's stomach, so that the other man reeled away, gasping, swiping weakly with a blow that Akrit deflected with his forearm. For a moment his hands found purchase: behind the knee, at the elbow. Then he had dropped his weight under Water Gathers and thrown him in a perfect demonstration of the warrior's art, a display of experience over youth.

Maninli's son landed well though, on one knee, and then lurched back onto his feet, drawing the axe back again.

But Akrit was a wolf once more, even as Water Gathers had been flipping through the air, and he came up under the man's striking reach, too close for the axe-blade, and clamped his jaws about his enemy's throat.

The rush of blood down his throat filled him with fire. He could not have said if he had planned to kill the other man, rather than just shake him into submission, but with that blood in his mouth a terrible rage rose in him: the Wolf's own fury. He shook and he worried and he slammed the man down, so that the axe bounced away and clinked against the altar. Water Gathers was scrabbling at his eyes with soft human fingers, but Akrit twisted and savaged and choked, until the struggles of his enemy grew weaker and weaker, lack of air, loss of blood. And he himself grew stronger. He felt the Wolf decant the man's strength into him, a ladleful at a time.

And when the son of Maninli was dead, he saw at last that his throw, his leap, had carried them both back into the circle of the stones, and he felt the whole world of the invisible poised above him, like a mountain waiting to fall.

He knew he should despair that he had done such a thing in this place. He knew he should cower in terror.

But he was born in the Shadow of the Wolf. He was the hunter, the warrior, the spiller of blood. Fear was not his way.

So he lifted his head to the angry, purpled skies and howled out his defiance, his triumph, and outside the circle the other Wolves howled too: Winter Runner and Many Mouths together, and the cry was taken up across the island, tribe by tribe, until every son and daughter of the Wolf was giving vent to that long, lonesome call: triumph and melancholy in one, the voice of winter, the cry of the Wolf.

Maniye had not looked back: the absence of her father in immediate pursuit was not enough to make her slow. He would be there right behind, she knew, or some of his people. If she slowed – if she let curiosity best her – then he would take her.

But then she was seeing the murkiness of the marsh ahead of her, the heaped earth of the island running out, and her straight course became a curve that brought others into her sight. She had thought that they would be looking at her: she had pelted between the stones, stirred up the gods. But no, they were still looking towards the circle, and a single fleeing Wolf girl was nothing to them.

And then she could not stop herself. She looked back, and saw that none of the Winter Runners was there. Instead they were gathered before the stones, and within . . .

She witnessed the last moments of the fight. She saw Akrit Stone River triumph over his enemy, and then throw his bloody muzzle up to the sky to give vent to his victory.

The other throats that joined with him took on a single voice that stabbed at the crowded sky and made it something that usurped all that it touched, driving the gods and spirits before it, pushing them away from their own place until only Wolf was left, ringing in every ear.

She felt it deep inside her, where her wolf soul was. She wanted to add her own howl to that chorus, to become part of the pack that she had just forsworn. The need was something external to her, and yet it was strong. She felt herself being shaken in its jaws.

But she put her head down and forced herself on through it, knowing only now: *I am my only master.*

Around her she saw the more timid of the others already moving for the causeway. The Coyote and the Deer, the stocky men of the Boar, they packed their tents and left, or else just fled and abandoned what they could not pick up in that moment. She could smell their fear, the rich savour of it. The Wolf was loose and gone mad, after a generation where they had lived mostly in peace even under the Wolf's Shadow. She saw a handful of men of the Eyrie simply take flight, Stepping up into the air in a clap of wings.

And she dashed past them all and through their camps, leaping over their fires and darting around their sleds and piled packs, and not one of them called after her or tried to stop her. She was Wolf, for all she was no part of what Akrit had done. She breathed out dread and trailed fear behind her.

Then there was another camp ahead, and she saw a sudden flurry of activity there: men and women in bronze-scaled mail spreading out, bearing short, curved knives and hatchets, hefting slender javelins. They did not scatter, nor did they reek of fear. The Tiger, she saw. This was the camp of the Tiger.

My people, and it was only when the first javelin flew that she realized they did not know her: they saw only Wolf, that had been their enemy before – and would be so again.

She twitched aside from the cast, and Stepped – knowing already that she was too close, that the next throw might pin her to the earth. Her panic sent her straight into her human form, abruptly running far faster than she was capable of on two legs, stumbling and tripping, hurtling head over heels.

Instinct took over then, and she realized only that she had landed on her feet, and that they were the feet of a tiger.

The Tiger warriors were staring at her, most of them, save for a couple still gazing out towards the circle. She forced herself into her human shape again, desperate to speak. 'Please! I'm you!' She had meant to say, *One of you*, or *One of yours*, but it

314

came out muddled. 'Please –' and the irrevocable step – 'take me with you.'

There was a woman there, the same tall priestess Maniye had seen in the circle. The others deferred to her, and her green eyes bored into Maniye's soul. There was a moment of stillness between them, each studying the other. Like the Bear, the people of the Tiger looked different to the rest of the Crown of the World. Their eyes, their sharp chins, their skins with just a touch of the coppery Plains colour. They wore their hair pulled back and braided into long tails, laced with gold and gleaming stones.

'We leave now,' the Tiger priestess declared. 'She comes with us.' And, at the snarling looks from some of her followers, 'There is a story here, and I will know it.' Not the most reassuring of words, but better than her turning Maniye away.

She was bitterly aware that she was abandoning Hesprec. She could only hope that he would be safe with the Bear tribe – surely they were proof against the depredations of the Wolf? If she could have carried him with her, she would, but there was no chance, no choice. The world brooked no delay.

The Tiger carried what she had taken for large shields or curved drums, but when they reached the water's edge, they turned them upside down and made boats of them. The eggshell things seemed far too fragile to trust her weight to, but everyone else there was larger than she was, and none of them hesitated.

She did, just for a moment, a heartbeat, looking back at the island, at the stones, at the unseen roiling host of spirits that was rising up like startled birds. She looked for something slender and serpentine, sliding towards her. She looked for a haggard old man with his bald head covered. She saw neither.

So she let herself be steadied in one of the craft, the priestess squeezing up beside her, embracing her close against the chill of her mail. Then the woman had taken up a short paddle, and she – and all the Tigers there – were making their way across the cloudy waters of the marsh, away from the howls of the Wolf.

26

'So what now?'

With the taste of Water Gathers' blood in his mouth he had been exultant, defiant. He had faced down the whole invisible world. He had howled, and the Wolf had howled back.

Now Akrit Stone River sat and stared into the fire, and felt the same leaden despondency that often came to him after his fights and rages. The world seemed a dark and uncertain place again. He had done a terrible thing. It had been a bold thing, when he was doing it. It had been what a Wolf warrior should do. But now it seemed more and more a terrible thing, and he wasn't sure what to do about it.

'The signs are . . .' Kalameshli looked grave and drawn, and yet with a new edge to him. 'The spirits of this place are in turmoil.'

We are all in turmoil. Let them for once experience how a man lives. 'I don't care about them,' Akrit made himself say. It was not true, but if he said it often enough then it might become true. 'I don't care about them, and they're too big, too far away, to really care about us. Isn't that what you've said? They'll just forget.'

The priest's shoulders rose and fell. 'This is where they come closest to the earth, where they can hear our voices. A deed done here in their full view cannot but bring repercussions. You are marked, Akrit Stone River. The powers of the world have marked you.'

'Let them. They mark great men, do they not?' The wise man avoided the attention of the invisible world, but it was a sharp-edged knife, if he could only avoid the blade and grasp the hilt.

Kalameshli's thoughts had probably run through the same twists. 'The gods—' he started.

'Only one of them matters,' Akrit said forcefully. 'Do I care that the Deer resents me? Do I care if the Boar carries ill will? Or even the Bear? How do I stand with the Wolf, Takes Iron? I thought . . . when it happened, I thought I felt him. I was inside the circle and I felt him there. And I had done the right thing, I knew it.' That blessed moment without doubts . . . but doubts always crept in, in the end.

'The Wolf is watching you.'

'What does that mean?'

'He is following your tracks,' old Takes Iron said. 'He is following to see where you will take him. If he finds you wanting, he will bring you down.'

'Or?'

The old priest's gaze was level. 'Or he will hunt alongside you.'

'Before this happened, I had spoken with other priests from other tribes. There have been many omens in this last year. It seems a testing will come to the people and to the land.'

'Are we to be that testing? Is it the Tiger war?'

Kalameshli took a deep breath. 'I think that there are only two ways to meet a test: swift feet, strong jaws.'

'Let the Coyote run.'

The priest smiled slightly. 'Before this day, you wanted to become High Chief because it was a role fit for you, and because you are a man who saw it within his reach.' He held up a hand to forestall Akrit's interjection. 'Before this day, you wanted to bring Tiger into the Wolf's Shadow, because you have never stopped hating the Shadow Eaters.'

'And now?'

'And now you *must* accomplish these things, or fall,' Kalameshli told him flatly. 'If you are the man who can do what he boasts, then you shall bear the future aloft. You shall wrestle it and cast it down. And if you fail at these things, if you are no more than just Akrit Stone River of the Winter Runners, then the spirits that marked you here will destroy you.'

'Do not fear for me.' But Akrit could not keep his voice entirely steady. Hearing his own uncertainty, he snarled. 'Fear instead for whoever took my daughter. Tell me you have news of her.'

'The Coyote saw her go,' Kalameshli said. 'She left with the Shadow Eaters. They will make for their strongholds in the highlands, and hide her there.'

'But?'

'Broken Axe has gone after her. He will track her, wherever she goes. He will steal her back or else he will tell you where she is, so that you can start your war.'

Akrit felt the world had become a torrent of water, carrying him along, carrying them all. 'And the other tribes?'

'Like the Wolf, they watch,' Kalameshli confirmed.

'But they must remember the war with the Tiger. Every tribe will have its warriors who fought in it.' Akrit stood up suddenly. 'You're right. This is the time to act, to seize the moment in our teeth and see if we can tear it free. Fail at this, fail at it all: that is what you're telling me.'

The priest nodded, gaze fixed on him.

'Tell them to gather their warriors. Tell them the Shadow Eaters have stolen my daughter. Tell them this is an insult to the Wolf, a sign that they mean to come down from the high places and rule over us again. Tell the people of the Wolf to ready themselves for a summer war.'

The Tiger priestess was called Aritchaka, and this was how her fellows addressed her. Later, Maniye learned that she had earned herself a proper name, what a Wolf would call a hunter's name, but amongst the priests of the Tiger such names were kept secret and used only within their own clandestine rites. She travelled with two male servants, Red Jaw and Club Head. They spoke seldom and stayed very close to her. Red Jaw had a sheath of javelins and a spear-thrower, and Club Head bore a knotted length of polished wood studded with bone and teeth. They wore sleeveless armour of square leather panels stitched together, which fell to their knees, while their lower legs were wrapped in cloth. There were livid marks striping their forearms. *Burns*, Maniye realized.

Aritchaka herself was clad in a cuirass of bronze scales, and she had donned a helm of the same metal with a red feather cresting it. At her belt was a curved knife and a short-hafted axe with a spike jutting backwards from the head. Altogether, the three of them cut as alien a trio as any Maniye had ever seen. She reckoned that even Hesprec would seem familiar and safe when compared to them.

Maniye had admitted only to the name 'Many Tracks'.

They travelled hard for the first day, pushing north and east, taking higher ground whenever it was offered. When necessary, they Stepped in order to climb, one or other of the men clawing his way up with a cord about his shoulder, then hauling the boats up after them. Maniye Stepped with them, without hesitation. Amongst other tigers, her tiger soul was like a comfortable garment. The idea of carrying a wolf body on her bones grew swiftly strange and unlikely to her.

They took the water road whenever it was offered, their progress following a string of lakes like stones on a necklace. Each time they did so, Maniye knew, they would be laying their scent to rest, forcing any keen-nosed pursuers to dither about the shore in order to hunt them down.

Still, there was one moment that she looked back, as they scaled a jagged-edged scarp of rock, and she spotted him: a pale wolf with dark shoulders, effortlessly keeping pace. She did not see him again, but after that she knew that Broken Axe would be there marking their trail.

She did not say anything to Aritchaka, for she was terrified that they would turn on her and drive her away if they thought she was a liability.

They pushed on hard like this for two days, putting much distance between them and any pursuers, before Aritchaka seemed to relax a little. On the night of the second day they lit a fire, rather than the four of them just Stepping to their feline shapes and huddling close together for warmth. Club Head built what looked like an altar over the little patch of flames, with a flat stone crowning it, laid out some fish on it and let them cook.

Aritchaka now regarded her impassively, loosening the sash at her waist and beckoning Red Jaw over to lift off her cuirass. 'Tiger girl,' she began, 'Wolf girl. What does the chief of the Winter Runners want with you, that he would tear down the gods to get to you?'

Maniye felt her chest clench. She had expected questions, of course, but not that they would be so well informed. A hundred lies squirmed in her mind: she had been a sacrifice; she had been caught spying or stealing; she was promised to the Horse Society and must return to them . . . But who could say how much this priestess already knew?

She took a deep breath, aware that she had already been silent for too long, and that her silence was the only sound aside from the crackling of the flames and the sizzling of the fish. All three of them were studying her intently, their eyes glittering in the firelight.

Without speaking, without acting, they stripped her of layer after layer of lies-that-might-have-been until she was left only with telling the truth. Or the truth as she knew it, which was all the truth she had.

'I am Stone River's daughter,' she informed them, seeing Aritchaka's eyes go wide in shock. The two men shifted posture slightly – first as if to ward against a threat, but in the next

320

moment ready to seize her, her role now transformed from refugee to enemy. And of course the Wolf told many stories about what the Shadow Eaters did with those they captured during their raids.

'He said that he got me on she who was once the Tiger Queen,' she forced herself to say.

Red Jaw hissed, baring his teeth, and Aritchaka cuffed him across the face – a movement so swift and without thought that it seemed mere force of habit. Then her hand lashed out and had Maniye by the throat – no, by the chin, turning her face slowly in the firelight, staring, staring . . .

Then the grip slackened, leaving Maniye gasping out, and still pinned by that green gaze.

'There is not much of her in your face. You look like a Wolf.' And yet Aritchaka was thoughtful, clearly troubled.

'Did you know her?' Maniye pressed.

'*Know* her?' The priestess weighed the words in her mouth before voicing them. 'She who rules the Fire Shadow People is also closest to the Tiger spirit. Whose will else should I obey?'

It took Maniye surprisingly long before she could say it. 'Will you tell me about her?'

'No,' came the swift answer. 'Or not now. There will come a time for many things.'

The next morning they had visitors. A handful more Tigers arrived, and with them came a stout, copper-skinned woman dressed in a long sheepskin coat of the Horse style. They appeared with a pair of stocky horses, shorter and shaggier than the beasts that Maniye was used to.

'There has been a change of plans,' Aritchaka explained to them. 'We have a third to come with us – the girl.'

The Horse woman nodded, unperturbed. 'Let her ride behind me. All she needs to do is hold on.'

The priestess took Maniye's shoulder, pulling her close. 'I had planned to withdraw to our lands carrying warnings of the

Wolf. Now it seems I shall bring them something more, no?' She stared into the girl's eyes. 'I see here no second thoughts or regrets. Do I see right?'

Maniye swallowed and nodded. There was a great deal in her mind about what she was leaving behind, but so few scraps of it were good and so much was baggage she was glad to shed.

She had never known her mother, for it had been right after her birth that Stone River had given the Tiger woman over to Broken Axe to dispose of. In all her years, the people of the Tiger had seemed nothing but a night terror, an enemy, the victims in tales of heroism in battle, a name to curse by, a byword for cruelties and dishonours since avenged. That they must exist, as a real people with a real history, she could surmise, but they had never seemed as such to her. Not until she saw them at the Stone Place.

Now here she was, leaving the Shadow of the Wolf, crossing its penumbra into that other Shadow that her mother had once cast.

The other Tigers would disperse by their own paths, leaving plenty of trails for any Wolf hunters to follow. They would go over rugged, rough country, by water and by rock, and yet still they might be overtaken by the swift feet of the Winter Runners. Maniye and Aritchaka, in contrast, would take a wider route along paths that the emissaries of the Horse Society had beaten out of animal trails, winding back and forth up the face of the highlands, through the dense forests to where the snow still lingered, and the Tiger held court.

The journey for her was a numbing one: holding tightly to the thick coat of the Horse woman as the two beasts picked their way up tracks that were nearly invisible, passing like ghosts through a landscape that grew ever more still and frozen the higher they climbed. The horses were astonishingly sure-footed, and the stocky woman whispered to them and chided them whenever they baulked, promising them rest and good feed and the respect of the Horse Society if they did their duty. She went in front, Maniye clinging gamely on, and behind came Aritchaka, riding with the ease of long practice, her boat slung from her saddle like a shield.

When the night drew in, there was always somewhere close that the Horse woman already knew: a cave, a secluded hollow, a skeletal frame of wood that she pulled hides over to trap their body heat. She never spoke to Maniye – probably sensing the uncertain position the girl currently held – nor gave her name.

They drew ever further from any lands that Maniye knew, travelling more east than northwards until the hills had become forested foothills, and the sun rose over a horizon toothed with mountains. They were south of the Bear lands, she guessed, but still climbing to where winter yet lingered, scowling down at the tides of spring that had driven it from the lowlands. Considering how matters stood between the Tiger and the Wolf, the image seemed appropriate.

Surely by now they had left any Wolf pursuit behind, and yet Maniye kept her eyes on the gloom between the trees, expecting at any moment to spot a pale wolf with a dark patch across his shoulders. In doing so, she began to notice other things.

The people of the Wolf built with earth and with wood, and while the Cave Dwellers lived beneath stone ceilings, such roofs were found and not made. Aside from monuments and monoliths, Maniye had never thought that anything substantial could be raised out of such uncooperative stuff. She had not known how her mother's people had made stone their slave.

There was not much to see at first, just traces of a people vanished from these lands. Sometimes there would be a pile of rocks that seemed oddly squared-off and regular. Once, butting onto the trail, she saw a big block, rounded a little by the weather but with its uppermost side still bearing grime-highlighted carving.

Then, one night, they stopped in what had been a tower before it became a ruin. The forest all about was scattered with dismembered fragments of stone but the lower level of the structure was still mostly intact – a jagged stump like a broken tooth. It was squat and square, with each corner buttressed out with fantastical carving. They had reached it after dusk, so Maniye had only the sense of it being a pale bulk between the trees, the stone seeming faintly luminous in the moonlight, despite the encroaching fingers of moss and lichen.

The Horse woman did her best to stretch some blankets over the uneven stones at the top, leaving them a cramped, dark space beneath, the ground under them lumpy and uneven from the detritus of the tower's collapse. Maniye gathered in all the driest wood she could find – for the rain had not quite been their constant companion, though a frequent guest. Still, she worked hard at it, because only for the last two nights had she been trusted to return if she wandered.

Once a fire was lit, Maniye had a chance to view their surroundings more clearly. The nascent flames threw a leaping, ruddy light across the truncated walls all around them, and everywhere seemed carved into images that led the eye one to another. She felt that, wherever she looked, she was immediately plunged into the midst of an unfamiliar story told using alien conventions. This carving had been intricate once, whole panels of the walls given over to abstract representations of forests where the spaces between each tree were deeper trees, and where the forms of men and women and beasts were constantly hinted at. If she let her eyes be led, she could see battles there, and hunting and the gathering of crops. She could discern worship and bloody sacrifice, the raising of great halls, the veneration of heroes and gods. And then she would become too absorbed and refocus her eyes, and not know what was truly there, or what had just been drawn out of her head.

'What is this place?' she asked at last.

Aritchaka gave a satisfied grunt, plainly waiting for the question. 'An outpost of . . .' a moment's pause, '*our* people. Your father's warriors destroyed it, burning its beams so that the stones fell.' Her face was fierce and angry in the firelight. 'There are many such places as this, relics of the golden days, the Days of Plenty.'

She meant when the Tiger had ruled, before her father and the other chiefs of the Wolf had broken them – in the days of Stone River's youth and the years before she was born.

Interpreting her expression, the priestess said, 'You yourself will have heard only the lies of the Wolf about those days. When we are at the Shining Halls, you will instead hear many truths.' After a thought, she added, 'And you will tell us many truths.'

The Shining Halls had been mentioned before: their destination was the stronghold of the Tiger that the Wolf's rampage had never approached.

'Will you go to war against my father's people?' Maniye asked in a whisper.

'Would you like that?' Aritchaka turned the question back on her.

Maniye regarded her across the fire for a long moment, and then nodded.

27

Asmander was not really surprised by the company they found at the campfire. Since leaving the Riverlands, his journey had become less and less the steps of a man in the physical world, more the passage of a figure from myth. He had hunted a vanished tribe on the Plains, and stood amongst the ruins of the Old Stone Kingdom. He had bared his soul to the gods of the north. He had borne mute witness as the Wolf tore through the heart of the Crown of the World and stood, howling, on its corpse.

Leaving the Stone Place, after that, had been interesting.

And in truth, he would not have known that any of it was unusual, save for the reactions of the locals.

For a variety of complex reasons they had taken the east road, once they had extricated themselves from the Stones and the marsh and its suddenly agitated denizens. The causeway had become a chaos of jostling and sudden violence, but water was no hindrance to a son of the Tsotec. He and Venater had taken turns in searching out a pathway of firm land for the other and Shyri to follow, both of them just as at ease in the marsh as they were on dry land, but neither of them able to bear the chill for a long stretch. Asmander wondered, later, whether that careful journey might not have gone differently had he not already squared himself with the local gods and totems. The spirit of a marsh was a poor thing to be on the wrong side of, if one were crossing it.

On the marsh's edge they had found a disintegrating little band of priests and traders and acolytes all come together to find their kinsmen and then depart. There they met the Coyote woman, Quiet When Loud, looking for her mate.

There were many there who were desperate, many who were grieving. Asmander was not truly sure who else the Wolves had killed – save that one of their own that everyone knew about – but every missing face seemed to provide cause to fear the worst. Likely there were another half-dozen such temporary camps about the edges of the marsh, each full of people looking for absent others.

Quiet When Loud was not panicking, but her eyes certainly lit up when she spotted the three southerners. Because that was a notably better reaction than they got from most of the locals, Asmander gladly wound his way to her.

'Where are you heading?' she asked them, and seemed satisfied with the answer. 'I will lead you east. My fool mate has set off already on some errand.'

'And you'd rather not travel on your own,' Venater finished for her, with a leer. 'You're so sure we're safer?'

Quiet When Loud gave him a simple frown that quite silenced him – it was a remarkable trick that Asmander would have paid gold to learn. 'But you're right,' she said, 'normally I would range to all the edges of the Crown of the World, either with Two Heads Talking or without. But right now . . .' Her look was troubled. 'I've not known anything like what happened back at the Stones. And everyone is talking of great change – all these priests gabbling about it. Not good change, either, to hear them. An escort would be welcome.'

Two Heads Talking had cut some signs, she revealed: the Coyote had a secret language of marks that they left for one another, the collective memory of a travelling people. Asmander did not say so, but he reckoned this was the closest to actual writing the north possessed.

They set off east, and made two days' clear travel before catching up with Quiet When Loud's mate. Approaching the fire, they found the Coyote sitting with the ancient Serpent priest, debating theology.

The wizened old man looked up at them, eyes glinting with mischief.

'Who is this that rides in on the back of the Snake?' he asked them with a crooked smile. 'Come, share our fire.'

Quiet When Loud sat herself down next to her mate. Wordlessly she took his hand in hers and held it a while.

'You've made good time, Messenger,' Asmander remarked carefully.

Hesprec's gaze was narrow, perhaps wondering what business had delayed the Champion at the Stones. 'And your path here has been solely to reunite these two children of Coyote? An act of benevolence that the cold gods of this land will, no doubt, entirely ignore.'

Asmander found a place across the fire from the old man, then glanced up at the others. 'You should bed down. No doubt we two will be talking a while.'

Venater grunted, cast a suspicious look at Hesprec, and then threw a blanket down on the ground. It was not his blanket – or had not been until recently. Asmander assumed he had made off with it during the confusion at the Stone Place. After a moment's consideration, Shyri laid herself beside him, tucking in close for warmth, as they had learned to do.

'How long is it since you saw the banks of the Tsotec, Messenger?' Asmander asked.

'The best part of two years.' Hesprec's wondering tone made it sound a great age. 'I guested with the Horse at Where the Fords Meet before I came north. But news finds me still. I know the clan of the Bluegreen Reach yet.'

'Do you know Asman, my father?'

'Not the man, though others of his line.'

Asmander smiled bleakly. 'If you do not know him, you do not truly know my clan, for he is a man alone – a singular creature.'

'And you, being his son, love and honour him,' Hesprec concluded.

'I am dutiful.' Not quite a confirmation, not quite a denial.

'And your father is no doubt a dutiful servant of the Kasra, as any clan head should be.'

'The Kasra is dead,' replied Asmander flatly.

The old man sat silently, watching him across the flames, digesting the news. What he knew of what occurred at Atahlan – of the division between Tecuma and Tecuman, the old Kasra's children – was hidden behind his veiled stare. Perhaps he already guessed at the need that had dispatched Asmander to this forsaken country, but the Champion only hoped he would not ask. To speak with a priest of the Serpent was like trying to navigate the shifting channels of the estuary itself. To *lie* to one would be far worse.

'Tell me of your own purpose here, Messenger,' Asmander fished.

'I came for word from the wise men and women of the north. And, thanks to the gathering at the Stone Place, I have it.'

'And what word did you find?' Asmander asked.

Hesprec sighed: just a simple sound but it sent a shiver down Asmander's spine that all the fires in the world could not have dispelled. That sound spoke of *ages*, great stone volumes of history that had come and gone, filled with the lives of men who thought that their 'now' was the only now that mattered.

'Do you know what it is like to try and see what the future holds?' the old man asked him. 'It is like looking into choppy waters at night, and trying to read the march of the stars reflected there, save that you can see only one wave's worth of them, just so small a span of the sky. How, then, can any man know with any certainty what is to come? You look, and you think, "Can it be? No, surely I am mistaken. That fragment I glimpsed, that looked all fire and broken things, that could have meant *anything*."' He was smiling but it was a skull's smile, especially on that near fleshless, parchment-skinned head. 'But if a wise man were to travel to many lands, and speak to the wise men of those lands – and avoid being sacrificed to the Wolf, which is always a danger, apparently – then a man might hear many views of the future, view many different handfuls of stars seen in the waters. And, from those tales and divinations and half-understood glimpses, a truly wise man might stitch together the whole cloth.'

Asmander was sitting very still, feeling inside him a deep cold that had nothing to do with the north. 'And what might such a wise man see?' he whispered. In truth, he wanted the Serpent priest to do what his kind normally did, snatching the revelations back at the last moment. He did not expect Hesprec to just speak on.

'When all those little fragments of tomorrow show fire and ruin, Champion, what then?'

'Tecuma and Tecuman . . . will it come to war, then? In truth, is that what it means?'

'And what would a river war mean to the Crown of the World?' Hesprec asked him. 'And, anyway, wars . . . there are always wars, especially here. Is it the war the Wolf now want to bring against the Tiger, then? Is it both these wars and more besides? What question must we ask of these signs, to put them in perspective?'

'What has gone before, that was prefigured by such omens?' Asmander asked promptly, earning an approving nod.

'The Fall of the Stone Kingdoms to the Rats,' came a voice from an unexpected direction. Shyri, who had been lying still and breathing easily as if asleep, now sat up without warning.

'What have you heard?' Asmander demanded.

'You think I could sleep with all this yattering?' she asked lazily. 'This one,' with a nod at the snoring mound that was

Venater, 'could sleep through the world breaking, but not me. Besides, what are you saying? That the end of the world is a secret just for you?'

Asmander threw Hesprec an exasperated look, but the old man was smiling.

'Daughter of the Laughing Men, welcome to our counsels. The fall of the Stone Kingdoms, is it? You've been there? You've seen their ruins?'

Asmander nodded along with Shyri, remembering.

'Then think on this: if I read these futures right, the doom they speak of is at least as grand and final as that. And wars on the River, or the spitting and yowling of wolves and tigers, all these disputes mean only that the people of *all* our lands will be at each other's throats when the axe falls on them, instead of standing together. The great enemies of history always thrive on chaos and rivalry: the Rat cult, the Pale Shadow, even the Plague People back in the very beginning – they could never have gained a victory if we were not forever turning against each other.' His tone had become bitter, bitter and old, a man whose withered hands are no longer strong enough to put things right.

'So if this axe must fall, who wields it?' Shyri asked. Even she seemed impressed, shorn briefly of the irreverence that was practically the air she breathed.

'Oh, I don't know. You think visions ever told anyone any-thing *useful*,' Hesprec hissed exasperatedly. 'You think there was a face of some warlord or sorcerer, and a map to where he lived, so that I could just go and poison his well or strangle him while he was still a child?' He laughed quietly. 'I cannot point the finger, Laughing Girl. I cannot say this leader of the Wolf will become the doom of the world. I cannot say that the rift between the royal twins in the Riverlands will be the spark to set the grass ablaze. I cannot say that it will not be the Horse, or a great union of the Plains peoples, or . . .' He waved a hand. 'I am like the god's offering: I see the knife and not the priest.'

'And your journey now,' Asmander said softly. 'The road east, that is because of these visions? You go to prevent this doom?'

'Wouldn't it be grand if that were the case? You'd be honoured to come, of course. You, the Champion, would have your part to play. Perhaps the fate of the world would rest in single combat between you and the enemy of all the peoples?'

Asmander felt a curious sensation inside him, a lifting, reaching feeling. *Yes*, it seemed to say. 'And can it be so?'

Hesprec laughed again. 'Oh, no, no. I have no idea what can be done – or if anything can be done. I have heard the wisdom of these lands. My place is back home, not haring off into the cold wilds like a fool. And yet here I am.'

'So why?'

'Because there is a girl . . . a young girl,' Hesprec said simply. 'She is fleeing the Wolf, and it is possible she has found safety, or perhaps she has found only danger wearing a different mask. And I want to *know*. I find I do not wish to return to the south without that knowledge, even though it is not part of the wisdom I came here to gather.'

'A girl,' said Asmander flatly. 'A girl of talents, of significance? Has she magical powers? Or she is so beautiful that men would give their all for her? Or a great warrior, perhaps? Or beloved of the gods?'

'None of that. Just a girl,' the old priest replied softly. 'But she saved my life – for her own selfish reasons, but nonetheless – and I find I do not wish to abandon her now. I am old. These fond foolishnesses are permitted me.'

Shyri made a derisive noise, and Asmander found himself perilously close to agreeing with her. 'This does not sound a fit task for a Messenger of the Serpent,' he said as strongly as he dared.

'Set not your foot upon the Serpent, lest it bite.' For a moment the old man seemed about to summon up a great aura of presence and power from somewhere, but then he smiled. It made him look older than ever for he had no teeth, not one. The soft lisping that prowled at the corners of his speech was more than just age. And he was mocking himself, because it was better to mock oneself than have the rest of the world do it.

'You are a long way from home, Messenger,' the Champion said softly.

'How observant you are.'

'And set to go further, you say?'

'It seems inevitable. And you will come with me, will you not? If I ask?'

'This one?' Shyri chuckled with a deep and earthy sound. 'He wears duty like a belt.'

Asmander nodded. 'I am tasked ... .' and then he caught the meaning behind her words: how a belt held in a man's desires; that he was trapped by his duty.

And there was Hesprec Essen Skese pinning him with a gaze full of pent-up years.

'You went to the temple when you were young, I'm sure. Your father, he's a man who remembers Serpent in his prayers, because it is the done thing. But you . . . what must it have been like to feel the mantle of Champion fall upon you, to know that *other* within your soul, that ancient shape scratching to be free? That it was *you* so chosen – not your father, not the votaries of Old Crocodile? It was the Serpent who showed you the path through the darkness in those days, am I right?'

Asmander nodded convulsively. 'You are, Messenger.'

'And now the Serpent calls to you in his hour of trial. Here is one of the Serpent's poor servants in need of your strong arm.'

'You said yourself, this is just some errand of your own.'

'And you were not listening. I said this is no part of my mission here in the north, but there is no breath I take, no thought that comes into my head, that is not the Serpent's business. If I owe a debt, it is the Serpent's debt to repay. Now, will you travel with me to the east, Champion?'

'He won't,' Shyri said derisively. 'You argue like a sick man, priest, all begging and wind and no strength. These words sway no one.'

333

'No doubt you're right,' Hesprec said. 'But here is the difference between the Sun River Nation and the peoples of the Plains, Laughing Girl. Our words are not just solitary stones thrown into the night. With our words, we build. What sways the heart is the sum of all the words that went before.'

Asmander sighed. 'You're right, of course. Messenger, it would be an honour.' He could hear it plain in those words that he thought it anything but, and yet the old man had played him, read him, moved him like a game piece. 'For I have walked the Serpent's back to escape the darkness. So now will I follow it one more time.'

28

The stronghold of the Tiger, that they called the Shining Halls, rose up a steep hillside, tier on tier, and all of it built from stone. Maniye had never seen so much worked stone in one place. There were towers three or four storeys high, and many of them intact. In places, a high wall ran intermittently. Even the lowest and plainest of the dwellings were of stone, and even they were carved, their faces boasting panels depicting human and animal figures intertwined, fighting one another, embracing one another. The upper corners of every building projected into the shapes of gargoyles, louring out over the broad thoroughfares that ran between.

Higher up the slope, the buildings became grander as well. Below were the homes of the lowly, the dens of the thralls, Aritchaka explained. Status and station was important to the Tiger: where one was born and what one could rise to. The higher dwellings were for warriors, for the priesthood, for the rulers.

Maniye had witnessed nothing in her life that might have prepared her for the great temple of the Tiger. It rose in leaps and bounds from a squat, square base, spiralling into towers that lifted claws to the skies above, the stonework coursing fluidly with the bodies of a thousand effigies. It should have been a chaos of mingling, contradictory shapes, but there had been a single mind behind it, so that the eye was led across this intricate fretted surface with a sure hand, images and scenes leaping into the mind.

The Shining Halls were certainly far grander than the village of the Winter Runners, and yet, as their tired horses passed beneath a gateless arch and under the eyes of a dozen armed Tigers, Maniye noted that there were fewer people here than the sprawling size of the place would suggest. As they made their way between the buildings, ever on upwards, she saw that much of the stonework had seen better days too. Some had been damaged and not repaired. In a few places there were signs of fire blackening. She was left with the impression of a culture defined by what it had come to lack, that once had been plentiful. She kept these thoughts to herself.

'You are taking me to your temple?' She knew the answer.

Aritchaka just nodded.

'And what will you do with me there?'

'Bring you before the Tiger,' came the short answer.

It had not escaped Maniye that some of the scenes that had leapt at her eyes from the stonework were of sacrifice, and intricately so: whole gatherings of Tiger priests officiating at the dismembering of those they would feed to their god. *The Shadow Eaters*, she thought. The Wolves believed they consumed more than mere flesh.

To the temple they took her, which Aritchaka said was also the seat of their ruler, the heart of their world. She felt many eyes upon her as she stepped under the great stone weight of it. They did not look kindly on her. They saw a Wolf.

Within the temple, there was a room of screens and fires. She had expected an icon, a carven tiger in mid-leap perhaps. Instead there was just an altar, a block of stone that was scored and cut. Behind it, a wall was carved over and over with repetitive shapes, and she saw the outlines of running cats there, each interlocking with the rest so that there was no part of the stone not coursing with a limitless cascade of them. Either side of her, the walls were fretted with a thousand holes, so that what remained was almost a lacework of stone, and fires were lit behind, throwing their light through that maze of gaps.

'What now?' Maniye could only whisper.

'Now the Tiger will come,' Aritchaka told her, already retreating. 'Now you will see what it is to be of the Fire Shadow People, the Tiger's chosen.'

Maniye heard the fires being banked, their light leaping higher. Shadows leapt and danced about her, running up and down the wall so that the constant progress of the cats seemed to falter, to change direction, their illusory movement chasing back and forth across the face of the carvings as though some terrified quarry was rushing amongst them.

Around her, the piecemeal shadows cast by the twin flames seemed to thicken and coalesce, and yet she was still waiting for some effigy to rise up, something like the iron jaws of the Wolf that she remembered from her home.

Not my home, she told herself fiercely. *I am of the Tiger now.* The traitor Wolf within her walked the lonely reaches of her soul and bayed at her, but she stopped her ears to it. Only now, here with her mother's people, could she admit to herself how alone she had felt since leaving the Winter Runners. Hesprec, Loud Thunder, these were not her people. She wanted to be with her own kind.

The shadows scurried and swayed about her. Although the fires were higher still, yet somehow the room was darker, until all those weaving spots and slashes of orange light seemed like embers on the very point of guttering out. As she watched, her eyes took in the circular dance of the shadows in her peripheral vision, and built shapes from it, so that the complex game of dark and light became abruptly the smouldering striped flanks of the Tiger – there in the room with her.

She fell to her knees, not through reverence but fear. Yes, the Wolf had touched her during her life, but that was a distant, dispassionate totem, a patient stalker always watching to see what she would do, what she could endure. The Tiger was immediate, fierce, predatory in another way entirely. Not for the Tiger the long hunt, the patient grinding down of fleeing prey. To be a tiger was to leap, to ambush, to strike suddenly and sure.

And can you? In her head, the voice was vast and purring, mingled with the low thunder of the fires. *What are you? But you do not know yourself.*

I am of the Tiger! she protested. *I am your own!* But the wolf was still howling deep inside her, and she lacked the means to drive it out into the cold night, and to sever it from her.

We shall see what my people call you, but I suspect it shall be 'prey'.

She wanted to beg, but that would be weak. She wanted to demand, but that would be presumptuous. She did not know what she wanted. She wanted to belong. Somewhere, she wanted to *belong*.

The red-lit shadows bunched and gathered, and in her mind the great beast sat up and regarded her indolently. *Do you think possessing my blood will save you?*

I have the blood of your queen! It was Akrit's own argument, but now she clung to it because she had nothing else.

But who truly believes that? The lazy, amused voice, always with a laugh hidden within it, and that laugh always cruel. *They know you for some mixed-blood foundling, and when your blood waters my altar, will it be any more red for all your heritage? Who will care? Who will know?*

'I will know!' she told it aloud, knowing that Aritchaka and the priestesses would be listening from where the fires were laid. 'I know who I am. Who else matters?'

Again that soft, dangerous laugh. *I so love human pride. I love the savour of it. I will certainly enjoy yours.*

There were chambers beneath the temple that never saw the sun, and that was where they put her. The torches that burned there only stirred the shadows; they brought the Tiger down

338

from its altar, let its smoky body pace instead the tangled network of buried spaces that she now had the run of. She was not a prisoner, not quite, for these were not cells. Still, when she encountered the steps leading up, there were always men of the Tiger tribe there, waiting to turn her around. Other times she could not find any steps at all.

Aritchaka came down sometimes. With her, she had thralls who bore food and drink: corn cakes and wizened little apples and stone jugs of dust-tasting water. When Maniye demanded to know what fate was intended for her, the priestess just cocked her head.

'We deliberate,' she said. 'We know what you claim to be, but a little Tiger blood – even a tiger's shape – does not make you *her* child. Are you some trick of the Wolf's? Are you just some child of two tribes who seeks to steal what is precious to us? Are you what you say? We have lit the low-smoking fires, and the smoke has provided no answer for us, not yet. And so you must wait.'

'How long?' Maniye asked.

Aritchaka gazed at her without expression. 'You may wish it had been longer, if the Tiger disowns you.'

Then she departed, leaving Maniye to the near-darkness.

She walked her buried domain on human feet. She prowled it as a tiger. It brought her no release. When she brushed against the unseen flanks of the greater cat that filled the space around her, she sensed its sudden snarl, the bared teeth and wide eyes, warning her off. Warning her not to pretend to something she had not earned.

Time slipped away from her. She could not say whether she slept when night fell, or whether she had been swept away from the rhythms of the sun, set adrift in this hidden world. After she had slept five times, with no clearer answer from Aritchaka, she began to despair. With the shadow-bulk of the Tiger looming at her back, she seized a torch and ground it into the stone at her feet, putting it out, swallowing up the shadows in a greater dark.

339

She crouched there in that blackness, her eyes slowly adjusting to the faint glow of more distant lamps. For a brief moment, though, the Tiger was pushed away from her, a creature of shadow that could not tolerate the utter depths of night.

In that black silence she put her hands to the stone of the floor, desperate for some reassurance that this was not the end, that she was not wholly alone and abandoned. Something moved there, she sensed. It might just have been her own pulse, but she felt the slightest of shiftings beneath her hands, as though something vast and far deeper shifted its coils as her prayer reached it.

She knew that she was fooling herself, and yet the idea was fixed in her mind now. Even as her eyes banished just enough of the darkness for the Tiger to slip back in, she felt stronger, more hopeful, less lonely. Even here in the Crown of the World ran the scaled lengths of Hesprec's god.

When Aritchaka came for her, not long after, she was ready.

The priestess's gaze was keen and searching, but she said nothing, merely beckoning Maniye to follow. There was a quartet of warriors there, in case she demurred. She recognized Red Jaw and Club Head amongst them, but they would not meet her eyes. Maniye could not read Aritchaka, but the manner of the men was curious, something of reverence, something of fear, yet they were plainly there to ensure she played her part.

They took her into a deep chamber where water welled up from a crack in the rock that had been smoothed and carved until it resembled a human face. Two thralls were present, men both, and they stripped and washed her, despite her protests. They kept their faces averted as much as they could, and would not speak a word to her, and the guards watched on throughout. At no point was there any hint of desire in any of them, or not any form of desire that might be consummated. They were treating her with the careful, dispassionate respect they might accord to one of their sacred carvings.

340

At the end, they gave her a shift of fine calfskin that was dyed near-black and set with rows of stones: beads of amber and green moss agate and three colours of tiger's eye, dense and heavy enough that she felt she had donned a cuirass of bronze. Aritchaka then reappeared, and set a circlet about her head – weighty enough to be gold – and anointed her with scented oils.

Maniye remembered what her father's plan had been: for her to come to the Tiger and announce her heritage; for them to kneel to her and accept her as their queen, somehow usurping their devotion and government simply by virtue of her blood-line. That was how the world worked for the Tigers, so Akrit Stone River had believed: no challenges, no consent of the tribe, just some sort of invisible fitness to rule conveyed by blood from mother to daughter.

In the way they treated her, she did not sense that they had accepted her as their ruler. A ruler, after all, was required to engage with her people. Maniye was being treated like a thing: a valuable thing but a thing nonetheless. And *things* were there to be used. They could trick her up in gold and shining stones as much as they liked, but even the most exquisite of *things* was still property.

She thought then of the Deer people. She had heard that they chose kings from amongst their number in spring, who lived well and wanted for nothing, beloved of all. Until the next spring, when they would take their happy, smiling king to the Stone Place and . . .

She could not tell if she was being welcomed as the scion of their lost royal line, or as a sacrifice for the Tiger's claws. She was wise enough in the way of the world to know these fates need not be mutually exclusive.

After all, she thought, *someone else has been ruling the Tiger since my mother was taken from them. How happy would they be, to find they have just been keeping a place at the fire for someone else? No, better to be rid of the newcomer, to denounce her and do away with her.*

She was being led upwards through the maze of nested stone, climbing towards the sun. Maniye made the resolution then that she would run – girl feet, tiger or wolf – if the chance presented itself. She would run, and head for Loud Thunder's house, wherever that was from here, or for the Horse Society, or even just walk all the way to the southern lands and speak them Hesprec's name, and hope . . .

But the Shining Hall of the Tiger had few windows, and it was busy with thralls and priestesses and people of the Tiger staring at her with a weird, unhealthy anticipation. They had a haughty grandeur to them, as if they did not see the broken carvings, all the small repairs that they no longer had the masons to perform. Here, wearing her Wolf's face, she was surrounded by the scars of the war the Wolf had brought against them, the wounds that an entire generation had not healed. Even now the lair of the Tiger echoed hollow to the tread of too few feet. Even now the work of a hundred hands was left undone.

She was still looking out for some opportunity to bolt when they led her suddenly into a far larger room, where the carvings seemed to have grown outwards from the walls, forming pillars and buttresses that leant in to support the great and intricate expanse of the ceiling. There were many already gathered there, yet the place felt empty still, resounding with the echo of the greater multitudes which had once graced it. There was a seat at one end, on a semicircular dais which rose seamlessly out of the floor and wall. The carvings surrounding it demanded the eye follow them: from all corners, a constant stream and progression towards that raised seat: thousands of human figures worked in miniature, bearing corn, wood, stone, weapons, tools, or else leading strings of thralls by the neck. They all of them faced that same empty seat, as though they were bringing the whole world to that point. It came to Maniye that the people of the Tiger set all they had in stone, immortalized and recorded and imprisoned there, save for the thing they valued most. Their soul, their heart, their god, they did not dare limit by trapping it in some rigid form: they knew the Tiger was smoke and flame and fear.

Many of the Tiger gathered there were priestesses like Aritchaka. They wore striped fur cloaks and ornamental cuirasses of stones and precious metals, and all of them were armed. The others of their people, also mostly women and all immaculate in furs and fine cloth, gave way to them deferentially.

Amongst them, she saw a delegation quite different in dress. She knew them as Eyriemen from the moment she set eyes on them, a band of haughty, hard-eyed men, their clothes embroidered with bone and feathers. Their leader wore a wooden harness about his shoulders, twin spars arching over him like the horns of the moon, the quills that decorated them turning them into perpetually spread wings. The Eyriemen's faces were tattooed on one side or the other, but they were careful to look at Maniye only through the painted eye. There was only one woman in their number, Maniye saw, and she looked at nobody. She wore a cloak of feathers over her plain shift, and there was a leather collar tight about her neck.

None of these things did Maniye understand.

Then she was standing before the seat, the throne, wondering what must happen now. Aritchaka was some steps away from her, and the guards also. The room was full of people, but she wondered how far she might get with a sudden surprise Step and a dash . . .

But there stood the throne, and it was empty still. Perhaps this was the test. Perhaps they were waiting to see if she would take what was hers by right.

That was a strange and heady thought. Surely it could not be so simple? To just sit down on that stone seat that all the walls of the room were marching towards? But if she did not, was she giving the lie to her own story? Perhaps *then* she would be transforming herself from queen into sacrifice.

By now she was very alive to the way that everyone in the room was watching her. It was not obvious, not an overt stare, but their attention was on her nonetheless. It was exactly the way that a tiger stalks its prey, she thought, subtle and subtle and again subtle, then suddenly the pounce. Sensing the minute shifts of stance and attitude all about the room as she drew closer to the throne, she became convinced that they were *not* waiting for her to seat herself there. To do so would be an unforgivable usurpation.

In her mind, that left only one possible fate they could intend for her.

She took a careful step back, trying to seem casual. Still that dreadful focused attention encompassed her, and it was the Tiger watching her through the eyes of his priesthood. It was there in the room with her: it was all the empty space that was not peopled.

I will run, she told herself. *I will be swift and sure, and I will run.* And she turned, ready to Step down onto her Wolf feet for extra speed, and saw him. A cry escaped her lips and died there. It was impossible!

There, in the doorway, standing between her and freedom; there, in the den of his enemies who should have cut him down in moments: there stood a lean Wolf-tribe man in well-worn leathers and furs, with ice-coloured eyes. *Broken Axe.* Broken Axe was here for her. Even the Tiger could not stand in the way of his hunting.

She pointed, but she could not say anything. Right then, she did not honestly know if anyone else present could see him. She would have believed anything.

He was smiling slightly, that expression that was becoming more familiar to her than her own would ever be. Of all of them, only he looked at her directly.

'Many Tracks,' she saw his lips form, and he took a few steps into the room. She saw the eyes of the Tiger people track him, then slide off him. They did not want to acknowledge him; somehow they could not deny him. Their warriors tightened their fists and scowled, yet nobody challenged him. And he advanced on her, step after step, like a terrible dream.

Then he had stopped, and everything had changed. The room had shifted around her, again like a dream, so that all the attention that had been moving between her and Broken Axe was abruptly elsewhere, following the great sea of stone figures until it reached the throne.

Maniye turned. It was now occupied.

The woman who sat there was hard featured, and there were scars on her hands and one on her chin. Her eyes were like green stones, lustrous as emerald, and as cold. Compared to the bright display of the priestesses, she should have seemed drab, wrapped as she was in a dark pelt. When she moved, though, she smouldered, and light gleamed and glittered in red bands within the fur, like fire in the deep woods.

It was plain to Maniye that the Tiger had spared no time in finding a new ruler, for this woman commanded their attention entirely. From the moment she took her seat, her hand lay on everyone in the room, stilling them. Even the proud Eyriemen kept their disparate eyes low.

'Come forwards,' she said, and that chill green gaze cut into Maniye. She took a stumbling step, knowing only that all chance of escape had been stripped from her. That cool gaze anatomized her calmly, tallying her faults and features, until the woman said, 'I see only *him*.'

There was movement at Maniye's shoulder, and she flinched as she realized Broken Axe had come up behind her. She still could not understand how he could be here.

The enthroned woman laughed at her reaction. 'It seems you make friends everywhere you go, Broken Axe.'

And Maniye felt like shouting at her, shouting at all of them, *Don't you know who he is? Don't you realize that he's the man who killed your* . . .

The man who killed my . . .

She felt something, some certainty she had lived with forever, fall out of her world. Suddenly the woman before her was different, entirely different in every particular, even though she looked exactly the same.

My mother . . .

'Now she knows me,' the Queen of the Tigers declared with satisfaction.

29

'What do they call you?'

In the now-emptied room the question hung in the air between them. The Queen of the Tigers had sent them all away: the priests, the warriors, the Eyriemen, even the thralls, save for Maniye – and one other.

By the door, a quiet presence, was Broken Axe.

'I am named Many Tracks,' she declared, seeing the slight twitch of an eyebrow when she glanced towards Broken Axe. 'But my name is Maniye.' Because, if this was really her mother, then here was someone she must give her true name to.

The Queen's face was rigid, her posture stiff, as though she was fighting to control something. Her eyes skittered across Maniye, unable not to look at her, yet never still enough to properly take her in. 'Always the Wolf way, the backwards way,' she murmured. 'To hide the birth name that means nothing, when it is the given name – the hunter's name – that tells the truth about us. That is why it is the secret name. They are fools, to reveal it so.' She stared at Maniye, seeming to steel herself. 'I am Joalpey,' she continued, and then, 'but I am called Strength Under Moonlight.' The words left her with a shudder, a concession born of customs alien to Maniye.

'Thank you,' the girl replied. She was waiting for some sense of connection to arise between them – mother to daughter. That was how it should be, she knew. That was how the stories had it, whenever estranged family found one another. They always *knew*. The connection of kin drew them inexorably together. She thought Joalpey was waiting for the same thing. There was a gap between them that was not mere distance though.

'They say you are my child,' the Queen of the Tigers declared awkwardly.

'They told me you were dead!' Maniye had not meant to say it. 'I lived all my life *knowing* you were dead, that my father ordered you killed, and that *he* did it!' jabbing a finger at Broken Axe. And then she rounded on him furiously: 'And why didn't you tell me? Any time, you could have said, "Your mother lives," and made all the difference to my life. I've lived in *fear* of you all these days. And you *hunted* me. Even at Loud Thunder's fire, when we were free of the Winter Runners, still you tried to take me back. Still you said nothing. *Why?*'

Broken Axe drew a deep breath. 'Why would I take you back to the Winter Runners? Because that was your home. Because it was safer than the teeth of winter. Why would I keep this secret? Because it *is* a secret. Because better Stone River believes Joalpey dead, and that he thinks any Queen of the Tiger he hears of is another woman. For my own sake, as much as hers.'

'I don't understand,' Maniye complained bitterly.

The Wolf hunter shrugged, suggesting that neither he nor the world were there simply for her to understand. 'I am the Wolf that walks alone,' he said simply. 'I am not Stone River's pack follower. I do what is right.'

'By whose reckoning?' she demanded.

'My own. That is the true path of the Wolf, not the leader, not the follower.' He spread his hands self-effacingly, as though embarrassed by how grave he sounded.

There was the scuff of a footstep: Joalpey had stood up, taken a step closer. Her presence was as demanding as a fire, and yet where was the heat?

One of Joalpey's hands moved a little, rising towards her daughter then drawing away. There was a thing she was not saying, perhaps not even letting her own mind light upon, but it was there in the chamber with them. Maniye felt it, that unspoken thing. It was What Had Been Done. It was the history of Joalpey's captivity amongst the Winter Runners, her humiliation and all of what she had endured. It was a history that had a sequel, though, and the sequel was Maniye.

'I feel nothing.' Joalpey's voice was fractured with emotion. *For you*, she meant. Maniye felt herself begin to tremble very slightly. She met her mother's eyes desperately and saw the same need there reflected back at her.

'You are my daughter.' It was spoken as though the words were alien to her. 'Broken Axe has vouched for it. After he took me away and swore to Stone River I was dead, he watched you grow into what you are now. He gives his oath that you are my blood.' The Queen brought her hands up before her, clenching them into fists over and over. 'But I look at you and see only a Wolf.'

'I can Step—'

'I know what they say. But it means nothing until you have cut a soul away and become one thing or the other. And you have a Wolf face, Wolf eyes.' Her own had gone very wide. 'I cannot see myself in you.'

'I fled the Winter Runners!' Maniye insisted. 'I want to be nothing of theirs.' But she was lying, of course. When she had passed Kalameshli's trials, she had been proud to take her place in the tribe. It was only when Akrit had revealed his plans that she had run. She was false to the Wolf, so why not to the Tiger as well?

'I kept Broken Axe here to remind me that not all born in the Jaws of the Wolf must be an enemy,' the Queen said softly.

'Mother.' And the word seemed as leaden and strange to her as 'daughter' had been to Joalpey.

'I will make you one of us,' the Queen declared, not as a threat but more out of desperation. 'You will train alongside our daughters. You will learn how to fight, and how to worship. You

349

will eat of our meats and dance to our music. You will learn our histories. With these flames I will burn the Wolf out of you, I will sever all his claims to you. And then I will know you, at the end. You will be mine: my blood, my child.'

As Maniye stood before her, she sensed that chasm between them, knowing only that Joalpey felt the need to bridge it even more than she herself did. Was that some way towards a mother's love? Maniye did not know. She did not have the real thing to compare it with.

She decided that it would do, that it was close enough. It was all the world would offer her, and she had seen enough of the world by now to know its meagre generosity.

The daughters of the priestesses and the families close to the Queen learned to fight, but it was like dancing. Growing up amongst the Winter Runners, Maniye had been resistant to being taught anything at all, and what she had been forced to learn had come only from Kalameshli, with his rod and the hard back of his hand.

She suspected that most children of the Tiger learned exactly like that, but for those close to the throne it was different. For them, there were ways of doing things. There were stories they were expected to know. There was battle.

They fought with long knives and with short-hafted axes, but they learned their fights one move at a time, and strung their moves together like beads, each flowing to the next. Their teachers – sharp-voiced priestesses like Aritchaka – emphasized the grace of each movement, the poise and balance: where the feet trod, where their bodies were weak. A student who took the wrong stance could expect to receive a hard shove to show her just where she had failed.

It was all alien to Maniye. More, the teachers regarded her with emotions ranging from bafflement to open dislike. The other students stared and whispered, repelled by her differences: wrong face, wrong skin, wrong hair, wrong eyes. And small, too:

350

smaller than girls three or four years her junior. Everything around her seemed set on making her admit defeat.

The girl who had hidden and skulked apart amongst the Winter Runners, the girl whose world had been an exercise in avoiding the notice of the powerful, she would have failed here. But she was not that girl any longer. Looking back, she could see that the actual privations she had thought she was escaping were small things. She had lived a life where she was fed and sheltered; not a thrall, nor fending for herself.

But when she had rescued Hesprec and fled, she had unwittingly broken out from a different prison: a prison of no choices. She had defied her father, and in doing so had become *someone* for the first time.

Maniye had spent a harsh winter becoming that person. Her flight from Broken Axe had taught her to think fast. Her months with Loud Thunder had taught her to shift for herself. She threw herself into her new surroundings with a will, watching every movement, listening to every word.

In the first ten days, everything she did was wrong. After that – well, she was learning for the first time what all the others had been practising for years. She did not know the precise, exquisite steps; she did not know the proper and exact wording for the tales. She recognized where the gaps were, though; she knew the limits of her ignorance. When she came to them, she did not turn back but just ran faster, leaping each gap as it appeared. She found in herself a swiftness and a sureness that meant she could keep to her feet: not able to beat the others, but not so easy to beat.

And when it came to Step, she found she was as swift and fierce as any of them, and as used to the tiger's shape. She could climb better than they, and run faster. Whilst they had learned and practised, she had been *living*. None of the Tiger's other daughters had been forced to test their skills against the sharp edges of the Crown of the World. However they might try to look down on her, they always found her eyes staring right back at them.

But always, when she reached deep into her soul so as to Step, there was the Wolf, that solitary figure. She pictured it out in the snow, banished from the fire, a little further away each time. And yet still there. She wanted it to go away, to pad off into the darkness and leave her forever. She wanted to step wholly into the Shadow of the Tiger. But still it lingered, howling mournfully at the edge of her attention.

Sometimes she woke from Wolf dreams, pack dreams, raging at the obstinacy of her own soul.

Sometimes her mother came to watch, and that was when she got it most wrong. Because suddenly there was a new thought in her mind: *I must impress her.* Those were painful times.

Her blood link to the Queen did not seem to be general knowledge, and Maniye herself said nothing of it. Her teachers must have been told *something* of why this Wolf-looking girl had been forced on them, but they remained close-mouthed. No doubt she was a constant source of speculation amongst her unwilling peers.

One day – and she had lost count, but felt it must be close on a month since she first came to the Shining Place – they were spared being put through their paces. Instead, they were brought before the Tiger.

Maniye was never sure whether this was some sacred date that nobody had mentioned to her, or whether the Queen had ordered it, or whether this was all because of a challenge between two of the priesthood. They were taken down to the temple chamber, though, and made to kneel and watch the scattered smoke and firelight dancing on that wall with its ever-coursing carvings. To Maniye, the presence of the Tiger was palpable, hanging in the air, moving restlessly from wall to wall. Glancing at her peers, seeing expressions ranging from fear to boredom, she wondered if they felt as she did. Could you really become jaded with that brooding, bloody-minded spirit? Or was her own mind just colouring the smoky air? Perhaps she cast the Tiger as menacing because she knew she would never truly belong.

She fought down that thought mercilessly. And felt a tiny spark of approval? So she told herself.

There was music then: fierce and rapid drumming on instruments of hide and metal, and shrill pipes, all issuing from hidden spaces about the temple. Two priestesses had stepped out into that Tiger-haunted space between the fretted screens. They wore much gold about them, though little else, and their skins were streaked and striped with eye-leading patterns of black. They carried knives like curved razors, and they began to dance. With her breath caught in her throat, Maniye watched them as they stepped around one another. Each move was between positions of perfect balance, each step moved the hands and the knife as they circled. It was the perfect expression of the clumsy lumbering that Maniye and the other girls had been lurching through. They were exquisite in every motion, eyes fixed on each other, moving through exacting passes with unthinking elegance.

Then the first blood was drawn and Maniye realized that it was actually a fight. Whether there had been some disagreement between them or whether this was an offering to the Tiger, she had no idea, but in a handful of seconds both women bore two thin lines of blood across their bodies, and the tempo of the contest was accelerating, without their movements being any less perfect.

And then they Stepped, and fought as tigers, and it was simply a continuation of the dance. Each flowed from shape to shape as advantage required, two feet to four and back, and never faltered. The keen lines of claws joined the thin scratches of their blades. Watching them – two masters of an art that she had only recently discovered – Maniye could only think, *How could these people ever have been beaten?* The Wolves had nothing compared to this, only the hard experience of a hunter, gained piecemeal.

But the Wolves had a different way, of course, for they did not fight alone. And she had seen herself how few in number the Tigers were.

She almost missed the moment when one of the women misstepped, in human shape with her blade held wide, and her opponent a tiger under her guard. Then she was down, the snarling beast atop her, jaws agape. Maniye expected her to die. She sensed the bloodlust of the Tiger all around her.

And the drums reached their crescendo and the pipes shrieked, and then all was still, and the tiger was a woman once more, stepping back from her adversary. Instantly, thralls were rushing forwards to tend to their wounds, and the loser was forcing herself to stand, proud before her god. Maniye was left wondering whether it had not, after all that, been merely a dance to long-rehearsed steps.

She felt as though she was back at the frozen lake with Loud Thunder again, and waiting for the thaw. Her mother came to see her, and she tried and tried, coming ten years too late to all these traditions. Never did Joalpey speak to her; never did she call for her daughter. Always her eyes seemed frozen with doubt and bad memories.

Maniye knelt in the room that was the Tiger's shrine, crouched before that apparition of smoke and imagination that was the closest her mother's people got to representing their god. The Tiger without spoke there to the tiger within. She felt the connection as clear and self-evident: *This is where I belong.* And yet the Wolf was written in her face and in her compact frame, in the way she spoke, in her blood. And the same Wolf was embedded in Joalpey's mind like an arrow.

She began to feel a terrible fear that she would never become either of the things within her. That, in the end, neither Tiger nor Wolf would have her. That she was lost.

She began to dream badly: confusing, tormenting nightmares of fleeing or chasing, though really it was herself that she both pursued and fled from. In her dreams there were no familiar places. Each seemed to take her further from anywhere she knew, from any sight she had seen. She was drifting away, inside her own head. She had been given a chance to belong: it had been within her very reach. Yet she was losing her hold on it, as though she had climbed and climbed only to fail within sight of the top. And that meant a long drop.

Maniye began to dread going to sleep. In the dreams themselves, though, it was waking that she dreaded. Another day where her mother turned away from her. Another day alone amidst all the people of the Shining Halls, because there was nobody she could speak with about this: not her teachers, not Aritchaka, not anyone.

Yet one morning she woke in the close stone cell where she slept alone – the other students would not have her in their dormitory because of her face and her twitching, whimpering nightmares. She awoke with the sense of a presence close by, quiet and still and buried . . . and he was there.

He sat beside her pallet with his back against the wall, awake but not quite looking at her. He seemed paler and older than ever, and the scales of his tattoos were so faded that they had almost rubbed away in parts. His skin seemed brittle, as though to reach out and touch him would break him into a thousand desiccated flakes. But then his eyes flicked towards her, and a delicate smile pulled at the corner of his mouth.

'Good morning, little Tiger,' said Hesprec softly. 'I came to see that you are well.'

She had her smile ready, and was hunting about for some mocking retort, some dismissive joke, when the tears came. Abruptly she was sitting up and weeping, holding him close, feeling the feather weight of his hand on her head, smoothing her hair.

30

'It is no great matter,' Hesprec told her.

'But how are you even here?' Maniye demanded.

'Does the Serpent not know all ways under the earth?' Hesprec looked at their close stone confines almost approvingly. 'Besides, I discovered some fellow countrymen whose aid I was able to enlist. Serpent provides, little Tiger.'

Maniye thought about the gods of Wolf and Tiger. Did they provide? They challenged, yes; they made their people strong by testing them and weeding out the weak. Which sounded admirable unless you spent your life terrified of weaknesses you could do nothing about.

Hesprec was watching her, reading each thought from the smallest change in her expression, or so his eyes suggested. 'Nothing lost, nothing forgotten,' he told her softly. 'Serpent seeks for old knowledge in the deep earth and brings it to light. Serpent's coils cradle learning now gone from the rest of the world, ready to proffer it to us when we are ready. Why do you think the world has to suffer ancient creatures such as I, mm? Only that we go amongst the people of the world with those gems of knowledge Serpent has dug in the deep earth of old time.'

'I don't understand you,' she told him, but inwardly she experienced a stab of envy at the comfort his god gave him. Then she felt guilty for it, because she was trying to grow close to the Tiger, not be seduced by some other way. Still . . .

She almost did not say it, hovering twice on the edge of voicing the words without letting them out, before finally giving way.

'I thought I felt . . . Serpent, I thought he helped me, once, twice. He? She?'

'Either. And most likely you did. Serpent's coils run beneath all the earth and, now you have met me, you may see them from time to time. You have become something that Serpent may notice.' He stretched. 'Now, there is a priestess who has said she would speak to me of visions.'

Maniye stood up suddenly, feeling betrayed. 'You're here for your mission! You're not here for me at all!'

Hesprec rolled his eyes, spreading exaggeratedly exasperated hands. 'Dear me, life is so simple in the Crown of the World that you can do one thing at a time only. I came here for you, and I am very grateful that your meanderings took me to a place where I might also advance the Serpent's business.'

'Hmm.' Feeling backed into a logical corner, Maniye folded her arms stubbornly. 'If the coils of the Serpent are everywhere, why does he need you?'

'Because I am a loop of those coils.'

It was past time for her to be gone to her studies, she realized. 'Will you . . . ?' She could still not quite understand how he was here, alive and unfettered. 'You will stay?'

'For a time,' he agreed mildly. 'I must find some path back to my home eventually, but for now I am here, and in no apparent danger from your kin, thanks to, if I might say so, a remarkable combination of good fortune and deft speech on my part. And you, of course.'

She started. 'Me?'

'Yours is a name to conjure by. When I gave it, they brought me straight before that remarkable woman who rules here. Why was that, I wonder?' His expression gave her no clue as to his private thoughts.

She wanted to answer him, but the whole business had laid a weight of secrecy on her ever since she had first left her mother's presence. She had grown used to it being that one piece of knowledge that was never spoken of – even amongst those who knew the truth.

Later, Hesprec was there as she tried to match the careful steps of the other students. In those slow passes she saw again the fierce duel between the priestesses: the same movements at a difference pace. It should have made her nervous, but instead every part of the dance seemed to fall into place that much more naturally: her bones now knew what it was all *for*. That was the day she Stepped and took her bronze knife with her, making the hard metal a part of her body, and finding it in her hand again when she retook her human form. The old Serpent's gaze upon her made her feel proud.

Just as nobody openly stared at her Wolf face, or speculated on her heritage, so Hesprec seemed to share in that peculiar invisibility. He could hardly be missed, that outlandish old man with his cloth-covered head and his corpse-pallor skin, and yet Tiger eyes slid off him in a willing conspiracy to pretend he was not there.

When Broken Axe made an appearance, which was rarely, he too was looked straight through, made to disappear by the collective consensus of the Tiger. Even the Eyriemen had a touch of it. At first Maniye saw this as an aloofness born of disdain. It was watching Hesprec that taught her otherwise. Somehow, as he passed amongst them, he taught her to look at her hosts anew and see the weakness she had taken for proud strength. They did not wish to see him, or Maniye, or any of these strangers walking freely in their halls, because they were all evidence of how the Tiger had fallen from the heights of its strength. She studied the carvings then, seeing past Queens seated with great ceremony while the world scuffed a path on its knees to their throne. The Eyriemen would not have stalked so haughtily through these halls in those days.

She understood, then, that the whole of the Shining Halls could not look at these foreigners without feeling the pain of old wounds, humiliations and indignities. Just as her mother could not look on her.

With that particular revelation, she found herself a high place, roosting up on the temple wall amongst the carved monsters: the petrified jaws and claws of tigers trapped forever halfway out of the stone. Just as she had once retreated to the high eaves of Akrit's hall, she perched there and stared down at the sprawl of buildings that was the Shining Halls. At night there seemed to be precious little about them that shone.

How long she stayed there, as the moon bellied up into the sky, she could not later have said. She only came out of the depths of herself at a scuffing sound nearby. Instantly she was a Tiger, keen-eyed in the dark, and she saw Broken Axe standing further along the wall from her, feet neatly balancing along the same ledge that she had taken as a roost.

'What do you want?' she asked sourly.

His eyes fixed her against the stone. Even now that she knew some inner part of him, she could not say just who or what he really was. He was the Wolf that walked alone. He did what he did for his own reasons.

'I wanted to see how you were,' he told her.

'Why would you want to do that?' she demanded. 'I thought you didn't need to hunt me any more.'

He shrugged, and then lowered himself until he was sitting close by, looking down. 'You are a strange creature, Many Tracks. You are something that should not have come into the world.' He said it matter-of-factly, without any sign that he intended to hurt her. 'To bring a thing into existence is to be responsible for it. Whose hands are behind the fashioning of you, then? Stone River, for sure. Kalameshli Takes Iron also, for his was the thought behind it. And your mother, too, for all she had little choice. And me.' Meeting her fierce glare, he shrugged again. 'Or do you not think so? That I saved your mother, there is the mark of my wood-knife in carving you. That I never told you, there is another. That you grew up believing I had murdered her, a mark there. I did not bring your shape from the wood, but I have helped finish you.'

'You're responsible for me?'

'In some small way.'

'You don't need to be,' she told him harshly. 'I – what? – absolve you. You are nothing to me. I am happy to be nothing to you.' It wasn't true, of course, and she felt they both knew it. He still frightened her, but she could not cut him away from her history. In that, he was right.

He stretched, prior to changing the subject. 'I have travelled from the Swift Backs,' he said, naming the closest tribe of the Wolf.

'You lie to them like you lied to the Winter Runners?'

'I lie to nobody. I am the Wolf alone, and I serve the Wolf in my own way. If they believe that I must be a slave to their path, it is not my place to enlighten them,' he said softly. 'Of all my responsibilities, the chiefest to me is that I tread a path that bears neither guilt nor shame. Those are the things that the Wolf cannot endure.'

'Did you . . . ?' Asking a question of him was putting herself in his debt, drawing back into his shadow that she claimed to be free of, and yet . . . 'What have you heard, of my f—of Stone River?'

'That he is strong with the Many Mouths now, and that the eldest son of Seven Skins has given many gifts to Stone River. That the Moon Eaters and the Swift Backs have exchanged many messengers, and it seems that they are halfway into Stone River's camp, each for fear that, if the other joined but not they, then standing alone they would fall prey to the rest. You know how Stone River got his name, Many Tracks?'

'I . . . the landslide.' She knew the story, of course: the most told tale amongst the Winter Runners, or at least of those recounted within earshot of her father. During the war with the

Tiger, Akrit had come to a battle in a canyon. He had lured the Tiger to where he had seen a great slope of loose scree and, when they had chased him, he had brought it down on them, killing many of their best. He had been barely older then than she herself was now.

'The words of the Swift Backs were only the first stones of the landslide,' Broken Axe told her. 'You know what I mean.'

For a long time she stared at him, and then she finally found the question that had been stalking her mind since she first saw him in Joalpey's throne room.

'How did it happen? When did you become . . . *not* a Winter Runner? Was it in the war?'

'I was just a boy during the war.'

'You didn't fight?'

'I fought. Boys fight, but they don't ask questions. They believe what they're told. I fought well, scouted well. That's what they used us for, mostly. Of all the youth of the Winter Runners, only I could walk alone into the trees and take back the night from the enemy. I was noticed because I killed Tiger warriors. When I left an axehead in the skull of one of their war chiefs, I was not much older than you. If you could have met me in those days, you'd not have found a more devoted member of Stone River's warband.'

'What happened then?'

'Afterwards, after the Tiger's power broke – when your mother had been captured, and they were forced to give tribute to Seven Skins and your father, there was a hunt. Stone River entrusted it to his best warriors – and I was one. Tell me, girl, how many tigers have you seen in your life?'

'Tigers?'

'Of wolves, there are many, but you will find few tigers in these parts or anywhere west of here. We were ordered to trap and kill every one of them we could find. We were told to strip the Tiger of its souls.' He gave her a bleak look. 'I cannot even say what might happen then, whether the Tiger souls must travel many miles to find a new body to be born into. And what if there were not enough? What happens to those souls then? And I thought about it all too long, what we were doing. And I knew that if I just did what I was told, and it was wrong, then being told to do it would not save me. If the Tiger himself should stand between my soul and a new life, and demand to know why I slaughtered so many of his kind, what could I say? That it was Akrit Stone River who gave the order? What would that matter to a god-spirit? More, what could I say to myself, when I asked that question of my reflection in the waters? So I became Broken Axe, the Wolf that walks alone. I thought Stone River would be angry.'

'Why wasn't he?' Because to Maniye, it seemed her father had always been on the point of anger.

'When I came back from the hunt, he saw how I had changed. He saw how the change made the others in the village feel about me. They knew me for a strong hunter and a warrior, so they feared it. And Stone River used that. He let me go my ways so long as I went his ways, too. He made me his huntsman, his messenger to other tribes, his fist to lift in threat against those who uttered words he did not wish spoken. And each time I weighed his orders, but mostly I did what he asked. Because it did not offend me, and because, for all a man wanders, having a home is still a good thing.'

She was going to ask it then, but he was already going on. 'And there was your mother, of course. Your father . . . you know what was done, what his plans were, for her, and for you. And after you came, he gave me that order: to take her into the forest, far enough that her ghost could not find its way back to the village of the Winter Runners. And to kill her, while she was in her human shape. He wanted her spirit to wander a long while before it could be reborn, if it ever was.'

'And that was wrong.'

A shrug, once more. 'It seemed so to me. And Stone River

never did understand me. He never saw that I was not his creature. He gave me the name of Broken Axe, but he never realized I was not his weapon.'

Her next question took much longer to emerge. She did not want to think about it at all, but it could not be kept down.

'And what my father did to her, was that not wrong?'

She forced herself to look at him, and caught the raw, hurt expression on his face. But he had no answer for her.

A few days later, a commotion summoned her from her solitary practice after the other students had gone. Since watching the duel between the priestesses she had been taking every spare moment to work through as much of the fighting dance as she could remember, over and over until every muscle ached.

The noise, to her surprise, was the Eyriemen. They hadn't seemed the boisterous types when she had seen them stalking about the Shining Halls previously, but now they had something to celebrate. Or else, she considered, they were making sure that their hosts appreciated them.

She followed the sounds of their rhythmic whooping and clapping until she found them outside the front gates of the temple. There were half a dozen of them, and they had a prisoner between them. She felt an odd twist inside her when she recognized the man as a Wolf.

It was not anyone she knew, no Winter Runner at all. From his dress and markings she guessed he must be a Swift Back: a short, stocky man dressed in furs and quilted leather. The Eyriemen had a rope collar about his neck, and his hands were bound behind him. They were pushing him about between them, sending him reeling from one to another, with kicks and blows whenever he stumbled or fell.

She watched, and told herself that she was glad, because he was a Wolf and an enemy. That was what any child of the Tiger would feel in her bones.

'A gift!' The speaker was the woman the Eyriemen had with

them, although, behind her, their leader held his hands up. 'The Wolf are growing bold again! They come sniffing up to your very walls. Be glad you have the keen eyes of the Eyrie to keep you safe! A gift for your queen, here!'

And then Joalpey was there, revealed in the opening temple doors with a dozen of her priesthood. At her arrival a little of the scorn went from the Eyriemen, though not all of it.

'You give him to me, Yellow Claw?' Joalpey asked. The Wolf had been forced to his knees.

'He is yours,' the Eyriewoman confirmed after a glance at her chief.

'Great are the hunters of the Eyrie,' Joalpey recited. 'All will have their reward.' The words were a shade less than sincere and, from her look, her alliance with Yellow Claw and the Eyrie was a difficult one. Two priestesses stepped forward and hauled the prisoner to his feet, manhandling him into the shadow of the temple at a nod from their queen.

Maniye held still, watching and waiting, but Joalpey's eyes never turned to her. The Queen re-entered the temple without ever glancing her way, although Maniye's gaze bored into her every second.

When she turned away, after Joalpey had gone from view, she was staring directly at the chest of Yellow Claw. The Eyrieman's gaze flicked over her, predatory and keen. His woman stepped forward to speak his words, but he yanked her back by her collar.

'So, this is the Wolf girl,' he said. A handful of his people were at his back, but he was a big man, and there was an aura about him of a strength more than physical, Maniye thought. He hardly needed his followers to give weight to his threats.

Nonetheless, she could not let that accusation lie. 'I am no Wolf.'

'You are no Tiger.'

'I am.'

'Your face says you lie to me,' Yellow Claw observed. He reached for her, as though to cock her head back, but she flinched away, feeling both her souls rise with a fighting anger within her. It was all she could do to hold a human shape right then.

'I lie to no one,' she spat at him. 'I am Tiger. This is my home. More so than it is yours.'

He angered quickly, the emotion darkening his face instantly. 'The Wolf girl is full of words,' he observed. 'They cram her mouth so much, they leak. Perhaps it would be a kindness if a hole was cut in her, so they could all fly free.'

She felt her feet slide into the ready stance she had been taught. Her heart was hammering, infecting her blood with fear, but she held his gaze. 'You challenge me?'

Yellow Claw sneered at her boldness, but there was an exasperation to him because she would not simply bow her head and back down. She thought of the only Eyriewomen she had seen, all of them meek, and haltered too, denied even the chance to give voice to their souls. *How are my mother's people in league with these creatures?*

A hand fell on the Eyrieman's arm: one of his compatriots, short and broad-shouldered, with half his face plain black and the other half painted a pale grey. White paint slashed a band across his eyes. It was a simple mask, but the sight of it awoke a deep fear in Maniye – a fear of something she could not name. He wore a drab woollen cloak of no particular colour, and beneath it his chest was bare, ridged with old, carefully inscribed scars.

The sight of him seemed to jolt Yellow Claw as well, for all the newcomer said nothing. He had the authority of a priest, though: a man who it was unwise to cross. For a moment, the leader of the Eyriemen warred with himself, but then he hissed between his teeth and stalked away.

The grey-faced man stayed on, staring at her with wide,

round eyes. She felt far more scared of him than she had been of his leader. Then he turned aside and nodded once, and she saw Hesprec standing there.

She did not have to ask the question, for it was writ large in her expression.

'This is Grey Herald, who spoke for me,' Hesprec explained. 'His word brought me into this place. There is yet remembrance in the Eyrie of the oldest tales, when the Serpent and the Owl Society stood shoulder to shoulder.' The words rang a distant echo within her, one of stories seldom retold. Tales of the soulless Plague People, and the loss of many things.

That night, she dreamt – a broken, twisted string of images informed not so much by Hesprec's talk as by the things he did not say. She was chasing after her mother, running through a landscape made as though the Shining Halls had been sunk deep within the earth. She called out Joalpey's name, and even her secret huntress name, but the woman still would not look back, rushing full-tilt through the broken, buried streets. Stepping to her tiger shape, Maniye ran and ran, but the distance between them only grew. A terrible convulsion in the earth's bones was occurring all around them, stone cracking, ornate carvings shivering into shards. Looking up towards the cavern sky – lit by some greenish radiance that emanated from precisely nowhere – she saw Hesprec standing atop one of the buildings, and others like him: men and women, old and young, and all with the tattoos of the serpent making tracks across their faces. Grey Herald was there too, and others painted like he was, and more still. They held their hands up as though warding off some presence that sought to intrude through the rock above.

And then she knew how she could catch up with her mother, and she had Stepped into her wolf shape, swift paws carrying her eagerly in the pursuit, but when she was at Joalpey's heels the woman looked back with a stricken, terrified expression, and Maniye saw that the shadows on all sides of her were other wolves, and that *she* had been what her mother had been running from all along.

Then she woke, because there was screaming, and it was coming from somewhere outside her head.

31

The bronze knife clattering to the ground at her feet was the loudest sound in the world.

Maniye had slept poorly these last two nights. It was not the dreams, though. It was the sound of the Wolf scout that the Eyriemen had brought in. The priesthood were torturing him.

The people of the Tiger knew that gods were not of the world: above it and beyond it, things of pure spirit. That was why they would not commit the image of their deity to stone or metal or wood. Smoke, shadows, these were fit intermediaries through which to glimpse the spirit world.

She had learned all this, of course. She remembered carefully committing to memory that, for a soul to be prepared for the Tiger, it must be brought to a height of spiritual awareness, drawn from the body until it was almost visible in the air. In her lessons, the logic of this had seemed unassailable.

And there were different methods of arriving at such awareness. The year-kings of the Deer Tribe had their every want sated until it was time for them to kneel at the altar; the Wolves hunted their Running Deer to exhaustion. Drugs, deprivation, death at the point of physical exultation; the gods could be reached in many ways.

For the Tiger, when it came to offer up its enemies, there was only one way. Fear and pain were the hammers they used to forge a fine sacrifice. And so the Swift Back writhed and wailed deep inside the temple, his voice carried out to all, echoing his despair along the halls and the corridors. And in the temple's heart, in the room of smoke and pierced stone, the Tiger licked its insubstantial lips and waited.

When he cried out, there was a distant echo deep within Maniye, the return call of her receding wolf soul. She hated it, yet it kept her awake. No matter how much she told herself that these were her ways now, still that lonely voice would not be silenced.

And now this: the dancers and their knife.

She had been up early, red-eyed, trailing towards her lessons, when four of the other girls had blocked her path.

'You,' said one who stood in front like their leader. Maniye had looked her in the eye and groped for her name. Imshalma, or something like that. Tiger names were still strange to her.

Maniye did not answer, merely waiting. She could sense the ill-feeling amongst them, and yet they were nervous, too.

'I understand you now,' said Imshalma or whatever her name was. 'I have watched you, all the days since you came. I have asked myself, "What is this Wolf they have brought among us?" There must be a reason, I knew, but I could not see it. But now I understand you.'

Maniye had no sense that her relationship to the Queen had become known to these girls, but plainly something had changed.

'I have seen our teachers watching you. I have seen the *Queen* watching you. I know you, Wolf girl. You are a test.'

Maniye's eyes narrowed. 'I am not a Wolf.'

'You are a test for us, to see if we possess the mind to be warriors. Our teachers have watched just to see if we would act against this enemy they have brought into our midst. They have been disappointed, because we accepted you so meekly. The Tiger is not meek. The Tiger takes his prey without hesitation, without mercy. So, I will take you. I will pass the test.'

That was when the daggers came out, one to stay in Imshalma's hand and one cast at Maniye's feet.

Maniye weighed the girl's words, hunting for truth and finding not a trace of it. But there was another possibility. There might be a test, after all.

'They are testing *me*,' she told the other girl. 'I am Tiger but they doubt me. And I have been meek. As you say, the Tiger is not meek.' She picked up the dagger, noting an eddy of movement through the other girls. Imshalma's eyes were a little wider than before, and Maniye wondered if she had been expecting the 'test' to be passed simply by making the challenge, perhaps thinking the Wolf girl would flee when confronted with a blade.

The Shadow of the Wolf clung to her, and it made them fear. Just as Wolf children grew up on tales of the Shadow Eaters, so recent history had given these girls plenty of reasons to fear the Wolf.

She shifted her back foot, dropping her weight lower. Her left hand came up before her face, fingers crooked, whilst her right held the curved blade extended at waist level. The mantle of her lessons settled on her, and for once she felt each part of her in its proper place. If Aritchaka had come by just then, she would have found no fault at all.

But the priesthood were not present to arbitrate. The other three girls had backed off to give Imshalma space, and it was just the two of them in the whole world. Maniye's opponent had adopted a counter-stance, blade held high and jutting forwards, offhand low, halfway to reaching for Maniye's weapon. The girl had been learning these stances and moves for years: her technique would always be better. If this was a dance, or the slow measured steps of a lesson, then Maniye would always be stumbling to keep up.

Some part of her mind had frozen – *What comes next?* – just as she sometimes found in practice. The animal inside her knew that she could not afford to be the one reacting, though. Even as Imshalma moved forwards, so Maniye's feet were already dancing. She passed backwards three quick steps, because over a short distance it was always possible to go backwards faster than the opponent could advance. That was Lesson One. Lesson Two was when she braced against her back foot, pushing herself towards her opponent as Imshalma was trying to close the gap. In the moment after, she had reversed her motion, but before she was within reach of that bronze claw, she Stepped.

She managed the pounce badly, the dagger nipping her across the foreleg, and her impact coming at an angle, so that she made Imshalma stagger without knocking her down. Then she had leapt off, ending up on the far side of her opponent, knowing that, without that dagger pinned, she could not stay within its reach.

They both Stepped in the same instant, Imshalma to Tiger, Maniye to girl, her blade sweeping so that it cut her opponent across the muzzle, sending the animal reeling away, pawing at the shallow wound.

She felt her heart racing within her. For a moment she was fighting against her own body, trying to settle back into her ready stance. If Imshalma had been able to break through her own pain to mount an attack, things could have gone badly. Instead she was retreating again, now on human feet and dabbing at a line of blood that traced the bridge of her nose and ran along one cheekbone. For a moment Maniye thought that her opponent lacked the will to go on, but then some metal came into the other girl's eyes and she was striding forwards, passing with the dagger, changing stances fluidly, all her years of practice flooding back into her.

Maniye Stepped, Stepped back, retreating before the darting bronze that kept coming for her. Abruptly her tiger eyes could not see a way past the blade. She tried a feint to give herself room, got her footing wrong and took a raking scratch across her forearm. She was aware that she had been backing up for too long – that she might hit a wall at any moment.

Something made Imshalma pause: it was Maniye's expression, all bared teeth and frustration and Wolf features. In that moment, Maniye struck back, slapping for Imshalma's knife hand, letting her own blade find the lines that she had been taught: belly, throat, armpit, flank. Imshalma fell back rapidly, and they both Stepped at once, pushing forwards into a grappling embrace of tigers, a lightning exchange of claws that marked both of them. Then Imshalma had twisted aside, shrugging out of the clasp and Stepping back to drag her blade past Maniye's eyes. It left a slight wound, a scalp wound, but the shock of it threw Maniye back to her human form, out of position and off balance. Imshalma had a hand bunched in the collar of her tunic, holding her down, with her dagger drawn back to thrust.

Maniye Stepped, without conscious decision, and got her teeth into the other girl's wrist. Had Imshalma held to her purpose she could still have stabbed and ended it, but instead she jerked away with a yell. Instead of holding – as every instinct was howling at her to do – Maniye broke away and made a snarling, defiant retreat, blood in her jaws. Her wolf jaws.

She Stepped to human instantly, standing in her best approximation of a ready stance, and Imshalma was still facing her, still nominally fighting, but the other girl's eyes were wide, the expression of someone whose fears have been made flesh: seeing the Wolf brought to life right there in the temple.

She found her balance, though, levelling her blade at Maniye once more, although there was a terror still lurking in her eyes. She would not back down.

Then there was only Aritchaka's voice calling out, 'Enough!'

The priestess stood at the far end of the passage, the same direction the four girls had come from. Maniye felt sure she had been watching there for quite long enough.

'Your dedication to your studies is admirable,' Aritchaka said, in a sharp-edged voice. 'However, I feel you both require more practice so as to master the proper forms. Have those injuries washed and tended to.'

Please don't tell her. Please don't tell my mother, but the words could not be spoken and Aritchaka's expression was stern.

Following a day of practice in which she did not look at or speak to any of the other girls – and they had returned the same cold courtesy – Aritchaka came to her as she was bedding down.

'Do not sleep. Tonight I will come for you,' the priestess instructed. She was staring, weighing what she saw, but her face could not be read.

'What is it?' Maniye wanted Hesprec there, because she dearly needed anyone who might be on her side. Although he was tolerated within the Shining Halls, his presence in the temple itself was very much on sufferance. He could not stay there long. She was alone.

'The Queen has sent for you,' Aritchaka told her. 'Tonight we feast with the Tiger. It is for the priesthood and the great families – but she will have you there.' She was unhappy about it. Maniye felt her own innards clench. What did this mean? Was Joalpey going to acknowledge her at last? Would the priesthood stand for it, if she did? Or was she herself to be offered to the Tiger? Would it be her screams next, now the extended torment of the Swift Back scout had finally been silenced.

After that, there was nothing for it but to watch the moon climb the sky and put the stars to shame, to name the constellations as they made their procession above, and wonder if any of them might be invoked to come to her aid. Within her, her twin souls roiled in a festering sore of fight and flight, keyed up to a danger that she could not assess or confront. The foot-dragging stretch between dusk and midnight was a long and lonely road for her.

And then at last she heard the soft scuff of Aritchaka's return. The priestess carried with her a robe of soft hide and a cloak of tiger fur, which lay heavy enough on Maniye's shoulders that she felt the Tiger himself was pressing down on her. Meekly, mutely, she followed in the woman's footsteps into the heart of the temple, into that same room of smoke and shadow where the insubstantial spectre of the Tiger dwelt.

She had expected there might be other students – those in favour or disfavour – or perhaps the priesthood all mantled in tiger-skin, but Aritchaka backed out again as soon as she had delivered Maniye there, and then it was just the two of them: the girl with the Wolf tribe face and the Queen of the Tiger people.

Joalpey, whose secret name was Strength Under Moonlight, forced her head around to gaze directly at her daughter. The muscles of her jaw clenched, but this time she did not look away. Her eyes just lanced and lanced deeper, as though Maniye was a boil.

She knows. Just one lapse into wolf shape, after resisting it for so long . . . but of course word had come to her mother. *Is this to be a reckoning then?* Maniye felt the Tiger cease his pacing and settle down in the darkness behind her, head resting on his paws, and watching. Something was to happen here: her twin souls knew it. She could almost hear the great cat's rumbling purr of anticipation, feeling it like a tremor in the ground.

Then there were servants: thralls, men with heavy collars bearing platters of meat. They looked at neither woman, merely trod about the chamber in fixed paths, eyes on their feet as if terrified of stepping astray.

'Sit with me,' Joalpey instructed. 'Maniye . . . Many Tracks . . . daughter, sit with me.'

She folded herself down alongside the altar and, after a moment, Maniye followed her example.

'Aritchaka and the priesthood hold the Tiger's feast, but the Queen takes her meat apart from her subjects,' Joalpey explained. She was watching Maniye as if the girl was venomous, or apt to become violently mad. 'But you shall eat with me. Please . . .'

Maniye took a sliver of meat: it was so tender that it seemed

374

to melt on her tongue, delicately spiced and rich with juices. She was suddenly aware of how hungry she was, having fasted since noon. Joalpey found a smile and forced it onto her face, picking at the flesh herself.

'They tell me you learn fast, devouring all they have to teach you,' she observed.

'I want to be of the Tiger,' Maniye insisted. 'I will do anything, if it means that.'

Joalpey regarded her doubtfully as the girl scooped up another slice of meat and tore into it. 'In this short time, you have made great advances, they say. You cannot walk the steps of the Tiger's dance, yet each footfall is not so very far away. You do not know all the cycles of our heroes and our deeds, yet you can tell a tale that is not so very far removed. And they say you Step well.' Her voice had gone hard on that word, but Maniye could see that she was fighting down the bitter edge in it.

Maniye opened her mouth again, not sure what she should say next. She longed for Hesprec's wisdom, to know what convoluted sequence of words would break down the barrier still between them. Surely there had to be some magic that could accomplish it.

'The Tiger's sacred meal,' Joalpey gestured. 'How do you like it?'

'Very well,' Maniye said, desperate to please, although it was true.

'You understand, then?'

The girl frowned. 'Understand?'

'That you eat the flesh of the Wolf.'

That was no great revelation: amongst the Winter Runners she had eaten wolf-meat many times. It was common, when a hearth-woman wished to become with child, that she would have her hunter mate kill a wolf and butcher its body for the pot. In that way the beast's soul would be cut loose, and might seek out a new life within her belly. Usually there was enough to

375

spare, and it was good practice to woo the Wolf's favour by gifting it to many. Still, the meat was tough and poor eating, not like the feast currently before her.

'This tastes like no wolf,' she remarked, around a mouthful, 'This is tender as pig.'

Joalpey regarded her intently. 'It is Wolf,' and this time Maniye caught the special inflection, and a sudden shudder of fright went through her.

With great willpower she forced the mouthful down, aware of sitting suddenly on a knife-edge. Yes, the Swift Back scout had stopped screaming at last. She had not asked what would be done with him after that.

'But, if he died . . .' The words were drawn out of her as though she had eaten a keen-edged thread along with the meat, and now it was being hauled back out. Humans were animals, animals were human. There was no line between them save the ability to Step. Souls passed one to the other. To eat of a deer that had worn a man's shape was no different than to eat of a mute deer that had not.

But Joalpey meant something different.

'His ghost . . .' Maniye got out, 'is here?'

'Yes,' the Queen confirmed calmly, and selected another morsel herself.

Maniye sat very still. Because this was a Tiger thing; this was a tradition of her mother's house. This was *how they did things* in the Shining Halls. But it was wrong, it was terribly wrong. Not eating the flesh of a man, for all beasts were men, but to eat his soul. To trap it within the yoked human flesh and to consume it – to give a mad ghost sanctuary inside your own body – was to fill yourself too full of souls – and she had two already fighting within her.

'This is how the Tiger is fed. He is a god. What do you think he eats? Other people do not understand this, but *we* know.'

And Maniye thought, *The Shadow Eaters, the Wolves call us. It is not just a casual name.*

Her hands shook. She thought that she could feel the dead Wolf's ghost squirming inside her. And yet . . . and yet the Tiger had padded up behind her, darkening the gloom further with its smoky presence, waiting to be fed.

There were rituals that they had tried to teach her, words and forms and steps. Aware that Joalpey's eyes were fixed upon her fiercely, Maniye stood, trying to master the hammering of her heart. She took a deep breath – and turned to face the god.

Her eyes saw only the dancing patterns of shadow that the fires threw against the wall, but her mind told her that these were the striped flanks of the Tiger, that the hot air was his breath. The knowledge, the utter *certainty* that he was immediately before her came like a blow, as though that sightless muzzle had suddenly nudged at her chest, rocking her back on her heels.

She could not remember all the moves, the gestures of invitation and propitiation, but she could guess and follow her instincts, just as Joalpey had said. The sequence was not long, and if she did not get every motion of it exactly right, she was never far away – hovering about it like a crow over a dying thing. With a mix of grace and awkward pauses she invited the Tiger to feed, to take the struggling soul of the Swift Back scout from between her lips.

As she imagined that vast maw gaping for her, she wondered what else it might take from her. She felt her own Wolf nature backing as far into her as it could go, tail between its legs, yellow eyes glinting.

When she turned back, with the dark tide that was the Tiger receding in her mind, Joalpey was standing there – close enough to touch. She was still staring – forcing herself to stare at the girl. One hand was raised halfway, as if to rest on Maniye's arm, but it had paused. For a moment – for a long, tense agony of a moment – she remained still, save that Maniye could hear her mother's ragged breathing.

'I want a daughter,' the Queen got out. 'I want an heir of my own blood. You are all the heirs of my blood, all that there will ever be . . .' The outstretched hand twitched, contracting into a fist. 'But . . . but . . . but I look on you and see it in your eyes, in your face. You have a wolf soul.'

'I have a tiger soul.' Maniye's voice was just a whisper.

'It is not enough,' Joalpey forced out through clenched teeth. 'Aritchaka has told you—'

'Aritchaka,' Joalpey hissed. 'Aritchaka has spoken for you. You are strong, she says. You are clever. You are brave. You are all the things a child of the Tiger should be. But I see these things in you, too, and it is a Wolf's strength, a Wolf's cleverness. I cannot change my eyes. I cannot forget them: Stone River and that loathsome creature his priest. And you *are* them. They sit in your face, and I cannot see you past them.' She took two steps away, convulsively. The hand that had been reaching out was now warding.

Maniye tried to voice something: a plea, a protest. What sound came out did not make a complete word.

'And they will use you against me,' her mother whispered. 'The Tiger tells me so. The Tiger tells me that you must be prey, if you are not his. What am I to do? I want to make you mine, but I cannot. I cannot bear you to be here. I thought I could face it, after all this time, but it still cuts me – it hurts just as it did.' She turned away, fists clenched by her sides, shaking.

Maniye felt the Tiger's breath still on her neck, its insatiable hunger for souls. *You must be prey, if you are not his.*

She fled then, while Joalpey was still wrestling with herself. Any later would be too late.

32

Shyri had been terrorizing the local wildlife, Stepped into her Plains form, a Laughing Girl indeed. The deer and squirrels and groundhogs and coyotes she scared up had no idea what she was. A long-limbed, spotted demon with swift and terrible jaws, she killed more by fright than by trauma, Asmander reckoned. She killed more than they needed, too, but she was enjoying herself, and he had no intention of stopping her. It was a bitter realization but, of the three of them, she was the only effective hunter in this country. He disdained to sully his Champion's shape for something as mundane as finding food, and neither Old Crocodile nor the Dragon could hunt in such cold. The year was supposedly getting warmer, but Asmander could only assume that in the Crown of the World that word carried some other meaning.

'Come south to our country,' Asmander had told the Laughing Girl. 'Come hunt the channels of the estuary or the banks of the Tsotec's head and then we'll see.' But she just laughed at him, and she was right to do so.

'I will,' she said, her grin widening from ear to ear as she made him gut and spit the spoils of her pre-dawn hunt. 'And I'll outdo you there, too. There is nowhere in the world my people cannot thrive.'

'Then why do you rule just a hand's breadth of the Plains,

and no more? Where is the great Empire of the Hyena?' Asmander demanded, nettled.

She put her face right in front of his, eyes to his eyes. 'O leaping Champion, we are a patient people. We are not hasty. The Plains are covered with the dust of those who have mounted greatness and failed to keep a hold. We have seen the Aurochs and the Horn Bearers, we have seen the Cats come and go. We will see these northern Wolves fall, and no doubt we will visit the ruins of your own great city one day. We watch you all claw up for the sun, and then burn, and we laugh. And when you have all fallen, then we will walk the carrion road of your failure, and we will rule.'

And she had him. He was staring into those wide eyes, struck to the core with the certainty of it all, the manifest destiny of the Laughing Men and the women who led them. He could see, vividly in his mind's eye, their dominion of bones, extending from the cold north to the deserts beyond the Tsotec.

And then she laughed delightedly and pushed him away, so that, off balance from squatting on his haunches, he tumbled backwards. For a moment he was a crocodile, twisting and whipping his bladed tail at her, and then he regained his feet and his human shape.

'You made it up,' he snarled at her. 'This is all your fantasy.'

'Maybe it is and maybe it isn't,' she grinned fiercely. 'But you recognized it for truth, didn't you? I think you even liked it. A strong woman to put her foot on your neck, eh? Is *that* your type, O Champion?'

Venater sniggered: there was no other word for it. Asmander glowered at the pair of them. 'Mock all you want, a Champion is chosen by the world. It is something you will never know.'

'A Champion can't even get his servant to gut a rabbit for him,' Shyri pointed out, not in the least put out.

'It's beneath him.' Asmander looked down at his own slick hands and smiled somewhat shamefacedly. 'You're right, I should really take him in hand.'

'Try it,' Venater growled.

They had been hiding out here in the woods near the Shining Halls for days now, in a shelter built of branches and leaves that had not been meant to last this long. Every so often, Hesprec appeared and assured them that all was well, but his business was not yet concluded. Questions about whether this Wolf girl of his needed rescuing or not were dodged nimbly, and then he would be gone. That the locals were aware of them seemed inarguable – yet nobody troubled them, nor invited them within the walls of the settlement either. And that was a shame, for the Shining Halls looked as close to civilization as he had come in a long while. In the manner of their building and carving Asmander saw an echo of his own homeland, and wondered what ancient architects had tracked north – or south.

'What's the point of him, if he won't cook and clean for you?' Shyri demanded.

'I'm not his mate,' the old pirate spat.

'Are you not?'

'Enough.' Asmander stood up abruptly. He didn't know what had alerted him, but something was definitely wrong.

The other two abandoned their quarrel instantly. Shyri Stepped smoothly, surging forwards into her high-shouldered hyena shape. Venater took up his *meret*, the greenstone edge of which he had been awake half the night sharpening.

A moment later Asmander spotted them: Hesprec returning, and this time not alone, for a small Wolf girl dogged his footsteps. The sight filled him with gladness. It meant they could move again, and it meant he could now fulfil his own mission, one way or another.

Hesprec had paused, struggling for breath. The girl addressed him briefly, and then she was a tiger, and the old priest a serpent coiling in her jaws. Seeing that – such trust between them – Asmander understood why the priest had demanded his reluctant entourage wait for him. He pushed further thoughts of his duty to the back of his mind.

Then the striped cat had flowed up the hillside towards them, hardly seeming to need footholds. A second later Hesprec was with them in human form, looking so worn out that Asmander felt he could have held the old priest up to the sun and viewed his bones through the man's skin.

'This is her, then?' he asked lightly. Stepped back to her human shape, the much-heralded girl seemed an insignificant piece of work.

'And now we go,' Hesprec confirmed with uncharacteristic directness. 'Forgive me for ruining your breakfast.'

'There are more rabbits,' Shyri said happily, 'always more rabbits. This is good hunting land.'

'A shame,' Hesprec remarked wryly, 'for we will be hunted.'

They set off as swiftly as possible, a Stepped Shyri leading the way. Asmander had asked for the honour of bearing Hesprec, the priest's whip-slender form tucked inside his tunic, next to his bare skin. The girl changed too, not to the tiger but into the compact form of a wolf, but he had been expecting that.

Asmander would have preferred to have the two Coyote traders with them, because the north remained a large, cold and complex place in which to navigate. However, Two Heads Talking and Quiet When Loud had abandoned their company as soon as they were close to the Shining Halls. The pair had shown little confidence in Tiger hospitality.

Even so, at first it was simply a matter of finding the best paths downhill through the trees, for it was more important to put distance between them and any pursuers than to be clever. As night drew on, then perhaps some application of cleverness might be in order, Asmander considered, and that was where they were more likely to run into trouble. Even a day out from their starting point they would still be well within the Tiger's Shadow.

And yet, as dusk fell, he was aware that all sign of civilization had been left behind save for the odd tumbled ruin. There was no great sprawl of farms and herdsmen here, as there would have been in the south. Asmander sensed that they would be re-entering the domain of the Wolf before too long.

Which brings its own special problems, he knew.

Shyri sniffed out a sheltered hollow, and they all bundled themselves together to sleep, going without a fire but building a shelter around them that would hold their body warmth near to them. Even so, they were all awake and shivering well before dawn.

'Early start it is, then,' Asmander declared, and he nodded at the Wolf girl, Maniye, who had not said a word to anyone yet.

'What's she good for, then?' Venater was more direct. 'She's what all this is about? Why?'

'Because it is my whim, and my will,' Hesprec told him sharply. Venater – no proper follower of Serpent – glowered at him but stopped short of any direct challenge.

'We are walking between fires, I am afraid,' the old priest said gently to Maniye, 'and yet we must walk.'

'Who is likely to be chasing us, and why?' Asmander asked him, posing a question necessary enough not to seem invasive, although he was burning with curiosity.

'All I know is that she came to me in the Tiger city,' Hesprec told him, 'and she needed to leave. That was enough.'

'You foresaw it,' Asmander decided.

The old man shook his head tiredly. 'If only the Serpent could speak so clearly to me. It seemed to me that life in the Crown of the World is seldom kind, and that the life of one half-Wolf girl has not been kind, and that such unkindnesses might not be shrugged away simply by exchanging one roof for another. And so I came to the Shining Halls, and waited. And I wish that I had not been needed there, and could have returned to you alone. But sometimes the Serpent moves in your innards, and you must learn to trust that movement, and follow it.'

'What was it, though?' Asmander asked plaintively. Somewhere in the question lurked the southerner's civilized horror of these northern people and their ways.

'My mother.' Maniye's voice sounded flat and dead. 'I found my mother.'

Looks were exchanged between the rest of them, and then: 'The Tiger did for her?' from Venater.

'Idiot, her mother must *be* Tiger,' Shyri hissed.

'Doesn't mean they can't—'

'Quiet,' Asmander hissed at them both. Maniye stared at them: it was as though, after a day's travel together, she was seeing them for the first time. 'You are as I thought men of the far south would be,' she remarked in a small voice, staring at him.

'As I said, the followers of the Serpent are special,' and Hesprec then named them all, though Asmander could see that the girl had problems with most of what she heard, traditions being so different in these lands.

'What was it about your mother?' Asmander rested on his haunches beside her, so as not to loom. He wanted to know whether there was some rescue they would need to enact, or if the older woman was dead.

Maniye took a deep breath. 'She did not want me,' was what he barely heard, the words scarcely venturing beyond her teeth. 'She would not look on me.'

Faced with that, he could only stand up and back off.

They achieved another day's hard journeying. At first they followed the Plains girl Shyri's best guess, and Maniye trailed behind on her wolf feet, mostly so she would not have to speak to anyone. Past midday, though, she came out of herself enough to object to the path.

'Where are you even going?' she demanded.

Shyri regarded her narrowly. 'Away.'

'Where would *you* head for?' Hesprec asked her gently. They had stopped to eat in the shadow of a great fallen stele, a carven obelisk that might even have marked some key Tiger tribe border.

'The further west we travel, the more the Shadow of the Wolf falls on us,' she warned them simply.

'These things are known: a stranger is always short of friends,' Hesprec said.

'Yet we may find some,' she insisted. 'If we find the river and follow it, there are the Horse traders.'

The old priest frowned. 'But your people . . .'

'We would brave the Wolf's jaws to do it, yes.' She closed her eyes, breathing in the land around her. 'Winter Runners or Swift Backs – if there were Wolf scouts at the doors of the Shining Halls, then they will be everywhere south as well. We could run into them at any time, but more and more so, the further south we tread.'

'Then what?' Venater demanded, sounding as though running into a few enemies on the road would be just the thing for him.

'North,' she said.

'What is north?' Asmander asked her.

'*Cold*, is what's north,' put in Venater. 'More cold even than this.'

She looked at him blankly, because this was a warm spring promising a fierce summer. 'Do you think Loud Thunder would help us, Hesprec?'

The old Serpent looked troubled. 'The Cave Dweller we wintered with, yes. The man he now is, after his Mother has taken him to task – that is a different man.'

'But?'

'But these are quite the most hostile lands I have ever travelled,' he admitted, and then added, 'Yes, even including the Plains, Laughing Child: your people have no monopoly on unpleasantness. So we will see if the Bear will take in the Tiger's quarry . . . and the Wolf's.'

'And then, Messenger?' Asmander demanded.

The old man plainly knew what he meant, though he looked so weary at the thought that Maniye could feel the weight of his age dragging at her, too. 'Then it will be time to look to the south's needs, Champion. And whatever I can do, I will do.'

They set out again, and this time Maniye, as wolf, led them. Shyri relinquished the vanguard with nothing more than a shrug of her shoulders. Her scent, when she Stepped, was harsh and strange in Maniye's nose.

Their path took them into broken ground, where the cover of the trees was patchy and unreliable. That was her error, she realized in retrospect. She was trying to find the shortest path, and thought this must also be the best.

When the attack came, it was unheralded: not a scent, not a sound until it was too late. She was running their little band across a rugged stretch of land creased deeply by the path of a stream that was still swelled by late meltwater from the northern reaches of the highlands. The crossing was difficult, the waters high and fast and hungry, too much so to swim in any shape. Shyri and Venater were already across, and Asmander was just about to make the jump, with Hesprec slung inside his tunic. Then there was a rush of wind – she assumed it was just that at first, but it grew louder and louder far too swiftly. Abruptly the sun was blotted from the sky by a vast shadow.

The great bird struck, coursing at head height over the uneven land, angling its wings as it took her, its talons, hot and strong as metal from the forge, seizing her about the body. She had time for one shriek – more of surprise than pain or fear – and she was airborne.

There were other birds, lesser creatures circling overhead, but the vast-winged eagle made them seem sparrows. It hoisted her into the air with ease, and the blustering beat of its feathers sent Asmander toppling from the stream's edge. She caught a wheeling glimpse of him kicking away from the rock, one arm out for the others to catch him, and then she was already too far from them, jolting and jostling in the air as the eagle shifted its grip on her. The points of its hooked claws snagged in her clothing and pierced through all her furs and hide, to prick at her skin.

In mid-air she had tried striking out at the eagle, thinking that she might be able to hurt him, and so bring him down. At the first blow, though, he simply let go with one claw, leaving her dangling wildly from the other over what was now a fatal drop. The message was clear.

She was not carried so very far, and she could feel the eagle beginning to labour, for all the great span of his wings. Could he have plucked up someone larger – Asmander or Shyri, perhaps? Venater? Surely not. But Maniye had always been small.

Abruptly the hard grip of those talons loosened and she yelled out in terror, before landing on hard rocks. The drop had just been a second's worth, and she found she had taken her tiger shape, four legs cushioning the landing as best they could. For a moment she was snarling, swiping at those around her, full of fighting spirit. Then the eagle landed on her back, driving her savagely to the unyielding ground. She twisted and clawed at him, but his grip was horrifyingly strong. A second later he had effortlessly shifted a claw to her neck, choking her, and she was again in her fragile human form beneath him.

He keened and shrieked, deafeningly loud, and people nearby were hurrying forwards. Even as she gasped and gagged, a noose was about her neck, pulling tight, and then his wings boomed in the air, lifting him up and then dropping him down a handful of paces away. She reached for the noose instantly, but hands were laid on her, hauling her to her feet. There was an Eyrieman on either side of her, twisting her arms back painfully: lean, hard men with half-painted faces.

The eagle stretched its neck back and spread its wings, a gesture of triumph beyond mistaking, and became a man: Yellow Claw. Of course, it was Yellow Claw.

'What do you want?' she shouted at him. Surely it was enough that her mother's people and her father's would be hunting her, and that neither meant her well? What did this creature want with her? 'Did she send you? Did the priesthood send you?'

'Nobody *sends* Yellow Claw,' the Eyrieman leader scoffed. 'Yellow Claw is his own master. Yellow Claw is a *Champion*, Many Tracks Wolf girl. Your people do not even know what that means.'

He spoke the word as Hesprec had, when referring to Asmander. There *was* something about the big Eyrieman, and there had been a similar sense about the black southerner, although the general strangeness of the latter's appearance had taken more of her attention. They both cast greater shadows than other men. *As though a greater spirit stands behind them?*

Yellow Claw's wings had taken them north to a high place, a stony shelf jutting high and sheer out of the trees, with the mountain slopes above. Here the Eyrie had carved out a roost for themselves within Tiger lands. There were at least a dozen warriors in her sight, and a handful of women. The former were eyeing her with brash stares; the latter had eyes downcast, some cooking, some mending or making things. With a jolt, Maniye saw that each woman's long hair was looped about her own neck like a halter: nothing they could not have undone with a little effort, but a mark of slavery nonetheless.

'As for what I want?' Yellow Claw muscled closer to her, so that she could smell the raw-flesh stink of him, feel the heat rising from his body. 'I want you, girl, and so I have you. So it is with all that the Eyrie's gaze lights on.' He was glaring at her from his war-eye. 'I have the little mongrel girl that Stone River is hunting, and that the Queen of the Tigers demands back. But I do not think I will give you to her, not yet. Not until I know what is so important about such a meagre-looking morsel. And then I will decide whether you should return to our faithful allies, or whether I fly you to the Eyrie as my prize, or whether I cast you from the heights to see if the Hawk will save you. I do not think that he would.'

He cocked his head at some of the women. 'Make sure that collar stays on her, or you'll feel my talons, every one of you. She's a valuable cur, this one – for now, she is. Fleeting Light, fly to the Shining Halls, see what they say about their missing mongrel. But don't take too long. You know how easily I grow bored. I might give this one the Hawk's test.' He thrust his tattooed face into hers, close enough that she could have bitten him, had she dared. 'Do you fly well, Wolf girl, Tiger girl? Do you leave many tracks in air? I didn't think so. Whatever god you speak to, ask him to make you useful to me.'

33

Maniye sat miserably, with a braided collar tight about her neck. A day had passed since her capture, and Yellow Claw was still awaiting the return of the man he had sent off to the Shining Halls. In the meantime she had been held here under the watch of the women, eating thin stew once a day. Right now she was watching two of the warriors play some sort of game. The Eyriemen had plainly camped here for some time. They had a row of wood-framed hides to shelter in, lined up against the rising rock furthest from the edge, and there were jagged stakes bristling at the one place where their bluff could be approached on foot from below.

Then there was their testing ground – or whatever name they had for it. They had hauled up a dozen tree trunks and then wedged or roped them to the rock so that they projected out over the sheer drop, jutting at various angles. The task must have involved a considerable effort, but then Yellow Claw would have had a band of fractious warriors on his hands, and an urgent need to find them something to do. She watched the Eyriemen play a game where they fought and wrestled at the ends of those precarious posts, darting and dancing to tag each other without having to resort to their wings.

A shadow fell across her: one of the women, come to check on her – or check that she was not escaping the rope. *Not that I would have anywhere to go. Yellow Claw was right. I can't make tracks on air.*

There came another little wooden bowl of stew, containing the last scraps of whatever the hunters had caught. The Eyriemen had a strict hierarchy of eating: Yellow Claw would be first, or whoever he had left in charge. Then, if he was present, would be the sinister Grey Herald, although Maniye had seen little of him, and he had shown no sign of knowing her. After that, the other warriors ate, jostling to be first with much joking and cursing.

Maniye ate next, and the women of the Eyrie were left to satisfy their hunger with whatever remained. A prisoner ranked above them, it seemed. At first Maniye assumed they must forage for themselves, but it was plain they were forbidden to Step, prisoners of this plateau even as she was.

'You were at the Shining Halls?' Maniye asked one. In truth they all had a similar look to them, these women: not in the features so much as the downtrodden expression that gripped them.

She thought the woman would ignore her, but the Eyrie girl paused and then shook her head quickly.

'But one of you was?' Maniye pressed. 'She even spoke for you. So she's your leader?'

The Eyriewoman's eyes widened in shock. Maniye was ready for her to flee, but instead she dipped her head closer and murmured, 'Yellow Claw cannot speak direct to the Tiger. There are only certain ways a Champion of the Eyrie may speak to such a woman, and still retain his dignity.'

'Threats and bullying?' The words came out before Maniye could plan them.

The Eyriewoman's look was solemn, though. 'If you anger him, you will find out.'

'Do you have a name?'

The question, coming out of the blue, seemed to take the woman completely by surprise. Maniye hoped perhaps she

391

might have an ally here: a fellow sufferer under the tyranny of Yellow Claw.

'I am Many Tracks – that is my hunter name.' She had so little to barter with. 'I am Maniye . . . I was born Maniye.' It was a great gesture of trust for her to tell that to a stranger.

For a moment words formed on the Eyriewoman's lips, but then they died and she backed off, as though Maniye carried something contagious.

Yellow Claw came back towards evening, strutting through his men, giving some of them a shove to remind them of who he was. Maniye had hated a lot of people in her time, not least her own father and the priest Kalameshli, but she decided there was nobody she had come to dislike quite so swiftly as this Eyrieman. He was strong, and marked out in that odd way that lent him a fierce grandeur, and his Stepped form was majestic and proud enough to put the other hawks to shame. And yet it was wasted, Maniye thought: great gifts given to a small man.

He stared at her with something of a sneer on his face, and she found she could read the sequence of his thoughts there quite easily. He was impatient; he wanted to start on her. He was – she realized, with a mouth abruptly dry with fear – wondering if there was sufficient chance that she was unimportant. If she was just being pursued as a criminal, a thief or oathbreaker or the like, then nobody would complain at her fate.

'So what are you?' he murmured.

She wasn't sure if he was speaking to her, or just to himself. There was a great temptation to blurt it all out: *I am the daughter of the Winter Runners; I am the daughter of the Shining Halls! I am not for you!* She could save herself the horrors of his touch, for this night at least. But if he learned that, how would he then use her? Would he sell her back to her father, or turn her against her mother? Or would he take her, anyway, and crow to his men how he'd had a Wolf chief's daughter and the child of the Tiger Queen all in one night?

That last seemed very plausible.

But his patience held, for now. The chance that there was some great value in her, which could be bartered for his own advantage, lent him a fraying line of restraint. A cruel man and a bully he might be, but no fool.

That night she did not dare sleep in case it was the hard hands of Yellow Claw that woke her. She lay and shivered, and tried to pick at her collar where it had been woven together. Or she made plans to creep to the edge of the bluff and find a way down, human hands and feet grappling with the jagged rock. And she did none of these things, because she knew that defiance from her, the wrong look, the wrong word, would cut that straining thread that held Yellow Claw back. An excuse was all he needed.

Late that night, with the moon high in a chill and cloudless sky, someone moved very close to her, sending a shock of fear through her. Yellow Claw? Or one of the women? The thought of rescue did not even occur to her.

And it was not rescue. Instead it was Grey Herald. She could make out his cloaked form, the moonlight pale on his bare barrel chest. He had sat down within arm's reach of her, and had done so with only one small scuff to betray him. His eyes watched her from their white-stripe mask.

'In the Other Lands dwelt all the People once,' he said, his deep voice soft, the intonation one of ritual and rote-learning. 'Where there was always game for a hunter's bow, and the water was sweet, where every tree bore ripe fruit, and there was no summer nor winter.'

She craned her neck to blink at him, because this fierce warrior was crouching there reciting children's stories with great gravity. His eyes were fixed on her so fiercely that she thought this bizarre recounting must somehow be the prelude to an assault.

'In those days the People had many shapes between them, and many souls, and great was the number of their Steppings and their forms, and all were of one people,' Grey Herald informed

393

her sincerely. 'But there were some amongst them for whom all these forms and all these souls were not enough and, in seeking more, they grew less and less, until they had no souls at all.'

'The Plague People,' Maniye breathed. The contrast between this man and his words was fading with the intensity of his telling. She felt like a child again.

'They had no souls,' he went on, 'but power they had, for they became sorcerers and bent the world and the spirits to their will. And they consorted with monsters that had come into the world, and that sought to devour all the People, all the mute brothers, every living thing. And so they were called a plague.'

He paused at that, as though lamenting the loss of such paradise days, and then sighed. 'Those of the People who escaped their devouring tide realized that the Other Lands were lost to them, and they begged the sun to lead them to a land where they might be safe from the Plague People. And the sun bent low and red to the earth, and those people who yet lived followed that light into another place that is these lands that are ours.'

He paused, and Maniye had to restrain herself from urging him to continue. It was an old tale, and she had heard it many times, in various incarnations. Not like this, though. Grey Herald spoke as though it was a true article of faith to him, deeply and direly relevant to every day of his living. This ancient tale had no dust on it, for him.

And she realized he was waiting for her to speak the next words and, though she did not know his precise way of telling it, she could bridge that gap.

'But the Plague People came after,' she said, and he nodded briefly.

'The Plague People came after,' he echoed, 'for they could not abide the thought of there being a land free of their hungers, be it never so cold, never so dry, never so barren. And as the last of the people crossed from the Other Lands to the lands that are ours, three there were, who turned to face them and held them back. And these three fought them from sunset to sunrise, and stood against all the monsters that the Plague People had compacted with. And on the next morning, the sun arose with such a fierce fire that it scorched the land away, all that stood between the Other Lands and our lands. And the sea rushed in, of such depth and such width that even the monsters of the Plague People could not cross it.'

And she realized that she was not the only listener. For all that he spoke quietly, there were more than a few of the Eyrie with their eyes open, tilting their ears towards Grey Herald to catch his words.

'And those few who had escaped their hunger spread across our lands,' the storyteller went on, 'and found that the game was scarcer, and the water less sweet, and that the winter brought cold, and the summer drought. And they fought, and they divided – from one tribe of many forms to many tribes each of a single Stepping.

'And of the three who had fought the Plague People during that long night, what of them?' He raised his eyebrows sharply at her. 'It is said those three, and all their children who came after them, kept the secrets of the Other Lands and formed brave societies to teach them, lest they be needed again. And they painted their faces in the colours of their enemies, to remind all who saw them of the old dangers. And they never forgot what had been lost. And each remembered who had stood beside them, be it never so long ago. So it is that there shall always be an understanding and a friendship and a shared burden between the men of the Owl and the Bat and the people of the Serpent.'

He uttered the last words very deliberately, staring at her intently, and Maniye's heart leapt. For the Eyriemen it was just a story, well known and well told. For her it was a message.

Hesprec. Hesprec, somehow. He is giving me hope.

***

Akrit had expected to meet resistance from the Swift Backs. They were a tribe that had few links with the Winter Runners and bad blood from a couple of generations back. When the Wolf had risen against the Tiger, the Swift Backs had not been easy under Seven Skins' leadership. Always they had followed their own paths, never where they were supposed to be. But still they were of the Wolf, and their lands were closest to the Tiger. He could not ignore them.

And the girl had been brought this way, for he had followed her trail this far, with his warband at his heels.

He had fought Water Gathers for the loyalty of the Many Mouths, and he had come with the expectation of more blood in his mouth before this day was out. Instead, he and his people were welcomed as guests. For once somebody was pleased to see them.

He and Kalameshli Takes Iron stayed the night in the long-house of the chief. Word was running through this part of the Crown of World like the wind: the Tiger was on the move. Hunting parties were coming down out of the Shining Halls, driving the game of the Swift Backs before them. There had been raiding parties, stealing both thralls and food. A burning stand of the Wolf's wood had been scattered and despoiled. Scouts and lone hunters were missing.

The Swift Backs were between the claws of the Tiger, Akrit found.

Word had come to them from the Stone Place, outstripping Stone River's own progress. They looked at him with a measure of fear, a measure of respect. He felt as though he could almost reach across to them, to take them in hand and make them his.

Despite it all, though, they were waiting. They watched him eagerly, but in anticipation of what he might become.

He went to see Takes Iron the next morning. 'What do they want? Should I have come here wearing Water Gathers' skin? Do they want the spirits to take flesh and kneel before me?'

The old priest grimaced a little at the words. 'They have heard stories, and tales grow in the telling.'

'I am less than they expected? Is that what you now tell me?'

Kalameshli took a deep breath, glancing sidelong about him in case any of the Swift Backs was too close. 'If word has come, then it will be word of all, the good and the bad.'

Akrit hissed through his teeth. In that moment he wanted to tear down the Swift Back village with his bare hands and scatter the earth of their mounds. 'The girl, still?' He had a terrible sense of a story being told here, one of the old tales: *The Chief who Hunted His Daughter.* And how did that story end? 'What do they expect me to do? Stride into the Shining Halls and seize her?'

'I think that is just what they expect.' Takes Iron shrugged. 'They have lived close by the Tiger's Shadow, all this time. Year after year they have watched it creep down from the heights to inhabit their woods. All this time, the Winter Runners have told stories of the Tiger's defeat. The Swift Backs have told stories of what they once did when they were strong.'

'And now they think they're strong again?' Akrit spat.

'I think, for the Swift Backs, every darkness has a tiger in it,' said Kalameshli, shaking his head. 'They want someone to rise up and lead the war against the Shadow Eaters, but they will not raise their spears unless they believe they can win. As the shape of the enemy has grown in their minds, so they need a great leader – one who does all he sets out to.'

Akrit turned his mind to the Shining Halls, remembering his one sight of the place when he was young. Yes, Seven Skins had driven the Shadow Eaters back to the highlands, but even he had not brought the fight to the very heart of their power. A dawn had come when even he had turned around and said, 'Enough.'

'Enough.' Akrit's voice echoed his thoughts. 'Give me the warbands of all the Wolf tribes, and I will tear down the stones of the Shining Halls gladly. But not now.'

He was still brooding the next day when a Swift Back scout came hotfoot back from spying out the edge of the Tiger's Shadow. There were warbands come down from the Shining

Halls, she said, and the craven panic that went through her people was pitiful to see.

But there was more: they were not come to raid the Wolf, the scout announced. Instead they were hunting strange fugitives. The scout had seen that with her own eyes.

Long before he had heard all, Akrit knew the truth, and he was calling for his people to hunt too.

★★★

Next day, Yellow Claw's messenger flew back on swift wings from the Shining Halls. He made his report out of earshot of Maniye, but she could watch them between the trunks of the testing ground. Yellow Claw was not exactly overjoyed with what he was hearing, but plainly his man had learned something. The Eyrieman leader's gaze slid across to her, again and again.

Then he came striding across the bluff towards her, slipping a copper knife into one hand.

'The Tigers are searching the forests for you. The priesthood women are all very upset you have gone,' he announced with a sneer. 'But nobody says why. So it seems I must dirty my hands with you, after all. Have you stolen something of value that you've hidden from us? Is it some secret you discovered, that they wish no one to know?'

Maniye just stared up at him stubbornly. She did not know why she was protecting Joalpey, after what had happened. The bond was still there, though, a new-forged link that could not be cut by just one pair of hands.

Yellow Claw sighed theatrically, raising his eyes to the sky. 'I will find this knowledge in you, even if I must cut you open and read it in your entrails,' he declared, matter-of-factly.

Still she said nothing. She would gladly have answered him with something scathing, an insult even, but fear kept her from it.

Then the cry went up from one of the Eyriemen, 'Coming up the path!'

Yellow Claw rolled his eyes at this distraction. 'I shall be brief, little one,' he told her, as though she was his lover, and then he strode over to a spot at the bluff's edge that must be the sole accessible point, with sharp stakes thronging on either side of a narrow gap. A handful of other Eyriemen had gathered there, some with bows, but Yellow Claw was plainly not impressed by what he saw. He was curious, though: Maniye could read that in him. And Grey Herald was speaking there, too, giving some quiet piece of advice.

The Eyriemen backed off, enough to allow the newcomers to reach the top of the path. Maniye caught her breath. It was *them*. Not the whole mob of them, who would probably have been riddled with arrows by now, but two had come. One was Hesprec, leaning on his staff, nothing but bone-stretched skin in the shape of an old man. He looked exhausted just to be there, even though he had surely been carried up the path in his serpent form. The other was the black man, the true southerner. He was Asman or Asmander, she could not remember which.

The young southerner rolled his shoulders, looking over the Eyriemen but mostly at their Champion. Yellow Claw was the same brute of a man he remembered from their journey to the Stone Place – perhaps his presence there had been required for some Eyrie supplication.

Asmander wore the proper regalia of Old Crocodile's chosen warrior, as he had fighting the Wolf, Sure As Flint. It did not make him feel any happier.

There were enough warriors here to do away with him without much of a fight, and he could hardly outrun a flight of hawks if things went badly. Hesprec seemed confident, though. Just two nights ago he had been in solemn conference with a shadowy figure who had flown in on silent wings, and departed the same way. From that he had conceived a plan, little of which he had been inclined to share.

The night after that . . .

Shyri and Venater were down at a camp at the base of the

slope, far too distant to provide help. Asmander hoped the pair of them weren't killing each other even now. Venater had been particularly bitter, saying the whole business was a fool's errand and that, when Asmander got himself killed, who would give him back his name?

'You will just have to beseech the Dragon to grant me health,' had come the Champion's dry reply.

There had been real anger and fear in the pirate's eyes, at that remark. The reaction had been oddly reassuring.

And he's right. This is a stupid thing to be doing. If the old man wasn't of the Serpent ... But a life spent in the Sun River Nation had taught Asmander to respect the priesthood. Their true intent was seldom obvious, and almost never what they claimed it was, but it was usually for the best. Or so they taught, at least, and history had borne them out.

What lay ahead of them was knotting his stomach. Not the challenging of Yellow Claw, but what that challenge might force him to do.

His head was full of Hesprec's words, the preparations they had made, the ritual he had undergone. He was frightened by it. Fear of pain and death was something he had the shoulders to shrug off – those were things outside him, and he knew how to brace himself against them. This new thing which Hesprec had gifted him with, though, it was buried within him, alien and eager.

'I remember you,' Yellow Claw said, eyes like stone for all he affected a mocking tone. 'No woman to do your fighting for you this time?'

'I thought I should leave you at least a small chance,' Asmander acknowledged.

'What do you want, Black Man? Or perhaps you have come here to learn to fly?' Yellow Claw's glance encompassed the nearby sheer drop that made up most of the bluff's edge.

Asmander managed to force out a snort of amusement, although he had decided on the way up that he was very much not fond of the heights that most of this cold country seemed built from. 'I'm here to fetch the girl.'

Yellow Claw went still. 'Why?' he hissed. 'What is this girl, that the world wants her? This ugly little Wolf brat?'

'She is dear to my friend,' Asmander said, with a sideways nod at Hesprec. 'And, besides, if not for her I would have not have been given this chance to challenge you.'

The Eyrieman laughed, and Asmander was not heartened to see that it was a genuine laugh, rather than something put on for his followers. 'I am the Great Eagle, Black Man. I am a Champion of the Eyrie. Nowhere in the Crown of the World will you see such a terror as me!'

'I am a Champion of the Sun River Nation,' Asmander told him mildly. 'I will fight you for the girl.'

There was a gleam of cunning in Yellow Claw's eyes. 'But we already have the girl, do we not? What does the Eyrie stand to gain, save painting our ground with your blood? But this your *friend*, this dead stick beside you, he can tell us the girl's value, yes? Why would he seek her, unless he plans to sell or use her? When you are dead, he will tell us all he knows. Or he will go to meet the Hawk.'

Asmander cocked an eye at Hesprec, and the old man nodded tiredly. Last night's business had clearly taken a great deal out of him.

'Enough bragging.' The south's Champion squared his shoulders and drew out his *maccan*. 'Let's fight.'

Yellow Claw made a derisive face. 'Look, your wooden sword has stone teeth. Is that so you will be able to eat when your real ones are broken, Black Man?'

The Eyrieman sauntered over to that snaggle of logs jutting out over the drop, plainly expecting dismay from his opponent at the sight. Asmander was forewarned, though, by Hesprec's informant. He had always known how this was going to go.

That didn't mean he had to like it.

Yellow Claw leapt out into thin air – the action of a maniac if he had not become an eagle at the apex, mighty wings shadowing the ground as he lazily flapped and circled until he found a roost atop the furthest pole, where he became a man again, balancing without effort.

'Come, Man of the River!' he called. 'Come bring your challenge.'

Asmander looked once more at Hesprec, hoping to see a suggestion in the old man's expression that the plan he knew of was only some small part of the Serpent's scheme. The pallid Snake priest looked ashen, though, drawn and haggard. His colourless eyes met Asmander's and there was no help to be found there.

The other Eyriemen were drawing closer, eager to see this foreigner beaten. Asmander reached the closest pillar and inched out along it, arms extended for balance. There, he managed to at least approximate Yellow Claw's enviable poise.

At the bluff's edge, the Hawk warriors were spreading out, and plenty of them had knives. There was no going back that way until the fight was over, and the only other exit was straight downwards. And, of course, Yellow Claw himself could just fly away.

The Eyrieman Champion had a knife in each hand now: long tapering blades of bronze, styled like feathers. Asmander found himself almost obsessing over their craftsmanship, which was beautiful, because the alternative was actually starting the fight.

But he had to fight. It was not about the girl. It was about being a Champion.

The step to the next pillar was a long one, but manageable. Beyond that, they were more spread out, some surely beyond a man's ability to reach without jumping. Yellow Claw was like his reflection, moving as he moved. The sun gleamed along the length of his knives.

The next step was more of a stretch, and Asmander was forced to teeter for balance as he made it, to jeers from the Eyriemen. Yellow Claw came rushing for him in the same moment. The Eyrieman had not Stepped, but just ran across the posts with great, sure strides that Asmander would never have been able to match. He had closed the distance between them in an absurdly brief moment, one dagger snapping out. Asmander could not just feint aside as he might have done on the ground. Instead he struck at the blade, stone scraping metal and deflecting the thrust, throwing them both off balance. Yellow Claw just took a long step to the next post, not even looking back, whilst Asmander swayed in place.

Time to shift the odds . . . and he Stepped.

The shape he took was something the Eyriemen did not know, and did not like now that they saw it. Asmander's Champion shape, with its sickle-clawed feet, its heavy jaws, was something beyond even their stories. Yellow Claw gave ground swiftly, putting a half-dozen posts between them, but Asmander was the Champion now: a new soul had taken hold of his limbs. A little distance was not going to dissuade him.

He sprang, the great strength of his hind legs sending him sailing forwards three posts, to land almost next to Yellow Claw with a scrabbling of talons, straight tail out for balance. The post gave dangerously beneath him, sagging towards the abyss. The Eyrieman swiped at Asmander's snout with a blade, but he was backing away as he did so, three jumps and the last one almost a fall. Asmander screeched at him, riding a wave of defiance.

He had one more chance, another spring with an almost flat trajectory, bringing him down to rake a post that Yellow Claw had just vacated. The Eyrie Champion was shaken, but he was not beaten. A vicious grin had forced its way onto his face.

'Very fine, Black Man,' he called, 'but can you fly yet? I think not!'

Before Asmander could pounce again, he had Stepped himself, hunching as an eagle on his own post, wings half-spread. The River Champion paused, muscles tense to spring, knowing that the bird would be in the air before he landed.

Then Yellow Claw was airborne anyway, his spread of wings

seeming to shadow the whole bluff, rising up with indolent slowness, untouchable, and then abruptly snapping into a dive.

Twin clutches of bronze talons stooped on Asmander like a sudden storm. He threw himself out of the way, almost missed his footing despite all the nimble balance the Champion's form lent him, and then the eagle was swooping for him again.

For a moment he was preparing to fight back, to risk everything to try and take the bird in mid-air as it came in. Then either his nerve broke or his rational mind told him that he must fail, and he was hopping away again, awkward and graceless – and pursued.

They went through the same game three more times, and by then Asmander knew that it *was* a game, that the Eyrieman was having great fun chasing him around and demonstrating his superiority to his followers. And it told Asmander what sort of a man he was, which was useful for what came next.

Yellow Claw broke off and settled on a further post, Stepping back to his human form with his arms outspread just as his wings had been.

'Well, Black Man?' he demanded. 'Have you learned to fly yet?'

Asmander assumed his human shape, breathing heavily. His heart was battling within his chest in what seemed to be a determined bid for freedom, but it was not the exertion nor fear of death at the talons of Yellow Claw. This was the plan. It was Hesprec's gift.

They had sat up late, that last night, and the old Serpent had looked into his soul. 'A Champion is touched by the invisible world,' he had said. 'There are paths that have been trodden once. Perhaps they might be travelled again.'

Asmander looked Yellow Claw in the eye and tried to find some cutting rejoinder, but no words came. He was drawn bowstring-tense by what he was about to try, and there was no room for wit.

He wanted to say, *Yes . . . Yes I have learned to fly.*

He Stepped. It was not to his Champion's fighting form nor to the low-slung water shape of Old Crocodile. It was to something else, something that Hesprec had invited into him: a new soul enticed into his body.

He could not say what it might look like through someone else's eyes. He knew only what it felt like: the feet that gripped the post beneath him were fiercely taloned, the barbs gleaming with the black lustre of obsidian. His arms were long and attenuated, hands reaching out until the last finger of each was longer than his whole body. When he shook them out, the webs of skin between them and his narrow body snapped sail-taut, twitching and rippling. His head was like a crested spear, forming a razor-edged beak longer than a man.

When he spread his wings, they were almost as vast as Yellow Claw's own. When he gave voice, it shook the peaks above them. He was something like a bat, something like a crocodile, nothing that the eyes of men had ever seen.

The transformation struck Yellow Claw as hard as a sword blow. He Stepped to his bird form, stuttered back to man, then bird again spreading his own wings and keening, but a moment later he was crouching on human feet, the two knives held out. His eyes were wide enough that Asmander could see the white all around them, could stare right into their depths to Yellow Claw's mean and bitter souls, and see his own reflection ravening back out of them.

Asmander beat his wings and pushed himself forward, gliding two posts closer to Yellow Claw and managing a creditable landing with his hooked feet and the fingers of his wings. Part of him was trying to exalt in this new form, but far more of him was terrified of getting it wrong. The body's shape knew the air, but there was an understanding that Yellow Claw had and Asmander lacked. Some things only came with practice. And the moment he slipped, the moment he looked a fool, his hold on the other man would be gone.

If it came to it, and if Yellow Claw fought fierce, then the Eyrieman would still win.

So Asmander came on strong, hop after hop, shrieking and thundering with his wings. He made that unfamiliar body into a death threat aimed straight at his enemy. *I too can fly! There is nowhere you can go I cannot follow.* And he thought: *If all my life I'd had mastery of the sky, uncontested, then would I be a brave man still? If I had the luxury of living where none could attack, of attacking only where I chose.* He was maligning the Eyrie, no doubt. Surely there were many brave warriors there, for they had to strive against each other to prove themselves. Their Champion, though . . .

And he made that final lunge. Yellow Claw was a man until the second before he struck, and then spread his wings and kicked away, flight over fight. Asmander became the Champion and caught him in the moment that he took to the sky. Sickle-talons raked across the eagle's body, ripping feathers and scoring lines of blood, and then the bird was free of him, wheeling and tumbling in the air, circling down awkwardly, one wing trailing. He was a man again as he landed, clutching an arm to his chest, bloody where the claws had raked.

For a moment Asmander wanted to stoop on him, to finish him off, but that was not the way between Champions – for all such niceties were probably unknown in the cold north. Instead, he Stepped back to human form, standing tall and proud and high.

'I claim my victory,' he called. 'Free the girl, and if I see a wing-speck in the sky following us, then I shall rise to meet it.' Empty words, but he gave them force.

34

Maniye cast more than one nervous look up at the sky as they scuffed and slid their way down the treacherous path that was the only land-bound escape from the Eyriemen's camp. There were clouds aplenty, eager to gift the world with rain, but she spotted no winged shapes wheeling against them. It seemed the Eyrie was licking its wounds.

They made wordless progress for some time. Hesprec was chancing the walk down, feeling his way with his staff and choosing his footing wisely – of the three of them, he never stumbled or slipped once. On her other side, Asmander seemed deep in thought, stealing a suspicious glance at her every so often. He must surely be brooding over the same question that Yellow Claw had asked: *Why her?*

Maniye wanted to ask it, too. She remembered the lie Hesprec had told the Horse, that he had come north to seek her out for a prophecy. Was he just repaying a debt? Her rescue of his old bones from the Winter Runners paid by his bringing this exotic warrior to defeat Yellow Claw?

Then the Snake priest croaked out, 'I imagine you must be full of questions.' He had paused to catch his breath, and she felt pinned suddenly by his gaze.

She should ask *why*, so she might know whether he was still on her side, or whether he would take up with his strange friends and abandon her.

She would not ask him. She would remain ignorant until their parting forced the knowledge into her. For all he was old and frail and strange, she wanted him to be her friend. She needed him.

So she asked of Asmander, 'What were those animals you Stepped to? Were those things of the south?' She already knew in her heart they were not. They were something special: part of that way he had of seeming bigger, weightier than he was.

He was already shaking his head. 'What you saw first, that was the Champion of the Sun River Nation.' He frowned at her expression. 'Just as Yellow Claw's shape was Champion of the Eyrie. You understand me?'

'Most of the peoples in these lands have no such thing, and the Eyriemen keep to themselves,' Hesprec suggested. They had all halted alongside him, within the cover of the treeline, to let him recover his strength.

'I am chosen,' Asmander tried explaining.

'By who?'

'By Old Crocodile. By the Tsotec – river of my homeland. By the spirits.' His hands made nebulous gestures. 'Just . . . *chosen*. And so a new soul came to me, or maybe it is a part of a greater soul that all Champions can touch.'

'You sound like you don't know,' she accused him, because he scared her a little, and she needed to challenge that fear within herself.

To her surprise, he grinned sheepishly. 'It is something that happens. Of course, you ask for it when you're a young warrior and learning to Step. Everyone does so. But why me? Who can say? I never felt I deserved it. And the Champion can be hard. The Champion has his own way to live, his own rules.'

'And you have a flying Champion as well?' Maniye pressed.

Asmander shook his head fiercely. 'Never before; most likely never again. It is in me, but I am not sure I will Step that way. Ask me when I'm next falling off a cliff.' Another bright grin, quickly on, quickly gone. 'The Messenger, he is the man who knows about that.'

Hesprec spread his bony hands. 'Entirely the wrong time of day to talk theology. Let me say no more than that a Champion's soul is more *open* than any other's. There are rituals, very old, very sacred, that can invite another soul in. It is as though . . . your soul has cousins and uncles, Asmander, and with the proper invocation he can be prompted to reach, to call out for them, to ask them to muster in his warband and hunt along with him. I was not sure it would work, not in this cold, harsh place where the Serpent's coils are few and far-flung. But it did, and I'm proud of you. You are a Champion for your people to take pride in.'

Asmander seemed to take the compliment awkwardly, waving it away. 'We should move on. I don't trust these Bird men.'

Hesprec managed a snort. 'If they wanted to catch us up, you think *I* could walk fast enough to prevent them?' He sighed. 'I wanted to walk down, for once. I thought going down would be easier. But it seems my many years will have to beg another ride.' He chuckled ruefully. '"Many Years", that can be my name here in the Crown of the World, Many Years and Many Tracks.'

'Messenger.' Asmander held out a hand, but Hesprec had been looking at Maniye.

'Gladly,' she confirmed, and took his fingers in hers. In a moment he had done his trick of casting himself up his own arm, the ribbon-thin serpent he had now become winding its way up the sleeve of her threadbare Horse-made coat.

She and the southerner set off down again. She wanted to be a Wolf or a Tiger, and make better time, but she was not sure she could run with Asmander's stalking monster beside her. *The Champion.* Hesprec had used the word as though it was Asmander's title, but the man himself had spoken of the Champion as though it was a different creature entirely.

'Did you come here seeking Hesprec?' Asking him anything

was an act of daring, and she fully expected to be rebuffed haughtily.

Instead he gave her a surprised look, and for a handful of moments there were frank emotions visible on his southern face, though she could not quite follow them. Then he gave her a smile that seemed slightly sad.

'That would have been a mission of great honour,' he told her. 'I should just tell you, "Yes", and have you think better of me. But it was not so.'

'Why, then?'

'If you had three days and a desperate need to sleep, I could tell you much about the Sun River Nation, how it is governed, and what threatens it. But these are problems you do not have in the Crown of the World: politics, taxes, hereditary rule. You are better off without these things.'

In truth Maniye found the words difficult. 'Is that where the child always gets what the parent had?' and then, at his nod, 'Then the Tiger have that.' She almost went further but caught herself, saying only, 'Their daughters become what their mothers were.'

'Hence you run from them,' Asmander noted drily. 'That, I approve of. They are much wiser, most of your tribes and villages here. Avoid such foolishness.'

'*Your* people's foolishness.'

'Exactly.' He was plainly making some joke for his own amusement, at his own expense.

'We have our own foolishness.'

'No doubt. That is how people are. Once they have food and drink and shelter, the next thing they must find is a quarrel.'

They carried on picking their way downwards, beneath the intermeshed needles of the trees. The southerner was a contradiction, a study in strength and self-mockery. She wondered what he would have been without the mantle of Champion weighing on his shoulders. Something less? Happier? The same?

Her eyes were still on the sky, waiting for Yellow Claw and his

410

warriors to return. She had forgotten her other enemies, and in her human shape she could not scent them out. How long they had followed her footsteps before striking, she never knew.

She said, 'Tell me about your priesthood,' feeling the slender serpent shift its coiled grasp about her wrist.

He opened his mouth to answer, but the wrongness struck her all at once, and she cried out: no words, just a warning. The instant they knew she had sensed them, there were wolves bursting out from cover, weaving between the trees with their jaws half-open, eyes burning her with their yellow gaze.

And she knew them. No strangers these, who might be fooled or reasoned with. At their head was Akrit Stone River himself. Her father had come for her.

She Stepped to her own wolf shape instantly and was away, feeling Hesprec shift awkwardly to stay clasped about her. Asmander had his stone-toothed sword out, eyes wide in that dark face, but it was plain the wolves were happy to avoid him and ignore him, if only they could have her.

She went scuffing and scrambling away between the trees, but the gradient was taking her further downslope any time she was not actively pushing upwards. The Winter Runners knew it, running below her, one or other of them pacing her at every moment, the rest closing the jaws of the trap. They were wolves: as a pack they could run forever. As solitary prey she could not.

It seemed to her that she had always realized it would end like this. These were just the last moments of a hunt that had begun the moment she had abandoned her home village. If she had only looked far enough behind her, she would surely have spotted the patient form of Stone River loping along her trail.

But still she ran. Like every hunted thing, she ran until they caught her.

She had lost track of Stone River, but Amiyen Shatters Oak was pushing towards her from down the slope, inching closer and closer. Then another couple of wolves were almost falling upon her, two young hunters shouldering at each other to be the one who caught her. They lost their purchase on the root-strewn ground, nearly taking her with them. She veered, and then was a tiger, clawing and climbing straight upwards swifter than Amiyen could follow, kicking dirt and mats of dead needles down at the wolf behind her.

Another of the pack was above her, had overshot her in trying to second-guess her course, but was now turning back. She saw the grey of an old wolf still strong, and her heart shot her through with dread: Kalameshli, surely? Stone River had brought the priest along, and why would he do that, unless the hateful old man had a special vengeance in mind for her?

They will give me to the Wolf. They will give me to the fire.

She turned back the way she had come, from tiger back to wolf as soon as she had found a level course, leaving Amiyen and Kalameshli and the rest scrabbling to match her shift in direction.

Then Smiles Without Teeth was there before her, a huge dun wolf with spittle-strung jaws. He lunged for her and she twisted aside, knowing that she was going to make it, that those teeth would close only on empty air.

But he Stepped as he lunged, the reach of his teeth suddenly extended by the length of his arm, and his huge hand got the scruff of her neck, and then he had her by the throat.

She was human again, no fangs, no claws, and he lifted her up with a triumphant grin. Then Hesprec flashed out from her sleeve, toothless jaws gaping right in the Wolf hunter's face, and he howled and dropped her, losing his footing and sliding away down the slope. She hit the ground on four feet, Hesprec on two.

'Asmander! Here!' the old man managed, a quavering cry that surely the Champion would never hear, and then he lunged desperately for her, knotting his scaled length about her even as she was off, wolf-shaped again, feeling the net close in on her.

Seconds later three wolves were nipping at her tail, each pushing at the others for a chance of being the one that brought her down, and she could scent the fierce, hot reek of the pack – not the individuals but the single creature they made when they came together. She dodged and danced between the trees, keeping her few heartbeats of a lead, but one stumble from her would finish it, and they were inexorably bending her path so as to bring her into the jaws of the others.

Then Asmander was amongst them in the Champion's shape, striking down with sickle-clawed feet and scattering them, shrieking out his challenge. The wolves bolted in all directions, one of them tumbling over and over down the slope, and Maniye was running, still running. Abruptly there was no other wolf behind her, and she was leaping free, of her own volition and not driven by their storm.

Two, three breaths the world allowed her, when she thought she was clear of them. Then Stone River pounced from the higher ground, the cunning old hunter who had guessed where the hunt would take her, and had waited, fresh and alert, for her to come to him. He struck her in the side, knocking her from her feet with his weight, and then he had his forepaws on her, pinning her to the ground, his breath hot and stinking in her nose.

He lunged, jaws gaping, but it was just to set them about her throat, not enough to pierce her wolf hide, but sufficient to jolt her back into her human form.

Then he was human too, looming, monstrous, one of her childhood's two tormenting demons. He hauled her up and, when she tried to twist out of his grasp, he slapped her across the side of the face, hard enough to loosen her teeth and blur her vision.

'Now,' he growled, and Hesprec struck at him desperately, first an open-mouthed lunge at his face, then whipping his body about Akrit Stone River's throat, a living noose that grew and grew, thickening and tightening as Hesprec Stepped and Stepped through a spectrum of greater and greater serpents, fighting for the strength to overcome this man.

Then Akrit had a hand about the snake's head and neck, as

413

he tried to wrench the creature away, and abruptly there was no longer a crushing serpent there, but just a fragile old man with his withered and impotent hands at the Wolf chief's throat.

Maniye was a tiger, in that instant, snarling and yowling and ready to defend her friend, but the old priest cried out, 'Run! You're their prize, not me!'

Even then she would not have gone, but another wolf was on her, jaws gouging long grooves in her haunches: Amiyen Shatters Oak had caught up with her. Without thinking, Maniye smacked the newcomer across the snout with a rake of her claws and was a wolf again, already darting away. She left Hesprec behind. She hated herself, but she left him.

But Shatters Oak would not be thrown off. Pelting through the trees, she felt that she had left the pack behind, perhaps even left Akrit behind, but the hot breath of Shatters Oak was always at her back. Now Maniye found herself remembering the Horse camp: how it had been Shatters Oak and her son there who had tried to kill her.

She tried for another sudden burst of speed, but she was too tired, and Amiyen was running a little downhill of her, forcing Maniye to spend her strength against the slope.

I cannot run like this much longer. She was slowing. When she had slowed enough, been worn down enough, Amiyen would strike. That was the Wolf's way.

So she turned to fight.

She was a tiger again when she turned, claws digging for purchase, given a tantalizing glimpse of a clear path beyond Amiyen when the other wolf overshot, but now she had decided to fight, it was a fight she would make of it. Even in this form she was smaller than Amiyen's wolf, but it was a closer match, and her position upslope had become a weapon.

She struck, and heard Shatters Oak's surprised yelp, and then the two of them were tumbling over and over. They bounced off a couple of trees, one that caught Maniye in the ribs, one that

414

bruised Amiyen's haunches, and then the wolf had scrabbled to her feet, snapping at Maniye's throat.

She sprang back, swatting at the wolf's muzzle as she did so. A moment later she was human again, knife coming out as she fell into a fighting stance. But it had only ever been a dance for her, and Amiyen was as determined to kill her as a woman could be.

The wolf regarded her with cold, hating eyes, and then Amiyen Stepped as well, pulling an iron hatchet from her belt.

Shatters Oak attacked straight away, three swift cuts with the axe, left, right, then a vicious hack across Maniye's midriff that had her leaping back. She made it a dance though, turning on the ball of her foot and driving back in, cutting down the line of Amiyen's collarbone, one hand up to catch the axe-wrist.

The slash fell short when Amiyen twisted aside from it with a surprised snarl, yet she had still drawn a thin line of red close to the other woman's neck. Catching hold of the axe was harder, though. Amiyen was stronger than she was, stronger than any of the Tiger girls Maniye had trained against. She had been taught all sorts of lessons about using strength against itself, but none of them were in her head right then, and her feet almost slid out from under her.

Instantly she was a tiger again, and she scored three lines across Amiyen's leg before the axe came down. Her Step had taken her in close, so the hatchet's haft slammed hard into her shoulder, and then Amiyen was a wolf with teeth of iron gnawing for purchase at the back of her opponent's neck.

Maniye bucked and threw herself aside, feeling those fangs draw blood yet not lock. She writhed out from under her enemy, turning back with a savage snarl, all finesse forgotten, looking for the wolf but finding the woman.

The axe threatened: she flinched back from it, and Amiyen kicked her beneath the ribs, bowling her over onto her back. The sudden wrenching pain yanked Maniye into her human shape again, gasping for breath that would not come, and Amiyen

415

dropped onto her, a hand at her throat, a knee crunching down on her knife-arm. She was smiling.

'Now I kill you, as you killed my son,' she crowed triumphantly. 'And your ghost shall rot in your corpse.'

Maniye tried to protest that she hadn't, but Amiyen's grip was choking off all the words in her throat. With her free hand she fumbled with that clenching grasp, but she might as well have tried to bend iron.

Then someone was standing behind Amiyen, though by then Maniye could make out none of the details. She heard the voice, though.

'Many Tracks didn't kill your son. I did.'

A voice she knew: Broken Axe's voice.

Amiyen had gone still, but not relaxed her grip. 'You? How could it be you . . . ? You were not . . .' But her eyes had narrowed and she must have been casting her mind back to the Horse camp. In amongst the twisted skein of scents that had knotted the air there, had she scented the spoor of Broken Axe? Surely she had . . . 'The girl was there. Iramey was on her heels.'

'Because he sought to kill her. And because you did.'

Silence from Amiyen Shatters Oak.

Broken Axe stepped round until Maniye could see him. He seemed eminently unhurried.

'Why would you?' Amiyen said at last. 'If I told Stone River you had turned on your own—'

'And if I tell him you would have killed his daughter, against his word?' Broken Axe raised an eyebrow. 'He will say I was doing his will.'

Maniye could feel Amiyen growing tenser and tenser, poised to Step, to spring. She tried to warn Broken Axe with her eyes, but he gave no sign of noticing her.

'And now?' Amiyen's tone was low and dangerous.

'Now you seek her death again. And you have no sons with you.' Broken Axe spread his hands wide. 'But here I am, Iramey's Bane.'

Amiyen screamed out her hatred, throwing herself off Maniye and Stepping at the same time, so that her hind claws gouged and tore at the girl as she scrabbled for purchase.

'Go!' Broken Axe snapped, and then he was a wolf as well, and the two were meeting each other, fang to fang.

And Maniye followed suit, running once again, wolf nose in the air to warn her of any of her kin who might be close.

That was how, much later, she found the camp of Venater and Shyri, who had been waiting with less and less patience for someone to tell them what was going on.

By that time, Maniye was half dead with running, sore-footed, hungry and parched with thirst. By the time she was ready to tell them what had happened, Asmander had arrived too, stalking into the clearing as the Champion, proud and terrible and strange. Only when he Stepped back did he show that he was just about as tired as she was.

His look at her was accusing, and she hung her head.

'I'm sorry,' she whispered.

'The Messenger.'

'There was nothing I could do,' she told him, and then, noting his expression, 'He was my friend! I don't know what he was to you, but he was my friend. My only one!'

Asmander looked as though he had a lot more to say, but he held it and he held it, and then it let it go, just breathing it all out and leaving behind a man who was calm and in control. 'We should move on,' he decided. 'Your Wolves, they will be sniffing after you with their long noses, yes?'

'Someone's coming,' Shyri said, standing up abruptly with a knife in her hand. Maniye Stepped instantly, but without deciding to what. Something within her chose tiger over wolf. Too tired to run, she would fight.

The three southerners were all ready to make a battle of it too, so she had to Step very swiftly and call them off when she saw it was Broken Axe.

He regarded them narrowly, taking in the foreigners.

'Your old man, the Snake,' said Broken Axe. 'Stone River has him. They will give him to the Wolf.'

35

'Who is this?' Asmander demanded, seeing only another Wolf. The air between Broken Axe and the southerners was tense as a strung wire

'Calm,' Maniye said, drawing their taut gazes onto her. 'Broken Axe is a Wolf who follows his own path. He keeps many counsels and we need to know what he can tell us.' She was sensing out the balance of power between the southerners: who cared about Hesprec, and who was spoiling for a fight.

'So speak,' Asmander said at last. 'If your people have the Messenger, tell us why they won't have shed his blood already.'

'They'll want to do it properly,' Broken Axe explained. 'The old man, he was due for the Wolf's jaws once before. They have no idol here to sear him on, but Takes Iron will do what he can to make it a proper sacrifice, to appease the Wolf. They say that, after what happened at the Stones, the Wolf's eye is fixed on Stone River right now. He's being measured. Anything he can do to win favour, he'll do.'

'Then they must've done it by now,' Maniye argued. 'A big fire, a few words, what else is there?' After her time spent amongst the Tigers, all the rituals of the Wolf clans seemed no more than brutal muttering.

'They would have to stop for it,' Axe explained. 'Stone River is on the move. They have come too close to the Shining Halls. Tiger scouts have been playing games with them, and they already fought off a Tiger warband – one that was also hunting you, like as not. There was a fight, wounds on both sides. The Tigers slunk back to the Halls to lick their wounds, but this is still Tiger land, and Stone River is making for another camp of his, heading west.'

'How far?' Maniye demanded.

'Less than two days for a wolf, but the old man is no wolf. With a halter about his neck he's no snake, either. So they must pull him on a sled, and that slows them. Slows them so that a wolf could catch them.'

Maniye stared at him. 'Would you lie to me, Broken Axe?'

'If it was the right thing to do.'

'And now?'

'The right thing to do is to tell you what I have told you.'

'Why?' Asmander demanded suddenly. 'Why do you care? Yes, I will do all I can to save the Messenger from *your* people, but why tell us this, save to trap us? Surely any sacrifice to the Wolf god must be music to you.'

'The Wolf I follow is in here.' Broken Axe tapped his chest. 'He wants no sacrifice. He needs no man to die in agony by fire. He wants the clean joy of the hunt, the fresh snow, the wide sky and the moon. He wants a simple life that isn't stained by other men's ambition and greed.'

It was hardly enough to win over Asmander, Maniye thought, but at the man's words the southerner nodded thoughtfully. 'If this is true, then we must travel now.'

'We must.' Broken Axe's nod took in Maniye and nobody else. 'Stepped, we'll overtake them. Can *you* run with the Wolf?'

'How will I find out save by trying?' Asmander replied. 'You two,' he turned to his southern companions, 'track us, and make what pace you can.'

Shyri, at least, looked rebellious at that, and who knew what pace she could keep up, but the life of Hesprec was apparently not something she was willing to exert herself for.

They Stepped then: Broken Axe, Maniye and the southern

Champion. Two wolves and a stalking lizard creature left the camp, heading west.

During that first stretch it was plain that Asmander could not only keep up, but could have sprinted far faster than they if he wanted. He was constantly having to rein himself in, cocking his head back towards them and scratching at the ground while they caught up. Then Broken Axe was human again and signalling a halt, though they had covered almost no distance. They were on the same slopes where the Winter Runners had attacked previously, and there was a stench in Maniye's nose: a personal scent, familiar and yet somehow changed.

'Why've we stopped?' Asmander demanded. 'You're going to camp here for the night?'

'I must retrieve something, that is all.' Broken Axe searched about, Stepping into and out of his wolf shape, until he had found the right place. Then he reached up with human hands and hauled himself into a tree, coming down again with something bulky draped over his shoulder.

Maniye, who had remained a wolf through all of this, knew it for a pelt. Some part of her was desperate for this to be the last remnant of Amiyen Shatters Oak, but it was not. The scent was familiar, but she could not immediately put a name to it.

'Dirhath,' Broken Axe supplied, and she remembered: a young hunter, scarcely more than a boy, strutting and unsure but desperate to win the approval of his elders. He had not yet won himself a hunter's name. Now he never would.

'He was caught by the Tigers, separated from the pack. They killed him, and his spirit is flown.'

'So . . . you skinned him? This is a Wolf thing?' Asmander enquired with a frown.

'I am still welcome amongst the Winter Runners,' Broken Axe said, though the echo to those words was, *For how long?* 'You, though, Many Tracks . . . let Stone River decide to Step, and catch the scent of the child who fled him, and you'll be theirs.' He nodded to her. 'You know what we will do with this.'

'I . . . have heard of it being done.' In stories, even in fireside recountings, but she had never witnessed it. It was a grisly thing, to wear two skins and carry another's scent. 'They will not think me Dirhath. I cast a smaller shadow.'

'Then do not been seen by them. It is enough that they scent what is familiar,' Broken Axe told her.

'And me? You have another magic skin for me, perhaps?' Asmander's tone suggested they did not do such things in the south, even in stories.

'You . . .' Broken Axe scratched the back of his head. 'I don't know what to do with you. I don't know this creature that you Step to. But I have watched you run. You're very swift, but you are not a Wolf. You will not match us for the long haul.'

'Will I not?'

'If you fall behind, go find your fellows. When it comes for us to bring the old Snake back, we will try and sniff you out. Perhaps we will have company when we return.'

Then he took the pelt of Dirhath, still sticky with the dead man's blood, and laced the paws together so that it could rest on Maniye's shoulders like a cloak, the unskulled head flopping and flapping behind her, the tail and hind legs dragging on the ground.

'We will not know human shape again until we have caught them,' Broken Axe pronounced.

Maniye nodded shortly, knowing that when she Stepped, her wolf form would be trailing the dead Dirhath's scent; that some part of him would be carried with her, not his ghost but something of him nonetheless.

They ran as the wolves run, that can travel night and day when they have to. For most of that night, Asmander kept up, although the scent of him told Maniye he was flagging, all his lightning speed nothing compared to the constant grind of their own progress. This was how the pack brought down the fleet deer: not being faster, but never slowing, never giving up, running the prey ragged and staggering, then circling for the kill.

In the end, Asmander slowed, then Stepped, resuming his human form on one knee, raising a fist at the dark sky, perhaps in frustration, perhaps in salute. It was only Many Tracks and Broken Axe now.

She had run from Broken Axe for so long, before. Now he broke fresh ground and she followed, although her nose already warned her of the passage of many of her kin. She knew that Broken Axe was right: the Winter Runners were not moving swiftly.

In her mind was no plan, and that was what frightened her most. She had no idea how Stone River would have set his people when she and Broken Axe came upon them. They might still be on the move; they might be camped. If camped, they might have all eyes watching the dark, every nose alert for the stink of ambush. Perhaps the Tiger was still on their trail, after all.

And even if they felt themselves secure, away from the diminished reach of the Shining Halls, would she still be able to go creeping amongst them undetected? What of those who had been mourning Dirhath? What of . . . ?

Her body ran on, tiring, tiring slowly, with a wolf's stubborn stamina. Her mind wheeled and battered like a trapped bird, but Broken Axe was always ahead of her, and so she followed, the second member of a pack of two.

She had feared him so much. He had seemed like Death to her, inescapable and always waiting. She still could not quite understand this drive in him to do whatever was right, not in the eyes of Wolf or Tiger or other people, but only his own. And yet he was surely the most gifted hunter she had ever known: a man swift and certain, sure in his judgement, at ease in both his skins.

It was that last she truly envied. She had three skins; none of them fitted her, and two of them were at war.

Then she would worry again about the choice still hanging

over her like a blade: Wolf or Tiger; Tiger or Wolf. Small wonder she would risk this much for a chance to rescue Hesprec and receive his counsel once again. Of all the world that knew her, perhaps only he did not care which path she took. Or he and Broken Axe.

Would he have taken me as a mate? That had been Stone River's drunken threat. *Would it have been so bad?* But make her the hearth-wife of Broken Axe, and she would never have got to know him. He would have been a mystery, more absent than present, close-mouthed and secret-eyed. Only this way could she have come to discover the man he truly was.

She lost track of the distance they covered, giving herself over to the long chase for its own sake, weariness her constant companion but not yet her master. Still, when Broken Axe finally slowed to a halt she was grateful. It was midday by then, the skies close with clouds, pregnant with rain on the very point of falling.

Broken Axe Stepped to his human form and beckoned her near, but she first took a moment to draw in a great breath of all the world's secret knowledge. She inhaled the forest and the earth, the sky and the distant peaks, renewing her connection with it all, finding herself again within its vastness. *I have been here, or close to here. This is known to me.*

With a leap of hope she found the answer in her mind. The Tiger had driven Stone River west and north. *Close to the lands of the Cave Dwellers. And Loud Thunder dwells on the border of those lands.* For a moment she had a desperate thought of rushing straight to that cave-house and petitioning the giant himself. Too far, though. Days more of running to take her there. Hesprec would not have that long to live.

In her nose was the scent of Wolf, but other scents too: other people. Stone River had found company out here.

At last she crept closer to Broken Axe, shifting from wolf to a woman with a heavy pelt about her shoulders. 'What is this place?' she whispered.

'A village of the Boar people,' Broken Axe explained. 'They

call themselves the Spined Sons – they were Roughback once, but split from them and came out here.' He plainly saw that Boar tribe squabbles were lost on her. 'They are few. Stone River's warband will have mastered them. He will be in the chief's lodge by now, served by the best of their women. The others likewise. To have stopped here, they must think themselves out of the reach of the Shining Halls.'

'Are they?' Maniye asked.

Broken Axe's face twisted. 'Once, the answer would have been no. After that – after the war – yes. Now? Hard to say. The Tiger stir themselves more than they used to.'

'So what will they . . . ?' Maniye felt a sudden clutch of anxiety within her. 'Have they done it? Have they given Hesprec to the Wolf already?'

Broken Axe shrugged. 'I think not. The Wolf is not in this place. Offer a soul up here, and it would end up on the tusks of the Boar, like as not.'

'But you can't be sure.' Maniye was thinking of every word that had been spoken before they set off, every wasted moment, of every step, when she could have pushed herself harder.

'I can only go and see how the land lies,' Broken Axe told her. 'And you must stay here and keep your head hidden. There will be scouts.'

'Wait.' A thought that had been nagging at Maniye was suddenly at the front of her mind. 'What about Shatters Oak? Does she still live?'

Broken Axe nodded grimly. 'She does, and if she found my back turned to her, and nobody else to see, she would kill me. But she will not strike before the eyes of others.'

'I thought it was *him*, that wanted me dead,' Maniye told him. 'After the Horse post.'

'He has many plans for you, but not your death yet.' Then Broken Axe had Stepped back to his wolf shape and went loping off through the trees towards the scents of Wolf and Boar, of hearth, and sheep dung and people.

Maniye Stepped, if only for the warmth and the security that a wolf shape gave her. She settled down low, belly to the ground and cloaked with another's scent, and she waited. It was hard, that wait: harder than the long run to catch up with Stone River and his warband had been. Left with nobody but her own company, she found herself looking into the great expanse of the future. *Rescue Hesprec.* Yes, but then what? Those smoke dreams of going south? Had that ever been a real plan?

Then Broken Axe was back, slinking through the trees before pausing to lift his muzzle and scent the air.

'They have him in the chief's house,' he confirmed after he Stepped, 'the largest of the huts there. He's not been well used.'

'But alive?'

His expression suggested there was not much difference in it. 'They are holding him cruelly. There is little kindness amongst the Winter Runners tonight.'

'And Stone River?'

'Your father broods in the chief's hut even now, but he's in his restless mood. Soon he will go out amongst his people, to remind them who he is. That will be your moment, if there is one.'

'What about the others?'

He waved a hand. 'They have the Boar to serve them. Some are guarding another prisoner, I think. Others raid the village larders, or they lick their wounds. All were on two legs when I saw them: after a fight, men love to tell each other how brave they were. You will have to be quiet and clever – just like back home.'

'Then let's do it.'

'Follow in my shadow; find a place where you are hidden but can watch me. When Stone River sets out, that will be your moment.'

She envied Broken Axe, who could walk between the Shining Halls and the Winter Runners so deftly. While he strode into the village of the Spined Sons, with only Shatters Oak to worry about, she had to find a path of shadow to follow. In this she was aided by the clouds that chose that moment to break over the village, bringing not torrential rain but flurrying late-season snow. Maniye took that as her cloak and moved in.

The Boar village was laid out in an oval of low huts, each one little more than a sloping roof that reached from the ridge pole down to the ground, with a floor beneath propped on posts off the ground, to ward off flood and vermin. Each had a firepit dug at its entrance, protected from the snow by the eaves. In most, there would not have been room for an adult to stand up straight, but the Boar crammed their families and their goods inside until there seemed to be not a hand's span of space left. The chief's hut was the sole building on a grander scale, so that a tall man could just have stood upright down the house's centre-line.

She made her way, shadow to shadow, wolf and tiger, feeling the chill of the snow on her pelt but blessing it for veiling her. She found herself a place to hide, where the earth under one of the huts had been eroded away just enough to fit a very small wolf.

The air was full of the sounds of people: familiar sounds. She could recognize voices, even: that was Bleeding Arrow, and there the deep rumble of Smiles Without Teeth. It was as though she had never left home.

In their own village, the sullen Spined Sons shuffled and scuffed about, seeking refuge with each other, shoulders bowed as they bore the unlooked-for burden of Stone River's warband.

Then the skins at the entrance of the chief hut rippled, and Stone River pushed his way out, snarling up at the snow. A human snarl, though: no keen wolf's nose to scent her out, not yet. She guessed he had been at whatever fermented gourds or mead the Spined Sons had stockpiled, for he had that ugly, belligerent expression she remembered from when he had been drinking. From the way he walked, this was not just a random

venture his feet were taking him on: he was looking for someone.

Let him take long to find them. She crept out from beneath the
eaves and covered the distance to the chief's hut like a shadow
herself. The skins barely moved as she burrowed beneath them.

The hut had a firepit inside it, the smoke coiling about the
centre-line above before escaping through holes at either end.
The slope-walled interior was red-lit by those sullen embers,
and beyond the fire she saw Hesprec Essen Skese.

Broken Axe was right: they had used him cruelly. The old
man was stripped to the waist, his body seeming just a bundle of
dry sticks held together by skin. The firelight played across the
bruises and marks that patterned his hide, where the warband
had had their fun with him. Now they had him strung up by his
wrists, hanging from the centre-pole. A cord was strung taut
from wrists to the halter at his neck, hoisting him onto his toes.
He was trembling, an old man at the very far shore of exhaustion. His eyes were closed.

She hurried over to him, Stepping as she did so.

'Hesprec,' she whispered. 'It's me. I'm here.'

One colourless eye opened and rolled over to stare at her. For
a moment he did not seem to believe the evidence of his own
senses, but then his withered lips crept into something like a
smile.

'Again? What bad habits you have fallen into.' His voice was
so faint that the popping of the dying fire almost drowned it out.

'Enough,' she silenced him. 'Now let me get you down.' She
had her Tiger-made knife of bronze, that she could now Step
with without any difficulty at all. What she did not have was the
reach. He was taller than she, his bound wrists higher still.

'I . . . I may have to climb up you,' she decided tentatively,
because he did not look as though he would survive a feather's
weight more burden.

And yet he nodded minutely, and closed his eyes again,

428

bracing himself as best he could. Still she held back because he was so frail, and she was afraid.

And then she heard a call from outside.

'Stone River!' Broken Axe's voice.

'Axe.' Her father. 'If you've not found the girl, get out of the way. I'm not in the mood for you today.'

Maniye froze, caught stretching as high as she could with her knife – which was nowhere near far enough. A moment later she was crouching in the shadow that Hesprec cast in the firelight, waiting for the worst.

Stone River shouldered his way in, obviously in a foul temper, and there was Kalameshli Takes Iron along with him, the priest looking scarcely happier.

'You've had enough time with the Wolf.' Akrit Stone River cast a look towards the flap, as though fearing to be overheard. Thankfully he did not consider that there might be an eaves-dropper already within. 'Time to tell me what he wants.'

Kalameshli looked sour. 'What does the Wolf ever want?'

'I ripped out Water Gathers' throat for him in the sacred place!'

'Not through design,' Kalameshli snapped.

'But it happened!' Stone River shouted back. 'And here we are. The first clash with the Tiger, in how many years? And we lose two and end up running away.'

'It was not—'

'Tell it to them, not to me. What do I need to do, Takes Iron? What is it the god wants?'

'I am only a priest. The Wolf never spoke clear and direct to anyone. But I think he is testing you. I think he is watching you.'

'And he's not impressed, eh?' Akrit growled.

Kalameshli did not venture an opinion.

'What, then? This old one?' And abruptly Stone River was standing right there, staring into Hesprec's hollow face, while Maniye crouched at the Snake priest's heels and tried not to breathe at all, not even to think.

'I've told you, not *here*,' Takes Iron said exasperatedly. 'This is not our place. The Boar is fat enough already.'

'We can make this *not* a Boar place,' Stone River mused. He had turned back to the fire and was fumbling with his belt. Maniye assumed he was about to piss in it, but there came no hiss of steam. 'Round them up and give them all to the fire: the greatest sacrifice the Wolf has tasted for twenty years.'

Kalameshli sighed. 'If we'd found a Deer tribe, then perhaps yes. We'd take whoever we could catch, and the rest would run. But the Boar . . . you know how the Boar people are. They bow their backs readily enough, but you can only push them so far. And we'd not get out alive if they all Stepped and came for us at once. You know that.'

Stone River spat, still crouching by the fire. His mood was not improved when Takes Iron went on, 'If you hadn't given the prisoner to the others . . .'

'They need to think we're winning,' Akrit told him sharply. 'What better way than someone to play with?' And then he turned from the fire. In his hand was an iron knife, its handle wrapped in skin, the heated blade glowing a baleful red. With a convulsive movement he thrust it at Hesprec. For a moment Maniye thought he would kill the old man then and there, and she had to fight down a scream, but then the flat of the hot blade was laid against the Snake priest's brittle ribs.

Hesprec made a sound. Not a hiss or a yell or anything so identifiable, but a whimpering noise of pure exhausted agony. It made Maniye sick to hear it, more even than the smell of burning; her nightmares would be haunted by that sound for a long while to come.

Then the chief of the Winter Runners, the would-be High Chief of all the Wolves, stormed out of the hut, taking his priest with him.

Again she was left with the impossible task of reaching Hesprec's wrists, but this time he got out, 'The halter, girl. That is all I need.'

And she saw it at once, and cursed herself for being so foolish. His hands were bound, but a snake has neither hands nor arms. She sliced through the thong that was looped about his neck, desperately delicately to avoid cutting him, even though she was on her toes to reach. A moment later he was a serpent, coiling and writhing lethargically on the floor of the hut.

The flap moved again, and she was in her Tiger fighting stance, blade raised, because if Stone River came back now there would be no avoiding it. She saw Broken Axe instead, though, nodding with brief satisfaction to see that she had got the old man down.

'Good work,' he said softly, and would have said more, but the air was rent by a terrible scream. It was a woman's scream, and what was worse was that it was not a first-scream, made from a first-hurt. It was the scream of someone who has been hurt and hurt, and held on and held on, and now cannot hold the scream in any longer.

There was a look that came to Broken Axe's face, then.

'They said they had a prisoner,' Maniye whispered. She was gathering Hesprec's sluggish form to her, bringing his cold coils next to her skin. 'A Tiger warrior, it must be.'

Still Broken Axe said nothing, but he did not need to. Another scream tore through the air, followed by a chorus of jeers from the same direction.

'We have to go,' Maniye told him. 'Please, Broken Axe. We have to go. We can't do anything. I have to save Hesprec.'

Then she flinched from the look he turned on her. Most of all, in that look, was disappointment. A revelation struck her then. The last time he had heard a woman of the Tiger scream, he had not acted to stop it then, only waited until later, and saved whatever he could. She had not known it before, but she saw how that delay had eaten into him, had made him the man he was: determined to follow his own path.

And yes, she must save Hesprec, or why else had they come? Yes, they could not save everyone. Perhaps a dozen Boar girls

431

had already suffered the same, perhaps a dozen of their menfolk too. The world was cruel and callous, as were its people.

But they were here, and that pain and shame and agony was here, and there was nobody else. She saw, in that moment, how very hard it was to be Broken Axe.

'I can run,' she said. He thought she was abandoning him, but that was not her meaning. 'I can run, fast as any. I will run for Loud Thunder's home and the lands of the Cave Dwellers. I will run from here, but I shall call out before I go. I shall call out to show Stone River he has failed and that the Wolf hates him. You must do what you must do, when they chase me.'

He weighed and measured her with his gaze, and then put a hand on her shoulder. 'I will bring the southmen to Loud Thunder, if I can,' he told her. 'Look for me there.'

'You cannot hide this from the Winter Runners,' she warned him. 'Someone will see you. They will mark you for death from now.'

'Nothing is forever,' and then he Stepped, always his favourite way of avoiding questions, and he was gone.

Maniye braced herself. *I can run*, she told herself, and she took off the skin of dead Dirhath and Stepped, feeling Hesprec wind himself tighter around her.

Outside, the snow was swifter, starting to settle. Perfect. Perhaps the Wolf really was on her side.

She bolted through the village and, as she cleared the last hut, she howled out a cry of challenge and knew that her father would recognize just who it was that called him out.

36

She did not see what Broken Axe did next, after that fractured moment when she had called out the whole of the Winter Runner warband. What went through her father's head then, she could not imagine. He had chased her, nearly caught her, lost her – and yet here she was again just outside his circle of firelight, howling her defiance.

And she ran, and did not see, but in her mind it played out: Broken Axe entering the hut where the warriors were amusing themselves with the Tiger woman. Perhaps they thought he had come for his turn. They would greet him. He would reply, jovial and easy, but with a tightness to his jaw they would not mark. Then he . . . would he kill the woman to put her out of her shame and misery? Maniye did not think he would. He was more than that. He would take his blade and bend towards her – and perhaps she would even recognize him, from the Shining Halls – and with one deft move he would sever the halter that held her confined to her human shape.

Then there would be a tiger at large in the village of the Spined Sons, angry and hurting. Perhaps she would hunt.

But others were also hunting: others were on the trail of Many Tracks. Even as her mind toyed with the thought of what the strength of Broken Axe might accomplish, her feet were speeding her further and further away from him.

And the snow fell thicker as she ran. Snow was of the Wolf,

who claimed winter for his own, his breath sent to test the world. When last she had been fleeing the Wolf's people, he had sent her this cloak of snow, but then her pursuer had been Broken Axe, who could not be thrown off the trail by a little adverse weather. Instead the snow had nearly killed her, a punishment for her disloyalty. Now . . .

Now the Wolf exhaled, and she fled into that shifting labyrinth of white, and felt that she had a god's favour. Her heart was hammering high, but there was a jagged blade of excitement lodged there, rather than the fear she had been living with for so very long. Let Shatters Oak rage, let her father curse, let Takes Iron mumble his platitudes. She had challenged the Winter Runners.

Despite the snow, her nose still guided her swiftly towards Loud Thunder's home, though it would be another long and draining trek across rugged country. She would tire eventually, she knew, but right then she felt as though she could run forever, like the wolf in the stars.

They were close behind her, she knew. She could not put names to them, but glimpses and instinct told her at least three, perhaps five, were on her trail. Would Stone River be one of them? Surely his pride would have urged him out. Was Broken Axe clear of the village by now?

She could not know, and she might never know. Running was all she could contribute to his success.

About her narrow wolf chest the bonds that were Hesprec's body tightened. He must be cold but she could do nothing about that. She had no pack for him to crawl into. Better the cold than the fire, if the worst came. If he perished even as she tried to rush him to safety, he would at least die in a fit form, and his spirit would pass on, and some hatchling serpent elsewhere in the world would inherit all that he was.

Abruptly there was a figure racing almost beside her, and she realized that she had been running for the long distance, whilst her hunters were flogging themselves in a quick sprint, desperate

434

to catch her up. Not Stone River, this; not Shatters Oak or Smiles Without Teeth, just some young hunter she could not immediately name, but he was snapping at her flanks, trying to force her aside to where others of the pack might intercept her.

She put on more speed, spending her strength, but he matched her, a boy who had not had to run and run as she had the day before. The snow waxed and waned, curtains of white shifting and drawing aside before her, but it would not hide her from this persistent youth. Perhaps he saw in her a chance to win his name, or perhaps he already had a name that was less than complimentary, and needed deeds to offset it. He was determined, though. His eyes were set on nothing but her. His breath was on her haunches, his teeth at her side.

Maniye kept her eyes fixed ahead, pushing herself harder. They were ascending a rocky slope, slippery with the snow that had drifted there, and she was hoping the other wolf might slip or stumble. Luck held with him, though, and he was forcing her to veer now, stealing her speed from her.

And then there was no more ground beneath their feet.

Maniye had seen it barely in time to react. The boy had not, too busy recounting his own legend inside his head. They had found a stream that had been cutting into the rocks for generations, a stone-scattered drop of ten feet to the shallow silver line of the water below. Maniye was a tiger the moment she began falling, landing four-footed and then kicking off on wolf paws again. Her pursuer lost his luck, though, landing heavily, all the breath gone from him, and she had vanished from his sight before he could recover.

Then she was running again in earnest, that long lope of the wolves, forcing herself always uphill. When her path found rocks and jutting heights, she scaled them, Stepping to tiger and feeling that extra tightness as Hesprec adjusted his hold on her, inch by frozen inch. She heard howling, once, but it was far away. The snow had eaten her tracks and her scent. The world had swallowed her up.

But although she was discovering the ground ahead rock by rock, drop by drop, she knew that this great trackless forest was the same one in which she had played chase with Broken Axe; the same one that she had stumbled through half-frozen to reach Loud Thunder's camp. She was closing with her destination, over so many miles, led by stray memories, by guesses, by hope.

And then, with a dawn grown ripe in the sky and the snow at last behind her, she was at a lakeshore. It was not frozen now although the snow had made a slush out of its fringes, shot through with the dagger-like fingers of reeds. A pair of herons took thunderously aloft as she skidded and scraped to avoid wetting her feet. And she knew it. She remembered this place clear as day, despite all that had changed. Here, Broken Axe had bearded her. Here he had given her a hunter's name.

And somehow her long run had directed her right, despite the snow, despite the great, great heedless spaces of the world. She was close now; still a long way to run, but she was close.

She drank gratefully, though the water was icy cold. Her stomach snarled at her, and so she Stepped and took out some of the dried meat, the nuts and wizened fruit she had taken from the Tiger.

'Hesprec,' she said softly. 'Eat. Snake or man, but eat.'

For a moment he did not move, remaining just a cold line tight against her chest, and then she thought it was too late. In that moment – even as her heart clenched – he loosened, dropped like a dead thing to the ground, and became a shivering, bluish-skinned man.

In that dawn's harsh, uncompromising light, he looked more corpse than living, so thin that she could barely think where any muscle could fit between skin and bone. That skin, always so pale, was crazed with lines, blotched with broken veins. His eye-sockets were bruise-dark and his lips were cracked, drawn back to expose the ravaged gums beneath. She took her coat off and draped it across the knobs of his shoulders. He clutched it to

436

himself, shivering uncontrollably, fumbling at the sheepskin lining with fingers like claws.

'Eat,' she told him, and then, 'I'll chew it up for you.'

He looked at her at last. She could just make out a smile on that face, and it was like the ruins of Tiger power she had seen on the way to the Shining Halls: an echo of a strength that once had been.

'Dear one,' he said. Just then the great bowl of the lake seemed very quiet, the morning holding its breath as Hesprec's own plumed white in the air. 'You are too good, but no need. No need.'

'Then . . .' She offered a strip of meat to him uncertainly but he made no move to take it.

'No need,' again, from those old lips.

'You have to eat.'

He just watched her, though. His eyes were the lake's pale colours, which were no colours at all, even the pink of their edges gone bloodless.

'Hesprec.' She tried to find some authority to invest her voice with. *Am I not a Wolf chief's daughter? Does my mother not rule the Shining Halls?* 'You have to eat . . . and then we'll move on. We'll go to Loud Thunder. He'll shelter us.'

He was shivering – or more like shuddering, the mess of angular sticks that made up his body jumping and spasming beneath the Horse-made coat. His eyes were steady, though, as if they had already severed ties with the rest of him.

'You need to go,' he said softly.

'We – *we* need to go. When you've eaten, we need to go. We're going to Loud Thunder. I'm saving you.'

'You must stop that, or it'll become a habit.' His ghost-smile again. 'But here I am, and I am saved. I am free. But I cannot go further with you.' He was so dreadfully calm despite the state of him.

'But your friends, the southerners . . .'

'They will have to understand.'

'No.' She could feel a child's wailing welling up inside her and fought it down stubbornly. 'You have to come, see . . . because, because you have to.'

'Maniye.' The uttering of her name was like a spell to silence her, to still her. 'The coils of the Serpent are endless, their loops everywhere. You see before you just one such loop. It has passed into the sunlight from the earth, and curved about its long, long course, and now the time has come for it to return.'

She stared at him, struggling to shake off the quiet he had placed on her until at last she came out with, 'But you still have to come with me. Step, and I'll carry you, and if, and if . . .' Her own voice was like a serpent fighting to escape from her control. 'If . . . then your soul will pass, and . . .'

'Did I not tell you, when we first met, that my people are different?' he said gently. 'We must do everything in a way that is ours alone. Even this. Especially this. The Serpent waits for me below, and I must return to the earth.'

'No, but—'

'Maniye.' Again that quietening spell. 'I am further from home than I should ever be, but some things do not care for distance. This is how it is for my people. Below us, the Serpent coils upwards through the earth towards me, and I must go to greet him. I have been his servant for more years than you can imagine. I look forward to meeting with him again. This is not the end, Maniye.'

'I know, but . . .' She had nothing she could say, and yet she was still speaking. 'But I rescued you! I got you out. I stole you from my father! And it's not supposed . . . it wasn't supposed to be—'

His hand on hers surprised her: colder than the water itself. 'I am rescued,' he said simply. 'You cannot know how great it is, the thing you have done in bringing me away from that place. Greater than all the pains and tortures that this body has been spared is what you have gifted to my soul.'

And at last her words had run dry. She collapsed to her knees beside him, holding him close, feeling his bird-bone fragility.

Then he was running like sand from her arms, dwindling and diminishing, casting off his humanity until he was that whip-slender snake she had carried for so long. It lifted its head, slit eyes bright, and she knew the cold must be biting into every scale of it.

'Goodbye, Hesprec,' she said, and the little reptile had found a crack between two stones and vanished into it. She wanted to believe that she felt the earth tremble with the smooth motion of unseen coils, as the god came for his servant, but there was nothing. The ground was frozen hard.

She ate then, chewing bitterly at the cold, tough meat, switching between human, wolf and tiger teeth to best gnaw it into pieces she could swallow. As the sun clawed its way free of its bloody birth and the new day began in earnest, the dawn found her sitting staring across the lake, but seeing nothing at all.

Broken Axe found her there, too, padding up with his fur bristling in the chill. For a long while he watched and waited, and no doubt he was piecing it all together. His nose would tell him Hesprec had been there, but was not there now, nor had left any track to follow. When he Stepped, his human face showed that he understood it all.

'Many Tracks,' he told her quietly, 'you cannot stay here.'

She just looked up at him bleakly.

'The southerners are close behind me,' he told her, 'but closer than that, the woods are full of hunters. I outran a warband of the Tiger to find you, and your father is not far off.'

'What then?' She looked at him through raw red eyes.

'There is only Loud Thunder. I have nothing else. We must run, now.'

She was sick of running. It solved nothing. She had run fit to make the gods proud that night, and still it had not saved Hesprec.

But when Broken Axe put out a hand, she let him lift her to her feet. When he Stepped, she followed.

The Tiger and the Wolf, he said, but it seemed to her that the further they ran, the more the world around them fell silent. Each rasp of her own breath echoed in her ears, along with the drumming of her feet and the constant drumming of her heart. The grand silence that had been spread out over the lake where Hesprec had gone to earth was following her, more surely than any hunter. It coursed past her and stilled all the sounds of the world.

She was falling behind, so that Broken Axe had to stop and wait, then stop and wait again. All that fierce fire that had given strength to her legs when she had escaped the Winter Runners seemed to have run out of her, and left only a void. Her mind thronged with all the words she had not said to Hesprec before the end. Everything around her, within and without, was defined now by absences.

And those absences, the holes in her world, they were growing and growing. She felt the ground brittle and hollow beneath her pounding feet, and that seemed entirely fitting: the Serpent that had burrowed there was gone now, and the space it had taken up was surely collapsing in upon itself. Even as she ran, she felt she was standing at the brink of something vast and cavernous.

There was a forest down there, a night-dark forest, as though it had grown within a great chasm in the earth. She was leaning over it, arrested at the very moment of falling. Things moved in the spaces between the trees: a hunt . . . it was a hunt. There was a tiger like smouldering embers. There was a wolf like a pale ghost. Each intended murder. Each was hunting the other, and each fled in turn. But they were closer and closer, hunters gaining with ravenous jaws agape, prey flagging and failing in its flight. And there was a light, a glaring brightness growing in the forest. It swelled and swelled, searing the eyes of her *mind*, not the eyes in her head, until it had eclipsed all the world, and she could see nothing, know nothing, be nothing, because she had to choose now, she had to *choose*, she had to know what she wanted to be . . .

When she came back to herself, the cold of the ground had leached into her bones. Broken Axe was calling out her name, his hands on her. His ice-water eyes were the first things she saw as she opened her own.

She made a questioning sound, little more than a croak. Moving her limbs, she found herself shaky and weak, barely able to sit upright.

Broken Axe's expression was closed, but his body thrummed with tension. 'Can you run?' he asked her. 'I've heard the Wolf calling.'

'What . . . ?' She wanted to ask him if she had been struck; she wanted there to have been an attack, some cause outside herself. She could not deny the knowledge, though. Her souls had fought: they were grown too great for her small body. They had fought inside her, and now they had withdrawn to lick their wounds, leaving her the strength of neither to help her.

'You fell,' Broken Axe explained shortly. 'You started shaking. There was foam on your lips, and your eyes were white.' He was keeping himself as calm as possible, so as not to pass his alarm on to her. 'Many Tracks, can you still run?'

'Yes.' But she could barely stand. Terror shot through her: not at the thought of being caught but at being unable to trust or master her own body. Every muscle within her was trembling, and the more the fear mounted, the more the strength ebbed from her limbs.

Without a word, Broken Axe had swept her up and in a moment she was clinging to his back, arms clasped before his throat and her legs about his waist. He spared no more effort on words, but began trudging on between the trees. She could read his mind though: a burdened man on human feet could never outpace wolves or tigers. There was no escape that way.

441

She wanted to tell him to leave her – his life was surely forfeit if he was caught, just as hers was. But strength to make such sacrifices was gone from her along with the rest. She just huddled into him, feeling his muscles shift beneath her.

They found the deer soon after: not the tribe but their mute brothers. Spring had come to the Crown of the World enough for the first bucks to be out gorging, and the hollow they found was one of their feeding grounds. At the intrusion, the half-dozen beasts fled, white tails flashing in the sun, and Broken Axe set her down.

'We need a new plan,' he told her. 'This place is thick with deer-scent. If I leave you here, can you hide yourself? Can you Step?'

She reached tentatively for the souls within her, then flinched away. Her expression was all the answer he needed.

'I will find help.'

'Loud Thunder?' She knew herself how far it was still to his cabin.

For a moment, Broken Axe didn't answer, and she realized that it was because he *had* no better answer. Even he was beyond the edge of his inventiveness.

'I will wait.' She was stronger now than she had been. If the Tiger or her father caught up with her, then she would find out whether she could run or not. 'Broken Axe . . .'

But she had no words to follow his name, and he understood. A moment later there was that pale wolf with the dark shoulders again, before he was off into the forest. She found shelter for herself amidst the roots of a tree, and husbanded her strength.

37

She heard wolves calling as she crouched there – not close, but not as far away as she would have wished. The Tiger she did not hear, nor expected to. Slowly her two souls slunk back to her, their power seeping grudgingly back into her limbs. She did not try to Step, in case playing favourites with them might trigger another rebellion. Denied their animal senses, she felt blind. There could be enemies all around and she could not scent them.

But then Broken Axe was back, far sooner than he should have been – and not alone. She leapt up, knowing instantly that he could not have found Loud Thunder in such a short span. Her body was flooded with the need to fight or flee.

He had found other allies, though. He had come with the southerners.

'They were on my trail,' he told her. 'The girl here, she tracks like a wolf.'

The Plains woman made a scoffing sound at that.

'Can you run?' Axe asked. It seemed to be the question that her life revolved around.

She did not know the answer, but she replied, 'I can.'

'Make for Loud Thunder's home,' he told her. 'I will run ahead to alert him. Perhaps the Bear will give us guest rights.'

And Asmander enquired, 'Where is the Messenger?' It was a yawning moment before she realized who he meant.

Saying the words opened up the wounds again. 'He is dead.' The Champion stared at her.

'I took him from the Winter Runners,' she said in a whisper. 'But he was hurt, and then the cold . . . I'm sorry.' She was not quite sure of the relationship between Hesprec and this man. They had not been old friends from before, but the black youth had shown the old priest immediate and unquestioning respect. She was very aware of how little she knew any of these southerners.

The news had struck Asmander like a hammer. 'A Messenger of the Serpent, dead?' he got out. Maniye wanted to remind him that Hesprec had been old. She had wanted to say how he had seemed at peace. The words would not come, though, and she doubted that they would have helped.

'We must . . .' Broken Axe started, but Asmander wandered off a few steps, unsteady on his legs. Maniye looked at the other two. The southern girl was grimacing, a spectator to someone else's awkwardness, but when she met Maniye's gaze she just shrugged. The other man, the big one with the long hair, seemed blithely unconcerned.

Broken Axe approached Asmander. 'What will you do?' he asked. 'Where does this leave you?' His clenched fists alone showed how aware he was of the valuable time lost.

'I don't know,' the Champion said, and then, 'It leaves me with my duty.' He did not sound glad about that. 'Why can the girl not run with you?'

Broken Axe frowned. 'It is her souls.'

For a second, Asmander just stared at him blankly before understanding dawned. 'One must be cut away. The Messenger could have done that.'

'I could do it,' Broken Axe said tersely. 'But first she needs to choose.'

'Why not Wolf?'

'What do you know about it?' Axe asked sharply.

'She grew up a Wolf, did she not? And you are a Wolf – there is no Tiger here. She respects you.'

The hunter scowled. 'Normally this is easy. Normally there is one soul that speaks of home, and one that speaks of the *other*. But Many Tracks . . . the jaws of the Wolf, the claws of the Tiger, each is as unkind as the last.' He took a deep breath, glancing over at Maniye. 'Southerner, where do you stand now?'

A flurry of conflicting thoughts passed across Asmander's dark face, but they were written in the fashion of his River Nation, and Maniye could read none of them. 'Don't ask me this,' he replied hollowly.

'I ask you to do what you believe is right,' Broken Axe said simply. 'I would value your help, if you will offer it.'

Asmander's expression was eaten up by something that Maniye could not quite discern.

His big friend made a derisive noise. 'Wolf, this is no business of ours. Keep your girl and your tigers, and your piss-cold north.'

Broken Axe nodded once. 'I understand,' he said, but then Asmander held a hand up.

'We will go with her,' he declared, to the obvious surprise of his fellows. *Why?* Maniye wondered. *Just because of Hesprec? Does he owe me that much purely because Hesprec valued me?*

'Thank you.' Broken Axe clapped his hand on Asmander's shoulder, making the southerner shy away from him. 'She will show you the way, and I will be with you, with help, as soon as I can bring it.'

'But will they help?' Maniye asked. 'The Bear, will they even care?' She felt far too fragile to have so much of the world concerned about her fate. The weight of it was crushing.

Broken Axe's face showed that he had no such certainty, but a moment later he was back on four feet and dashing away, vanishing into the trees in a moment.

*

'What's she good for, anyway?' Venater demanded. 'Right now the only use for her that I can see is as lunch when our food runs out.'

'Enough.' Asmander kept his eyes on the girl ahead, because she didn't seem at all as sure of where she was going as she had claimed. She hadn't Stepped either, trusting neither of her souls. He guessed that mere human senses were inadequate to the task of navigation.

'Enough?' growled the old pirate behind him. 'The First Son of Asman has a duty to his father, and yet here he is up in the cold north, helping orphans.'

'She's not—'

'I don't care. Her parentage is like those knots your Snake priests tie, that nobody can undo. So why's it *our* problem?' All of this certainly loud enough for Maniye to hear.

'It's your problem because the First Son of Asman told Broken Axe we would do this,' Asmander snapped back at him. 'I am your only problem, Venater.'

'You've got one thing right, then.' The man spat disgustedly. When his voice was stilled, Asmander found that he missed it. Snarling with Venater had at least kept his mind busy and not asking itself the same question. *Why are you* really *doing this?* Going near that question was like touching a raw wound.

Broken Axe will be back soon, he reassured himself. *Then I will not have to make the choice of what to do.*

They were making poor time, at the girl's plodding pace. *Unless she trusts herself to Step, a three-legged wolf could catch us.*

Shyri was bored. She sauntered past Asmander on four feet, hackles high, and then Stepped right next to Maniye, making the girl start.

'So,' she said, chewing at a piece of gristle, 'Broken Axe . . .'

'What of him?' Maniye mumbled.

'You and he,' the Laughing Man girl continued, 'he's your mate?'

'No!' Maniye told her.

446

'No – or not yet?' Abruptly Shyri was in front of her, walking backwards directly ahead of the girl, putting that grin in her face. 'Maybe I'll make him mine.' She shot Asmander a look. 'Strong man, doesn't talk too much . . . I'll bet he'd fight, too, but not too much. Men like that, they like being broken—'

'Enough!' Asmander got out.

She stared at him with exaggeratedly owlish eyes. 'Have I shocked the Champion with my talk?'

'Aim your barbs somewhere else.'

She smirked and slunk aside, letting Maniye stumble on. 'You are Broken Axe's Champion now, are you?'

'And you are very brave to mock a man who isn't here,' he told her sharply, and caught a look of genuine hurt on her face for just a moment before she covered it. 'Broken Axe is a man who says he will do a thing, and then does it. Not for gold or meat or favours, but because it must be done.' He surprised himself with those words: before they came out, he had not realized how much the other man had impressed him. *If the Wolf only had Champions . . .*

Shyri's face darkened, and no doubt she had a spectacular put-down ready on her tongue, but then Venater snarled, and a moment later he had coursed past them and into the trees, his low-slung shape glittering black with scales. Asmander Stepped to the Champion immediately, baring black stone teeth, and Shyri was a hyena. Only Maniye remained on human feet, clutching her bronze knife.

They heard the surprised yelp of something – Asmander didn't know the animals of this land well enough to guess – but Venater came slouching back to them soon enough. When he Stepped back, his face was frustrated.

'Just one,' he reported. 'One, and fled.'

'One what?' Asmander demanded. 'The Wolf?'

'Cat,' Venater said. 'Stripes. The other one.'

'And gone to fetch his friends,' Shyri pointed out, 'since you let him get away.'

Venater gave her a sour look. 'Maybe I wanted them to come and put an end to this stupid thing we're doing.'

'Girl, can you Step?' Asmander demanded.

Maniye wouldn't meet his eyes. For a moment he thought she would at least try, arms clutched about herself and teeth bared. Then she was shaking her head, and shaking all over.

'Then we'd better keep going. We run, and hope Broken Axe is coming back for us.'

Then it was just the hard march onwards, their pursuers devouring the distance towards them as inexorably as the sun kept sinking towards the horizon. That morning she had said her last words to Hesprec. The evening would bring the Tiger.

Maniye tried to keep her gaze focused before her, but the corners of her eyes betrayed her. The woods seemed full of fire-striped forms; the deepening dusk made tigers out of every shadow.

And she was slowing all of them.

I must trust to my souls.

If she fell now . . . but if not now, then a mile later. Unless she Stepped.

She reached inside of herself. She felt as though she was looking into one of those pits her father's people dug to keep prisoners in. At its base, the lean forms of her souls paced round and round, cramped by their captivity, snapping and snarling at each other and at her.

Obey me, or I die. But perhaps they wanted her dead – to part company with each other and fly free of her corpse.

Then, from how far away she could not say, she heard a wolf give voice, high and lonely, at the moon. The Winter Runners or just mute brothers? At the sound, the wolf within her leapt for freedom, and she Stepped, or tried to Step, only the tiger began fighting her, clawing at her insides. She stumbled and fell, briefly sleek and grey-furred, then bruising her human bones again.

448

She heard Venater curse her furiously, then Asmander had yanked her upright on her human feet.

'Go,' he said, but at the same time Shyri announced, 'They're here.'

A tiger leapt up before them, springing from the gathering dark to stand proud atop a rock. Another crouched on a tree trunk, while the spaces between the trees rustled with the passage of their bodies. How many? She could not know.

For a moment the Tigers were coming for them, but then Shyri had dropped to four feet, and Asmander was the Champion without warning, exploding into his terrible, alien shape right beside her so that she fell back from him – all the claws and scales and jagged teeth of him. Only Venater had retained his human form, a short-bladed club in one hand. He looked fearsome enough in any shape. Maniye saw the lead Tiger abruptly turn its aborted lunge into a casual pacing. The Shadow Eaters were clearly not so sure how the souls of these foreigners would taste.

And then Aritchaka was standing right before them, resplendent in her bronze mail and her feather-crested helm. Maniye caught her eyes for a heartbeat, and saw regret there, but not enough to stop her leading the hunt.

'You have a thing of ours,' she called out, and her warband padded all around them, never still, never clearly seen.

Asmander was human again, toothed sword slanted over one shoulder. 'She says you mean to kill her,' he observed.

'She is claimed by the Tiger.'

'Life too short to go over everyone who's claimed her,' Venater grunted. They all ignored him.

The Tiger priestess took a careful step forward. 'Foreigner, do not make us paint our hands with your blood.' She sounded genuinely solicitous. 'We have no grievance with your people.'

'Fair point,' Venater nodded.

Maniye felt the world beginning to tilt against her once more, to nobody's surprise. In the handful of heartbeats when there was still talking, not fighting, she reached inside herself again, facing the tortured eyes of the two beasts trapped within her.

Wolf, carry me, or I will cut you away. With my last breath I shall go gladly to the Tiger's mouth, as one of his own.

She sensed the snarl of canine teeth at that, the pain and the resentment.

Shyri had Stepped back now, if only because, if there was talking, she wanted her fair share. 'Well, longmouth? Who speaks within you now? Your Champion? Your father? The Axe one? The Serpent?' She was watching the shifting circle of the Tigers close in on them imperceptibly.

Tiger, let me ride the Wolf or I will cut you away. If Aritchaka catches me, it shall be a wolf soul the Tiger feasts on. Was that even a threat? But she heard the yowling in her ears, the hiss of displeasure.

'We fight,' Asmander declared flatly. He did not seem very happy about it. 'We keep her from the Tiger.'

'But *why?*' Shyri asked, but then the ground shook, and something like a mountain cut loose from the ground had thundered out of the trees, bellowing its defiance; and dancing about its feet was a pale wolf with dark shoulders. Loud Thunder and Broken Axe had arrived.

The Tiger scattered, but in the next moment they were attacking, springing out from the darkness. One tried to leap on Loud Thunder's haunches but he spun on the spot to face her, roaring, so that the Tiger almost fell over her own feet trying to get out of the way. Instead she met Venater, who did his level best to skin her alive with that short stone blade of his.

Then there was another, a man of the Tiger, leaping up on four feet to land before Maniye on two, a studded club cocked back to strike. She skipped aside from the blow, knife angled ready for the Tiger dance, the fighting style of his priesthood. The sight of it gave him pause: the men did not learn that dance but they feared it. Then Shyri had jumped him from behind and torn a ragged mouthful from his shoulder.

450

The clearing was alive with leaping shadows. She heard the screech of Asmander's Champion as it pounced into the midst of the Tiger, scattering them, chasing them here and there. Loud Thunder was holding two or three off, the Tigers' claws and knives not even managing to penetrate his hide.

Broken Axe went rushing past her, pausing to snarl at her through bloodied fangs, and she knew it was time. She confronted the two beasts within her, reminded them of her dire threats, and Stepped.

For a moment they were rebellious, writhing stubbornly in her grip, but then she had forced her will on them, her blood hot with the violence of the moment. Stepping, she followed after Broken Axe, her nose telling her instantly that the sharp, alien scent of Asmander was on her other side as they dashed into the treeline. Behind her she heard the weird heckling cry of Shyri, that hunting call of a distant land cackling out of the darkness.

Almost immediately the reek of tiger was strong and close in her nose. She veered away, unseeing but hearing the sudden rush of it as it tried to ambush her. A moment later the dark shape bolted out behind her, raking at her flanks but falling short, hissing a challenge.

A thing from nightmare dropped onto the tiger, leaping so high that it seemed to fall out of the branches above. Asmander's curved claws ripped in, but Maniye heard the splintering of ribs simply under the force of his landing.

Then the Tiger were on their trail in earnest. The woods seemed full of them: with brief ember-bright glimpses of their striped bodies, their moon-gleaming eyes. The fear that hammered within her was the Wolf's generations-old terror of the Shadow Eaters who came to devour their souls.

Asmander was gone now. She had no sense of when, just that something had dragged him away. Then she was battling her way through denser trees, swerving and scrabbling, knowing that Broken Axe was off to her right and getting more distant. In a sudden panic, surrounded by that peopled darkness, she

Stepped to her tiger shape to climb and leap, hoping to make better time through the tangle, trying to break out into the open where her wolf speed would count.

It was a mistake. In that moment of change her souls clashed inside her, ripping at one another, and she tumbled over, shocked onto two human feet, jarring hard off a tree trunk and landing on her knees.

When she looked up, she was not alone. The sight of the woman who had come so far to kill her hurt like a wound inside her, one that would not close.

Joalpey, Strength In Moonlight. 'Mother.'

The Tiger Queen looked down on her. The curved blade was in her hand, but for just that moment she made no move to use it. Around them the woods seemed abruptly quiet, as though both of them had been abandoned by their allies.

'I will not go with you,' Maniye told her.

Joalpey nodded, and then one foot slid back and she was in her fighting stance, ready for the dance of tigers. Maniye felt herself fall into a mirroring pose, but there was a cold blade of fear in her, because to fight she needed her souls, and she could not say if either would answer her call right then.

Joalpey was moving as soon as she had made her stand, bronze edge flickering forwards in curved paths through the darkness, so that it was more an idea in Maniye's mind than a sight in her eyes. She let the shape of her mother's body tell her where the knife would go next, slipping aside into a crouching pose and bringing her own blade up in an arc that would have driven it into the other woman's armpit if she had stayed still. Joalpey made the smallest shift to her footing, Maniye's point missing her by an inch that might just as well have been an arm's length, while Joalpey's own blade drew a long red line down the girl's arm.

And even as Maniye stepped back, stabbing at throat height with a hand slick with her own blood, her mother became a tiger, springing even as she Stepped. She launched herself under

Maniye's strike, knocking her smaller prey off her feet and slamming down on her.

The bruising pain of it seemed to knock Maniye's mind askew even as the breath was driven from her. She was clawing and biting furiously at the big cat atop her, snapping with a wolf's yellow teeth, digging in hooked tiger claws, digging in with the point of her blade, even as she fought to keep Joalpey's own jaws away from her. She Stepped and Stepped, swift and uncontrolled as a spring flood, her fluid form denying her enemy a target.

Then her mother was knocked away with a yowl of surprise, as another of her people bowled into her, his fur bloody. Venater's reptile shape uncoiled from the dark in chase, saw-tooth jaws tearing open the injured tiger's entire flank. Then the pirate had bloated into his human shape, kneeling over the Tiger hunter with hand upraised before driving his razor-edged blade down, three hacking blows to butcher the beast with no mercy given. When he stood again, gory implement in hand, his eyes were on Joalpey. His grin looked like death.

Maniye fled, though right then she was not sure who she was fleeing from. She hit the ground on wolf paws, hoping that her mother would take up the southerner's challenge.

She did not. Instead, she was pounding after her true target, and Venater, for all his fearsome skill, could not keep up with them.

But Maniye was faster: allow her twenty breaths of clear running and she must pull ahead of Joalpey. Ten breaths and no more conflict within her or even—

All of that was tangled in her mind when Joalpey leapt at her and caught her a raking blow down her haunches. The pain seared through Maniye and she stumbled, losing her speed, lurching desperately to get back onto her feet again. The tiger was off balance too, her lunge overextending her. One more time, Maniye fled.

Then there was a new shape coursing alongside her – Broken

Axe keeping pace with effort, with blood in his teeth and down his sides.

Something passed between them, an understanding, and if she had the time to take human shape she would have told him not to do it. But he was already turning, Stepping into a man with his axe drawn back. She heard the hissing scream of a woman as the iron blade bit, shocked out of her tiger form by the sheer pain. Not her mother, which meant that . . .

She had slowed without meaning to, waiting for Broken Axe, and that was when Joalpey caught up with her. Maniye saw only a flurry out from the dark, and then she had thrown herself aside, a leap the wolf was not capable of, so that she landed on her hands and knees, rolling and kicking to try and get up, her knife lost, even as her mother approached.

The hot breath of the tiger was on Maniye and she froze, reaching for any other form but the helpless, naked one she had been born to. The Tiger Queen was a shape of fire-splashed darkness, her eyes seeming to glow from within.

Then she was a woman once more, her knife levelled at Broken Axe as he returned.

'Why?' Joalpey asked him.

'For the same reason I saved you from the Wolf. Because it is right. Will you not honour my judgement?'

There was a battle on Joalpey's face just then, but she lost it when another pair of Tigers slunk out to stand beside her, one limping and the other with a torn ear.

'For all I owe you, you were too late,' she told Broken Axe. 'You cannot heal the scars they left. And she is just one more scar.'

Something stayed her though. Her history with Broken Axe allowed Maniye two more breaths. The Tiger was fierce behind Joalpey's eyes, but the eyes were human still, somehow penning it in. Not for Maniye; she would not defy her god for something as trivial as her daughter. She wanted Broken Axe to flee now though. She did not want his blood on her claws, his soul in her teeth.

Then Asmander stepped out, a shadow from the shadows, smudged darker with blood here and there, and his sword jagged with missing teeth.

'We're leaving now,' he announced to the world, his voice ragged with weariness, but still trying to sound light and mocking. 'Let the Tiger fill its belly somewhere else.'

Joalpey's face twisted and she Stepped, snarling, but Asmander met her shape for shape. The ear-splitting screech of the Champion tore through the forest, sending the Tiger Queen skittering backwards.

Axe's hand yanked at Maniye's shoulder, and then they had seized the opportunity the southerner had given them, making a straight line through the trees, away from Joalpey, and hoping there were no more Tigers lying in wait.

Asmander caught up with them moments later, those long reptile strides easily outpacing them. By then, Maniye's husbanded reserve of strength was almost gone. Since the three of them had set off to rescue Hesprec, it felt as though she had never stopped running. Axe was stumbling too, and she did not know how much of the blood that painted his pelt was his own. Asmander kept in front of them, leading them, guiding them downslope, darting between trees. Of the others – of Loud Thunder or Shyri or Venater – there was no sign.

Maniye realized a moment later that Axe was straying further from her. *Don't go back to fight them*, she pleaded inside her head. That seemed just the sort of thing that either of the men would do. She felt that if she was left on her own, she would simply collapse, that only their presence was pushing her on.

But Axe was not heading away – he was coming back now, trying to reach her, but Asmander was in the way. Asmander was herding her, pushing close, rushing her ahead. When Axe got too close, the Champion snapped at him. In the midst of her

455

headlong flight, Maniye could not work out what was happening.

There was a scent on the wind, a familiar one that spoke of hearths and food, so that she found a last cupful of strength to push her onwards. It was a testament to how tired she was that the smell of home seemed reassuring to her: the smell of the Winter Runners and the Wolf.

She realized too late – even as the jolt of fear shot through her, grey bodies were passing on either side of her. She heard a yelp and a snarl from Broken Axe, but there were two or three Wolf hunters between him and Maniye already. She turned, trying to reach him, but there was Asmander – in the form of the indomitable Champion – shrieking into her face, driving her away.

And then he was human, his stone-toothed blade still in hand, calling out, 'Broken Axe, run! Run now!'

Maniye tried to do just that herself, but Smiles Without Teeth was on her already, powering her to the root-knotted ground and digging his teeth at her neck, trying to force her to change form. She thought she heard Broken Axe shout her name, but there were half a dozen wolves roiling around her already, and more vanishing into the dark to look for him.

One of the pack was straightening up, casting off its pelt and its hide and taking on the much worse guise of her father. Right now, though, those familiar and hated eyes were not on her. They were fixed on the southerner.

'So,' spoke Akrit Stone River.

'You will remember our words in the Stone Place,' Asmander spat out tiredly. 'You had killed another chief inside the circle, but you had lost her. This was what you wanted.'

'You take a long time to honour your bargains,' Stone River told him.

'But honour them I do. And you will find me the Iron Wolves my lord needs, the invulnerable warriors of the north.'

Hesprec. Maniye felt all of her grief and loss anew, because *this*, this was why Asmander had been travelling behind her. And then he must have met with Hesprec, his Messenger, the man he respected and followed without question.

And then Hesprec had passed on; she had saved the old man from her father but not from time or cold. And Asmander must have been left wondering then where his path led. And he owed her nothing. He had not journeyed all the way from his far homeland just to chase around after a mongrel girl.

'I will be High Chief as soon as the Moon Eaters recognize me, and you shall have your warriors,' Stone River replied carefully. 'There will be many young hunters eager to prove themselves. Why should they not see your homeland and taste its joys? I am Stone River. I keep my bargains.'

And Asmander should have looked triumphant, Maniye thought. He should have been delighted at himself for outwitting all the Crown of the World to thus win his prize. But instead he looked only sick, either at the world or at himself, and he nodded as though he was accepting a punishment.

38

She had slept. In the end sheer anxiety had not been enough, and exhaustion had overpowered it. When she awoke, she was within a tent-space built about a tree, sheets of hide stretched out over the lowest branches to give the temporary dwelling a shape. She had half expected them to string her up, as they had with Hesprec, but instead there was just a collar and a thick braid of rawhide that led to a stake of iron dug into the ground. It represented wealth, that stake: enough iron to make four or five knives or a couple of axe-heads. She was being treated as a thing of value, but as a thing nonetheless.

Asmander had betrayed her. But then Asmander had never been loyal to her. The reversal still hurt her though. She was the centre of her own world, after all. She had not stopped to think that she was only peripheral to the lives of others. For a moment, when they had all been together running the Tigers' gauntlet, she had seen them as some kind of hero-band out of the stories: Bear, Wolf and exotic foreigners bound together by mutual respect to triumph over all comers. But that had been a foolish thought, and if she had not been so young she would not have entertained it.

Time to grow up.

And to grow up she must cast aside childish things. Such as having two souls.

Trapped in her human form and unable to favour or discipline either of them, she felt them pace about within her. She was her own cage and they were her prisoners, forced into a proximity that neither could live with. She felt a desperate need to return to childhood: it seemed to her now a carefree time of freedom when she and the different sides of her nature had lived together in harmony and joy.

'I cannot choose,' she told the world. 'I am both. If I was only one, I would be just half of what I am. How can I be asked to choose?'

As if summoned by her words, Akrit shouldered his way through the flap of the tent and paused to survey her. He loomed large in her memory, but right now he seemed even larger.

'There you are,' he told her, as though he had simply mislaid her for a moment, rather than chasing her all across the Crown of the World.

She stared at him sullenly, and he sat down cross-legged before her, even smiling just as if this was a much-sought meeting of old friends. 'I've lost a lot in chasing you,' he told her almost jovially. 'I've had warriors killed by the Tiger, and you've turned Broken Axe from me, too. If you liked him so much, you could have had him. I told you that.'

Still she said nothing, shuffling away from him until her leash pulled taut, her back against the sagging hide of the tent.

'What?' he asked her quite frankly. Her fear seemed to baffle him.

'Why?' she whispered. 'Why go so far? I am grown. I am not tied to your hearth.'

'You are of my blood and I have a use for you,' he explained patiently. 'You are a tool of mine, a thing that I brought into being when I had your mother. And I need you to fulfil my destiny.'

'Destiny?' she echoed.

'Takes Iron is sure that there is a destiny at work. There are strange things happening in the world – can you deny it? All the

459

people of the Crown of the World feel a change, like winter. And you were at the Stones. You know what happened there. A great destiny has come to the world – and it is mine.'

'It is not mine,' she got out.

'You are its,' he told her. 'You are a part of it. A Tiger and a Wolf child, and my only child. Who could doubt that the world meant you for a purpose?'

She stared at him. At first she could not even imagine what he was talking about, so much had happened to her since that night.

His smile was encouraging, though. It invited her to meet it with one of her own, though she refused to.

He rose in one smooth motion, rolling his shoulders and stretching. 'You will do what you are told,' he said mildly. 'When you leave me again, it will be to do my bidding. You will see this is the right thing to do. But you were ever a slow child, and disobedient.' He loomed over her, and she saw the glint of a knife in his hand. When he hauled her up she thought he would cut her, but he just sawed at the laces of her shift until he had stripped the clothes off her back. 'Even grown,' he told her, 'you are still a child in your mind. So you must be made to serve.' And he had dropped her and taken up something that had been lying near the tent flap, something she had not noticed before. A thin switch of birch.

'I want you to recite back to me what I say,' he told her. His hands sent the switch keening through the air, not touching her yet but the mere sound sending a rush of fear through her. 'You will speak it back, and back, and back until it is from your own mind you are speaking. Let us start with something simple. You will obey your father in all things.'

Even terrified, she scowled at him.

'Yes, I had thought that would be hard for you. It always was, and I was too soft before. I did not see how you would grow, or else I would have been firmer. Tell me: "I will obey my father in all things."'

460

Even as she was deciding to resist him, he struck her. The thin line of the switch seared across her arm and back and sent her to the floor, not with the force of it but with the pain. The thin wood of the whip had been split, and stones braided into it. A single lash stung like a dozen bees.

'Tell me,' he said again, and still in that terribly calm voice – not at all like him, in fact. This was Stone River possessed by his own destiny.

She would have spoken, but the sudden agony of the blow had driven her voice from her, and so he struck her again, laying down a second weal across her back. This time she shrieked – no words, but somehow he read in that sound the confirmation he was looking for. Perhaps he was not wrong to do so.

'Again,' he said, and drew back the lash. When she bared her teeth at him, he put twice the force into his next blow, hard enough to splinter the switch against her, leaving her sobbing and hunched in upon herself.

Stone River sighed with mild exasperation, and went to fetch another switch. She had already seen that there were half a dozen lying there in the shadows of the tent's edge.

'Now . . .' he began.

'I will! Please, I will!' broke from her lips. She had not meant to say it, had not wanted to, but the traitor words got out somehow and hung in the air between them.

'Well, now,' he said, plainly pleased, and swished the new whip through the air, getting a feel for it. 'Tell me how you will go to the Tiger for me.'

She stared at him because plainly he was mad. But of course he could not know all those bitter things that had happened since she had last escaped him.

'I can't,' she said into the silence, and when he raised the switch she went on, 'I can't! I can't! It doesn't work, I can't go to them!'

'You will go to the Tiger,' he said with more force. 'You will tell them who your mother was. I know how they are ruled.

461

They cannot but make you their leader, because you are the blood of their last one. That is the way of the Tiger, everyone knows.'

And it came to her, even as the lash rose again, that she had found the limits of him, the walls that hedged his mind. For this was what he had been told of the Tiger, and he had never questioned it or tried to find out more about it. His ignorance was his hearth, and he had never explored the darkness beyond.

And he struck her again and raised another torn stripe on her human skin and, although the leash restrained her physically, whatever had held her back inside now snapped. She screamed then, but she was screaming defiance at him. 'I have been to the Tiger! The Tiger want me dead because I am yours! My mother lives and rules them, and she will not accept me as her daughter, nor would I be yours! But you will never rule the Tiger through me, because they reject me! They will eat my flesh and my soul if I fall within their power one more time!'

He had brought the whip up for another strike, but now he was frozen, staring at her. '*Alive?*' he hissed, and then he did break free from his enclosed ignorance, leaping from stone to stone in his mind until he spat out 'Broken Axe!' seeing past the man's recent betrayal to that far greater one.

'He was never yours!' she hissed at him. 'He was always his own, and I will not be yours either.' It was as if, somehow, her mind and her mouth had forgotten the whip and the pain, just for that moment.

But Akrit did not strike again. This much she could say for him: within the little domain of his thoughts, he was no fool. Already he was planning. 'You will serve me,' he said, whether to her or to the world, she could not say.

The switch was lowered. Akrit's eyes narrowed. 'There is a destiny. I tore out Water Gathers' throat in the ring of stones, and the spirits stooped low about us, watching. You ran beneath their gaze, too, that day. You are marked by them, as am I. Marked for great things. Or for a great doom. So I must show the Wolf I am worthy, and to do so I must use what the world has given me.' His gaze rested on her again. 'It has given me you.'

'Have you never thought,' she got out, 'that perhaps we just did those things, and the spirits don't care?'

He struck her three times with the full force of his arm, though his hatred and anger, which would have made the blows a real terror, were concentrated elsewhere, considering his next move. Once she lay twitching and whimpering before him, though, he barely seemed to notice her, departing again, already calling for his priest.

Maniye was left to herself, after that, in a gloom that seemed lit up by the burning stripes Akrit had laid across her back. She could hear exchanges about the camp, sometimes a snap and snarl of disagreement, once what sounded like a full-scale skirmish between two of them. Akrit's warband was fraying. They had come this far with him, and they had been bloodied by the Tiger, and now they must be looking to their leader and wondering. Some would be thinking of challenge. Who would be the first? Smiles Without Teeth was too loyal, Shatters Oak was a woman, but others would be asking themselves if their own time had come.

The wait seemed to go on forever, any sense of time's passing taken from her, without the sky to mark it. The hurt from her whipping dulled, like embers dimming but never quite extinguished. She slept a little, but fitfully, then was awoken by her father's voice barking loudly outside the tent. He was giving orders, rousing the warband to move. Shortly after, a pair of hunters came in and uprooted the metal stake between them, not looking at her. She could have named them both but they were working very hard at pretending that they could not see her, even as they hauled her out at the end of her leash.

The Wolves decamped so quickly that Maniye guessed the Tigers were still stalking somewhere nearby. She had a feeble hope then, for if they were to move at full pace, surely they must run as wolves, and free her to do the same. Then she would seize the first chance she had, and she would be gone from them, trusting to her feet once again.

A moment's thought told her it could not happen. They had baggage with them, hides and tents and provisions, and loot from the Boar village. They had a pair of travois that they bundled their burdens on, to be hauled by the younger hunters. Of the rest, many did Step, running ahead or falling away to either side to keep an eye and a nose ready for any enemy, leaving a handful to stay with Maniye and the baggage, led by Smiles Without Teeth.

Smiles stooped low to speak in her ear, putting her in his shadow.

'Stone River says he wants you to live, for now,' he told her. 'But he says, "If she runs, break her leg."' His dark eyes pinned her. 'I asked him, "Why not do that now? No running then." But he says there's too much we need to carry already. But I will – give me the chance, girl, and I will.'

She fully intended to meet his ugly gaze, but the deep rumble of his voice pitched itself right to the fear in her mind, and she could not. He took her leash himself, his hand almost eclipsing the metal stake.

Her wounds were dressed roughly, leaving her feeling as though they had lit a fire on her back. Then they headed westwards, away from the Tiger, and there was no talking between them. Despite their loads, Akrit's warband set a swift pace, further reinforcing Maniye's suspicion that the Tiger were not keeping to their own places now. *And I have caused that somehow. I am a weapon so fierce that my mother cannot let her enemies grasp me. I am the spark that sets the fire.*

But that was merely a sop to her own vanity. Even helpless, she was trying to spin a tale that gave her some sense of control. She had been swept before the rush of events like broken wood in the river during the spring thaw.

Akrit dropped back occasionally. He would encourage Smiles to keep up the pace, but his eyes were ever on Maniye. When they camped that night, the stake was hammered in again, but she lay out in the open, surrounded by wolves on all sides, without any true camp being pitched.

Several of the warriors had been sent ahead. *My father has a plan.*

Some time during that same night she woke into a darkness relieved only by the fire's last embers and a sliver of cloudy moon. A man stood over her, and she recoiled, assuming it must be her father. Then, for a mad moment, she thought it was Broken Axe, for it lacked Stone River's broad bulk. This was an older man, though, shorter and leaner, and one she should have known sooner: Kalameshli Takes Iron.

She was not going to speak at first, although he must know she was awake. He just watched and watched, though, and at last she got out, 'You must be very happy, Takes Iron. You were right all along. I am no true daughter of the Wolf.'

'Nor of the Tiger yet.' His voice startled her, for she had not expected an answer. 'You were wolf enough, when you were caught.'

'Your chief is a fool,' she said softly, wondering if any other was awake to hear. 'He needs me to be a Wolf, so as to be his own, yet he thinks the Tiger would follow me if I was not a Tiger?'

'He has cherished some dreams a long time.' Takes Iron did not say 'too long' and yet it was there between his words. Maniye frowned, because she had never heard him even come close to criticizing her father.

'The Tiger will not have me anyway, no matter how much Tiger I am,' she added bitterly.

'I think your father understands as much,' he agreed. His eyes had never left her, and she felt a crawling sense of unease born of that rigid scrutiny.

'Then what?' she hissed.

465

She saw Kalameshli's shoulders rise and fall. 'His thoughts are close about him now. The eyes of the Wolf—'

She made an exasperated noise, because Akrit himself had told her all that, and it gave her no clues as to what her father would actually *do*. In the wake of that, she heard someone nearby stirring, woken by her frustration. Kalameshli melted away into the dark silently, and in the morning she was not sure she believed any of it.

They travelled two more days, moving with all the speed the travois could manage, swapping bearers and scouts, and never giving Maniye the least chance to escape. When Smiles was not holding her leash, the job fell to Shatters Oak, the other veteran amongst them. She was a worse captor, if anything. Smiles Without Teeth was a man of little imagination, and able to plod along in silence for hours without growing bored or fretful. Amiyen Shatters Oak had a harsher streak to her. Even if Maniye had not killed her son, she had still been *there*, connected to that death by a trail of blood. Amiyen would yank on the lead viciously, hauling Maniye close, her teeth almost to the prisoner's ear.

'When we catch Broken Axe, we're going to skin him,' she would hiss. 'Kalameshli says he has spat on the Wolf, so his ghost can't be allowed to leave his body. We're going to wear his human pelt and leave his flesh for the coyotes. He'll never come back as wolf or man.' From her first sally she had realized that simply threatening Maniye herself with pain or death would barely register, Akrit having already run her to exhaustion on that front. Instead, she noticed the flinch when she first brought up Maniye's ally. 'He will come,' she had crowed. 'He'll come for you, do you think? I will be waiting. When he's ours, I'll wield the knife myself. I'll beg Kalameshli for the chance. I am owed, girl. We'll roast him alive on the fire and feed you his human flesh.'

She was endlessly inventive in the fates that they had in store

466

for their former kinsman, each of them whispered viciously into Maniye's ear. It was a pastime the woman never tired of.

At last they stopped, because they had caught up with the hunters Akrit had sent ahead. They had been crossing open land, following a young river's descent out of the highlands and onwards west, but there were more trees ahead. Maniye had lost all track of where they were: without her wolf nose, she felt disconnected by so much travelling.

At the edge of the trees and in the crook of the river, a fire was already going and the hunters had not been idle. There was a mess of wood there, and they were building something too small and irregular for a dwelling. When the travois party arrived, Kalameshli took himself off to view it immediately, mostly to berate them and have them dismantle much of it.

They had been hunting, too, because there was a pit dug and within it a sow and a boar were pacing angrily, leaping up at their captors whenever a human face showed itself. At first Maniye feared she would be thrown in there too. Instead, the big tent-shelter they had originally kept her in was reassembled here, and she was leashed inside, kept blind to what was going on without.

Her ignorance lasted only until nightfall, for most of which time she had simply lain there, feeling the ache in her legs and feet, the taut tugging of the welts across her back, not even trying to uproot the stake. Kalameshli's voice came to her, calling instructions peevishly, and the harsh shout of Akrit when something went wrong. If anything, the tension between the Wolves was spun tauter than ever. Maniye had been desperately looking for any sign that someone was getting close to standing up to her father – for surely any challenger would have no particular interest in her fate – yet Stone River's reputation still held them in check.

Then, once the noise and mutter outside had died down into

uneasy sleep, Akrit and Kalameshli backed into the tent. The priest glanced at her once, her father not at all.

'Two pigs are no sacrifice,' Akrit stated. He had brought a brand with him, and he jammed it into the ground for its light. 'The scouts say the only people close to here are the Horse, who they fear to touch.'

'Well, they are wise,' Kalameshli murmured. 'If we are to war against the Tiger, we would be fools to seek more enemies. The Horse are dangerous, not because they have many warriors, but because they have many friends—'

'All this I know,' Stone River cut him off sharply. 'So, not even a hunter of the Deer or some Boar woman out looking for mushrooms. Then you know the answer to your question.'

And Kalameshli's eyes slid inexorably to Maniye, sitting up and staring at them. 'This also is unwise,' he observed.

'I have asked you for wisdom but your well has run dry,' Akrit told him flatly. 'I can feel the Wolf's breath on my neck, old man. He is waiting for me to prove myself to him. I need to show him that in me are all the qualities he values: that I am fierce and strong; I baulk at nothing.'

'There are other qualities that the Wolf values. Loyalty to kin—' Kalameshli started, trying to sound mild but the strain in his voice betrayed him.

'Yes, loyalty!' Akrit interrupted. 'And she has shown none! So she deserves none. She fled the tribe. She stole meat from the Wolf's own jaws. She has been the guest of the Shadow Eaters! The Wolf must be hungering for her.'

Kalameshli glanced at her, the fire catching his eyes. 'Akrit, as I am your friend, this is not the way.'

'She will be given to the Wolf.'

What Maniye felt was some terrible variant of relief. Her fears had come to pass. The nightmare that had chased her all the way from the village of the Winter Runners had caught up with her. Outside the tent they had been building an altar: jaws of wood in imitation of the iron teeth of home. They would burn her inside them, and the Wolf would consume her.

But Kalameshli continued shaking his head. 'She is your kin,' he insisted. 'No god will protect a kinslayer. Is this what you will have the Wolf see?'

Akrit even smiled at that. 'But I will not be a kinslayer. Because you are my priest, and you shall carry the flame.'

The older man's face went dead in an instant, utterly without expression. 'It cannot be done,' he said quietly.

'You'll do it,' Akrit told him. 'As I am your chief, you will do it. Because the Winter Runners need me, Takes Iron. I will make us first of all the tribes, and I will make the Wolf the first of all the peoples. It starts here, with this. This is how I show the Wolf what I dare. This is how *you* show the Wolf your loyalty. Don't think he isn't watching you as well.'

Kalameshli would have argued further, but Akrit abruptly grabbed him by the robe, yanking him forwards in a clatter of little bones.

'Do not challenge me,' Stone River growled into the old man's face, and then dropped him, the old priest falling to his knees. A moment later Akrit had stomped out of the tent, the parting of the hide flap giving Maniye a glimpse of the flames outside.

Kalameshli got to his feet and stood there for a long time, long after the brand had burned out, thinking in the darkness, and then he, too, left.

39

'So what makes him High Chief, then? He has to kill the others?'

Before now, Venater had shown no interest whatsoever in the Crown of the World. He had happily fought against the place's natives, but even the Stone Place had barely impressed him. Now, though, he seemed suddenly interested in the ways of the Wolf.

Asmander would rather not have spoken of it, but at the same time he knew that silence would only encourage the old pirate. Sensing weakness was meat and drink to the Dragon.

'I don't think so.' His voice seemed remarkably conversational, to his own ears. 'He has not killed the chief of these . . . Swift Ones? Swift Feet, Swift somethings. And there is some other tribe he says will join him. It is these Moon Faces who are not decided. He needs to impress them, I think.'

'Better than *your* lot,' was Venater's verdict. 'When you told me what that was about, I thought it was arse backwards both ways.'

Shyri smirked at that, eyes flicking between the two of them. Seeing Asmander being baited came second only to baiting him herself in her list of pastimes, or so he surmised.

'All that ceremony. Fasting, invocation, sacrifice, just to make someone Kasra, but you've already decided who gets to do it: always the eldest brat of the last one.' Venater was watching him keenly for any crack in the facade.

'You'd rather everyone fought until only one of them stood?' Asmander asked him with a superior look. 'That is how life is amongst the Dragon?'

'No ceremony, no certainty.' Venater grinned. 'When we get back, maybe that's what I'll do: cut a few throats and make myself chief. About time I settled down with a few wives.'

Asmander glanced at him sharply, fighting down a flare of real anger, and found himself meeting the pirate's amused stare. More bait, always more bait, until he found himself lunging at it.

'I would think those women would rather cut their own throats than settle down with you,' he managed, knowing it for a weak rejoinder.

'You don't understand what women want,' Venater replied, still coolly jabbing away with a patience that said he could do this all day.

'Who would not want to lie with the son of Venat,' Shyri added slyly. 'The muscles of his arms are like hard melons. His teeth are so yellowed you'd think them nuggets of gold,' and then, just as Venater was about to expand on her words with more of his attributes, she added, 'Alas for his name, though: it has entered its second childhood. Have I got it right?'

The old pirate found himself abruptly on the other end of the joke, snarling at her, which bred only laughter.

Asmander did not join in.

'Well, what now, longmouth?' she pressed him. 'You trust this Stone River to give you your due, now he's got his cub back?'

'We move like his shadow. When he travels to visit these Moon Faces – no, Moon Eaters – I will follow his tracks. I will remind him of his promise.'

'And if he just sends his hunters out to kill you?'

'Then I will kill his hunters until he remembers his promise,' Asmander said dully.

'And if he sends his Iron Wolves, his great warriors that even the Sun River Nation has heard of?' she pressed.

'Then I will see whether they were worth me travelling so far. And perhaps I will die.' *Killing one was hard enough.*

'Is that really it?' Shyri asked.

He could not tell what she meant. 'Dying?'

'Why your chief sent you here, your . . . Tecuman?'

'My Tecuman, yes. But it was my father who sent me.' And enough said about that. Asmander must be a dutiful son and do what he was told. Even when he was told to cross the whole world in search of a mad myth. *Who would have thought the Iron Wolves were actually real?*

Not for the first time he wondered what had happened back home since he set off upriver. Perhaps Tecuman had defeated his sister. Perhaps he was dead. No word would have come to him here, in these cold lands.

'Well,' said Venater, eyeing him. 'You've done it, anyway. Think of the look on the old man's face when you bring him what he asked for. Like something out of that story.'

Bizarrely, Asmander knew exactly the story he meant, or what sort of tale anyway. There were many variants, but there was a young man given an impossible task by someone supposed to be their ally – stepfather, uncle – yet finds some way to complete it. The hero's return was always a triumphant scene of virtues rewarded, and evil unmasked. Somehow Asmander did not feel that his own exploits would fit into that pattern.

But he said, 'Yes,' trying to make himself sound enthusiastic. 'I will have done my duty.'

Shyri snickered at that, and he glared at her. 'The Laughing Men know nothing of duty, then?'

'There are things you must do, and things you must not do. We know this.' Her smile was blithely unconcerned with his feelings. 'You river people find it so complicated, so hard to tell one thing from another. You use so many words.'

'Loyalty,' he snapped at her. 'Duty. Family. These are just words to you?'

She exchanged a sidelong glance with Venater, as though the

472

two of them were conspirators in Asmander's torment. 'All words are just words. They are not the things they are used for.'

Asmander opened his mouth to argue, then found her point too unexpectedly philosophical to make headway with. This was the sort of talk the Serpent priests debated in the temple.

Venater had at last grown bored. 'Home soon, anyway,' he suggested.

Asmander nodded.

'Gratitude of the Kasra, I reckon. Or half a Kasra, anyway. Good way to make your mark, that. All those snapping fools at your Tecuman's feet, each one giving all their strength to fighting the next man for the least scrap from his table. And in you come, Asmander the Champion, with your Wolfguard, ready to swear the iron savages into your Kasra's service. Good way to make everyone realize you're on top.'

'Is it?'

'Not as good as biting some throats out, true, but – oh, no, you're all too *civilized* for that. As if it wasn't always the best way.'

'Enough, Venater.'

The old pirate merely chuckled. 'Now what your man really needs is Dragons.'

'He has them. Or do you think your people will be in rebellion against the whole of the Sun River Nation, when we return?'

'*Half*,' Venater corrected, almost absently. 'And we might. Hadn't thought of it, but we might. Even if not, though, your man has us, but he doesn't *have* us. There's not-fighting-against, and then there's fighting for.'

He was angling for some concession, but Asmander was not in the mood. 'If the Dragon have betrayed Tecuman, then I will send you out to kill them. To kill your own kin until they kill you.'

Venater went still. It was not really the kinslaying: the Dragon were notorious for simply not caring about all sorts of concepts that were the basis of human life everywhere else – even in the Crown of the World it appeared. It was a threat of a new order from Asmander, though. It was a promise to abuse the old pirate's freedom more harshly than before.

'I'd be careful what plans you make,' was Venater's quiet pronouncement.

'Because one day the Dragon will rise up from the delta and ravage all the Tsotec?'

'One day, maybe.'

Asmander's smile was like a knife. 'But first you must learn how to work together. You must stop killing each other over petty slights and women. You must become more than murderous children, Venater – become more like us. And you never will.'

And there was the spark, alight again in the old pirate as though it had never gone out. There was the fierce, fighting rage that Asmander remembered from when he had fought and bested this man. And this time Venater was not drunk and suddenly woken into a fight. This time he was fresh, and ready to bloody his hands.

'No reaver of the Dragon would shed so much skin as to be like you.'

'Reaver is a fancy word for a thief. Even *her* people are more honest.'

'What?' Shyri had been following the exchange keenly, plainly not sure how serious they were.

For a moment Asmander wondered if he could bait either into a real fight. *And why?* But he knew why. Venater trying to kill him was something that was simple and comprehensible. He would welcome the Dragon's teeth in his throat, or his own claws in the old pirate's gut.

'I will forget your name,' he spat.

Venater's fists were clenched.

'What's that supposed to mean?' Shyri complained.

'You will be a child forever. I will cast your name out of my

474

mind.' Asmander tried to make every word a javelin to hurl at the man. 'There will be none who can give it back to you.'

'But I know what his name is,' the woman put in, baffled, ruining Asmander's moment of triumph. 'I even know what it was before you did whatever thing . . . you just made a new sound on the end of it. That's just some stupid river thing. It isn't *real*.'

They were both staring at her now. She glanced wide-eyed from one face to the other and for the first time seemed genuinely off balance.

'It is? That's a thing you can *do*?' And, as they continued to stare at her, 'You people are crazy.' But she sounded impressed, too, as if she had finally found a secret of the river worth knowing. 'So what happens if he's stuck with his baby name forever?'

Venater went for her, but she was absolutely ready for that and Stepped away from him, reviling him with her high cackle. Venater had Stepped too, and now he was very still, a long black shape with scales that glittered in the firelight, its blue tongue lashing the air angrily.

Shyri had achieved what she had set out to, though. She had cut the tension between them, playing the pair of them. No doubt she thought she was doing the right thing.

And we all know what comes of doing the right thing.

She was grinning, and her self-satisfaction irked him like sand under his eyelids, like broken shards underfoot. Even as she opened her mouth for some witticism he pushed himself up from the fireside and sloped off to the dim periphery of its light, sitting there alone. He thought one of them might come after him, told himself he didn't want them to . . . then was honest enough with himself to admit just why he had stopped short of the deeper darkness. *Conduct unbecoming of a Champion.*

Another sore point.

He took his *maccan* from his belt, letting his fingers touch lightly alongside the sharp stone teeth, finding any loose flakes, investigating the gaps left by those that were missing. He had a

475

pouch of new blades – obsidian from home and flint that he had knapped here in the Crown of the World. He set about repairing and replacing, a constant duty with such a weapon but one that he hoped would settle his mind.

His father would be very proud of him, or at least that was the ideal. Tecuman would smile on him for returning home with such a savage and indomitable bodyguard. Yes, Asmander had done well.

He worked patiently and carefully, fingers delicate in placing the razor-edged flakes. Still his mind did not clear, but surged and roiled like rapids in flood. Then, after plenty of time had passed, there came the scuff of a footstep nearby. Not Shyri but Venater.

'What?' the pirate demanded bluntly.

'Is it not you who have come to me?' Asmander asked him, his hands still busy at work.

'Let it go,' Venater advised. 'I would.'

'Would you?' No sense in denying what was eating at him.

'Don't you think you did it right?'

At last Asmander's fingers stilled and he looked up, saying nothing.

'You know what I think?' Venater went on, squatting down on his haunches.

'No doubt you will gift me with it.'

The pirate smirked. 'You did it right. You surprised me. I didn't think you had that in you. But you led her right to her daddy. You got what you were after, no matter how. That's good. That's the way things are done in proper places. My people know that. The Wolves know it, too, I reckon. It all worked out perfectly.'

'And that's what you think?'

'Why wouldn't I? Why wouldn't anyone? Life's a killer. The only way you win is be a killer back, twice as hard. Biggest bastard at the end of the day wins the morning.'

Asmander looked into his face: lantern-jawed, traced with

lines and scars, the eyes like flints, long greying hair bound back. There was more going on behind that face than the barbarian whose words he aped. Who else would believe that, from somewhere in there, a keen intelligence was peering slyly out? Not the learning of letters nor the mysteries of the priests, but a man who knew people, if only because it was easier to kill them if you did.

'So we rejoice,' the Champion half asked.

'I do.' Venater grinned. 'Does you good to be more like a real man, like me.'

Asmander stood up suddenly, the *maccan* clutched tightly in one hand, the other knotted into a fist. Venater just leered up at him, utterly unworried.

Asmander took a deep breath. 'You've always known, haven't you?'

'Since you got back from selling the girl? I know you, Son of Asman. I've had to put up with you all the way from the Riverlands. When you're pleased with yourself, I know it – which is rare enough 'cause you're a gloomy streak of piss. When you're eating yourself up inside, I know that too. And you are now. So just say it.'

'I believe I am having second thoughts.'

'Oh, how terribly civilized of you.' The pirate mocked his tone perfectly. 'Did you even work out *why* yet? I take it you don't think it's really about the girl. Tell me you've not decided you love her or something.'

Asmander shot him a sharp look. 'She's not my type. It's not *her*. She's nothing to me.' Actually speaking the words made him feel better than anything else that evening. 'I owe her nothing.'

'It's the old Snake, then? Because he liked her, you have to?'

Again Asmander shook his head. 'Maybe you don't know me so well after all.'

Venater just frowned at that, like a hunter who has lost the trail. *Because he is, in the end, just enough of what he seems to be: a bloody-handed old man of the Dragon who would not understand.*

477

And Asmander smiled at the pirate, because it was good that there were constants in the world, even if some of them were evil ones.

It was not Hesprec. It was certainly not Maniye. Oh, he sympathized with her, but that was life: duty and loyalty and family and society, all cages within cages. Believing in freedom was just a knife the girl had made and given to the world to cut her with.

Except . . .

In his mind was a man he had barely met, who had uttered only a handful of words. But those words! The Wolf had no true Champions, but there was a man who should have been one. When he had spoken, the soul within Asmander had resonated with what he had to say. He had no shackles on him to drag him down, to make him less than he should be.

As I have lessened myself.

In the end, it was because Asmander felt bitterly ashamed of disappointing Broken Axe, a man who should mean less to him than a stone underfoot.

Venater sighed. 'Knew it was too good to be true,' he muttered, and then, 'Oi, Laughing Girl!'

Shyri ventured over, looking from one to the other. 'You two lovers finished your spat, have you?'

'We have,' confirmed Asmander.

'He's got something to tell you,' Venater leered.

There was a tiny fraction of a moment when her expression was unguarded, but then the usual snide smile was back in place. 'Oh?'

'He's going to get that girl back.'

Shyri laughed, head thrown back. Then, realizing nobody was joining in with her, she stopped. 'No, he's not. That would be a stupid thing to do.'

'No argument here about that,' agreed Venater.

'Or here.' Asmander sighed. 'But it is true, even so.'

She tried another laugh, but the resulting sound was an

uncertain one. 'There're more than a few of those Wolves there, Iron or not. Is the great Champion going to fight them all?'

'Who can say? Perhaps they will line up for me sideways on, like in the carvings.'

Venater snickered at that, but Shyri just frowned.

'Well, then, when do we go? What is your plan?'

'I have no plan. *We* do not go. I go. With my lack of plan.' And then, 'You'd go, too, would you?'

'Someone has to watch and laugh,' she replied defensively.

He stood. The time for it was now, he realized, or he might change his mind. 'Thank you.'

'Don't thank me.' She tried to back off, but he caught her wrist before she could do so, and held on for a moment before she tugged it free. 'You're stupid. You want to die so much, let *me* open your throat.'

'So kind an offer, but I owe that honour to Stone River's Wolves.'

'Then tell us where we can meet you.'

He almost laughed at that, but she was desperately serious about it, just as he had been. 'So now you think it's a good plan, and it will work?'

'No, but tell us anyway.'

'I have nowhere to suggest for you.' Asmander spread his hands. 'This is not my land. What can I say?'

And a new voice broke in, a girl's voice, 'Let me say it for you then.'

They all three whirled round to confront her, and for a moment Asmander thought it must be Maniye herself, somehow free and come to accuse him. He found himself looking into a different face, though: a strange face and yet one that he knew.

40

The Tiger came to her in dreams, but only to express its disappointment. As she slept, her mind was wandering out in the dark, with only the fire-glimmer of her mother's god to light her way.

You should have tried harder to cast out the Wolf within you, came the low rumble of the Tiger's voice. *If you had only pleased your mother more, she would have taken you in. You could have been the golden child of the Shining Halls, if only you had been better.*

And when she fled from it, into the darkness – on human feet, for the leash restricted her even in her dreams – there was the Wolf, a greyness shifting through the midnight forests of her imagination.

You could have been High Chief's daughter, it growled. *If you had truly wished, you could have been one of my children and run with my pack. Instead I will feast on your soul.*

And still she fled, but the two of them were always with her, snarling at each other and at her.

She *knew* it was a dream; that was the worst part. She fled and she fled, knowing it for one of those inescapable dreams that would pursue her to the very shores of waking. And, at the same time, the Tiger and the Wolf were truly within her and still at war. She knew that some men and women had dreams that told them the future or let their souls speak to the gods. When Maniye dreamt, she spoke only with her own fighting souls as they grew more and more savage within her. In the dream, her feet bled and her skin was lashed with briars, yet still they made her run.

Then there was something ahead that was not just gloomy ghost-forest or the shades of remembered hills. She saw open water and an island crowned with stones: the Stone Place, and yet not quite. At first she stumbled to a halt at the water's edge, finding no causeway there, and the Tiger and the Wolf came to her and loomed above her, their eyes like stars in a clouded sky, baring their teeth like the curve of the moon.

But something glimmered within the water that was not a mere reflection, and she saw scales sliding past scales there, reflecting rainbow colours even in the darkness. As the animals inside her howled and spat, she stepped out over those measureless depths and, wherever her feet touched, those looped coils rose from the depths, ridged and somehow dry, and bore her weight. Each step was taken with a faith that she could not imagine copying in her waking life, but the Serpent was there for her each time she entrusted her weight to the waves.

And she found herself on the island, which was so small that two men lying head to foot could have spanned it, with a handful of tumbled old stones, as if it was what the Stone Place had once been in the unimaginable mists of time, before it had grown into what it was now. The Tiger and the Wolf were swimming after her now, for the Serpent would not consent to bear them.

You should have cast out the cat from you! came the vicious cry of the Wolf. *And now you will burn!*

And from the Tiger: *What mother could want a creature such as you! What are you if you will not make up your mind?*

Something rose in her with that barb, as though she had acquired a third soul from somewhere, possessing the strength to face down the other two. 'I am Maniye! I am Many Tracks! And I will walk my own path, and I will be nobody's slave!'

And she woke to the sound of her own voice crying out, and

found herself staring into the eyes of Kalameshli Takes Iron. The old priest was kneeling beside her, far too close for comfort, and she shrugged and elbowed herself away from him until she was right at the tent's sloping edge, at the limit of her leash. He stayed where he was, illuminated by a strip of moonlight shining through the open flap.

'You were calling out to the Wolf,' he observed.

Maniye bared her teeth at him. 'There were three gods in my dream, old man. It was not the Wolf that helped me when I was in need.'

'The Wolf does not help,' he replied, surprisingly mildly. 'The Wolf wants us to be strong. We cannot be strong if we live our lives on crutches. The Wolf chases away the summer stars and brings the winter: you know this. The Wolf sends the ice and the snow, and makes the game scarce. And the other tribes grow weak, as they shiver by their fires, and only we remain strong.'

She could not say where the next revelation came from, but the words were on her lips already. 'There are two ways of seeming strong: to build yourself up or to throw all others down. But only one of these is truly a way of being strong.' The thought felt like sacrilege, but it tasted like truth on her tongue. She imagined Kalameshli's face darkening, because he would not value that kind of truth. She thought he would reach for a switch and beat her just as her father had, and so she burst out, 'What does it matter? You'll burn me anyway, tomorrow or the next night.'

'It may not be so,' Kalameshli said quietly.

But she knew him of old. If he held out any hope to her, it could only be so that she would grasp it by the sharp edge and cut herself. 'You will do as Stone River bids you,' she said. 'And you will do it joyfully. You have always hated me for what I am. This chance now must be a thing made from your dreams.'

And he replied: 'How can you think that?'

She was silent a long while, feeling that she had not understood, that he had said one thing and her ears had misheard it entirely. And yet he was sitting there peacefully with no angry words, no blows. And this was the same man who had whipped her through her trials, pacing after her with dreadful patience, and waiting for her to fail.

'You have hunted me my whole life,' she told him. 'I lived each day in fear of you. When I came to Step, you knew I went as a tiger where no one else saw. And you hated it.'

'Of course,' he snapped, as though this was too obvious to need saying.

'And you hated me for it because I offended the Wolf.' She had wanted to say 'your Wolf', but it was her Wolf too, no matter how she might fight it. 'So you punished me at every chance you got. Don't blame me for seeking a life outside the Winter Runners. Blame my father. Blame yourself.'

'You idiot child,' he began, with an edge of familiar anger that she welcomed. But then he continued: 'I drove you hard so that you became a strong child of the Wolf. I tried to whip the tiger out of you because, if you had slipped just once and been a tiger before the eyes of the Winter Runners, they would have torn you apart.' And abruptly his voice was fierce with emotion, though he forced himself to keep it low. 'So you *had* to be forced to be a Wolf above all things, no matter what! I drove you to make you strong, you stupid girl!'

'But not so strong as to break away from your hold,' she challenged him. 'Not so strong that I couldn't still be a thrall in Stone River's mad plans that could never have worked.'

'If the woman really had been dead, they might have worked. If she dies now, they still may.'

Maniye felt a stab of pain and outrage. *My mother!* No matter how she had left the Shining Halls, no matter that the Tiger were probably still hunting her with murder in mind, she had found her mother once. She felt a loyalty there, where Akrit stirred nothing in her. Perhaps it was just a loyalty to the ideal mother she might have dreamt of, rather than the all-too-real father that she knew.

'I have seen your altar, priest,' she told Takes Iron. 'The Tiger Queen will outlive me.'

'Perhaps not.'

'I heard my father. He thinks my death will win him the Wolf's love.'

'*A* death – but perhaps not yours. I have spoken to him. Another throat has bared itself to us now. I will make him spare you.'

'What other throat?' Maniye demanded, and he told her.

The clash of champions, open combat under the sun, that was one way for the Sun River Nation, yet there were others. When his father's people had surprised Venat's pirates, they had blown no trumpets to alert their foes. Sometimes an attack must proceed by the moon's rules.

The moon was too grand and bright for his liking, but there was plenty of the cloud that seemed never to leave these northern skies. So it was that the light faded in and out, and great bands of shadow passed over the world, as though Asmander lay in clear water as vast fish swam above.

Well, he had only this night, so no sense complaining about his preferences. The world did not care.

And it would be cold. Even with this 'summer' they were so proud of, even with the clouds to hug the day's heat in, he was under no illusions. He had clothed himself and donned his armour, and then clothed himself again, layer after layer, and still knew it would be cold.

There was a fire within the Champion: it hunted under sun or moon indifferently, burning up its strength for warmth, for speed and strength. But Old Crocodile, he was a creature of the warm days of the south who loved nothing more than to lie in the sun on the banks of the Tsotec. Show him the cold air of the Crown of the World and he grew slow in mind and body.

And yet, Stone River had set guards all about his camp – scouts who were men and scouts who were wolves – and left one gate wide open, unbarred and unwatched. There was a slender whip of a river that curled into his camp at the forest's edge before passing under the trees, and that would be Asmander's road.

The wolves' noses were keen, but the water would disperse the scents of both reptile and man. How good were wolf eyes in the dark? Asmander could not say, but Old Crocodile saw well by moonlight and possessed keener senses besides. Many had been lost beside the Tsotec because of a shadow or a log with hidden teeth.

Asmander had warmed himself as much as he could, and sealed in that warmth with hides and furs and cloth. When he Stepped to that long, ridge-backed shape, the hoarded heat of his human body would be the only fire he had to warm himself with. Old Crocodile would provide no more for him.

Enough, he told himself, knowing that now he was simply taking up time to avoid having to act. *Go now.*

And so he did, sliding headlong into the river, Stepping even as he went, so that he barely made a ripple. Gliding in the waters with only his eyes and nostrils above the surface, he felt the thickness of his clothes become a barrier within that crocodile body, keeping out the chill of the river. He let the current carry him, drawing silently near to where the Wolves had their camp.

The Champion would have ambushed them – every one of them. How many of the Wolves could he have fought, catching them unprepared and without their iron hides? All of them? Probably not, and yet the Champion was nothing if not confident in his own abilities.

He had stood in the dark, after leaving the others, on the brink of calling that shape to him, and decided it was not permitted. He had committed a shameful act, unworthy of what he was. It did not matter that he had fulfilled his duty to his family, or to Tecuman. The Champion held him to a higher standard. Until he had lived through this night, he was locked in his body with only Old Crocodile for comfort.

Knowing this in his heart, he did not call for the shape of the Champion, in case he was right and it would not come.

He could scent the camp as he drifted closer, just a little sculling with his tail aiding the flow of the water. His eyes, half-closed so as not to reflect the firelight, marked the presence of sentries along the bank. Old Crocodile brought the news of them to him with a rumble of hunger: any warm, living shape by the water's edge spoke to the animal within him. He fought that instinct down.

And if the wolves looked into the river, even in the full lambent paleness of the moon, they would see only a log drifting . . .

He left himself glide a little further, well past the ring of sentries that Stone River had posted in case the Tiger was stalking. There was a grand fire that the camp was built around, and with a structure of stones and wood set before it. There were tents pitched – neat little things that spoke to him of economy and warmth – and there was a larger and more untidy shelter strung about one of the trees. That must be Stone River's domain, surely? And yet it seemed a rough piece of work, with gaps where the cold would creep in and no sign of a fire inside.

He slowed himself and his long form drifted towards the riverbank, where he clawed into the mud for anchorage. The cold of the water had begun seeping into him and he would have to get out soon, to return to his human shape and restore some heat.

His nose was telling him a lot, but he did not have any memory of the girl's scent. The big tent looked too flimsy to be a prison but, still, where else to keep a prisoner? There was also a big pit up where the ground rose away from the river, but that stank strongly of pigs. Would they put the girl in such a place? Asmander realized he had no idea if such a thing might be done in the Crown of the World.

He had been hoping they would just have her out in the open, tied to a tree or similar. But then this was a test, after all, and the world expected him to exert himself. Nothing was supposed to be *easy*.

Except . . .

Except, looking towards the treeline, surely there was something there? Old Crocodile was not so good at seeing distances in the dark, so Asmander let himself slide back into the water. With a sinuous ripple of his spine, he let himself ease closer, passing invisibly through the heart of the camp before beaching himself once again. The cold was beginning to slow him now. He must make a plan and act on it.

There was a prisoner tied there. It was almost as if he had dreamt it, and the dream had become real. There, from the nearest tree, was a captive hung by the wrists. And yet it was not the girl. Within his barrel body, Asmander's heart stuttered.

A man: Broken Axe.

'You have him?' Maniye demanded.

'He crept into our camp, but we were waiting for him,' Kalameshli confirmed. 'He will say nothing, but I know he came for you.' The moon caught the old man's raised eyebrow. 'Is it for your mother that he would save you?'

'My mother cannot live with the fact of me,' Maniye said bitterly. 'And Broken Axe . . .'

'If you have grown an affection for him, you should have become his mate when your father offered the match,' Takes Iron observed with that mocking tone she was used to from him. 'He will surely die now. Amiyen demands to wield the blade: she claims a right of vengeance against him.'

'Amiyen and her son would have killed me, once they found me,' Maniye told him flatly. 'If not for Broken Axe they would have done so. She is no loyal hunter of Stone River.'

The old priest nodded slowly. She could still not believe that he was just sitting here speaking with her. Where had the savage tormentor of her childhood gone? Why did the man *care*?

487

'So Stone River believes that the Wolf will welcome Broken Axe's soul as a gift?' she enquired.

'Broken Axe will die – as all who turn against the Wolf must die,' Kalameshli replied equably. 'But because of that—'

'Broken Axe *is* the Wolf,' Maniye hissed fiercely. 'He is the Wolf that walks alone. He is a man unto himself, not a creature that needs the crutches of others like my father does. You think the Wolf will be glad when Broken Axe's blood is shed? The Wolf will curse Akrit Stone River seven ways.'

Kalameshli sighed, exasperated. 'Girl—'

'My name is Many Tracks. Broken Axe gave it to me.'

He slapped her. In the dark, she barely saw his hand move before the hard boniness of it exploded against her cheek.

In the startled silence that followed, Kalameshli spoke slowly and patiently. 'Broken Axe will die. If he is weak and a traitor, he will die for that reason. If he is strong and a rival to Stone River's power, then it is fit he will die for that. Let the Wolf decide what taste his soul has. But, with that sacrifice, it may be Stone River will be satisfied.'

But this time Maniye felt that she had wisdom, and it was the priest who indulged in foolish fantasies. 'If he finds more to barter, then he will trade it all, and get whatever value he can. He would cut a thousand throats if he thought the Wolf would place a great sign on him to make him known as High Chief. You know this, Takes Iron.'

And he did know it. She could see it from the defeated slump of his shoulders. Still he tried to argue: 'He has listened to my counsel for many years. He has heeded me since before you were born. He will heed me now when I tell him you must be spared.'

'Why?' she asked simply, and then to clarify, 'Why would you even try? You say you have tried to make me strong? Old man, you have tried to break me all my life.'

'That is how it is with iron as with men,' came his almost-whisper. 'They must be taken to the point of breaking, beaten, hardened, tempered. Only then can they be strong enough to take an edge and not to shatter. With iron and men both, that is how it is. I have always tried to make you strong, stronger than the rest. I have tried to make you such a thing as the Wolf might be proud of.'

And the word, *Why?* was on her lips again, but then there came to her some words of her mother's, when the woman had been least able to stand the sight of her own daughter, because of the captivity and the treatment that had ushered Maniye into the world. *I cannot forget them, Stone River and that loathsome creature his priest.* And here was the priest, cursed by her mother for exactly the same deeds as Akrit himself.

And she understood: staring on Kalameshli, she saw it all, the secret that even her father – that her father most of all – could not know.

Broken Axe had been ill used. The moonlight touched the bruises the Wolves had laid on him in capturing him, and there was a noose drawn tight about his neck. He was strung up by his thumbs to a branch, high enough that he was on his toes trying to keep his own weight from tearing at his arms.

He was guarded, but the woman standing before him had no eyes for Asmander. Instead her venom was turned entirely on her captive. Words drifted on the air, hissed in an ugly mutter: she was telling Broken Axe how he would suffer. They would give his soul to the Wolf and to the fire, yes, but she would bring him plenty of pain before then.

Asmander was still creeping along, belly to the earth, just a long low shape that took one slow step at a time as he neared. He would have to find his human feet soon enough: even the ground was chilling his innards like ice.

And then he was as close as he dared, and he Stepped so that he was still lying low to the ground, arms splayed out, hands still in the mud, thick clothes all dry as if he had never been in the river at all.

489

He understood the woman: from her words, she had a right of vengeance for a dead son. It was a debt that would be understood over all the world. In the Sun River Nation a parent's grief might be bought off, but here in the Crown of the World they were more true to themselves.

To interfere with a right of vengeance was the wrong thing to do, but Asmander felt he had the curious luxury of already having placed himself beyond honour. And he could not leave Broken Axe.

He shifted closer, crouching low on all fours. There were plenty of Wolves in earshot but none watching: this woman's vengeance was personal and private. When she struck out at Axe, marking him with her knife, that was a matter between the pair of them, and Asmander was an unwelcome eavesdropper.

But he would have to kill her instantly and noiselessly. One cry or shout of warning would set the whole camp on him.

He saw Broken Axe notice him, as he rose up behind the woman: just a flicker in the man's eyes, hurriedly masked.

A blow from his *maccan* would not suffice, he reckoned, and he had no expectation that he might creep close enough to gag the woman and cut her throat. She was a warrior, and likely she would manage to shout or wrestle herself away from him.

This left him one option: not sure by any means, but it might serve. This was a trick he had been taught by the Serpent priests: something that was common practice amongst them, but came far harder to all other people.

He was standing behind the Wolf woman now, watching as she slammed a fist in under Broken Axe's ribs, raising nothing but a stubborn grunt from her victim.

Gingerly, Asmander extended a hand, until he could have touched her shoulder. In his mind he was trying to think through that exacting set of translations he would need: something closer to mathematics than mere Stepping. And again he was putting things off, despite the danger should any of the Wolves happen to glance this way.

The woman made his mind up for him. She caught sight of his hand in the corner of her eye and began turning, her mouth open.

He Stepped, throwing his shape forwards along the line of his extended arm. For Serpents this was easy: their legless nature divorced them from the human shape almost entirely. A crocodile was closer to a man, but still different enough that, if Asmander fought hard, he could twist himself so that his outstretched arm exploded out into the gaping jaws, his head merging into his shoulder, his body whipping out into the long, saw-scaled tail, even as he lunged forwards.

His jaws snapped down across the Wolf woman's head and arm with all the force he could give them, and the falling weight of his body – more than human – took her off her feet. He wrenched her savagely about by the grip of his myriad teeth that were hard and sharp as onyx flakes. He felt her neck break, her skull crush inwards. Her blood was warm and maddening in his throat, awaking Old Crocodile's hunger savagely. He was hard pressed not to give in to it and simply feed.

She had died in her human shape, he knew. Her flesh was a prison for her ghost, and to eat of it would be to invite madness. He shook his head until the mangled body fell clear of his jaws. He could feel her ghost stuck between his teeth, caught there like a fragment of meat.

Then he was human again, and cutting Broken Axe down. The renegade Wolf had no words for him, but there was understanding in his eyes. That was all the reward Asmander needed just then.

He could have Stepped to the Champion's shape then, for he felt he had regained enough of his honour to do so. He could have called out all the Wolves and seen how many it would take to bring him down. He wanted to finish what he had come for, though: retrieve the girl and get her away. Moreover, he wanted to live.

He shared a moment's silent communication with Broken

Axe, and the Wolf nodded towards that big, haphazard tent. *There.*

The two of them crept about the periphery of the camp, whilst nearby there were plenty of Wolf eyes turned outwards, watching for the wrong enemy. Axe had stepped to his wolf shape, slinking like a grey shadow, crouching in stillness when the pale stripes of the moon passed over him.

Then he had frozen, one warning look cast backwards to warn his follower to do the same, and now someone was emerging from the tent. Asmander recognized the Wolf priest, in his coat of bones, and guessed that he had been conducting some ritual to prepare the girl for sacrifice. The old man paused, looking up at the sky, and there seemed something dejected or defeated about him.

The world is full of stories, Asmander reflected, willing the man to be on his way. *Yours does not concern me.*

And then the priest was gone, hurrying off towards the main fire, his face crossed with lines of worry. Asmander made to go forwards, but another look from Broken Axe stopped him. As the wolf slunk into the tent, Asmander crouched in the shadow of its entrance, hand on his *maccan*.

He heard a gasp from within, and then murmured words. He hoped that, in rescuing Broken Axe, he had gained an ambassador to Maniye, to speak for him.

Then Axe was at the flap again, a hand stretched out, and Asmander passed over the flint edge of his knife, without needing to be asked.

That was when the woman's body was found. That was when the Wolves discovered the absence of Broken Axe.

41

She had not wanted to believe it at first. As soon as she thought of the secret, she had tried to rid her brain of it, as though it was yet another soul jostling for room there. But the idea refused to go and, looking into the shadowed eyes of Kalameshli Takes Iron, she saw the confirmation. She knew, and he saw the knowledge in her.

She could destroy him, or at least she could try. If she convinced Akrit of what she had intuited, then he would turn on his own priest. What price angering the Wolf then? If he killed Takes Iron, the other tribes might even abandon him altogether. Killing priests was as bad as killing kin.

Although she had spent all her years hating him, now that she had that weapon in her hand – the weapon he had handed her, hilt first – she did not know whether she wanted to harm him with it or not.

He had backed out of the tent, stiff with the knowledge of what she could do to him, and she had turned away from the intruding moonlight and tried to think. This might be her last night before the Wolf took her in his fiery jaws. She wanted to have some of it to herself.

But no, she heard his tread again, coming back to her, this time padding in the shape of his god. She curled in upon herself, screwing her eyes shut, as if she could simply unmake him and unravel all his history back to the beginning.

'Many Tracks,' a voice addressed her.

Her heart jumped within her chest. It was not Kalameshli.

She scrambled to sit up, and there he was, impossibly: Broken Axe himself. A surge of emotion leapt inside her that she could not anatomize.

He ducked out for a moment, and came back with a sharp flint, sawing away at her collar with swift strokes. She wanted to question him but, if there was a tale to be told, this was not the time. She could not understand how he had got free and then walked through the camp of his enemies to come to her. She knew only that he had.

Then she was loose, and she felt both the tiger and the wolf within her leap up, clamouring for her attention. For an instant her own shape slid through her hands, and she felt herself losing control of it, her twin souls about to battle each other there and then. Her Serpent dream had lent her a little control, though, as if its invisible coils were still hobbling them. She took them each by the scruff of the neck and held them apart in her mind.

Then there was a yell from elsewhere in the camp, and Broken Axe bared his teeth, that grimace becoming a wolf's snarl as he Stepped. She copied him, finding her wolf feet, and the two of them were out of the tent and into the open air.

She scented him instantly: the southerner. He was crouching by the tent flap, but Broken Axe stood beside him, and so she understood that somehow the dark man was here as her ally, not her enemy. She would trust Axe's judgement.

There were more important matters right now, for the Wolves were coming.

It was just a couple of them at the moment, but their cries had woken up all the camp. There were vital seconds in which confusion would run from Wolf to Wolf – surely the Tigers were attacking! Then they would look to their prisoners and all would be lost.

There was one who came as a wolf, and the other as a man. Perhaps hoping she would just flee, Broken Axe threw himself at

494

the first, snarling and snapping out of the shadows, the two of them rolling over and over. The second paused, a hatchet already to hand, eyes flicking from the two fighting animals to Maniye herself. He was a hunter called Thorn Foot, one of Akrit's cronies since forever.

He lunged at her, letting his companion trust to his own luck. He was coming in with an open hand though: grabbing rather than attacking, just as if she was still the girl he remembered. She got her teeth into his fingers and shook her head savagely, and he howled with pain. Bones ground between her jaws. Then the axe came up, a swift feint at her that sent her skittering back, his blood in her mouth – and Asmander cut him down.

The southerner made his rise from the shadows flow into the downward-cleaving arc of his sword: a single fluid motion. The stone teeth of the weapon sheared into Thorn Foot just where his shoulder met his neck, and the man was snuffed out just as swiftly, live meat to dead meat in an eyeblink. The taste in Maniye's throat was abruptly that of a corpse.

'Go, now!' Asmander urged. Broken Axe had seen his opponent off, sending the other wolf running with his tail between his legs. The whole warband was converging on them, though. They were in the heart of their enemy's little domain.

Maniye had a sudden vision of herself ending up with the altar at her back, the whole escape attempt nothing more than a means to bring her to sacrifice.

'With me!' The southerner was haring off through the camp. He was still a man, not even in his fighting shape.

Broken Axe shared a look with her, wolf to wolf, and she saw that neither of them had a better idea.

She saw a wolf leap at Asmander, enraged beyond all telling by the foreigner's intrusion. He caught the animal with a smooth upward swing that barely seemed to interrupt his sprint, yet cast his attacker away trailing a spray of dark droplets. Others were massing into a pack, though, and there would be archers. Even the greatest warrior in the world could not fight all of Stone River's hunters together.

And yet she followed the southerner, Broken Axe coursing alongside her. There were jaws nipping at her heels and she saw an arrow darting almost lazily above her, close enough that she could have jumped and caught it. She could hear her father's furious bellow.

A man came at them with a spear, driving it for Broken Axe's side. Axe twisted away, almost belly to the earth to avoid it, and Maniye leapt into the attacker's face, snapping jaws one moment, then Stepping to her tiger shape to slap him down with her greater weight, raking him a little with her rear claws even as she kicked away.

But there was nowhere to go, and Asmander was at bay now, his back to the river. Still, he was calling to her, calling to both of them: 'With me! With me!' An arrow clipped his arm and hung in the thick fabric of his coat.

And by then there were enough of the Wolf close behind her that all she could do was head towards him. All her options in this whole doomed venture had narrowed to that.

'Step,' Asmander yelled, 'and hang on!' He had slipped his blade away and was reaching out with empty hands.

Broken Axe reached him first, clasping wrist to wrist and being yanked closer, and then Maniye just threw herself forwards. For a terrified moment she did not think she could resume her human form – the souls within her twisting in rebellion – but then she slammed into Asmander, arms about his waist, hard enough to knock him into the water.

She felt him Step. His body thickened suddenly, her grip slipping and scrabbling over ridged and rugged scales. She thought she would lose her purchase on him altogether, but then she had hold of a stubbly limb, her legs wrapped about the strong barrel of his torso. He was driving forwards into the water with great flexing contortions of his spine. She could barely snatch a breath of air, held underwater half the time. Arrows and even spears were lancing into the river like murderous kingfishers. She saw at least one strike solid against Asmander's armoured back but simply glance away.

And then they were out of the camp, even though there were wolves trying to pace them along the banks. With the current and his thrashing strength, Asmander was making them run hard to keep up with him. All the while the banks grew higher, the forest more snarled.

From then on, simply getting herself a half-breath of air was all Maniye could concentrate on.

The next she knew, she was lying half-conscious in the forest by the riverside, soaked through and chilled to the bone. Dawn was still some way off, and someone was trying to prise her out of her clothes.

She kicked and spat, Stepping into a very sodden tiger, her back arched and hissing. It was Broken Axe, she realized. He lifted his head, plainly listening for any suggestion they had attracted attention, then held up a tunic and a coat, dry clothes produced from somewhere. He himself was as bedraggled as she was.

She regained her human form with a quick nod, and stripped away her river-ruined clothes, struggling into the new garments, which were far too big for her. Broken Axe had acquired dry leggings and a thin tunic, and was now tugging them on unselfconsciously. After she had the coat firmly wrapped about her, she realized that Asmander was still with them, wearing several layers less than he'd sported before.

There was something important that had struck her about him during that mad river-ride, but it was gone from her head now.

'We can't risk a fire, of course,' she guessed. 'So what happens now?'

'If you're fit enough, we travel,' Broken Axe told her. 'The southerner has somewhere to go.'

'Does he?' Maniye fixed Asmander with a hard stare. 'What do I think about you, Son of Asman?' His title came to her even as she spoke. She hoped that using it made her seem even a little more intimidating.

'Think what you want.' He shrugged. 'But come with me.'

'You're going to trade me to the Tiger now?'

'I was not sent to make bargains with the Tiger. My father sent me only to the Wolf,' he replied candidly. 'I had been promised what I needed, in return for you. Long before I even met you was that promise made – back at the Stone Place when your father went mad.'

'He's always been mad,' she told him darkly. 'So what now?'

'Now I do not have what I needed. Nor will I obtain it.'

She shivered, and Broken Axe hugged her to him. She twitched away from him at first, because the stripes on her back hurt, and because she didn't know what she thought about him. He was warmer than she, though, and sharing that with her.

'We will need to move soon, wherever we go,' Axe murmured.

She nodded jerkily. 'So why?' she demanded.

For a long while he remained silent, his dark face unreadable, then just tilted his head towards Broken Axe. 'For him.'

Maniye did not know what to make of that, and she suspected that Axe didn't either, but it was said now, and apparently there was to be no more explanation. 'So what was it your father wanted anyway? Furs? Timber?' She was trying to remember what the Horse had been carrying south on their great barges.

'Warriors: the Iron Wolves,' Asmander explained with a fragile smile. 'Where I come from, they are a myth to frighten children. Perhaps I shall go home and say they are no more than a myth indeed.'

'And where would you lead us now?' Maniye was reaching inside herself for strength, finding it bleeding back into her limbs slowly.

'This river will take us to a Horse Society camp,' Asmander told her. 'My companions should already be there.'

'The girl with the laugh and that big man who hates every-one?'

'Just the same.' His grin was startlingly white. 'And there will be another. One who very much wishes to meet you again.'

She didn't like the sound of that at all, but at the same time she had no sense of malice from him. His perverse humour was back, which meant that he was done with straight answers.

Soon after, they were setting off along the river. Maniye won-dered how far the Wolves were ranging; how her father's new rage had manifested itself. She wondered about whether the Tiger had turned back for the Shining Halls, or whether the Fire Shadow People were also trailing her, clashing with their Wolf enemies. The world was cast in fog, and the only way she could discover what was out there was to go to it.

Maniye thought she could not be so far from that very outpost she and Hesprec had fled to at the beginnings of winter. When she asked, Broken Axe confirmed that would likely make any Horse they found to be of the same clan or family or band of the Horse Society. This gave her a little heart, as she recalled their small kindnesses before: the clothes and the warning.

They followed the river at Asmander's behest. When she trusted herself to Step, Maniye's wolf nose told her once more where she was, and how to reach places. She felt that she had been travelling in darkness, both night and day. Now finally there was a little sliver of light. She tried to look within herself to find the root of this new hope. Her passage through her father's hands had broken some hold on her that he had still possessed all this time, even when she was sitting at her mother's feet in the Shining Halls. She had seen him for the man he truly was. Even whipping her with his switch, he had been a thing dimin-ished: not the ogre of childhood nor the all-powerful god-chief. Even as he had expounded his plan for the Tiger, which could never have worked, she had seen further and understood greater mysteries. He was nothing more than a man.

And after that had come the revelation gleaned from Kala-meshli. Hurrying along the path of the river, Broken Axe and Asmander at her side, she felt a control of her own destiny that had been lacking for a very long time.

And then the Horse were ahead, and this was not the trading post, though she knew by now that it was the same river. Instead, they had arrived at a point where the river was shallow and wide. There the Horse Society were camped in force and busily engaged – with two dozen of the Boar and Deer – sieving and trawling the sands of the shallows with nets, for their own mysterious purposes.

The three of them were spotted at a distance: a black man with two wolves trotting at his heels. She saw that the Horse people included a fair number armed with little curved bows and spear-hafted axes that would surely give even a bear pause. They recognized Asmander, though, and the arrows were returned to their quivers. Soon after, as Maniye's party neared the camp, the other two southerners turned up and with them a figure whose bulk put even Venater into shadow.

Maniye broke into a run, Stepping to her human form so close to him that she almost collided. 'Loud Thunder!' She was aware that many of the Horse had stopped playing with their nets to watch, but she decided that she didn't care what others thought. 'What are you doing here?'

'The Sons of the Bear travel where they like,' he replied, somewhat defensively. He had his axe in hand and wore foul-smelling armour of grease-hardened fleeces: a Cave Dweller ready for war.

'I don't believe it,' Venater was saying to Asmander. 'You actually came back with her. I was heading south today, maybe tomorrow. I was going to tell old Asman that his favourite son had died attempting something stupid, just to see his face. You ruin everything, you do.'

Asmander shrugged. 'The Crown of the World has no short-age of stupid ways to die. You'll get your chance.'

And the woman, Shyri, cackled and smirked. 'Ignore him. He was fretting all this time for fear you'd take his name with you to the Wolf's belly.'

Maniye ignored the southerners and their banter. Instead she drew Loud Thunder aside, because him, at least, she was glad to see.

'Maniye Many Tracks,' he addressed her. 'Running again?'

'Always.' She felt her whole life since the Testing had been one long flight.

'Not from Broken Axe these days?'

'Not any more.'

His look caught her utterly by surprise with its childlike happiness. 'Good, that's good. Broken Axe, he's a good friend. You, you're a friend, too. It's not right for friends to fight.'

She nodded at that. 'You came when he called – when the Tiger was attacking?'

He shrugged, looking almost embarrassed. 'I am all sorts of stupid sometimes, the things that I do.' He went wandering off towards the fire, where some of the Horse were cooking. 'For many days since the Stone Place I have been teaching war to the men of the Bear. Very slow, very dull. Much more interesting to follow Broken Axe.'

That made her laugh as she followed him. 'Surely the Bear don't need teaching how to fight?'

He grimaced. 'We brawl, we are rough with each other, we hunt. But fighting? That is hard work. Hard work does not come easy to my people.'

'And your Mother chose you for this?'

'Because I once fought. After the Tiger was beaten . . . so many warbands in the Crown of the World then, working for meat, for mates, for glory. I was young.' He sounded very apologetic. 'We went many places – me, Broken Axe, Peace Speaker, Storm Born, Restan Bastard.' Across Thunder's broad face, a gentle tide of memories washed like a lake's shallow ripples. 'We went all over, even to the Plains when the Lion were still trying to rule. But always we returned . . . or most of us. Peace Speaker, he was killed, and Restan too. And Storm Born went south. He was mad, though. He had destinies like a dog has worms, that one . . . But I fought, so they make me a teacher of war.' His expression showed exactly what he thought about that.

'And now you've run away from your Mother again,' she divined, and the Cave Dweller cast his eyes sideways, as though the rest of the Bear might spring out from the Horse tents to accuse him.

'I have not forgotten what I was told,' he mumbled. 'I have come here because I am concerned for my old friend Broken Axe, that is all.' His display of nonchalance was unconvincing. 'And also for my new friend, Many Tracks.'

She stared at him, unable to tell how serious he was being.

She found inside herself a sudden desire not to be important. She remembered Hesprec joking with her about prophecies and destinies, and how she had wanted there to be some mystic star above her head – one that would give her a purpose in the world. Now she was wiser. She had witnessed Asmander fighting the purpose his father had laid across his shoulders like a yoke; she had seen how Broken Axe lived, who knew no destiny but the dictates of his own heart. She had known how it felt to have others risk their lives for her. Perhaps she had yearned for the eggshell crown that was a destiny, the year before, but now it was summer and she was grown, and childish things were left behind her. That the world had a purpose for her, she had no doubt, but the chief use most of it seemed to have for her was as a corpse.

Thinking further on that, she had it in her mind to warn Loud Thunder that he should go back to the quiet of the highlands, to his lakes and his cave. Akrit Stone River had killed bears before.

She thought she had said it, then, but from his puzzled frown she realized that her words had not come out properly. A moment later she was swaying, as the tiredness of several days descended on her. She waved off his huge hands as they reached out to support her. She was fine; she was well. She was just weary, so very weary. All that time she had spent locked tight about herself, binding herself with iron bands to keep out the fear and be ready for the least chance. She had been strung taut for so long, and now she could relax, just for a while.

And within her the Tiger leapt and seized hold of her. Abruptly her mind was in its jaws. She felt its fangs bite, its claws raking and ripping at her, as it tried to get at the Wolf. The Wolf had the other half of her, worrying and dragging at her entrails so that she clutched at her stomach, the pain now so intense that she was sure she had been torn open then and there.

She dropped, very distantly feeling herself fall into Loud Thunder's hands, whilst her two souls ran madly about her mind and body, stalking, ambushing each other, skirmishing furiously and then breaking apart. Her limbs were twitching and shuddering and there were distant voices crying out in alarm, advice being offered. She felt something forced between her teeth and she gnawed and savaged at it, feeling wood splinter against her gums.

When she came back to herself, every part of her hurt. She was within a tent and, for a dreadful moment, she thought she had not escaped her father after all, and that the fire that glimmered in from outside had been lit in the mouth of the Wolf's effigy. The tent was smaller and neater, though, and the memories came back to her piecemeal: this must be in the Horse fishing camp.

All was quiet outside. No doubt there would be a few Horse sentries watching through the dark hours, but the rest – all the people that her presence had somehow drawn together – would be sleeping.

She felt gingerly within herself for her souls. She had a sense of Tiger and Wolf glowering at each other from opposite ends of her mind. They had run themselves ragged within her: every muscle hurt from where she had thrashed and strained, and there was a fierce knot of pain within her skull. For now, though, those beasts within were exhausted, and she was free to step out under the stars.

The Horse had no walls here. There was nothing between her and the world beyond.

Her father would be hunting her, somewhere out there. He would find this camp soon. Probably her mother's people would as well. She was the loose end that everyone wanted to tie off or cut away. Left to herself, she might go mad, run ragged across the hills by her two natures. To simply walk away from anyone who could help her was something close to suicide. But she did not really believe that any of them could help her. None of them possessed that kind of wisdom.

She took a deep breath, knowing it was time for her to leave. The anxiety that had descended when she spoke with Loud Thunder remained with her. She did not want these people to come to harm, and harm seemed to be all she had to gift the world with. She had spent a winter with Loud Thunder, lived on his hospitality and become his friend, and yet she dragged him before the claws of the Tiger. She owed Broken Axe far too much, not least for all the years she had hated and misjudged him, and he had been caught by Stone River because of her. Even the southerners had risked far more than they should: rough Venater and snide Shyri had fought for her. She even felt she owed Asmander, who had changed his mind in the end.

She owed it to all of them to leave.

She reached for the shapes that twisted inside her, but she could not say what might happen if she favoured one or other of them right now: better let them sleep. Instead she padded off on bare human feet, weaving her way through the tents, and away from the river. She could only hope the sentries would not cry out an alarm at seeing someone *leaving* the camp.

There was a shape in the darkness, eyes glinting in the fire-light as it watched her. For a heart-stopping moment she thought it was a wolf; that her father was already *here* and about to take her. Then she saw it was just a dog – one of Loud Thunder's dogs, in fact, Yoff or Matt. The animal's gaze was on her, but it made no sound, nothing to wake its master. If it could think like a man, no doubt it would be glad to see her go.

A few more steps, and the last of the tents rose before her. The air was full of quiet breathing, a few snores, the crackling of guttering fires . . . and her name.

'Maniye.'

Not a voice she knew: a woman's voice – no, a girl's. Maniye crouched, reaching for a knife she didn't have. A small figure was standing close up, seemingly sprung from nowhere.

'There you are, Maniye.'

Her eyes slowly gathered in the firelight, picking out details from the shadows before her. This was a girl a little younger than she, but very different. A girl of Asmander's people, she assumed: dark of skin and with a pale headscarf pulled over her hair. She wore a shift, and an over-large winter coat above it, though the summer night was mild. Her face seemed a little familiar, as if Maniye had once known the girl's mother.

'I don't know you.' Maniye was still motionless. Inside her, she could feel the first stirrings of her souls reacting to the surprise.

'But I know *you*, a little at least,' the girl said, taking one small step forwards.

She must be one of the children that the Horse trade for, Maniye realized, recalling something of this sort she had been told. 'You were at the trading post? Or you've heard them talk of me from Thunder and the southerners?' *Is it just because she's of Asmander's people that I think I recognize her?*

The girl nodded. She seemed to be very amused about something, but then Asmander behaved like that too, so maybe it was a Riverlands habit. 'I wanted to talk with you.'

'Why?' And then, because she did not want to get drawn into a rambling conversation with a stranger, 'I can't.'

'Please, do not leave until we have spoken. It's very important.'

Maniye bared her teeth. 'What's it to you?' she hissed. 'I need to go. It's safer for everyone.' Even that was more than she should have said, but that maddening sense about the dark girl was drawing out the words. It was not that she was like Asmander: in fact, the more Maniye studied her, the less like Asmander she became, and yet the more familiar.

The girl took another step, as careful as if she was approaching a wounded animal. The firelight touched further on the brown of her skin, striking rainbow colours there. Maniye started in surprise: there were patterns tattooed onto her skin, gleaming where the light revealed them – endless loops of scales that wound about her forehead, cheeks and neck.

The sight brought a lump of loss to Maniye's throat, for of course someone already *had* died for her. 'I have to go,' she whispered.

'Maniye, there's no need.'

'Don't use my name! I don't know you. I owe you nothing!' Maniye was fighting to keep her voice down, sure that there must be people stirring into wakefulness in all the tents around them.

'But I owe you, Maniye. I owe you more than a life can repay,' the girl told her solemnly. 'Won't you sit with me just a little, and talk? And if you still want to go, you can be gone long before dawn. But I hope you will stay, for me.'

Maniye opened her mouth, and what came out was: 'You look like . . .' Her legs were suddenly unsteady. 'You came to find him, didn't you? You came looking for Hesprec Essen Skese.' Abruptly her heart was pounding in her chest, and just drawing in a breath had become a struggle. The far horizons she had set her aim at contracted to the here and now. She lurched into a gap between the two last tents of the camp and sat down there, almost collapsing. 'You're . . . you look like him: granddaughter, or granddaughter's daughter, or . . . ?'

'We are close. Not as close as we should be, I sometimes think.' Still the girl seemed amused, and Maniye had a horrible feeling that nobody had told this child about the old man's death.

'I'm sorry,' she got out.

'Of all things, you have no reason to be sorry.' The girl sat down beside her, hugging her knees for warmth.

'He was taken by my father's people. I tried to rescue him but . . . it was too late.'

'It was not,' the girl told her with absolute assurance.

'He . . . they had hurt him. He was weak, and we ran so far, so fast, but it wasn't enough.' Inside her, the Wolf was howling mournfully at a remembered moon, while the Tiger lay smouldering in shadow, its head down on its paws. The simple thought of all she had gone through had cowed them both. She was not weeping, she refused to, but inside, her souls mourned on her behalf. 'I thought I could do it.'

The girl's thin arms encircled her cautiously. 'Ah, forgive me. I am too cruel,' she whispered. 'I am too fond of jokes that amuse only myself. Maniye, none could have done more than you did. A death in the mouth of the Wolf is a death for all time. Preventing that is all that the world asked of you, and you did it. You have no weapons against time and old age.'

Maniye stared at her, bewildered by the words, the tone. The girl's light voice was speaking as though Hesprec's ghost was in her.

'I don't understand,' she whispered, staring into the other girl's eyes, seeing there such a weight of experience and wisdom and dry old humour that she could hardly stand to look.

42

The dark girl sat beside her, at the edge of the camp. The fires were behind, the measureless night extending before them. There were wolves in that night, and the sullen shadows of tigers, but for once Maniye had no thought for either. Knowledge was echoing inside her, making her head ring like a bell. She had come to the brink of Revelation, that deep understanding of the world that changes all things. It was not something that she was equipped to deal with. A great many things she had once thought were immutable had become fluid and uncertain through just a handful of words.

'I told you, when we first met, that my people were special,' the strange girl told her, grinning with bright teeth. 'You were asking then – you thought southerners were dark, burned black by the sun. And, as you see, we are.'

'Hesprec wasn't.' Because Maniye could not bring herself to say, '*You* weren't,' as if such things were everyday matters.

The girl shrugged, smiling. 'And, if I have the chance to grow old once more, then, when I am old and my skin grows loose and brittle on me again, I shall seem pale to you once more.'

'And . . . and then?' Just a whisper, from Maniye. This felt like either madness or the sort of lore that gods guarded jealously.

But the girl continued, quite unconcerned with supernatural retribution. 'And then I shall find myself somewhere alone, and at the end of my body's strength, and I shall seek peace and go find the Serpent beneath the earth. And I shall touch his coils, and partake of our mystery, and I shall be born anew and be young once more, just as I am now.'

'As a boy – a man, I mean?'

Again that carefree shrug. 'Who can say how matters may fall out? I did not know, this time, if I would succeed. I thought that it might be a final death, despite all your bravery. The Crown of the World is a long way from those places where the Serpent is strong. But my faith is rewarded: he is beneath the earth even here.'

And Maniye could restrain the question no longer. 'How many times?'

'How often have I shed my old skin?' The girl's eyes glinted as she looked at her.

'Yes, are you . . . ? You told me, during the winter, of the Oldest Kingdom that your people lost at the start of the world. Were you . . . ?'

'Was I there?' The girl laughed gently, and it was that sound which made her Hesprec. A young throat, but an old laugh. 'No, no, I'm not so old that I laid any pair of eyes on those wonders . . .' And then she grew reflective. 'But I spoke once with an old, old priest who did, or so he said.'

Maniye felt an almost crippling sense of time, for here was an ancient being in the body of a thirteen-year-old girl, speaking in awed tones about one who had been *truly* old.

And at last Hesprec sighed, and admitted, 'Eight times, now, and that is plenty of years enough.'

'Were you a man or woman? First of all, I mean.'

'You know, I'm not sure I can remember.' Hesprec shook her head. 'A little of the memory sloughs off with the skin, each time. We shed our childhoods soon enough.' She looked up, finding the moon in the sky just as that pale crescent cut its way out from the clouds. 'And will you leave now?'

'Leave?' For a moment Maniye could not think of what she meant.

'You were planning to go. Because you did not want to hurt people, I think.'

'I . . .'

'The Tiger has been here, but two days ago.'

Maniye stared at her.

'They came asking after you,' Hesprec continued. 'None was there then whom they might have marked. But their queen was with them.'

An uncertain, shocked sound escaped Maniye as though she had been stabbed. 'The queen . . . ?'

'She did not announce it, but these eyes of mine knew her,' the girl confirmed. 'And no doubt there will be wolves howling beyond the camp soon enough.'

'Then I must leave.'

'Leave in the daylight. Leave with me.'

'Why?'

'Because I owe you a debt. I know that some of the others have fought for you, for their own reasons, but I owe you my life twice over, and what I can do for you, it shall be done.' Hearing so young a creature make so solemn an oath should have seemed absurd, but there was a current of certainty in Hesprec's voice that most people could have lived a hundred years and not achieved.

'You can't help me. My father and my mother hunt in vain, because I will destroy myself. My body has three shapes and they are at war. I don't know what to do. I don't know how to save myself.' And all her resolve had crumbled with the words, leaving her voice shaking. 'I have too many souls, and they're tearing me apart.'

Hesprec put a youthful arm about her shoulders and hugged her close. 'The Serpent hides many secrets, and the Crown of the World contains more than one seam of wisdom. There are . . .' And then the girl trailed into silence, cued by a change in the way Maniye held herself. 'Or perhaps you have thought of something,' Hesprec finished quietly.

510

Maniye looked at her, feeling as though she had donned the halved face of an Eyrieman: wolf eye, tiger eye; tiger eye, wolf eye: her souls jostling behind her visage. But, yes, her own words had sparked a thought, an unlooked-for avenue of enquiry.

'I will stay,' she said softly. 'For now, I will stay.' There was a conversation she needed to have and she was not looking forward to it.

In the morning she watched as Loud Thunder made a fuss of his dogs, teasing them and scratching under their jaws and throwing them scraps of fish. She could never quite get used to dogs: the language of their bodies was so like wolves, and yet so different. Time after time she thought they were attacking Thunder for real, and then it became clear they were only playing after all.

After that – for she was still working up courage – she watched the Horse and their fellows wading about in the broad, shallow basin of the river. She realized by now that more than one set of eyes was fixed on her, watching to see what she would do. There was an awareness in Broken Axe's look that suggested he knew she had been on the point of fleeing overnight, and of course there was Hesprec. She had thought that the Serpent priest's eyes should have been a fixed point, some part of him that he would carry forward, shed his skin as he might. Instead, the dark girl looked back at her from wide eyes of bright copper, and there was nothing of Hesprec in that gaze at all.

A shadow fell across her, as she stared across the water. She glanced up, then further up, for this was a tall man of the Horse, long-boned and even-featured.

'Blessings of the morning on your road, child of the Wolf,' he intoned formally, bringing his hands together before him. He was keeping a precise distance between them, and she reckoned it was calculated as the reach of her arm if she had a knife to wield in it. That this long-boned, broad-shouldered man should be so wary of her was almost funny.

511

She opened her mouth, trying to think of something equally elegant to say in reply, but what came out was, 'I know you.' She was abruptly back at the Horse outpost on the Sand Pearl, where she and Hesprec had gone to seek passage south. There had been a fat man leading the Horse back there, but when the Winter Runners came hunting, it had been this tall, fine-featured youth who had come bearing food and clothes and warning.

He nodded solemnly. 'I have been a servant of your host, during another season. I am—'

'Alladei, Hand-son of Ganris,' she recited. A moment later she felt herself colouring, for to remember the man after so long seemed oddly embarrassing. He was striking, though, and she remembered thinking so the first time she had set eyes on him.

His eyes widened, but then he nodded. 'You do me much honour. You are the one they call Many Tracks. Welcome to our camp. *My* camp, as my hand-father has trusted me with this expedition.'

She nodded cautiously, still aware of the respectful distance between them. 'What is it the Horse has travelled so far for?'

'Travel is life and breath to the Horse,' he declared. 'But here is where we gather magic stones.'

She blinked. 'Magic . . . ?'

He reached into a pouch and came out with a thumb-nail-sized orb of translucent gold. 'They love these so much on the River that they will shower us with wealth for them. They love stones of all kinds: turquoise, serpent-stones, tiger's eye. But for magic, they must have the river-gold, these sun stones. Look, this is a cursed one.' He held it out to her. 'There is a little demon caught within it. With this their priests can do great magics.'

She squinted closer, seeing in the murky depths of the stone a tiny hunchbacked shape, a suggestion of veined wings, a tangle of thread-thin legs. *A fly?* She reached out to touch it, and he pulled the stone back hurriedly, holding it to his chest as though it might give him some protection from her.

'I'm . . .' Maniye managed a weak laugh. 'I'm not going to hurt you.'

'Such was never my thought, but we know by now that there are those who would hurt many to reach you. Would they risk the enmity of the Horse Society to do so? Who can say?' He gave a sad smile, but she felt a chill run through her.

'I cannot stay.'

'You are our guest. *My* guest, since my hand-father has trusted me with this expedition. I shall shelter you as befits a host, so shall my family and all who heed me.'

'And, as I am your guest, I cannot stay,' she completed.

'I would we might meet in happier times.'

She thought it was just a Horse pleasantry, but his eyes were still on her, and abruptly she felt uncomfortable.

'I must . . .' And she had spotted her quarry now, out beyond the tents along with his fellows. 'I'm sorry, I must . . .' But Alladei was nodding, saving her from hunting down further words.

Asmander was performing some sort of dance with his sword. It was not like the Tiger dances, intended to be interlaced with the leaps and raking claws of an animal. Instead, she watched as he and his stone-toothed weapon moved about one another, performing an exercise in balance. Asmander killed invisible foes for her, the sword curving and striking, but never still, and he never still at its other end, so that they seemed equal partners in the fight.

The other two were nearby: southerners together. The laughing woman had been watching the dark man intensely, and now she turned the same keen gaze on Maniye. The big old warrior was just lying on the ground with his eyes closed, letting the morning sun warm him.

When one of his strikes brought him round to face her, Asmander stopped his practice and just waited for her to approach, his weapon still to hand. His face was unreadable, save that he did not look happy.

Standing out of reach of a strike from that jagged blade, she took a deep breath and met his eyes. *It's time we spoke.*

He nodded curtly, not needing her to say the words. 'Go, find some other to bother,' he told his friends.

'Hmm?' Venater opened his eyes, registered Maniye, then waved a hand idly. 'I'm comfortable. *You* go, if you want.'

'And I want to hear her put her claws in,' Shyri said pleasantly. 'So speak, Wolf girl – or Tiger girl, is it? Tell the Son of Asman what you think of the honour of the Riverlands.'

Asmander scowled at her, but his face was composed as he turned back to Maniye. 'So, speak.'

In truth, ever since seeing him in the Wolf camp she had baffled herself over what she might say to him, whether she should condemn or thank him, or just ignore him. But now her life was easier, in this small way. Now she knew exactly what she must say.

'I don't want to talk about that – any of that,' she told him. Now her life had contracted into a single knot and she could not indulge herself in raking over history. 'What was that thing you Stepped to, there in the camp?'

'That?' Asmander frowned. 'That is Old Crocodile. That is the shape of my people, the Patient Ones, lords of the river.'

'And that's a . . . this is something that exists, where you come from?'

Venater snorted, eyes still closed: 'Is she stupid?' And Shyri snickered.

'Why would she know?' Asmander chided. 'This land is too cold for Old Crocodile. But, yes, they are common all along the Tsotec – the river of my people.'

'Then what is the other shape you take?' Maniye demanded of him.

'That is the Champion. I told you so before.'

'But what is the Champion?' she demanded. 'I have heard the Eyriemen talk of their Champions. I saw Yellow Claw take on

514

the Great Eagle's shape, when you fought him and when he snatched me from the ground. So what is *your* Champion?'

Understanding her at last, he nodded. 'It has many names, like your hunters do. The Champion is Running Lizard, he is Killing Claw, Swift Reaver. But he is no beast that is known to men. The Champion comes from deep time, the priests say, a shape from the days before our fathers ever fled to this land. He came to me and he chose me to bear its soul. It is a great burden, a great glory . . .' His voice trailed off, because Maniye was staring at him fiercely.

'Then it's true,' she hissed. 'I didn't think of it before, but it's true. You have two souls. You live with two souls.'

'The soul of a Champion is not like . . .' And he was shaking his head. 'No, I know why you ask, but this is not what you seek. You are torn between Wolf and Tiger – they are in balance within you, so that neither can chase the other out. When the Champion's form comes upon me, Old Crocodile shifts himself aside. He knows not to contest his kills with such a creature.'

Maniye found herself baring her teeth at him, because this was her idea, her only *idea* about what was happening to her and how it might be controlled. 'I will tell Hesprec. He . . . *she* will find a way to help me, with this,' and she was off, running back into the camp and looking for the priest.

She had only just tracked the Serpent girl down when a deep horn was sounded by one of the Horse sentries. They had spotted a pack of wolves breaking from the treeline.

She could not imagine what Alladei would say to Stone River when the wolf warband Stepped into human form within a spear's cast of the camp. To her, the man's options seemed brutally simple: hand Maniye over or bare his throat to the Wolf.

But perhaps the Horse Society always enjoyed more options than anyone else. Alladei went out to speak to Akrit, and he invited the Wolf over to his fire to talk.

Stone River came with Kalameshli and a hunter known as

Sunset Spear. That Smiles Without Teeth had stayed back with the warband gave Maniye something to think about. Had Akrit told his strongest supporter to stay behind to keep the rest in line? How unruly were the warriors of the Winter Runners becoming?

She had intended to hide herself away – perhaps even to flee unnoticed if the chance arose, but Alladei himself found her and guided her to the fire where her father was waiting. He was polite but he was firm. He had Broken Axe there as well, and Hesprec – though hers was not a face Akrit would recognize any more. Loud Thunder and the southerners were close by, within earshot but not within the circle at the fire – without a voice.

The Horse people made a great show of hospitality: they had milk and meat and honey for all their guests, and Akrit was served first, his status explicitly acknowledged. In all things Alladei was the gracious and compliant host, until the formalities were observed and Akrit spoke.

'You have something of mine,' he said shortly. 'The Horse are not thieves and I know they will return what they find if they know it is already promised to another.'

Alladei nodded thoughtfully. 'I will not insult you by pretending I do not know of what you speak,' he replied slowly. Indeed, Akrit's glower at Maniye was unmistakable.

'Then let me take her, and let me go.'

'Set out your claim to her.'

Stone River stared at the Horse man narrowly. 'She is of my tribe, and is fleeing my judgement. I am chief of the Winter Runners. I am High Chief of the Wolves.' Though many expressions about the circle said *Not yet*, none gave voice to the objection, and Akrit smiled at that. 'The Horse are welcome in the Crown of the World. I know they will do what is right.'

'Well, it is not for a foreign visitor to your lands to argue the laws of the Wolf,' conceded Alladei calmly. 'As you see, I have her in my hands, and now you ask me to give her up to you. Gladly would I do so, but I find a wall between us, which I

516

cannot fetch her through,' And, seeing Akrit's impatience at his speech, he continued, 'You are my guest, Chief of the Winter Runners. She also is my guest. My duty to her is unyielding.'

Stone River snarled and started to say something heated, but Alladei went on, more forcefully, 'The duty of host to guest is known to all peoples, in all lands. I would be cursed if I forsook it.'

The Wolf chief was colouring with anger, but Kalameshli leant in and murmured something that restrained him. At last he got out, 'And how long is she to remain your guest?'

'I suspect your coming here will prolong it,' Alladei said, with every appearance of regret.

'A guest that brings trouble to her host is no guest.'

Alladei spread out his hands, appealing to the sky and then to the horizon. 'That is not a distinction that any god will make when my soul is weighed. I have taken her as my guest. I must live with that. I told the Tiger the same.'

Akrit went very still. 'Did you so?'

'They were equally unhappy with my words.'

Maniye kept her own face devoid of expression, knowing that any words Alladei had given the Tiger had taken place before she had ever become his guest, but of course Akrit could not know that.

'The Horse would be unwise to anger the High Chief of the Wolves.'

'The High Chief of the Wolves would be unwise to cut himself off from the Horse, or to give the men of the Horse more reason to aid the Tiger. All know the Shadow Eaters – that is your term? – are now down from their high places. We of the Horse have traded with Wolf and with Tiger freely, as we trade with Boar and Deer, with Seal and Hawk, and even with the Bear sometimes. Many are the goods we bring from all the lands south of the Crown of the World and, of all the families of the Horse, my hand-father Ganris heads the greatest. So let us not rattle spears, my guest.'

Maniye's abiding memories of her father were of his short temper, but here he mastered his rage, husbanding it until he could use it. 'So what says the Horse?' he demanded.

'Amongst my people we have found ourselves in this position more than once,' Alladei said patiently. 'It is my duty, as Hetman here, to see if the grievance between my guests may be settled by trade or by promises. I would have to know the faults laid at the feet of Many Tracks.'

Hearing her hunter's name mentioned, Akrit's lip curled, but he did not try to strip her of it. 'I do not choose to recite her wrongs again,' he replied, affecting boredom, 'save to say that, wherever she travels, she raises enemies against the Wolf. How is it that she now turns the Horse against me?' And now a little genuine frustration was leaking into his words. 'For that alone, I would hunt her down.' Then Kalameshli touched his arm, cautioning him, and he subsided. 'There is nothing to be offered by you that can cool my need to have her. The Wolf demands her.'

'And if I was to take her away from the Wolf, and from all the lands of the Wolf?' Alladei asked softly.

Stone River frowned. 'Away where?'

'Out of the Crown of the World, to other lands where neither Tiger nor Wolf hold sway. To Where the Fords Meet, joy of the world, or to the Riverlands that lie further still. She can work no ill to you if she is so far beyond your horizon.'

Maniye expected her father to throw those words back in Alladei's face almost immediately, but though his face twisted darkly, he said nothing for a few precious seconds. Even for such a short time, that idea was something he considered.

Have I truly become so much of an annoyance to him that he would simply be glad to see me gone? she thought, with sudden hope. *Or say an embarrassment rather than an annoyance. He cannot use me against the Tiger, but so long as I am alive and free in the Crown of the World, I am something that another tribe could use to shame him. Yet if I am gone . . .*

But Akrit was shaking his head. 'It cannot be. How could I believe she was gone,' *unless I saw her corpse*, was the unspoken addition that perhaps only Maniye heard. Alladei was opening his mouth, perhaps feeling that he could press his case further, but then Akrit added, 'And, even if she were gone, what about the other betrayer?'

'Of whom do you speak?' Alladei was baffled.

'Of me,' Broken Axe put in. 'He speaks of me.'

'I do,' Akrit agreed. 'I do not know how the men of the Horse regard oaths, but this man swore many times to do my service, and yet he betrayed me and lied to my face. In the lands of the Wolf, that gives me the right to his pelt. How stands that behaviour with the Horse?'

'It . . . is not recommended,' Alladei said, glancing at Broken Axe. He was instantly on more unsure footing now that a real crime had been named. 'How do you answer?'

'These claims are true,' Broken Axe acknowledged, 'and my reasons for doing so are nothing that would satisfy the Wolf. But if it is I whom Stone River has run so far to catch, then let him hunt *me*. Let the girl go south. That is fitting. I have made all this come about. Let him hunt me alone.'

He said it with such careless calm that Maniye was almost angry with him. Seeing Alladei about to answer – perhaps even to condemn – she burst out, 'I'm not going south.' Everyone was staring at her now, but she squared her shoulders and went on. 'Stone River has not caught me for two seasons, he will hunt me for two more, and two more after that. And I will run beside Broken Axe, and I will kill the Winter Runners if they are at my heels – just as I will kill the Tiger.' They were brave words, as wildly overstated as if a coyote had threatened a bear, but she said them with absolute conviction. 'So I will run and be free, or I shall die hunting for my freedom.'

Akrit stared at her and she waited for the raging, the hard words and invocation of the Wolf. Instead she saw a strange sadness there, quite alien to his usual expression. For just that moment – never before, surely never again – he was looking into other futures, where he and she had not grown so far apart. He was seeing the daughter he might have had, and might have valued.

She held her breath, but already his face was turning sour. 'It seems you cannot bring harmony to your guests,' he growled at Alladei.

'Then my guests must leave in their own time. If Many Tracks will run, then I may not stand in her way,' the Horse Hetman stated. 'As I am your host, I swear that, before tomorrow dawn, she will be gone. As you are my guest, swear that until then you shall camp beyond an arrow's flight from my fire, and make no move against her.'

Akrit said nothing, but his eyes roved the camp, plainly weighing up the prospects of forcing the issue. His warband were surely fiercer fighters than any the Horse could muster. They had iron to strengthen them. They comprised a number close to that of the Horse. Surely it was only the guest bond itself that was now holding Akrit back and, if he returned to his warriors, would that deter him?

But Maniye saw that, of the men and women of the Deer and the Boar who had been assisting the Horse, most of them had a weapon to hand. They had clubs and spears, and some had bows; they had axes and knives, and of course they had horns and tusks. With their numbers added to the Horse, the odds against the Wolves were much poorer, worse than two to one. Maniye felt as if the ground beneath her had shifted in some strange, foreboding way. The Deer and the Boar had once been subjects of the Tiger, and they were subjects of the Wolf tribes now: farmers and gatherers and fishers bowing the knee before the greatest hunters of the Crown of the World. But they were many, even so, and here they had come to work for the Horse, learning foreign ways like *resistance*.

Nothing was revealed on Akrit's face, to show that he had made the same observation, but he nodded and said, 'You have my word on it, as your guest.' And with that, Maniye had another sunset gifted to her, another night in which to plan.

When the Wolves had left the Horse camp, she went straight to Hesprec, because she had one last chance to free herself from her shackles and her rebellious souls. And if she could not do that, then she would not even be able to run.

43

Hesprec heard her out, as Maniye presented her plan. She had so little to work with, just odd scraps of things the Serpent priest had said, and a few things he – she – had done. Most of all she remembered how the old Snake had come along with Asmander to free her from the Eyriemen. Was that the moment the idea had been planted in her mind?

'You made him take another shape when you took me from the Eyriemen.'

'Asmander? Yes, I did.'

'You gave him another soul.'

'We invited one in together, he and I.'

And Maniye gripped the other girl's hands and said, 'Then do it for me.'

Hesprec regarded her warily. 'The gods of the River, their totem, their souls . . . there is a flexibility that I think you northerners do not possess.'

'I could not choose when the choice was before me. Now . . . they are running wild in me. Asmander said that the Champion was a chief of souls, a ruler.'

'I suspect he did not say such words,' Hesprec noted with a small smile. 'But yes, you understand it right. The Champion's soul is of a different order.'

'Then that is the way I can stay who I am. I cannot retain my mind with two souls. I cannot drive one of them out. Even if both could be cut away from me, they would take *me* with them, and leave . . .'

'Do not speak of that. It is too late for such things . . . perhaps it was too late before we ever spoke in the pit, back in your village.'

And Maniye considered Kalameshli and all his tests and his cruelty. *He was trying to drive the Tiger out of me. He was trying to force me to make the choice.* 'Then . . .' But she had no words to go after that 'then'. They had all been spoken.

But there was a contemplative expression on Hesprec's young face. 'Take this dilemma to one of your Wolf priests, they would say it cannot be done: there are no Wolf Champions. Take this to a priestess of the Tiger, she would say the same.'

And hope had leapt into Maniye's mouth: 'But the Serpent is ancient and wise, and his people know better.'

Hesprec's eyes held no assurances, but something had hooked the Snake girl's interest. And so emerged the words: 'I cannot promise you that it can be done, but together we might *try*. If the Serpent will offer up his secrets; if you will follow where I guide you; if you are strong enough; if, indeed, this thing is possible at all. But it cannot be done quickly, and it cannot be done here.'

'Where, then?' Maniye demanded. Already she was feeling tremors through her, as her souls stretched and shouldered against their confinement and against each other. Another attack from them was on its way, she knew.

'We will be petitioning the invisible world,' the Serpent girl announced, with an echo of the elder Hesprec's grandeur of speech. 'That Stone Place of yours is too far, but there will be others: places where the sky reaches down to touch the earth, or where the depths of the earth are laid open to the sun. Places where the priests have gone, generation on generation. Some ancient stone or a hill or a cave – some place visited year on year, yet where nobody would ever *live*. Some place so old and strong that people have forgotten why it was first picked out, knowing only that it has always been there.' She smiled fondly as she spoke, and in her eyes Maniye thought she could see the reflection of ancient shrines beside a southern river, of deep ravines where the coils of the Serpent moved within the rock.

So Maniye thought hard on all she had been told, and then she sought out Broken Axe and explained what Hesprec was looking for. Who knew the Crown of the World better than he?

'A place like the Stone Place,' he echoed. 'Some place near here. A sacred place; a spirit place.'

'And not the place of any one god,' she added. 'A place of great spirits. There must be somewhere.'

'And you will flee there, and hope Stone River does not follow you.'

She saw his intention in his face. 'And you will be with me, to guide me.' *And you will not try to lead my father away, and shed your blood for me.*

A moment's battle of wills, with her meeting his stony gaze and refusing to look away, and he nodded tiredly.

He surprised her then, because he knew of no place of ritual anywhere nearby; this was not his land and he had only a passing familiarity with its ways. Instead, he moved amongst the people who had been working for the Horse. They were men and women who had long hunted and foraged the riverside here, and all the lands around. They were nervous around Broken Axe, as well they might be near any Wolf. Maniye realized that she herself had not even considered asking them: Deer and Boar, what could they know?

But that was Stone River inside her, like yet another soul. Seeing them through Broken Axe's eyes, she discovered just how much of her father was embedded within her. Hearing him speak to them, simply as one human being to another – something she could not imagine any of the Winter Runners doing – she was disappointed with herself. *I will never be myself until I rid my mind of him.*

In the end, they were directed to a broad-framed old Boar

man whose long hair was mottled light and dark grey, and whose cheeks were tattooed with tall upward-pointing darts.

'There is a place,' the old Boar had conceded, once he understood what Maniye wanted. 'There is always such a place. Only a fool would seek these places out, save on certain days, and then only by certain ways. But of course there is a place. A high hill, with two fallen stones and one still standing. The Eyriemen bring their dead there sometimes, and lay them out on high platforms for the crows to pick apart. My people bring offerings when the year turns towards winter. Our priests approach with their faces masked by the skins of the Boar – when I was young, I witnessed this – but we shun the place at all other times. The Path of Fallen Stones, we call it. It has been there longer than my people – perhaps longer than any people. It is a place for spirits to dwell, not men.'

He had told them where they would find these stones, which hills to head into, which winding path would lead them there. His expression said plainly that he thought them mad.

'None who go there escape being changed,' he warned, but to Maniye this sounded more like a promise than a threat.

'You have been kind to me, even when you had no reason.' Maniye had not wanted this conversation with Alladei. She was clawing for control of her own destiny, though: even the kindness of strangers could not go unquestioned.

The Horse Hetman looked slightly embarrassed, hands out as though to defend himself. 'I have risked, it is true,' he admitted. 'When I tell my hand-father what choices I have made, he will either embrace me or turn his back on me. But if we bow our backs even once to the Wolf – or to anyone – then they will always hold the lash in their hands whenever they come to us. The strength to run far, the freedom of all horizons, that is the creed of the Horse. Where other people try to tame us, to bar our way or make us their slaves, then they will find that the Horse too can fight.' He said the words proudly, and just for a moment she saw there the man he was waiting to become, the man his father perhaps saw in him. 'But the Horse understands profit, also. Your friend the Serpent, she has promised. I have sent men south already, with certain words and secrets she has given me. Great are the rewards for my family, whatever should befall this solitary son. I do not regret standing up for you.'

'You're a fool, then.'

He shrugged. 'Perhaps I am wise beyond my years.'

'I have brought too much trouble to you,' Maniye muttered, biting at her lip.

'Yes, you have.' Alladei grinned suddenly. 'To hear Stone River tell it, you are a trouble to the whole world. But perhaps only a little trouble for all that. Over the winter, our wise people were speaking of a great trouble. The Serpent girl tells me she has heard the same wherever she has gone, from the River to the Crown of the World. I do not think they were speaking of you, Many Tracks.' He shook his head. 'Change is coming upon us like the north wind from the mountains, like the sand wind from the south. So I will be kind to a strange girl who doesn't know what skin she should wear, because who knows what will grow from that seed tomorrow? And because I think that being kind to Stone River is like planting a seed in dust.'

'You Horse are very stupid.' She tried to say it venomously, like Shyri would, but her voice shook and she heard herself sounding close to tears.

'Not all of us – just me, perhaps.' He was still smiling. 'How will you outpace your father when you leave here?'

'Somehow.'

'You cannot run south, leaving this land as I suggested?'

'I would. I cannot.' With the very thought, the souls twisted inside her. She felt unsteady on her feet, her human form momentarily alien to her. 'I would not last. I need to . . . to cut, or . . . They are both too powerful within me now. I cannot cast either of them out, yet I cannot keep them within me . . .' She looked at him, wide-eyed. *I've said too much. These are secret things.*

There was only sympathy in his face. 'Then there is one more favour I can do for you, to help you on your way.'

Towards evening a messenger arrived, a young hunter of the Winter Runners, who had tracked cold news from post to post across the north until he had finally picked up the trail of his chief.

Akrit Stone River listened without reaction as the breathless youth recounted it all, standing rigidly straight and obviously fearing an angry response. Stone River just stared, though – not at the messenger but into the distance of his own imagination, and then he dismissed the youth and turned to Kalameshli, the only other listener.

'What do you think now,' Akrit asked, 'of the Horse plan to let the girl flee southwards, and thus be forgotten in the Crown of the World? You spoke for it, after we departed their fire.'

The Wolf priest nodded wordlessly.

'And you see now why it cannot be. But I think you should have seen so before.' Abruptly Akrit's rage – like his knife, never far from his grasp – was rekindled. 'Even you – the girl pulls even you from me.'

Takes Iron said nothing.

'Or perhaps you'd say it is I who push you?' Akrit demanded, working up his anger further. 'But this is what it is to be a Wolf: to be strong, to drive my own path through the world, never to be led or herded or penned. You have always taught so. Each year of new hunters, this is the message you put into their hearts. This is the truth about the Wolf, that we are the strength of the world. I have only sought to be that strength! And this girl – my own daughter! – goes about the world unpicking my work, smearing my deeds, placing ill words in the mouths of those whose support I rely on. Even you!'

'Akrit,' Kalameshli said softly. 'You are my chief, I am your priest. We are old friends, you and I.'

'And yet she is here between us! You would protect her from me, if you could.'

'There is no need—'

'There *is* need! If there was ever doubt, then now we see the need. I am called, Takes Iron. I am *summoned*. On the shortest night, I am summoned so that all the tribes can meet to choose their high chief. And who summons me? Otayo of the Many Mouths, the son of Seven Skins. He who gave his voice to me after I killed his brother, and now he declares he must *choose*, and the other chiefs must *choose*, and no doubt there are half a dozen who they shall choose between, where once there would only be one. *One*, Takes Iron! And it is because this girl shames me that they do not already have my name in their mouths!' He lifted his fists as though to strike the old priest – or the world at large. 'What shall they say, then? Here is Stone River whose girl-child flouts him. Why should a man rule the destiny of the Wolf when he cannot even control his own get?'

'We will take her again,' Kalameshli murmured. 'Bring her before the other tribes with a halter about her neck, if you will.'

Something like a laugh escaped from Stone River. 'And can I even hold her, if I take her?' He was speaking too loud – enough for all the rest of the warband to hear. 'I have had her in my hands already, and where is she now? Vanished and fled to her many allies! If I tried to parade her before the tribes – if I dug a pit for her a hundred men deep, or built a cage of iron without a door – she would be gone in the moment I sought to bring her forth. She would be rescued from the earth by moles, or spirited away by songbirds. What is she, Takes Iron? Is she even my child?' He was so caught in his ranting that he missed the old man's flinch. 'No capture this time. I'll tear her throat out myself. She is no kin of mine. She is a thing of the invisible world, a changed child, a thing as soulless as the Plague People. When I go before the tribes I will throw her pelt at their feet – be it wolf or tiger or human.'

Then the voice of Smiles Without Teeth boomed out, 'She's

moving!' and Akrit Stepped instantly, darting over, with his eyes shining in the last rays of the sunset.

Two horses had broken out from the camp, heading west. One small figure, one greater one, they were already moving at a gallop.

Akrit threw back his head and let out an air-rending howl, and then forced himself into his human shape, and into human thoughts. Undue haste now could mean defeat later, and Maniye might have more friends waiting for her – perhaps Tiger friends.

'Weapons and armour, as much iron as you can carry, and leave the rest!' he roared. 'Let us be Iron Wolves, fast as you can, and then we shall run them down.' No wolf could outrun a rider in the short term, but wolves ran on when laden horses tired, especially on the uneven ground of the Crown of the World.

In what seemed a few heartbeats, the warband was on the move, picking up the track of the horses, knowing them through their scent even though they had ridden off into the concealing dusk. There was the spoor of Broken Axe. There was that of the treacherous Maniye, plain to every nose. Silent and grim the pack went after them, murder on their minds.

Only after they had gone did Maniye herself come out from one of the Horse tents. She wore a quilted coat dyed in faded colours of red and mauve, a garish and much-darned garment. Her original coat was now fast receding on horseback, worn by a Horse girl only a little larger than herself.

The deception would not work for long, but she was hoping for Akrit's fury to take him a long way from the Horse camp before he realized it. The riders had a good head start and were making off across open country. When their pursuers came close they would Step, and four unladen horses would outstrip all the wolves in the world. They had undertaken this task without complaint when Alladai had asked it of them. Hesprec had purchased a great deal of loyalty from the Horse Society, it seemed.

The rest of the camp was packing up now, ready to return to the trading post, where the Society would have the numbers to withstand the rage of the Winter Runners if need be. Alladai was dismissive about such a confrontation, and yet at the same time he was going among his people, enjoining them to be brave. Maniye worried for him.

But her path and his must separate for now. She was departing for the sacred place, this Path of Fallen Stones. She was going to confront the madness in her souls, to conquer it or to be conquered.

'Are you ready?' The new Hesprec was at her side, teeth gleaming as she smiled. The young energy that ran through her now was the most alien part of the Serpent's transformation. Maniye was amazed at how much of the elder Hesprec's character had simply been a factor of the years that burdened him, and that his rebirth had stripped away.

The others were already gathered. Broken Axe and Loud Thunder were talking quietly – she saw the Bear grin, a boyish expression that only emerged when he was happy and with his old friend. To see it was almost a relief: if the big man was to risk himself, it would at least be for Axe, and not for Maniye herself.

The three southerners stood apart, and Asmander's eyes flicked between the two women as they approached.

'Messenger,' he said, and glanced at Maniye again, not quite guiltily. 'I am here to serve you.'

Hesprec nodded. 'Champion, always I am glad of your company, but do not confuse my path with your own.'

Asmander lowered his eyes. 'When I was told you were dead, I knew despair.' There was a wealth of pain in his voice, a sudden open wound, but Hesprec held a hand up to forestall him.

'No more of that,' she said. 'Enough has been said. If Many Tracks will challenge you, then that is her business. What about your fellows though, Champion? Are they so happy to walk in your tracks?'

'No,' Venater snapped immediately, arms folded.

'Quiet, you,' Asmander told him. 'You are my shadow until I set you free.'

'And you, laughing sister?' Hesprec asked.

Shyri smirked. 'No sister of yours, old man, whatever face you now wear. But I am not yet bored of this river-boy and his stupidity. I will stay.'

Alladai came next. Hesprec clasped her little hands in front of her and he matched her.

'May your road be smooth underfoot,' he intoned, and then, 'though that is a poor blessing for the Crown of the World.'

'May the earth carry your burdens,' Hesprec matched him, 'and the Serpent's back lead you home.' She tugged her scarf tighter over her hair.

'Many Tracks,' Alladai called out. 'We'll meet again. Stay well.'

She carried his parting smile with her a long way, once they had set off.

44

Moving north again, a day's travel took them to the sacred place of the Boar. At first they were following the river into the woods but then they broke off into tangled, cluttered country, hunting for the tracks they had been told of. Broken Axe sniffed out the scent of boars and led them to a narrow trail half overhung with the knotted branches of trees.

They should have moved faster, for even Loud Thunder could make a good pace when Stepped. Maniye had hoped to take the trail on wolf feet, to range alongside Broken Axe with her nose open for danger. When the time came, though, she could not do so. She took a deep breath to Step, and instantly those two souls were welling up like pus inside her, poisoned and corrupted, pressing and swelling against her. She fought them down though they racked her body, forcing themselves up in a mouthful of bile and trying to make her vomit one or the other out. She was a prisoner of her human shape.

So they were limited to a human's speed – and less even than that, for Maniye felt feverish, shivering. The fits came and went, each one tearing at the tenuous hold she was keeping on the world.

And the going grew harder and harder, the upward slope of the land weighing on her like stones. She was awash with sweat, her heart skipping and dancing to rhythms that seemed to ape those of the Tigers' dance. There was a pressure within her head born of too many eyes trying to peer out from the same two sockets.

She did not stop, though. Even though she knew that she was slowing them all, she would not call out for aid, and she would not give in to herself. Whenever the ground tilted up beneath her, she went on all fours, climbing with human hands and feet where she would have leapt like a tiger not so long before. When the land was flatter, she stumbled and lurched along, with the wolf inside her snarling and clawing for the freedom of the far horizons.

But then the way was more steep than not, and the forest was rising upwards ahead of them, following the slope of a hill.

'Hold!' called the high voice of Hesprec. 'Not another step until I've studied our way.'

'Our way is up,' Venater pointed out.

Maniye squinted upwards, and there, within her sight, rose a hill crowned with stones – and not just the three the Boar had mentioned. There was a clutch of enormous boulders, as though some giant spirit had plucked them from the mountains and set them down here where they had no business to be. She thought she saw more, too: odd suggestions of regular lines that might have indicated the work of man, but overtaken by enough time to bury them. And there were ridges running around the hillside that almost seemed like . . .

'There's a path,' she croaked. 'It goes round, round and round and up.'

Venater made a disgusted noise. 'That's not a path, not for people who want to get anywhere fast. We'll go straight up.'

'We will not,' Hesprec said quietly but firmly. 'We will approach this place as its creators intended. Perhaps they were wiser than we. Certainly they were wiser than you.' She raised an eyebrow at Venater, who loomed over her, big and mean enough to tear her in two. The old pirate just looked surly, though, and took a step back.

The path spiralled up the hill, in and out of trees at first, and then they had left the forest behind, climbing out of it onto rocky slopes, with each lessening turn bringing them closer to the huge stones above. Squinting upwards past the glare of the duskbound sun, Maniye's mind jumped back and forth: natural or made; made or natural? She could not decide which. The greater boulders were too vast to have been moved there, too unworked to have been intended. And yet, as they drew near, her earlier conviction returned to her. Someone had built here once, laid stone on stone just as she had seen in the Shining Halls. She remembered the intricately carved stonework of the Tigers, and how so much of it had fallen to ruin. Whoever had made this hill their temple had done so in an age that made all the works of the Tiger seem mere follies of yesterday. The earth – the grass and moss and mounded soil – had almost completely swallowed all signs of it. Only the occasional protruding block remained there as mute witness; a certain regularity that led Maniye's gaze along the secret, hidden lines of the place.

She remembered how the Stone Place had first seemed to her, with the spirits louring low in the sky, their twisting scrutiny anchored to that island in the swamps. As they approached the summit, she knew this was a kindred place. Not so grand, surely, but perhaps older. Those spirits that dwelled here, sleeping within the earth or spread across the wide sky above, they were powers that had been drifting away from human affairs for centuries. Yet there was strength here: she felt it in the hairs at the back of her neck; in the clutch of her bowels. Or else she was simply desperate to believe so, because if there was nothing here then all Hesprec's lore and wisdom would accomplish nothing.

The three stones themselves seemed almost nothing. One stood, barely more than a man's height; two were fallen, and one of those cracked in two. Together they formed two sides of a triangle inside a little round space that was half walled off by the mounded boulders. This small stretch of mystery was what their long spiralling progress had led towards.

Feeling the strength of those quiescent spirits, though,

Maniye knew that Hesprec had been right. To approach as the Boar did; to approach as the ancient architects had intended, that was how to win one's way to the sacred site without gathering the ire of those whose power suffused the place. If they had just scaled the hillside as Venater had suggested, then they would have reached the top amid an invisible tempest of offence. Any ritual conducted against that anger could only have gone badly wrong.

And now they were at the top, and Maniye collapsed onto her knees at the summit's edge, looking around her at where those old, old stones cut through the turf like loose teeth. They had been carved once, but time had smoothed over whatever message human hands had incised in them.

Hesprec, though, was looking downwards with a speculative air.

'One might wonder just whose hands raised this place, and when,' the Serpent girl murmured, echoing Maniye's own thoughts. Her copper eyes were narrowed in thought, and Maniye could see the world as she did, just for a moment. The spiralling path that encircled the hill was like the coils of a serpent, so that they now stood at its head, here where the stones were. And was that just a coincidence or was this some distant, cold splinter of the Serpent's history that even Hesprec did not know of?

'So you're going to go straight on with this business, are you?' Venater demanded.

The Serpent girl shook her head. 'Preparation is ever the friend of the ritualist.'

'What's that even supposed to mean?' the pirate demanded.

'It means priest business,' Asmander decided. 'And we have travelled far and, while the Messenger works, we will sleep, save for those who watch.'

'And when the Wolves sniff out the truth and come for us?' Shyri asked.

Asmander put a hand to his ear. 'What's that I hear? Laughing Girl wants to take first watch? Then, of course, she must.'

'Dung-eater.'

'Not laughing now?' Asmander challenged her.

She shrugged. 'At least you're not moping and groaning about your honour any more. Selling that girl to her father was the one clever thing you ever did, and after it you were no fun at all. I prefer you when you're stupid and happy.'

Venater smirked. 'You didn't know him back home. He's all smiles half the time, and about to cut his own throat the rest. You try being his slave, see how much fun it is.' And then, seeing Asmander's gaze on him, 'What?'

'A slave?'

'Slave with no collar's still a slave,' the pirate replied with a rebellious look.

'Enough,' Broken Axe intervened. 'Laughing Girl, you keep watch with Loud Thunder until the moon's high. I'll see out the rest of the night with one of these Rivermen.'

'That means you, then,' Venater told Asmander, stretching.

The Champion eyed him with half a smile. 'Of all the slaves in the world, you are the least satisfactory.'

'There are worse ambitions.'

Maniye had wanted to put herself forward to watch out part of the night. It had hurt when Broken Axe had overlooked her, though she knew she would not have been capable of it. In a sudden reversal of perspective, she understood how he saw them all: they were his pack, his tribe. They were here because of an odd network of loyalties, but all focused on making one of their number well again. While she was weak, Broken Axe had arranged the pack around her, their strengths covering for her. When – *if* – she was strong again then he would lean on her to precisely that degree that she could endure. That was how he led, and that was how a Wolf leader ought to.

Lying on the cold ground, huddling close with Hesprec's

slight form tucked against her, and Asmander's back against her own, she indulged a fantasy in which Axe, and not her father, had risen to become chief of the Winter Runners. How the world might then have been different! And her own life, how might that have gone if her father had been no more than a strong hunter of the Wolves . . .

But without Stone River and what he had done to her mother, surely there would be no Maniye Many Tracks. Knowing what she now knew about her origins, perhaps there would just have been Akrit, childless. Her wolf soul would have found some other body to be born into, her tiger soul likewise. The unlikely and traumatic combination that had given rise to *her* would never have arisen. If she had a destiny at all, she shared it with him.

And she shivered, and tried to sleep, but she was still awake when Loud Thunder pushed his mountainous way in to share their warmth. Only then, with Broken Axe lying alert atop one of the rocks, his muzzle on his paws and his ears cocked, did she find a little rest.

Her sleep was troubled with dreams, but then she had been their plaything ever since she came to the Shining Halls. Asleep, the cages of her souls were thrown open and they ran about the spaces of her mind, hunting one another, hunting her too. Their battlefield was every place between her home village and this hilltop, all jumbled together inside her mind. She had expected to dream of great spirits, to be touched by the powers that inhabited this place. They did not come, though, and she was left to her own mercies until morning.

Dawn's light found Broken Axe pacing restlessly about the hilltop, scrambling up to find a high perch, then dropping down again. When enough of them were awake, he Stepped into his grim-faced human shape.

'I scented tigers overnight,' he confirmed. 'I didn't see them but they were out there, down at the treeline.'

'Then why didn't they attack?' Shyri asked. 'They weren't shy about it last time, and we don't even have a cave to hide in now.'

'Two, maybe. Three at most,' he informed her. 'Scouts, but they'll be back in force. Tonight we'll have to face them, I think, if we're still here. So tell me that we won't still be here.'

Hesprec looked unhappy. 'The Serpent's path involves many twists—'

'Just plain words,' Broken Axe told her flatly.

She pursed her lips in exasperation before snapping, 'You want words you can understand? Then know this: what Maniye is seeking, it cannot be done. Neither amongst Wolves nor Tigers is such a thing known. Even if she were of the Eyrie, say, or one of the Patient Ones, it could not be achieved without cleansing and ritual, fasting, meditation and the goodwill of her totem – or her totem*s*, I suppose. None of this has been accomplished in the whole history of the world.'

Faced with that statement, Broken Axe blinked. 'Then what are we doing here?'

'I am of the Serpent, who were the first people in this world to undertake a great many things. And so perhaps I will be the first to accomplish this, if Maniye remains strong.' She held up a hand to forestall his next question. 'But it will take *time*. Maniye must go on a great journey, one that laughs at all her wanderings until now. I need water to be fetched for me. I need a fire going. Champion, do you know the Seven Figures?'

Asmander grimaced. 'Perhaps I can remember them.'

'Do your best. Scratch them on stones – big stones. Make a circle of them. And after all that is done, and after I have washed and prayed, and let the spirits of this place walk into and out of my mind and grow accustomed to my scent, then perhaps I will be ready.'

Broken Axe sighed, sharing a look with Loud Thunder. 'So, by noon? Midnight? Winter?'

'Every word you speak drives it further away,' Hesprec told him darkly.

★

Asmander had finished scratching the Seven Figures, or at least as well as he was ever going to. They were part of every child's education, or of those who got an education. The Snake priests taught them as an aid to contemplation, as the basis for the written script of the Sun River Nation. They were a relic from the Oldest Kingdom – that lost land the Serpent people still talked about with such bitter nostalgia. *Ah, yes, what a land we had, what magic and majesty, before the coming of the Pale Shadow People . . .* It came to Asmander now that a great deal of what he had so faithfully learned as a child had not served particularly to prepare him for his present circumstances. There had been, for example, a notable paucity of information about surviving the cold north.

There had been too many tales of heroes, and too little on how to act like one when the time came.

He set to repairing his *maccan*, which lost its teeth as often as Old Crocodile but sadly could not grow new ones on its own. He was almost out of the gum he used to reattach them, and it came to him that he had no idea what materials the Crown of the World might furnish for providing more. It was unlikely to be a problem that the Wolf tribe ever needed to solve.

He glanced back at the three great stones. Hesprec was kneeling there, hands on her knees, her head bowed. *Chains of obligation.* Axe felt himself responsible for the girl because of something to do with her mother. Thunder was here out of loyalty to Axe, and perhaps because he liked the girl also. Hesprec was bound to Maniye by cords of obligation. *And I . . . ?* It was time to admit that Asmander had so far made enough of a mess of his life that serving Hesprec seemed the only honourable path. *But, as paths go, probably not a very long one. And, like all storied heroes, my death seems unlikely to be a private matter. I have invited my friends along.*

Even with this thought there was a footstep nearby, and then Venater squatted beside him. Asmander studied his leering face: the heavy jaw, the cruel, flinty eyes, the broken nose never quite set right. There was a majesty to this man's ugliness that the heroes of old might kill for.

'The Wolves will be with us long before nightfall,' the old pirate offered.

'It seems likely.'

'And the Tiger are already here – so says Axe – and more on the way. Reckon they'll fight each other? We'll have a good view of it.'

'I think that they will mostly fight *us*,' Asmander decided quietly. 'Each other as well, but they will throw their greatest strength into seizing the girl.'

'We should just let them take her.'

'I am not arguing.'

Venater sighed. 'You are, though. Because of the Snake and Broken Axe.'

'Well, then I suppose I am.'

Venater nodded philosophically, chewing away at a strip of jerky. 'This is the bit,' he spoke around a wad of soggy meat, 'where you tell me the Serpent possesses some great magic in this place that means somehow we win.'

'That would be a good thing to be able to tell you, yes.'

'Or that this thing that the Snake girl is doing turns out to be real knife-point magic at killing wolves and tigers.'

'That doesn't seem likely, does it?' Asmander continued at his task, but cocked an eye at the other man. 'Did you have something else you wanted to say?'

'I wanted to say how stupid it is to have so many grown men wasting their time over one mad girl.'

'Were I a priest, I would write your words in the Book of Truths so as to last for all times. Alas, I am not, so they will be lost when we all get ourselves killed by angry northerners.'

Venater snorted, but there was a coal of anger behind his eyes still, a look of resentment.

Asmander sighed. 'I think it is time that we were honest, you and I. My father felt the hook of envy when the Champion chose me. It was something he himself had sought all his life, yet never found.'

Venater grunted.

'And he has used my Champion well in pushing the interests of our clan, but there was ever a distance between us from that day on. A distance he would not speak of, and so it grew. And I think we both know that, in sending me to find the Iron Wolves, there was more than a little hope that I would not return. As with so many of my father's plans, he wins every way. If I do not come back, he is rid of me; if I return with Wolves, then he gains in Tecuman's eyes. If I return without them, I lose that same respect.'

'He's a clever bastard, your father.'

'You say so little I can argue with that I feel disappointed.'

'You'll get to argue with the Wolves soon enough. We all will.'

Asmander laughed briefly. 'The famed Iron Wolves! If only I could tell my father: they are real, yes. Also: they want to kill me. And they are just men – even as we are men. They eat different food and follow different gods but, like men everywhere, they quarrel with one another, and their stupid quarrels end in bloodshed. How like us they are – almost as bad as the Dragon.'

'*Nobody*'s as bad as the Dragon,' Venater stated with pride.

Asmander tried another laugh, couldn't manage it, and so took a deep breath. The Champion stirred within him watchfully, sensing a moment of crisis coming but one it could not help him with.

'I am now ready to fight,' he declared.

'Not sure about that,' the old pirate jibed. 'Give it another ten years.'

'I was good enough to defeat you.'

He had been expecting an angry response, but Venater just looked away, his mouth twisted.

'Yes, yes, you were drunk and half asleep,' Asmander prompted.

The pirate shrugged.

'But we have walked a long road together since then. And I have gained great joy from knowing that you would cut my throat while I slept, every night we have been together, if only you were free to do so.'

'You're right there.'

'But we are here now in this stupid land, and I am proud to have you with me for one more dawn, Venat, though it seems likely there will not be another.'

'Speak for yourself,' the pirate snarled. 'I'll still be . . . still be . . .' His jaw worked. 'What did you call me?'

'You heard.'

In the quiet falling between them, the laughter of Loud Thunder rolled in from across the hilltop, startlingly loud and intrusive.

'What am I supposed to do with that?' Venater – *Venat* – demanded.

'Whatever you want. That is the point of freedom.'

'Why would you . . . ?'

'Because I remember fighting you, at the mouth of the Tsotec. Because I should have killed you – or not killed you. You were mine. I should not have let my father chain you.'

It took the smallest motion for Venat's stone blade to appear in his hand. 'And if I slice you open right now?'

'Then we will fight, and I would welcome it.' Asmander felt himself tense, feeling the Champion crouch about his shoulders, awaiting its moment.

'It's a long way to the River,' Venat said softly.

'Not too long for you.' He could not read the other man at all, had no clue whether to expect an attack. But then Venat shook his head, looking oddly lost, and a moment later he had turned away and was picking his way towards the treeline, weapon still in hand and his tread uncertain.

'And you should go too,' Asmander told the air. And sure enough there was Shyri, dropping down from her eavesdropping post atop one of the boulders, and Stepping back to human as she did.

She just looked at him, blinking a few times. 'How could you let him go?'

He knew she wasn't talking about the loss of Venat's blade to help them in the fight to come.

'The right thing to do,' Asmander muttered. And then Broken Axe howled, loud and long. Relieved of further explanations, the Champion rushed over to see what had emerged from out of the trees.

They saw the Wolves: Akrit's warband, that had plainly not been fooled as well as anyone had hoped. There was a good score of them there so far, some in one form, some in another. A handful of those who wore a human shape were clad in shirts of metal: the Iron Wolves whose fame had spread all the way to the banks of the Tsotec.

Look, Father! thought Asmander drily. *It's your army. What can I buy them with now, though? The only thing they want is my blood, will that do?*

'They've started.' Broken Axe was abruptly at his shoulder. For a second Asmander thought he was simply stating the obvious, but then he glanced back to see Hesprec and Maniye sitting together between the stones.

The Wolf grimaced. 'How long do Snake rituals take in your land?'

'It varies. Sometimes they are over in as little as three days.'

'And your big friend's gone.'

'He had pressing business elsewhere.'

'Do you southerners ever give a straight answer to anything?' Broken Axe asked exasperatedly, eyes still fixed on the warband below.

'Yes. I am here and I will fight, for Hesprec and for you,' Asmander told him flatly.

He earned a curt nod. Perhaps there might have been further

words, but just then Shyri was calling out, 'I see tigers, many tigers coming!'

Asmander attempted a brittle smile. 'So: everyone is here. We can start now.'

45

Maniye and Hesprec sat in the shadow of the stones, in this spirit-heavy place, with a fire burning between them and with Asmander's glyph-carved pebbles arranged between the bases of the monoliths, the standing one and the two fallen. Hesprec had covered Maniye's hair with a shawl of bright-dyed Horse linen. She had mixed up an ink of charcoal and water, and had dabbed it on Maniye's face, tracing the dotted path of coils there, making them sisters, light and dark. And Maniye told herself that she could feel the hill shift and shudder minutely beneath her as the Serpent rose within the earth, summoned from its unthinkably distant southern haunts, from its sunning places alongside the warm river. For the coils of the Serpent ran everywhere – had she not felt its presence and seen its rainbow scales in dreams? She might dare to hope so if it would help her now.

'You and I, we will go on a journey,' Hesprec told her softly.

Maniye was aware of her other friends moving – spreading out around the hilltop, sudden tension in them. As though she was truly connected via the coils in the earth, she knew that Akrit Stone River was nearby, and that Joalpey the Tiger Queen was close. The jaws that had been gaping for so long were preparing to snap shut, and she was where the teeth would meet.

'There is a landscape known only to the wisest,' the Serpent girl whispered, 'in whose number, of course, I count myself.'

Her voice was slow and rhythmic, becoming almost hypnotic. 'It is not a land of rivers and marshes or of deserts and plains, or even of cold northern mountains and the jagged teeth of broken rocks. It is a landscape of gods. That is where we must travel to petition for your soul.'

And the yowling of the Tiger cried out its warning from the trees, chilling Maniye's blood. She shivered and made as if to jump up, but Hesprec reached about the fire and caught her wrist.

'You must listen to nothing and nobody save for me. If our friends fail, then we will be caught and killed here, because our own minds will be far away, gone in a direction that nobody else can ever follow. Our souls will be with the gods, and whether that is a good thing or a bad depends on how you comport yourself before them. So you must attend to me or you will be lost, understand?'

Maniye nodded.

Hesprec's eyes flicked sideways. 'The Stone Place would have been better,' she sighed. 'Two or three could have stood off an army on that causeway. Here, well, we are sheltered and the hill is steep. Perhaps our handful will keep them back for long enough.'

There were raised voices now: the sound of men working themselves up for the fight, swearing the oaths and boasts that prefigured bloodletting. Maniye forced the sounds from her head and looked straight into Hesprec's copper eyes.

'Now I will tell you something of this land we must travel to, and thus you will see it in your mind and let it become real to you, and this shall become our steed to take us there.' The Serpent priestess was still gripping her hand. 'Are you ready to see your gods for what they truly are?'

Matt and Yoff were very still, very focused. There was none of the running about and yapping that might have been expected of them. Their master was going to war, and they understood it. Their eyes were pinned on the enemy down below.

Loud Thunder wore his stinking armour of grease-hardened hides, surely enough to deter the noses of any number of wolves. His great axe, with its weighty copper head, rested over his shoulder as he peered down at the Winter Runners. Beside him, Broken Axe seemed a frail figure, even with an iron hatchet in his hand.

'Down there they look like little ants,' the big man grunted. 'I think they won't look much bigger when they get here, eh?'

Broken Axe couldn't raise a smile.

The Wolf pack was at the treeline, scaling the hill, ignoring the twisting path and scrabbling directly up the steep side, using human hands and feet. It was heavy going for them, especially those wearing coats of iron. Loud Thunder looked around speculatively, hauled up a decent-sized stone in both hands and bounced it down the hillside with a roar. The Wolves scattered to either side of it, but when they started up again, their ascent was slower, and they spread themselves out more.

Another few stones failed to hit any of them, and then they were past halfway up, whereupon Stone River halted and shaded his eyes, looking up at them.

'Broken Axe, I see you there,' he called out, and one by one the other Wolves paused, waiting. They were just outside the distance where they might have rushed the two defenders.

'It needs no good eyes for that,' Axe replied, still weighing his hatchet in his hand.

'Shatters Oak is dead.'

'I saw it,' Broken Axe conceded.

'It was she who wanted your blood. I have claim to it, for you've betrayed me and the Wolf. But I'll let you go – and your fat friend, too,' Stone River told him. 'You're not why I'm here. I can forget the bad blood between us. You've made a mistake. All men make mistakes. Wise men seek to amend them.'

'I did make a mistake,' Broken Axe admitted.

'Go then. Mend that error of yours. The girl is nothing to you.'

'That's not the mistake I meant.' Broken Axe took a deep breath. 'My mistake was not calling you out, ten years ago and more. How far have you chased, just to catch one frightened girl, Stone River? We both know you have no claim on her. Yet because she has defied you, you cannot walk away. That is your mistake, not mine. My mistake was turning my back on the man you became back in the war.'

'The war with the Tiger,' the chief of the Winter Runners echoed. 'You don't remember how it truly was.'

'I remember enough,' Broken Axe replied harshly. 'Now come, if you're coming. Or go.'

He was almost too slow; he had been focused too much on Stone River, but a handful of the Wolves on either side had been inching up the hillside, drawing slowly nearer. Only Loud Thunder's roar saved him as the Cave Dweller Stepped, bulking out into a bear that seemed to blot out the sun. Then there were three warriors clambering for him, fighting to get close enough to Step and close the last of the distance on wolf paws.

Maniye was in a shadowed land of undulating hills that fell away in every direction she looked. Above her was the night sky, but the constellations were not those she recognized. Instead the stars drifted past one another, hunting the sky for . . . she could not say what for, but there was something threatening about those mobile motes of gleaming light. She was terribly afraid that they were hunting for a way *in*.

'This is the Godsland,' came Hesprec's soft voice. 'This is the secret known only to my people, and some few others. This is what we saved.'

'Saved? From your Oldest Kingdom?'

'Before that, even. We took this into our hearts and carried it away from the lands we had lost to the Plague People. And then we burned all the land behind us, so that they could not follow, and the sea rushed in to fill it. This is the land of souls, Maniye Many Tracks. When we die, this is where our souls return, and whence they depart to be born again. This is the heart of our dream.'

Maniye knew she still sat atop the hill, with the three stones about her. She knew that what she saw was built from her own imagination and Hesprec's hypnotic voice. And yet, with her eyes closed, she saw it: it was as real to her as the world of grass and trees and the sun which she had left behind.

'You are not alone,' Hesprec told her, and she realized it was true.

Close beside her was a shadow standing under that restless dark sky. Eyes like green gems regarded her imperiously, and fire rippled down the great beast's flanks in shimmering stripes. A tiger. *The* Tiger. The suggestions, the mere shadows and breath she had seen within the Shining Halls, were nothing to it. Seeing the beast before her, standing so close, she could barely breathe. Its scale and magnificence exerted a pressure in her mind. Away from it, a thousand half-seen reflections seemed to recede in all directions, mirror-tigers, each one of them less and less like the original as it fell further away.

It regarded her imperiously, and distantly she heard Hesprec ask her what she saw, and her own voice stammer out an answer.

'Look beyond. Find another hilltop. What do you see?'

To think was to move her gaze, to look was to travel. The hilly land was crowded, she now saw. Every hilltop had its master, surrounded by myriad shades of itself. From the feet of the Tiger, now she found herself before the Wolf. A stare composed of moon-silver pinned her, crouched almost between its paws. The gape of its teeth could have swallowed the sun.

'Good,' came Hesprec's dry tone in her ear. 'But, tell me, what lies beyond and between? Whose domain is nearby?'

'You must know.'

'I cannot know. The Serpent's lair is far from there. You have gone to your own place in the Godsland. I may not travel there.

Maniye, listen to me. Because you saved my life not once but twice, I will tell you the secret of the world. I will tell you what no other priest or chief or sorcerer would wish you to learn. It is power, this knowledge, if you can only use it. But then again, all knowledge is power if it is not wasted . . .

'So tell me, what do you see near the Wolf? Turn your back on him and search the nearest hills.'

'I see . . .' There was a lean, half-starved shape looking back at her from the next peak, like Wolf's thin shadow. 'There is Coyote there.'

'Of course, Coyote that would be Wolf if he could,' Hesprec confirmed, amused. 'But further, look further.'

'I see . . .' There was an animal beyond, something like a big-eared dog with a spotted hide, but quite unlike the creature that Shyri Stepped to. Maniye described it uncertainly, but it seemed to make sense to Hesprec.

'That is the hunting dog of the Plains. His people were Wolf tribe once, before they were driven south. Find yourself at the feet of the Tiger once more. Surely there will be something there . . .'

She sought out the Tiger, thinking that it must be on the next hill, or the next. But when she found it, she had lost the Wolf, skipping over a vast gulf that lay between them. The hillsides about the Tiger were strewn with other cats, large and small. She saw Lion watching her with haughty stare, and the sly, cruel smile of Jaguar, and others still, but none to her purpose, not even the great sword-toothed cat that was the Lion's Champion.

'Where is the creature Asmander Steps to? Where is his Killing Claw?' she demanded. 'You must know the path that leads there.'

'No, no, no,' Hesprec broke in. 'That is not the way of the Godsland. Open your mind to me and hear my words. The Godsland is the land of the possible. It is the landscape of every animal that is and ever was, perhaps every beast that there could be. Travel from the Tiger and you shall reach first those beasts that are its brothers and sisters and cousins. Travel on from them, and you find totems like them, but less like Tiger, you see? So travel the land between Tiger and Wolf and tell me what you find. Surely there is some unknown shape lurking there that will be your Champion!'

And Maniye walked that land, hill to hill to hill, and she saw cat-likes and wolf-likes, and many shapes in between that were like nothing she knew. But many of them were small, more hunters of mice than of men. There were no giants, no savage killers that she could find, and between the two halves of her being was that great yawning darkness, where she could find nothing at all.

Asmander crouched atop the boulder-strewn side of the hill. He could hear the voices of Axe and Stone River shouting at each other. Perhaps that was the tradition in the Crown of the World, before a formal fight. He'd heard the same went for the Plains.

'Perhaps you should insult them,' he suggested.

Shyri shrugged. She had pulled out some armour of layered linen, which had been folded almost flat inside her pack, but now hung on her in starched panels: a cuirass and plates hanging down to her knees. To his eyes, it made her seem younger and more fragile.

'Insult who?' she asked.

Asmander had been noticing shifting movement at the treeline for a while and, even as he opened his mouth, he heard the calls of the great cats to one another. He narrowed his eyes, watching for that first move, wondering if he would leap down amongst them, or if he would let them come to him.

Then Shyri yelled a cackling battle cry, and dropped past him with her axe descending. He heard the furious snarl of a tiger from right beneath his feet and realized the enemy were already upon him; that the Shadow Eaters had ghosted right up to the stones without him seeing.

He did not hesitate, jumping down from the boulders and Stepping halfway, so that what landed before a startled Tiger

551

warrior was the Champion, rattling its quills and shrieking like death. His opponent was a man, a cat, then a man again, thrusting at him with a spear, but Asmander leapt at him, springing high over the lunge and coming down across its shaft, shattering the weapon and knocking its wielder to the ground. There were more coming at him already, just flurries of movement in his peripheral vision, so he kicked the disarmed spearman hard in the stomach, catching him just as the man Stepped to his tiger shape and bowling the striped cat down the hill.

Shyri had her bone-crushing teeth about a tiger's foreleg, shaking her spotted head back and forth as it raked its other claws down her side. Then both of them had Stepped away, the Plains woman's axe sweeping past the northern warrior's face as the Tiger retreated, ruined arm held close.

Another woman came for Shyri with fluid movements like dancing water, cutting at her with the curved bronze edge of a knife. The Laughing woman skidded away, losing a foot of hillside, but then Stepped and went for the throat, teeth snapping just short of her target before finding herself facing off against a tiger considerably bigger than she was.

Asmander was about to go to her aid when he saw that one of the Tigers had gained the top of the rocks, with nothing between her and their quarry but a jump down. With a hiss of anger he took three quick steps and leapt, clearing the vertical distance in a single bound and landing off balance beside his enemy. She flinched away, but a moment later she was on him, claws hooking at his hide and her jaws gaping wide. She was going for his throat, but all she managed was to graze the flesh over one shoulder before he sank his own teeth into her. She Stepped, using the shifting of shapes to twist from between his jaws: this was the Tiger priestess who had led the hunt against them the time before. Then she had got her knife into him, just a glancing line of pain down his ribs. In an instant he had followed her, striking down with the stone points of the *maccan*. She swayed out of the way of the blow, sliding to one side in a

552

move that put the point of her blade at his gut. Striking down, he caught her forearm with the heel of his off-hand, ramming the pommel of her weapon into her leg and trapping her arm against her own body. Before he could use the leverage she had pushed a hand into his face, almost toppling him from the rock. She was a tiger in the next instant, and he was the Champion again.

Shyri was facing three – two big cats keeping her at bay, and a man beyond them with a fistful of javelins. They had all dropped some way down the hill, closer to the treeline.

The priestess swatted at him a couple of times with a paw, trying to put him off balance, but suddenly he had no time to fight properly. He struck out with his feet, not trying for a dis-embowelling stroke with his claws, but simply kicking the tiger hard under the ribs, spilling her from atop the rock and hope-fully winding her. Then he had leapt out into space.

He let his mind fall into the Champion's well of calm, reach-ing out for a feeling, a way of experiencing the world . . .

The breath leapt in his lungs. His great leathery wings caught the air and he shrieked for the sheer joy of it, the hideous cry of the shape that Hesprec had sent against the Eyriemen. He dropped onto the tigers like a monster from the old stories and they scattered, darting back for the trees.

'Back to the rocks,' Shyri yelled – there might have been some gratitude in her eyes, but there was no time for it to form proper words. A moment later and they were both Stepped and run-ning again. There was a cry from Maniye – he heard it clearly, not of shock or pain but a wail of lament. For a terrible moment Asmander thought that Hesprec must be hurt. Even as they scaled to the base of the rocks, though, he heard the Serpent priestess's voice calling out.

'Laughing Girl, come here now!'

Shyri, human once more, met Asmander's lizard eyes.

'That's not a good plan,' she declared.

Asmander forced himself back to humanity, though the

Champion resisted him, knowing bloodshed was coming and wanting its share. 'You must go,' he got out.

'But—'

'The Serpent calls, and you must go. That is how it is.'

'For you, maybe.'

'Shyri, please.'

She looked frightened, but not for herself. Fearing what his own face might show in answer to that, he let the Champion take hold of him again, assuming his post atop the rocks once more, watching Shyri weave her way around to reach the others.

The Tiger were coming out from the trees again, only a handful, but there was only one of him.

Broken Axe was swift, as man or wolf. He danced and darted
and yet never fell back. The blows of his enemies cut through
the air past him, and the iron edge of his hatchet was quick to
respond. Stone River watched one of the younger hunters try
him – darting in on four feet, all snarls and defiance. Broken
Axe met the youth in the same shape, twisting aside from his
teeth to worry viciously at the back of the boy's neck, flipping
him over and sending him rolling down the hill. His next assail-
ant got close and then Stepped to human, bringing the grey
edge of a knife towards Broken Axe's gut. Nimble as a warrior
half his age, Axe got his shoulder beneath the upward-cutting
blow and guided the attacker's knife-hand away. His own
weapon lashed in, not a killing strike but a powerful blow with
the flat to his opponent's temple. Stone River's warrior collapsed
to the ground, stunned or worse, while Broken Axe still stood.

And no wonder, for he was fighting in the shadow of the
largest Cave Dweller that Akrit had ever seen. The huge Bear
had not shifted an inch since the skirmish began. Three Wolves
had gone up against him, with spears and axes and fangs, but all
of them had fallen back limping and mauled. Arrows and throw
darts had not even penetrated the monstrous creature's hide. At
the Bear's feet were two dogs fighting with the coordination of
warriors, lunging out from behind their master's ankles to snap

and bark and growl, a constant threat and distraction to any enemy that might dare come close.

On open ground, the entire pack could have descended on them, surrounded them and dragged them down – even the Bear. With the tumbled stones lending them a hard flank, the Wolves could not concentrate their numbers to finish the fight. Broken Axe stood in the Bear's shadow, and to enter the Bear's shadow meant broken bones.

Stone River had hesitated, on seeing that great mass of muscle and hair and claws blocking the way. He was not reckless; he wanted his followers to wear the monster down first – though there was precious little sign of that happening as yet.

'Bear-killer,' he snapped, and one of his warriors handed him the weapon. It was a favourite of the Wolves: long-hafted with an inward-curving iron blade honed to a razor edge, and terminating with a piercing point like a beak. The Horse called it a falx, but the Wolves knew it as the bear-killer. And killing a bear was what Akrit needed to accomplish.

But now it was the turn of Smiles Without Teeth, and if Akrit's most faithful follower was smaller than the Bear, still he was the strongest of the Winter Runners. He loped up the slope with another couple of hunters to back him, stopping outside the Bear's reach to survey his enemy.

Arms spread wide, the Cave Dweller reared up on his hind legs and bellowed, and Smiles seized his moment to dart in. He Stepped as he came close, dropping down to one knee and striking in with his axe, with the other two Wolves right behind him. Broken Axe was there too, though, lunging forwards even as Smiles's blow went swinging in. Their hafts locked together, deflecting Smiles's stroke up and away, but for a second Broken Axe was left exposed to the next hunter in.

Akrit hissed in triumph, envisaging the death-stroke before it happened. The dogs got in the way, though, snapping and leaping at the hunter so that he flinched away, striking too late.

The Wolf's knife ripped into the side of one of the dogs,

opening the wretched creature up. It was a meagre victory, but Akrit heard his follower cry out in triumph nonetheless. It was the last sound he made, though, for then the Bear saw what he had done. With a roar of fury the Cave Dweller came down on him, all his awful weight concentrated in his forepaws, splintering the man's bones like kindling.

It will be me, then. Akrit hefted the bear-killer in one hand, then Stepped and was heading up the hill at a run. Before him he saw Smiles Without Teeth Step and go for the Bear's legs with his teeth, forgetting that there was a human mind behind that mountain of animal power. The Cave Dweller Stepped to meet him, kicking him in the stomach hard enough to bowl him over, then swinging furiously with that great axe of his. The blow had been meant for Smiles, but the other hunter got in the way as he lunged at Broken Axe with a spear, not paying attention to anything else. The Dweller's axe-head caught him across the shoulder and chest, shattering his arm and spinning him away.

Then Smiles was back. His iron coat had kept him from any real harm, just a solid bruise where the bigger man had kicked him. He had his axe upraised, ready to bring it down with all the power both mighty arms could manage.

He had always sought to win his battles with strength, had Smiles Without Teeth, and amongst the Winter Runners it had sufficed.

The Cave Dweller stepped back into his bear shape and slapped a claw-studded paw with crushing force under Smiles's strike. The blow hooked the Wolf off his feet, hurling him away with the bear's vast strength and sending him through the air like a stone, end over end. Just as the ground fell away from the hill-top, so Smiles Without Teeth seemed to fall away from the ground, falling *upwards* until the world remembered him and brought him down. From that impact, iron could not save him.

Stone River spared a brief second's regret for the death of his friend, but then he was standing before the Bear himself, and that became all of his world.

Broken Axe had recognized him and was trying to close, but another pair of young Wolf hunters was at his heels, diverting the traitor's attention as they snapped at him.

The Cave Dweller's paws came thundering down, the huge beast truly fighting mad now. Stone River pushed himself aside, scrabbling against the slope of the hill, feeling the breath of that near-miss twitching the hairs of his pelt. Then he was a man again, the bear-killer blade of his falx sweeping in, too close and too soon, so that the beak-point barely grazed his foe's back and the cutting edge glanced off that thick hide. Then the Bear was a man once more, towering over Stone River still, swinging the axe down in a wide arc.

Akrit Stepped to slip beneath that swing, got his teeth briefly into the Bear's unprotected shin, then backed off. To lock his jaws would be to fix himself where his enemy could find him. The copper axe swung down again, its great weight of metal swooping through the air swift as a bird. Stone River tried to twist aside again, but the other dog was in his way, and the two of them went down in a snarling tangle of limbs. Furious and desperate, Stone River ripped at one of the animal's forelegs, tearing a great bloody gash there. He knew the axe would be coming for him again, so he darted before the Cave Dweller, under the swing, Stepping as he came round.

He had wolf speed in a man's shape just in that moment, and he threw it all into the strike, the arc of the falx cleaving the Cave Dweller in the hip. The cutting edge was foiled by the larded goat-fleeces the big man wore, but the point dug in deep, not a killing wound but a slowing one.

His enemy Stepped again, seeking the greater mass of the bear shape to protect him. Akrit was ready for him to rear up in anger and expose his belly. Instead the Cave Dweller stayed low, swiping at his tormentor and baring his great yellow teeth.

Akrit could see his path clearly now. He had fought men and he had fought tigers – yes, and other wolves – and once or twice he had fought bears, though none as massive as this. He swung again, making a great show of the powerful two-handed blow, and the bear – with its man's mind – swatted the falx away.

Akrit took the force of that blow, but he took it as a gift, spinning the weapon about at its balance-point, so that it came in twice as fast from the other side. On all fours, the bear had only one paw at a time to act with, already overextended from its first parry.

Akrit put all his strength into that blow. Had a man ever before killed a bear this size with a single stroke? Perhaps he would be the first.

He felt the clean bite of the blade as it chopped the beast's hide and slammed deep into the flesh beneath. He had been aiming for the neck, but his enemy's movements or the fickle ground had left the weapon deep in the bear's shoulder and back, the tip surely in amongst the creature's ribs. The Cave Dweller roared again – but Akrit heard more pain than anger now, a desolate, terrible sound.

The beast reared up, and if Akrit had not been ready he would have lost his weapon. As it was, the Bear's own motion ripped the falx out of his flesh, releasing a gout of blood that painted the rocks around them.

For a heartbeat Akrit stood in the Bear's shadow, falx already arcing inwards again, and braced for the crushing impact of those claws. Then the Cave Dweller dropped back on to all fours again, with a whimper, and the falx's course raked across his muzzle.

Stone River would have finished it, if not for the dog. The beast was at him without warning, leaping up to his chest, teeth hungry for his throat. Akrit Stepped, took the animal by the scruff of its neck and simply flung it away. He was already flinching from the Bear's expected retaliation as he turned back, but the Cave Dweller was shambling backwards, lurching and limping. Instead, before him stood Broken Axe.

'Go,' the traitor shouted to his injured friend. Stone River found himself grinning, because he *had* defeated the Bear, because he was about to kill Broken Axe, and after that he would have one of his people open his daughter's throat – and then none amongst the Wolves would ever doubt his strength.

And Broken Axe's eyes passed from Stone River to the eleven Wolves who could still fight, and he nodded philosophically.

'So be it,' he said. 'I call you out, Stone River. I challenge you.'

Akrit shook his head. 'We will tear you apart, traitor.'

'Who is the traitor?' Broken Axe called out. 'Here we stand, two men born of the Winter Runners, and which has betrayed his people? What are my wrongs? That I have gone my own way, and helped a girl who chose to do the same.'

'And what do you suggest are mine?' Akrit knew he should just strike, but he wanted Broken Axe to *know* that he was wrong before he died.

'You have placed yourself above the Wolf,' Broken Axe declared, and loud enough for all to hear. 'You have followed a dream where the Crown of the World was in your shadow, and you have ever sought to make it real. You sought to rule.'

'To rule in the Wolf's name!' Akrit snapped, feeling the tension stretch the moment until surely the pack would flow past him to bring Broken Axe down for his killing stroke.

'In *your* name. In *your* name you have shed blood at the Stone Place. In *your* own name you have sought to dig up the war with the Tiger. You have ever sought to be a taller man than you are, and to do so you have piled up the bodies of others. That is not the Wolf's Shadow you cast, it is your own.'

'Bring him down!' Akrit snapped.

The tide of grey bodies . . . they milled and moved about, but did not advance. Those in wolf shape whined and kept their heads low, and the men would not meet his eyes. If Smiles Without Teeth had been there to set an example . . . But Smiles was dead.

'You are not fit,' Broken Axe said, each word heavy as a stone.

560

'I challenge you. For the leadership of the Winter Runners, I challenge you.'

Maniye kept searching from hill to hill and yet, whenever she turned back, there was the Wolf or there the Tiger, the twin poles between which her life was strung, picked out by the light of an unseen moon. Between them, the landscape of gods and monsters was shrouded by eternal night, denied to her. If Hesprec spoke the truth, here was the country that stretched from Wolf to Eagle, from Tiger to Serpent, to Asmander's Swift Lizard. In that dark there were great beasts of time and legend waiting to gift her with their souls. She felt she was tethered, even as her father had once leashed her. Her realm was just a small circle of light in that great midnight landscape. She could not break free from her heritage. And within her she could feel her souls uncoiling, pressing against the walls of their prison. This was *their* place far more than it was hers. Here was where their strength arose from. Here they were stronger than she was. Once that understanding filtered through to them, she would not be able to keep them tied within her. They would break free from her, break away from her, and then . . .

And then there was noise and shouting, all too close, intruding from the world outside so that she lost her image of the Godsland, lost that sense of the great spirits standing close by. The wheeling stars drew together to become the fire, and she jerked away from it, feeling the ground tremble as though the whole hill was stirring.

But it was not the hill. It was Loud Thunder. The huge man sat slumped by the fire, his skin and the fleece of his armour glistening with his own blood. His face was clenched up like a fist but, when he met her eyes, he still tried to smile.

'He's a fast one, your father,' he murmured, just a rumbling in his chest. 'And my Mother will not be pleased with me.'

Maniye leapt up and went over to him, but the sheer scale of his body – and his wounds – dumbfounded her. She did not know what could possibly be done. It was like trying to heal the land itself.

'Back to the fire!' Hesprec yelled at her. 'Maniye, we'll have no other chance than this. You have to find the Godsland again!'

'But he's hurt!' So obvious a statement, and yet what else could she say?

Hesprec shook her head frantically. 'If not now, then you're lost. Maniye, please!'

That shadow-landscape was still there, in the back of Maniye's mind. And yet Loud Thunder was right here, with Yoff whining and sniffing at him, the dog as helpless in his misery as she was, and . . .

She sensed the vast breadth of the Godsland. For a moment she was falling back into it as both her souls tore at her. Vast and without boundaries, the tether fraying that had kept her at the feet of her totems. Her legs lost their strength and she collapsed, knotting her hands in Loud Thunder's goat hides.

Hesprec was still calling her name, but when she tried to find the Serpent priestess, all she saw were those stars, that land.

'I . . . I see,' she got out. 'I am there, and I . . .' She was moving away from the Wolf, crossing towards the Tiger, passing through the valleys of wolfkin, moving into the fiefdoms beyond. There was the vast shadow of the Bear, a hill atop a hill. She could see all the shapes in between, the succession of beasts that she could pass through, in order to turn a wolf into a bear, a bear into a wolf, a wolf into a tiger . . .

'You must go on without me,' came Hesprec's whispered voice. 'But I understand now. I will help you. I will help Loud Thunder too, if he can be helped. Trust me. Find your new totem.'

And then, from a greater distance still, the distantly heard summons of the Serpent girl: 'Laughing Girl! Come here now!'

Can I choose the Bear as my champion? But Maniye knew she could not, for it had its people already, living and dying and being reborn: animal to human, human to animal in a constant round. She must find some great warrior-spirit in the space of Bear and Wolf and Tiger that would make her its avatar.

And she searched and she searched, and the tether was back, its cord stretched longer, and yet still she was leashed, and what time was there, if Loud Thunder had been taken from the fight?

And the world opened up for her.

Perhaps there was a tether still that would have kept her from the lands under the Eagle's wings, or the lazy shadow-river where Old Crocodile basked, but abruptly she was let loose into the land beyond, a land of a thousand thousand god-spirits, each one showing its claws and sharp fangs to her. She was in the great empire of the killers, where before she had been bound to the little village domains of a mere handful. The profusion of shapes about her bewildered her. There were shadows of beasts that never were, or were no more. There were bears greater than the Bear; wolves that doubled and redoubled the Wolf; there were cats that overshadowed the Tiger, with teeth longer than falx-blades. And there were hyenas as great as horses, gathered next to Shyri's spotted and high-shouldered, laughing god.

Asmander watched the Tigers approach, sliding in shadow up the hillside. He had Stepped to his human shape and calmed his breathing, feeling the familiar grip of the *maccan* in his hands. As they picked up speed, closing the distance, he rediscovered his winged soul, spreading his great vanes so that he became the cloud that blotted out the sun, his shadow like an eclipse, screaming at them in his hoarse, harsh voice. And then there was the Champion, crouching atop the rocks, exuding its invincible confidence, master of all the killers of the earth.

And they slowed, not one of them wanting to be the first, and when they had slowed enough, they stopped. Probably they thought they were still too far off for him to pounce on them, though they were wrong.

There were some javelins hurled then. He danced aside from two of them, then one came in that was sent high – enough to land close to where Hesprec was. And so Asmander sprang up, Stepping to catch it in human hands and cast it back, then landing back on the Champion's scythe-clawed feet. His return throw had been wild and awkward, but he had still made an impression.

Then one of them was suddenly human, a stern and handsome woman armoured in bronze plates, an axe in one hand and a knife in the other. She had about her a sense of command, and before that solemn gaze Asmander regretted his showmanship, and Stepped so that he could hear her with human ears.

'I am come for my daughter,' the Tiger Queen told him.

Asmander made an awkward face. 'I know that.'

'Why stand in my way, Black Man? Why do you harm my people? What is this to you?'

'It's complicated,' he admitted, keeping a narrow eye on where those people of hers might be fanning out to. 'I don't care for your daughter; I would throw her to you myself. But she is beloved of one I respect, so I am here.'

In the Tiger's face he thought he saw a spark of pride that, even in defiance, her daughter had found strong allies. What she said finally, though, was, 'I am not afraid of you. Take as many shapes as a sorcerer, and I am still not afraid of you.'

It was not what he had expected from her. It was not what her followers had expected either, to judge by the sudden uncertainty amongst them. Asmander racked his brains to remember what he knew of the woman. What had Maniye said . . . ?

'You have heard the Wolves howl,' he observed. 'They have come for her, too.' There was a flinch in response, though the woman covered it well.

'Then stand aside so that we may take the girl before they do. Or would you fight us on their behalf?'

Asmander grimaced. 'Not any more.'

'I do not fear the Wolf,' she spat at him, though he heard the hurt in her voice.

'I would hunt Stone River for you, if I could,' he decided, for surely that would be the correct action. 'But what little honour I have left is committed to another's service. So fight me, Queen of Tigers. I shall come down to you.'

He relinquished his greatest advantage, just slipping to the ground rather than leaping down amongst them. The Tigers were still bunched uncertainly there, held back by what they were hearing and seeing. He had them spellbound.

And their queen gestured them away. 'I am not afraid of you,' she repeated.

'I do not want you to be,' he confirmed. 'I want you to fight me. That is what I am meant for. I have tried other purposes in my life. I have proven ill-suited for them.'

He got a smile from her then, just a faint one, but it was well worth the effort. Then she was before him, settling into a fighting stance with the ease of long practice, knife held low, axe across her body. He followed suit, *maccan* sloping at his shoulder, his right foot back, knees a little bent.

He had the reach, but she struck as he tried to use it, her axe hooking his weapon away and then the dagger darting in. He gave ground, back and sideways, trying to use her own hold on the axe haft to drag her off balance. She was a step ahead, though, the knife still driving for him, persistent as an angry bee. He swept a foot towards her legs, forcing her to step away, and followed up with a strike cleaving at where her neck and shoulder met, moving to complement the *maccan*'s weight and balance.

She passed through those moments of the duel as perfectly as a dancer, eyes always on his face, matching aggression with aggression, yet calm as still water. He could not land a blow on her.

It was an admission of defeat of sorts, but he was the first to Step.

He took the Champion's shape, leaping abruptly so as to come down on her with his talons. Instantly she was a tiger ducking beneath him, so that when he landed she was almost behind him, a woman once more and her axe hacking towards

565

his neck. He was a crocodile then, belly to the earth and lunging forwards with open jaws. She vaulted him, came down on his back as a tiger with her claws drawn in. She lost her grip a moment later, the Champion kicking her off and pursuing. He took a rake across his flank and another along his snout. For a moment he had her, the deep bite of his jaws fixed at her neck, his clawed hands hooked into her striped hide. There was bronze beneath that fire-and-shadow fur, though, and then she was a human woman twisting from his grip, her knife drawing a shallow line across his leg.

The Champion loved her, Asmander could feel. Not he himself, not his human heart, but the Champion was smitten. It wanted to kill and devour her, but it was love nonetheless.

Then the rest of the Tigers were there. In that moment, when she had been within his jaws, their loyalty had overcome their honour and they rushed forth. Abruptly he was surrounded. Their queen stepped back, face a mask of frustration and anger, but she did not call them off.

He fought; of course, he fought. The Champion gutted one with a rip of his claws. Old Crocodile's jaws closed on the leg of another, as his armoured back shrugged off the blow of a stone-studded club. He spread leather wings and cowed them in his shadow, forcing them to fall back. Then Aritchaka tackled him from behind, wrestling and reaching until she had his throat gripped in her arms, bearing down his suddenly human body as another fought his hand, contending for a hold on the *maccan*.

47

Stone River glared back at his followers, willing them to descend on Broken Axe and clear the way to reach Maniye. They would not. Some would even look him in the eye, and still not rush to support him. Even Kalameshli would not come at his bidding. Their faith in him had been unravelling ever since the girl had run away, and every twist and turn of the trail had eaten into Akrit's place in the world until the footing beneath him was suddenly treacherous.

Kill the girl, that was the answer. Even if another's hand held the knife, the girl must die at his order. He would show the Wolf and the entire world that he was not to be denied, not even by his own blood.

But Broken Axe still stood in the way, and though he was a smaller man than the Cave Dweller had been, he cast a longer shadow. Broken Axe, whose name was known to all the Winter Runners and many beyond: the great hunter; the Wolf who walked alone.

Every legend needs an ending, Stone River decided, and hefted his bear-killer.

He went in with a savage scything cut. Broken Axe Stepped swiftly, ducking forwards under the stroke – so close that the iron edge must have split some hairs on his back. He struck Stone River's chest with his forepaws, going for the throat, knocking the man to one knee. Axe came at him again, fangs glinting, and Stone River met his leap with the bear-killer's haft, throwing him off and lurching back to his feet.

He was already bringing the falx down. Broken Axe's wolf shape seemed to leap straight into the oncoming blow, and for a moment Akrit thought it would be as simple as that. His enemy Stepped back to human, though, the handle of Axe's hatchet staying Stone River's stroke, and Axe's free hand curling about the shaft. Against the pivot of Akrit's own grip, Axe pushed the falx up and back, yanking it half out of his adversary's hands and twisting violently, so as to lay the shaft across Stone River's shoulders and neck, bending him forwards.

Akrit Stepped: either that or be at the mercy of the hatchet. He left his falx in his enemy's hands, turning even as he found his wolf feet, to chew at Axe's hamstrings. He got a boot in his muzzle for his pains, but he dodged aside from the hatchet-sweep, drawing a little blood with his teeth as he snapped at his enemy's hand.

Then Axe was a wolf as well, pale with a dark flash about his shoulders, bucking up to get his jaws to the back of Akrit's neck. Stone River beat him to it, and for a moment they were chest to chest, twisting as each tried for the throat of the other. They slipped sideways, and went tumbling over and over down the hillside, scattering the rest of Stone River's rebellious pack. Then Broken Axe was a man again, trying to pin Akrit down with a human's greater weight, his blade coming up.

Akrit squirmed out of his hold, teeth ripping into Axe's fore-arm. The hatchet went spinning away but, quick as water, there was a bronze knife in the man's other hand. It drove in, once, twice, and snapped against the iron that lay within Akrit's Stepped form.

Stone River returned to his true shape, getting a hand about Broken Axe's neck and throwing him downslope, towards the trees. His hand found a familiar shape beneath it: his falx had come downhill too, ready for its master to reclaim.

He lunged with it, finding his enemy unarmed and still

568

regaining his feet. The attack was hurried, though, the long weapon tangling with the outlying branches of the trees, and then Akrit had a wolf at his throat again.

He beat the animal away with a solid blow from the falx's haft, but already Axe was a man once more, his arm snaking about the weapon, his weight dropping suddenly to remove it from its owner's hands for a second time. His other hand found Stone River's face, the thumb groping for an eye.

Akrit dragged his opponent down on top of him, and he ripped clear his strong iron knife from its scabbard and drove it into Broken Axe.

He saw realization come to Axe, as the blade sank deep under his ribs. The blood went out of the man's face, just as it was coming out of his body.

Akrit knew he should fall back then: less for fear of any last trick of fists or jaws that his enemy might manage, but to give Broken Axe a chance to Step, to let his soul go to the Wolf. Instead he wrenched the blade sideways, sawing viciously within his enemy, giving voice to his hate.

Axe's hand was at his throat, but the grip was weak. Still, there must have been strength left somewhere in the man because, with a great shuddering heave, he became a wolf at last, even with the terrible wounds Akrit was carving into him. Shuddering, he dropped off Stone River and fell over onto his side, panting once, twice, and then no more.

Akrit lurched to his feet, the reddened knife held high. 'Well?' he demanded of his people, for surely now they were his forever and forever. But they just stared with wide, frightened eyes.

In the distance, Maniye could hear voices as if echoing across the far hills. There was the Laughing Men girl, Shyri, demanding to know what she was supposed to do . . . saying that someone was fighting and that he was fighting alone against . . .

And someone was in pain, the small sounds of a great, great man sorely wounded, cursing through gritted teeth, hissing and snarling – and sometimes the sounds were those of a vast bear on the point of madness, and sometimes of a man just the same.

And Hesprec, that strange young girl's voice that was still Hesprec's voice, was speaking calming words to both of them. And the dog with its agitated *Yoff! Yoff! Yoff!* But there was no answering *Matt! Matt! Matt!*

And the hilltop, that real hilltop with the stones, in the world of men and beasts . . . Maniye felt as though it was the one stationary point, and that all the rest of the wide world, from the mountains to the southerner's vaunted river, was being slowly twisted about that anchor.

There were many great beasts she had passed now that she could tread the road of possibilities between her souls: bears and huge wolves, great cats and other hunting beasts never seen before by human eyes. They were like ghosts. She could not reach them or make them real, call out to them as she might. Nothing was interested in answering her summons, and the world twisted tighter and tighter about its centre.

Something must surely tear, and soon.

And, with that thought, something did.

The more she had sought a new soul, the more her two natures grew restless. The further she had hunted away from the Tiger and the Wolf, the more the animals within her had clawed and howled to be let out.

And now, with a great heaving vomiting rush, they broke free of her, shattering the bonds she had placed about herself, leaping from her shadow to become things in their own right. A tiger and a wolf: the bitter mother, the callous father.

And they would fight each other: they would fight forever, but first they would finish their work of destroying her. She was where the Tiger and the Wolf were united: she was the halfway creature that neither could bear to let live.

And so she ran across that uneven landscape, stumbling and tripping over her two bare feet. Behind her loped the beasts that had escaped from her mind, her own souls hungry to seize her in their jaws and tear her in two.

And worse was what she knew herself to be: an empty vessel that thought it was a girl; a soulless thing no better than the Plague People in the stories. How could she be real when even her own souls wanted to consume her?

But still she ran, the instinct stronger than reason or religion. She skittered fleet-footed across the Godslands, and the gods looked down, disinterested, and turned their muzzles and their snouts away from her frantic cries for aid.

And at last she could run no more, scrabbling halfway up a steeper hill that was far from any landmarks she might recognize. She slipped back down, feeling her nails break and skin tear; railing at the terrible frailty of a mere human form; knowing the hot breath of her own birthright as it prepared to devour her.

And so she turned, standing at bay at last, and saw those two familiar shapes pad out to confront her, one grey as shadow, the other flickering with red embers. These were the beasts of the wild, the killers and eaters of men, the howlers and snarlers in the dark: the Winter Runner and the Shadow Eater. And she had nothing but blunt human teeth and clawless human hands.

They closed with her lazily, keeping a distance between them, the wolf to her right, the tiger to her left. Her feeble hands clawed at the substance of the Godsland for aid.

There was something hard under her fingers.

Her hand closed on it. That was what her hand was for. She hefted the stone and in a heartbeat she had thrown it, hearing the wolf yelp from the unexpected impact. That was what her arm was for.

She had been crouched and cowering. Now she forced herself to stand tall, to stand on her own two legs. Her hands were reaching again, drawing the shadows into other shapes, as though even those mute things had soul. She had a knife; she had a spear; she had a club; she had a bow.

But the two beasts were still closing in, though there was something cautious in their step now, a hint of wariness.

'I am not yours.' Her voice sounded tremulous and high, but it was the only voice in all the Godsland.

She had a stick in her hand now, which was just a slender wand. She lifted it high. Part of her had caught its breath at what she was about to bring into this place of spirits.

'You are mine!' she challenged them, the wolf and the tiger. 'You were born from me and you shall go back to your place! I am your master. You shall hunt at my bidding, or not at all!'

And she struck the stick against the ground, and it blazed forth with fire.

She saw its light gleam back from their startled eyes. She saw it race across the Godslands, and the lesser beasts there shied away from it. Only those great, implacable creatures of myth she had come to seek were able to stare without any fear at the spectre of a human hand holding a blazing brand.

'I am Maniye! I am Many Tracks!' she yelled to her recalcitrant souls. 'And you are mine! You are no more than my shadow!'

And she brandished the flame at them, first one and then the other, forcing them backwards, showing them that she was strong.

She knew what must be done now, though she could not have said how this knowledge came to her. She planted the brand in that dark earth and stepped past it, letting her two-legged shadow stretch long and tall across the undulating ground. And, where it touched them, it showed the two beasts before her to be no more than shadows themselves: wolf, tiger, human, all three just the shapes that the firelight cast outwards from her.

And when they were back inside her – when she knew she had mastered them in this place, and they would not drive her mad any more, or fight each other within the confines of her skull – only then did she turn back towards the fire.

On the far side of the brand, the flaring light was reflected in

572

two eyes bigger than her fists, on teeth like ranks of knives. A beast had come down from its hilltop to gaze at her, at long last.

The *maccan* was twisted free of Asmander's hand, its stone teeth gashing the fingers of the man who took it from him. He saw a knife curved like a claw raised up above him. Kicking out won him a second's respite as he got a heel into a Tiger woman's knee, throwing the whole tangled knot of them off-kilter. But then they had him again and he stared into the narrowed eyes of his killer.

Something black came amongst them then, like a long streak of night speckled with the glint of stars. Yellow teeth flashed in its jaws, shearing at flesh and leaving ragged wounds in their wake; claws dug and ripped and pried, prising the scrum apart as though opening a clam.

Aritchaka still had Asmander firmly by the neck, but abruptly his limbs were unencumbered, and he gripped her arm, twisting it away. Her knife jabbed at him, but it slanted off the quill-scales of the Champion as he slipped from her grasp just in time. Then she had fallen back along with the others, forming a loose ring of warriors and tigers with their queen in the centre, facing the Champion and his Dragon.

Venat Stepped, rolling his broad shoulders, weighing the greenstone *meret* in his hand. The weapon of a chief, Asmander knew: lesser warriors would use bone or wood or flint, not the hard jade rock that took long seasons to craft and retained its edge like nothing else. How hard it must have been for the man to bow his head, to relinquish his name and become a servant to a boy. When Asmander had given it all back to him, he was sure the old pirate would kill him, or try. Some part of him had been hoping for it.

And now here he was, with his back to the rocks, his unnerving grin towards the Tigers. Those coal eyes of his took in the fire-shadow stripes of them, the shining bronze plates of their mail, the feathers cresting their helms.

'Don't we look pretty,' he spat disgustedly.

Asmander Stepped, feeling the Champion still just a breath away and eager to resume the fight. 'Did you forget something?' he managed.

'That's how they do gratitude in Atahlan, is it?' Venat bared his teeth: maybe a smile, maybe not. 'How are you still alive, boy?'

'I keep finding old men stupid enough to save my life.'

Venat squared his shoulders as the Tigers expanded their half-circle, taking their places on both flanks. One had a javelin drawn back to throw, and the big cats were drawing themselves up to leap.

'Last time, I promise,' Venat assured him.

Asmander Stepped again, the Champion's bow-taut form closing about him. The Tigers flinched back a little, confronting the alien majesty of that shape as though they were looking into the sun. A Champion's soul burned fierce and free, torn from the deep time when its avatars had once walked the earth.

And then it happened; they felt it, every one of them. The ground did not shake, but each of them, Tigers, Venat and Asmander himself, they all shifted their balance slightly and all at once. Something had changed.

Something new had come into the world.

'What are you waiting for?' Standing over the body of Broken Axe, one foot planted on the dead wolf's blood-matted hide, Akrit Stone River bellowed to his followers. 'Go get the girl, bring my daughter to me! Or is there another who would challenge me?'

And they were still staring, and only then did he realize that they were not staring at *him*. The Winter Runners stood in awe of something, and it was not their chief. Old Kalameshli Takes Iron's old face was slack behind its tattoos. There was shock in his yellowed eyes, and there was fear, but there was something else to be read there too. Akrit was abruptly aware that it was *reverence*.

When he turned, he half thought he would behold the Wolf himself. What came down from the hilltop was grander and more terrible even than that.

It walked like a bear, on flat feet, with curved talons that gouged the earth where they touched, and it possessed a bear's heavy-shouldered bulk – not quite the size of the Cave Dweller Akrit had just dispatched, but not so far from it. The monster's head was not the squat muzzle of a bear, though, but a long, grinning gape that had a great deal of wolf in it, were it not for the size. Those were jaws that could reach out into the night sky and pluck down the moon. Its eyes held the gold fire of the sun. Its pelt was black as a panther's, with a shimmer-sheen of silver to the dense hairs, and its tail lashed the air like a cat's. There was something of a tiger's grace to it, too, despite its size.

And, more than that, there was an aura that surrounded the creature, of something more than natural. As it advanced down the hill, Akrit backed away until he was almost amongst his followers, for there was a terrible cold radiance that seemed to limn the creature, perceived only by the mind.

The creature had halted at Broken Axe's body, staring down at it, and Akrit was half convinced this prodigy must have been sent by the Wolf himself to bring home the soul of his fallen son. For the first time in a long while he had a stab of doubt, beginning to wonder if he had done the right thing.

And the huge monster Stepped, and it was just slight Maniye standing here, gazing with gleaming eyes at the dead animal, at the empty vessel that had once been Broken Axe.

Akrit was finding it difficult to draw breath. He had reclaimed his bear-killer, hands clutching white-knuckled on its haft. *There she was!* He had only to rush her now and he would be rid of her. And yet, if he shed her blood, the whole world would denounce him as kinslayer. None of them would *understand*.

575

'Kill her,' he croaked. 'Takes Iron, Tree Striker, any of you, kill her. Kill her! Kill her *now*!'

At the sound of his voice, Maniye glanced up and looked him in the eye. She was shaking, and if it was grief that had struck her, she wore it like armour. It was a grief that peeled her lips back from her teeth, and made of her expression something terrible and savage.

She was saying something – he could not hear what it might be. She was speaking, and then she cocked her head as though something answered back.

But she was *his* child, disobedient and wayward as she was. She was *his*. He bared his teeth at her, and saw their history reflected in her eyes; her life spent under the shadow of his hand. And he knew he could master her again, and he hefted his falx. If it had served as a bear-killer, it would serve well enough to bring to heel whatever Maniye had become.

Then her eyes narrowed, and she Stepped.

She had not believed it possible until she saw the body: only a wolf with a dark flash of fur across its shoulders, but just as the spirits here were an invisible presence, so the death of Broken Axe left an absence, a gap in the world. There was a man who had walked with Wolves and Tigers, who had fought alongside the Bear. There lay the Wolf who walked by himself, owning to no master save his own judgement. There was the man who had saved Maniye's mother from the hands of the man who still called himself her father. There lay the man who had hunted her across the Crown of the World; the man who had been her friend in the Shining Halls and who had fought for her freedom, even though it had cost him everything.

There lay the man who had given her a name.

And at last she looked up at Akrit Stone River, who was staring at her with his face clenched into such a tangle of hate and fear, horror and rage that surely the knot of it would never come undone unless it was cut straight through. He was pointing at her, making demands of his warriors, of Kalameshli and of the world. And for once the world was not listening to Akrit Stone River. For once, the sun and moon did not move about his drives and wants and ambition. Instead, the world was watching *her*.

'Can I do this?' she asked, as though Broken Axe might hear her. Within her breast, the tiger and the wolf that she was inheritrix to were both waiting. They did not strain against her any more; there was no rebellion left inside them, and if there was a madness in her, it was of a different order, a thing divine.

'Can I face him?' she whispered. A lifetime of blows, of spite, of callous little cruelties spread before her like a path of thorns. She looked on Akrit's face, and he still meant *Fear* to her, as if her frightened, beaten past could have its own separate soul. If he raised a hand against her, she would cower back, she knew it.

But the voice rose up within her – the *other* voice as vast and measureless as the horizon, and it told her that she could.

'My father,' she murmured . . . but of course he was not her father, he had never been her father. He was only the man who had tried to make her *his*.

Her heart was rattling in her chest – her human heart – but she made herself meet Akrit's eyes, forced herself to do so as though she held a knife to her own throat. She had intended defiance, but there must have been some yielding emotion on her face, because his eyes gleamed and he brandished the weapon at her, the blade that had carved up Loud Thunder, in the hand that had struck down Broken Axe. Here was the man who had harried her mercilessly back and forth across the Crown of the World.

And so she Stepped, and called that Champion whose lair she had found in the Godsland. Its form enveloped her, the iron strength of its muscles, the thick leather of its hide. She stretched, and felt a sullen, enduring power in every sinew, felt her new claws rake furrows in the earth, licked the jagged fence of her teeth with a black tongue.

The great weight of it, the sheer power of her new shape, made Akrit Stone River take a pace back as she closed with him. She tried to build on that: rearing up and stamping on the ground, bellowing in a voice not like a wolf's or a bear's or any animal's. His eyes were very wide, but he held his ground, and then abruptly he had Stepped again, darting to one side and then towards her flank as a big grey wolf. She turned on the spot and swatted at him, missed his fleeting shape and then felt the nip of him at one side. His teeth closed on nothing but thick tufts of her pelt, and a moment later she lurched at him, bringing her bear-claw feet down where he had been and forcing him to back off.

But she could not fight well. Asmander, despite all his winged glory, had never flown. Just so for her: the shape was unfamiliar, its tolerances and capabilities unknown to her. For all her new body's strength and speed, she was like a woman drunk and unable to use it to its fullest, slipping, overreaching, chasing the swift-footed wolf but never catching him.

He would realize that soon, she knew. So far he was surely congratulating himself on his nimble speed. But he was no fool, and when he understood . . .

And again he was a man, the falx biting down towards her, but he had made the move too swiftly, still unnerved by the Champion's reek of deep time that cloaked her. She shouldered into him, the haft of the weapon bouncing off her ribs, and then he was down, rolling frantically to get out of her way. She charged him, lumbering forth with a sudden access of speed, but he was Stepped and out of reach long before she got to him. They faced one another, both panting. Downslope their audience was the Winter Runners and Kalameshli. Upslope, Hesprec was standing in that gap Broken Axe had held for just long enough. The Serpent girl would die too, if Maniye failed.

She growled and slashed at Akrit, batting with her claws like a cat, sending him scuffling backwards, but then he was at her again. He rushed straight into her jaws, it seemed, but, as she snapped at him, he was past her, dodging up the slope. For a moment she thought he was after Hesprec, and she wheeled clumsily. He was only after height, though, Stepping back to human for that leap, then to wolf form for the extra distance its lighter frame would lend him, and then he was a man once more, and on her back.

She reared up onto her hind legs, snarling: it was exactly what he wanted. The hard wood haft of his falx slid under her throat until he had a hand at either end of it. His arms were only just long enough to manage it; to put a collar about that great neck.

But in the next breath, the neck was not so great, and he was pulling her human head against his mail-clad chest, the weapon's shaft crushing into her slender throat.

And yet he held off: he did not make that final twist or pull that would finish her. Instead he roared at Kalameshli. 'Bring your knife, priest, now! Finish her! Give her to the Wolf!' And she realized that, enraged as Akrit was, he did not want to bring the curse of kinslayer down upon his name.

Her mind was very calm then, somehow. The Champion was at the back of it, awaiting its moment, passing on to her mouthfuls of its strength. She gazed down at the Winter Runners, and met the eyes of Kalameshli.

The old priest shambled forwards, the little bones of his robe clicking and rattling. He had an iron knife in one hand, a piece he must have crafted himself, sweating at the forge as he acted out that secret knowledge known only to the Wolf. Akrit held Maniye rigid, just able to breathe, unable to give voice to more than a choke . . . but her eyes spoke.

Kalameshli stood in front of her: the other scourge of her childhood who had whipped her and pushed her and challenged her. The man who had known of the Tiger in her heart, and hated it, but never told her father. And she had hated him back – with reason! – for a long time, but at least she knew *why* he had been that man.

He had been like iron, hard as his name, through all her childhood. There had been no love, no give in him. Now he looked like a wretched, defeated shadow of himself.

'Akrit . . .' he murmured. 'Not your daughter's blood.'

'Do it!' Flecks of Stone River's spittle arced close past Maniye's face.

The old priest raised his knife and lunged forwards with it, a movement so jerky and sudden that both Akrit and Maniye assumed he had stabbed her – instead of forcing its leather-wrapped hilt into her hand.

She could not sever Stone River's mail, she knew, not even with iron on iron. He wore no helm, though, and she stabbed back past her own shoulder with the blade, close enough to draw a line of red across her own ear. It bit solidly into Akrit's face and abruptly he was screaming, and the pressure was gone from her throat.

And the Champion was waiting for her, just like family, gathering her up in its might and power, and she swiped at Akrit with a paw and sent him tumbling back down the slope.

He scattered his own men gathered there, but then found his footing, staggering upright with half his face clad in blood. He screamed at her; he raged, and she raged right back at him.

And he was charging her again, first as a wolf to make up speed, and then as a man, with falx raised high. He was the chief of the Winter Runners; he was the terror of her childhood.

She looked down on him – yes, *down*! – and realized that the fear had gone from her at last. She roared at him in a thunderstorm of sound that slowed and slowed him further, until he stumbled to a halt outside of her reach. He looked into her beast's eyes, and saw that she was not his any more.

She advanced with one stomping step after another, swinging her head and baring the daggers of her teeth. Something went out of him then, as though his mastery of her had been his last crutch, and now she had broken it. He had nothing left to hold him up.

He backed off a couple of awkward steps, and then he became a wolf, fleeing like a swift grey shadow for the trees. He did not reach them.

Maniye could not have kept up with him, but another had been waiting for her chance. A form of fire and shadow dropped upon Akrit, raking and savaging, and then it was a woman in bronze mail with knife and hatchet, and then a tiger again, her teeth crushing, her claws ripping until the weak points of his iron hide gave way. And sometimes he was a man, fumbling desperately against her savage jaws, and sometimes he was a wolf shuddering as she stabbed and stabbed at his grey hide. But it was the end of him, in either shape. And so it was that Akrit Stone River came to die.

He died a wolf, in the end. His soul would not be a feast for the Tiger. And that was the best that could be said about the demise of Stone River.

When she had done, Joalpey stood and confronted Maniye, first looking up into her great amber eyes, then down, into her human ones. The Tiger Queen's reddened weapons were still in her hands and there was a fighting tension in her to match.

Maniye took a deep breath. 'Do you seek to kill me, now?'

Joalpey just stared at her, still wound up for bloodletting. From around the hill slunk her Tigers: Aritchaka and a handful of others, on two legs and four.

'If you feared that I might be a weapon used against you,' Maniye continued, 'then the hand that would have held that weapon is no more.' She was very aware of the Winter Runners bunched together and nearer to her than the Tigers were – inching closer, too, as though they were going to stand alongside her. That threw her, because she had expected nothing but enmity from them. Apparently she was still theirs, when Tigers were about. Without her father to feed them his hate, they smelled the Wolf on her.

'If it is just that the sight . . . the knowledge of me,' Maniye went on, hearing her voice shake slightly, 'is impossible to live with, after what was done, then . . . Then you have killed the man who did it. I ask you to leave the hatred there with his corpse. Do not bring it to me. I have not earned it.'

And the Tigers Stepped back and forth, shifting to keep the Wolves in sight, and then again as a handful of people descended from the hilltop. Hesprec was there and the three southerners, and last of all came the slow and limping figure of Loud Thunder, a great bear with a single dog at his heels. The balance of power shivered and danced between them all: a ring of three warbands, with Maniye at their centre.

At last Joalpey took a long breath. 'It is not over,' she declared.

Maniye felt the Champion looming large in her mind, ready to come to her aid. 'Let it be over,' she urged.

'He – *he* is part of this.' Joalpey jabbed with her knife, and it was Kalameshli Takes Iron that she singled out. 'I will have this man's blood. I will have his soul for the Tiger.'

And, of course, she was right. Of course, the old man had played his part. Maniye was living evidence of that.

She glanced back at Kalameshli. The priest was staring levelly at Joalpey. Would he go forth and meet her, knife to knife? Perhaps, and he would die. He was old and, though he was strong, he was no warrior.

He had saved Maniye, at the end. She had left the iron of the knife behind when she Stepped, but not the memory of his actions. If he had remained true to his chief, she would be dead.

Maniye wanted Hesprec's wisdom and Broken Axe's calm. She had only herself, though.

'It is your right, to ask it,' she replied quietly, thinking through all the words she might say. 'How can I say that you're not owed your revenge?'

'Then give it to me,' Joalpey demanded.

'Because I owe him my life. I owe him that debt. And because he is my kin, my blood. Because he is my father. The very act you are owed vengeance for is what put me here – what made me.'

582

'What are you saying?' the Tiger Queen growled.

'I cannot ask you to forget, but I am asking you, just this once, to stay your hand. For no other reason than your daughter asks it. I have nothing more than that, nothing to bargain with save for that.'

For a long, silent moment Joalpey said nothing, and all eyes were on her. Her lips twitched once, a muscle clenched in the corner of her jaw, her hands tightened on the hilts of her weapons.

At last she spoke. 'What is this new shape you have, daughter? Is it some Champion of the Wolf that you have called out of the darkness? Is this what will hunt my people when the moon is high?'

And Maniye found she could answer, for that was the one thing she had a full understanding of when she returned to her body from the Godsland.

'I am a mother to wolves,' she said softly. 'I am sister to cats. The blood of bears and hyenas runs in my veins. If I am a Champion of anything, it is of all the beasts that rend flesh with tooth and claw. No one tribe has a claim on me. I am for all the Crown of the World and beyond.' Saying the words and knowing the truth behind them, she felt a sudden thrill of joy.

'And whose flesh will you rend?' Joalpey asked her.

Maniye took a deep breath. 'Whoever lifts a hand against my people.' *And who are my people? Everyone and no one. Whoever I decide.*

The Tigers were watching their queen doubtfully, sensing the shifting emotions within her. Asmander and Venater were poised to fight, Maniye recognized, and Shyri as well. The Wolves were strung as taut as bows.

Hesprec, though: the dark girl caught her gaze and nodded, just the once. Centuries of watching the world gave the small motion weight. Hesprec, at least, felt that Maniye had found the right words to say.

And then Joalpey took another long breath, and cast her knife down before her, point first into the earth.

'It is over,' she declared, and a great invisible burden seemed to slough off her shoulders. 'For you, my daughter, I grant this. Let the old man be kept far, far from the lands of the Tiger, and I will renounce my claim on him. I grant you this, because there is nothing else that I can give you. I have nothing else for my daughter but this.'

The words were said without remorse, flat and empty of feeling, but Maniye's hide was thicker these days. They did not sting her as they once might.

48

Up here in the highlands the winter was gathering its pack, ready to go hunting in the lowlands. Maniye could hardly believe that, back in those lands she called home, summer had only just spent its store of days. What a time to be travelling in this hard, cold country!

But she had been called to where few outsiders had ever gone. Of all the people she had ever known, perhaps only Broken Axe had travelled into the high country of the Cave Dwellers. Perhaps not even he had been summoned here by their great Mother.

Long months had passed since the death of Stone River, of Broken Axe . . . and of much else. At the autumn equinox she had gone to the Stone Place and shown herself to the priests of all the Crown of the World, who had already heard rumours of what had come into the world. She had stood before them in that great bear-dog shape, burning with the strangeness of it, walking the circle of the stones on feet the world had not known since before the memories of man. And then she had stood before them as a small Wolf girl of tangled provenance, and seen in their eyes the fear and speculation. They had thought that she would come to hunt them, or to challenge them, or to rule over them. The most ambitious had thought on how to use her, the least on how to destroy her. She had seen it all in their eyes.

And they would grow used to the idea, and perhaps she

would only be the first, for Asmander had told her that he was by no means the only Champion of the Riverlands. Hesprec said that when she stood in the Godsland and looked into those moon-round eyes, a new door had opened.

At the Stone Place there had been too many questions, and she had let most go unanswered. Only those which would have tied her to one place, to one tribe, had she rejected outright. Those who simply said she would be welcome, that she could be their guest, she thanked. Those who came to her with their allegiance . . . well, that had become complicated.

And there had been a command. Only one had been strong enough and self-contained enough to make demands of the new Champion of the north, but when the Mother of Bears demanded her presence, Maniye went to her.

Here she was now, up in the mountains, many days' travel past Loud Thunder's home. Here she had come, passing through high prairies already past their brief and frantic time of bloom and growth, following the streambeds until she came to cliffs that were pocked with caves.

Lone Mountain had greeted her solemnly. He was just as she remembered: taller even than the bulk of his people, and wearing linens and wools of bright colours to mark him out. The look he gave her was that of an equal: no deference for what she had become, but nothing in his eyes to acknowledge that the crown of her head did not reach much past his navel.

She had tried her authority, then, surrounded by these huge people, overshadowed on all sides, virtually underfoot. She had demanded to see Loud Thunder first, to know how he was healing. And they had frowned and shuffled and exchanged looks over the top of her head, but at last they had given in, with poor grace, and taken her to him.

He was on his feet again and well: well enough for her to feel a wash of joy come over her. She had known men crippled by lesser injuries, but Hesprec had more than one lifetime of healing lore at her disposal, and she had done well with treating those fresh wounds. He still limped a little, and sat stiffly, one hand resting on Yoff's loyal head.

They spoke of many things: of his Mother and her plans; of the journeys of his youth; of those waiting in her future. And then word had come that she was wanted, that the woman who ruled these high lands was growing impatient. So here she now sat, cross-legged at a fire, while the Mother of the Cave Dwellers regarded her thoughtfully. The woman was even greater than Maniye remembered: a huge, slope-shouldered shape clad in the hides of a score of animals, stitched and overlapping.

'I thought you'd be bigger,' the woman muttered, almost a complaint. 'Show me what you have with you.'

So many times, Maniye had been asked that. There had been plenty who had wanted her to perform for them: to dance from shape to shape just to prove that she could. She remembered what Asmander had said, when he was asked the same, and she knew it to be true. The Champion was not for casual display. It was not called on lightly.

But she guessed that the Mother did nothing lightly, and so she Stepped into the shape of the Champion, her bear-dog, and crouched there, head raised a little above her paws, looking the huge woman directly in the eye.

Eventually the Mother nodded, not seeming daunted, but just weary. 'All I've heard is true. Take it away.'

'Mother,' Maniye said, when she had Stepped back, 'I have heard it said that you see the future.'

The great woman snorted derisively. 'No art to that,' she muttered. 'Tell me the sun will rise and you've told the future. But some see further. Some have better eyes. That old Snake who was at the Stone Place back in spring, he had good eyes, and good ears too, for he listened to every tribe.'

'Hesprec said something was coming,' Maniye agreed, 'something bad. He said that everyone he spoke to had some piece of it, some glimpse. And you, you've seen the same?'

The Bear Mother grunted. A child came in just then – ten or

587

twelve, and taller than Maniye – with a wooden platter of meat and fish hot from the fire. For a while the big woman just ate, as though she had entirely forgotten her guest, but at last she grudgingly invited Maniye to join her, her calculating eyes showing that she had been turning over her thoughts.

'Something, yes. Enough word, enough signs. Birds flying out of season or on new paths, news from the Seal that the fish are schooling differently, flowers in bloom not seen for a lifetime, too many bad dreams, too many frightened children. And so we know something comes, but we're blind as to what. So we try to prepare.'

'You had Loud Thunder as your warleader?'

The Mother laughed. 'And what use did we have of him? Some half-hearted lessons in war to our hunters, and then he must go chasing across the Crown of the World after his lack-wit Wolf friend. And yet . . . so many changes in the world, and one of them sits right before me now. And so perhaps that was what we chose Loud Thunder for: to see that you became what you have become. You see? Prophecy is even easier if you offer it after the event.' She worried some more meat off a goat leg and chewed thoughtfully. 'I had thought a war between the Wolf and the Tiger might be the start of it, but now it seems this will not be.'

'With Stone River dead, there is none left so very desperate to be High Chief over the Tiger's corpse. Perhaps the Wolf begin to see that they need none,' Maniye said. 'And the Tiger keep to their places, for now.'

'And this you have accomplished?'

The girl shrugged. 'It is just a madness that passed from the world when my f—when Stone River left it.'

'And the Coyote and the Horse bring word and trade,' the Mother mused. 'And who knows what tomorrow's tomorrow may bring?' She leant ponderously forwards, casting Maniye in her shadow. 'And now what will you do, little one? For I hear you make the people of these lands nervous.'

'The chiefs fear that, if I am not theirs, I will threaten their power. They make me their guest, they speak kind words to me, some even offer themselves or their hunters as mates. But when I tell them I am not ready to settle, I see the worry in their eyes. The Wolf tribes, yes, and the others, too. I am too new in the world, and they remember Stone River and see him in me. They think I am ambitious.'

'And of course they have no reason to think so?'

'I cannot control what young fools do,' Maniye snapped bitterly.

The Bear Mother chuckled deep in her throat. 'How disappointed they must be, those bold hunters, when you send them away.' Her eyes narrowed. 'Or do you?'

'Most times, they will not go. They skulk like dogs at the edge of my firelight, or hunt and bring me meat and hides.' One or two at first, and then a handful, and surely there were more on the way: misfits, mystics and bravos out for glory and adventure, and all of them had decided that their best trail was the one left by her new footprints. They came to the Champion and offered their weapons in her service. And so the chiefs of the Crown of the World grew more nervous, and Maniye could not keep from wondering what she might gain if she mustered these followers. What sort of power could she become, with a warband at her back?

And even before the equinox – where she had stood before those chiefs and priests and seen that she had gone in their eyes from being a bringer of peace to a harbinger of strife – she had seen her path. She wanted to give no man cause to strike out at her but, more, she wanted to give herself no way to yield to temptation and strike first. She was no daughter of Stone River but she had grown up in his shadow, and that shadow moved in her mind sometimes and whispered about what she might do.

'When I first fled the Winter Runners, I had a plan. The Snake priest and I, we would fly south to his homeland. I know a man who brings a handsome offer to any Iron Wolves who might come to aid his chief, there by the river they love so much. I will go south for a time. I will go with Hesprec and the southerners and any who will follow me. I remember Broken Axe telling me that, when he was young, he and Loud Thunder did just that, fought battles and had adventures and saw strange lands. Now I shall do the same. And when I come back to the Crown of the World, it will be more ready for me, I hope.'

'When you come back, it may need you.' There was a great deal of foreboding in the Mother's voice, but Maniye just shrugged.

'I've had enough of being gifted with futures. None of those I was offered ever appealed to me. Broken Axe, he made his own – and so will I.'

Acknowledgements

The usual suspects, of course: my agent Simon, Peter Lavery, Julie Crisp and the rest of the crew at Tor, without any of whom this book would not have come to pass.

Also, having worked at some places that treated being a writer as akin to contracting leprosy, I am very grateful to Blacks Solicitors of Leeds for being both supportive and flexible.

Finally, I am also enormously thankful to the many, many people who have supported my writing thus far. Sometimes writing can be a very lonely business, and someone just saying hi on Twitter or posting a humorous insect video on Facebook can take a lot of the gloom off.

extracts reading groups
competitions books new
discounts extracts
competitions
books
new
events books
new extracts
new titles reading groups
interviews
events extracts
discounts
new books events
events new
discounts extracts discounts
www.panmacmillan.com
extracts events reading groups
competitions books extracts new